Laughing Boy

LAUGHING BOY

BY

OLIVER LA FARGE

HOUGHTON MIFFLIN COMPANY
The Riverside Press *Cambridge*

PRINTED IN THE U.S.A.

DEDICATED

TO

The only beautiful squaw I have ever seen in all my life, whose name I have forgotten

INTRODUCTORY NOTE

THIS book is a work of fiction. I have tried to be as true as I knew how to the general spirit of Navajo things, to customs and character, but all personages and incidents in the story are fictitious, as well as places. I have used some real place-names applied to imaginary places, or else have shifted them a hundred miles or so. There are about thirty thousand Navajos, most of whom have at least two descriptive names; it would be impossible, then, to invent names for all my characters and not hit upon some real ones. So I have frankly borrowed from names I have heard, or those listed by scientists. But neither whites nor Indians are real.

I have been as accurate as possible about ceremonies, rites, and customs. If occasionally I have taken liberties, I plead a writer's privilege. Any innovations I may have made are none the less true to the general pattern of Navajo ideas.

This story is meant neither to instruct nor to prove a point, but to amuse. It is not propaganda, nor an indictment of anything. The hostility with which certain of the characters in it view

Americans and the American system is theirs, arising from the plot, and not the author's. The picture is frankly one-sided. It is also entirely possible.

O. LA F.

NEW ORLEANS, 1929

Laughing Boy

LAUGHING BOY

CHAPTER I

I

HE was riding the hundred miles from T'o Tlakai to Tsé Lani to attend a dance, or rather, for the horse-racing that would come afterwards. The sun was hot and his belly was empty, but life moved in rhythm with his pony loping steadily as an engine down the miles. He was lax in the saddle, leaning back, arm swinging the rope's end in time to the horse's lope. His new red headband was a bright colour among the embers of the sun-struck desert, undulating like a moving graph of the pony's lope, or the music of his song —

> '*Nashdui bik'é dinni, eya-a, eyo-o . . .*
> Wildcat's feet hurt, *eya-a, eyo-o . . .*'

Rope's end, shoulders, song, all moved together, and life flowed in one stream. He threw his head back to sing louder, and listened to the echo from the cliffs on his right. He was thinking about a bracelet he should make, with four smooth bars running together, and a turquoise in the middle

— if he could get the silver. He wished he could work while riding; everything was so perfect then, like the prayers, *hozoji nashad*, travelling in beauty. His hands, his feet, his head, his insides all were *hozoji*, all were very much alive. He whooped and struck up the Magpie Song till the empty desert resounded —

> '*A-a-a-iné, a-a-a-iné,*
> *Ya-a-iné-ainé, ko-ya-ainé* . . .'

He was lean, slender, tall, and handsome, Laughing Boy, with a new cheap headband and a borrowed silver belt to make ragged clothes look fine.

At noon, having no money, he begged coffee from a trader at Chinlee and went on, treasuring his hunger because of the feasting to come. Now he began to meet Navajos of all ages, riding to the dance. The young men bunched together — a line of jingling bridles, dark, excited faces, flashing silver, turquoise, velveteen shirts, dirty, ragged overalls, a pair of plaid calico leggins, a pair of turkey-red ones. Some of them were heavy with jewelry; Horse Giver's Son wore over four hundred dollars in silver alone; most of them had more than Laughing Boy. They stopped to look at his bow-guard, which he himself had made.

'I am a good jeweller,' he said, elated; 'I make silver run like a song.'

'You should make a song about yourself,' they told him, 'and teach the burros to sing it.'

'Have you had any rain up by T'o Tlakai?'

'No, it is just like last year. It is the devil. The grass is all dried up and the sheep are dying.'

'They had a cloudburst over by T'isya Lani. It washed out the dam.'

'It washed out the missionary's house, they say. His wife ran out in something thin and got wet, they say.'

'*Ei-yei!*'

Tall Hunter and his wife drove past in a brand-new buckboard behind two fast-trotting, grey mules. He owned over five hundred head of horses, and his wife had thick strings of turquoise and coral around her neck.

'His brother is in jail for stealing cattle, they say.'

'What is jail?' asked Laughing Boy.

Slender Hair explained: 'It is something the American Chief does to you. He puts you in a room of stone, like a Moqui house, only it is dark and you can't get out. People die there, they say. They haven't any room; they can't see anything, they say. I do not like to talk about it.'

Laughing Boy thought, I should rather die. He wanted to ask more, but was ashamed to show his ignorance before these southern Navajos, many of whom wore hats like Americans, and who knew so much of Americans' ways.

They raced. His horse was tired, but it won by a nose, which was just as well, since he had bet his bow-guard. Now he had six dollars. He hoped there would be gambling.

Tsé Lani showed a distant bonfire in the dusk, with mounted Indians moving in on it like spokes of a wheel. About two hundred young men came together half a mile away, making their ponies prance, exchanging greetings. Crooked Ear carried the ceremonial wand. Now they all lined up, with the dull, red sunset behind their black figures. They started going like getting off to a race, right into a gallop, yelling. Over by the fire was shouting, and another line tearing towards them. The world was full of a roar of hooves and two walls of noise rushing together, the men leaning forward over their horses' necks, mouths wide. '*E-e-e-e-e!*' They met in a great swirl of plunging, dodging horses, and swept on all together, whooping for dear life, with the staff in front of them, almost onto the fire, then dissolved with jingling of bits, laughter, and casual jokes as they unsaddled by the pool.

The steady motion of excitement was slowed then, in the last of the day, by the rocks and the piñons, by the reflection of the sky in the pool where flat, vague silhouettes of horses stooped to drink. The voices of many people, the twinkling of fires continued the motif, joining the time of quiet with elation past and to come; a little feeling of expectation in Laughing Boy's chest, a joyful emptiness, part hunger and part excitement.

He tended his pony minutely. The little mare had had two days of loping; shortly he wanted to race her; three days of rest would not be too much. She was his only horse; he had traded two others for her. She was tough, as a horse had to be to live at all in the North country. He ran his hands down her withers, feeling the lean, decisive muscles. In all that section, from Dennihuitso to Biltabito, from T'o Tlikahn to T'o Baka, where he knew every horse by sight, she was the best, but she would meet some competition here. He felt as if she were his own creation, like the bow-guard; at least he had selected her, as he had chosen the soft blue turquoise in the ornament. Little, compact, all black save for the tiny white spot on her forehead, she had the ugly Roman nose of character. She was like an arrow notched to a taut bowstring — a movement of the hand would release level flight swiftly to a mark.

He was thinking some of these things, half hearing the noises of the people. Just like the prayer, 'travelling in beauty.' It would be good to be a singer as well, to express all these things through the prayers. He would like to know many of them, to learn to conduct the Mountain Chant, and know all the beautiful stories behind the songs and ceremonies inside the Dark Circle of Branches. That would be really on the trail of beauty; to work in silver and turquoise, own soft-moving ponies, and lead the Mountain Chant. Just thinking about it was good. It made him feel cool inside.

'*Hozho hogahn ladin nasha woyen* ...
In the house of happiness there I wander ...'

All the time he was passing his hand along the pony's neck, along her back, feeling the lines of tough muscles.

'*E-ya*, Grandfather, are you going to dance with the horse?' Jesting Squaw's Son called over to him, 'food is ready.'

'*Hakone!*' He returned abruptly to the quick-moving life of the dance. 'I can eat it. I did not know you were coming.'

'I came when I heard you were to race your mare. I think there is money to be made, then, and I want to see her race.'

They went up arm in arm into the crowd, pushing their way into the circle around one of the fires. Busy housewives gave them coffee, the big pot of meat was passed over, and a flat, round loaf of rubbery, filling bread. The meat was the backbone of a yearling calf, boiled with corn. It was good. He munched joyfully, feeling his empty stomach fill, wadding himself with bread, washing it down with bitter coffee. A couple of Americans carrying their own plates dipped in gingerly. A Hopi, having collected everything he could possibly eat, sat down officiously beside them to air his school English and his bourgeois superiority.

II

A small drum beating rapidly concentrated the mixed noises into a staccato unison. Young men gathered about the drummer. Laughing Boy might have eaten more, but he left the fire immediately with Jesting Squaw's Son. Some one led off high-pitched at full voice,

'Yo-o galeana, yo-o galeana, yo-o galeana . . .'

By the end of the second word the crowd was with him; more young men hurried up to join the diapason,

'Galeana ena, galeana eno, yo-o ay-e hena ena . . .'

They put their arms over each other's shoulders, swaying in time to the one drum that ran like a dull, glowing thread through the singing, four hundred young men turning loose everything they had.

A bonfire twenty feet long flared to the left of them. Opposite, and to the right, the older people sat wrapped in their blankets. Behind them, men crouched in their saddles, heads and shoulders against the night sky, nodding time to the rhythm, silent, with here and there a reflection of firelight on a bit of silver, a dark face, or a horse's eye.

Twelve girls in single file stole into the open space, moving quietly and aloof as though the uproar of singing were petrified into a protective wall before it reached them. Only the pulse of the drum showed in their steps. They prowled back and forth before the line of young men, considering them with predatory judgment.

Laughing Boy at the back of the crowd looked at them with mild interest; he liked to watch their suave movements and the rich display of blankets and jewelry. One caught his attention; he thought she had on more silver, coral, turquoise, and white shell than he had ever seen on any one person. He speculated on its value — horses — she must have a very rich mother, or uncles. She was too slender, seeming frail to dance in all that rich, heavy ornamentation. He wished she would move more into the firelight. She was well dressed to show off what she wore; silver and stones with soft highlights and deep shadows glowed against the night-blue velveteen of her blouse; oval plaques of silver were at her waist, and ceremonial jewels in the fringe of her sash. Her blue skirt swung with her short, calculated steps, ankle-length, above the dull red leggins and moccasins with silver buttons. The dark clothing, matching the night, was in contrast to the other dancers, even her blanket was mainly blue. He felt animosity towards her, dark and slight, like a wisp of grass — only part of a woman. Her gaze, examining the singers, was too coolly appraising. Now she was looking at him. He threw his head back, losing himself in the singing. He wished he, too, had an American hat.

Her mincing steps took her out of sight. Jesting Squaw's Son's arm was over his shoulder, and on the other side another Indian, unknown, but young. Their life flowed together with all those others, complete to themselves, merged in one body of song, with the drumbeats for a heart,

'*Yo-o galeana, yo-o galeana . . .*'

Song followed song with a rush; when one ended, the next took up, as though the whole night would never suffice to pour out all that was in them.

Some one plucked at his blanket; then with another, stronger pull it was snatched from his shoulders. He whirled about. The men near him snickered. The frail girl held his blanket up toward him, mockingly.

'*Ahalani!*' she greeted him.

He stood for a moment in feigned stupidity. He did not want to dance. The devil! Then with a sudden lunge he snatched the blanket. It was no use. She hung on with unexpected strength, digging her heels into the sand, laughing. The men on either side were watching over their shoulders with open joy.

'What's the matter? I think your feet hurt, perhaps. I think you are bandy-legged, perhaps.'

Girls didn't usually say these things. He was shocked. Her clear, low voice turned the insults into music, bringing out to the full the rise and fall of a Navajo woman's intonation. All the time they tugged against each other, her long eyes were talking. He had seen girls' eyes talk before as they pulled at the blanket, but these were clear as words. He wanted desperately to be back among the men. He nearly pulled her over, but she hung on, and her eyes seemed to be making a fool of him.

Suddenly he gave up. She led him around behind the men, not speaking to him, uninterested. He pulled his end of the blanket over his shoulders, assuming the conventional pose of resistance, setting each foot before the other reluctantly, in response to her dragging. He watched her closely, but her grip did not slacken. Out in the clear space she transferred her hands to his belt. He pulled his blanket to his chin, masking enjoyment in a pose of contemptuous tolerance, like the other men dancing there.

The solemn turning of the couples contrasted with the free release of the singers: this was a religious ceremony and a rustic, simple pleasure, the happiness of a natural people to whom but few things happen. They were traditional and grave in their revelry.

According to the etiquette, whenever there is a rest, the man asks what forfeit he must pay; by the length of time taken by the girl to get down to a reasonable figure, he gages her liking for his company. The music paused an instant for singers to catch their breath. He made a feeble attempt to get away, then asked,

'How much?'

'Ten cents.'

The prompt answer astonished him. He paid the forfeit, still staring at her, chagrined, and furious at the blank, correct impassiveness of her face, at the same time noting delicately chiselled features, set of firm lips, long eyes that in their lack of expression were making fun of him. Ten cents! Already! With a splendid gesture he swept his blanket round him, stalking back to the singers.

He was set to lose himself in the songs, but he watched the girl drag out a man nearly as tall as himself. Instead of dancing in the usual way, they held each other face to face and close to, each with one hand on the other's shoulder. It was shocking; and why had she not done it with him? But she had let him go the first time he had asked. She had insulted him, she was too thin, and probably ill-behaved.

III

Jesting Squaw's Son's arm was over his shoulder, his ears were full of the beat and uproar of music. He was a man among men, swinging with them, marking the rhythm, releasing his joy of living in ordered song.

'Nashdui bik'é dinni, eya-a, eyo-o . . .'

A late moon rose, cool and remote, dissociated. They brought another tree up to the bonfire, standing it on end a moment so that the hot light played on its dead branches; then they let it topple over and fall, sending up in its place a tree of moving sparks into the blackness.

Night passed its middle and stood towards day. The girls moved off together in single file, blankets drawn over heads, worn out by the night of unremitting dancing. The older people fell rapidly away. Inert forms like mummies stretched out in their blankets by the embers of the feast fires. Most of the young men gave in, leaving about a hundred knotted in a mass, still hard at it. They surrounded the drummer, an older man, intently serious over drawing forth from a bit of hide stretched across the mouth of a jar rapidly succeeding beats that entered the veins and moved in the blood. He played with rhythm as some men play with design; now a quick succession of what seemed meaningless strokes hurried forward, now the beat stumbled, paused, caught up again and whirled away. Devotedly intent over his work, his long experience, his strength and skill expended themselves in quick, wise movements of the wrist, calling forth a summation of life from a piece of goatskin and a handful of baked clay, while younger men about him swayed and rocked in recurrent crescendos.

Night stood towards morning, now night grew old. Now the first white line was traced across the east far away, outlining distant cliffs. Now it was first light, and Dawn Boy was upon them. The drumming stopped; suddenly the desert was empty and vast. Young men, whose bodies felt like empty shells and whose heads still buzzed with songs, moved down to drink at the pool.

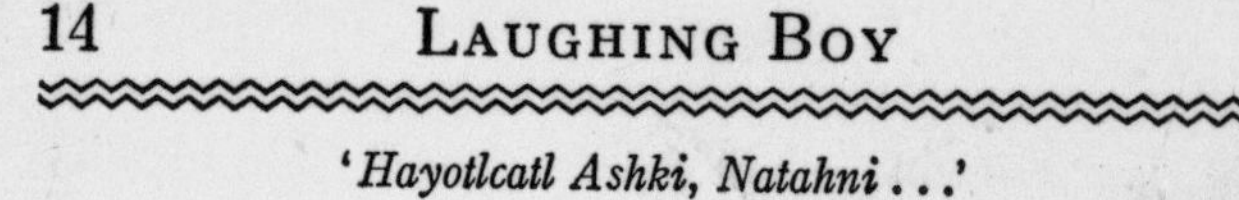

'Hayotlcatl Ashki, Natahni . . .'

Laughing Boy breathed his prayer to himself, feeling a moment of loneliness,

'Dawn Boy, Chief . . .'

He rolled up in his blanket. When he rode his horse in the races, people would see; he would ride past the people, back to T'o Tlakai, with all his winnings. That girl was strong for one who looked so slight. He would make a bracelet about her, thin silver, with stars surrounded by stone-knife-edge. His horse came to stand by him. He roused himself to look at it, struggled awake, and dragged out the corn from under his saddle.

He pulled his blanket over his head. All different things melted together into one conception of a night not like any other.

CHAPTER II

I

Some one was calling him,

'*Ei shichai, ei-yei!*'

He opened his eyes, staring upward at the face of Jesting Squaw's Son that laughed at him as he sat high above him in the saddle. The face was in shadow under the circle of his stiff-brimmed hat, cut out against the gleaming, hard sky. The sun was halfway up.

'Wake up, Grandfather! Big Tall Man is going to play tree-pushing against everybody.'

'*Hakone!*' He was up at the word. 'Give me a smoke, Grandfather.' He climbed up behind his friend's saddle. 'Come on.'

They stopped for coffee at a hogahn near the pool, where the woman of the house mocked him for sleeping late.

The people were gathered in a little box cañon, where fire had destroyed a number of scrub oaks and piñons under one wall near a seep of water. There they were dividing into two groups, according to whether they backed Big Tall Man or Man Hammer, the policeman from over by T'o Nanasdési. Hill Singer rode back and forth between, collecting and announcing the bets. Most of the money was on Big Tall Man, and there were few takers. Laughing Boy could not place any. He saw that girl sitting among the neutral spectators.

'Who is that girl,' he asked Slender Hair — 'the one who had so much hard goods on last night?'

'She is called Slim Girl, I think. She comes from down by the railroad track, from near Chiziai, I think.'

Big Tall Man and Man Hammer moved up to two dead trees of roughly the same size. Hill Singer and Hurries to War were judging. Now they pushed and strained at the trees, digging their feet in the sand, heaving shoulders. Big Tall Man's tree began to crack; then suddenly it went over. People exclaimed and laughed. After that nobody more wanted to play against him.

Then they had wrestling for the young men. Laughing Boy bet a little and lost a couple of dollars. There was a tall man wearing an American shirt and trousers and a hat, who made a great deal of noise about himself. He beat one challenger easily. Laughing Boy recognized the man who danced so outrageously last night.

'Who is that?' he asked.

'That is Red Man. He comes from down by the railroad.'

'He is too skinny. I am going to beat him.'

He challenged Red Man.

'How much will you bet on yourself?'

'I have three-fifty and this bow-guard.'

'That makes eight-fifty.'

'The bow-guard is worth more; it is worth ten dollars.'

The man looked at it judgingly. 'Well, it is worth eight. That makes eleven-fifty. Why don't you bet your belt?'

'It is not mine.'

'So you are sure you are going to lose, I think?'

Laughing Boy did not like this Indian. 'No; I'm going to throw you right away.'

'*Ei-yei!* Then bet the belt. See, mine is better than yours. It has turquoise in it.'

'All right.'

They piled up the stakes: three-fifty and a bow-guard against eleven-fifty, belt against belt. The belt was worth money, but it was ugly, Laughing Boy thought. He did not like this man. He knew how to dance improperly.

They stood face to face. They laid hands on each other. As he felt the man in his grasp, Laughing Boy saw all red. He and his enemy were alone in space with anger. He heaved with all his skill and strength, like one possessed. The other grunted and strained, then suddenly gave way — a fall.

Red Man arose puzzled and angry. He went at the next bout seriously. He would have liked to foul, but he was afraid of Hurries to War. Laughing Boy, staring over his opponent's shoulder, saw Slim Girl's face as she watched, half smiling. Again he ceased seeing, his jaws clamped fiercely together, he gripped close and lifted, then over — now! A fall, and a hard one.

Red Man was shaken, and came into the next bout without confidence. The fall he got was worse than the others.

'Take the goods,' Hill Singer told the winner.

'Put up your horse, and try again. You might get your belt back,' Laughing Boy mocked.

'We are going to play *Tset Dilth* on the fourth night, then bring your belts.' Red Man was feeling the back of his head.

'I shall be there.'

Laughing Boy gathered up his winnings. He looked around. Slim Girl had disappeared. He was hungry. He hunted up Jesting Squaw's Son.

'It is noon. Let us go eat.'

II

Many visitors were at the hogahns scattered about Tsé Lani. There was much food and much talk. Where they went, they reclined on sheepskins, while two small naked boys brought ears of corn as they were roasted, and calm women set broiled goats' ribs and corn bread before them. They ate at leisure, having a pleasant feeling of being at a party, yet at ease, and enjoying their appetites. Gossip was exchanged; they discussed crops, sheep, rain, and horses.

'I hear you have a horse to race,' a man said to Laughing Boy.

'Yes, I have a good one.'

'A man brought a tall bay over from Tsézhin; it is very fast, they say.'

'We shall see. I shall bet on my horse.'

'Where did you get your bow-guard?'

'I made it.'

'I'll give you six dollars for it.'

'I don't want to sell it.'

The man changed the subject. 'Did you hear about Red Goat? His wives put his saddle outside the door, they say.'

'What had he done?' somebody asked.

'He drank whiskey; he spent their money on it, so they say.'

'They were right, I think.'

'I have never tasted whiskey,' Laughing Boy said; 'what is it like?'

'It tastes bad, but one feels good. Then later one has a headache.'

'It sounds like *t'oghlepai.*'

'It is stronger. I'll give you eight dollars for that bow-guard.'

'I don't want to sell it; it is lucky.'

'That turquoise is no good, and the work is not very good.'

Laughing Boy looked bored. 'Give me a smoke, Grandfather.'

'The turquoise is too green. Eight dollars is a lot.'

'Eight dollars is nothing,' he answered loftily, with a pleasant remembrance of his winnings.

'Here, I have nine-fifty. That is all I have.' The man held out the money.

'No, I really do not want to sell. I would not sell it for a horse.'

'It is a fine bow-guard. If you make many things like that, you will get rich.'

Everything was well, Laughing Boy thought. He had money now, and a belt that was ugly, but could be sold to a trader for fifty dollars. People praised his work. That girl was only an incident; one should not let oneself be ruffled so easily.

It was good to lie in the sand talking a little, borrowing smokes now and then. Now that he had money, he would buy tobacco when he came to a trading post. Meantime he thought he would hunt up those two Americans to see if they would give him one of their big, white cigarettes. Perhaps they would buy his belt; they were travelling just for fun, people said; they must be rich. Perhaps, too, they would have sweet food, canned goods, and coffee with much sugar in it. He called his friend.

'Let us see if those Americans will buy my belt. Let us see what they will give us.'

'Good.'

They rode off sitting sideways on Jesting Squaw's Son's unsaddled horse, heels drumming softly on opposite sides, humming a song together.

III

The Americans, a rich Eastern tourist and his guide, were tired of feeding stray Indians, of whom there had been a plague all day. They set out to ignore these two who descended gravely upon them, but the double line of silver plaques about Laughing Boy's waist caught the tourist's eye.

'Ask him to let me see those belts,' he told the guide, and then, in baby-talk American's Navajo, 'Your belt — two — good.'

Laughing Boy sat down beside him. '*Nashto, shadani* — give me a smoke, brother-in-law.'

It is rude to call a man brother-in-law, and like most Navajos, he enjoyed using the term, and teaching it, to innocent foreigners. Americans were good fun. This one gave him a black cigar, cutting the end for him and holding out a match. It nearly killed him at the first whiff, only medicine-hogahn experience in swallowing smoke enabled him to keep a calm face.

'This is good!' He passed it over to his friend, who habitually inhaled deeply. 'It is like the magic tobacco Natinesthani gave the magician. We have nothing like this. Try it, elder brother.'

He tried it, cautiously at first, the tiniest puff, then a good lung-full that clutched his agonized insides like talons. Desperately he fought back tears and a choking cough, while Laughing Boy struggled with almost equal difficulty to keep a straight face. By a heroic effort he let the smoke out slowly. Then, with a sigh that disguised relief as critical enjoyment,

'Yes, little brother, that is very good tobacco.'

The tourist was fingering Laughing Boy's belts, pulling them around. The Indian thought of pulling in turn at his necktie, but decided it would be poor business.

'Ask him how much he wants for the one with the turquoise in it.'

'How much do you want for the one with the blues, Grandfather?' the guide asked.

'A horse, perhaps.' He puffed gingerly at the

cigar which Jesting Squaw's Son passed back to him.

'I'll offer you a nickel, perhaps.'

Both laughed.

'You say, how much.'

The formal gambits were over. The guide cocked his head, pursed his lips, and looked critical and rather disgusted. 'I'll give you twenty-five dollars.'

'No, no.'

'How much, then?'

He took it off. 'This is a good belt. These stones are good. The silver is heavy; Mexican silver. That is good work. Seventy-five dollars.'

The guide grunted, and threw a pinch of sand on it in token of its worthlessness.

'What does he say he wants?'

'He says seventy-five.'

'What's it worth?'

'Up to about sixty, I guess. Them's good stones.'

'Get it for less if you can.'

Laughing Boy passed the cigar back. His friend, who knew a little English, whispered, 'He says sixty, I think, that he will pay.' He blew out on the cigar to use up as much as was possible.

Laughing Boy asked the guide, 'Where do you come from?'

'From Besh Senil. We are going to the Moqui.'

'*Ei-yei!* That's far! Why do you want to see the Moqui?'

'We want to see them dance with snakes.'

'They are crazy to do that. Our dances are better.'

'Perhaps. Well, this man says your belt is pretty good, and he will give you forty for it. No more.'

'No, seventy, no less.' He buckled it on again.

'Perhaps we can give you forty-five, but that is all.'

Laughing Boy took the cigar again. It was a long time burning down. He wondered if he would die and be brought to life again, like the magician who smoked with Natinesthani.

'What does the Indian want?' the tourist asked.

'He still says seventy; it's too much.'

'Get it if you can.'

Laughing Boy whispered, 'What are they saying, Grandfather?'

'I'm not sure. That one who speaks Navajo says "too much," I think. The pink one says "get it."'

The guide spoke to them. 'This man says he will give you fifty because he likes your belt. He cannot give any more.'

'No, I do not want to sell. He does not want to

pay what it is worth, he is just talking about wanting it.' The cigar was done at last. He rose.

'Oh, give him what he wants!'

'How much, Grandfather? You say.'

'Sixty-five, perhaps.'

'He says sixty-five. Looks like he won't come down no lower.'

'I'll take it.'

'He says he'll take it.'

Laughing Boy handed over the belt. 'Grandfather, do you know this paper money?'

Jesting Squaw's Son considered the bills. 'Yes, these with tracks here in the corners are fives. These with little sticks and the man with long hair and the ugly mouth on them are ones. This with the yellow back, I do not know it. I think it is no good.' He had been stung once on cigar coupons.

At last the sum was made up, with ones, fives, and the silver dollars which they preferred.

'Ask that man,' Laughing Boy told the guide, 'to give us another of those big, black cigarettes. They are good.'

The guide translated.

'My God! I thought it would make them sick. Here's one for each of them.'

'Good. Now, Grandfather, give me some cigarette papers.'

The guide forked up. As they shook hands all around, elaborately, Navajo fashion, the Americans' faces and voices seemed to grow very distant and uncertain. Riding away, Laughing Boy sighed deeply.

'Let us go to a quiet place. I want to be sick.'

'I too.'

Later, at sunset, they went to wash at the pool, dipping up liquid silver and lilac in their hands. They lay back against the rock watching the sun go down, the shadows and lights on the water, the distant fires and people moving. They had slept, they felt very empty, clean, and peaceful.

'Shall we try making a cigarette with that tobacco?'

'Not yet, I think. Go tend your horse. It is time to eat again.'

'I go. I hope there will be much gambling after this.'

CHAPTER III

I

THE dance of the second night was much like that of the first, although perhaps a little less exuberant. He entered once more into the river of song, and was happy, yelling his head off, save that he kept on being conscious of that girl. While she was dancing, he would forget about her, but when he saw her looking for another partner, he would be uneasy until she had made her choice. He noticed that she did not dance with Red Man. Halfway between midnight and dawn, the women having departed, he fell out, to sleep by a fire.

They rode down to Ane'é Tseyi that day, where the dance of the final night would be held. He rode behind Jesting Squaw's Son's saddle, leading the mare. He hoped they would find a place with some grass for the animal, and reflected that in any case, now, he could afford to buy corn. The long, hot ride, hot sun, hot wind, unrelieved, weighed on them somewhat, combining with lack of sleep to make limbs sluggish and eyes heavy. It was a relief to ride into the narrow cañon of their destination, to rest in a strip of afternoon shade. Laughing Boy took the horses down to the windmill for water, and staked them out in a corner where uncropped spears of grass stood singly, each inches from the next, in brown sand. A beaten track toward an oak tree and a break in the rock caught his eye. A spring, perhaps.

He followed it. Behind the oak, currant bushes grew in a niche of red rock like the fold of a giant curtain. At the back was a full-grown, lofty fir. A spring, surely. Behind the fir a cleft opened at shoulder height into transparent shadow. The footholds were worn to velvety roundness in the sandstone; at one side a pecked design showed that long before the Navajos had swooped upon the land, a people of an elder earth had known this entrance. Laughing Boy climbed lightly in.

It was a stone-lined pocket, scarce twenty feet across, narrower at the top. One went forward along a ledge at one side, shouldering against young aspens, then slid down a rock face into a curving bowl, with a seep at one lip from which silent water oozed over moss and cress into the bottom. Spears of grass grew in cracks. By the tiny pool of water in the bowl was a square of soft turf with imprints of moccasins. He squatted there, leaning back against the rock. Here was all shade and peace, soft, grey stone, dark, shadowed green, coolness, and the sweet smell of dampness. He dabbled his hands, wet his face, drank a little. He rolled a cigarette with crumpled cigar tobacco. This was good, this was beautiful.

Away above, the intolerant sky gleamed, and a corner of cloud was white fire. His eyes shifting lightly, the edge of the rocks above took on a glowing halo. He amused himself trying to fit it back again, to get the spot the cloud made back against the cloud, playing tricks with his half-closed eyelashes that made things seem vague.

'*Ahalani!*' The two-toned greeting came from a voice like water.

He returned to himself with a start. Slim Girl stood poised on the edge of the bowl, above his shoulder, water-basket in hand.

'*Ahalani, shicho.*' Dignified, casual.

'Move over, wrestler, I want to come down.'

He observed her small feet in their red, silver-buttoned buckskin, sure and light on the rocks as a goat's. She seemed to be hours descending. She was business-like about filling the basket, but she turned utilitarian motions into part of a dance. Now she knelt, not two feet from him, taking him in with the long, mischievous eyes that talked and laughed.

She is a butterfly, he thought, or a humming-bird. Why does she not go away? I will not go — run away from her. He thought, as he tried to read her face, that her slimness was deceptive; strength came forth from her.

'Now, for ten cents, I go.'

He blinked. 'I save that to get rid of you to-night, perhaps.'

'I do not dance to-night. There is trouble, a bad thing. I come from far away.'

He thought he had better not ask questions. 'To-morrow there will be horse-racing, a chicken-pull, perhaps.'

'And you have a fine horse to race, black, with a white star and a white sock.' He grunted astonishment. She smiled. 'You are a good jeweler, they say. You made that bow-guard. You sold Red Man's belt to the American, they say, for sixty-five dollars.'

'You are like an old wife, trying to find out about everything a man is doing.'

'No, I am not like an old wife.'

They looked at each other for a long time. No, she was not like an old wife. Blood pounded in his ears and his mouth was dry. He pulled at the end of his dead cigarette. At length,

'You should stay for the racing. There will be fine horses, a beautiful sight.'

'I shall stay, perhaps.'

Her rising, her ascent of the rock, were all one quick motion. She never looked back. He stayed, not exactly in thought, but experiencing a condition of mind and feeling. Loud laughter of women roused him, to pass them with averted eyes and go forth dazed into the sunlight.

II

The last night of the dance was a failure for Laughing Boy, for all its ritual. He tried to join the singing, but they were not the kind of songs he wanted; he tried to concentrate on the prayer that was being brought to a climax, but he wanted to pray by himself. He quit the dance, suddenly very much alone as he left the noise and the light behind him, strongly conscious of himself, complete to himself. He followed a sheep trail up a break in one cañon wall, to the rim, then crossed the narrow mesa to where he could look down over the broad Ties Hatsosi Valley, a great pool of night, and far-distant, terraced horizon of mesas against the bright stars, cool, alone, with the sound of the drumming and music behind him, faint as memory. This also was a form of living.

He began to make up a new song, but lost interest in it, feeling too centred upon himself. He sat noticing little things, whisper of grass, turn of a leaf — little enough there is in the desert at night.

'*Yota zhil-de tlin-sha-igahl . . .*'

His song came upon him.

'*A-a-a-ainé, ainé,*
I ride my horse down from the high hills
To the valley, *a-a-a.*
Now the hills are flat. Now my horse will not go
From your valley, *a-a-a.*
Hainéya, ainé, o-o-o-o.'

Slim Girl sat down beside him. His song trailed off, embarrassed. They rested thus, without words, looking away into the night while contemplation flowed between them like a current. At length she raised one hand, so that the bracelets clinked.

'Sing that song.'

He sang without effort. This was no common woman, who ignored all convention. The long-drawn '*Hainéya, ainé, o-o-o-o,*' fell away into the lake of darkness; silence shut in on them again.

On the heels of his song he said, 'My eldest uncle is here. I am going to speak to him tomorrow.'

'I should not do that if I were you.'

He rolled a cigarette with careful movements, but forbore to light it. Again they sat watching the motionless stars above the shrouded earth. No least breeze stirred; there were no details to be seen in the cliffs or the valley, only the distant silhouettes against the sky. A second time her hand rose and her bracelets clinked, as though speech unannounced would startle the universe.

'You are sure you are going to speak to your uncle, then?'

'Yes.' The second self that is a detached mentor in one's mind recognized that he would never have talked this way with any other woman. Etiquette had been left behind down in the narrowness of Ane'é Tseyi.

'Perhaps you will listen to what he says, I think; perhaps you will not. Perhaps your mind is made up now.'

'I am thinking about what I intend to do. I shall not change.'

'We shall see then. Good-bye.'

She rose like smoke. He called a startled 'Good-bye,' then began to follow at a distance. He stopped at the rim of the cañon, where the noise of singing that welled up from below passed him by as he stood watching her dark form, down to the bottom, along by the grove where his camp was, and beyond into the shadows.

He went back to the far edge of the mesa. He did not want to sleep, not ever again.

'Now with a god I walk,
Now I step across the summits of the mountains,
Now with a god I walk,

Striding across the foothills.
Now on the old age trail, now on the path of beauty
wandering.
In beauty — *Hozoji, hozoji, hozoji, hozoji-i.*'

The deep resonance of the prayer carried his exaltation through the land. Then he began to analyse her words, finding in them nothing save unconventionality, no promise, and his own he found laggard and dull. Was she playing with him, or did she mean all he read into her brevity? Was she thus with other men?

'I ride my horse down from the high hills
To the valley, *a-a-a* . . .'

He was up and down, restless, no longer on the path of beauty, yet tormented by a new beauty. Far away, high-pitched, he heard the faint '*Yo-o galeana, yo-o galeana,*' and the thudding drum. He walked to and fro. My mind is made up, I shall make things as they should be. Now with a god I walk — or is it a game, looseness?

Suddenly he fled to sleep for refuge, rolling in his blanket by a high place under thickly clustered, brilliant, unhelpful stars, falling asleep with the feeling of vastness about him and clean, gracious silence.

III

He woke to a feeling of expectation, and made his Dawn Prayer with all the gladness that his religion prescribed. He could not wait to see his uncle and have the matter settled before they went to the trading post for the races. At the same time, his own certainty told him that his eldest uncle, his mother, and all her kin were only wanted to ratify a decision already made. What was, was; he would announce what he wanted to do, not ask for permission.

Now he stood on the rim above the cañon, bathed in sunlight, while below him in thick, visible shadow unimportant people moved, horses stamped, smoke rose from tiny fires.

His uncle was staying down by the trading post with Killed a Navajo. He started off without breakfast, leading the pony, and sorely tempted to mount and gallop those few miles, but the thought of the race and the pleasure of winning restrained him. I'll win for Slim Girl, he thought with a smile, and burst into song, lustily pouring forth keen delight from tough lungs over the empty flat. The dusty walk and hot sun, the heat that lay over the baked adobe and dull sage-brush, troubled him not at all. The bleak, grey parts of the desert have a quintessential quality of privacy, and yet one has space there to air one's mood. So Laughing Boy sang loudly, his horse nosed his back, a distant turtle-dove mocked him, and a high-sailing, pendent buzzard gave him up as far too much alive.

Killed a Navajo's hogahn was well built, of thick-laid evergreens over stout piñon poles. Looking in through the wide door one was conscious of cool darkness flecked with tiny spots of light, a central brilliance under the smoke-hole, vague outlines of reclining figures, their feet, stretched towards the centre, grotesquely clear. He stood in the doorway. Some one spoke to him, 'Come in.' He shook hands all round. They offered him a little coffee, left over from breakfast, and tobacco. He made himself comfortable on the sheepskins beside his uncle in the place of honour.

One by one the family went about their work; the children to tend the sheep, Killed a Navajo down to the store where he did odd jobs, and was needed to-day for distributing free food, his younger wife to preparing a meal for the many guests expected that day, his first wife to weaving, outside. Laughing Boy's cigarette smoke went up in shadow, was caught in a pencil of sunlight, disappeared, and gleamed once again before it seeped through the roof. A suggestion of a breeze rustled the green walls. He studied his uncle's face — big and massive, with heavy, high-bridged nose and deep furrows enclosing the wide, sure mouth. Under the blue turban wisps of hair showed a little grey. Across his cheek-bone ran the old scar from which he took his name, Wounded Face. It was an old eagle's head. Laughing Boy was a little afraid of it.

'My uncle.'

'Yes, my child.' The old-fashioned, round silver earrings shimmered faintly.

'I have been thinking about something.'

They smoked on. A black-and-white kid slipped in the door, leaped up and poised itself on the cantle of a saddle. Outside was the rhythmic thump-thump-thump of a weaver pounding down the threads in her loom. A distant child laughed, some one was chopping wood — sounds of domesticity.

'I have been thinking about a wife.'

'You are old enough. It is a good thing.'

He finished his cigarette.

'You know that Slim Girl? The one who wears so much hard goods? She danced the first two nights.'

'She is a school-girl.' The tone was final. 'She was taken away to that place, for six years.'

'That is all right. I like her.'

'That is not all right. I do not know how she came to be allowed to dance. They made her stop. Water Singer let her dance, but we stopped him. She is bad. She lives down by the railroad.

She is not of the People any more, she is American. She does bad things for the Americans.'

'I do not know what you mean, but I know her, that girl. She is not bad. She is good. She is strong. She is for me.'

'You come from away up there; you do not know about these things. Nor do you know her. What is her clan?'

'I do not know.'

'Well? And what makes you think you can go out and pick a wife for yourself like this? The next thing I know, you will jump into the fire. I tell you, she is all bad; for two bits she will do the worst thing.'

Laughing Boy sat up suddenly. 'You should not have said that, you should not have thought it. Now you have said too much. I hope that bad thing follows you around always. Now you have said too much. Ugh! This place is too small for me!'

He ran outside. He needed space. People were beginning to arrive; there was laughing and shouting around the trading post. He went off rapidly to get by himself, too proud to run before people. His mind was boiling; he wanted to hit something, he was all confused. This way he went on until at last he reached a small butte that offered protection. He tore around the corner.

Slim Girl was walking towards him, cool and collected. Her brows rose in surprise as she stopped. He came up to her uncertainly.

'Sit down; there is shade here.' They faced each other. 'You have seen your uncle.'

His hand fell forward in the gesture of assent.

'And he spoke to you.'

'He said bad things. I am angry with him.'

'And towards me?'

'You came here on purpose to meet me.'

'Yes; I knew that when you had seen your uncle, you should see me soon.'

'What my uncle said will stay with him. He has made a bad thing, it will follow him. The track of an evil thought is crooked and has no end; I do not want it around me; I do not keep it going. I have only good thoughts about you.'

'Your mother will never send some one to ask for me. You must just come with me.'

'Wait; what is your clan?'

'I am a Bitahni; and you?'

'Tahtchini; so that is all right. But I have nothing to give your mother, only one horse.'

'I have no parents; they died when I was at school. I belong to myself. All this' — she raised the necklaces, turquoise, coral, white shell and silver, one by one, then let them fall back together — 'is mine. All this' — she touched her rings, and shook her braceletted wrists — 'and much more is mine. They left it for me. Now I do a little work for the missionary's wife there at Chiziai; she pays me money, so I grow richer. I shall give you silver to make jewelry, and I shall weave, and you shall have fine horses. You can make money with them, and we shall be rich together.'

The long, talking eyes looked into his now, with nothing hidden. He felt her strength, this woman who could talk so straight, who made the direct road seem the only sensible one. It ceased to be strange that they sat and talked about love, while elopement became obvious and commonplace in a scheme of things the whole of which was suddenly miraculous.

After a while she said, 'We shall go to-night, after the races.'

He reflected. 'No, I came here to gamble. I told Red Man I would play against him. If I do not do it, he will say I am afraid.'

'He is crooked; he will take your money.'

'That makes no difference; I cannot back down now. If I let this go because I was afraid to lose, what would I be? If I refused because of you, what kind of a man should I be for you?'

He saw that he had spoken well.

'It will be time for the races soon; you must go. I go the other way round.'

He was in a new and more profound daze returning, but yards that had seemed miles were passed as inches. He floated over the ground, he was a walking song.

CHAPTER IV

I

THE horse-races were to be held in the latter part of the afternoon; during the hottest time almost everybody took a siesta, while those who were entering horses tended to them. Jesting Squaw's Son joined Laughing Boy in going over the black pony. They discussed the other entries, agreeing that competition would be severe. A man from Navajo Mountain, in old-fashioned fringed buckskin shirt and high leggins, had brought a dun mare, said to be swift as thought. Jesting Squaw's Son had seen her; she moved beautifully, he said. From Tsézhin came the undefeated bay, and the local contender, a big iron-grey, had a good reputation. Its sire was an American stallion, it was long in the quarters, and relatively heavy-boned; Laughing Boy thought that in a short race-course — the usual Navajo track is under a quarter of a mile — it could not do justice to itself.

Laughing Boy planned to bet a little on the saddle-changing race, and put the rest of his money on himself. His friend would bet here and there, though mostly on him.

'Are you going into the chicken-pull?' Jesting Squaw's Son asked.

'Why not? That one race won't tire my pet.'

'But the chicken-pull will come first, they say.'

'That's bad. Why is that?'

'That man from Tsézhin, his horse got loose, they say. He is out tracking it. So your race will be held last, to let him be in it.'

'The devil! Then I can't go in the chicken-pull. I won't risk having something happen to spoil this one. And you?'

'I shall go in.'

All the time they talked so, Laughing Boy was thinking, how do I do this? I am talking about the same things, thinking about them. And I am the man who is going away with that girl to-morrow. I am going away with Slim Girl. I feel like shouting. I am not as all these people.

Jesting Squaw's Son noticed something in his manner. 'You seem very eager, my friend.'

'Why not? Is not all well? I trade everything I have, two ponies, a blanket, five dollars, for this one because I love a fine pony, because I think this one is better than all that. Then I come down here, and right away I make nearly ninety dollars, when I began with nothing. Now we have a race. Nothing is more beautiful than galloping as hard as you can. I do this thing, that I love, on this pony that I bought for pleasure, where many people'—and one person, oh, beautiful!—'may see and speak well of me. If I win, I double my money, for doing what I enjoy. If I lose, it is only what I never had until yesterday.'

And whatever happens, I have won more than all the money and hard goods in the world.

He meant what he said. Jesting Squaw's Son nodded.

There was a shot. The pony jumped. Then two shots together, from somewhere over to the right. Hastily tethering the animal, they raced to their camp to get their bows. People were running all about; women gathering around the camp-fires, packing up bundles, men snatching their weapons and making towards the noise. Three more shots had been fired, about ten seconds apart. The men did not rush towards the firing as Americans would; they went rapidly, but keeping a sharp lookout, and ready to take cover. Some one shouted that a Hopi had killed a Navajo; some one else called that it was Americans. Now they heard a burst of quick shooting, both rifles and revolvers, at a greater distance. Topping a slight ridge, the two friends saw the Navajos just ahead, nearly a hundred already, in an irregular, slightly crescent-shaped line. They came up and pushed to the front. No one was talking.

About twenty paces in front, facing the crescent, stood Tall Old One, the district headman, and an American from the agency in army hat, riding-breeches, and leather leggins. The American had a rifle and a revolver. Behind these two, in open order, stood Man Hammer and Left Hand, policemen, and a Hopi and a Tewa policeman, all with rifles. The latter two wore parts of khaki uniforms. Over to one side a Navajo leant against a tree, looking sick. Blood ran down his sleeve and dripped from his fingers; at his feet lay a revolver. Farther back another policeman, Mud's Son, stood guard over a handcuffed Navajo, and, partly hidden by a clump of bushes, somebody was stretched out on the ground.

The American official and the Hopi were acutely conscious of the fact that several hundred Navajos were thinking that these aliens had started something, and if only the native officials would step aside it might as well be finished now. They also knew that those same officials were aware of this feeling, and sympathized with it. There were a couple of dozen rifles and revolvers in the crowd, and at that range a bow is just as effective. The Indians were all looking at the wounded man; he made an ugly exhibit.

The Tewa policeman shifted from foot to foot and grinned. The situation might become serious, but he thought it would work out all right, and he devoutly hoped for an arrest involving a fist-fight with a Navajo. Tewas punch; Navajos kick, scratch, and pull hair. For several centuries the Tewas' official profession was fighting Navajos.

Nobody knew quite what had happened. A Navajo was arrested, and one was wounded. There was a dead man, but they couldn't see of what tribe. The older men hoped there would be no trouble; nothing to bring soldiers into the reservation; the younger braves all wanted to start something. Men began to sidle off to the left and right, slowly carrying the horns of the crescent farther around the police. In time, they would have them surrounded.

Tall Old One called: 'Wait! Make no mistake! Everything is well and you have no cause to be angry.'

They obeyed him, and the tension relaxed slightly.

A man said, 'There come some more people.'

Another cried, 'An American is hurt!'

People felt better immediately.

'Two Americans — look!'

They began to talk excitedly, and some of them smiled. The government man let out a sigh and threw his gun across his left arm. Man Hammer said something cheerful to Left Hand.

The newcomers arrived from the direction of the burst of shots that had been fired last. Thin American, the trader from Tséchil, and an unknown Navajo supported between them a badly wounded man who swore slowly and steadily. Behind them a Tewa supported another American official, who limped.

They set the wounded men down by the handcuffed Navajo, the Tewa lined up beside his fellow tribesman, and Thin American came to talk with the official. After a minute of discussion, he interpreted to Tall Old One.

The headman stepped forward.

'Hear me, my friends. You know how bad it is to drink whiskey, how it makes you crazy. You know how Washindon has forbidden it. Now the American here, this man whom you have seen brought in, came here to sell it. That Navajo' — he pointed to the handcuffed one — 'came with him. That was bad. So American Chief sent these Americans and policemen to stop it.'

As he talked, Thin American translated to the agency man.

'Already one man was drunk; that wounded one over there by the tree. See what it did for him. When we started to arrest them, he began to shoot. He killed that Hopi you see back there.'

So it was a Hopi killed. There were more smiles.

'Now he and this man, the one who helped to

sell it, and that man must all go to jail. You know it is right. There is nothing to upset you; there is nothing to spoil your races. After all, there has been a Hopi killed, and two Americans wounded; now an American and two Navajos go to jail for a little while. That is not so bad.'

The trader suppressed a smile as he skipped translating this last remark, saying only, 'He's letting 'em think that Indian will only get a light sentence for shooting the policeman. Best leave it at that.'

Older men remarked, 'That is right, that is well said. Let us have no trouble.' Some of the young men grumbled, but others asked them, 'What would you do? You can't fight Washindon. Do you want them to send soldiers in here again? Shall we go into exile again?' It was news, an incident, something to talk about. The crowd became just a lot of people, watching the first aid, and talkative.

'Have the Hopi and Tewas take off that dead man,' the trader advised; 'they'll never forgive you if you leave a corpse for them to take care of; spoil their party and make 'em leave. They're plumb scared to death of a corpse. Look how those Navajo policemen are edging away from it.'

Horses were brought up, the wounded and prisoners mounted. The Pueblo policemen slung their comrade's body across a saddle. The party rode off, leaving Tall Old One and the local police to return to their games.

The first Tewa remarked to the other, 'No fight.'

'No. But it would have been more shooting, anyhow.'

'Some day, perhaps, we arrest an American, unwounded.'

'Some day, perhaps.'

They looked at their knuckles.

II

The two friends returned to the pony.

'What is this whiskey?' Jesting Squaw's Son asked. 'I am always hearing talk about it. They say it is so bad, yet they try so hard to get it.'

'I do not know. They all say it is very bad. It makes you crazy, they say. It must be like eating jimpson-weed I think.'

'It made that man crazy. He tried to fight alone.'

'M-m. It made him brave, I think. But it stopped his sense. When a thing like that happens, a number of men coming against you, you run away first. Then you can get behind something and start shooting.'

'Anyhow, he killed a Hopi.'

'*Ei-yei!* He shot straight! But jail is very bad, they say.'

'Well, that's just for a few months, and he will have that to think about. When he comes back, people will think well of him.'

The call sounded for the first race, which was the saddle-changing relay. They separated in the crowd, which split into two parties according to whom it backed. Laughing Boy put two dollars on a group of active young men with a short-coupled pony that looked as if it could turn smartly and not get flustered.

The ponies were saddled and mounted. The cinch-strap was carried through the ring of the girth, then up to the horn, where the rider held it fast with one hand, a finger of which also hooked in the reins. The other hand held a quirt ready to strike. The men were stripped to breech-clout and moccasins, slender, golden-brown bodies, the bodies of perfect boys, under the dark colour a glow of red showing through.

Now! The ponies scampered, people shouted. The horsemen flashed to earth, bringing their saddles with them, the ponies were wheeled around. Bare arms and backs rippled as the new saddles were swung on, the cinch-strap caught through, held to the horn by the same hand on which the new rider swung as he leaped to the saddle, the horse already in motion under him.

A man's foot slipped. Every one laughed and cheered. It was a close race. Now the last men were mounting. The one on the team Laughing Boy was backing lost his grip on the strap, and the saddle turned under him. He wrenched it back, throwing his weight in the stirrups, then clinched his legs under the horse's belly. But he had thrown his mount out of its stride, and he lost by a good length. They laughed more, and called jokes to him,

'Grease on your fingers, Grandfather! You should have held the strap in your teeth!'

Laughing Boy went to pay his bet. They were organizing the chicken-pull. The chicken was a salt-bag half full of dirt. A piece of blue cloth tied around its neck was the head; two bits of red at the bottom corners were the legs. Whoever threw the head over the line, a hundred yards away, won five dollars; each of the legs brought two.

Laughing Boy drifted around the edge of the crowd, gay and excited. Never had there been such a four days! He had an eye out for Slim Girl, and saw her at last, sitting slightly apart from a group of women. Their eyes met, then he moved away.

Red Man hailed him. 'You are racing a horse, Grandfather?'

'Yes.'

'I hope you win. I shall take it all away from you to-night.'

'All right.'

He turned out of the crowd to avoid him; the man made him feel disagreeable. Towards him walked a pinto pony with too-long ears, carrying Half Man, his father's brother. Laughing Boy watched him sorrowfully as he approached, considering the withered arm and leg, the wasted appearance of this man, and remembering Wolf Killer, the tall, cheerful brave he had known as a boy, before the Ute arrow grazed the right side of his head and, by some strange Ute magic, shrivelled the left side of his body.

'*Ahalani*, nephew. Are you here alone?'

'Yes. It is good to see you.'

'Are all well?'

'All are well, but there has been very little rain this spring.'

'Too bad. The chicken-pull is starting. Aren't you in it?'

'I have only one horse; that I am riding in the last race.'

'You should be in it. I should have been in it at your age. This horse is all right; take it.'

He dismounted clumsily, taking a walking-stick from behind the saddle. Laughing Boy felt his eyes sting.

'*Ukehé*, Thank you.'

Navajos almost never say thank you, save in return for very great favours; ordinary gifts and kindnesses are offered and accepted in silence. They regard our custom as obsequious. The word was startled out of Laughing Boy by the occasion. Half Man understood, and avoided his nephew's gaze as he limped away, the fingers of his useless arm hooked into the front of his silver belt.

The chicken was buried in loose earth, so that just enough of the neck of the sack stuck up to let one get a good grip. A referee stood near, armed with a long horsehair quirt; as each horseman rode past, he swung full force across the animal's rump, thus ensuring an honest gallop. Laughing Boy cantered up in his turn, tried to hold his pony in, felt it leap to the smack of the whip, and reached too late for the prize. He watched the next few tries, rode back, argued with Slender Hair about his place, and went at it again. He was leaning well down from the saddle before the quirt fell, he could have touched the ground with his fingers. Smack! and the pony jumped slightly sideways. The chicken was out of reach. He swung back to his seat and rested. Horse after horse came by, well in hand, then leaped to the stroke of the whip, or shied away from it. The horsemen swooped, swinging incredibly low, reaching amazingly far out, in a haze of dust.

Ya-hai! E-ya-hai! Ei-yei! Straight Fingers had it. Straight Fingers galloped for the line. All the young men rose in their saddles, their elbows were spread forward, their knees clutched, their quirts fell on willing ponies. Those who had been waiting just for this headed him off, the others caught up with him. It became a big, spinning wheel of mounted braves, horses' tossing heads, and dust. Laughing Boy saw Straight Fingers just ahead of him, clinging to the chicken's head, while some one else held both its legs. He took a lick at the next horse in front of him, saw it carom, and reached for the prize, yelling. Somebody cracked him over the head with the butt of a quirt; somebody else tried to pull him off. He defended himself, wrestling with the man who had grabbed him, while the two ponies plunged, then both let go as the mob swirled away from them.

Straight Fingers broke away, and threw the head over the line. Somebody else threw over both legs. Laughing Boy and the stranger, a young fellow with a mustache, laughed at each other.

'This has been a lovely day!' said the young man.

'Yes, a perfect day!'

'Aren't you the man from T'o Tlakai who has a horse to race? Is *that* the horse?'

'I'm the man. This is not the horse.'

And I am the man whom that girl loves, I am the man who is going away with the magic girl.

III

The man from Tsézhin had found his horse; now the last race was called. Laughing Boy placed everything except his bow-guard in bets. If he won, he would have nearly two hundred dollars. Now he stripped off his clothes to his breech-clout, settled his headband, and adjusted the light hackamore around his horse's nose.

They gathered at the starting place, good horses and eager, with shiny coats, erect ears, and quick, small hooves. Hurries to War, the starting judge, cautioned them. Laughing Boy saw Slim Girl, halfway down the track, watching him.

Here I am doing just this, and these others do not know who I am. They do not know they are racing against the man who goes with her tomorrow. Oh, I must win, I want to win, I must win!

He made a very brief prayer, and patted his pony's neck. 'Little sister, we must win. Do not fail me.'

They mounted. He felt the warm, silky hide between his knees, pushed her up to the reins and felt the play of muscles. Counting for the start;

he leant forward, held his breath, raised his quirt. Go!

Arrows from the bow — no other simile. At the tearing gallop, flat-stretched, backs are level, the animals race in a straight line; all life is motion; there is no body, only an ecstasy; one current between man and horse, and still embodied, a whip hand to pour in leather and a mouth to shout. Speed, speed, but the near goal is miles away, and other speed spirits on either side will not fall back.

E-é-é-é-é! His left hand, held forward, would push the horse through slack reins, his heels under her belly would lift her clear of the ground. *E-é-é-é-é!*

A quiet, elderly Indian let his hand fall. The ponies cantered, trotted, were turned and walked back to the finish.

'The black mare was first.'

He rode off to his camp, to dress. We won. I am rich. Was there ever such a day? And to-morrow I go with that girl. Oh, beautiful! I wish it were to-morrow now. About a hundred and eighty dollars. My pet, my little black pet, well done. I wish it were to-morrow.

CHAPTER V

I

LAUGHING BOY went off alone to wrestle with gods: Slim Girl turned to loneliness as a tried friend and counsellor. To be with herself, complete to herself, that was familiar reality; distraction and strangeness was to be among many, to consult. On a high place she sat down to think, not facing the greatness of the desert, but where she could look on her gathered people, made small and impersonal below her. Long habit and self-training had made her cool and contained; she did not like to admit that she had need of mere emotion, and when she did allow herself a luxury of feeling, it had to be where none could spy on her. It was not that she would make any demonstration; she just did not want to be looked at when she was not quite mistress of herself. Now her isolated, high position put a physical difference between her impulses and those of the people in the valley, making them visibly superior. She lit a cigarette and relaxed.

If she did not watch out, she would love this man. She did not intend to love any one; had she not learned enough of that? He was necessary to her; he was the perfect implement delivered to her hands; he was an axe with which to hew down the past; he was a light with which to see her way back to her people, to the good things of her people. She held him up against the past, matrons and teachers at school, platitudes and well-meaning lies. And now, for all their care and training and preaching, she was 'going back to the blanket,' because under the blanket were the things worth while, and all the rest was hideous. With her knowledge and experience, with what the Americans had taught her, she would lead this man, and make for them both the most perfect life that could be made — with an Indian, a long-haired, heathen Indian, a blanket Indian, a Navajo, the names thrown out like an insult in the faces of those who bore them, of her own people, Denné, The People, proud as she was proud, and clear of heart as she could never be.

There were to be no mistakes, and no chances. She could tie this man to her as surely as any prisoner; she would follow her clear plan to its victorious end. She had conquered herself, she had conquered circumstance; emerging from the struggle not American, not Indian, mistress of herself. Now from the Americans she took means, and in the Indians would achieve her end. Not such an amazing end, perhaps, but strange enough for her: a home in the Northern desert, and children, in a place where the agent's men never came to snatch little children from their parents and send them off to school. They would be Navajo, all Navajo, those children, when the time came. This was her revenge, that all the efforts of all those very different Americans, to drag her up or to drag her down into the American way, in the end would be only tools to serve a Navajo end.

It made her happy to think of that man, Laughing Boy. He was more than just what that name implied; one felt the warrior under the gaiety, and by his songs and his silver, he was an artist. All Navajo, even to his faults, he would teach her the meaning of those oft-repeated phrases, '*bik'ê hojoni*, the trail of beauty'; through him she would learn the content, and she would provide the means.

Yes, this was her man, as though he had been made expressly for her, strong, straight, gay, a little stubborn. He had character, she would develop it. And she would bind him. There would be no second wife in her hogahn.

'Patience,' she told herself; 'you are not in the Northern desert yet. You have a long road to travel yet, full of ambushes.'

She had no intention of herding sheep and slaving away her youth in a few years of hard labour, herding sheep, hoeing corn, packing firewood, growing square across the hips and flat in the face and heavy in the legs. No; she had seen the American women. First there was money; the Americans must serve her a little while yet; then, after that, the unmapped cañons, and the Indians who spoke no English.

She sat perfectly still, looking at nothing and hating Americans. She had not turned herself loose like this in a long time. Some young man, far below, was singing a gay song about the owl that turned her thoughts to Laughing Boy; she relaxed and smiled. This was something happy to think of. He came like the War God in the song, she thought, and began to sing it haltingly, not sure of the exact words —

> 'Now Slayer of Enemy Gods, alone I see him coming;
> Down from the skies, alone I see him coming.
> His voice sounds all about. *Lé-é!*
> His voice sounds, divine. *Lé-é!*'

That is he, she thought, Slayer of Enemy Gods. He would be shocked to hear me say it, to hear a woman sing that song.

She went on to the formal ending, 'In beauty it is finished, in beauty it is finished,' then changed it, 'In beauty it is begun. In beauty it is begun. Thanks.'

That is a good religion, as good as Christianity. I wonder if I can learn to believe in it? One needs some religion. At least, I can get good out of its ideas. If he is that god, what am I? White Shell Woman? Changing Woman, perhaps. I must mould and guide this War God I have made. I must not let him get away from me. None of the bad things must happen; I must make no mistakes. I am not a Navajo, nor am I an American, but the Navajos are my people.

II

The sun was low; the shadow sides of cliffs became deep pools of violet seeping out across the sand. She rose and drew her blanket about her, composing herself for contacts with intrusive humanity. Down the steep trail her little, moccasined feet sought the sure footholds lightly. Above her feet, the clumsy deerskin leggins were thick; the heavy blanket gave a quaint stiffness to her body. Wrapped so, her feet and head and slender hands alone showing, she became pathetically small, a wisp; but her thoughtful eyes were not pathetic.

The American guide hailed her as she passed his camp, using her school name, 'Hi, there, Lily!' She dismissed him with a measuring glance that made his backbone feel cool.

'God-damnedest la-dee-dah squaw I ever run acrost!'

She had little appetite, but camped with a group of distant relatives all too ready to look askance at her, she took pains to do the normal, which was to sup well. She helped with the cooking, dipped into the pot of mutton, drank coffee, then rolled a cigarette. The Indians joked and laughed without reducing the speed of their eating. Chunks of meat and bits of squash were scooped, dripping, from the pot, to be compounded with bread into appalling, mouth-filling tidbits. Three coffee cups and a Hopi bowl served for all to drink in turn; a large spoon was purely a cooking implement. They sprawled on a half-circle of sheepskins within the open brush shelter, facing the fire, chattering and joking. Still in holiday mood, they heaped the blaze high, lighting up the circle and throwing lights that were ruddy, soft shadows on the bushes roundabout.

Some of them prepared to sleep. Visitors dropped in; more coffee was made. Slim Girl drew apart, into the darkness, and rolled up. Over there, a chink of light showed in the blanketed door of a big, earth-covered winter hogahn. Singing came out of it, rollicking, running songs. They were gambling there; Laughing Boy would soon be penniless. She smiled at the thought of him and his stubbornness. The bushes rustled faintly. From where she lay, she could see a clump of yucca in a fixed pattern against the sky. The voices by the fire became distant. The stars stooped near.

'In beauty it is begun. In beauty it is begun. Thanks.'

CHAPTER VI

I

At first light, before dawn, the desert is intimate, and each man feels the presence of others as an intrusion. Blinding colour has not supplanted soft greys, uncertain forms; cliffs harsh by daylight, and thunderous-walled cañons loom soft with wells of coolness. The east is white — mother-of-pearl — the world is secret to each one's self.

Slim Girl, sitting apart, watching the slow increase of visible forms, looked towards the gambling hogahn. She heard them announce sunrise with the Magpie Song, and, after the last ringing 'It dawns, it dawns,' saw the straight dark forms coming out, moving away; some alone, some together talking, their voices intruding upon the hushed world.

She rose to intercept the path of one. He stood before her, answering her smile with a smile, tall and straight and shameless as he let his blanket fall to show — no silver belt, no jewelry, only the lucky bow-guard on his left wrist.

'Take this bow-guard, now, to keep. By first cold moon you will hear from me again. My uncles will look for you, or I shall.'

'So they won everything?'

'Everything.'

'Horse, belt, money?'

'Horse, belt, money. I go to T'o Tlakai to make silver.'

'You were foolish.'

'What else could I have done? And it was fine play! I was happy. We sang, all night we sang. We made new songs about ourselves. Now I must work.'

She was prepared for this. 'You are not a man yet, I think.'

That gave him a start. 'Why do you say that? That is not a good thing to say.' Losing the goods meant little, but if losing them meant losing her, the world was a loom of lies.

'You are like a child. You are happy now, so you forget what you wanted before.'

'What thing?'

'Where is the love-song now? "Now my horse will not go From your valley, *a-a-a*,"' she sang.

'I tell you, I have nothing now. I have not even a horse. Nothing.' He struck his right hand across his left in emphatic gesture.

'I tell you, you do not have to pay for me. I have no mother. If you come, you must come now.'

'I am a man. I cannot come to you with nothing. I cannot let you buy me.'

'Look at me.' She shook herself so that her jewelry clanked. He heard the sound, but his eyes were upon hers. The east was banded with orange, red, and purple. 'Look at me.' Her eyes were long and narrow, and deep enough to absorb a man. 'I am rich. I shall give you silver and turquoise to work, horses to breed, till you too are rich. Must I tell you twice?' Her eyes were more beautiful than springs among the rocks. 'You have spoken to your uncle; you know what he said. Your mother will give you no sheep, no horses for me. If you want to come with me, come now. I cannot wait until first cold moon. You cannot cache me in a tree until you are ready for me. You have your manhood and your weapons; if you are not good enough with them, nothing can make you good enough. Come now.'

He was a long time answering, searching and searching her eyes. At last, 'It is good. Get your horse.'

She thought she had stood for twenty years with a rifle pointed at her breast. Her face did not change; she walked away slowly. He saw that full day lay golden along the tops of the cliffs, and the sky was brilliant; from the camps he heard the noise of departure, bustle and low voices and laughter that to an American would have seemed furtive.

I am like Natinesthani and the magician's daughter, he thought, but I have no sacred tobacco. I have just myself and my bow. I wonder what medicine will she give me? I shall make a bracelet that is like her walking; she is silver strong as iron. When I have horses again, we must both come back to T'o Tlakai. There is good water in Tseya Kien Cañon, that is the place for our hogahn.

He rolled a cigarette. The freshness would leave the air soon. Already he felt tired.

She rode as well as she danced or walked. Her pinto pony tossed its head, working against her light touch on the reins, ringing the tinklers on its bridle. That girl on that horse — *ei-yei!* Reaching him, she smiled, and he forgot his fatigue. He walked tall and proud beside her, one hand on her stirrup, not caring who might see.

II

Red Man sought out Wounded Face where he stood at his pony's head, talking to Killed a Navajo. Despite a certain jauntiness, he did not look like a gambler who had just won a small fortune. He addressed the older man rather abruptly,

'Grandfather!'

'Yes?'

'Are you not the uncle of that man who won the horse-race, the one from T'o Tlakai?'

'I am. What is it?'

Red Man had meant to go slow, but his words were jumping out on him. 'Did he speak to you? Has he told you what he planned to do?'

Wounded Face and his friend suddenly lost all expression; they became wooden.

'I do not know what you mean. We talked together yesterday. What is in your mind?'

'He has gone to Chiziai. He has gone — he has gone — he has not gone alone.'

'He went with the woman who was stopped from dancing?'

'Yes.'

'Well?'

'Do you not know about her?'

'I have heard a little talk; I do not know anything. She is rich; perhaps it is a good marriage, I think.'

Red Man saw that Wounded Face very much wanted first-hand information. 'I live not far from Chiziai. I know, not just talk. She lives alone, she does no work, she is rich. The Americans make her rich, for badness. She is two faces and two tongues. You see her clothes and her skin, and hear her voice, but all the rest inside is American badness. I know. Hear me, I know.'

He had managed to be gay all night; he had been the cheerfullest of all the gamblers, the readiest singer, the pleasantest loser. Now suddenly it all went back on him. He moved his lips, and found he did not dare speak. He raised his hand to his mouth with two fingers outstretched, and thrust it forward — two-tongued. He struck his heart, then raised his fist before his face and brought it down rapidly — heart that kills with a knife. He struck his heart again, then brought his right fist down on his left hand — like a stone — making the gesture with all his force. He repeated how she made her living; in sign talk it was frightfully graphic and coarse.

'That is enough, Grandfather,' Wounded Face said. 'You did well to tell me.'

Red Man departed.

'Shall we ride after him?' Killed a Navajo asked.

'No. That is what that young man wants us to do, I think. You saw him, how moved he was. We have heard something of what he says, but still, he had reason to lie. Besides, it would be no use. He is like me, he is like his mother, and his father. You know them. When it is something serious he makes up his mind; you cannot move him unless you can convince him. I have six nephews, he is the best of them.' Wounded Face stood with his hand on his saddle, staring at the stirrup. 'Well, we can only wait. Do not speak of it, my friend.'

'I hear you.'

He mounted swiftly, and rode off at a trot.

III

It grew hot when the sun was halfway up. Laughing Boy's last sleep seemed years ago. From time to time he looked at her as one might drink at a spring, and her occasional speech was like rain falling. She rode in triumph.

Abruptly he stopped, gazing first at the trail, then over to the right, while with a hand on the bridle he stopped her horse. He said in a sure voice, 'Get off your horse.'

She did not quite know why she obeyed so immediately. He took off saddle and bridle, tied a thong about the animal's lower jaw, then stood for an instant, one hand on the withers, head raised high. She saw his lips moving, and was afraid of his intent face and a hard, excited look about his mouth. With a quick gesture he strung his bow, and before she could speak to him, mounted and was off, galloping. There was nothing for it but to wonder and wait.

She knew by the sun that he had not been gone over half an hour, but it seemed more than she could stand to wait longer. Her feelings alarmed her; was she falling in love? She saw him rounding a butte, trotting, driving two more ponies ahead of him. This, she thought, was madness. Truly, she must take him in hand. She rose as he drew near.

'What have you done? American Chief will put you in jail.'

'No; it is all right. That man' — he gestured toward the butte — 'I did not hurt him much; besides, he is a Pah-Ute. He took this horse from my brother last year. He is bad, that one. He lives up beyond Oljeto. I saw him at the dance. Now I have something, to come with you. He was a bad shot, look.'

He showed her proudly a long, shallow scratch on his forearm.

'And the belt?' She pointed to the silver at his waist.

'I do not know from whom he stole that. It is a pretty good belt.'

They laughed together.

Immensely alone in that white stretch of adobe desert, they rode side by side, like two men, like friends. It seemed to Laughing Boy that she promised freedom and astonishing companionship; her small mannerisms, her casual remarks, were unconventional without consciousness; it was good. The ponies stepped out well despite the heat, the bridle jingled, the spare horse, with high head, pranced alongside, obedient to the rope. He sat slackly in the saddle, leaning back, flicking his pony's quarters in rhythm to his song.

They stopped seldom, ate little, and rode fast. It was hard on her; she was not accustomed to missing meals and sleeping where night happened to catch her, but she knew better than to complain. His easy toughness, his enjoyment of momentary comfort, were a compensation for her, and at night, camped beside a tiny waterhole, she listened to his singing.

She was tired and stiff. Already she had been alarmed, worried, tired, and hungry for this man. With a sudden fear, as she looked at him across the fire, she realized that she loved him. She had started something she could not stop, then. Well, it was all right, it was good. If only he hadn't gone off after that Pah-Ute, it wouldn't have happened; it was that waiting without understanding; it was that imperious warrior who gave her orders and was suddenly stronger than she, and apart from her. That had done it. While he sang, she looked at his hands locked across his knees, at the bow-guard on his left wrist. When he loosed his shaft, the bowstring had snapped down across the leather on the inside; towards her he turned the lovingly worked silver on the back of it. The shaft had gone true, into the shoulder, between the neck and the butt of the aimed rifle. She shivered.

He stopped singing. She rose and sat down again close beside him, and waited. He made no move. She knew now that these next few days when she would be with him alone were desperately important to her, but she was meeting with a restraint blended of tribal custom and ignorance for which her knowledge of the American's world had not prepared her. It was beyond all other necessity to possess him fully now while the trail was single and straight, but he was a religious man, schooled to obedience of absolute conventions.

She thought. He was unused to her originality; she delighted him, but she came close at times to alarming him. She must go slow in all things. She would wait. The effort her decision cost her was so great that it frightened her. Perhaps, she told herself, it is a good thing to have to wait. I love him, but I must remain mistress of myself and him. This is good for me.

She wanted to touch his face with her fingertips, to brush his hair with her lips. When they galloped together and he sang exultantly beside her, she wanted him to swing her to his saddle.

There is very little gesture of tenderness in Indian experience, but she thought she saw latent in him the same desires, promising herself days to come when she would teach him many things. She thought to herself, I shall complete him with my knowledge. I shall make a god of him.

IV

The town of Los Palos shimmered in the heat. A lot of adobe houses and frame shacks pushed carelessly together were beaten down by the sun. Behind them was a strip of irrigated green like a back-drop, alfalfa, corn, beans, cottonwoods, alfalfa, corn, cottonwoods, a mile long and a few hundred yards wide. Rich, deep, cool green was not part of the desert landscape; it was something apart that the sands held prisoner. The mean little town was a parasite on the goodness of the water; here water and earth and man made beauty; there man and mud and boards created squalor.

A few yards of concrete and some blistered paint made a gesture of civic pride at the railroad's edge. A two-story hotel, compounding Spanish mission with cubism, was a monument of the railroad's profitable beneficence. From a rise where the trail crossed the railroad track, a little way to the west, it all compounded into a picture; the dejected town with its dominant hotel-station, the green strip behind it, yellow-grey sand, and farther, dancing buttes in the mirage.

Laughing Boy's attention was divided. 'Do these iron paths run all the way to Washindon? That is a beautiful place; there must be much water there. I have never seen so many houses; how many are there? Five hundred? I should like to go there. Are there many trading posts, or just one? Those are rich fields. Can one come here and see the iron-fire-drives?' He silenced himself, ashamed at having shown himself so carried away.

'Let us not go there now,' she told him quickly; 'it is better that we go first to my hogahn. The horses are tired.'

'You are right. Are there more than five hundred houses?'

'Yes, a few more. The iron-fire-drives goes by many times a day; it goes that way to Washindon and that way to Wide Water. Any one may see it. Come now.'

They gave the town a wide berth, trotting east past the end of the irrigated land along a trail between two buttes. About three miles farther on, where the clay walls widened again to face the southern desert, an adobe shack stood in the shadow of one wall. Behind it a tiny spring leaked out. Here they dismounted.

'But this is not a hogahn, it is a house. Did an American make it?'

'No, a Mexican built it. He went away to herd sheep, and I took it.'

He stepped inside. 'It does not smell like Mexicans.'

'I have been here a long time. Yellow Singer made the House Song for me. Is it not good? The door is to the east, like a hogahn.'

'Yes, it is good. It is better than a hogahn, I think; it is bigger and the rain will not come through. It will be good summer and winter.' He hobbled the horses. 'There is not much grass by that spring; we shall have to find pasture.'

'There is a little pasture just down there you can use. You must not let the horses run all over the place; this is American country. The Navajo country begins across the railroad track. There is good pasture just this side of Natahnetinn Mesa, enough for many horses. You must keep them up there.'

She lit a fire in front of the house.

'You have no loom. There is no sheep-pen.'

'I have been alone. I have had no one to weave for, and no sheep.'

'How do you live?'

She was laying the big logs over the first flame.

'I work a little bit, now and then, for the missionary's wife in the town. She is a good woman. Now I am going to set up a loom, and you shall have a forge.'

He thought that something was wrong. Her face was too blank. 'Not all missionaries are good, they say. There used to be a bad one at T'o Nanasdési, they say.'

'No, not all of them are good; but this one is.' She spoke musingly. 'His wife pays me much money. She is not strong; I am.'

Her strange, pensive smile troubled him. He thought how beautiful she was. He thought again of the magician's daughter. He did not care what bad magic she might do to him; just she was worth all other things.

Sprawled out on his saddle-blanket, he watched as she brought food from the house and began to prepare it. Her movements were like grass in the wind. He eyed a banquet of luxury — canned goods, tomatoes, fruit.

'Perhaps when we go into the town to-morrow we can buy some candy.'

She thought, he must be kept away from town. I must think of something. 'I have a little here.'

'Sticks with stripes on them?'

'Yes.'

He sighed luxuriously. The food on the fire smelt good. It was cool. With a couple of ditches one could make a good cornfield by that spring, and plant peaches, perhaps. If they were to have food like this all the time —— It was important to find that pasture for the horses, he must tend to it to-morrow. The town could wait. A swift movement caught his eye, lifting the coffee-pot aside. *Ei!* she was beautiful.

V

They talked as they ate, lounging, while night filled the valley.

'Do you speak American then?' Laughing Boy asked. 'Is it hard to learn?'

'It is not hard; we had to learn it. They put me in a room with a Ute girl and a Moqui and a Comanche; all we could do was learn English. Sometimes some Navajo girls sneaked out and talked together, but not often. They did not want us to be Indians.' She rested on her elbow, staring into the fire. 'They wanted us to be ashamed of being Indians. They wanted us to forget our mothers and fathers.'

'That is a bad thing. Why did they do that?'

'Do not talk about it. I do not want to think about those things.'

When she had put away the dishes, as they lit their cigarettes she said, 'If ever they come to take a child of ours to school, kill her.'

'Is it like that?'

'Yes.'

'I hear you.'

They lay side by side against the wall of the house, watching the fire. Her shoulder moved closer to him. He said,

'Tell me your true name.'

'My name is Came With War. What is yours?'

'My parents named me Sings Before Spears. It is a good name. Yours is good.'

'Why do they always give women names about war?'

'They have always done it. It brings good fortune to the whole People, I think.'

She moved so that she touched him. Sings Before Spears!

He asked her, 'Have you any relatives here? Some one must get a singer to make the prayers over us. There are the four days after that to wait; that is a long time. Let us have them end soon.'

She caught her breath and looked at him despairingly. He felt a wind blow between them while he met her eyes, a hollowness behind his heart. He clenched his left hand against his side, repeating slowly,

'Four days is a long time to wait,' and then, almost inaudibly, 'Oh, beautiful!'

She looked away, wanting to laugh, to cry, to swear, and to kick him. He could not know; how could he know? She examined the line of his chin, the set of his lips, so very Indian in their fine chiselling and faint outthrust. Devices ran through her mind. This was a Navajo. This was something her missionaries and teachers never dreamed of. This was part of what she loved. She set her nails into the palms of her hands. Patience.

'I have a friend near here who will speak to a Singer to-morrow. He will be here to-morrow night.'

They smoked again. At last he said, 'I do not think I shall sleep in your house now. I think it will be well to sleep up there.'

'Yes; that will be better.'

He got his blanket. 'I shall forget the trail.'

He loomed above her, in the play of darkness and firelight. She saw all the strength of the Navajo people embodied, against the sky, and she felt ashamed before it.

'Four days is not long, Laughing Boy.'

CHAPTER VII

I

EARLY in the morning she got Laughing Boy off with the horses to find pasture. When he was well away, she put on American clothes; high-laced shoes, an outmoded, ill-fitting dress, high to the neck, long-sleeved, dowdy, the inevitable uniform of the school-trained Indian. It was a poor exchange for barbaric velveteen and calico, gay blanket and heavy silver. She had deleted from the formula a number of layers of underclothing; the slack, thin stuff indicated her breasts with curves and shadow; a breath of wind or a quick turn outlined firm stomach, round thigh, and supple movement, very little, but enough.

It began to be hot when she reached the wretched 'dobes and stick hovels on the outskirts of Los Palos, among the tin cans and the blowing dust. She stopped by a dome of sticks, old boxes, and bits of canvas.

'*Hê, shichai!*'

Yellow Singer crawled out into the sun, blinking red eyes.

'Hunh! What is it?'

His dirty turban had slipped over one ear, his hair was half undone. He sat looking at her uncertainly, his open mouth showing the remnants of yellow teeth. She noticed his toes coming out from the ends of cast-off army boots.

'Wake up. Were you drunk last night?'

He grinned. 'Very drunk. You lend me a dollar, perhaps?'

'You keep sober this morning, perhaps I give you a bottle.'

'Hunh?' He focussed his attention.

'I am going to be married this afternoon. I want you to come and sing over us.'

'Coyote!' He swore, and then in English, 'God damn! What do *you* want to get married for? What kind of a man have you caught?'

'You talk too much, I think; it may be bad for you some day. You come this afternoon and sing over us; I shall give you a bottle. Then you keep your mouth closed.'

He read her face, remembering that her grandmother had been an Apache who, in her time, had sat contemplating the antics of men tied on ant-heaps. And he knew this woman pretty well.

'Good, Grandmother,' he said respectfully, 'we shall come.'

She left without more words. In the town she had shopping to do — food, a jeweller's simple tools from a trader, a can of Velvet tobacco and big, brown Rumanian cigarette papers. Then she drifted idly to the post-office, sauntering past it in an abstracted manner, not seeing the men who lounged there. One of them immediately walked off in the other direction. She continued down the street, till it became merely a strip more worn than the land on either side of it at the edge of the town, where she entered a small, neat 'dobe house. In a few minutes he followed, closing the door behind him.

He wore a clean, checked woollen shirt, the usual big hat, and very worn, well-cut whipcord riding-breeches. He was of good height, light-haired but tanned, with rather sad eyes and a sensitive mouth. Even now, when he was plainly happy, one could see a certain unhappiness about him. He threw his hat on the table, put his hands on his hips, and drew a breath as he looked down on her, smiling.

'Well, you're back on time.'

'Yes, why not? Didn't I tell you?' She held out her hand to him. Speaking English, she retained the Navajo intonation.

He sat down on the arm of her chair, and ran the tip of his index finger along the curve of her throat. 'That's a terrible dress, about the worst you've got. I'd like you to get some good clothes.'

'How will I do dat? Do you tink I can walk into dat store, dat one down dere, and dey sell me a dress? Will one of dose women, dey make dresses, work for me? You talk silly, you say dat. Maybe I give you my measure, maybe you write to dat place in Chicago, hey?'

'Sears Roebuck, my God! Well, it's not such a bad idea. All right, bring me your measurements.' He leant over to kiss her.

'Don't start dat now. I got to go back soon now.'

'What the hell?'

'My husban', he makes trouble, dat one. I can' stay away right now. Soon maybe.'

He heaved a sigh of exasperation. 'Listen! you've kept me waiting a week while you went off on that trip. Now you put me off again. You're always putting me off. I don't think you've got a husband.'

'Yes, I have, an' he's a long-hair. You know dat. Don't I point him out to you one time, dat one? You want him to kill me, hey?'

'Well, all right. To-morrow, then.'

'I can' do it. It ain't I don' want to, George. I can', dat's all.' She passed her hand along his cheek, slowly. 'You know dat.'

He kissed her finger-tips. 'Day after, then, Tuesday. That's flat, and no two ways about it. I have to go back to the ranch Wednesday; ought to be going back now. You can manage; I think

you can manage anything you want. Understand? Tuesday.'

She studied him. He was difficult, this man. Now you had him, now you didn't. There were different kinds of Americans; this one came from the East; he was easy, and he was hard. Well, she could manage almost anything.

'All right, dat will be nice, I tink. I'll be glad to come den. So you go get me two bottle of wiskey now, to take home, den I fix it. Tuesday.'

'That old souse! I wish he'd fall over a cliff and break his damned neck.'

She smiled at him. 'I wish dat too, sometimes. But he ain't a bad man, dat one. He has been good for me.'

'I suppose so.'

'Now get de wiskey.'

'Kiss me first.'

II

She thought hard on the way home. The difficulties are beginning already. My path is beset with ambushes. And this is hard. Four days — Monday, Tuesday, Wednesday, Thursday, too late. Oh, no, Laughing Boy, I must bend you. I cannot be robbed of this, I have a right to it. Now I've got to manage, I, Came With War. I have earned this, I think. I am afraid of you, Sings

Before Spears; I do not like to be afraid. I shall conquer you, or else I'll herd sheep. I cannot be conquered. God give me help — hmph, that God! Well, I know how. I make my own trail of beauty. I know what to do. I am strong, Laughing Boy, Laughing Boy.

She was dressed as a Navajo again when he returned from Natahnetinn. He inspected the jeweller's tools which she spread out for him, praising them, while she set to preparing food.

'They were talking about you in the town today,' she told him.

'How was that? I do not understand.'

'That Pah-Ute, the arrow went in farther than you thought. He went to Nahki Zhil trading post; there he bled to death. He told them about you. Now American Chief has made an order to put you in jail.'

'Perhaps we had better go away from here, then.'

'No, they will not do anything; it was only a Pah-Ute, they say. Only if you come into town and they see you, some policeman will take you then.'

'I am sorry. I should have liked to see that place. However, some day they may forget.'

'People have long memories for some things.'

Yellow Singer and his wife came just at the end

of the afternoon. He watched them walking, with their long shadows rippling over the unevenness of the ground and the occasional bushes.

'What are those coming? They look like Pah-Utes, perhaps. They look like Hunger People! What rags!'

'They are Navajos; that is Yellow Singer. They look like that because they are poor, that's all. He has come to sing over us.'

There was something about those two faces that made Laughing Boy uncomfortable, as though a black veil had been pulled in front of them. They were people who would have unpleasant laughter. Both of them looked at him with open curiosity and an expression of understanding that bothered him. As they exchanged formal greetings, these two seemed to be extending to him a sympathy which he did not want. Then Slim Girl came out of the house dressed in her richest costume, and they were expressionless. Then, too, Laughing Boy was not concerned any more.

Yellow Singer's wife handed a medicine basket to Slim Girl, which she filled with the corn mush she had prepared. The singer placed it in the correct place on the floor of the house. Laughing Boy entered carefully. He was thinking hard about what he was doing; he was putting forth every effort to make it good and beautiful. He thought about the gods, about Slim Girl, about the future. It was all confused, because he was excited. He wished House God would come to stand over them; he thought Hunting Goddess would be a good one for her, or Young Goddess, or White Shell Woman. Now Yellow Singer's wife was leading her in. Under his breath, 'Oh, beautiful!'

She was thinking of many things at once; her excitement was deep down like a desert river under the sands. Now I really have a husband in my house. When this is over, it will be a test between us. I ought to feel all sorts of things, marrying like this now. You are handsome, Sings Before Spears. You do not know how much you are mine.

She sat down on the rug beside him. Yellow Singer divided the mush in four directions. Now he was praying for them. Laughing Boy concentrated his thought. Unreasonably, the girl was terrified lest something might happen. She was madly impatient. Now they partook of the yellow corn, ceremonially, and now it was Laughing Boy's turn to make a prayer. He sang the prayer to House God with solemn emphasis:

'House made of dawn light,
House made of evening light,

House made of dark cloud,
House made of he-rain,
House made of dark mist,
House made of pollen . . .'

Yellow Singer's wife, fat and sleepy, sat in the corner. She was vaguely sorry for that young man. She rolled a cigarette, wishing he had not chosen so long a prayer.

'In beauty it is finished,
In beauty it is finished.'

The confident, solemn voice ceased. He looked at Slim Girl. Now they were married 'in a beautiful way.' It might seem a little furtive, that ceremony without relatives, almost without guests, but now the gods had married them. Slim Girl was staring back at him with wide eyes.

Yellow Singer's wife stretched bulkily. 'Now let us feast.'

The old singer grinned. Slim Girl regarded them dreamily until her husband spoke to her,

'The guests must feast.'

She brought forth a banquet — canned tomatoes, pears, plums, beans, candies, pop, white bread. She heated the coffee, and set it out with plenty of sugar, and cups for all. On one side she put down a bottle of what looked like water.

'It is a feast,' said Yellow Singer.

They all started eating. The old man took some of the clear liquid, and passed it to his wife, who drank and offered it to Laughing Boy.

'What is it?'

'Whiskey,' Slim Girl spoke quickly; 'he does not know how to drink it.'

'I should like to try it.'

'It is good; you should take it, Grandfather. We all like it.' Yellow Singer chuckled.

'I do not think he can stand it,' Slim Girl said thoughtfully.

'Let me try it. It is right that I should find out about these things. Give me the bottle.'

He saw that her eyes, watching him, were speculative, with something hidden in back of them. He thought she was measuring him.

'Give it to me.'

'Wait. You are not used to it; let me fix it for you. I can make it taste good.'

She took out an orange and a lemon, that she had had hidden behind the water jar.

'What are those?'

'That is called "lanch." This yellow one is "lemon"; there is no word for it in Navajo. They are American fruits; they grow on trees, like peaches.'

She made a stiffish drink in a tin cup, sweetened with a great deal of sugar.

'You never did that for me,' Yellow Singer muttered to his wife.

'I shall do it for you, that thing — when you are as young and handsome as he is.'

They watched him with grinning interest while he tried the drink. Slim Girl was inattentive.

'But this is good! This is better than that red boiling water, I think.' He nodded towards his bottle of pop. It began to glow in his stomach. 'What is it doing to me?'

'It is beginning to do its good, little brother.' The medicine man pulled at the bottle in sympathy. 'By and by you will love it, that feeling.' His wife reached for her share.

Slim Girl stood up. 'The sun is setting. If you take much more of that now, you will not find your way home. Here is a bottle for you to take with you.'

Inside the house it was half dark, and the doorway framed the clay bluffs opposite, painted with sunset. She rearranged the blankets and sheepskins for reclining against the wall, and there relaxed, smoking a cigarette. He finished his drink, liking the flavoured sugar in the bottom of it.

'Sit over here, and let us talk a little now.'

He placed himself half-sitting, half-lying beside her.

'That is queer, that drink. I feel queer here,'

touching the hinge of his jaw, 'as if something were squeezing my teeth. But it is good; make me some more of it.'

'Not right away.'

'It would be good to sing, I think. Let us sing some very beautiful prayers together. Everything is good now.'

'Let us just think for a little bit, now we are married.'

'Now we are married. Why are you looking at me like that? I do not understand you all the time, what your face means.'

'I like to look at you, Sings Before Spears.' Her hand fell into his, he felt her beside him. Something told him that that was only half an answer. He touched her face with his finger-tips. She was studying him intently.

Then she kissed him. He did not understand it; her face suddenly near his, against his, distorted so close to his eyes, her eyes run together. He was held tightly, and something wet, at once hot and cool was against his mouth, with a tiny, fierce imprint of teeth. Vaguely he remembered hearing that Americans did this. He did not understand it; he had a feeling of messiness and disgust. He tried to move away, but she held him; he was pressed against the wall and the sheepskins. She was fastened onto him; he could feel all her body, it was entering into him. There was something uncontrolled, indecent about this. Everything became confused. A little flame ran along his veins. The world melted away from under him, his body became water floating in air, all his life was in his lips, mouth to mouth and breath against his face. He shut his eyes. His arms were around her. Now, almost unwittingly, he began to return her kisses.

III

Slim Girl was asleep. Laughing Boy was very tired, but there was no rest for him. It was black inside the house; here no night wind blew through the leaves of the hogahn wall, no stars looked down through a smoke-hole. He found his tobacco and stole outside.

The cold night wind blew against his skin. His eyes rested among the shadowy forms of the buttes; he looked up at the thick-gathered, cool stars. It was like laying a cold knife-blade against a burnt finger. It was right that they gave women names about war; he understood that now.

His feet took him up onto the high place above the spring, where he had slept before. There he made himself comfortable with his back against a piñon trunk, smoking. Everything was whirling within him: it was necessary to put his thoughts in order. He had never imagined it was anything like this. He had lived the intimate life of the *hogahn*, he knew the camp-fire jokes; but there was never a hint of this kind of thing. It might be just American tricks, but he thought not. No, it was she, her power. She was stronger than iron or fire. That drink was medicine, but she was not medicine; it was just she herself. That blade of grass of a girl, that little Slim Girl, she could make his belly turn over inside of him, she could make his interior dissolve. He sat wondering at her and at himself. So very uncontrolled, at moments he felt ashamed, but mostly it was wonder. That girl was like one of the Divine People. One should not forget one's self, but this was a beautiful thing.

He had fought, and sung, and raced horses, and known the uplift of the great dances; he was old friends with hunger, cold, fatigue, and suddenly contrasted feasting and comfort; he had lived out to the tips of his fingers, but this was something that made everything else turn thin and shadowy. That was her magic, perhaps, and it was wonderful, it altered life: that she gave complete fulfilment, where everything else was partial. Her house was better than other Indians' houses, her food was richer than other Indians ate, and she fed one's spirit with a perfection that only she could give. Hunger was dead where she was. She was not like The People; life with her would have to be different, but the trail was beautiful.

His cigarette was long dead. Boy Chasing His Arrow had moved far across the sky. Drowsiness mingled itself with his thoughts, blurring them, while the night wind blew upon him. His doubts and wonderments faded and thickened into sleep. Sleeping, he dreamed a dream. Perhaps the sight of the ragged, wretched singer and his wife had put it into his head. It was not much of a dream, not elaborate.

He sat by the hogahn fire, and his uncle was telling the end of the Coming Up Story. He did not really see much, but he knew it was his uncle, and he felt angry with him for what he had said about Slim Girl. He knew that the other children were there, and that the snow coming through the smoke-hole melted in the air, and fell on the fire with little hisses. It was his uncle speaking, it was Wind God speaking in his mind; they were the same. None of that was clear; only the old, familiar words came to him, very definitely, spoken with emphasis, as when one wants to impress a lesson upon children.

'Slayer of Enemy Gods came to the Hunger People, they say . . . He said, "Now I am going to kill you, because you are bad for my people."

Hunger Chief said, "If you kill us, nobody will be hungry any more, nobody will care about feasting. They will not go out and hunt for good food, venison, and fat prairie-dog. Nobody will want to go hunting," he said,' they say.

'Slayer of Enemy Gods said, "Then I shall let you live," they say.'

He heard Talking God call in the distance, 'Wu, wu, wu, wu!' Then the god called again, nearer. He knew he was asleep, and tried to wake, to meet the god coming. He was terrified lest he should be asleep when the god called for the fourth time. He had an idea that he had put himself asleep deliberately, against the god's will. The call sounded for a third time, just outside the hogahn. Talking God was out there, standing on a bent rainbow, in company with many other Divine Ones. He had shut himself up in a pitch-black place with no entrance; he had locked himself away from the gods under a blanket of dark clouds.

With a desperate effort he woke, sitting up, gasping with relief. His eyes drank in the dawn, the open space, the tree, the clay buttes, things apart from his dream. Over across, a turtle-dove called, 'Hoo, hoo, hoo-hoo-hoo.'

CHAPTER VIII

I

SHE was still asleep inside the house. He stood looking down upon her in the half-light. She seemed frail, childish, and sweet, with the shadow under the eyelids, her mouth faintly drooping, her figure reduced to almost nothing beneath the blanket. He thought of that drama of strength and weakness, of conquering and being conquered, fitting it to this small person, soft in sleep. Now that he was looking at her, he had no reservations; it only seemed a miracle that she should be his. He wondered at the mere chance it was; Slender Hair speaking to him of the dance and the racing, coming to Tsé Lani, this little incident and that, until out of nowhere that which might never have been entered and became the core of his life.

The sun would be up soon. He went to meet it.

> 'Dawn Boy, little chief,
> May all be beautiful before me as I wander . . .'

She woke happy, watching him under lazy eyelids as he stood outside the door, naked save for his breech-clout, with the level sunlight touching the edges of his flanks and ribs, making a golden reflection where his upraised arms bunched the muscles at his shoulders. She thanked God and the gods indiscriminately. Whatever happened now, this could not be taken away. She shifted the blanket, closed her eyes, and assumed sleep.

He sat down beside her, a little nervous about her awakening. Her eyelids quivered, she yawned deliciously, she stretched her arms like a kitten playing. She sat up and smiled at him, seeing his face brighten as he responded.

'Have I slept so late? I shall get your breakfast as soon as I have fixed your hair. You should see it.'

He felt of its disarray, with the queue hanging lopsided, then he grinned at her. 'Your own is just as bad; go look at yourself in the spring.'

She reached over to a shelf and took down a small mirror, which she handed to him. He looked at himself in it; this was fascinating but a little disappointing. Finally she took it from him.

'Come, now, dress, and do up my hair.'

He had often exchanged that service with his brothers and sisters; it was a pleasant and friendly act. He had watched his mother and father together at it, one leaning against the other's knees, laughing when the brush pulled too hard, and he had seen that they extracted some pleasure from it which he did not know. Now he understood that, and the sheer domesticity of it delighted him.

He felt really married, settled, a man who would soon have children, and speak as one of established position, no more a boy.

Breakfast was welcome when it came.

'To-day you must get me the wood for a loom,' she told him. 'It is a long time since I have woven, but I have beautiful blankets in my mind. I shall weave and you shall make jewelry.'

'No, to-day, before we do anything, we must make a sweat-bath. This is all different, here. We are starting off new. We must make ourselves clean, we must make a fresh start. And, besides, how can you weave? You have no sheep.'

'I shall buy wool in the store in town. They sell good wool there; the people round here bring it in.'

'Why do we not raise sheep? I have some in my mother's flock I could get.'

'Who will keep them? You will have your horses and your jewelry; that will be plenty. I must always be going in to work for that missionary woman.'

'I do not like your working in there.'

'Why, have you some bad thought?'

'No, I have no bad thought. But a house is empty when the woman is away.'

'I used to work for her every day; now I only work sometimes. She gives me good money. It is because of her that you will have silver to work with. To-morrow, when I go in, I shall bring you Mexican silver. And those days you can go tend to the horses. By and by, when we have made much money with your jewelry and horses and my weaving and work, we shall go back to your country. We shall go back rich. Is it not a good plan?'

'You have spoken well. Here, I do not know about these things, but you know, and your words are good. It is enough for me that I have you. It is not just that we are married, but we are married all through; there is not any part of us left out.'

'No; there is not any part of us left out. And you do not want a second wife, Laughing Boy?'

'No — no!' The extra-emphatic, three syllable negative, '*É-do-ta!*' long-drawn-out, with the decisive sign of the right hand sweeping away. 'Have you a sister you want me to take? If you want help here, in the hogahn, I will get one, but she will not be for me. She will be in the way. You are enough for me; perhaps you are too much for me, I think.'

Quickly she kissed him. He felt embarrassed, and loved it.

He had to teach her the ritual and song of purification, but, with faint childhood memories to aid her, she was quick to learn. Her close attention pleased him, and it was a pleasure to hear her sing. He was only sorry for her, that she had for so long been denied these things, and angry and puzzled at the schools and the American life that had forbidden them. In the end, he taught her songs that she had no business knowing, quite aware of what he did, as a kind of unavowed tribute and token of the special quality he felt in her.

II

After the steam bath and the water and the foaming yucca-suds, it was good to lie with hair spread out, drying, and talk vaguely of things to be done, and now and again to touch her. Great achievements completed themselves in a phrase. He drew the design of a bracelet in the sand; he braided his hair and mimicked the nasal speech of a Ute. They fell to talking of the ways of different tribes, the old wars, and the present semi-hostility between the Navajo and the Pah-Utes.

'There is not often trouble with them,' he told her, 'but we do not like them. They live wild up in that country beyond Oljeto, where they are hard to catch, and they steal things. Mostly they trouble the Mormons; the Mormons are afraid of them, they say. Since I was a little boy, only once we had real trouble with them. Then one time we

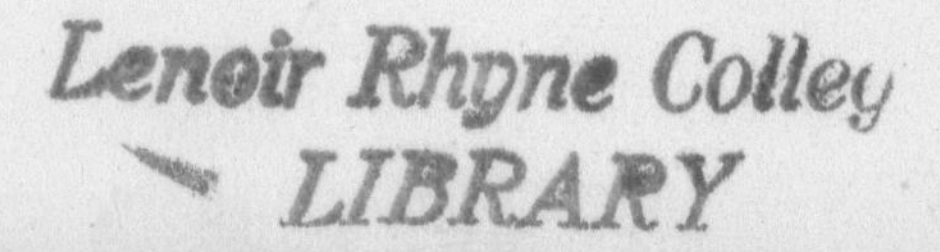

went on the war-path for them. I went on the war-path that time.'

He felt proud of the part he had played, and wanted to tell her about it.

'That was three years ago; I was just about full grown. Blunt Nose, he made the trouble, that one. He was chief of a band of them; he lived up beyond Naesjé Cañon, near Tsé Nanaazh. That is wild country, almost in the mountains. He was bad.

'He used to kill Mormon cattle all the time, a cow, and a cow, and a cow, here and there. He needed to keep no sheep. He did the way he pleased. He wore two pistols, and had a gun on his saddle, they say. He would ride down the middle of the trail, and not turn out for any one.

'One time he heard the Mormons had sent for soldiers, so he left their country alone. Then he sat quiet for a while, but his people got hungry. A Pah-Ute will eat almost anything, but there is very little up there. That is why the Navajos leave them alone; there is nothing in that country but a few Pah-Utes and a few antelopes. You cannot make anything out of the skins of either, so we let them alone.

'Well, now Blunt Nose decided to try mutton. He came down by Jahai Spring where Hungry Man lived. He had all his braves with him. They started to run off Hungry Man's sheep. Then The Doer came along. You have heard of him? He is the one who killed those two Americans; his father was Generous Chief, the one who never was captured when The People went into exile. So The Doer came along; he saw that man's wife, where she came running. He rode up, he started shooting at those men. They shot back at him. They were too many for him; he rode away and they chased him. But he killed one.

'Then Blunt Nose was angry. He killed Hungry Man, and his two children. He ran off the sheep. He went back into the Naesjé country.

'The People around there gathered together to hunt him, but the trader at Oljeto told them not to. He told them to wait while he wrote a paper to American Chief at T'o Nanasdési. So they did that. Meantime Blunt Nose was talking. He learned that there were no soldiers in the Mormon country, but he said he liked mutton. He said no Coyote could kill one of his braves and not be punished; he said the Coyote People would pay for what they had done. He talked like this all around; he talked brave, calling us that name.

'In a little while he came down again. But they had men on watch, they made smoke signals. A lot of people came together and went after him, so that he had to make a big circle, around by

Oljeto, to get back. When he went past the trading post, he shot into it. He did not hurt any one, but he spoiled some tin cans and broke some windows. Then, on his way home, he crossed the bridge over T'o Atsisi Creek. It is a big wooden bridge that you can ride a horse over; Washindon had it built. They sent two Americans to show how it should be built.

'Well, he came by this bridge. He was angry, so he burnt it, that man. And he got some sheep, and went home.

'Then the trader wrote another paper, a strong one, and sent it to American Chief. Meantime The Doer was getting up a war-party. The People were angry; they wanted to kill them, all those Pah-Utes. So American Chief wrote a paper saying that he was getting up a war-party of Americans who would do the fighting. He said to have good horses ready for them, and that the Navajos must not start fighting or there would be soldiers. That was what he said.

'He tried to talk to Dokoslid over the talking wires, to get the war-party, but a man down by Besh Nanaazh had cut some of the wires to mend his wagon, so he had to wait a day to fix them. Meantime he sent a rider with this paper.

'The rider came by Gomulli T'o trading post. His horse was lame and he was tired. I was there with a good horse, a roan. Yellow Mustache was the trader there; he told me to carry the paper. He told me to ride hard. He said I would be paid.

'I rode all day. I rode at night until the moon set. I rode after it was all dark, but I was afraid of the spirits. Then I made camp. The next morning I saw a fresh horse, so I caught it and rode on. The sun was about halfway up when I saw Oljeto. And right then the Pah-Utes saw me. They started after me, and I went as hard as I could for the trading post.

'I could hear them shooting at me; I could hear their bullets. I was very much afraid, but there was nothing to do except ride hard.

'Then I felt something hit me. It made a dull thump; it did not hurt. I thought, "I have been hit in the bottom of my spine. In a minute it will hurt. Probably I shall die, I do not want to die." That way I thought.

'I thought all that all at once, then I felt behind, but there was nothing. Then people began shooting from the windows of the trading post, and the Pah-Utes went away. I rode up to the door and got off, wondering if I should fall. But I was all right. There was a bullet in the cantle of my saddle; that was what I had felt.

'We waited five days for the American war-party; meantime they got some good horses together. Blunt Nose was around all the time. People gathered together in groups of ten to twelve families, or more, like in the days when we were always at war. Then those men came.

'There were eight of them. They all had badges on their shirts, like policemen, only not quite the same. One of them was a fat man; we did not see why they brought him.

'They said they wanted four Navajos to be trackers. The Doer was to be head tracker. There were two other young men, and then they took me. They said they would pay me a dollar a day. That was a new idea to me, to be paid for hunting Pah-Utes. I thought you just hunted them.

'We tracked them for three days without seeing them. They tried to make us go at night, but we pretended not to be able to follow the trail. When The Doer told them that, they believed him. It was not an easy trail. Their horses were not shod, and they went a great deal over bald rock, they turned and doubled, they dragged branches behind them.

'We did not get much to eat, we could not make a fire. Those Americans brought a brown, sweet candy, and a little, dried-up black candy in boxes, something sticky. These we ate; you could go a long time on them. Then we had some dried corn.

We started at first light; we went till it was quite dark. During the day it was hot among those rocks. We were hungry. It did not seem that we were following Pah-Utes; we were just following tracks in the sand, or little scratches on the rock, and some day we should come to the end of them, and something important would happen. Now the only thing in the world was those marks. When you saw one where you had not expected it, it seemed to shout at you.

'But we were gaining on them. On the fourth day they were much fresher, those tracks. We were close to them. Then we saw a couple of them, on lame horses, and we chased them. They had to cross a deep arroyo; when they went down into it we raced, hoping to catch them at the bottom of it. But they got up the other side; they just came up that side when we got to the near edge. Right away they started shooting. They shot at that fat man.

'Right away he fell off his horse. He landed on his stomach, and as soon as he landed he began to shoot. He shot between his horse's legs. He hit one Pah-Ute in the leg and one in the arm. Then we knew why he had been brought along, that fat man.

'We wanted to kill them, but the chief American said that they had to go to T'o Nanasdési to be punished. Their horses were no good, so they put them on those two young men's horses, and sent them back with them and one American to Oljeto. That left me and The Doer. I had never seen him before, that man, but everybody has heard about him. I was anxious to do well in his eyes.

'In the afternoon we came to the mouth of Yotatséyi Cañon. The trail was fresh and clear. The Doer told them that the other end of the cañon was halfway up Napani Mountain, to our right. It went in a big curve, he said. If they got out there, we could never catch them, he said. So he told them to send three men with him, and he would take them straight across there. He would reach it by nightfall, he said. Then, in the morning, we could start in from both ends and catch them, he said. So they did that. I stayed with the four at the lower end. I thought about there being still ten Pah-Utes, but I did not say anything. I did not want to seem afraid, if The Doer was not.

'We went a little way into the cañon and made camp. The chief American lent me a pair of magic tubes that he had, that you put to your eyes, and they made everything far away look near. I watched with them until I saw The Doer's smoke signals. He signalled that they had had a fight, and the enemy were coming towards us. So we watched, but we saw no sign of them. It was dark soon after. We watched all night.

'When it was getting near dawn, but no light as yet, we started on foot. As soon as there was a little light, they sent me along the top of the talus along one wall, to look out for ambushes. The cañon was about five hundred paces wide; the walls were at least that high. The chief American watched me with those tubes. I would wave my hand, as a sign that I saw no one, and they would come forward, strung out across the cañon.

'It was full light when we got near where the cañon turned the corner. I went on ahead again, very slowly. I could look down into the sand and see the tracks that we had been following so long. I felt very much alone. I knew that man was watching me as I crept; that made me feel a little better. My father told me that the war-path was like stalking mountain sheep, only more exciting. I thought that there was more to it than that. Mountain sheep do not shoot back at you: mountain sheep are not people who are thinking about you just as hard as you are thinking about them.

'Then I saw them. They must have made camp up in the middle of Yotatséyi; now they were coming to try to get out this way. There were nine of them, in single file, riding carefully and watching. So I signalled to the Americans, and saw them take cover. I made myself as hard to see as I could. Suddenly I thought that I was enjoying myself a great deal.

'They came around the corner; now I looked right down on them, from behind a bush. One of them, looking around, looked straight at my bush. He was searching for people hiding. I thought that that bush was not nearly thick enough. His eyes passed on, and for just a moment I felt weak.

'Then the Americans started shooting. So I stood up and gave the war-cry and started. As I was shouting, I thought, they will hear the Coyote howl and know he's a Wolf. There was a brave just below me in a buckskin shirt with beadwork on it, and a hat with a silver hatband. I noticed all about him while I shot at him. I wanted to kill him; I wanted it to be known that I had killed one. I saw my arrow in the air a long time; I saw it strike. He fell off his horse. Then I saw that he was not dead, and I was glad. I do not know why.

'There were five of them down now, and the others put up their hands, so the Americans took them prisoners. One had been killed over in the other end of the cañon.

'We went back to Oljeto, and they paid us as

they said. Then we had ourselves purified from the blood, and we spent several dollars on canned food. I bought a big paper bag, as big as a hat, full of all different kinds of candy, and went home, and we all ate it.

'When I was telling about what happened, I got to the part about thinking I was shot, and I started to laugh. I could not stop, I just laughed. So they started calling me by that name. That is all.'

Slim Girl said, 'I am glad you are a man like that.' She thought to herself, he is a warrior. That was worth ten thousand schools. He must have been about eighteen. Where is basketball against that?

III

Before supper there was the well-mixed drink again, with its attendant elation and the curious feeling at the back of his teeth. He finished the brew.

'I should like to take some more of that.'

'That is not a good thing to do.'

'Why not?'

'If you take too much you become foolish. You grow old before your time.'

'That would not be good. Perhaps it would be better not to take any. You do not take it.'

'It is not every one who is able to drink it. It is not meant for women, that drink, it is for men. If I take it, it makes me sick quickly. It is all right for you, you are strong. It just makes you feel well, doesn't it? You like it, I think?'

'Yes, I like it. I think it is good for me.'

'It is good for you.' And she told herself, 'I shall tie you with it. It is another hobble around your feet, so that you will not go away from me.'

CHAPTER IX

I

TIME passing and corn growing cannot be seen; one can notice only that the moon has become so much older, the corn so much higher. With a new life almost more regular than the old, yet far more thrilling, with a rich supply of silver and choice turquoise, with horses to trade and a cornfield to care for, and all the world made over new, time for Laughing Boy went like a swift, quiet river under cottonwood trees. For him, life — which had never been a problem — was solved and perfected, with none of Slim Girl's complication of feeling that such happiness was too good to last. Had he sat down at T'o Tlakai to compose a song of perfection, he could not have imagined anything approaching this.

It had always been a pleasure to him to work in the corn, to help make the green shafts shoot up, to watch them dance, and contrast their deep, full green with the harsh, faded desert. Among his people corn was a living thing; to make a field beautiful was not so far from making a fine bracelet, and far more useful. He drew the precious water into his field thriftily. At its corners he planted the four sacred plants.

Slim Girl did not understand it at first; she had rather wanted to bar it as entailing unnecessary labour, but decided not to say anything. He saw that she thought it dull, drudging work. He did not try to explain it to her directly, but told her the story of Natinesthani and the origin of corn, and taught her the songs about the tall plant growing. When the stalks were past waist-high, he took her to the field at evening, while sunset brought the drab clay bluffs to life with red, and a soft breeze made the leaves swing and whisper. He made her see the whole field in contrast, and the individual hills, the slender plants and their promise, talking to her of Corn Maiden and Pollen Boy, and of how First Man and First Woman were made from corn. Her eyes were opened to it then, as much through understanding how he felt as through what she objectively beheld. After that she worked with him a little, to please him, although she never cared for the backbreaking toil in itself.

His silver sold well. His craftsmanship was fine, his invention lively, and his taste in turquoise most exacting. It was strong, pure stuff, real Northern Navajo work, untouched by European influence. Other Indians would buy it in the store, and its barbaric quality caught the tourist's eye. Slim Girl got in touch with the

Harvey agent, finding him a ready buyer at good prices. She liked to think, then, of the many places along the railroad in which strangers were paying for her husband's work.

She had learned not to care much for general opinion of herself, and was surprised to find that this tangible evidence of her mythical husband's existence, this visible means of support, made a pleasant difference in the trader's attitude towards her, and eventually in the looks she received from men throughout the town. There was a surprised feeling that she must have been telling the truth about herself, and a grateful decrease in attempts to scrape unwelcome acquaintance with her. As for George Hartshorn, her American, he developed an increased jealousy that she knew how to use.

To complete her idyll, she wanted to weave, and she found it harder than she had expected. She had been taken to school young, before she had become skilled, and now it was almost all forgotten. Laughing Boy even had to teach her the names of her tools. She wondered, as he watched her struggling with the stubborn warp, if he were laughing at her inside himself, if she seemed ridiculous to him. Many times she would have given up had it not been for her natural determination of character, and for knowing how anomalous and incomplete to him was the house in which the woman could not make a blanket. She dearly longed to reconstruct that scene, but after just a little her back would ache, her forearms grow heavy, and in the backs of her hands would be sharp pains, while the threads were like demons to outwit her. The patient, monotonous spinning was pure torture, and she knew little or nothing of dyes.

Of course, her first blanket was an ambitious one, elaborately designed. The conception was simplified in the making, and the finished product was a quarter of the originally intended size. When she cut the sorry object from the loom, and looked at it, all crooked, irregular, and full of holes, she could have cried. She hid it from him. Many of her later attempts, not fit to go under a saddle or be sold, she destroyed, but this was the first thing she had made. It was a sad failure, but she could see what it was meant to be, and she kept it.

She wove perfectly plain strips that might serve to be sat on, and even many of these were hopeless. At times, despite her husband's encouragement, in his absence she would curse fluently in English and yank at the strings. Few things could make her lose control of herself thus; she wondered at herself for continuing. It was an offering to her belovéd and, unconsciously, an expiation for a guilt she had not admitted.

II

On a day when the corn was nearly ripe, she went to work in the field. Tiring, she sat down to rest where she could watch two stalks, with their silk just showing against the sky. Low on the horizon the beginnings of a storm darkened the blue. She called Laughing Boy.

'Show me how they draw the corn in the sand-pictures.'

'I do not think I should show you that. You are a woman, and you have never seen the true gods in the Night Chant.'

'Perhaps you are right.'

He was making a decision.

'I shall show you.' He drew in the sand. 'We do it like this. Here is blue, here yellow. Here are the tassels, the silk.'

'Why do you show me?'

'You are not like ordinary people, you have a strength of your own. I do not think any harm will come to you.'

She looked from the conventionalization to the growing stalks; she divided the threatening sky into a design. Her first, elaborate blanket had been a built-up, borrowed idea, her later ones were uninteresting accidents. Now she saw her work complete, loving it and the task of making it. Now she really had something to tell her loom.

She was impatiently patient with the dyeing and spinning, needlessly afraid that she would lose her inspiration. When she was ready, she worked so steadily that Laughing Boy warned her of the fate of women who wove too much, and forced her to let a day go by. Her muscles were much tougher now, and her fingers had grown clever and hard among the strands.

She managed for him to be away with his horses during the last two days, when she finished it. He had not yet returned when, a little despondently, she locked in the selvage, unrolled it on the frame, and sat back on her heels to smoke and look. She did not see what she had conceived. She did not see a living design, balanced and simple, with mated colours. She saw thin, messy workmanship, irregular lines, blunders, coarsenesses. At one place she had forgotten to lock the blue into the green weft, sunlight showed through. The counting of stitches was uneven. The blanket was not even a rectangle.

She went quickly away from the house, walking hurriedly and smoking fiercely.

'I am not a Navajo; it is not given to me to do these things. Mother was happy when she wove, she was beautiful then. I cannot make anything, and he is gifted. He will despise me in the end. Being able to make something beautiful is important to him. He will feel his house empty without the sound of weaving. They said I was gifted, that man who came that time. "My child, just stick to the things of your people and you will do something. You have it." "Mr. Waters is a very famous artist, you must pay attention to what he says, my dear. He expressed himself much pleased with your pictures. I am sure the whole class is proud of Lillian to-day." Those crayons were easy. Perhaps he would like that. But I want to weave. There is nothing the matter with me. No use. *God damn it to hell! God damn me! Chindi, mai, shash, Jee-Cri!* Well, let's go and look at it. There's his pony in front of the house. Come on.'

He had taken down the blanket and was pegging it out carefully. All he said was,

'Where are your wool cards?'

She brought them, two implements like very sharp curry-combs, used to prepare the wool for spinning. She sat down to watch him, thinking, 'Perhaps I shall get very drunk. That might help.'

He carded the face of the blanket energetically, so roughly that it seemed a gratuitous insult even to her poor work. The very coarseness of her spinning served his purpose, as the sharp teeth scraped and tore across the design. She wondered if he were trying to efface it. He stood up.

'Now come here and look.' He put his arm over her shoulder. 'You have thought well. The picture is beautiful.'

The scraping had torn loose a long wool nap, almost a fur, fluffy and fine, that covered all the errors of the weaving. The sharp edges were lost, but the lovely combination she had dreamed of was there, soft and blurred, as though one saw it through tears. She could see how good her conception had been, how true and sure. She had made a beautiful thing. She looked and looked.

He loosened the pegs and turned up the untouched side. As he turned it, he jerked at the corners, throwing the uncertain weave out of shape. It looked like a child's work.

'I am not telling you a lot of things. I am just letting you see something. I think you understand it.'

'I understand. You will be able to put my next blanket under your saddle, and be proud of it. Thank you.'

III

After that there were long, flawless days when they were at home together, he at his forge, she at her loom, time passing with the thump of the batten, the ring of the hammer or rasp of the file. There were chatter and laughter, songs, and long, rich silences. Work then was all love and inspiration.

She had known a good many different kinds of pleasure, but this was a new richness, something that did not exhaust itself, but grew, a sharing of achievement, designs, colours; fingers, hands, and brain creating, overcoming. There was the talk and hummed songs. There was a great deal to be silent about. It came to her as she was weaving the coloured threads to her intent, Why was this not enough?

This is it. This is the thing I have always wanted. There is nothing better; why endanger it. Why not let that man go now? Why not just do this?

The batten thumping down on the weft, the hammer ringing on white metal.

As long as I keep on my way, there is danger. I could never go back to what used to be now. This is what is worth while. A hogahn in the Northern desert would be beautiful now.

Sure fingers interlocking dark blue and black, driving the toothed stick down over the juncture.

I cannot stop halfway now. I am making a

new trail of beauty. When I get through, it will be wonderful. Nothing will ever have been like our life.

Lifting the treadle to let a line of crimson follow the shuttle through the design.

We shall command money, money will command everything. I have herded sheep, their dust in their lungs, hot, a little girl howling at the sheep. We shall be above that. *Aigisi hogahn hojoni.* A little girl watching old Light Man drive by to his summer camp in a buckboard behind two spanking pintos.

A tiny touch of white brings the red meander to life, and deepens the thunderous background.

Navajo women are growing old when Americans are just getting really strong. I am not going to turn into a fat old squaw. My dear, my dear, will you be gay when you are old? Your silver is beautiful. Is anything in the world worth the risk of separating your forge and my loom?

The blue shuttle goes under six warp strands, the black, coming under two, meets it. A close weave looks like a true diagonal.

Are you afraid now, Came With War? I can handle these men. I make my own trail, and I do not stop halfway. I shall make something perfect, that nobody else has made. If I stop now, I might as well stop work on this blanket, after all it cost me to learn to make it. I shall pay myself back for everything that has been.

A single weft strand has no thickness at all, and a blanket is long. It needs patience to finish it, and to make it beautiful, one must not be afraid of the colours.

Laughing Boy, having done his thinking and made up his mind, did not mull over his decision, any more than when he had started a bracelet; he worried whether it ought to have been a necklace. If he did think of other forms, it was only in reflecting that after this was done he would make more, and always more.

You make your dies out of iron files, you get some small piece of iron from a trader for your anvil. In a hard wooden board you cut depressions for hammering out bosses and conchos and hemispheres for beads. When you have bought or made your tools, and have your skill, you go ahead. You make many things, rings, bracelets, bow-guards, necklaces, pendants, belts, bridles, buttons, hatbands. No two are alike, but they are all of the silver, or of silver and turquoise.

Having what he had, he went ahead with living. There were many days, all different, some of high emotion, some of mere happiness, but they were all made of the same stuff; there was one element beautified in all of them. So he worked, content.

When he had made something that had truly satisfied him, he would give it to her, saying, 'That is for you. There is no use selling that to Americans, they do not understand.'

It always pleased her, but she would appraise the jewelry carefully, checking it against their mutual profits, his sales and horse trades, her blankets, and what she brought from the town. If it could be paid for, she put it away, otherwise she required that it be earned. Her primitive banking won his astonished admiration. For her, it was a happy symbol that their fortune, however earned, should be stored in things of beauty.

And every day, at the end, the sun went down and the harsh horizons dimmed. Then there was the magic drink ready for him, and after that a banquet. They spoke dreamily in the firelight, side by side, and knew a great intimacy. They were not two individuals, but two parts who together made a whole, and there was no cleavage between them.

CHAPTER X

I

The first time Laughing Boy rode away to Natahnetinn with the horses, he rebelled against the need to leave their tiny valley, and against the prospect of recurring trips, some of several days' duration. But very shortly he found that, no matter how much in love, a man needs both time to himself, alone, and in general periods of being away from the sphere which is permeated by the influence of a woman. He had a use for these days alone. After all, at the end of a day the sun always set, and it was less than half the time that a strayed animal, a bit of trading, or the need of moving his herd kept him away overnight.

Here he could ride the range and sing. Here it was that he thought of the best designs for his silver. It was beautiful, too, watching the long-maned ponies in the good grass, or coming down to water. Then there was the trading, meat and drink to a Navajo — patience, bluff, deception, penetration. It was so pleasant to sit down with another Indian for a long morning of smokes, gossip, and business, learning all the news and driving a close bargain. Very few of his people ever came by his house, and those were mostly specimens like Yellow Singer. He did not want any one there; that was a place apart, just as here he always had the feeling of a secret knowledge he could not share, something beyond the comprehension of the men he encountered.

He listened to the gossip, jokes, and talk about women that was frank enough, seeing in it all that they had no idea of what he knew. He did not try to speak of his wife, knowing that he could never tell them about her, nor yet make a pretense of speaking as if she were just a wife, as they did. Few ever asked after her, and then in a tone of a certain constraint, though their words were formal enough. He had expected something of the sort, after what his uncle had said; she broke the rules and upset things. If they knew her, she was troublesome to them. Of course they resented the disturbance of their minds, and called it bad, with tales that grew in telling. So he sat, as it were, on the edge of their domestic discussions. When it was a matter of horses, he came to be listened to with respect. Every one agreed that he knew horses, and that he was an excellent trader; when he was speaking about a horse he was trying to sell at the moment, nothing he said was believed.

Trading was brisk and profitable. His own

people were active enough in it. Hopis came down that way, and occasionally a Zuñi would pass by. A tourist company in Los Palos was having a good season; they found it convenient to tell Slim Girl that they wanted so many ponies delivered on such a day. They often got fearful cat-meat, but always sound, and profitable for all with the Easterners paying two dollars a day.

His profits went back into the herd. One by one he was getting himself animals that satisfied him, that made him happy to touch and proud to ride them. When the day came that they went back to T'o Tlakai, they would bring fine blankets and much jewelry on splendid horses. He made a pair of brass-mounted saddles, and began, little by little as he earned the silver, a squaw's bridle that should be envied from the San Juan to the Little Colorado.

Those days afield ceased to be penalties. As he settled in the saddle at dawn, it was rather like reëntering the old, familiar life into which he carried the enchanted quality of the new. The trail to Natahnetinn was still cool; he loped and enjoyed himself. There would be the action of rounding up a loose pony, the pleasure of feeling a neat-footed horse under one, chance meetings, talk, and trade.

Almost best of all was to sit on a knoll, smoking

and watch the animals feed. One never sees a horse so well as when he is grazing close by, intent upon the grass, oblivious of the man. Then one sees how he moves his ears, how he blows through his soft nostrils, how his casual movements are made. He moves from clump to clump, making his selections by standards of his own, never still, yet entirely free of the restlessness of a stalled horse. It is the essence of pastoral life. Cigarette smoke rises lazily in the hot air, the sun is comfortable upon one's bones, the gently moving animals make peace.

He did his thinking then, detached from his emotions, mildly introspective, reflective. He would weigh each thing and value it, go back, retrace, and balance. It was one thing to have made up his mind, another to know exactly where he was — the difference between setting out on a new trail and marking down all the landmarks of the discovered country. The horse shifted from clump to clump, making soft noises, hooves in sand, and crunching. Cigarette smoke wavered and turned with breezes too soft to feel, the movement of the heat in the air. Thoughts became pictures, changing slowly.

He had accepted Slim Girl's difference and unconventionality, but for some time still she occasionally startled him. He wanted to understand her; he thought he was sure of what she was, but yet admitted that there were things about her that were beyond him. And for some reason, he always resented the idea of her working in the town. Not that it was a novelty for Navajos to work for Americans, or that he had any means of taking an attitude towards menial labour. His people had owned slaves in the old days; a few still survived, but he had no particular idea of the position of a servant. Yet he wished she would not go there. Then again, he sympathized entirely with her idea of amassing a fortune. Perhaps it was just because the town and its Americanism were part of an unknown world, perhaps because when she returned from there she seemed so tired, and once or twice he had surprised in her eyes a puzzling look, a look of a man who has just killed and scalped a hated enemy. But it was no use his trying to form an opinion. He did not know his way here; with only his people's judgments and measures, he could decide nothing. He certainly could not expect everything to be the same. As well expect, when one had ridden beyond Old Age River, into the Mormon country, to turn and still see Chiz-na Hozolchi on the eastern horizon.

On those few occasions when she warned him that the missionary's wife would want her to stay overnight, he did not like to come home. He tried it once, and found that the house without her was a long song of emptiness. Usually he would stay with some friends on the reservation, feeling a little patronizing towards their family life, slightly disturbed only by the presence of their children. Those nights he missed his drink, finding himself with but a poor appetite for supper, and with little desire for talk. Their food seemed coarse to him nowadays.

Aside from all other things, going away was worth while for the sake of coming back, well tired, to be greeted at the house. It was so different from coming back to T'o Tlakai. There was a thrill in riding up to the door, particularly when he came on a newly traded, yet finer horse. Or it was a real source of pleasure to bring in a string for the tourist company, whooping at them as they debouched from the narrow place between the bluffs, herding and mastering them at a run, into the corral, conscious of Slim Girl leaning in the doorway, delightfully aware of her admiration. There would be news, talk, and all the magic when the sun began to set. Quite often he was first home. He would amuse himself by arranging things for supper, piling wood, drawing water. He learned to handle the can-opener. Then she would come through the opening; he would see her pace quicken as she noticed his horse in the corral, and he would sit back, smiling, to receive her smile.

II

One day he raced home before a thunderstorm that caught him just at the end, first a fine spray, then such a drenching as one might get from buckets, then the spray again, and a pale sun that had no warmth. The valley was all in shadow when he reached the house; he was wet and cold. She had not arrived yet. He built up the fire, and then, searching for coffee, came across the bottle. That was just the thing. But no, he decided, it is she who understands that, and went on looking for coffee. He found the package, empty. Well, he would try a little whiskey.

There was no fruit in the house, so he poured himself about half a mug of clear liquor. Bah! It was filthy-tasting stuff.

'Mule's water!' he said.

But even that little taste was warming. He sugared the whiskey, held his nose, and bolted it. First he felt sick to his stomach, then he began to feel better. *Ei-yei!* There was a fire in the middle of him, he was warm all over. He was walking on air. He rolled and lit a cigarette. He began to feel so well! He sang,

'Now with a god I walk,
Striding the mountain-tops . . .'

That was the way to take it, it was fine stuff. He wished Slim Girl would come soon. He thought of many things to say to her. He would make her see how he felt about her, how beautifully he understood her. She must know what wonderful things he knew how to say, how perceptive he was. She must stop thinking about all those things she was always thinking about, and drink some of this, and sing with him. There would be such love as never had been in all the world before. To-morrow he would bring his horses and they would ride to T'o Tlakai, and if that missionary's wife said anything about it, he would shoot her and tie her scalp on his bridle. It was foolish working for her, when his jewelry and his horses were so entirely sufficient. Life in T'o Tlakai would be a dream. He could see just how beautiful it would be. A little more whiskey would be good.

It went down more easily, a second half-mug, nearer full than the last, on his empty stomach.

'T'o Tlakai and children.' He said out loud, 'I want some children.' And began to feel sorry for himself. Then he began to feel sick. He felt very sick. Everything was dark and whirling, and he was miserable. He fell upon the floor, hiding his eyes to see if things wouldn't stay still. Immediately the floor began to rise on end, higher and higher; soon he would be pitched against the wall. He opened his eyes, the floor went back to level, but the whole business span. Then he was racked. The world heaved and bucked, waters roared in his ears. Then he went out completely.

She, too, was tired when she came in, having been kept back by the storm. She looked down on him, heaved a sigh, and then smiled as a mother might whose child had done something forbidden and hurt himself just enough to learn a lesson. Very gently, she pulled him so that his head lay in the ashes. One arm fell across his spew. She put the uncorked bottle beside him, where he would smell the stuff when he came to. She nodded to herself. It was well enough, lucky to have happened just like this. It would teach him. The place did not smell very well. She took some food and a blanket, and went up to the tree on top of the bluff.

III

The corn matured and was harvested. Seedling peaches that he had set out began to lose their leaves. First frost appeared in the night. The season of thunderstorms had passed; now was the time when one might say the names of the gods. Laughing Boy, riding herd, felt the tang in the air and touched his bow. This was good hunting weather, if one could go to the mountains. Down here there was nothing save the usual prairie dogs, coyotes, and jack rabbits. He began to feel restless.

One day he met two braves dressed in all their best and fanciest, one on a roan and one on a pinto. His own horse, freshly caught, was prancing as he rode up to them; theirs were lively.

'*Ahalani!*'

'*Ahalani*, Grandfather!'

'Where are you going?'

'To dance at Chilbito. And you, say?'

'Just riding around. I have horses here.'

'You have a good horse.'

'He is pretty good. I got him from a Hopi. Let us race.'

'Good. How much will you bet?'

'Five dollars.'

'That is too much for us; bet three.'

'Good. To that tree there?'

'All right.'

Hé! His horse did well. Too bad he didn't have the bay. '*E-é-é-ya!* Come on now, my horse, come on, Grandfather!' Three horses tearing neck and neck, three men bent over their manes, urging. The pinto was nosing ahead. Laughing Boy pressed in his heels, his belly drew tight with the thrill of motion.

They hurtled past the tree, the pinto slightly ahead, and drew rein, laughing.

'You win, Grandfather.'

The man received his money.

'I am sorry I did not have my bay horse here. He is much faster than this one.'

'Bring your bay horse to the dance. There may be some racing, I think.'

'What dance is it?'

'A Night Chant. Wind Singer is leading it.'

'I shall think about coming.'

'It is only a five-day dance. It is for Twice Brave; he has not much money, they say. You had better come soon.'

'What made him sick?'

'He looked at his mother-in-law; he spoke to her, they say.'

'*Ei-yei!* How did that happen?'

'They lived near each other. When his wife was away, she got his food for him, they say. He came too soon and saw her. She covered her face, but he spoke to her, they say.'

'He spoke to her! He is crazy, I think.'

'Perhaps he is; he does strange things. When the missionary at Tsé Tlchi used to serve beans, a lot of us went to hear him. He held a sing every seven days, and afterwards there were beans, but there was no dancing. We followed the Jesus

Road until he stopped giving us beans. Then Twice Brave went back and stole a lot of red *t'oghlepai* that he had, it was something to do with his religion. It was good. But when he had drunk a lot of it, he went and made his horse drink it. He put the bottle down its mouth and made it take it, the way he had seen an American do. He made his horse crazy, just like a man. I saw it. It couldn't walk straight. And now he has spoken to his mother-in-law, they say. So he has a bad toothache. You should come to the dance.'

'*Ei!* I should like to see that man. I shall come if I can.'

He was glad that the season of the great dances was returning. As he rode home, he thought that it would be good to see the gods once more, perhaps to know the holy fear and exaltation when one swallowed the sacred arrows inside the Dark Circle of Branches. He loved the gatherings of people, the huge fires, and the holy things. There was religious experience and high thought, and then there was sociability on a large scale. Sometimes there were horse-races or a chicken-pull or gambling.

He had not thought about these things for so long, or at least he had thought of them distantly, himself apart. As a blanket and its design before dawn is seen, but has no colours, then with clear light grows vivid in red and green and yellow, so the feeling of his tribe swept over him. It was exhilarating.

IV

He spoke about it to her after supper. 'There is to be a Night Chant over at Chilbito, by Tseye Buckho. There may be racing.'

'How long will the song last?' There was no reason in the world why they should not go. She was searching in her mind, and found only that she dreaded it.

'Only five nights. It is for Twice Brave; he is not very rich, they say.'

'We do not want to go, I think. Let us wait for a complete one.'

She understood herself as she spoke; she was jealous of his people, of something they had in common which she could not share.

He looked at her inquiringly, catching a tone of earnestness in her voice. She had no reasons, yet very much did not want to go. He saw that it mattered to her.

'Perhaps you are right. We shall wait.'

'I think that is better.'

Both understood.

It was puzzling, though. He wondered about it as they sat there. He wanted to understand her.

He told himself: 'If she wants me to know, she will tell me. I do not think she knows herself. I have made up my mind, there is no use hesitating on the trail. I make her my life, let her be my life. I do not know why she does this thing, but I know what I think of her. If I knew just what was in her mind, it would be worth thinking about, it would tell me something about her. Now there is so much of her I do not understand. I know what I want, that is enough.'

He watched her in the firelight, her slender lines, her oval face of sleeping fires. The trail of beauty lay within this house; not all the songs and horses in the world were worth this minute.

CHAPTER XI

I

THE life apart enclosed him again. If some encounter with Indians bound for a dance, some reminiscent incident, brought on a momentary restlessness, he did not have to deal with it. It simply expressed itself in the smug feeling that what he had was so vastly superior to anything in their philosophy. He was a little sorry for those people. When he felt like that, he would stir his pony to a lope, with his head high, uplifted, thinking of Slim Girl, of some little thing to say or do for her. He was a young man very much in love, a young man with his mind made up to love.

At the beginning of the month of Little Snow, he surprised her by bringing an Indian home with him. She was disturbed and uneasy as she prepared the extra food. There was no reason to be bothered; just because something had never happened before did not make it a bad sign. Underneath all her self-confidence was a feeling which she refused to recognize, that this life of theirs hung by threads. Really, in her heart of hearts, she was surprised that everything ran so smoothly. Little things upset her.

Long-haired and hatless, the man's pure Navajo costume, the heavy look of his jewelry, indicated the Northern country. Laughing Boy called him cousin, and questioned him about people and things at T'o Tlakai and all the Gyende district. The eager voice and the old, familiar names, the home things: she was afraid of all those people, those words. Life was lonely here. Perhaps if she were to keep him, she would have to give up and move back among his own kind. She observed to herself that this man, who was to bind her to The People, seemed to be driving her yet farther apart from them.

When they were alone for a minute, he said, 'Why did you not give me my drink? Why did you not offer him one?'

'That drink is medicine that I know. You must leave it to me. There are things that must not be done about it, just like prayer-sticks and sacred cigarettes.' As she spoke, she prepared a stiff dose. 'That man must not have it or know about it. You must not speak of it unless I say you may.'

'Good, then, I hear you.' He drained it off. He had missed it.

'I was afraid you would speak of it before him.'

'I thought about it. You had some reason, I thought. So I waited.'

She nodded.

'He is my uncle's son; not Wounded Face at Tsé Lani, another one from T'o Tlakai. His sister is sick. They are going to hold a full Night Chant, ten nights. They want us to come, he says. Mountain Singer wants me to dance in it; it is a song that I know well. I have been in it before when he led.'

His voice told her, 'This time I want to go. Now you must do something for me.' She saw that it would be a mistake to oppose him.

'Let us go, then; I think it will be a good thing. I shall be glad to see your country and your people, and a big dance like that is always good to go to.' There was under-pleading in her voice, but he knew that this was a gift to him. 'When is the dance to be?'

'At the full of Little Snow Moon.'

It was obvious that he looked forward eagerly to the visit. This was to be her test that was coming, one more test, and she felt there were enough already. She excelled herself in tenderness and charm, and strengthened his drinks. His response to her was evidence of a steadily burning fire that would momentarily lull her doubts. In every act and word and look he seemed to testify his steadfastness, but still she was uneasy.

On the night before the start for T'o Tlakai,

they sat late by the fire. He spoke eagerly of his own country, while she answered little. The colourful cliffs and cañons, the warm rock, the blue masses of distant mountains ——

'When it gets all hot there in the valley, when it is sunlight in the little crevices, and everything you look at seems to jump out at you, you look over towards the east. Just above the rim of the cliffs you see Chiz-na Hozolchi Mountain. It is far away, it is blue and soft. Even when the sky is blue as turquoise and hard as a knife-blade, it is soft, and more blue. You will like that country.'

Is he trying to persuade me to stay there? Perhaps we shall have to, in the end. I shall need all my strength.

'It will be fine when we ride in together. We shall have two good ponies. They will envy our jewelry. They will envy my saddle-blanket that you made me.'

And they will know about me, and his own people will talk to him.

'They are good people. You will like them.'

They are my enemies, more than if they were Utes.

When he fell silent, he would touch her arm with his finger-tips. Then he would speak again, staring into the fire as a man will when he is seeing something, but always turning to look at her, almost shyly.

She relaxed, relieved of her fear. I am a fool. I am a crazy damned fool. I am the centre of all that he is thinking. He is all tied up in me. He cares for this and that, but I am the door through which it all comes. Listen to the way he is talking, see how he looks. We can go to a thousand dances and he will still be mine. Not all The People in the world can take him away. If he is ever lost to me, it will be I who have lost him.

She moved over and leant against him, her head on his shoulder. 'I think your country will be very beautiful. I shall be glad to see it. Your people will not like me, I think, but I do not care, if we are together.'

II

Slim Girl's idea of travel on horseback was that one should ride during the cooler part of the morning, rest out the noon downpour of light and heat in a shady place, and use the last of the day to find the nearest friendly hogahn. There could be none of that now, she knew. Her man was a Navajo and a horseman; when he settled in the saddle, as the sides of his calves touched his pony's barrel, and he felt the one current run through them, there was always that little look of uplift. Probably half of the waking hours of his life had been spent on a horse's back, but not the longest day could destroy in him a certain pleasure in even the workaday jog or mechanical, mile-eating lope of a good pony.

She thought of this, as they skirted Los Palos in the dawn, and sighed, foreseeing heat and fatigue, stiffness and soreness in unromantic places, all to be concealed from this man of hers. He did not even know that it was necessary for one to be toughened to the saddle; he thought people were born that way, if he thought about it at all. She wondered, doubting, if any of the exaltation of their first ride to Los Palos would carry her through this.

It was not so bad as she had feared. At this late time of year it was hardly hot even at midday. Her weaving and occasional hours in the cornfield had hardened her somewhat. The high-cantled Navajo saddle he had made for her, with its seat of slung leather over which a dyed goatskin was thrown, was more comfortable than one would have thought possible. The miles stretched out before them, shrank, and were overpassed. She was tired in the late afternoon, thirsty from dust, silent. She watched this man who rode before her, so easy in his saddle, so at home, going back to his own country.

She no longer had her own, different background. She was afraid because of him. It was no longer she who was strong, leading, marking the places for him to set down his feet. Now it was she who must fumble, uncertain, and he who must hold her up. What hobbles would she have on him now? It was all right, that he felt all for her, that she was the centre of things, but how could she be sure when his own people and his own things spoke to him? There was nothing to do but wait and be watchful, and meantime a little mouse was gnawing at her heart.

They spent the night at a friendly hogahn. There, too, he was at home and she astray. She saw his natural sociability expand in the evening gossip, and she learned with surprise that he had an established place among these people, who looked at her faintly askance. He was already known, and his opinions on horses were listened to with respect.

She had been drawn to him first just because of these things. She wanted him as a link between herself and just such as these people. But more, terribly more now, she needed him, himself completely hers with no fragment left out, and so they had become her enemies.

Yet there was plenty with which to comfort herself. Their opinion of her changed visibly when they learned that it was she who had woven Laughing Boy's saddle-blanket. The red background, with the black and white interlocked fret of the heat lightning, was a gay and handsome thing. The women examined it, felt its weave, and spoke highly of it. There was an evident, kind-hearted relief at this proof that she was regular.

More important was the subtle difference, the special quality of her husband's attitude towards her when compared with their host and his wife. In that house was the usual peace and understanding of an Indian's home, but there was none of that faint reverence and intimate desire that she felt when Laughing Boy spoke to her. She knew she should be proud and happy, but sleep was long in coming as they lay in their blankets about the dying fire.

The second day was like the first, save that, instead of growing stiff and sore, she grew stiffer and sorer. Her fears rode with her behind the saddle; she wondered after her old, arrogant sureness.

They made camp for themselves, having come to a section where no one lived. She was unhappy in mind and body, not overjoyed at their roofless stopping place and the prospect of a cold night, nor pleased with bread and coffee and a little dried meat. After supper they sat in silence, smoking and looking into the coals. She thought that silence was inimical.

At last he said; 'I shall set a trap back there by those rocks; we should have a prairie-dog for breakfast. They are good. I know you do not care for this food we just had. You are used to better.'

'I do not mind. You must not think about me.'

'I wish you had brought some of that whiskey. Since you have taught me that, everything is flat without it. There is no salt in things. I missed it last night, and I do now.'

'I brought some. I did not know you wanted it. Here is about enough for two drinks. You will have to take it just plain.'

'That is all right. Give me some, then.'

He drank his dose eagerly.

'There will be none of that at T'o Tlakai,' she told him.

'That is all right. It does not belong there; it is part of the new world you have made for me. I do not think I could go back to just living, like these other people.'

She thought to herself, that is well enough, while we are alone. You will lose the need for the drink in the time we are there, perhaps you will forget about it.

None the less she felt better, and noticed that the night was beautiful with stars. After all, camping thus was part of her people's heritage. She was doing a Navajo thing. Her blanket sufficed to keep her warm; she fell asleep as soon as she closed her eyes.

As they went farther north, at first the desert rather appalled her. She was accustomed to the southeastern part of the Navajo country, grey bluffs, and grey rolling plateaus and harshly monotonous, distant mountains. Since she had known fertile California and the bustle and comfort of the places where civilized man gathers together to domesticate the scenery, she had never been able to feel any deep liking for the empty desert and the hostile fury of its silence. Now they were come among warm, golden cliffs, painted with red and purplish brown and luminous shadows, a broken country that changed with the changing sun, narrow cañons, great mesas, yellow sands, and distant, blue mountains.

They rode along a defile, scarcely a hundred yards wide, whose walls, twice as high, looked as though they had just drawn apart, and might decide to close again. Scrub oak, in the bottom, clustered along a running stream. The place was full of shadow. Looking up, one saw magnificent, dark firs growing along the ledges and hanging valleys. Up there, the ruddy rock, touched by the sunlight, became dull orange and buff, with flecks of gold, and a golden line where it met a flawless sky. Their horses' feet made a tiny, soft noise in the sand. Nested on one ledge was a village of the long-vanished Old People, square little stone houses high up, with black spots of doorways that watched the cañon. Laughing Boy pointed to the ruin.

'Yota Kien,' he said. 'Some of the Divine Ones live there, they say. The two brothers came here when they were looking for Talking God, they say.'

They stopped to rest and water the horses. She looked about her, feeling the quiet, absorbing the place. She had a sense of rest and of growth. She had not known that one could feel intimate about anything so grand.

He brought her to a high place late one afternoon, a spur of Dzhil Clizhini. It had been a fatiguing, scrambling climb, with one piece to be done on foot, alleviated by the increasing growth of jack pine and spruce. At length they trotted along a level, following a winding path under firs. There was a short stretch of broken ground, grey, knobbed rock, oaks whose branches one had to duck, a tumbling little gorge at the left, with the smell of water. They were shut in by trees.

He drew rein, motioning to her to come up beside him. She did so, crowding past the twigs that hemmed in the path. Right before their horses' feet the cliff fell away, some fourteen hundred feet, and there, under their hands, lay all the North Country. It was red in the late sunlight, fierce, narrow cañons with ribbons of shadow, broad valleys and lesser hills streaked with purple opaque shadows like deep holes in the world, cast by the upthrust mesas. The great, black volcanic core of Agathla was a sombre monstrosity in the midst of colour. Away and away it stretched, jumbled, vast, the crazy shapes of the Monuments, the clay hills of Utah, and far beyond everything, floating blue mountain shapes softer than the skies. She drew back in the saddle.

'When any one comes here, even if he has been here many times, it hits him in the face. Wait and look, by and by you grow until you can take all this inside of you. Then nothing can make you angry or disturb you.'

They sat in silence, looking, absorbing. He dismounted, added one to a cairn of stones, and squatted, gazing out. There was something about it that made Slim Girl choke. It made her want to cry.

The trail led down over the face of the cliff in an alarming manner, a test for sure-footed ponies.

Below, it was all thick shadow. Their animals, stepping delicately, were taking them down from sunlight into late evening.

You, too, have your magic, your strong medicine, Laughing Boy, and I think it is greater than mine. This is what I want you for. Some day we shall put our two magics together; some day you will bring me here, to have this always. You will bring me, if it does not take you from me first.

III

At length they were reaching T'o Tlakai, riding down a slope of bald rock into a valley about three miles square, surrounded by moderately high cliffs. Here and there, at their feet, were clumps of scrub oak, peach trees, and the marks of summer cornfields, where water seeped out under the rocks. Along the north cliff was a long ledge, with the rock above it rising in a concave shell of light reflected under shadow. Along the ledge stretched an imposing ruin of the Old People, at one end of which, where there must be a spring, a strip of grass showed very green. Down the middle of the valley spindly cottonwoods marked the course of the wash. The rest was dull and colourless — sand hills, sand, rocks, sagebrush, greasewood, some sheep. Nearly in the centre were five hogahns, two square ones of leaves, deserted now that winter was at hand, and three dome-shaped mud ones. The framework of the medicine-lodge for the dance had already been set up. There were a good many horses tethered around the settlement.

It did not look like much, but she found it threatening, inimical. She wanted some sign; it would have been a relief if people had come buzzing out as they appeared over the brow of the rock, if there had been shouts of anger, anything. The houses were more than a mile away still. Would they be clever people or stupid, hostile, friendly, or resigned? Were they able opponents or could she conquer them? The quiet houses fascinated her. Just she against all those, against everything here, these rocks, these underfed trees, those far-off mountains, the little bushes. She had fought against worse, but this meant so much. The horses seemed barely to crawl.

Ahead of her, Laughing Boy was singing a hymn, half aloud:

'Dawn Boy Hill rises,
Jewels Hill rises,
White Corn Hill rises . . .
Those people their fields, my fields, now
they rise all beautiful before me!'

CHAPTER XII

I

DURING the greetings, Laughing Boy took stock. With entire confidence in his wife's ability to win over these people, he carried himself as though he had no faintest idea that there might be strained relations between them, but in his mind he was calling the roll of his family. Wounded Face, sitting apart in his blanket like a sleepy eagle, was against him. Spotted Horse, the younger uncle, was waiting; meantime he intended to be cordial. Spotted Horse would follow somebody's lead, whoever spoke most commandingly; afterwards, if the issue were unpleasant, he would mildly deplore it. His mother was against him, but she too waited, not declaring herself, not closing her judgment yet. His sisters took no position, but welcomed the stranger and did their best to make her at home because she was his wife. Bow's Son, his brother, and Bay Horse, his brother-in-law, both evidently thought he had made a fool of himself, and felt hostile towards her. Bay Horse could be discounted; he did not belong to the clan, and the taboo which forbids a man's looking upon his mother-in-law kept him away from the family circle most of the time.

Out of the corner of his eye, without seeming to pay attention, he watched Slim Girl with relish as she said and did exactly the right things, giving an excellent impersonation of just any attractive woman.

Now Jesting Squaw's Son dismounted before the hogahn and stood beside him, looking anxious and hesitant. It was plain to see that he was concerned only lest there should be some estrangement between them, lest an alien life might have made a gulf. Friendship stood firm and true. So they embraced and wrestled and spoke loudly to each other.

He faced his father last, and most anxiously. Two Bows had held back from the others; his was an awkward position in this matter. Long days of teaching the jeweller's craft, hunts together, lessons in the trail and the bow, work shared, had brought them very near to each other. They were father and son, and they were close friends. Laughing Boy admired and emulated the old warrior, and he could confide in him. Two Bows saw some of himself bearing fruit anew in the young brave. And yet, in a matter like this, his rights were only those of courtesy — to Laughing Boy's own clansmen, to his mother and her brothers, was the decision. He could only watch for the time when his purely personal influence might turn the scales. Now, he said nothing. His son could feel fondness and sympathy there, but whether approval went with it he could not tell.

II

Laughing Boy had been half-afraid lest, like Friend of the Eagles, or Reared in a Mountain, he would find that his own people seemed dirty and smelled badly when he returned to them. Secretly, even a little shamefacedly, he considered the life that he was living perhaps not so far removed from that of ordinary Earth People as the Eagles' home in the sky, or the mother-of-pearl and turquoise dwellings of the Divine Ones, but still something apart, like the magic country at the end of Old Age River. He had waited somewhat anxiously for his first impression, and found that his home was delightfully as he had imagined it. Everything was the same; it seemed a miracle. That which had been intimate and dear was so still, only now nothing was taken for granted, but every commonest detail leapt to him with new vividness.

There were constant little surges of delight in his heart over trivial, minor things — a shadow across a cliff, the bend of a cottonwood, the sheep coming in at evening, their silly, solemn faces all about the hogahn — why should they have changed? A man does not realize that he has changed himself, or only partially recognizes it, thinking that the world about him is different; a familiar dish has become no longer enjoyable, a fundamental aphorism no longer true; it is a surprise, then, when his eyes and ears report unchanged, familiar impressions. So the wonderful sameness of things, the unfailing way in which expectation was fulfilled, were proofs of something beautiful in the order of the world. It was glorious to pick up the threads of talk where he had dropped them, discussing the old, well-worn subjects casually and in detail, as though they were still inlaid in his life, with just a little seasoning of the attitude of one who has been farther and seen more.

One could see that his family had expected some outlandishness. Now they were puzzled; some disappointed, and some pleased to see how normal and Navajo were Laughing Boy and his wife. Her blankets spoke for them with many tongues, and the solid evidences of their prosperity, all Navajo, nothing bizarre or American, but good honest silver, turquoise, coral — 'hard goods' — and handsome Indian ponies.

He watched Slim Girl, seeing the shutters closed behind her eyes, correct, sure, in hand, doing just the perfect thing. He was swept by constantly recurring waves of pleasure in her, and felt, as he sometimes did, a faint fear of that detached self-command. Slowly they were being forced to accept her as really belonging to the People. It pleased his dramatic instinct, as well as the strong sense of privacy he had concerning their relationship, to play up, being very normal, and letting no look or gesture suggest that they two came from a land of enchantment.

Knowing her well, he could see that she was at high tension, and secretly watchful. He had no idea that that strain, that painful vigilance, was above all for himself.

When he was alone with his father, he showed him the silver-mounted bridle and some of his other jewelry. Two Bows turned over the harness, feeling the surface with his finger-tips.

'I have nothing more to teach you — that is well done.' He tapped the cheek-strap. 'I should not have thought of using that design that way.'

From Two Bows, such praise made it hard to keep a quiet, modest face.

Jesting Squaw's Son came back in the late afternoon. They drifted off together, with arms over each other's shoulders, until they came to rest under the scrub oaks behind the peach trees. They discussed this and that, vaguely, trailing off into silence, playing with twigs and pebbles, running their fingers through the sand, occupying their hands. At length Laughing Boy looked at his friend and spoke:

'I do not talk to those people. Some of them have their minds made up, some of them will not understand. I do not think you will know what I am talking about, but you understand me. I want you to know.

'I have been down Old Age River in the log, with sheet-lightning and rainbows and soft rain, and the gods on either side to guide me. The Eagles have put lightning snakes and sunbeams and rainbows under me; they have carried me through the hole in the sky. I have been through the little crack in the rocks with Red God and seen the homes of the Butterflies and the Mountain Sheep and the Divine Ones. I have heard the Four Singers on the Four Mountains. I mean that woman.

'It sounds like insane talk. It is not. It is not just because I am in love. It is not what I feel when I am near her, what happens to my blood when she touches me. I know about that. I have thought about that. It is what goes on there. It is all sorts of things, but you would have to live there to see it.

'I know the kind of thing my uncle says. It is not true. We are not acting out here, we are pretending. We have masks on, so they will not see our real faces. You have seen her blankets and my hard goods. Those are true. Those are just part of it.'

Jesting Squaw's Son answered, 'I have seen the blankets and the hard goods; they sing. I am happy about you.'

He felt better after that, he cared that his friend should know, and, in contradistinction to the others, telling him did not lessen the rare quality of the thing described. He returned to the hogahns feeling better able to act his part.

He found the evening meal most enjoyable as he watched the good ways and mannerisms of his family. Among them he could make out a growing perplexity. What had that old man told them to expect? A word slipped from his brother to his younger uncle gave him the cue, filling his heart with glee. When he got a chance he whispered to Slim Girl,

'What my uncle said — they expected you to have no manners. They were waiting for you to act like an American, and give them something to talk about.'

He lolled back on the sheepskins, laughing inside himself. A smile shadowed the corners of his wife's mouth.

III

Slim Girl watched the ceremony with interest, feeling in a pronounced fashion the mixed emotion she had towards so much that was going on about her. It might be a weapon to destroy her, for the very reason that it was a summation and a visible expression of many things in her people's life that mattered to her. She had a sneaking suspicion that the family had gone to the expense of a full Night Chant largely because of the effect they thought it might have on the erring member.

It was sometimes absurd and sometimes quite beautiful. The masked dancers were grotesque, but there were moments by firelight when their shapeless heads and painted bodies, their rhythmic, intent movements, became grand and awe-inspiring. The long and repetitious prayers were often monotonous, chanted to dull, heavy music, but in the worst of them there were flashes of poetic feeling. Her American education had dulled her sensibility to the quick, compact imagery of a single statement, leaving to the hearer, the evocation of the picture intended that forms the basis of Navajo poetry. Still, she caught it sometimes,

> 'By red rocks the green corn grows,
> Beautifully it grows . . .'

She saw it, and the terse implication that takes for granted all that the Indians feel about corn, contenting itself with merely calling forth that feeling.

She tried to think that these things were native and close to her, but found that she could only observe them objectively. She was foreign now. She could sympathize with their spirit, but not enter into it. A door had been closed to her, and at times, even standing here among the other spectators, in the heart of the Navajo country, she was swept again by a hopeless nostalgia for the country and the people, forever lost, of her dim childhood.

When she had been a very little girl, she had trembled with terror and awe at the sight of the very gods coming into the circle of people. Out in the darkness one heard their distant call, repeated as they came nearer, until with the fourth cry they entered the firelight. They danced and sang there, majestic and strange; then they vanished again to return to their homes in the sacred places. Now they were just Indians whom she knew, dressed up in a rather silly way. Like many unreligious people, she kept slipping into the idea that these worshippers were pretending to be taken in by the patently absurd. Most of the adult spectators had been through the Night Chant initiation; all of them knew that the gods were no more than men in masks; how could they be so reverent? What was her devout husband's ecstasy, or his devoutness, when he himself put on the painted rawhide bag trimmed with spruce and feathers, pretending to be Talking God?

She remembered the sacrament at school when she had been Christian. She had known that the wine came from the vineyard of an Italian who was a Catholic — something vaguely wicked — and that the bread was just bread. She knew the minister for a nice man whose wife rather bullied him. Yet she had believed that Christ's blood appeared in the wine, or something like that, and had been uplifted when she partook of it.

A Klamath girl had cried bitterly before her first communion. It came out that she feared that eating Christ would make her conceive. In a legend of her own people, Raven had made a woman conceive that way. The minister had been very patient with her, and afterwards the other girls had made fun of her.

The casual way in which the minister handled the jug of wine when it came used to shock her, yet when he raised the chalice, his face would be inspired. He knew it was just the Italian's wine and himself, but he had not been pretending.

These Navajos were just like that. She couldn't make it seem reasonable to herself, but she understood it. And what effect would it have on Laughing Boy?

During the day she occupied herself with the women's work of preparing the semi-sacramental ceremonial foods. She knew very little, indeed, about the ancient ways of cooking, but her sisters-in-law taught her. They were prepared to like her. Her bad reputation had reached them only vaguely, and already they were discrediting it, so that she became to them some one somehow belonging to a larger world, said to be dangerous, hence superior. Now they found her ignorant in this matter, humble, and anxious to learn. She was normal, then, what their slight experience had taught them to expect of returned school-girls, who were always to be pitied. They were delighted to make her their protégée and have the feeling of taking this woman of the world under their wing. Her warm response was not all acting, either; it was not often that women of any race were friendly to her without reservations.

Their mother, she saw, was merely conscientiously fulfilling the ceremonial requirement that every one should feel kind towards every one else during the days of the dance. That atmosphere of '*hozoji*' pervaded the whole camp with a sweetness that was saved from being laughable by the deep devotion behind it. The time of trial was not yet. Slim Girl had some cause to be happy, and so fell in with the general frame of mind, finding a certain reality of meaning in the eternally repeated 'trail of beauty,' 'walking in beauty,' of the ceremony.

In a sentimental way she played at believing her people's religion, and indeed began to find some truth in its basic doctrine, but when she attempted to extend acceptance to the forms which she observed, her sense of the grotesque made it a farce. Meantime she was conquering these people; some were her friends already; her enemies were checked and nonplussed. The opening skirmishes, at least, were hers. She was moving ever more in the stream of Navajo life. She did have cause to be happy. The religion might remain meaningless to her, and probably always would, but the underlying concept of the active force of '*hozoji*' became real.

IV

The men who took part in the dance kept pretty well by themselves. For several days she did not speak to her husband. It was during the fifth afternoon that, seeing him go over where the sun warmed a rock to snatch some sleep, she followed and sat down beside him. She dreamed, watching his face. She loved him so much. There was that love, enough in itself, and then there was so much more. As she had hoped, after all, he was the means of returning to the good things of the Navajo, the good things of life. She could not lose him. What would happen when the dance was over, when it was time to leave, when old Wounded Face showed his hand? She was dependent on this man, her husband; she could not lose him.

She smoked and waited. At length he woke. She reached out and drew her fingers across the back of his hand.

'You must not do that.'

'Why not?'

'I am thinking about the Holy Things. I have to concern my mind only with them. You should not have come here.'

'Is it bad to think about me? Are your thoughts of me not — *hozoji?*' She smiled.

He remained grave. 'They are *hozoji*, but they are not all of it. When I think about the whole, I am thinking about you, too. I give thanks for you. But I must not just think about you and forget all the rest. Now, go away.'

'I see.'

She went softly. Two voices spoke within her; one, that this was the beginning of destruction; the other, that this meant nothing; indeed, that it was a good sign that her presence could disturb him so. Overriding both opinions was a feeling that, unless she was the whole for him, she could not be sure of holding him, and her imperiousness rebelled at being ever subordinate.

And still the ceremony was only half over. What would the remainder bring? She watched the changing rites. The ninth night passed, and the tenth day. She marvelled at the men's endurance; they had periods of rest, but there were night vigils, and for Mountain Singer, endless preparatory prayers. He did not seem tired; rather one would say that he drew rest and strength from his songs. She was sorry for the sick girl, a passive bundle of blankets inside the medicine hogahn, sadly in need of quiet and fresh air.

During that last day visitors began to arrive, until two or three hundred were camped in the valley. There was a slaughtering of sheep and wholesale boiling of coffee and tea. Slim Girl was kept gratefully busy helping in the preparations. The tenth night, with the rite of the Grandfather of the Gods, was the climax.

It was a fine spectacle, the many dancing figures in the firelight, their strange masks and the dull earth-colours, blue, red, white, yellow, black — a broad white zigzag across a black chest, a red figure on blue, outlined with white, standing out in the half-light of the fire. The dancers were never more intent, the chanting more ecstatic. There was real dramatic quality in the entrance of the Grandfather. She was interested, excited. These were her people, putting themselves in touch with eternal forces by means of voice, strength, rhythm, colour, design — everything they had to use. They were creating something strong and barbaric and suitable, and still beautiful.

'In beauty it is finished,
In beauty it is finished,
In beauty it is finished,
In beauty it is finished!'

V

The next day was one of let-down and much sleeping. By dusk, most of the visitors had ridden away. After supper, Laughing Boy's mother and uncles went over to one of the deserted summer hogahns. He finished his cigarette and followed. Wounded Face returned and spoke to Two Bows, who went back with him. Mountain Singer rode in, dismounted, and joined them.

So she was not to be allowed to fight for herself. None of the others at the fire paid any attention; not even casting an extra glance towards Slim Girl. She remembered vaguely that, when a marriage-contract was under discussion, it was the correct thing for the girl concerned to go well away from the house. She supposed that some such etiquette could be invoked to cover this occasion. It would have to do. She slipped out into the darkness, watching to see if her going caused any commentary of exchanged looks. Then she went swiftly away from the hogahns, past the corral, where she deliberately startled a herd-dog into barking.

She circled behind to come up on the summer hogahn, carefully now, thinking of the silent feet and quick ears of her people, feeling herself clumsy, her limbs managed by indirect control. She crouched in the shadow of the back wall, clutching her blanket about her for warmth, praying that her teeth would not chatter. She was clearly conscious of the beauty of the night, its stars and sharp cold, the smell of sage and sand, the faint rustle of leaves on the hogahn.

They were lighting a fire. When it was burning well, they gathered close to it, so that peering between the leaves and branches she saw them as dim, significant masses with their faces faintly shown, identifying them. Mountain Singer was in the place of honour, with his back to her; on his left sat Walked Around, Laughing Boy's mother; on his right was Spotted Horse. Wounded Face was next to him, facing Laughing Boy, and Two

Bows sat a little bit back, near the door. She summed them up to herself, wishing she could be present to use her skill and have her share in the approaching conflict. It was not fair. She wished she could see Mountain Singer's face; that old man's influence would be emphasized, now that he was just through conducting the chant, and her husband with serving him as acolyte. He was the leader of the Tahtchini Clan in this section; his importance was shown by his seat of honour in this conclave of people to whom he was only distantly related. Spotted Horse did not amount to much. Walked Around hated her, personally and with fear. Wounded Face was set against her for more general, but weighty reasons. As for Two Bows, she could not tell. He had a quality of understanding which might make him her friend or her most dangerous enemy. In any case, he was here only as a privileged outsider.

The fire began to make warmth, and tobacco was passed round. Nobody spoke for several minutes. Then Mountain Singer said:

'We are thinking about my younger brother here; we are thinking about what he should do. We have come here to talk it over with him.'

They went on smoking. They were sombre bundles of shadow, in their blankets, with faces of people faintly seen. Wounded Face spat out a grain of tobacco. 'My nephew, we do not think it is good, this thing you are doing. We have talked about it a long time among ourselves. We know about that woman, that she ——'

Laughing Boy raised his head. 'You have said those things once, uncle, and I have heard them. Do not say them again, those things. If you do, there will not be any talk. Tell yourself that I have heard them, and know what I think of them. They were said in Killed a Navajo's hogahn. I heard them there. Now go on from that.'

They talked, watching the end of their cigarettes, or with the right hand rubbing over the fingers of the left, as though to bring the words out, or touching each finger-tip in turn, with their eyes upon their hands, so that the even voices seemed utterly detached, the persons mere media for uttering thoughts formed at the back of nowhere.

'Perhaps you are mistaken, I think, but I do as you say. You are making unhappiness for yourself, you are making ugliness. You are of The People, the good life for you is theirs. It is all very well now while your eyes and your ears and your nose are stopped up with love, but one day you will look around and see only things that do not fit you, alkali-water to drink. You will want your own things, and you will not be able to fit them, either, I think.

'It is all very well that you deceive the younger people with your clothes and hard goods and manners, but we can see that all the time you are apart. And you are just a light from her fire, just something she has made. She has acted and spoken well here, that one. She speaks above and below and before and behind, but she does not speak straight out forward, I think.'

'We live like other People.'

'Even your beginning was like Americans. You talked about it with each other, you two arranged it face to face. You had no shame. She caused that. Have you been married?'

'Yes.'

'Who sang?'

'Yellow Singer.'

'Did you look at him? No, I think. You looked at him with your eyes, so as not to fall over him when you walked past; did your mind see him? No, I think. If you think now about him, you will see him, perhaps. You will see what is left of a man when he leaves our way, when he walks in moccasins on the Americans' road. You have seen other People who live down there. Some of them are rich, but their hearts are empty. You have seen them without happiness or beauty in their hearts, because they have lost the Trail of Beauty. Now they have nothing to put in their hearts except whiskey.'

Slim Girl winced.

'Those people cannot dance in a chant and do any good. You would not want Yellow Singer to hold a chant over you, it would not bring you *hozoji*.

'You say live like The People. Why do you live apart, then? Does she not like to be with The People, that woman?

'I have spoken.'

Laughing Boy made a gesture of brushing aside. His uncle threw his cigarette butt into the fire with an angry motion.

Walked Around leaned forward. 'What my brother says is good, but it is not all, what he has said. I have watched you, how you go about. This valley T'o Tlakai speaks to you with tongues, I think. When you look over to Chiz-na Hozolchi you hear singing, I think. You hasten to speak with your own people, you like to use your tongue for old names. You care more to talk about our sheep and our waterholes — your waterholes — than we do. You belong with us, and we want you. We want good for you. When you are gone, we know that you are away. That woman keeps you from us. Why does she do it? If she means good towards you and we mean good towards you, why should she be afraid of us? Perhaps because she wants to make you into something else, she does it. Perhaps because if you were among us you would see straight.

'She has no parents, no uncles, that she should build her hogahn near them. There are plenty of the Bitahni Clan here; let her come here. Come and live among us, your own people. Perhaps then, if she is not bad, we shall see that we are wrong, we shall learn to love her, my child.'

Clever, clever, you bitch!

Laughing Boy moved his hand again.

Wounded Face took up the word. 'You are young, you do not like to listen.'

His voice was level, but he was angry; there was tension in the hut. That was good; if they showed anger they would lose him forever.

'You do not intend to hear what we say.'

Mountain Singer interrupted him. 'His father taught him to hunt, to dance, and to work silver. His father knows him best of us all, I think. Grandfather, what is in your mind?'

This was more important than anything heretofore.

Two Bows spoke slowly. 'We have all seen his silver, her blankets. We have seen him dance. We know, therefore, how he is now. We know that, now, all is well with him.

'A man makes a design well because he feels it. When he makes some one else's design, you can tell. If he is to make some one else's design, he must feel it in himself first. You cannot point a pistol at a man and say, "Make heat-lightning and clouds with tracks-meeting under them, and make it beautiful."

'My son is thinking about a design for his life. Let him tell us, and if it is not good, perhaps we can show him.'

'You have spoken well, Grandfather.'

'Yes, you have spoken well.' It was Spotted Horse's only contribution.

They all shifted slightly, watching Laughing Boy. He spoke without hesitation, but selecting his words precisely.

'I had not spoken, because I thought all your minds were made up. Now I shall tell you. I heard what my uncle told me that time; I saw Yellow Singer and those others down there. I have thought about all those things. I have not just run in like a crazy horse. Everything has been new, and I have watched and thought.

'I have been with that woman many moons now. I tell you that I know that those bad things are not true. Hear me.

'It is true that our life is different, but we are not following the American trail. Do not think it, that thing. She is different. She does everything as we do, more than most school-girls; but she is different. You have seen our silver, our blankets; if you come to us you will see how everything is like that. It is beautiful. It is the Trail of Beauty. You will just have to believe me, it is something I never imagined, we have nothing here to compare with it, that life. We do only good things. Everything good that I have ever known, all at once, could not make me as happy as she and her way do.

'Look at me. I am older than when I left here, I know what I say. My mind is made up. I do not want you to be angry with me; I do not want you to be unhappy about me; I do not want you to tell me not to come back. You may not believe me, but I want you to wait.

'It does not matter. I know. I have spoken.'

VI

Her triumph was real and urgent, but now was no time for indulging it. She walked back to the fire circle as though, from her waiting place apart, she had just seen the counsellors returning. It was time to go to bed; she found her place on the sheepskins inside the hogahn. It was stuffy and warm in there save for a faint draft of air in under the blanket that closed the door and out the smoke-hole, and a coldness that seeped through the ground from outside, where the finger-tips of one hand had touched the floor.

That is how he feels, then. All mine. I can do anything. *Ya*, Wounded Face! Then, if I am so sure of him, why not come to live here? It is dangerous there. What a strange idea: when I am most sure I can do as I want, I give it up. Hunh! We have made almost a thousand dollars in ten months, counting the horses he has now. Everything is going perfectly. George eats out of my hand. I am strong.

She was becoming drowsy and making pictures. There was a story she remembered faintly, how Nayeinezgani did not kill the Hunger People. An allegory; her Slayer of Enemy Gods could not kill them, either. She could do away with them.

I have seen more than you and all you People, I know more. I shall lead you on the trail.

I, Slim Girl, Came With War.

CHAPTER XIII

I

THEY rode away from T'o Tlakai in gay company — Bay Horse and Bow's Son, Tall Brave from T'ies Napornss and his wife, and half a dozen others, men and women, returning towards T'o Tlikahn, Tsébitai, and Seinsaidesah. It had turned sharply cold, the ponies went well; they played and raced, showing off their jewelry and best clothes and horsemanship — all young people. Bay Horse smoked on a dead twig, blowing out clouds of breath.

'See my new magic! I take this twig, and it is a lighted cigarette.'

'*Ei-yei,* Grandfather; see if you can swallow all your smoke.'

They came to the foot of the slope leading to Gomulli T'o trading post.

A man said, 'Let us go buy some crackers and canned fruit.'

'It's too cold. Some coffee would be good, I think.'

'Maybe Yellow Mustache will give us some,' Laughing Boy said. 'Why did he not come to the dance?'

'Yellow Mustache is not there any longer; he has gone to Chiezb'utso. The man there now is called Narrow Nose.'

'What is he like?'

'He is no good. When we put things in pawn, he sells them before we can buy them back. He is small; inside himself he is small.'

'He tries to be smart with us, but he is not good at it. His word is not good.'

'He thinks we are fools. He ought to look at himself.'

Laughing Boy broke into the chorus of information — 'Wait a moment!'

He rode over to Jesting Squaw's Son and whispered in his ear. His friend smiled.

'I am thinking about coffee. I can make him give us all coffee free, I think. Who will bet?'

'I know you,' said Bay Horse, 'I won't.'

Bow's Son whispered to Slim Girl, 'He is like this. They are like this, those two, when they are together. They are not for nothing, their names.'

'I will bet two bits, just to make a bet,' Tall Brave said.

A stranger offered fifty cents. Laughing Boy gave each of them his stake.

'Now, you all go up to the post. Go in. Do not buy, not anything. None of you know me; if any one else is there tell him not to know me; but you all know my grandfather here. You, little sister,' he looked at his wife, 'stay here.'

They rode away while he advised with his friend. Then he explained to Slim Girl, and took her silver bridle. After a slow cigarette he said,

'When that shadow reaches that stick will be time, I think. I go.'

Gomulli T'o trading post stood on a flat, bare shoulder of sand and rock, a level space of half a dozen acres, rising to the west, falling to the east. There was a corral with sides six feet high, and the L-shaped one-story house of stone and adobe with a corrugated iron roof. Around it was nothing green, nothing varied, just sand and rocks, some tin cans, part of a rotted blue shirt. There was no relief. In summer the drenching sun searched out its barren walls; in winter the wind was bleak around it. It was just something dumped there, a thing made by man, contributing nothing, in the midst of majestic desolation. Beyond its level were red-brown cliffs, dull orange bald-rock, yellow sand, leading away to blend into a kind of purplish brown with blue clouds of mountains for background. This did not belong; it was crushed and empty.

Besides the ones belonging to his own party, Laughing Boy noted two other ponies hitched by the corral. He made his fast with a bow-knot, the animal being rather unenterprising and not having learned how to untie them. He looped the reins over the saddle-horn and sauntered to the door of the store, trailing the bridle carelessly, and adjusting his recently acquired hat. It was a stiff-brimmed felt, with the crown undented and the string tied under the chin, Indian fashion, becoming him well. He gave it a wicked slant.

The store was a square room with a counter around three sides; in the fourth the door and a small window. Another door in the back led to the rest of the house. Now the room was rank with tobacco smoke and the heat of an iron stove. The Indians lounged along the counter, leaning on it with their elbows, talking or staring at the goods on the shelves. He recognized the owners of the two ponies — Stinks Like a Mexican, an old rogue with his hair cut short to the level of his ears, who had worked for the railroad, and Long Tooth, the policeman from T'ies Napornss.

He stood in the door.

Bow's Son regarded him blankly.

'Where to, tell?'

'To T'o Tlakai, for the dance.'

'The dance is over; we come from it.'

'*Chiendi!*'

'Where from, tell?' Tall Brave asked.

'Chiziai.'

'That's far!'

'Yes. You tell, where do you live?'

'T'ies Napornss.'

He drifted to the far end, where the trader sat, feet on the counter, chewing listlessly. The man was partly bald, with drooping, pepper-and-salt mustaches and a stupid, narrow face. He looked stingy and ignorant, not bad.

An unsuccessful dry farmer, he had bought a poor post, sight unseen, and come out to make quick money from the ignorant Indians. Somehow it didn't work. They fooled him and exasperated him until he strove frantically to outcheat them, and that didn't work either. He had no idea of how to attract their trade, nor of how to circumvent their sharpness. It was always like this. Two men had been there since he opened the store in the morning, making one nickel purchase, and now none of these others wanted to buy. They just wanted to talk. They thought he was running a God-damned club.

Laughing Boy sprawled against the counter, clicking a quarter against his teeth. His face was vacuous while he studied the ranks of tin cans. This part came natural to him. He thought idly that it was six months since he had been in a store. It was too bad Yellow Mustache was gone. Yellow Mustache would have welcomed him, and probably given him some candy.

'What kind of candy have you?' He spoke in the baby-talk Navajo that they use with Americans.

'Round-soft-ones, hard-clear-ones, and brown sweets.'

The man was not really at home even in the trade language. He was a little hard of hearing; it hampered him in learning.

'How much are the round-soft-ones?'

'Two for a yellow.'

Laughing Boy examined his change carefully, and put a dime on the counter. 'Give me a blue's worth.'

The trader let four gum drops roll toward the customer. 'Give it to me.' He reached for the dime.

Laughing Boy held onto it. 'Haven't you any twisted-sticks?'

'No.'

'I don't want those.' He put his money back in his pocket. 'Give me a smoke.'

Narrow Nose eyed him for a moment, as though he would like to see him shrivel. Policy was policy. He slid a half-empty sack of Stud and some papers along the counter.

'Match, brother-in-law.'

'You have some.' He pointed to the Indian's shirt pocket.

'I need those.'

'Well, you go to hell!' Narrow Nose swore in English with that fatuous confidence of not being understood.

'*Juthla hagɔ ni*,' Laughing Boy paraphrased softly, half as though interpreting to himself, half as though throwing it back. The insult, in Navajo, is serious. There was a laugh.

He lolled against the counter, lit his cigarette, and puffed at it critically.

'I think I buy that saddle. Let me see it.'

'I'll take it down if you really want it.'

It hung from a rafter, among other saddles, quirts, bridles, pots, Pendleton blankets, ropes, silk handkerchiefs, and axes.

'Let me see it. My saddle is worn out. I need a new one. I want that blanket there, I think, and four red cans of tobacco, the kind with the preacher in the long black coat on it.'

'Can you pay for all that?'

'I give this in pawn.'

He clanked the bridle onto the counter. Stinks Like a Mexican drew nearer.

'I want that handkerchief there, I think.' He nodded toward a silk one. 'And a knife that shuts.'

The trader got up, feigning reluctance. The way the man had made up his mind to buy was typical. He hefted the bridle — ninety to a hundred dollars. Things were looking up. If he got his hooks in this, in return for thirty dollars' worth of goods —

'Where do you live?'

'Chiziai.'

'Where's that?'

'Down there.'

Indians edged up to handle the silver. Narrow Nose turned to the policeman, who spoke a little English.

'Where's Chiziai?'

'Lo Palo. Mebbe-so lailload tlack side him sit down. Him come flom dere now, me sabbey.' He didn't quite know what was up, but he wasn't going to spoil it.

'Los Palos, hunh? I know.'

'I came up for the dance, now I go back. In Eagles' Young Moon I shall come back and take out my bridle.'

That sounded good. Five — six months, likely he'd forget it. Likely it wouldn't be here.

'Is he speaking true?' The trader asked the store in general.

Bow's Son held up the bridle. 'This is the kind of work they do down there. It is not like the work up here, not like my father's jewelry,' he lied. Bay Horse and Tall Brave agreed. Narrow Nose knew them and Two Bows well. He believed them.

'Good, I take your bridle.' He reached for it, wanting to feel its possession.

'Wait a moment; put down the goods.'

He assembled them laboriously. 'Forty-one dollars and one blue.'

'How?'

'Saddle, twenty-seven; blanket, ten — thirty-seven; tobacco, six blues; handkerchief, two dollars; knife, twelve bits; forty-one dollars and one blue. I make it forty-one dollars.'

Laughing Boy strung out the bargaining stubbornly, until he heard singing outside. The trader had stuck at thirty-five dollars.

'Good, I take them.'

He started to push over the bridle; Narrow Nose had his fingers on the heavy silver. Jesting Squaw's Son and Slim Girl entered together.

'*Ahalani!*'

'*Ahalani, shichai!*'

The two men strode up to each other, Laughing Boy still clutching the harness. The trader's hands felt empty. They hugged each other, wrestled, went through a huge pantomime of friendship.

'It is good to see you, my friend!'

'Very much it is good to see you!'

'*Hozhoni!*'

'*Aigisi hozhoni!*'

'What are you doing here?'

'I came up for the dance, but I am too late, they say. What are your news?'

'I have just got married. This is my wife, she comes from Maito.'

'Good!'

Narrow Nose thought he must be progressing in the language, he could understand most of what they said. Usually when they talked among themselves, he could not follow, they seemed to mess it around so. He had no idea that they were using baby-talk for his special benefit, any more than it occurred to him as unusual that a man should be bringing a bride to live in his settlement, instead of going to hers.

Jesting Squaw's Son shook hands with his other friends there, as though he had just come back from a trip.

'I have just finished building our hogahn, over towards T'ies Napornss. We are going to make the House Prayer in a little while. I want you all to come now, we shall make a feast afterwards. You, my friend, you must come. Come now.'

He nodded at Tall Brave, who started to the door with a couple of the others.

'But I am making a trade here. I must finish it.'

'You can make a better trade with the trader at T'ies Napornss. He is a good man.'

Narrow Nose swore to himself. He wanted that bridle, and he wanted that new couple's custom. Jesting Squaw was well-to-do; she would give her son plenty of sheep.

'I give you a good trade. Stay here and finish it.'

'I go with my friend to feast, I think. All these people are going.'

'Yes,' Tall Brave struck in from the doorway, 'it is time to eat.'

'Why don't you buy food and feast here?'

'I have food there, coffee and meat and bread. Why should they buy food here?' Jesting Squaw's Son told him.

The trader made a quick calculation, involving about a dollar and a quarter.

'I will give you coffee and crackers and some canned plums. How is that?'

'*Ei-yei!* Then we shall stay.'

'He must be a good man to deal with,' Laughing Boy said solemnly.

Narrow Nose called through the back door,

'Make about three quarts of coffee, quick, and put jest a little sweetnin' in it. Bring out ten cups.' He set out two boxes of saltines and four cans of plums. 'Now, give me the bridle.'

'I think I get something more, a rope, perhaps. You are a good man to buy from.' He laid the bridle on the counter, but hung onto the reins.

Narrow Nose climbed onto the counter and pulled down a length of rope. 'This is good.'

'No, I want horsehair.' With his mouth full.

'No horsehair.'

'Rawhide, then.'

He had to search under the counter for hide ropes that Indians had made. Laughing Boy went over them minutely. The coffee came. The Indians wolfed down the food and drink, and tipped up the cans to drain the fruit juice.

Laughing Boy said, before he had swallowed his last mouthful,

'I do not think I want those things.'

'Hunh?'

Drawing at the reins, he made the bridle seem to walk off the counter.

'Hey, stop!'

He turned at the door. 'Another time, perhaps.'

'Hey, by Gawd!'

All the Indians streamed out, with the trader

after them. Laughing Boy was off at a gallop, his wife and Jesting Squaw's Son close behind. The rest followed, whooping and swinging their ropes and whips. Narrow Nose stood in the sand.

'Hey!'

Inside the store, Stinks Like a Mexican collected some tobacco and a handkerchief. He slid through the door, and vanished around the corner of the house.

'God damn a red devil!'

The Indians went fast; already their singing was distant. It was cold. He stuck his hands into his pockets and stared after them.

'God damn a red son of a bitch!'

CHAPTER XIV

I

IT began to snow on the morning of the third day of their trip home, not far from Kintiel. The ground, where it had any dampness in it, had been frozen since the night before, and they had hurried under a threatening sky, having still a good day's ride before them. The storm came down like timber-wolves, rushing. A mountain-top wind sent the dry flakes whirling past, stinging their ears and the sides of their faces; there was no sun, they could see only a few yards ahead of them. Pulling their blankets up over their heads, they guided themselves by the wind at their backs.

An Indian takes the weather passively, accepting and enduring it without the European's mental revolt or impatience. Comfort and fat living had changed this to some degree in Laughing Boy; he was unusually aware of discomfort, and resentful, rating the blizzard as colder than it was. Slim Girl was simply miserable. They did not speak, but jogged on, punishing their horses.

Time passed and the wind slackened, so that

the snow about their ponies' hooves stayed still, although the fall of flakes continued. Laughing Boy was preoccupied with thoughts of the road, but his wife contrasted this ride with the other time when they had ridden this way together. First it is the top of a stove and then it is an ice-machine, she thought; yet I am beginning to love it.

Cliffs loomed before them, duskily blue with snowflakes rebounding and zigzagging before they touched the rock. The snow was beginning to drift.

'These are not the right cliffs,' he said; 'the wind must have shifted, I think. I was afraid it would.'

'What shall we do, then?'

'I think this is Inaiyé Cletso'i; we follow to the left.'

'Why not camp here?'

'We must find firewood. We might just sleep here and not wake up. Come along, little sister, perhaps we shall find a hogahn.'

They continued, he fully occupied, she miserable with nothing to do save follow. Sometimes the snow whirled up at them, sometimes a flaw would sting their faces with fine, white dust. Their heavy blankets felt thin as cotton over their shoulders.

'There's a hogahn.' She pushed forward.

'*Hogay-gahn*, bad. Do not stop here!'

'What do you mean?'

'Don't you see it is deserted? Don't you see the hole in the north side? Some one has died here. Come along.'

She sighed in anger, gritted her teeth, swore under her breath, and turned her horse back. Nothing on earth would make a Navajo stop there; he would not even use the dry timbers for firewood to save his life. Well, it was part of the rest.

'We are coming somewhere now,' he called to her.

'How?'

'I smell smoke. There, you can see.'

It was a well-built hut beside a corral. Smoke issued from the hole in the roof. The dome of daubed mud and untrimmed logs looked beautiful just then. Laughing Boy shouted at the door, and a middle-aged man crawled out.

'Where are you going?'

'To Chiziai.'

'You are out of the trail; it is far.'

'This snow confused us.'

'Where from?'

'T'o Tlakai.'

'Where's that?'

'Between Seinsaidesah and Agathla.'

'*Ei-yei!* You come far! Just beyond, there, is a box cañon. There is shelter and feed. Put your horses there, Grandfather. Drop your saddles here, I shall bring them in. Come in, Grandmother.'

They lost no time over the horses, and crawled gladly into the smoky, fetid, warm hogahn. There were the man, two women, four children between eight and fifteen, and two dogs. The space was a circle some twelve feet in diameter — the average size; with the people, the fire in the middle, saddles, cooking utensils, a loom and blankets, it was well filled.

'You live at T'o Tlakai?'

'No, at Chiziai. My parents live there. There was a Night Chant; for that we went. It was a full ten days' chant. Mountain Singer conducted it.'

'Beautiful!'

'Yes.'

The elder wife served them a pot of boiled mutton and corn, with a chunk of the usual tough wheat bread. They ate readily. It flashed through Laughing Boy's mind that he had not enjoyed a meal so much since his arrival at Tsé Lani, but then he thought that that was silly. The foods to which he was accustomed!

II

They were storm-bound for all the next day. He was anxious to be home again, now that the restraint of the ceremony and after-ceremony was ended. He wanted to have Slim Girl to himself, at leisure, and to enjoy their own special kind of life once more. So he was impatient and ready to find fault.

It was a long time since he had been confined in a winter hogahn, with its crowded things and people and close-packed smells. Their house at Los Palos was always aired. At T'o Tlakai it still had been warm enough to leave the door unblanketed during the day, and he had spent most of his time in the brush-walled medicine-lodge. He found it too close here, and was made self-conscious by fearing what she might think of it.

The modern Navajo diet, boiled mutton and tough bread, tough bread and boiled mutton, a little corn and squash, coffee with not enough sugar, tea as black as coffee, had none of the delicacy of the old ceremonial dishes. He went outside only on rising, when they all rolled in the snow (it had never occurred to him to warn Slim Girl of that custom, but she followed suit without a sign), and again for half an hour to look at his ponies. The thick air inside weighed upon him;

he felt dull after a heavy breakfast, and had no more appetite.

Then there were the lice. His wife had rid him of them, conquering his sincere belief that they were a gift from Old Couple in the World Below to enable people to sleep. He had rated that as one of her minor magics. No new ones had got on to him at T'o Tlakai, but in this crowded place they stormed him. He was not used to being bitten, so he was tormented, and he scratched a great deal.

His host asked him naïvely, 'You have many lice, Grandfather?'

He caught his tongue in time, answering, 'No, but they nearly froze yesterday. Now they have waked up again, and they are hungry.'

Slim Girl gave him a look of approval and sympathy, with a little gesture of scratching furiously at herself. He smiled.

The afternoon and early evening were better, for his host recounted the second part of the Coming Up story to his children, the part about the Twin Gods, Slayer of Enemy Gods, and Child of the Waters, which Laughing Boy loved best. He noticed that Slim Girl listened intently. Some day he would be telling his children. It seemed a long time for them not to have had any, but he really did not know very much about these things. It was the woman's business; the children were hers. after all. She would arrange it in due time, according to her wisdom. He drowsed and was soothed by the tale of the familiar, strange adventures, the gate of the Clashing Rocks, the trail over Boiling Sands, Monster Eagle and Monster Elk and Big God, lightning-arrows and cloud-blankets. After supper the close air drugged him; his eyes were nearly closed as he listened to the last of the myth.

The snowflakes, drifting through the smoke-hole, fell into the fire with little hisses. The even voice went on, telling the end.

'Slayer of Enemy Gods came to the Hunger People, they say . . .'

But it was not his dream, there was nothing portentous about this voice. Slim Girl had slain the Hunger People. He smiled and listened, cradled in drowsiness, distantly conscious of a louse biting him, and comforting himself with the thought that to-morrow all that would be attended to, to-morrow they would be home again. These poor people, they could not know. He half-opened his eyes, seeing his wife's thoughtful, delicate face, and said, as sleepy people will, much louder than he realized,

'*Hasché Lto'i!*'

'What was that, Grandfather?' asked the man.

'Nothing.'

'I thought you said something about Hunting Goddess.'

'No, I said "*hashkê yei itei,*" the gods are brave.'

'Unh! That is well said.'

Slim Girl reflected. Hashché Lto'i was one of the few real goddesses, but she had nothing at all to do with the Coming Up story. He had covered his slip neatly, that man of hers. He was no child They two would go far, far, under her direction.

The story-telling ended, and the flakes had ceased falling through the smoke-hole. To-morrow would be clear. The banked fire became a dull redness, scarcely glowing.

III

They covered the fifteen miles home at a racing pace, on a morning of clear, brilliant air and dry, fresh snow. They both felt glorious, released from the cramped hogahn, glad to be approaching their goal. Though she had no great endurance, Slim Girl rode well, and now, with their ponies prancing in the cold, played tricks and frolicked on horseback as Indian men and women rarely do together. They both yipped and waved their arms; she snatched his hat, and threw it for him to pick from the ground on the run; he swung low under his pony's neck and sent an arrow skimming ahead of them. Before they reached it, the special quality and privacy of their home reached out to them, and they were almost definitely conscious of reëntering their own way of living as though one entered an enclosure.

He admired anew the fireplace, with its smokelessness, its draft that set the flame quickly blazing, the heat thrown out from its shallow back. She prepared food while he tended to the ponies. The house became warm, but the air was sweet, the adobe walls and clay floor were clean, and now, with lively appetites, they smelt the good food cooking. She sat back from the fire while things stewed and bubbled. Kneeling beside her, he kissed her — to him perhaps more than anything else the act symbolic of their life apart — and they smiled at each other with grave pleasure. For a minute she was limp in his arms, then she pushed him away with an affectionate, scolding word and returned to a pot that was boiling over. He lay back on the sheepskins, watching. Domesticity, his wife, his home, perfection.

The loom-frame hung near the door; on the other side was the anvil. The place was permeated with an excited happiness, fulness, completion. Had any religious-minded Navajo, sensitive enough to the reiterated doctrine of *hozoji* to feel it without words, entered that place, he would have felt that he had, indeed, entered the 'house of happiness.'

CHAPTER XV

I

THE winter passed as swiftly as the summer; more so, in fact, for, feeling more sure of herself, Slim Girl consented to a social life. They went to various dances, becoming better known among the Southern Navajos, who began to accept her as entirely one of themselves. Learning with practice better and better how to avoid being different in a way that troubled others, she was able to be one of them without the fatal appearance of reserve and effort. By a slow process, she saw, Laughing Boy really was bringing her back into her own people. She consented out of policy to undergo the Night Chant initiation, the scourging with yucca leaves, the demonstration of the masks, and having done so found, surprised at her own naïveté, that it was a genuine source of satisfaction to her. Knowing that something of the true substance was forever lost to her, she surrounded herself as much as possible with the trappings of Navajo-ism.

There were obstacles and interruptions: a double life carries heavy enough penalties, and a past is a past, particularly if its locale is much the same as that of the present. Red Man, the wrestler of Tsé Lani, sophisticated and self-willed, was present at many of those dances. Slim Girl had never given him more than hope, and even that, he felt, more because he served a purpose than for anything else. She had used him. Now she belonged to this rustic, who had humiliated him, and who obviously did not know what it was all about. Red Man was too good an Indian to bear much resentment for the wrestling defeat, but it served the purpose of preventing him from amusing himself by explaining to Laughing Boy just what he knew about his wife. Besides, he shrewdly suspected, such a recital would be dangerous in the extreme.

So he adopted an attitude of smiling implications, of 'I could an I would,' that was as effective as possible for making trouble. Laughing Boy remembered the dancing at Tsé Lani, and he felt disturbed. Watching Red Man, it came upon him that, remarkable though his wife was, she was subject to the same general laws as other people, and he was fairly sure that he was not the first man she had known in love. Many things suddenly aligned themselves in a new way to assume a monstrous form. He became very quiet, and thought hard.

Slim Girl saw it immediately, not knowing what

he was thinking, but feeling the reality of her peril. At that dance, she paid no attention to it, continued as ever, and treated Red Man with cool friendliness. At home, she managed to bring him into the talk, told Laughing Boy how he had sought to marry her once, and described with entire truth an ugly scene with him at Tsé Lani. Her husband listened, and was gladly convinced.

Her past was her past, he thought; he knew enough of her to know that it had been more than unhappy, and that she had put it resolutely behind her. There was much suffering, many bad things, of which she never spoke. Some day, perhaps, she could tell him. In any case, he believed what she did say, and even had the case been otherwise, that was all dead.

The next time they met, he contemplated the man, and guessed at the dimensions of his soul. Taking an opportunity when they both were taking horses to water, he rode up beside him, sitting sideways on his barebacked pony, one hand on the mane, one hand on the rump — a casual pose for a careless chat. Red Man greeted him non-committally.

'Grandfather, let us not run around things, let us not pretend,' he said. 'You have not said anything, but you have said too much. Do not pretend not to know what I mean. If you like what you are doing so much that you are willing to fight about it, go on. If not, stop it. I say, not just do less of it, or do it differently, but stop it entirely. That is what I mean. I have spoken.'

Red Man studied him; he was plainly in deadly earnest. He might just as well have acted instead of spoken — those men from up there have not yet realized the power of police and law. Among Navajos, the reasonable and acceptable way to have done, had he acted, would have been from ambush. Red Man felt he had had a narrow escape. He emphatically did not like what he was doing that much. Time would inevitably bring sorrow to the fellow.

'I hear you, Grandfather.'

II

These occasional absences of from three days to over a week made complications in Slim Girl's arrangements with her American. His trips in to town from his ranch were made on business that was, as often as not, conjured up to excuse himself to himself for seeing her. Each rendezvous would be arranged the time before, or by a note left in the little house, which she was supposed to visit at fixed intervals. Now it was occurring, as never before, that he would demand her presence on a certain date, only to be told it was impossible. Increasingly, as her love for her husband gained upon her, he suspected part of the truth, and tormented himself with jealousy. That husband, whom he had always regarded as rather mythical, seemed in the past few months to have become exacting. In moments of honesty towards himself, he writhed at the acid thought of being used by a squaw for the benefit of herself and some low, presumably drunken, Indian.

He rode into Los Palos through the bottomless mud and wet of a spring thaw, only to find a note on the table:

DEAR GEORGE

My husband make me go too dance I will come day after tomorrow afternoon. pleas not mind.

love

LILLIAN

The poor fool cursed, got drunk, and waited over.

That had been a very pleasant dance; they had ridden part of the way home with as likable a crowd as the one that rode from T'o Tlakai to the trading post. She still tasted the flavour of it as she changed into her Sears-Roebuck dress and set out for Los Palos. Laughing Boy had surprised on her face, once or twice, that look of triumphant hatred when she returned. He would have been astonished could he have seen her now.

She looked back on their house, on the corral and the still leafless young peach trees, visualizing the dance, her people, and him. Her face was tender, almost yearning. Then she turned away towards the town, and braced her shoulders. For a moment she smiled, a war-path smile, and she was hard. Her upper lip curled back, showing her small, even, white teeth. Then her expression was blank; that passive look upon her oval face that made one turn to it again and again, wondering what deep, strong thoughts were going on behind the lovely mask.

He was in the house before her. She braced herself again at the door, then blotted everything from her eyes, becoming a happy, pretty woman with nothing on her mind. He rose as she entered. He did not answer her smile or move to touch her; that meant there would be a scene. Oh, well!

'Look here, Lillian, this is getting too thick. Here I come in here just to see you — we made the date, didn't we? — and you've gone prancing off to some dance. It won't do. I don't ask so much of you, but you've got to keep your dates, do you see? Don't make me suspect you . . .'

She hated scenes, loud voices, turmoil, protestations. God damn this man. *Juthla hago hode shonh.* She sat still, looking at him with wide, hurt eyes and drooping mouth. By and by he ran down.

'You tink lak dat about me! You tink I forget everyting! What for you tink dose tings, hey? I'm sorry I go away. I do it because I got to, you see? My husban', he tink someting bad, I tink. So he act mean, dat man. But you know.'

'The trouble is I don't know. I wonder about you. I wonder if you try at all, or just do what's handiest for you. I've got some consideration coming to me, you know.'

The man was truly jealous, he was miserable, she had him right in the palm of her hand. She didn't have to say much, just let him do it. After he'd got rid of all this, the fact remained that he loved her, and that was all that mattered.

He drew her towards him, she sat on his knees, her hands on his shoulders. He bent her face back and stared into her eyes. They were deep, deep, and swimming. There was a look in them that thrilled him, a look that must be true. Now there was an imprint of real truth in her words and gestures, and the fierceness of her kiss.

She was not acting any longer, she did not have to pretend this. There was no more falseness in it than there is in an arrow leaving a bow. She hated him. On him she had concentrated all her feelings towards Americans in general, everything that she had ever suffered. In him she was revenging herself upon them all. Her kisses were weapons, her tendernesses were blows struck in the full heat of battle. She was revenging herself, and she was acquiring the means to her perfect life.

Bound by those hours of happiness, he could not break away. These days, he gave her more money than he ever had before, more than he could well afford, seeking to bind her to him, knowing that that was no way to arrive at truth, but craving, if she were lying to him, to be lied to so well he would be convinced. He made many efforts to improve her, feeling how remarkable a woman she was. He wanted her to read books, but her distaste for them was deep and sincere; he wanted to make a superior American out of her. He would have liked to raise her to a position in which he could respect himself if he married her.

She was afraid always that he would ask her that, but he was not quite so lost. She kept him at tension, administering happiness and unhappiness carefully, accepted his increased gifts, and in her mind shortened the time of waiting. But it did not make a smooth road to travel.

III

She was beset by difficulties and entanglements, but she was conquering them one by one, even turning them to her use, as though she were taking weapons from her enemies. She could shape and bend men, she could control her destinies in theirs. In her thoughts, she tasted in advance the happiness of the goal towards which she aimed, and she felt her power, power, power; and so, as far as she could tell, she was happy.

Her weaving was winning Laughing Boy's unstinted praise, and, to her surprise and great satisfaction, becoming a source of income. The trading post in Los Palos would pass on to her occasional orders from tourists or people in the East. If she had been willing to weave the entirely un-Indian pictures of actual objects that so many tourists demand, she could have had all the work she could handle at fancy prices; but she refused to do anything, or use any colours not purely Navajo, and she strengthened her husband in his natural reluctance to stamp shapeless strings of swastikas, thunder-birds, and other curiosities on his silver. She was precious about it, as she was about all Navajo things. It was one piece with her eagerness to speak familiarly of everything familiar to them, to participate in every phase of their life, to acquire completely the Navajo gesture. When they were rich and lived in the North, she thought, she would make herself an influence for preserving all native ways; she would use any power they acquired in combating Christianity, short hair, shoes, ready-made trousers, and the creeping in of American-derived words. Already she had amused her husband by insisting on calling coffee by its old, cumbrous name of little-split-round-ones, instead of the much easier '*coghwé*,' that had been taken into the language.

Laughing Boy's reputation was spreading. The Harvey agent had made her a tentative offer for them to come to Grand Cañon. In the beginning of spring, at planting time, they moved forge and loom outdoors again. At sunset, laying aside tools, or coming in, tired and at peace, from working in the soft earth, they sang together.

Now was the time when ponies began to grow fat, and the desert was all one mass of flowers. Remembering a good thing from her school days, Slim Girl brought in great bunches, Indian paint brush, fireweed, cactus blooms, and a hundred others, and stuck them in tin cans about the house. This puzzled Laughing Boy at first, but later he caught on, and enjoyed grouping them, with a good feeling for arrangements of masses of colour, but little interest in the blossoms as such.

There was movement in the desert. Horse-trading picked up again. The first sprouts of corn came through the ground, the peach trees began to put out leaves; one of them triumphantly produced a blossom. The days slipped by. Life was settled, serene, monotonous; there was no detail of it that one would wish to change.

CHAPTER XVI

I

Any married couple, no matter how perfect the match, will undergo a critical period of strain, and these two were no exception. For all the dances, winter was a hemmed-in time; repetitious days indoors were a searching test of companionship. Slim Girl went into town, Laughing Boy sallied forth to watch over the herd; but they moved out of the home atmosphere together only for those eight or nine ceremonies.

They were attempting a difficult thing. They needed not only to see occasional outsiders when they were apart, new faces made attractive by the mere fact that they break the sameness, but also the presence of a third person when they were together, that their solitude might retain its value, and their unity refresh itself from the sense of the outsider's foreignness.

This same life, so closely together, will make people unusually sensitive to each other's moods; sometimes, if they are fond of each other, almost morbidly so. He did not answer that question; perhaps he thinks it was stupid. She handed me that cup of coffee abruptly; perhaps I have offended her in something.

They came through it remarkably well, and still deeply in love. But Slim Girl, watching her husband with close attention, felt him change and was troubled. Feeling less sure of herself, she was over-careful, and betrayed more than ever that reserve of something withheld that belonged inevitably to her double life. Each increased the other's uneasiness; it was a circle.

He did not read himself. The melting snows refreshed the pasturage, the grass grew tall. He gathered his scattered horses, shifted them, and watched them fatten. His peach trees grew, his corn was well above the sand. All these were good things, and in each he rejoiced as he enjoyed each detail of his day, the far riding and the loom before the house door, his wife's talk, the ring of his hammer. Each thing was good, and yet the whole was dull and devoid of savour.

Laughing Boy knew well enough that people wore on each other, and that every couple underwent a period of adjustment. He knew that in many households, when the man became seriously restless, his first wife would arrange for him to take a second, to preserve the home. But such was hardly the case here. He was by habit one who faced issues squarely and thought them out tough-mindedly, but now in the back of his head were many thoughts, safely hidden from himself, from which unease, like an infection, flowed through his system.

He did not realize that he was studying his wife critically, as one might an opponent. Once or twice, to his own surprise, he caught himself about to become annoyed with her over little or nothing; once or twice, away from her, building up a quite unreasonable sense of wrong. Then he would be disgusted with himself, and alarmed. The process was really natural enough; being profoundly dissatisfied with something in her which he refused to recognize, the feeling sought to give itself outlet by picking causes of annoyance which could be admitted.

She had always foreseen a period of difficulty and settling down, and was prepared to adapt herself to it, but now she did not know what was needed. She thought she was sophisticated, she thought she knew all about men, and all about herself. She thought she had penetrated to the ultimate truth. She knew only a little of life, not all of herself, and of men there was a half which she knew through and through, and a half which she was just beginning to discover. She wondered if the time had come at last to give up her American and go North. But this was a bad year for them; wool, and hence the sheep which they would have to buy, had risen, while horses, blankets, and jewelry sold badly. The tourists were unusually few. And here she had her one sure source of income.

Then she had a fatal thought. She was learning, from herself and from Laughing Boy, how much more there is to love than what is covered by its lowest terms. She was thinking things out by herself — particularly when she was weaving — like a philosopher. With the realization of the other things that are needed to make love worthy of itself, the bare fact that her husband and herself were in love with each other ceased to be sufficient. She wondered if, by falling in love when she had thought to make a deliberate choice, she had really known what she was doing. She wondered if life with this man, who was sometimes silent and strange, sometimes stupid, and sometimes irritating, might not be dismal in that wild homeland of his.

She did not really believe in her own doubt; it was purely an intellectual concept; but the dominant motive in her life for so many years had been the determination to move coolly towards a predetermined, sure success. Had she studied Napoleon in that California school, she would have admired him, and she might have been warned by him. Now, looking back on her past triumphs, she decided to wait until she made surely sure.

Just a few months more, a year at the most, and George was making a lot of money in sheep. Some of that would come in handy.

II

As summer approached, Laughing Boy became restless and more worried at his own condition. Had he offended a god, he wondered. He took a sweat-bath, sang, and tried a fast. It did not seem to make much difference.

He made up his mind one morning when he was leaving to round up three ponies for sale. Slim Girl had seemed abstracted; he had noticed her watching him curiously, seeming nervous. She had been like that various times lately, yet what could he say about it? It was just an impression. He felt sullen, snapped at her. Her hurt surprise made him miserable. As he mounted his horse, he thought, 'I must surely find a singer.'

There could be no doubt that he had done some unconscious wrong, deserting the Trail of Beauty. Forces of evil were preying upon him, he was no longer immune from bad thoughts. Stated in the American idiom, he decided he must be sick.

It was the merest chance that he met Yellow Singer walking along the trail with a bundle over his shoulder. Laughing Boy debated consulting him, and decided against it: not that ugly man.

'*Ahalani*, Grandfather,' the medicine man called to him; 'wait a minute.'

'*Ahalani*, Grandfather, I wait.'

The old rogue was standing straight and walking briskly; one saw that he was a tall man. Laughing Boy smelled whiskey.

'I see that you need medicine, little brother.'

'Unh! Why do you think that?'

Yellow Singer noted the grunt and followed his lead. 'I dreamed last night that when you were at the dance at Buckho Dotklish, you put those prayer cigarettes wrong. They fell down into the sand. Now they have put a spider's web into your brain.'

'You are right. I am not well.'

He nodded wisely. 'So I went and got the remedy for you. I am ready to make you all right. You are a good young man; it will be my pleasure to make you all right.' He glowed with benevolence.

Evidently this man had more power than one would think. 'How much will you want?'

'Twenty dollars.'

Laughing Boy considered. It was not a high fee. He counted out six dollars in coin, and pulled three plaques from his silver belt. 'There, that is really worth more.'

The old man hefted the metal. 'All right.'

'What must I do?'

'You must go to a place alone, you must wash your hair. Then pray to the Divine Ones whose cigarettes you offended. Then take this remedy.'

Out of the bundle he took a bottle of red liquor, looked at it a moment, and then, benevolence conquering, took out a second and handed them over.

'What is this?'

'It is a special kind of whiskey. It is very holy. The Americans drink it; it is so good they try to keep any one else from having it.'

'How do I take it?'

'When you have prayed, just start drinking it. By and by you will feel your mind becoming all right, your heart will be high. Then you will sleep. When you wake up, you will feel badly, but if you take some more, you will feel all right. One bottle should be enough. Put the other away until something tells you you need it.'

'I see.'

'I shall go on the trail to Buckho Dotklish, and make a charm there, to prevent any more bad things coming to you from those cigarettes. Tell no one about this, above all no woman. It is very holy and secret; if you speak of it, it will do you harm. It will make you jump into the fire.'

'I see.'

'If you need more, let me know. I may be able to get you some.'

He rode to his usual camping place by Natahnetinn, and went solemnly about the prescribed ceremonial. Then he tasted the drink. It was unlike the white whiskey; not so bad, but still pretty bad — low-grade, frontier tanglefoot rye, dear at a dollar a bottle.

After the first few drinks it came easier, but it did not make him feel very happy. As he grew drunk, he longed more and more for his own country, and for a truce from the constant feeling of the presence of alien things. About the time it grew dark, he stopped drinking and walked up and down. At first he sang, then he was silent.

Liquor, taken in solitude, sometimes has this effect. Along with a megalomaniac sense of his central position in the universe, a man grows bluntly honest with himself. All the secret, forgotten, stifled thoughts come out of the closet in his mind, and he must face them in turn, without a saving sense of proportion. This now was Laughing Boy's portion.

I am not happy in the house at Chiziai. It is too lonely, too strange a life; no one ever comes. We see people only at dances. That American town, what is there there? What is this preacher's wife? The look in her face when she returns

— I do not know. There is something wrong, always something hidden. She is always hiding something. Let us go North, go North, to T'o Tlakai! Oh, my mother!

When I told her about her weaving; when we rode together that time, then she needed me, then I, too, was strong. We were happiest then, both of us. She is stronger; it is she who leads me.

I am afraid to speak to her.

He stopped short and clutched his hands together.

Why? I am afraid to lose her. Am I losing myself? Oh, I do not know, I do not know; this life she has had, this wisdom of hers. What went on before? Who was the man, and what does Red Man know? Perhaps if I spoke to her, she would say no. She makes her own life. I am losing myself. And I cannot leave her, Came With War, Came With War. Oh, no, can't leave her. She would say 'No,' and I should say 'All right,' and then I should be dead.

How long will it be before we are rich enough to suit her? Why will she not herd sheep? All women do. I do not know. This American life she has led, she will not leave such things. It is my enemy. Our life is not good enough for her.

She wants so much money. A year, another year, who knows? So long, long. When will there be children? We should have had children. I want children. I want to go home. What is happening to me? I am losing myself. She holds the reins and I am becoming a led horse. Two, three years, all like this, and Sings Before Spears, who was a warrior, will have ended, and there will just be that part of a man which worships a woman. Not the rest of him, just heat. A bow-string without a bow. Only good for a woman to tie something with.

I need some more medicine.

Another stiff drink sent him over the border-line into incoherent plans for performing wonders. Three or four more put him to sleep.

He was in pretty bad shape when he awoke, late, with the high sun beating upon him. He went down to the arroyo and dabbled in its shallow, unfresh water. He was not as sick as the other time, but he was sick.

'When you wake up, you will feel badly, but if then you take a little more, you will feel all right.'

He would try it. The smell made him feel worse. He poured some into a cup, returned to the arroyo and weakened it with water. Then he downed it in one straining gulp. He did feel better. Perhaps he might take a little more, he thought, reaching for the bottle, and paused with it half-tipped for pouring.

No. He was remembering last night, and that had been terrible. He put it down, and stared at the ashes of his fire.

'Coffee,' he said aloud.

He drank a lot more water when he went to fill his pot. The heat of the flames was unpleasant to him; he was beginning to feel badly again, and wanted a drink. He put a lot of coffee in.

That had been all true, what he had thought last night, but incomplete and exaggerated. He was homesick, he was afraid of losing her, but what kind of man could not wait a few years, three at the worst, for so reasonable a cause. She was wise, she was right, and he was sure she loved him. Well, then?

The whiskey now, this magic. It did drive the clouds out of his thoughts, but it made everything appear twisted.

He lifted the coffee off the fire. It was strong. Without waiting for the sugar, he tried to drink it, burning his tongue.

It was not magic. It was just something like jimpson-weed. Under its influence he had seen himself, but there was nothing holy about it. He remembered quite clearly how he had placed those cigarettes in a crevice in the rock. There had been nothing wrong about it. That old coyote had made a lucky guess, and followed it up with lies to make money, that was all.

He saw a very clear picture of Yellow Singer and his wife as he had first met them, sober, and reaching for the bottle; he saw other scarecrow Indians he had met in this American's country. He looked at them, and behind them saw incoherently the great, ominous cloud of the American system, something for which he had no name or description.

That was another thing about which Slim Girl had been right, that drink. She knew how to tame it. She had the secret of how to prevent American knowledge from doing harm; she made it serve a good purpose.

He set down his cup of coffee, picked up a rock, and deliberately smashed the bottle. The liquid ran into the coals of the fire, caught, and for a moment the dampened sand burnt with a blue flame. That startled him. To drink something like that! He threw in the fragments of the bottle, in the bottom of which were still a few drops, and watched the blue light flicker briefly above them.

He drank another cup of coffee, with sugar, then unearthed the second bottle from its cache. That had cost money, much money. Well, he'd had his money's worth. From now on he could think without the help of blue flames. He poured it over the fire, and the drenching put the fire out. Eh! This was strange stuff!

To try to round up horses seemed out of the question. He stretched out in the shade of the rocks, craving sleep, his limbs feeling as though he had been through a furious wrestling bout. The sky was too blue, it hurt his eyes; the circling of a distant buzzard made his head ache. He turned over and fixed his gaze on a crack, studying it, sleepy, yet unable to keep his eyes shut.

Yellow Singer and all his kind were bad. They were like an offensive smell. But a smell came from a carcass. Those people were the way they were because of the Americans. The town of Los Palos in the drenching sunlight, quiet, dead-looking beside its irrigated fields. What was it? Something in the air, something that perverted the world. Where they were was no place for Earth People. They had done something to Slim Girl, one could see that, but she seemed to have risen above it. But they were bad for her, too. It was beyond him.

He smoked, and at length slept fitfully through the noonday heat, wakened now and again by flies, to drowse delightfully and return to sleep. In the late evening he went to where a waterfall in the arroyo made a trickling shower bath. The water refreshed him; he was hungry once more, and felt better.

What he had thought last night had been true, but unbalanced; and all this about Americans had been just because he felt sick. He had always known Americans, traders and such, they were all right, just people of a different tribe. He stretched out, fed, smoking, surprised at his desire to sleep again. It would be pleasant, it would be beautiful, returning to T'o Tlakai rich, very rich, with her, and to settle down somewhere near there and have children. They needed children. Meantime they would make their way together. Oh, beautiful.

III

Next morning he felt better. The drunkenness and the emotional outburst had cleared his system. In pouring out the liquor, he felt that he had destroyed a bad thing; the enemies in his head had indeed proved to be nothing but cobwebs, and they were gone. Like the man who burned the tumbleweed when the Eagles were afraid of it, he thought.

He rounded up the three horses he wanted, good ones. Only the best horses sold this year, and they did not bring so good a price. He rode home contented, quiet, and determined to do better with himself.

He found his wife waiting before the door.

'I did not know you were going to be gone so long; I have been lonely without you. Bring in your saddle while I get supper. I am glad when you come back.'

'I am always glad to be back.'

'As long as you feel like that, I shall continue to be happy.'

Why should he worry himself about this woman? And why should he worry about anything else as long as he had this woman? He slapped the ponies' flanks to make them run around the corral. He looked at his growing corn, and as he broke the little mud dam across his irrigation ditch, he felt the coolness of evening seep along his veins as the bright water spread through the narrow channels. Clay bluffs were not as fine as painted rock, there was too much adobe in this sand, but it was a fair place. The fire gleamed before his house, he heard the flow of water and the occasional stamp of a horse in the corral.

Slim Girl brought out the bottle and an orange.

'Do not make the drink, little sister, I do not want it. I think I shall try not taking it.'

She kept herself from looking at him. She was troubled.

'All right.'

What was this? Probably nothing. When one

walks on the sheer edge of a precipice, the meaningless fall of a stone over the side momentarily stops the heart. She studied him while they ate. She began to talk with him gravely of the life they were to make together, of the happiness that was in store for them.

He said to himself, 'She was bothered when I refused that drink, the way she looked at me afterwards. She is nervous about me. I have done that, by acting as I have. Now she is trying to tell me how she really is; she is talking true; I know. I have wronged her.'

She saw the last trailing clouds pass from him. That evening was perfect, so perfect that, with his doubts banished and the feeling of intimacy upon him, he almost told her everything he had done and thought, but he postponed. It was the last of its kind for many days.

Like an ancient magician who, by saying the forbidden names, evoked genii whom he could not then drive back, Laughing Boy had given form to thoughts which were not to be forgotten. Unhappily for himself, he was no fool, and of an honest habit of thought. There was love in that place, and sometimes happiness, but if a religious-minded Navajo had entered there, he would have felt that the air was empty.

IV

Slim Girl continued weaving despite the poor sales, because she found relief and, one might say, a confidant in her craft. And then, they two, working side by side, reconstructed at least the outward signs of the harmony that was gone.

He eased his soul by shaping the half-stubborn, half-willing metal. It is a matter of patience, from the lump or the coins to the bar, from the bar to the bracelet. This, the most precious and beautiful of metals, is the easiest to work. That is a gift of the gods. Slow, slow, under successive light strokes the bar becomes longer, flatter, thinner: it is struck and it grows towards its appointed shape.

I am impatient these days, I get tired of the finishing. One must have one's mind made up to it from the start, from four Mexican coins to the finely finished ornament; one must see it as it will be, and not stop short of what he has seen.

Having woven about a foot of blanket, the head-sticks of the loom are lowered, and the finished part is rolled around the foot-sticks, out of sight.

This is like time. Here, this little part showing, where I am weaving, is the present; the past is rolled up and gone; there are those empty warp cords above me. The weft is like handling a nervous horse; I lead the blue strand gently to the green, or it will break; I hate to break a strand, the knot where it is mended will always show, a blemish. But then, I pound the fork and the batten down hard, hard; they lock the weave and that much more is past.

He was curving the strip of flattened silver. This bracelet is coming out just as I thought of it. One must know his design before he starts; when this strip was still four coins, I knew that there would be tracks pointing one way from each end to the centre, clouds at each end, and that stone where the tracks meet. How do I know it? Not all men can; what is it I have? The Mexicans are lazy, their money is pure, soft silver; the American coins have something in them to make them hard, they are hard to work with. Those Americans!

Her fingers were deft, and she pulled at the warp like a harp-player. I am not sure I like this pattern, but it is too late to change it. No, it is a good pattern. Should I unravel all I have done, when it grows so slowly? When the blanket has been started, it is too late to change. The man who is always coming back to where he started, to figure out another road, will never get far from home. I wish I could just think my design and have it woven at an American mill. No, I don't; it is because I toiled over them that I love them.

The turquoise is the important thing in this

bracelet. I looked at it and saw the setting for it. But much of the time now I cannot think well, I am not myself. I have no design for myself, I do not know the nature of my jewel. I am hammering a piece of silver, and I cannot stop hammering, every day is another stroke; yet I do not know what it is to be. In the end it may be just a piece of good metal pounded flat. I do not know my design.

This blanket is like the other things. I am always being uncertain now. It is all like this blanket. Shall I unravel it, when I have been so long in getting so far? The design is set, a blanket with a broken design would be absurd, a failure. The only thing to do is to carry it through, with softness and with strength. My design is set.

CHAPTER XVII

I

As summer drew to a close, Laughing Boy took to spending more time than was necessary with his horses. Sometimes he would crave company, and, if he found it, would be sociable and garrulous; at other times he kept very much to himself. No one who met him then for the first time would have named him 'Laughing Boy.' Locally he was known as 'Horse Trader,' and latterly one Indian had applied to him, in jest, the name of the legendary character 'Turns His Back,' which bade fair to stick. Partly he liked to be away from home because of the chance of a happy return. If she were waiting for him, if she had not been in to town, if he was tired from the long ride and at peace with himself, the old spell would surround them. If she was just back from that work of hers, or if she came in after he did, she overtired, brooding, and a little nervous, it was a failure. Once or twice they quarrelled; she had an amazingly sharp and clever tongue. The quarrels ended in reconciliation and passion which exhausted them both without bringing peace to either.

On one day, when autumn had begun to take

the weight out of the noon sunshine, he sat basking on a hillock, smoking, with his pony beside him. He was lazily content, and comfortable enough within himself not to mind the sight of a human approaching. He felt like talking to some one.

The jogging dot drew nearer. Still looking black, the motion of the shoulders told that it was an Indian. Yes, and probably a Navajo, with a flaming scarlet headband. Laughing Boy sat up straight. He knew that bald-faced chestnut, he knew that swing of the whip hand. He made sure. He was surprised, curious, and delighted. What brought his friend so far from home? He rose to his feet. Jesting Squaw's Son slowed from lope to trot, to a walk, and stopped beside him.

'*Ei-yei*, my friend!' Laughing Boy took his hand. 'It is good to see you!'

'My friend.' He smiled, but he dismounted slowly, and his eyes were hurt. 'I am glad to find you.'

'Sit down. A cigarette?'

'Yes.'

'Where are you going?'

'Just riding around.'

'What is the news at T'o Tlakai?'

'All well. Your people are all well. Your sister, the one who married Bay Horse, has a son. The other one has just married Yellow Foot's Son.'

'Good.'

'There has been good rain, and the traders are paying twenty, twenty-five cents for wool.'

'Good.'

'And you, tell?'

'All well. Our goods sell well, the corn was fine this year. All well.'

They smoked.

'It is good to see you.'

Jesting Squaw's Son made no answer. Laughing Boy studied him; he was too quiet.

'What brings you so far from home?'

'Nothing, just riding around.'

'You will come to our hogahn?'

'Yes.'

They finished their cigarettes, and sat looking at nothing. There was a pleasant, afternoon feeling that tended to make talk slow, the smell of the warm sand, quietness. After about five minutes, Laughing Boy said:

'You might as well show me your true thought. It is all around you like a cloud. It is what you are thinking of all the time you are talking about anything else. You are hurt. What hurts you, whom I have called friend, hurts me.'

'You are right. Give me tobacco.'

He rolled another cigarette and smoked it through before he began to speak.

'You remember that joke we played on Narrow Nose at Gomulli T'o? Do you suppose we did anything bad by accident? Did we start any evil working?'

'What makes you think that?'

'You remember, I said I was bringing back a wife from Maito. That made me wonder. I went to Maito a little while ago.' He was looking at the tips of his fingers. Now he paused.

'We wanted to trade a cow for some sheep. Your brother and White Goat and I were riding along. We saw a Pah-Ute driving a cow he had taken from the Mormons, so we took it away from him. There is no pasture for cattle up there, but we heard of a man at Maito who kept a herd. So we took it down to him. His name is Alkali Water.

'The cow was pretty thin. We were there three nights trading on it.

'I saw his daughter. At the end of the first day I knew that I had been born only for her, that that was what I had always been waiting for. I was all one piece, everything in me was to one purpose. I do not know how to say it.'

'I know.'

'Yes, you know. That is why I am here. I know now why good men sometimes have to do with other people's wives. I have learned a great deal about myself.

'I shall not try to say what she looked like. What would be the use? She was not small, like your wife; she was strong. Her eyes and mouth were beautiful, she was beautiful, and you could see beauty inside her by her eyes and her mouth.

'We stayed there for three nights, for three nights and two days I was watching her and listening to her. I think she felt as I did; we did not speak to each other, hardly at all. When we went away she looked at me.

'I waited a few days at home. I was very happy; I did not know such happiness could exist. Then I returned to Maito. I wanted to see her again, to be sure, and to find out her clan before I asked my mother to ask for her. I did not want any one to be able to object, as they might, since she did not live near us.

'I cannot make up songs as you do, but I made up a pretty good one. I sang all along the trail. I neared her hogahn galloping and singing the Wildcat Song. She was coming out along the trail towards me. I galloped close to her and reined up short, in a handsome way. She came beside my horse and laid her hand on its neck.

'"My friend," she said.

'I was so happy then that there is no name for it. There was no earth under me, I had no limits. Then she went on.

'"You must go away, you must not see me again. I must not see you," she said.

'I asked, "Why?"

'She said, "What is your clan?"

'I told her, "I am an Eshlini."

'She lowered her head, then she looked up again. Her face looked calm, but her eyes were wounded. "I, too, am an Eshlini," she said.

'We touched hands, and I rode away.'

Jesting Squaw's Son bowed his head on his knees. Laughing Boy felt his throat hurt, and yet in a curious way he felt better than he had in a long time. He was taken out of himself; he needed something like this.

'I could not go home then. I rode to T'o Atinda Haska Mesa, and went up to the top of it. I have been there a day and two nights. I did not eat. Why should I?

'At first I did not even think. I was just wild at first. All I could do was remember that happiness, that had been for nothing. I felt like asking her to come with me even so. I frightened myself. Am I an animal? Would I sleep with my sister? I did not know what to do. Why could she not have been a Tahtchini or a Lucau or an Eskhontsoni? But it was not her fault. And could I curse my mother because she was not a Bitahni or a T'o Dotsoni or a Nahkai?

'Then I got myself calmer. I could not have her. I made up my mind to it. I accepted it. But I still loved her. I still do. I still remember that happiness.

'That is very bad, it is beastly. My heart must be bad. I am frightened. Perhaps I should kill myself. Why not?

'I came here to see you. I did not want to go home to all my people. Perhaps you can help me. That is all.'

Laughing Boy stared into the ground. He was shocked, and his heart was wrung. He had never imagined that such a thing could happen; had it been told him of some unknown man, he would have supposed there was something bad about him to start with. It was such a disaster as an angry god might send, as though one heard in some legend, 'He went mad and fell in love with a woman of his own clan.' But his friend was good, all good. He knew what he was suffering. He remembered his feelings those first days at the dance. He thought hard. They must have sat for half an hour there before he spoke.

'Do not kill yourself. And do not feel ashamed, do not think you have sinned, or your heart is bad. No, you have shown it is good, I think. It would be bad if you kept on wanting to marry her, but what has happened to you is not something you do yourself. It is as though you were shot with an arrow.

'I nearly went away with my wife without asking her clan. We spoke directly to each other, without shame, when we saw there was nothing else to do.

'It is not your fault that you were shot. Suppose you had starved for a week, and some American, trying to be funny, the way they do, offered you fish to eat. If you ate it, it would be bad, but if your belly clamoured for it while you refused it, could you be blamed? No, you would have done a good thing, I think. You have done a good thing, a very hard thing. I think well of you.'

Jesting Squaw's Son gazed at him searchingly, and saw that he meant what he said.

'I think you are right. You have cured me of a deep wound. Thank you.'

'Let us start home. There are some of my horses in that little cañon, we shall get one, and turn yours loose. It looks thin. There is pasture there, it will not wander.'

They caught fresh horses, and Jesting Squaw's Son exclaimed at the height of the grass, which in some places grew over a foot, in clumps. There was some like that at Dennihuitso, and in Kiet Siel Buckho, but not at this time of year.

They jog-trotted towards Chiziai, silent most of the time, talking occasionally.

'Up there, now, they do not call you by your old name,' Jesting Squaw's Son said, and hesitated. Even when he is a close friend, one is not free about discussing a man's name before him.

'I am not surprised.'

'They call you "Went Away." Your uncle calls you "Blind Eyes."'

'Unh! He would. Well, I am changed, it is right that my name should change.'

Jesting Squaw's Son trailed his rope to get the kinks out of it. Coiling it again, 'But they miss you. You will always be welcome.'

'In the end, we shall return.'

'You live close to the Iron Trail?'

'On the other side of it.'

'*Ei-yei!* A good place?'

'You will see, a fine place, but we cannot turn our horses out there, as it is Americans' country.'

'But you are near the Zuñis, too.'

'About a day's hard ride that way. I trade with them — horses for turquoise.'

'Have you any children?'

'Not now. We have a plan. We are making much money now, we are working as hard as we can. You would not believe how fast we make it. In a year or two we shall return to T'o Tlakai; we shall have perhaps fifty, perhaps sixty hundreds of dollars, in money and silver and horses, I think.'

'*Ei-yei!*'

'We shall be very rich. With that to start on, we shall be rich all our lives. We shall have our children then, we shall have a beautiful life. It is her idea, she thought of it. She takes care of the money, she trades with the Americans. She is remarkable.'

'You must be very happy.'

'I am.' He meant it.

II

Laughing Boy showed off the town, the irrigated strip, the railroad to his interested friend. Most delightfully, a passenger train went by; Jesting Squaw's Son sat his bolting, bucking horse with his head over his shoulder, his eyes glued on the marvel. His presence changed everything. Laughing Boy led him through the narrow place between the clay bluffs to his adobe house, the corral, the ditches and the hummocks of the summer's field, the sapling peaches. Jesting Squaw's Son admired, and a pain ran through him that there was not his own house and fields, and his own wife waiting by the fire.

Slim Girl came to the door. The autumn nights were already cold enough for the cooking to be done indoors. She greeted the visitor correctly, hospitably, and saw that her husband, although he seemed grave, was at peace with himself.

At the first moment when they were alone, Laughing Boy explained the situation, watching her anxiously. She nodded her head.

'Poor man, I am sorry for him. We must help him. He is going to get over his love, I think. He is already reconciled to it. It is that in combination with the other that worries him, I think.' Her husband, after a moment's thought, agreed. 'Now this is what we must do; talk about what will keep him interested, talk about things you have done together, talk of what will remind him of the good taste of life in his mouth. Do not try to make him laugh, do not try to comfort him. We shall show him new things. I shall give him some of your drink, I shall talk about the Americans. Now, I think, he is keeping one thing in his mind all the time, we must make him let go of it. Do you see?'

'Yes, that is very good.'

Truly, his wife was a remarkable woman, so wise, so right. Hearing his friend returning, he kissed her quickly.

That evening was blissful, so harmonious that in the middle of it Jesting Squaw's Son excused himself, went down to the corral, and cried into the shoulder of the first available horse. A horse, warm and silky, is very nice to cry into when it stands still. The tears came readily. He had not cried before.

He stayed for three weeks, riding the range with Laughing Boy, watching the silversmithing, going down to see the trains pass by. He spent an entranced and delighted afternoon behind a bush, watching three negroes shoot craps, and nearly frightened them to death when he stood up suddenly, not five feet from them, bow in hand, to go away. He forgot about Alkali Water's daughter for hours at a time, until she became a curious, sad memory. He gave much thought to his hosts.

The novelty idea had been a good one, and they had plenty to offer, from the railroad and the cocktail, with its taste and surprising effect, to Slim Girl's talk of Americans. At night she spoke of their ways, of California, and of the other nations of people like Americans of whom she had heard, across Wide Water, toning down the more amazing things to credibility. They compared her knowledge with their experience on the reservation, and discussed the Americans' works, the good and bad things their coming had brought to the Navajo. They talked about the posse that hunted Blunt Nose, and stories of old times and the soldiers. That would lead to old wars with the Utes and the Jicarillas and the Stone House people, and they argued whether they gained or lost under the present enforced peace. Laughing Boy and Slim Girl enjoyed themselves enormously.

It was cold enough for a blanket over the shoulder, the day that Jesting Squaw's Son and Laughing Boy rode out to the pasture and caught his horse. Laughing Boy was sad at his friend's departure. They mounted their animals and clasped hands.

'I shall wait for you in the North.'

'We shall come, but I hope you will visit us here again.'

'I hope you will come too soon for that. I have lived in your house, I have seen you. You are both happy, I think; you are both in love. But you are afraid. All the time you are enjoying yourselves you are watching for something over your shoulders, I think. I do not understand this. It is what I saw. This life of yours, it all looks like The People's life; only her going into town is strange. But it is not just she, it is you both that are not living like us, I think. I do not know what it is, but you are wearing moccasins that do not fit you. The sooner you both come back to your own people, the better, I think.

'I shall be waiting for you. You have restored my life.'

'It will be a good day when we meet again.'

It was a pity he was gone; he had been such pleasant company. They had been too much alone, and he had cured that. He had misunderstood it, too. He wanted to see his wife and talk about their guest. He hurried home.

CHAPTER XVIII

I

It had come round to the beginning of Little Snow Moon again, a time of year when horses, seeking feed, are likely to wander. Laughing Boy kept close watch on his herd, and was little surprised, on one day of high wind that covered the tracks, to find a stallion, a three-year-old, missing. It must have been gone for some time; he was unable to find it in the immediate district, and soon lost its trail completely. Returning to his house, he made preparations to be away for a week in search of it; the animal was valuable.

Slim Girl procured chocolate and other dainties for him. The weather was no longer warm, he could not tell where he might camp, she felt that he would undergo hardships. But, as he said, one could not let as good a pony as that wander at will in a country entirely populated by connoisseurs and lovers of horseflesh.

Four days passed in vain. On the fifth, acting on the tip of a Hopi mail carrier, he picked up its trail north of Winslow. The next morning he found it, scarcely fifteen miles from Los Palos.

It had no mind to go back to the herd. At first

sight of him it began walking as it grazed, then, seeing him draw slightly nearer, broke into a trot, and thus all morning, matching its pace to his, kept a quarter of a mile between them. He tried to edge it towards the left, but it seemed to guess his intention, taking advantage of a butte that prevented heading off to break sharply right and gallop furiously a mile in the direction of the railroad. It was never panicked, never too hurried, expending always just enough effort.

As he pursued, Laughing Boy admired. The chestnut stallion was coming into its strength, gleaming, round quarters, bunched muscles at the juncture of the throat and chest, a ripple of highlight and shadow on the withers, arched neck, pricked small Arab ears, bony head, eyes and nostrils of character and intelligence. It was one of those ponies, occasionally to be found, in which one reads a page of the history of that country; a throwback to Spanish *Conquistadores* and dainty-hooved, bony-faced horses from Arabia.

Midday was warm, sandy dust rose from the trail in clouds. Laughing Boy munched raisins and chocolate as he rode, remembering when the men on the posse had offered him the same rations. That girl, she was a whole war-party in herself! The stallion balked at the railroad tracks, considered, and cleared them with a nervous leap.

Now Laughing Boy thought he had it; the dingy suburbs of the town, on the far side from his hogahn, made a half-circle before them. He advanced cautiously. It was a question of getting it cornered so that he could dismount, for Navajos do not rope from the saddle. Now the stallion began to rush, and the work became fast — a break to the right, Laughing Boy, pouring leather into his pony, headed it, then left, and the houses turned it again. A desperate race to prevent a desperate attempt to break back across the tracks; it wheeled again, straight between two houses, stallion and mounted man going like fury, to the admiration of an old Mexican woman and the clamorous terror of a sleeping cur.

The stallion drew away from him, and he slowed his pace. It cantered past an adobe house standing alone under two cottonwoods, and, just beyond, fell to grazing in a little hollow. Laughing Boy advanced cautiously, using the house as cover. He figured that he could dismount behind it, and with a quick rush corner the animal in the angle of two wire fences protecting irrigated fields. The pony was already moving into the trap, unconscious of the wire.

He rode at a walk, close along the mud wall from which the sun was reflected with a stuffy, muddy smell. As he passed the window, he looked in, and reined his horse so suddenly that it reared, while his heart stopped for a moment and his whole body was a great choking. An agonized, clear voice cried out, inside,

'*Sha hast'ien, sha hast'ien codji!* — My husband, my husband there!' And a man said, 'My God!'

Before he had started thinking, he wheeled and rode madly for the door side. As he came around the corner, an American, hatless, came out, saw man and horse coming upon him, jumped aside and stood for a moment. His hands strung his bow without conscious willing. The man began to run towards the town. Arrow leaped to string almost of itself, hands and arms functioned, drew, released, but the excited pony would not keep still and the missile went wide, to the right. A second was in the air before the first landed, but it passed just over the man's shoulder, hard by the ear, startling him into an amazing leap and burst of speed. There was something ridiculous about it which calmed Laughing Boy. He steadied his pony and shot with care. The arrow struck just below the shoulder, the American fell doubled up, almost turning a somersault, picked himself up, and with a last effort rounded the corner between the outermost houses at the end of the straggling street.

Calmly, he waited before the house. Afterwards there were going to be terrible feelings and thoughts, but now he knew what was to be done. His face showed no particular age, young or old; it was hardly the face of an individual, rather, of a race.

Slim Girl stood in the doorway, neat, dressed in American clothes.

'Come here, little sister.' Voice even and impersonal.

She walked slowly. For the first time since he had known her, he saw that her self-possession was only a surface. She looked as though a searing light were shining before her, showing her Hell. She stood beside his saddle.

'Did you kill him?'

'No, I hit him in the shoulder.'

This was the fourth arrow. It was right that such a thing should happen by fours. The gods were in it.

'You have killed us both, I think.'

She did not answer. He looked at her eyes, then avoided them; not from shame, but because there was too much in them. He did not want to begin to realize yet. He must keep his head. He thought how beautiful she was, and began to feel the greatness of his loss.

'You understand what I am doing?'

Again she did not answer.

He notched the fourth arrow meticulously, drew to the head, released. The twang of the string echoed and reëchoed over great spaces. At the sound, he became aware of agony pent up behind his mind like high waters behind a too-slight dam, about to break through and carry away. At the same time, with the instant of releasing the string, he saw her open right hand pass across the face of the bow, her left arm rise. Now she stood, smiling stiffly, her eyes her own again. Her right hand was still in front of the bow in a stiff, quaint gesture. There was blood on the tips of the fingers. The arrow stood, through nearly to the feathers, in her left forearm.

He saw her as at a great distance. This was all wrong, something impossible had happened. She held her arm up rigidly, her lips remained set in that stiff smile. In a moment she was going to speak. The feelings and realizations were coming upon him. He lifted the reins and rode slowly around the corner of the house.

The stallion watched him nervously.

'Go your way, little brother.' He watched the animal as he rode past, then he contemplated the ears of his mount. 'You are saddled and ridden, but you are better off than I. This would be a good world if we were all geldings, I think.'

II

The pony, wandering unguided, brought him slowly within sight of his house. He turned it aside, making a wide circle to come to the high place by the tree from the other side. The house, the field of corn-stubble, the five struggling peach trees, the corral, all very dear, stood like unanswerable refutations in the long streaks of afternoon shadow. As the sight of the perfect, familiar body of some one just dead, or the little possessions, the objects just set down, ready to be picked up again as always, again and again render that death incredible, so was the sight of these things to Laughing Boy. Her loom stood under the brush sun-shelter before the door, with a half-finished blanket rolled at its foot. Unbelievable, not true, only — it was so. He went through the past day, searched the farther past, as though by travelling it again he could find where the false trail branched off, and reduce this calamity to an error.

Ten thousand things told him that what he had learned was ridiculous, but it always led again to the window in the adobe house and the clear frightened voice crying, '*Sha hast'ien, sha hast'ien codji!*'

Now it was time to think, but an hour or more passed before he could prevent the beginnings of thought from turning to frantic revolt. Prayer helped him. He got himself in hand and rolled a cigarette.

Now I must choose between her and myself. If I stay with her, I lose myself, really. I am a man. I am a warrior. If I do not give her up, I become something else from what I have always been. The world changes, the good things, the bad things, all change for me. And they change for the bad. I cannot shoot her again. I cannot do that thing. If I leave her, I am still I, but I and the world are dead. Oh, my friend, my friend, your choice was so simple, you were lucky. The arrow only grazed you; it has gone through my bowels. And when it came my turn to send the arrow back, I missed.

Oh, well named, Came With War, Came With War, oh, beautiful! Why do they give women names about war? I know all about that now. My uncle was right. I cannot go now and see their faces. Kill myself. That would settle it. But not now, not in this place. If it keeps on being like this, I shall do that, in my own country. Came With War, Came With War, Slim Girl, you coyote, you devil, you bad woman.

I must go away. I cannot stay with her. She is worth everything in the world, but there is something in me that I have no right to trade for her. That is what I must do.

He struggled for a long time, facing this decision, until it sank into him. The sun was low, the little valley between the buttes was all shadow. He had not seen her return, and hoped she had not. There would be begging, talk, tears — terrible. If she were not there, he would just take his things and go; the missing goods would explain.

It was all too much for him. He felt as if he were shaken by high winds. That little house down there was a place of waiting torment. He stood, clutching his hands together and weaving his head from side to side. This was far worse than war. He turned to the gods, making the prayer of a man going alone to battle:

'*Shinahashé nageï, nageï, alili kat' bitashah . . .*
'I am thinking about the enemy gods, the enemy gods, among
their weapons now I wander.
A-yé-yé-yé-ya-hai!
Now Slayer of Enemy Gods, I go down alone among them,
The enemy gods, the enemy gods, I wander among their
weapons.
Touched with the tops of the mountains, I go down alone
among them,
The enemy gods, the enemy gods, I wander among their
weapons.
Now on the old age trail, now on the path of beauty walking,
The enemy gods, the enemy gods, I wander among their
weapons.'

It was apposite, and it helped enormously.

Now it was not merely he battling with these terrific things, now the unseen power of good would uphold him. Leading his horse, he went down slowly to his house.

CHAPTER XIX

I

THERE were her tracks, wind-blurred in the sand. She must have come straight home, arriving before he reached the high place. With dread he entered the door, grateful for the half-darkness inside. She had got back into Navajo clothes, moccasins, skirt, and sash, but her blouse was only pulled over the right shoulder, leaving the left arm and breast bare. Did she think —? He saw her as an enemy.

'I am going away.'

'All right. But first pull this out; I am not strong enough.' She held out her arm with the arrow through it.

He stared at it, and it made him feel sick. He was frankly avoiding her face, but he knew that the blood was gone from beneath the bronze surface, leaving it yellow-white with a green tinge under it. He kept on looking at the arrow, his arrow, with his marks on it.

'You must come out to the light.'

She rose with difficulty, steadying herself against the wall. He supported her to the door.

The arrow had passed through the flesh of the

under side of her arm, just missing the artery and the bone. The shaft stood out on both sides. From the barbed, iron head to the wound there was blood in the zigzag lightning grooves. The roundness of her arm was caked with dried blood and already somewhat swollen. To the one side was the barbed point, to the other were the eagle feathers and the wrappings. He took out his knife.

'I shall try not to make it wiggle,' he said.

'What are you going to do?'

'Cut it off just by the hole; I can't pull all that through your arm.'

'It is a good arrow. Pull it through.'

There was never another woman like this one. 'Do you think I would use this again?'

He held her arm very carefully, he cut with all possible gentleness, but the shaft moved and moved again. He heard her take in her breath and looked quickly to see her teeth clenched on her lower lip. She should have been a man. Every dart of pain in her arm went doubly through his heart. The wood was cut short, just above the wound.

'Now,' he said, 'are you ready?'

'Pull.'

He jerked it out. She had not moved. She was rigid and her eyes were almost glassy, but she had not made a sign. He still knelt, staring at her, at the fresh blood welling, and at the red stump of the arrow in his hand. She was brave, brave.

She whispered, 'Get me some of the whiskey.'

He gave her a stiff dose in a cup. She emptied it at once, and sighed. A little colour came back.

'It will be dark soon. You had better go now. I can take care of myself. But before you go, know this: whatever you have seen, I love you and you only and altogether. Good-bye.'

She handed him back the cup. As he took it, their fingers touched, and he looked into her eyes. Something snapped inside of him. He fell forward, his head close to his knees, and began sobbing. She laid her hand on his shoulder.

'You have been hasty, I think. One should not turn up a new trail without looking around. And you have not eaten, you are tired. This has been hard for you. In a minute I shall heat some coffee, and we can talk straight about this.'

II

The night was plenty sharp enough for a fire indoors. Under her directions he prepared canned goods and coffee, but neither of them did more than toy with the food. He had a feeling that she was going to find a solution for them; the experience that they had just shared had changed everything again, he didn't know where he was. Landmarks shifted too quickly, he was in a turmoil once more, with his determinations to be made anew.

She asked him to roll her a cigarette; then,

'Make the drink as you have seen me do, only make some for me, too.'

He hesitated.

'Do not be afraid of my medicine.'

He muttered a denial and fixed the drink. She sipped at hers slowly. She needed strength, for she was nearly exhausted, and there was a battle to be fought.

'You cannot know whether a thing is good or bad unless you know all about it, and the cause of it. I do not try to say that what I have done is good, but I want to tell you my story, that you do not know; then you can judge rightly.'

He hardly had expected her to come so directly to the point. He prepared to sift lies.

'Roll me a cigarette.

'I have to begin way back. Hear me.

'When I was still a little girl, they took me away to the all-year school at Wide Water, as you know. They took me because I did well at the day school at Zhil Tséchiel, so they wanted me to learn more. I told you how they tried to make us not be Indians; they succeeded pretty well. I wanted to be American. I forgot the gods then, I followed the Jesus trail. I did well, then, at that school.

'While I was there both my father and mother went underground. My mother had no brothers or sisters living, and I was her only child. I saw no reason for returning to The People. I was an American, with an American name, thinking in American.

'I grew up. I wanted to work for Washindon on a reservation, like that Papago woman who writes papers for the American Chief at T'o Nanasdési. But I could not get that work right away, so they said I could work for a preacher at Kien Doghaiyoi — you know that big town? The Americans call it Oñate.'

'I have heard.' He was studying her intently. Her voice came low and toneless; she spoke slowly, but behind it was something intense.

'I went there, about three years ago. I loved the Jesus trail; I thought it was very good to work for a preacher. That way it was.'

She stared into the fire as she took a sip of liquor.

'He was a good man, and his wife was very good. He did not let her have much to say. I worked pretty hard, but it was all right.

'I learned some strange things. I learned about

the bad women — they make their living by lying down with men, just any men who will pay them. Some of them were Americans, some had been schoolgirls like me. The preacher used to preach against them sometimes; I thought, he did not need to do that. Something had happened to their faces, their eyes; their mouths were terrible. They were like something in a bad dream. That way I thought.

'Then by and by I fell in love with a man. He was big and good-looking and he talked pious. He was a cow-puncher; he worked on a ranch near there. Lots of American girls liked him. When he paid attention to me, I was flattered. He was wonderful, I thought. We should be married and have a ranch together; it was almost too good to believe, I thought.

'I was frightened when he wanted me to lie with him, but he made me feel all right. He knew all about how to make women forget themselves, that man.

'Then I saw I was going to have a child. The next time he came to town, I asked him to marry me quickly. He made promises. Then he didn't come to town again, so I went to the ranch where he worked. He was angry when he saw me there. He offered me money, but I said I wanted marriage.

'I became frightened, I begged and I cried. He got very angry, he called me names. He said to get out of his way, he couldn't be bothered with a "squaw." That is a word Americans use to mean Indian women; it is contemptuous. I learned a lot then; right then I was not so young as I had been, I think.

'I went back to the preacher's. I was not afraid to tell him, but I was ashamed. I could not be calm about it, it was hard to say. I just walked in on them and said:

'"I am going to have a child. It is that man's. He will not marry me."

'They were astonished; then the preacher looked angry. He called me bad. He asked what good all my training had done me; he called me ungrateful. He said a lot of things. If I had waited until he got through, his wife would have spoken, and they would have taken care of me, I think. But I was finding out that every one said one thing and did another. The Jesus trail seemed to be a lie, too. I told him that. I threw his religion at him. Then he said all sorts of things about me, and ordered me out of his house.

'My money was soon gone. I went hungry. I thought I had shame written all over my face. But even then I was strong; I thought that the world had beaten me now, but I would keep on fighting and by and by I would beat it. But just then I was desperate.

'Then those bad women spoke to me. They took me in and fed me; they were kind, those bad women. All my ideas were turned upside down now. I did not care. My heart was numb. I learned their trade. I did what they did. In a few months so, with the baby in me, that made me very sick. They took care of me, those bad women.

'I suffered much pain, the child was born much too soon, dead. I was glad.

'When I was well, I went back to work among them. I had thought a lot, I learned a great deal. I saw how this new life was bad. I saw the faces, the empty hearts of those women, kind though they were. I hated all Americans, and I made up my mind that an American should pay for what an American had done. I remembered my true name. I would have gone to my people, but I did not know how, and I wanted to be paid back. I had my plan.

'I noticed one thing — that the men, when they went with those women, liked to be helped to fool themselves that they were with another kind of woman, that they were loved. I did not look like those women yet. I looked young, and decent. They liked that, those men. By then it meant nothing to me; it was just as if I cooked them a meal. It had nothing to do with love, nothing to do with what you know.

'I watched for my chance, and by and by I saw it — a man from the East, that one. He had good manners. He was lonely. And he did not have the poor ideas about Indians that most of these people have, that man.

'I was very careful with him. I did not do any of the things those women usually do to get money away from a man and be rid of him quickly. I acted as innocent as I knew how. He said he was sorry to see me leading such a life. I caught him. He was in Kien Doghaiyoi three nights, and all three nights he came to me. I found out all about him.

'Two weeks later he came back, and I saw him again. I had him, I thought.

'Ten days after that I came here to Chiziai. I had money. I took that house where you saw me. I watched and waited. He lives a day from here. On the fifth day he came in. I managed to meet him when he was alone. He was surprised and glad. I asked him to come to my house in the evening. I had food and much whiskey for him, so that finally he went to sleep.

'When he woke up in the morning, that was the test. He felt badly then, and ashamed to wake up in the house of a bad woman. I handed him his money, two hundred dollars, and told him to count it, that it was all there. Then I gave him coffee, and a little whiskey, and then food. He asked how much I wanted. I said I was not doing this for money. Then I gave him a little more whiskey, and so I kept him all day. I did not let him get drunk, and I acted like a good woman who called him friend.

'The next morning he said he had to get back to work. He said he would see me when he came back to town, and he wished I was not what I was. He was lonely, that man. These were not his people, these Americans here; they did not talk the same. Like a Navajo living among Apaches.'

Her voice was taking on a timbre of triumph.

'I said, "You will not find me here."

'He said, "At Kien Doghaiyoi, then."

'"No," I said, "I am through with all that. I only did it because I had to. I hated it."

'He asked how that happened. I told him about half the truth and half lies, to make it sound better, saying I had been bad only a few weeks. Now I said an old Navajo whom I had always known was come for me; I did not love him, but he was a good man, and I was going to marry him. But first I wanted to see him — the

American — I said, because he had been kind to me, because he was not like the others. So I had come here for just a few days, I said.

'He thought a little while. He said, "Stay." He said he would give me money. I pretended not to want to take money from him; I made him persuade me. I was afraid he might ask me to marry him, but he was not that much of a fool. Finally I said, "All right."

'I had conquered.'

There was a strong triumph in her voice at that last phrase; now it returned to the level, slow, tired speech.

'I told him I could not just live there, a Navajo woman. It would make talk, men would annoy me. It would be better if I married the old Navajo and lived near by, then I could meet him when he came to town. With whiskey, I said, that man could be kept happy. I said he was old.

'He did not want it to be known he was providing for a Navajo woman, so he agreed. He gave me fifty dollars.

'There was no Navajo.'

She paused. 'Roll me a cigarette.' She smoked it through, then resumed:

'I was not happy. I was provided for, I was revenging myself through him, but I was not living. I wanted my own people. I was all alone. That was why I made friends with Red Man. He is not good, that man. He did not care if I were bad, he hoped I might be bad with him. I never was, but I kept him hoping. With him I remembered the ways of The People, I became quick again in their speech. He helped me much. He is not all bad, that man.

'The People looked at me askance. I was a young woman living alone, they did not know how, so they made it up. They do that. Your uncle knows that talk. This went on for over a year. Then I saw you, and everything changed. I had thought I was dead to men, and now I knew I loved you. With you I could live, without you I was already dead.

'I was right. Our way of life, to which you have led me, my weaving, our songs, everything, is better than the Americans'. You have made this.

'I had enough, but I thought I could have better. I wanted it for you; you were giving back to me what the Americans had robbed from me since they took me from my mother's hogahn. I thought it right that an American should pay tribute to you and me, I thought it was the perfection of my revenge. After what had happened to me, things did not seem bad that seem bad to other people. So I kept on. I did not tell you, I knew you would not like it.

'I thought it was all right. What I did with him had nothing to do with what I did with you, it was just work. It was for us, for our life.

'And I did not want to herd sheep and grow heavy and ugly early from work, as Navajo women do. I wanted much money, and then to go North and have children with you and stay beautiful until I am old, as American women do. I was foolish.

'Then I saw your face in the window, and the world turned to ashes, and I knew that there were things that were worse than death. That is all, that is the truth. I have spoken.'

She sank back, exhausted, with closed eyes. Laughing Boy lit a cigarette from the fire. Then he said:

'I hear you. Sleep. It is well.' He squatted in the doorway, smoking.

III

He was at peace within himself. Now at last he knew his wife, now at last he understood her, and it was all right. Error, not evil. Something inimical and proud in her had been destroyed. He was tired, emotionally drained, but he could let his smoke curl up to the stars and feel the cold air penetrate his blanket, calmly, while he thought and knew his own mind. He had a feeling, without any specific reason, that he should keep a vigil over Slim Girl, but he became so sleepy. He went in by the fire, pulled sheepskins about himself, and slept.

In the morning he brought her food and tended her wound. After they had eaten and smoked, he spoke.

'You have lived in a terrible world that I do not know. I cannot judge you by my world. I think I understand. You have deceived me, but you have not been untrue to me, I think. Life without you would be a kind of death. Now I know that I do not have to do what I thought I had to, and I am glad for it. Now I know you, and there is no more of this secret thing that has been a river between us.

'As soon as you are able, we shall go North. If there is a place where you have relatives, we can go there. If not, we can go to T'o Tlakai, or some place where your clan is strong, or wherever you wish. We shall get the sheep that my mother is keeping for me, and we shall buy others, and we shall live among The People. That is the only way, I think.

'Understand, if we go on together, it is in my world, The People's world, and not this world of Americans who have lost their way.'

They kissed.

'I shall be happy with you anywhere that you wish to take me. As you have said, there is nothing between us now. You have made up to me, and revenged me, for everything the Americans have done to me, My Slayer of Enemy Gods.'

'You must not call me that; it is wicked to call a human being by such a name.'

She answered him with another kiss. He thought he had never seen her look so happy. For the first time since he had known her, she looked as young as she was, a year or so younger than himself. Her face was full of peace.

They fell to planning. Reckoning their resources, they concluded that they had amassed the astounding sum of three thousand dollars in money, goods, and horses. He did not want to take what came through her lover, but she said:

'No; I took it like spoils in war. It was war I made with him. And you made it yours when your arrow struck him. And we both paid for it, I think.'

'Perhaps when he gets well he will send policemen after us.'

'No, I know him. He will say nothing; he will be ashamed, I think.'

CHAPTER XX

I

DURING the interval, Laughing Boy moved most of his horses a couple of days' ride farther north, not far from Zhil Clichigi, where he penned them in a box cañon in which there was a spring and still a little feed. He bought provisions at a trading post on the road to T'o Hatchi. Slim Girl had confessed to him that the story about the warrant out for him on account of the Pah-Ute had been a lie, but, all things considered, she felt it best that he stay away from town. He said that it had seemed a little odd that there should be so much trouble over a Pah-Ute.

'No,' she said, 'they do not want any shooting.'

'That is true. Whenever there is cause for a fight, they want to send men to do the fighting, and only let us come as guides, like that time with Blunt Nose. They must be very fond of fighting, I think, and they have not enough of their own, so they do other people's fighting for them. It is a good thing and a bad thing.

'I do not understand them, those people. They stop us from raiding the Stone House People and the Mexicans, which is a pity; but they stop the

Utes and the Comanches from raiding us. They brought in money and silver, and these goods for our clothes. They bring up water out of the ground for us. Wc are better off than before they came.

'But yet it does not matter whether they do good things or bad things or stupid things, I think. When one or two come among us, they are not bad. If they are, sometimes we kill them, as we did Yellow Beard at Kien Dotklish. But a lot of them and we cannot live together, I think. They do good things, and then they do something like taking a child away to school for five years. Around Lukachukai there are many men who went to school; they wear their hair short; they all hate Americans. I understand that now. There is no reason in what they do, they are blind, but in the end they will destroy everything that is different from them, or else what is different must destroy them. If you destroyed everything in me that is different from them, there would only be a quarter of a man left, I think. Look at what they tried to do to you. And yet they were not deliberately trying.

'Well, soon we shall be where there are few Americans, very few. And we shall see that our children never go to school.'

'Soon we shall be where there are very few

Americans'; that thought was constant in his mind. He was very happy, it was like a second honeymoon. He had kept all the good things of life, and he had saved himself. He saw that his wife depended on him; she was very tender and rather grave. He understood her gravity, in view of her wound and all that had happened. Soon in new surroundings there would be cause for only happiness. A little readjustment, a little helping her into a less comfortable life, but her courage would make nothing of that.

She was very tender and very grave, and she was thinking a great deal. That crisis like a blast of white light had shown her life and herself, it had ended her old independence. She had unravelled her blanket back to the beginning, and started again with a design which could not be woven without Laughing Boy, and she knew that there could be no other design.

It would not be easy at first to be competent and satisfactory up there; to make herself accepted and liked, to do the dull things, to watch sheep and make her own bread. But she would, and she could. They would go to Oljeto, Moonlight Water, a pretty name and a pretty place, if a childhood memory were true. She had relatives there, and it was far from the long arm of the Americans — wild country, with the unexplored fastnesses towards Tsé Nanaazh and the Pah-Utes. That would be better than dealing with his relatives at T'o Tlakai, and it was near enough for visiting.

'And we shall see that our children never go to school.' She echoed that, and she longed for them — his children. But the thought gave her pause. Now that she was thinking as true as she knew how, for her salvation, she wondered if she still could have a child. She was young, but she had been through a lot. After that one terrible time, instructed by the prostitutes of Oñate, she had never put herself in danger of it — or had she? She cast back carefully in her mind; she was not sure. It was possible that she could, possible that she could not. The thing stared her in the face like a risen corpse.

Then what could she do? Have him take another wife, who would bear them to him. Then in the end he would love that other. He would not, of himself, ever want her to go away, but that other would scheme against her, the mother of his children. What would there be in the world for her, a barren Indian, having lost Laughing Boy? An unlocked door in a street by the railroad track, or death. Only death.

There must be children. After all, she was only frightening herself with a chance. When she was quite well, and rested, in their new home, she would put it to the test, and it would come out all right. So she was grave and very tender.

II

When her arm was almost well, Laughing Boy brought three of his best horses to the corral. They prepared to move in beautiful, clear, cold, sunny weather following a first light snow, the slight thawing of which assured them of water. Their goods made little bulk — well over a thousand dollars in silver, turquoise, and coral, several hundred dollars in coin, his jeweller's kit, her spindle, batten, cards, and fork, half a dozen choice blankets, some pots and pans and provisions. They carried a good deal on their saddles, and packed the rest, Navajo-fashion, which is to say badly, on the spare pony. They set out with fine blankets over their shoulders, their mounts prancing in the cold, their saddles and bridles heavy with silver and brass, leading the pack-horse by a multi-coloured horsehair rope, a splendid couple.

After a period of worrying, she had reacted, partly by deliberately living each day for itself only, partly by a natural and reasonable swing to optimism. So they were both gay as they rode, and chattered together of the future. Oljeto had been agreed upon for their new home. It was a good winter camp, he said, and he thought that at Segi Hatsosi or Adudjejiai, little over a day's ride distant, he could find an unclaimed fertile strip for summer. There is good water there, even in dry summers.

'You have seen the stone granaries we build,' he said. 'The rock around that part breaks easily into squares, there is lots of good adobe. I can build you a house as good as the one we just left. We shall make a tunnel like that for the smoke from the fire, and we shall have one of those wooden doors that swing. There will be no house like it around there, except the trader's at T'o Dnesji.'

She smiled. 'And a window?'

'Yes, but we cannot have that clear stone in it. We shall put a membrane across it, that will let in light, I think, but you cannot see through it.'

'That will be good enough.'

They came into the mouth of Chizbitsé Cañon. Here and there were fragments of petrified trees, all colours, some dull, some reflecting like marble, the many shades made brilliant by the thin blanket of snow around them, and the clear sunlight.

'*Ei-yei!* It is a place of jewels!'

They slowed from a jog-trot to a walk, looking

about them at the reproductions of trunks, rings, branches, exact even to the way the snow lay upon them, beautiful in colour, and somehow frightfully dead.

'There is a piece I could use.' Laughing Boy dismounted and picked it up, marbled in ruddy blue and yellow. 'I can cut it up and polish it, and use it in rings and bow-guards.'

'Yes, it will be a new thing, if it is not too hard to work.'

They searched for a few minutes for more good fragments, then he mounted, shouted the pack-horse back onto the trail, and they rode on.

III

Red Man, on his way to trade at Jadito, rode past the mouth of Chizbitsé. He had not breakfasted, but the clear weather, the liveliness of his new horse, kept him cheerful. He looked up the cañon, saw them, and thought,

'Those two!'

He crossed the cañon-mouth and stopped where a rock hid all but his head and shoulders. He was swept by an emotion of many factors which time and much mulling over had compounded into one.

I helped that woman, I took care of her. I ran her errands, I made life possible for her. I loved her, in a way. I knew she was bad with Americans, but she would never do it with me. I deserved it from her. She made a fool of me instead. Why not me, too? Always putting me off and getting around me. And then that fool came out of nowhere and she gave him everything. Him! And he threatened me. *He* told *me* what to do.

All this through many months had become a single feeling. They were riding slowly, leaning towards each other, talking. Faintly, he heard her laugh. There was a pack-animal in front of them — they were going on a visit somewhere, very rich, with a pack-horse.

He thought, 'There goes the man who may send an arrow into me some day.' It made the small of his back squirm.

He took up his rifle, aimed high for distance, and fired. The gun had not been cleaned for several weeks, his hands were cold, and the pony moved. He fired three times, then ducked low behind the rock, and began riding.

Laughing Boy heard the shots, turned, and ducked as two bullets snapped close to him, before he saw Slim Girl slump forward in the saddle. He threw his arm about her, caught her rein, and drove the horses to a gallop. The pack-animal, startled by the rush behind him, raced ahead. When you have only a bow, and an unseen person or persons begins shooting liberally with a rifle, it is no time for gestures of valour or revenge.

They rode thus for about a mile, and then, still seeing no one behind them, drew rein. Here the cañon was wide, and on one side a cleft led into Chizbitsé Mesa, up a slow incline. In there he turned, until at the end of the box cañon sheer cliffs stopped them.

Slim Girl was silent and quite limp as he lowered her from her saddle and placed her on a couch of blankets. Once at ease there, she moaned and asked for water. Her eyes were narrowed and her lips drawn slightly back. He made a fire and melted snow, she drank eagerly.

The bullet had gone clean through her; she was soaked with blood. He did what he could to staunch the flow, and arranged her as comfortably as possible. Occasionally she moaned, then said quite clearly:

'No. I will be brave. Give me a cigarette, and raise my head a little.'

She had scarcely strength to smoke, and she began to cough.

'This is the end, my husband, my belovéd.' Her voice was faint, and she paused after every few words. 'Do not try to avenge me. Promise me that.'

'I promise.' He knelt facing her, unmoving, with lines in his face like carving.

'I think this was meant to happen. Perhaps it is right, I think. After all that had happened to me, perhaps I could not have had children. The Americans spoiled me for a Navajo life, but I shall die a Navajo, now.' She spoke very slowly, with long waits while she lay with closed eyes and her hands clenched. 'I have saved my soul through you. I have been very happy with you. This last little while, I found myself, I found truth with you.' She broke into coughing, and then was silent for almost five minutes.

'I say all this so you shall know that it has not been in vain. You will go on and live and remember me, you have changed because of me; in you I shall live.

'I have come home. I shall die at home, I shall be buried like my People. It is *hozoji*.'

He had no words at all.

'I love you so much. Kiss me.'

He bent over her, her arm clutched about his neck, he lifted her shoulders against his chest. Her eyes were closed and she kissed him with cool, closed lips of love, not of passion.

She opened her eyes, drew back her head, and smiled at him. Then she said in a clear voice,

'Nayeinezgani!' — Slayer of Enemy Gods.'

And so speaking, smiling, died.

Then she is dead. Then it is all over. But

just a little while ago we were laughing together and picking up stones. We were so happy together. Now it is all over. But we had everything arranged, we were going North, we had all our goods, our silver, our blankets. I was going to make her a ring with that purple stone. I was going to build her a house. Now it is all over. There is no sense in it. *Ei-ee*, Divine Ones! *Ei*, Slim Girl, Came With War!

He threw himself upon her body and pressed his mouth to hers. Her lips were cold, she was cold and inert all over. It was inhuman, it was dead. He drew back and rose to his feet with a revulsion of fear, then grew calm.

This is not she, not Slim Girl, Brave Alone, not Came With War, not my wife. This is something she left behind. It is dead, it never had life; it was she inside it who gave it life. I am not afraid of it, and can I ever be afraid of you, oh, beautiful? I shall be calm, I shall bury it, a Navajo burial.

He knelt beside her body and began to sob. After a while he thought, she would not like me to do this. I must bury her before it gets dark. It will snow soon. All alone I went with her, alone I lived with her and knew her beauty, now I alone shall bury her. She was not meant for common knowledge, she was not part of ordinary life, that many people should partake of her.

IV

The pack-horse had disappeared, but before going it had, like a wise animal, rolled its pack off. He collected all their goods and divided them into two equal parts. Most of the time he was not really thinking, but dully following out with slow movements what seemed to be a foreordained course. It occurred to him that the riches that came through the American ought to be thrown away, but he remembered what she had said about that. In jewelry and blankets it had been transmuted. He picked up one of the heaps of coin. That was a lot of money. They had suffered a lot for it, she had suffered so much. He set it down again.

The farthest corner of the cliffs made a niche about twelve feet square, in which the rocks came to the ground sheer, or slightly overhanging, without talus. Here he carried her, and set her in the farthest recess. He walked carefully, avoiding bushes, observing all the requirements, in so far as was possible for a single individual. Over her he put her blankets, at her head, food, by her hands, her weaving tools, cooking implements at her feet. He covered her form with silver and turquoise and coral and coins. As he arranged her, he prayed. Then he looked about for fair-sized slabs, of which there were plenty roundabout, in the talus. He began to bring them, covering her. He had placed the first few, at her feet, when he straightened up and stood still. He walked to his own pile of goods and looked at it. Returning to her, he found her arm under the blankets, and took from it a thin, gold bracelet that she had bought in California. From his own goods he set aside the finest saddle-blanket of her weaving, an old trade blanket, a coffee-pot and coffee. Bundling all the rest together, he carried it to the grave and spread it over her. Slowly he took off his heavy silver belt, his turquoise and coral necklace, his two bracelets, his garnet ring and his turquoise ring, his earrings of turquoise matrix, laying each one gently upon the heap. He changed his old bow-guard for one he had made at their house. Remembering something, he went to his pony, took off his silver-mounted bridle, and added it. With difficulty, he forced the thin gold circle up over his right hand, taking some of his skin with it: it was but little wider than his wrist, it would not come off easily. Then he continued covering her. It began to snow, in large, soft, slow flakes out of a grey-white sky.

It was nearly dark when he had laid on the last stone, and he began to be aware that he was weary. Blowing cigarette smoke four ways, he stood in prayer for a minute or two. He untethered her pony and led it into the niche. It stood patiently by the pile while he notched his arrow and spoke the requisite words. The string twanged, the shaft struck, the pony leapt and fell partly over the tomb. Those clear-cut things, happening rapidly, were out of tempo with everything else; they put a period to it.

CHAPTER XXI

I

Now began the four days of waiting. But just waiting was not enough; there had been no women to wail for her, no outcry of bereaved relatives; he would make it a vigil, all the four days should be one prayer. This was not an ordinary death.

It was quite dark, and the snow still drifted down like waterlogged leaves falling through water. He rebuilt the fire till it blazed, arranged the saddle-blanket and his saddle for a reclining place, pulled the trade blanket about him, and began the vigil, staring at the distant blacker place in the blackness of the cliffs behind the snowflakes that marked the niche.

He tried to pray, but his mind kept wandering, reviewing incidents of their life together, happy and unhappy, but so full of life, so charged with her personality. He would forget that she was dead, he would just be thinking about her. The cold coming through his clothing would wash along his skin, a flake would touch his face, and he would remember.

Now it is all over. Let it be altogether so. That horse is lucky; well, we shall go with her, too.

He got his pony, took his saddle in his hand, and went back into the niche. The animal was nervous and wild with the darkness and the cold and the smell of death. It would not stand still. Later it was to occur to him as part of the remarkableness that he went unhesitatingly into that place after dark, but now he thought nothing of it. Now he was not a Navajo terrified of the dead, not an Indian, not an individual of any race, but a man who had buried his own heart.

He selected his arrow.

'... It has not been in vain. You will remember me, I shall live in you.'

Wind God had spoken her words in his mind. She would not like this. He put back the arrow in his quiver, and led the horse out to the fire. There he took off its rope, and hobbled it.

'Go see if you can find food and water, little brother. Go away and be happy.'

He returned to his vigil, collecting a large pile of dead wood for the fire, and making himself as comfortable as possible with his blankets and his saddle. He began to feel some fear, conscious of the nearness of her tomb, being so very much alone in that narrow cañon. He set himself to the task of realizing what had happened, and conceiving a continuing life without Slim Girl. It was not easy; he spent a long time in rebellion, or in a mere thronging of bitter emotions that made him throw his shoulders from side to side.

Jesting Squaw's Son had been lucky. But in the end he was better off, because there had been that year and a half. Not for anything would he lose that. He began remembering again — it was a kind of anodyne — until he came back to the inevitable starting point. Then it was worse.

After some hours he grew calmer, partly because of fatigue. The disaster was accepted and familiar; he told himself that he could see the life ahead growing, in a way, from what had gone before. Nothing could ever make him forget; what he was and always would be, what he did and thought, would always be conditioned by Slim Girl. The remainder of his life would be a monument to her. All this could not be changed or taken from him, he would never lose its mark. That was a comfort.

He was thinking this way with his intellect, it did not really go inside of him. It was still just platitudes.

He became more aware of things about him, the cold, the fire, the snow. Flakes fell into the flames with little hisses, and he remembered his dream.

'Slayer of Enemy Gods' she called me. But Slayer of Enemy Gods spared the Cold Woman and Old Age Woman and Poverty People and

Hunger People. She tried to kill the Hunger People; I thought she could. If we had not tried to do that, we should have been living happily within the Navajo country long ago. She was too daring, she wanted perfection.

By whatever means she got it, we had perfection. But it could not have gone on. We are not divine. Or I am not; she had made herself above Earth People. What has happened to me, it is like what happened to many people long ago. It happened to Taught Himself and the Magician's Daughter, to Reared in a Mountain when he went through the homes of the gods, to Eagles' Friend when he went to the sky. They went away and saw something better than they had ever known. They did not try to bring something too good for earth back to earth. But they did not — lose — Slim Girl.

His head fell forward on his knees and he stopped thinking. He was exhausted, and shortly fell asleep in that position. He woke when he began to fall over, very cold, and thought he must have drowsed. The fire was low. The snowfall ceased and dawn came limping.

The first day was sparkling, crisp, and sunny. The first day was one of stunned, dull realization. He wandered about uncertainly and drugged himself with detailed, long-drawn-out memories.

And in the end, he would return to the beginning of his circle and stand or sit motionless and groan. It was a long day and a strange one; later he did not remember it clearly.

The second night he tried hard not to sleep, but it was hard, with cold, hunger, fatigue, and the fire. He dozed a good deal, and his memories became very accurate dreams into which slowly would creep a sense of horror without reason, until he woke, not knowing he had slept, continuing the thought and the mood. He tried to pray, but it was chiefly ejaculations and the names of the gods. It was an endless and terrible night.

Daylight, when at last it came, was a release. He shook himself, thinking, 'I must be calm, I must think clearly. This is no time for wandering without getting anywhere.' He quieted himself for a time, achieving a state of apparent resignation which enabled him to pray, but the oft-repeated *hozoji* sounded hollow. He did not really think there was anything beautiful; he was just acting as he thought he ought.

Plenty of people had died in his neighbourhood; there had been mourning and grief, when every one had stayed close to the hogahns for four days. But this was different. He had seen the bereaved, he had seen real sorrow upon them, but he could not believe that they had felt as he did.

He was alone in more than the physical sense. No one, not even Jesting Squaw's Son, could come near him. All his life, wherever he was, however long he lived, he would remain alone. It would always be like this. The one companionship in the world had gone; when the sun has been destroyed for a man, what comfort is there in a world of moonlight?

He had nothing to do in the cañon save tend his fire and think. He would get hold of a thought, work it over and over until he lost all sense of proportion towards it, and finally put it in a phrase or a simile, so that it obtained substance and could not be dismissed.

He hated to watch it grow dark; he felt afraid of the night. He did not want to be shut into that little space of firelight with all the things he was thinking. Alone, alone, all life alone, all life carrying this pain inside himself. He might as well die. But she wanted him to live. It was the third night, and he was approaching the stage of visions. Outlines of things dimly seen in the starlight changed and assumed startling forms. He became the audience listening to unseen people arguing as to whether he ought to kill himself or not. He knew he ought to live, but he could not control which side might win.

He couldn't always follow very well what was

going on. Extraneous things intruded themselves. There were people all around, pitying him. It was being insisted upon that loneliness and pain were not worth enduring for a whole lifetime, without purpose.

'But I have to live for her,' he said aloud, and thought hard about her.

Then he saw her, standing on the other side of the fire. He started to his feet, choking with all a Navajo's terror of the walking dead. He was dissolved in fear, but she was gone. He was alone, the voices were gone, the people. He sat down, trembling, and quite wide awake. Evidently he did not want to die, but he had no will to live; he did not know himself, it would be wrong to make a decision now. Little by little he grew drowsy, and dozed in snatches. Perhaps her coming was a good thing; one would not expect her ghost to be like other people's.

This, too, became a discussion outside himself. The spirits of the dead are bad; if they walk, it is for destruction. She is different, she would come to protect him. She would lead him to some frightful end. But no one could imagine blue fire coming out of her eyes and mouth. It went on and on. There was an outline of something he had not seen before, it moved and he felt his scalp crawl. Then he let out a deep sigh and relaxed. It was a bush, some little distance away. Dawn was coming.

A little water and the clear sunshine revived him for a time, but soon he was tired and miserable again, listlessly occupying himself with gathering more firewood, bringing a branch at a time, setting aside without interest those that would do for making a sweat-bath. Later, he thought of that day as the day of treason. He protracted his occupation, being meticulous about finding all the wood in one section before moving to the next. He thought of the eventual bath, which should wash him clean of the taint of death; he wished it might wash out his mind. He thought that if he never had met her, he would be happy now, remembering Slender Hair riding by and telling him of the dance that was to be, remembering himself riding, singing, down to Tsé Lani, the firelight and that girl, remembering what chance, what meeting of eyes in a crowd, his uncle's tactlessness, had put an end to a young man who had no cares.

The thought stayed with him as he wandered about kicking up the snow for bits of dead wood. He knew that it was an entity in itself, and saw it as a tall old man who leered as he walked beside and slightly behind him, a bad, strong old man. The old man kept at him about it, that he had been a fool, that he should have avoided all this. And he thought, in answer, that it was too late now, why couldn't he be left alone? He tried to explain to himself, to the old man, that he couldn't have helped doing what he did. He himself, as a third person, repeated that all the suffering was worth while for the happy months, but the old man only sneered. He tried to get himself in hand, and think of a new design for a belt, but that was useless. He would walk around for a long time without looking for wood at all. Picking up his pony's tracks, he followed them out into the main cañon until he saw the horse in a sheltered place under the east wall, then, realizing how far he had gone from the place of vigil, hurried back. Everything had gone to pieces, he did everything wrong. The old man had waited for him, he was triumphant over this breach of observance.

Nightfall was at least a change. Having plenty of wood, he built the fire up high, and went to some trouble to make himself comfortable. This was the fourth night, he was more or less out of his head. The old man had long ceased to be a personification and become a reality; he got in under the same blanket and hammered, hammered at him about the unfortunate past. Laughing Boy saw an empty, drifting future, always with this old man. He saw himself a long time from now, and the dead boy who had ridden down to Tsé Lani crying across a gap full of darkness to the empty husk of a man who had destroyed him. He tried to call on the gods, but there came only Hunger People, Old Age, and Cold Woman. Yellow Singer and his wife were there, looking sorry for him in that unpleasant, understanding way, like the day he was married. They all looked at him that way. He saw the stricken face of Jesting Squaw's Son, and thought, 'You too have received the wound, but you were lucky, the knife was pulled out as soon as it was thrust into you.'

The old man was pulling at his bow-guard. There was something around his right wrist, and that seemed to be being pulled too. The old man said,

'Where did you get that bow-guard?'

'I made it.'

'I'll give you six dollars for it.'

'I don't want to sell it.'

He did not really speak, but the words were saying themselves for him in answer to the old man, from a great distance, all the way from that hogahn by Tsé Lani.

The old man went on, 'That turquoise is no good, and the work is not very good.'

The work was good. He touched the silver

with his right hand, to show the four-points-with-three-points design. But it was not that design, it was not the bow-guard he made at T'o Tlakai, it was that one he made at their hogahn, the one with stars-following.

He said out loud, 'This is the one I made when she was weaving. I will not sell it.'

He felt the thing on his right wrist; it was the thin, gold circlet. He saw her hand and arm under the blankets, he saw the tomb in the dusk, and her face as he bent over it, so still. His in-turned torment was obliterated by the memory of that exalted agony. He remembered her last kiss, and her voice, and the mound of her blankets and jewels above her. His arms clutched about his knees, his left hand closed around the foreign bracelet, and he began to weep, tears pouring plenteously. As though they were rain on the desert, a coolness spread through him, a sense of majestic beauty.

He threw his arms wide, looked up, and began to pray,

'House made of dawn light,
House made of evening light,
House made of dark cloud,
House made of he-rain . . .'

The old man was gone, and the Hunger People and all the rest. He stood up, stepping back from the fire, stretched out his hands, and his prayer rose in powerful song,

'*Kat Yeinaezgani tla disitsaya* . . .
'Now, Slayer of Enemy Gods, alone I see him coming,
Down from the skies, alone I see him coming.
His voice sounds all about,
His voice sounds, divine.
Lé-é!
'Now, Child of the Waters, alone I see him coming . . .'

He finished, and stood with high head and hands still held forth. A log on the fire fell in, the flames leapt up, slightly dazzling his sight. When it had cleared, along the level of his finger-tips he saw a line dividing a deeper from a lesser blackness. The line spread right and left, and now along its upper edge a white glow appeared and widened; the sky above was changing from black to blue, the cliffs of the far side of the main cañon were silhouetted against the coming day.

'*Hozoji, hozoji, hozoji, hozoji!*

'Dawn Boy, Little Chief,
Let all be beautiful before me as I wander,
All beautiful behind me as I wander,
All beautiful above me as I wander,
All beautiful below me as I wander.
Let my eyes see only beauty
This day as I wander.
In beauty,
In beauty,
In beauty,
In beauty!'

He let his arms fall. 'Thanks!'

He rearranged the fire to make a lasting, small flame, enough to melt snow in the coffee-pot for drinking and refreshing his hands and face. He looked over towards the niche, a shadowy place; the rocks on each side of it were touched irregularly with sunlight.

I nearly lost you, little sister, but now I have you for always.

He began praying again, quietly and earnestly, not in set terms, but according to his need. He had come out of that closet in himself now, and things had fitted back into place. He was grave, and there would be many times when he would go by himself to feel a belovéd pain, but regret for the knowledge of happiness that had made that pain possible was ended. He had a clear conscience to pray.

He built his sweat-lodge, and, since it was hard to get mud out of the frozen ground, covered it with blankets. In the mid-afternoon he put in the hot rocks, stripped, and entered. He had made it good and hot; he sat in there chanting as long as he could stand it, then he burst out, rolled in the snow, and dressed hastily. He felt infinitely better. He looked at the sun, low in the west; the fourth day was ended.

He felt clear-headed, peaceful, washed, and

very hungry as he tracked his pony. The animal greeted him with a whinny; its legs were stiff from the hobbles, and it had fallen off from lack of feed. He rode back to the camp, and tethered it while he broke his fast with coffee. Then he saddled and mounted. Before he rode on he turned towards the niche and sat still until his mount jerked at the reins.

But we shall never be far from each other, he thought, always alone but never lonely. As he rode away he repeated, 'In beauty it is finished, in beauty it is finished, in beauty it is finished. Thanks.'

II

It was nearly dark when he climbed out of the head of the cañon onto the top of So Selah Mesa. He urged his pony along the level going, anxious to get to the settlement in Jaabani Valley as soon as possible. There was only a day-old moon, and a cold wind blew across the open. It was a talking wind, a voice of sorrow in the growing darkness, and Laughing Boy had been too long alone. He wanted a respite from self-communion; he wanted company and things happening, the old life, support. He was homesick for old, familiar things.

This cold plateau was nowhere, a waste land

separating the human world from the enchanted. It was always dark here, and a cold wind blew, and there was always a small moon setting.

I shall be whimpering in a moment, he thought. I am unworthy of myself and of her. Do I forget everything? It's because I am cold and hungry. I might sing. He began,

'I rode down from high hills...'

but the high-pitched love-tune affronted the night. He stopped, with a catch in his throat.

I will not cry. This is not a thing to cry over; it is a beautiful thing, to be thought of gravely. I devote my life to it, not just cry. He began to chant, in a deep voice:

'With a place of hunger in me I wander,
Food will not fill it,
Aya-ah, beautiful.
With an empty place in me I wander,
Nothing will fill it,
Aya-ah, beautiful.
With a place of sorrow in me I wander,
Time will not end it,
Aya-ah, beautiful.
With a place of loneliness in me I wander,
No one will fill it,
Aya-ah, beautiful.
Forever alone, forever in sorrow I wander,
Forever empty, forever hungry I wander,
With the sorrow of great beauty I wander,
With the emptiness of great beauty I wander,

Never alone, never weeping, never empty,
Now on the old age trail, now on the path of beauty
I wander,
Ahalani, beautiful!'

It was a prayer. He ended with four solemn *hozoji's* that seemed to travel out from him and fill the darkness. That is a good song, he thought. I shall sing that often, at evening, when I am alone. But I wish we would get to where there are people.

It had been night for more than an hour when he came to the edge of the mesa, looking down into Jaabani. He saw the little pin-pricks of fires, very distant. Then, as he watched, near them another began, and grew, until a tall flame rose, throwing light all about it. He heard a drum beat and faint voices singing, and saw around the blaze a wide circle of branches, and people moving. They were beginning the last night of a Mountain Chant, the ritual within the Dark Circle of Branches.

'Come on, my pet!' His horse began slowly descending the trail in the starlight. As they went down, he sang his song again. This was very good. When Reared in a Mountain returned to his people from the homes of the gods, he taught them these prayers and songs, and they held the Mountain Chant for him, because he was unhappy among them. Even so was he. He was rejoining his people in the presence of the gods. Ah, if she could have been here!

The singing grew louder, the triumphant songs. Now he could make out the words. They were completing the magic of the tufted wands. He drew rein a few yards from one of the camp-fires, tasting again the sense of his isolation. Then he dismounted.

Only a few people remained outside the circle, but he found a hospitable pot of broth, some chunks of mutton still in it, bread to dip, and coffee.

'Where do you come from, Grandfather?' the woman asked.

'From Chiziai.'

'Where are you going?'

'To this dance.'

'That is a good saddle-blanket; who made it?'

'My wife, she weaves well.'

'Is she here?'

'No, she stayed behind.'

III

The brush fence enclosed an oval some forty feet across, in the centre of which blazed the bonfire, higher than a tall man. All around the edge sat people, several hundreds of them; they were happy, their faces were grave but joyful. At one end were the singers.

Now Red God came into the open space, leading a file of dancers, the Grandfather of the Gods, who guided Reared in a Mountain through the homes of the Divine Ones, who saved him from the Utes. With his plumed sticks and his sacred insignia, Red God led the dance before them.

Talking God and South God and Young Goddess came before them with dancers, and all the place was full of sacred songs. They were leading good dances, with good music.

The magicians came in and planted the yucca root. They sang and danced about it; the yucca grew, it became tall, it flowered. In midwinter the enchanted yucca bloomed before them. These were the magics that the people of distant tribes brought to the first Mountain Chant. Now the magicians placed the board and the disk of the sun on the ground, the people all shouted, 'Stand! Stand!' The board stood up on end, the sun rose to the top and set slowly; four times the sun rose and set by magic; then the board lay flat again.

A man, stripped to his breech-clout, danced before a basket. Out of the basket an eagle feather rose; it danced up into the air, to the height of the man, and there it moved backward and forward in time with him.

Jesters came in, dressed as Americans and Mexicans, and made the people laugh. The spirits of the ancestral animals, hovering over the brush circle, were made happy. Laughing Boy, sitting among friendly strangers, smiled at them and said,

'It is good!'

The great central fire and the small fires that people made for themselves, kept the place warm. He had eaten, he was comfortable. He did not realize how sleepy he was. At times the details of what he was watching became blurred and he drowsed deliciously; but he was permeated with the general feeling of the prayer, and he looked upon it as he had when an uninitiated child.

Young men painted all white with black forearms, foxskins hanging from their waists, came in with the magic arrows adorned with breath-feathers. This was the holiest part; this was the charm that the Tall Gods taught to Reared in a Mountain in their divine home. The young men danced, they swallowed the arrows and shouted in triumph; these were the very acts of the gods.

Laughing Boy felt a deep sense of peace, and rejoicing over ugliness defeated. The gods danced before him, he felt the influence of their divinity. The naked youths danced with torches, they bathed in flame, they leapt through and through the fire. He had been bathed in flame, he had been through a fire.

The past and the present came together, he was one with himself. The good and true things he had thought entered into his being and were part of the whole continuity of his life.

It was beginning to dawn, the last prayer came to a close. Quietly, the people left the enclosure. He went to where his horse was tethered and rolled up in his blanket. Sleepily there, he kissed the gold bracelet, saying,

'Never alone, never lamenting, never empty. *Ahalani*, beautiful!'

THE END

Peaceable Lane

By KEITH WHEELER

SIMON AND SCHUSTER · NEW YORK · 1960

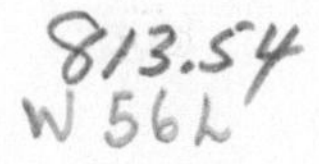

Published by Simon and Schuster, Inc.
Rockefeller Center, 630 Fifth Avenue
New York 20, N.Y.

Library of Congress Catalog Card Number: 60-12580
Manufactured in the United States of America
W

ALTHOUGH THIS NOVEL DEALS WITH A REAL ISSUE LATELY PRESSING UPON AMERICAN SOCIETY, THE CHARACTERS, PLACES AND EVENTS PRESENTED HERE ARE IMAGINARY. RESEMBLANCE, IF ANY, TO REAL PERSONS, PLACES OR EVENTS IS ACCIDENTAL.

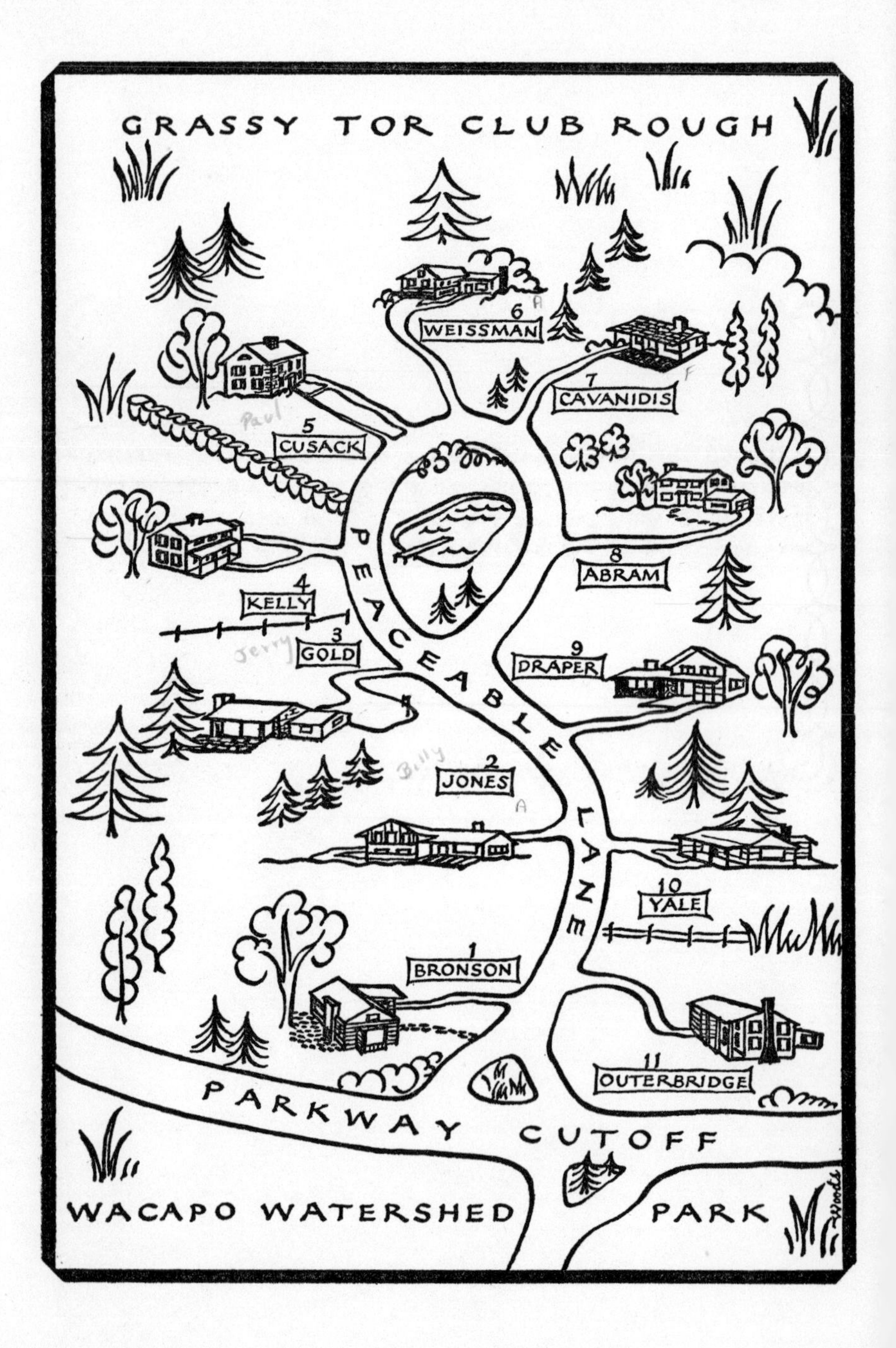
GRASSY TOR CLUB ROUGH
6
WEISSMAN
7
CAVANIDIS
5
CUSACK
PEACEABLE LANE
8
ABRAM
4
KELLY
3
GOLD
9
DRAPER
2
JONES
10
YALE
1
BRONSON
11
OUTERBRIDGE
PARKWAY CUTOFF
WACAPO WATERSHED
PARK

Book One

1

MATTHEW RICE JONES was in no shape to recognize a portent, still less to deal with one, on that Sunday afternoon in May. It was a bright day in the fullness of spring, and Matt was collapsed on an aluminum lounge in his back yard, living out the last gentle melancholy of a Sunday hangover. To ease the process, a Bloody Mary was balanced on the arm of the chair and the makings for more were close at hand on a table beside him. The sun, filtering down through the fresh green canopy of the maples, was soothingly warm on his body, while the first page of the New York *Times* lay athwart his nose as a shield against the hurtful light. The morning's real agony was past and he no longer feared relapse.

He reflected that spring was the best season for such slightly shaky Sunday reverie. Later, in July and August, the back yard would grow too torrid, and reasonable defense against a hangover would be possible only in the air-conditioned master bedroom. Really no better than fighting the same good fight in winter—saving that in midsummer Bill and his friends would probably be outside instead of in the playroom bombarding Matt's skull with the seething racket which seemed, unaccountably, as necessary to them as air. It occurred to Matt that probably the reason Bill did not need an air conditioner of his own was that he was nine years old and, unlike his father, did not yet include sporadic Saturday-night lushing among his excesses.

Matt Jones was an average medium-young man, enjoying a degree of material success slightly above average, suffering no troubles which a few fewer bills and a little more money couldn't have cured. He had one car, two seasons out of date, a mortgage which caused him alternate pride and distress, a blond wife whom he loved and who loved him, and a son they both adored with a bottomless outpouring of proud affection. Matt's health was admirable, except on days like this, and his disposition was sunny except when he occasionally got to worrying, without much real excuse, about going to the poorhouse.

Life thus far had tended to be more generous to him than demanding of him. Except for the war, when being uncomfortable or brave or scared were endemic conditions shared by everybody around him—or being in love with his wife or wholly bound up in his son, which were generally happy emotions—he had never been forced to deal with the basic raw stuff of human passion. He harbored no hatreds, felt no violent commitment to any controversial cause. Nothing ever had forced him to the hard business of making an exact definition of his place in the human cosmos. He felt no powerful obligation to the generality of mankind except to look upon it, for the most part, with good will. Matt was thus ill equipped to deal with what would begin to happen to him this day.

It was not difficult to take the measure of his returning peace. His stomach's unease could be felt yielding to the therapy of the Bloody Mary. No necessity for dangerous exertion threatened until Ellen would call him to cook the steak. The summons was still pleasantly remote and, in any case, he was fortified by knowing that ministering to a steak outdoors was work that could be done sitting down. A large element of his content was the knowledge that the office and its demands were still hull down over the horizon, sixteen hours into the healthful future—perhaps more if the New York Central behaved as lackadaisically as it often did. It promised to be a day which would not require him to move much, a day in which most things and people would come to him and would, by and large, prove more pleasant than otherwise.

In fact, he thought comfortably, I feel a lot better than I probably deserve. The thought was an error, for it set him musing on what he did deserve. Here lay danger. Suddenly he remembered the source of the hangover. They had gone to the spring dance at the Grassy Tor Club up on the hill. Had he had a good time? A good time! How much booze did it take to build a head the size of which he had started this day? He had believed himself clinically safe from pain, but now the thought of the night before plunged him into shuddering gloom. He could remember a long succession of flushed, jovial, laughing faces, but they tended to fuzz out into unidentifiable blurs. I must have bought a drink or two, he thought. A drink or two, nuts; I must have bought drinks for the entire membership, not to mention the caddies. It was too late now to back out of the memory process; all he could remember for sure was a parade of bar chits all bearing the bighearted signature of M. R. Jones.

He opened his eyes and, looking downward under the tent of newspaper, regarded his right hand with loathing. It's a damn wonder you haven't got writer's cramp, he thought.

Why hadn't Ellen done something about it? She, who kept a grip on sobriety even on expansively gay occasions, should have had the sense to put a clamp on him. She knew his fatal, fuzzy compulsion to grab a check before anybody else could make a gesture. But this was familiar and humiliating ground and he knew it; with a wince he acknowledged that she had probably tried. She had tried before, but the results were usually the same.

Recollection of one irritant led inexorably to another. Quickly, with his hangover making a comeback, Matt was wallowing in a sea of fiscal miseries any one of which seemed ample to swamp him. What had set him off this time? That was easy: Saturday's letter from the mortgage company. The Jones acre had been assessed upward again, the second time in two years, and the bank wanted him to know it would need another $30 a month from now on, plus an immediate $348.39 to bring his escrow account for taxes into mesh with reality. He wondered irritably why, when the mortgage people wanted more money, they always so meticulously calculated it down to the odd penny. Probably a kind of high-class financial gamesmanship, he reflected sourly: even the most outraged victim could not fail to see that a Shylock who weighed his pound of flesh so exactly must hate to claim it at all. Obviously this new tax increase was not the mortgage company's fault. They were merely acting as agent to reap the inevitable consequences of his own rashness in voting in favor of a new wing on the Wacapo Consolidated School. He groaned softly; no wonder he had got stewed.

Naturally, then, he was forced to recall that the grace period on a $532.71 premium payment to Prudential Life would run out on Tuesday. Life-insurance companies, he thought dismally, are as beady-eyed as mortgage bankers when it came to watching pennies. It did his mood no good to reflect that that was probably why they had so many pennies while he did not. Take it all together, the forthcoming month ought to be one of the blackest since October 1929. Not that every month wasn't more or less alike. It was only that each one seemed so when it got there. Wouldn't you think that once in a while—not all the time, but once in a while—she would buy hamburger?

He winced at an at first unidentifiable blast of human noise, and then, peering fearfully under the newspaper, realized that his resolutely untidy son and a raucous accomplice, Benjy Abram from across the street, were charging around the house in pursuit of a football.

"Catch it, butterfingers!" Bill Jones screamed. He launched a wobbly pass and Benjy charged downfield on a collision course for Matt's refuge. Matt cringed as the flailing young cannonball came down on him, jerked his legs toward safety and then felt his burdened skull seem to split as the football came down on the bridge of his nose, where there was no protection except the newspaper. He gasped, instinctively thrusting a protective arm toward the Bloody Mary makings.

"Hey!" he yelled. "You monsters trying to kill me?"

Benjy pulled up, abashed at the sign of hostile life. Bill, better aware of the enemy's fundamental impotence, approached and blandly retrieved the football. There was no outward sign that he was even aware of a parent, not to mention a parent who had just been assaulted.

"Try it again, butterfingers!" Bill yelled as he coiled himself into an approximation of a New York Giants passing quarterback about to heave a long one.

"Stop!" Matt yelled, then lapsed into a pleading tone. "Look, son, your father is suffering. Why can't you go play in Ben's yard?"

"Because my mother chased us out already," Benjy said. "She said we were too loud and, besides, the Vogelmans are there."

"She's right. You're too loud. Besides, you're about four months out of season. Now, go somewhere and play with dolls or something. Excuse me, gentlemen, I didn't mean dolls. But what I do mean is go somewhere; that's an order. You understand?"

"Aw," Bill protested, "you won't let us play in the street."

"Well, think of something. Go read the funnies."

"We did already," Bill said. "Besides, you only brought home the *Tribune* and the funnies are square."

"I don't feel up to discussing English usage today, son, but I've told you before I don't want you to use that word 'square.' While I'm at it, you can stop saying 'all that jazz,' too."

"Everybody else says it," Bill said reasonably. "Do you want me to talk like a sq——?" He stopped in time and regarded Matt with momentary doubt. Matt sighed and felt the press of parental responsibility but knew that this was not the day to cope with it.

"Look, son," he said, sinking to bribery without further fight, "you and Ben find something quiet to do—remote, too, if you can manage that—and I'll blow both of you to the price of a Good Humor, the de luxe kind."

The opposition was fully attuned to the Good Humor man's schedule and had been, for the last fifteen minutes, subconsciously awaiting the tinkle of his afternoon bell. They consulted through extrasensory perception, brightened, decided to surrender, collected and departed in peace.

"I knew he'd pop for it," Billy muttered as they left. Matt heard and shuddered.

Matt wondered what had become of his feeling of well-being and sought to win it back. He tried the paper for therapy but found no help there, nothing but woe compounded. Disgustedly he tossed the paper aside and tried to sink himself again in the serenity of the day. Upstairs in the maples a pair of bluejays squabbled in preparation for making love and settling down to summer domesticity. He looked but could not find them in the leafy canopy. He let his gaze drift across the back half of the

Jones acre and felt the old, never-failing stir of satisfaction in ownership. The dogwood is great this year, he reflected; funny, some years there's hardly a flower and then the next year they're loaded. It's a lovely place to live, he thought—if you can just keep your mind off the taxes.

From somewhere came the high-pitched whine of a lawnmower engine, now near, now receding, as whoever was guiding it moved back and forth across his lawn. Probably Zack, Matt thought. Nobody's gardener would be working on Sunday, and nobody on Peaceable Lane mowed his own grounds except himself and Zachariah Gold, who kept up the mortgage on the acre to his left. I don't know why it should seem funny for Zack to mow his own lawn, he thought idly, except that he's a Jew and it seems to me that Jews are apt to put more store on the appearance of status than goys are. But then, what the hell, I'm the only Christian around who mows his own, so I don't know why it's any odder for Zack to do it.

He turned his head as the mower's whine grew louder and saw Gold's tall, heavy figure moving steadily up the slope toward his turn-around point at the meandering row of hemlocks which, to an untutored eye, might have seemed to set off the boundary line but which, actually and deliberately, tended to obliterate it altogether. The hemlocks represented an act of collaboration between Matt and Gold, and both regarded them, rather smugly, as a shrewd strategic counterattack against the relentless way their properties had of proliferating work that had to be done. They had bought the hemlocks together in their first summer as lawnmower operators. Then they had planted them back and forth across the line, calculating the spacing according to what they hoped was a scientific theory of anticipated growth, with an eye to reducing as much as possible the expanse of lawn that would have to be mowed.

Now Matt could see Gold guiding his machine up to their cooperative grass inhibitor. Gold wore shorts but was bare to the waist, the hair across his chest showing blackly even at this distance. Gold looked up, took a hand from the machine and tossed a casual wave at him. Looks hot, Matt thought, and on impulse straightened up and yelled. Gold shut off the engine and came leisurely across the grass, taking off his glasses to mop away a film of sweat against his cotton shorts.

"You trying for a heart attack and a tan both this early in the year?" Matt asked. "Sit down and cool off and I'll make you something." He gestured with his own half-full glass. "It's got calories plus other restorative properties."

"Uh huh, looks like you're in convalescence," Gold said. "Got the pain under control?"

"It's getting there," Matt said, "barring a setback now and then." He arose, found a glass, peered into the ice bucket and saw with satisfaction that its contents were still solid.

"It's good," Gold acknowledged, sipping at the drink as he settled into another chair, "although it would take a genius to make a bad Bloody Mary."

"I wasn't trying to win a ribbon. Zack, how come you mow your own lawn?"

"Two reasons," Gold said equably. "Number one, I can't afford the eighty bucks these Italian barbers would charge for it and I don't know any ignorant college boy or old country peon I could con into doing it for less. Second—this one may be vanity—I need the exercise. I don't play golf, so I have no defense against a tendency to pad my gut muscles with lard."

"I should have been able to figure that out for myself," Matt said, wondering at the same time whether Grassy Tor's attitude toward Jewish applicants had anything to do with Gold's not playing golf. Matt had been a member for a year before he had begun to be aware of that attitude and he had not yet shaken off the feeling of discomfort the discovery had given him. "It was idle curiosity, you and I being the only do-it-yourself grass barbers in the neighborhood."

"Why do you?"

"Same reasons, same order of importance. Only I suspect the second reason impresses me less. Lard doesn't stick to me; I worry it off."

"What about?"

"About everything. It's oversimplifying, but you could sum it up by saying I worry about not being able to afford a gardener."

"Well, it isn't going to kill us to cut our own grass," Gold said.

Matt Jones and Zachariah Gold were casually and comfortably friends. It was an undemanding relationship but probably closer than most friendships on Peaceable Lane, whose eleven householders were not much given to intimacy. It had grown up out of the accident of living side by side but had flourished on solider fare. Either might have been hard pressed to define it but, though markedly dissimilar in appearance, temperament and background, they recognized in one another an essential similarity of generous decency and tolerant regard for their fellow men.

Their talk was desultory, in tune with the day, the lazy pleasure of a slowly sipped drink, the languor of Sunday afternoon in spring. Gold jibed at Matt mildly for his failure thus far, as elected chairman of the street's community swimming pool committee, to get the pool ready for summer. Matt defended himself on the ground that another neighbor and committee member, John Ainslie Outerbridge, had not yet hired a life guard. Matt asked whether Gold's taxes, like his own, had been raised, and, comparing the similarity of fiscal damage done them, they exchanged well-worn opinions of resigned indignation at government's merciless banditry. When David Bronson, Matt's next-door neighbor on the other side, appeared distantly in his back yard, Gold was moved to observe that he had heard Bronson was trying to sell his house.

"That," Matt said, "is a sign of spring as sure as robins. Every year, on the dot, Bronson tries to sell his house. How about another of these?" he asked, jiggling his empty glass suggestively. "One wing and all that."

"Not me, thanks," Gold said. "I still have what looks like a quarter section to go. Besides, I spent a virtuous Saturday night. I don't stand in your need."

"Okay, Zack, take it easy," Matt said as Gold raised his heavily muscled bulk and moved off toward the hemlocks.

The lawnmower coughed and began to howl. I'm glad I had the forethought to barber my own hay yesterday, Matt thought. I'd never have been able to face it today. Lying back dreamily, he heard a door bang and saw his wife coming toward him across the grass, tall, clean-limbed, blond, with usually, somehow, an aura of freshness and warm light about her. He watched the flow of movement of her legs and breasts against the pale cloth of her dress and felt a vague but pleasurable stir of lecherous interest. It could turn into something more than vague pretty quickly, he thought, and wondered, half shamefaced, how she would feel about it now in the middle of the afternoon. Well, what's wrong with the afternoon? he thought defensively. My God, married fifteen years and still raunching after the same woman. There's another mystery for you, he thought; why is it a hangover brings out the horniness in you? You'd think it would be the other way around. He watched her approach with approval, forgetting that she was probably coming to call him to unwelcome duty at the grill.

"How are you, good-time Charley?" Ellen said, smiling down at him with a sympathy belying the insult. "Coming back to life?"

"Don't nag me, darling," Matt said comfortably. "You know how I am—a jump from the undertaker." He eyed her speculatively. "How would you like to go make love?"

"Wow!" Ellen said. "You don't remember? Twice before breakfast?"

"We did?" He looked at her with astonishment.

"I've never understood how you can manage to look embarrassed and complacent at the same time." Ellen grinned. "You can stop blushing; I know I'm married to a Sunday-morning satyr, but I like it. But it's time to eat. Billy says if we don't stop starving him, he's either going to run away or complain to the police."

"Dutiful son," Matt said. "Grateful too. Good thing he doesn't know about the Juvenile Aid Society or he'd have them on my neck too."

"Do you think you have the strength to burn the steak?" Ellen asked. "After all you've been through?"

"Now who's blushing?" Matt grunted. "I guess I can face it. Did you light the fire?" With a feeling of dangerous experiment, he gathered his lanky parts together and managed to come upright. Ellen picked up the tray of makings and they walked to the cedar shakes and fieldstone pile of the Jones castle.

Matt found the salt, pepper grinder, clove of garlic, the heavy knife he liked and the steak laid out on a wooden tray. He inspected the meat, noting with approval that it was thick, dark with age, veined with fat. Another thing about her, he thought, she's found out how to pick a porterhouse. He went out to the fire in the stone grill, thoughtfully tonged on a few more lumps of charcoal, and spread the coals out in a gray-ashed bed of heat. Absorbed, his thin, assured but somehow gentle face intent, he watched the fire for a moment before driving the fork into the heavy slab of meat and dropping it on the grill precisely where he wanted it. At once the meat sizzled hotly and sent up a preliminary haze of aromatic smoke.

Ellen came from the house and put a drink on the stonework. "Here," she said. "Not that I think you really need it."

"Thanks," he said. "Fetch me a chair, will you, honey? How about you?"

"Got one made already," she said. "I'll be out in a minute, just as soon as I finish the salad dressing."

The telephone rang. "Damn," she said. "I wonder who that is. Not one of those twenty-minute party post-mortems, I hope." She started into the house.

"It better not be: this cow will be on the table in less than that," Matt said dangerously to her retreating back.

"I know: if it can't walk to the table you won't eat it. Don't worry, I'll cut her off, whoever it is."

But she did not, and Matt, guiding the steak toward the precise degree of pinkness, grew first anxious, then irritated. At last, when she had not returned, he lifted the meat from the fire and sounded his indignation.

"Hey!" he yelled. "You want to eat ashes? And where's Bill? Billy, hey, Billy! Ellen! Come on, knock it off." Had there ever yet been a time when a steak was ready and anybody else was? "Hey!"

"Stop squalling," Ellen said, coming from the house. "We're ready—that is, almost. Billy's in the bathroom washing off the barnacles. Everything's ready. Bring the steak."

"Where were you?" Matt asked irritably. "The damn thing is a cinder already."

"That was Laura."

"Oh, the Cusack, I should have guessed. I thought you were going to cut her off."

"I was, but you should have heard her. You know what she said?"

The nearing hoofbeats of Jones, Jr. taking the parts of both Matt Dillon and a thousand bloodthirsty Comanches in pursuit down the stairs put a stop to that subject.

"I want that part," Billy announced, breaking off the war whoop to point an imaginary scalping knife at the tenderloin. "No salad, Mom. I hate salad. Gimme a little potato. No butter, I said no butter. Aw gee, jeepers!"

"You'll take butter and like it," Matt said.

"Jeep-e-e-e-e-r-s!" Billy moaned and writhed in his chair as though in the last agonies of butter poisoning.

"Butter—and like it," Matt said. "I'm sorry, Ellen. It looks like the Cusack revelation will have to wait. Tell me after the tribes are back on the reservation."

"I love steak," Billy announced loudly. "Can I have some more?"

"May, dear, not can. May I have some more?" Ellen said.

"All right, may," Billy said agreeably. "But can I have some more? That piece there." He stabbed at the tray with his fork.

"Look, son, neither your mother nor I have even had a chance at a bite yet," Matt protested. "And how about those potatoes?"

"Aw, I hate butter," Billy said reasonably. "And I love steak."

"You used to call it 'snake' before you got grown up the way you are now," Matt said, reaching for the carving knife. "This is the last—the last anyhow until you do something constructive about those potatoes. What did Cusack have on her—you should excuse the expression—mind, Ellen?"

Ellen frowned. "The Bronsons are selling their house."

"I know. Zack was talking about it."

"Was he? Why didn't you tell me?"

"What's to tell? Bronson is always selling his house. The only difference this time is, so Zack says, he probably will sell it."

"To a Negro?" Ellen said. "Did he tell you that?"

Matt's chin dropped. "To a what?"

"To a Negro."

"You mean like Clarice?" Billy demanded, showing interest.

"Let it go, let it go," Matt said, sounding a note of warning for Ellen. "Come on, son, give those potatoes a break, hear me?"

"I did. I ate most of them." Billy sounded aggrieved, as befitted a man with more important things to do. "There was a black man and lady at Bronson's today. Not black exactly. Kind of brown. The lady's pretty."

"You saw them?" Ellen asked.

"Sure. They were there twice this week. With some white man the first time."

Matt and Ellen Jones, dumfounded as often before by the realities which seemed to catch up effortlessly to their son without bothering to intercept his parents, turned as one to regard Billy with something like apprehensive respect.

"Eat those potatoes!" Matt roared.

"I did. Can I go, Mom? Can I be excused?"

"May, dear, not can. May I be excused?"

"Okay, may," Billy agreed.

He was gone, and Matt looked at his wife. "How is it we managed to father a tornado?" he asked above the receding clatter.

"You fathered it, remember?" Ellen said primly. "Anyhow, I would rather it was a tornado than a zephyr. He makes me envious, not to say proud."

"I'm proud of him. In fact, I practically melt when I look at him, but I'm not going to let him know it too often. He's about two up on me most of the time the way it is. Let that kid get the upper hand and he'll run this place. Take the way he appears to have been casing the Bronsons—and that reminds me, what did the Cusack have to say anyhow?"

"He runs the place anyhow," Ellen said, taking things in order. "Laura said Mrs. Weissman told her the Bronsons have an offer from a Negro."

"What makes her so sure? I can't say I'm a student of Laura Cusack, but if I can voice the findings of casual observation, let me say she's off her rocker about seventy per cent of the time and the other thirty she's just plain mean."

"No, this came from the Weissmans. You know how Mr. Weissman is; he knows everything that goes on. And remember Billy."

Matt sat back and considered for a moment and then let his head fall back and the laughter roll out.

"A colored family! Straight across the street from John Ainslie Outerbridge! Oh, brother!"

Ellen frowned.

"Matt, I hope you're out of last night's laughing jag. Straight across the street from the Outerbridges is next door to us."

2 In 1776 Major General Charles Lee, commanding the only readily available relief force in the Continental Army, camped in the Chappaqua hills above White Plains and seemed strangely unable to hear General George Washington's frantic appeals to come across the Hudson and help fight off Lord Cornwallis. Some hundred and eighty years later the memory of Lee's studiously tranquilized behavior inspired a quaint place name for a suburban street at about the same spot.

The street was called Peaceable Lane. In the summer of which we speak, late in the 1950s, Peaceable came to seem a misnomer, denying both its sylvan setting and the hesitant hero of 1776.

The events which made Peaceable Lane possible in the first place had begun long before the English-born General Lee first migrated to the American colonies. To pick a year arbitrarily, the process began in 1669 when a tavern keeper named Easton, being land-hungry, joined a syndicate assembled under Colonel Caleb Heathcote. The colonel, a redoubtable land buyer, engineered a transaction under which a Mohegan sachem named Wampus did "absolutely give, grant, bargain and sell, alien, enfeoff, release and confirm" the township of Newcastle to Heathcote and associates forever. The price for the township, all five thousand acres of it, including "messuages, tenements, gardens, orchards, arable land, pastures, feedings, woods, underwoods, meadows, marshes, lakes, ponds, rivers, rivulets, mines, minerals, fishing, fowling, hunting and hawking, rights, privileges, hereditaments, and appurtenances" came to a hundred pounds sterling, "current money of New York."

Easton's share, relatively overpriced at five pounds sterling, came to one hundred acres of hillside lying above the headwaters of the Bronx and Saw Mill rivers.

Long afterward the residents of Peaceable Lane suffered nostalgic envy when one of their number, a scholarly immigrant from Vienna named Dr. Wolff Abram, discovered that the first taxes levied there, as fixed in the patent granted by King William III, came to six pounds, four shillings a year on the entire township. By the time

Dr. Abram unearthed this bit of fiscal history, he and his neighbors were paying an average of $1200 taxes on their houses and one-acre lots.

In the process of time most of the Easton acres were chipped away, but, notwithstanding a Mohegan habit of selling the same land several different times to different buyers, the Easton heirs contrived to hang onto a dozen acres of homestead.

They held to this birthright through all assaults. The most vigorous came in 1882 when a Minneapolis plunger named Graham, fresh from cornering the corn market in Chicago, came East in triumph and set about carving out his own barony in the Chappaqua hills forty miles from Wall Street. Graham put together a domain of four hundred acres, raised a thirty-five-room castle on a central hilltop and called it Grassy Tor. His pleasure in this lordly fief suffered only one flaw. The current Easton, a crabbed type who distrusted outlanders, refused his offer of fifty dollars an acre and stubbornly held to his land. This thrust an unkempt enclave into the lower slopes of Graham's tailored hills.

Graham died broke and without issue in 1905. Six years later Grassy Tor was sold for taxes to a Presbyterian charitable foundation and became a home for wayward young women.

Meanwhile, as the city of New York grew bigger and thirstier, its water department reached ever more greedily into Westchester County, seizing lakes and damming streams, adding thousands of acres to the vast watershed system based on the Croton Reservoir. Grassy Tor and the Easton enclave acquired a buffer state in the form of a thousand acres of watershed park land. The park was named Wacapo for the small lake it enclosed, which the water department proposed to enlarge with a dam. By this time, 1938 or thereabouts, it was generally forgotten that Wacapo Lake had got its name from a Mohegan squaw who had dwelt on its shores around 1680. Wacapo had been a notorious counterfeiter of wampum. So prodigious was her output of funny money, shaped from bone and stone instead of the licit quahog clamshells, that almost alone she forced the Dutch Council of the New Netherlands to pass an act devaluing the Indian currency.

Now her namesake park, barred to corruption by either commerce or human habitation, abutted Grassy Tor along a rutted road which meandered over the hills from Mount Kisco in the northeast to Ossining beside the Hudson on the west. Another byway led from Grassy Tor through the park to Chappaqua and the New York Central Railroad.

For a long time the serenity of Grassy Tor and its environs escaped violation while first the bulldozers and later the restless frenzy of traffic thrust themselves out from the city along ribbons of parkway. The Saw Mill Parkway was out of sight and even beyond hearing to the east, and the Taconic State Parkway, though nearer to the west, imposed nothing worse than a sibilant hum of movement. The few well-heeled exurbanites who had come up-county in the twenties and thirties to find gracious isolation on four-, five- or fifty-acre estates felt comfortably shielded from intrusion.

Hard times are notoriously hardest on charitable works, and the Presbyterian foundation did not recover from the depression of the thirties. Its trustees were regretful but relieved in 1940 when a syndicate of the exurbanites made an offer for Grassy Tor. Soon Graham's uplands had been converted into one of the sportiest eighteen-hole layouts in Westchester, and the castle's salons and verandas echoed to the jovial sounds of exurbanite relaxation rather than the complaints of girls who hadn't managed to get married before they got pregnant.

It was not until 1946 that a multiple great-grandson of the original Easton at last relinquished the enclave. He no longer needed the land, having by then brought the Easton line back to tavern keeping with a package store and beer parlor with attached filling station in Chappaqua. He sold out to a White Plains builder and developer named Riccetti. The price he got, $1500 for each of the twelve acres, amply justified his grandfather's earlier distrust of Graham.

Builder Riccetti was already profiting from the postwar baby boom, the rush to the great cities for profitable employment and the concomitant rush out of them for *Lebensraum.* But precisely because of the rush, Riccetti was being forced to cast ever wider for virgin land accessible enough to commuter stations to be added to the bed shed of Manhattan. He had coveted the Easton enclave as ideal dormitory space and was pleased when he got it.

Most of the township was zoned at a two-acre minimum, but Riccetti believed he would reap more ultimate profit by building for a new class of commuters. He saw the future in young or nearly young Manhattan executives on the way up, men who had prospects but could not yet venture much beyond $30,000 in providing the kind of surroundings they hoped their families deserved. Riccetti obtained a zoning variance which permitted him to build on one-acre plots. The affronted exurbanites opposed his request and, when he pushed it through against their wishes, darkly suspected that he had got to somebody on the township council with a bribe or worse. In fact, he had.

Riccetti's surveyors laid out an S-shaped street with its upper loop coming full circle to enclose a small communal park where, as an added attraction, he proposed to build a swimming pool to be owned and operated by and restricted to the residents. His architects were already growing famous for skill in combining modernity with the appearance of tradition and settled charm. They laid out the new street to furnish an illusion of even more space. No picture window set by Riccetti—all Thermopane naturally—would look into another. The houses they planned and Riccetti built were of clapboard and brick, shingle and stone. From outside they seemed to be authentic salt box, Dutch colonial or Georgian. Inside—it needed no saying for those who knew him—any Riccetti house would have radiant heating, fireplaces in living room and playroom as well, all-electric kitchens with built-in deep freezers, dishwashers, washers and dryers, high-speed incinerators and television set into the paneled walls of the vinyl-tiled family rooms.

Riccetti's sound performance was not confined to building. He had been born on a farm in the Veneto, below the foothills of the Dolomite Alps, and he owned a countryman's veneration for the things of the earth. He took care that his bulldozers did not rip out or fatally root-prune the tall oaks and maples which had been growing there when the oldest Easton was young. Even the underbrush of native dogwood was preserved so that ever after his street was a place of glory in the spring.

So knowingly did Riccetti build that as soon as grass began to heal the bulldozer scars, his eleven houses settled into the landscape as though it had long been used to them. Even the apprehensive exurbanites now grudgingly approved of how well he had wrought. But they were still nervous at the thought of who might move into such small holdings.

"They're pretty nice little houses, I'll admit that," Grant Macmillan told a special meeting of the Grassy Tor membership committee, of which he was chairman. "But they're going for a top of thirty-two five. The way the country's booming you can get some pretty odd ones at those prices today. You know what I mean."

They knew indeed, and it was decided to send a small group to see Riccetti and suggest the advisability of a restrictive covenant to keep up the standards of the Grassy Tor neighborhood. It was Macmillan's idea that the committee should be headed by Harry Strauss, who, as everybody knew, came from a family which had been in America since the War of 1812 and who, as everybody also knew, was, in addition to being a perfect gentleman, the only member at Grassy Tor who was indisputably worth a million dollars. Not to put too fine a point on it, Macmillan said, it wouldn't hurt Riccetti to see that Grassy Tor's concern for Peaceable Lane was definitely not a matter of discrimination.

But Riccetti, possibly because getting that zoning variance had cost him $3000 and he was still smarting at the memory, was not having any of this nonsense either.

"You're not kidding anybody," he said, looking straight at Harry Strauss. "I know what you're worried about and the hell with it. You don't want Jews in here. Well, you don't have to tell me you wouldn't want a dumb Catholic dago either. I can tell you this: this dago will sell to who I damn please." Then, perhaps not actually intending to rub it in, he added a virtuous afterthought. "Besides, them covenants ain't legal any more. I can't see you people coming up with the price of a lawyer if I put a covenant on this street and get hauled into court over it. No, sir, I ain't about to break the law."

When it came to naming the transmuted enclave, Riccetti commissioned his sixteen-year-old daughter Rose, promising her a car of her own the day the last house would be sold. Rose, then a senior in the White Plains High School, soon afterward heard of the diffident General Lee while on a field trip around the county with her American History class.

"A peaceable fellow, Lee was," said her teacher, pointing out Grassy Tor as the approximate site of Lee's camp. "He hated war."

It came to Rose in a flash. "That's just exactly right," she crowed. "Peaceable Lane. It sounds wonderful. Just wait till I tell Daddy!"

3

As MATT JONES was nursing the steak on his back-yard grill, then despairing as it passed the point of perfection while his wife was still on the telephone, a scarlet Jaguar roadster wheeled onto Taconic State Parkway and went flashing south. Within seconds the car had finished playing tag with the speed limit and, with a smooth surge of power, was plainly raising hell with it.

"Trying for another ticket, honey?" Through the rush of wind around the open cockpit, the voice of the woman beside the driver fell somewhere between irritated affection and exasperated anxiety.

His quick grin flashed at her. Then his eyes were back to his driving, expertly seeing all things at once, the freeway ahead, the receding scene in the mirror, the instruments on the dash, continuously registering and correlating everything that might affect the Jaguar's swift passage.

"I'm watching," he said. "I'm watching. Trust Papa."

"I'll trust you right into jail someday," she said.

"Promised the sitter we'd be back by five. We'll make it," he said, his voice rising above the wind. He fell silent, giving an intent, joyous concentration to the car.

At this swift pace only the car was spectacular. But, had it been at rest, anyone encountering its occupants would have seen the woman first. It was not only her costume, although it was notable, a loden-cloth car coat with its hood trimmed in mink. The coat concealed her figure, but the face, framed by the oval of mink and wisps of glossy black hair whipped by the wind, was arrestingly beautiful. Her mouth was rich and sensuous. The mouth and the lustrous huge eyes seemed at first to make all of her face. But there was more. Those who had time and the chance to study this arrangement of features, particularly the man beside her, were not likely to grow weary of it. Over a dozen years he had painted her a hundred times and unfailingly found new ways of seeing her vivid beauty.

The man himself was worth a second look. The face, a triangle wedging down from wide-set, confident eyes and high cheekbones to a mobile, somehow arrogant mouth, was instinct with vitality. He wore as distinctly as a garment an air of sureness, a controlled, catfooted daring forever ready to flare into recklessness. Here were two vibrantly handsome human beings, and both were Negroes.

Far ahead a glint of sun on metal seemed to suggest the possibility of a state patrol car. He studied it, narrow-eyed, and then, deciding, eased the pressure on the accelerator. The Jaguar's speedometer dropped smoothly from trembling at the hundred mark, down to ninety, then eighty and seventy and sixty, until it settled quietly on a legal fifty. The driver turned a pleased, inquiring look toward the woman.

"You liked it, Margo?"

"Why ask? You know I liked it. I would like the moon, too—and I'm just as likely to get it."

He laughed exuberantly.

"You'll get this one, baby."

"We thought that once before. Remember?"

Sudden, sullen anger darkened the man's expression.

"I know. But not twice. I take what's unavoidable, but only that much. Nobody's going to put the freeze on me the second time—not after I think I'm in."

Pride and worry chased one another across her face as she studied him through the wind-lashed fringe of mink.

"You're so tough." It was a simple statement of conviction. "It scares me. Nobody gets everything they want."

He grinned at her. The anger was gone again, wiped away by a flash of warmth.

"I do. Never forget it. I got you; anything else is easy."

She was silent, wondering as often before, caught somewhere between pride and fear, why it was that anger, more than anything else, seemed to nourish and enrich this man. Others of their race, she knew, either made peace with circumstance and learned to live with it, not necessarily in craven humility, or were destroyed by it. But not Lamar Winter; there was no compromise in him, nor would he consent to be destroyed. The color of their skins enforced a second place among men; he would have none of it, and the struggle, instead of crushing his defiance, seemed to fulfill it. She felt a puzzled glory in him, but he frightened her as well. She would follow where he led, but fearfully; she would have been content with less and felt safer with less.

"I made him an offer while you were daydreaming out the picture window. I'll bet you another mink coat he's going to take it."

"Oh." All at once the daydream bred a nightmare fringe of terror. So long as it had stayed within the wish-world of wistful impossibility it had been harmless. Now he was giving it reality, and in reality lay the vulnerability to danger. "Lamar, stop this thing. I can't think or talk the way you drive." The Jaguar had gone up again under the goad of the driver's foot, and the needle was hovering over the ninety mark. "Please, Lamar."

He flashed an indulgent grin at her and let the pressure ease; the car slowed until he braked it smoothly and it rolled onto the grassy shoulder of the parkway.

"We're plumb solid stopped, baby. You can start talking—thinking, too, if you want."

"Don't be smart-alecky. You know you scare me."

"Okay, I scare you. But I love you too. That's why I'm going to get this house for you."

"Will he dare? I mean dare take your offer?" The creamy face was taut with strain.

"You don't understand." Winter's lips curled. "This one's a pigeon, our kind of pigeon, the only kind we can use."

"You mean a liberal? I didn't think so."

He laughed. "Hell, no, baby. That Bronson's about as liberal as a Klan kleagle. But he's something more useful. He's hungry enough to be greedy. And he's sore enough at his neighbors not to give a damn. For us that kind are like diamonds."

She was silent, brooding. Winter's cocky confidence was infectious and tempting; she wanted to share it. But there was her own dark awareness of ancient taboos. She wanted to believe it, but there remained that old reluctance to tread on forbidden ground.

"But we'd have to live there—with them. Will they let us?"

"The hell with them." Unemphatic, the statement came flat, hard, final.

"That's easy to say. But even today . . . those kids in the yard . . . staring at us. It's not only their parents. But what about the kids? What about Tod?"

Winter's face softened and he took her hand gently.

"Margo, listen, you've got to face up to it. We can hand ourselves any number of reasons for wanting that house. For me it's reason enough that you want it and we have a right to it because I can afford to pay for it. If it was just you and I, it would be that simple and I'd still take it on those grounds." He grinned wickedly. "Just to let the bastards know I could, if for no other reason. Still, for you and me it's a luxury; we could get along without it. Tod can't; for him it's a necessity."

"But . . ." She was fumbling for it, trying to make him feel the reality of her fear, knowing, helplessly, that he would refuse to acknowledge it.

"Look, Margo," he said patiently. "I grew up on the south side of Chicago. You know that and know what it was like. No kid of mine is going to grow up in Harlem. . . ." The mercurial dark face was brooding now, revealing a nagging disappointment. "Especially not Tod. He's not tough enough."

"This may be worse," she said. "Have you thought of that? Do you think he's tough enough for this . . . if those people, those children, decide to hurt him?"

"Those little punks?" Winter sneered. "Ma'am, those are well-bred white folks' kids. He won't have to be tough."

He hoped he meant it, wished he believed it. But where was the way out? His son was soft, he knew it, soft and easily wounded. He wondered how it was that Tod had failed to get from him the wiry, resilient fiber that alone made it possible to live in this world and to whip it on its own terms. Tod Winter was a good boy, he acknowledged that, but being good was not enough. It wasn't enough to survive in Harlem. It might not be enough here, but he would have to take his chances. Maybe it would come to him yet, he thought; maybe somehow his son would find the fierce, proud will that made living possible.

"Lamar, these people aren't going to take us sitting down—just like that. You know they're not," she said, breaking into his reverie.

"The hell with them," he said again. "They're going to have to learn to take it from somebody, sometime. It might as well be now and from us."

"I don't know. . . ." She shook her head stubbornly. "They could make it hard . . . especially for Tod."

"Look, baby, all they have to learn to do is leave us alone. I ask no more than that, but I'm damn well ready to see we get that."

"You're only one."

"One's enough."

She sighed. "I hope you're right. How much did you offer him?"

"What he asked. Thirty-six thousand clams."

"It's an awful lot of money. Can we afford it?"

He laughed, happily this time. "Don't worry about money, baby. Never worry about money as long as Papa's around. Not so long as I'm worth a thousand bucks a painting and up—and the stock market keeps acting the way it does. I made it easy for him—twenty thousand cash on the barrelhead, no second mortgage."

"How about the rest?"

"That's easy. Any bank will jump at the chance. Don't worry about it, Margo. I researched this one."

"It seems terribly high. Is the house worth it?"

"Hell, no," he said. "To a white man it wouldn't be worth within four thousand of that. I know that and he knows it, and we both know the other knows. That's part of it. Bronson's a thief, but exactly because he is, he's also my pigeon."

She shook her head. "I can't help it. It seems dangerous to me. I wish it didn't. Isn't it there somewhere that man you work with lives? The advertising man?"

He grinned at her. "Sure, that's where Matt lives, all right. He does indeed. Not just in the neighborhood—but right next door. It isn't entirely accident either. I'd had that broker fella, Fox, looking for a place up here. And I snooped a little myself out of curiosity because I knew Matt lived there. I liked it and mentioned it to Fox and he poked around a little, not really expecting anything, I guess. But he found a soft spot—and so then we had to go ahead and see how soft it was." He watched her expectantly, ready for her protest.

It came. "Oh, Lamar. Can we do this to him?" She frowned. "And there's something else. I don't like that man Fox and I don't really think he likes us. Do we have to have a white broker?"

"I'll go at that one backward," Winter said. "We don't have to like Fox, but we got to use him. I don't like him either; he's a slippery bastard. But we'd never get to first base—even with a guy like Bronson—unless we had a white broker out in front. I know it and Fox knows it and that's his business. Then the other part. Matt. How's it going to hurt him? Besides—you know this—there aren't enough soft spots not to grab one when you get it. It won't hurt Matt; at least it shouldn't."

"But what if it does? You know what I mean. How do you think he's going to take it—a client, a man you work with?"

He sobered momentarily. "I know, and I thought about it. Don't think I didn't. As for the client part, it doesn't matter much. They bring me a lot of work, but you know I don't have to beg for work. If Matt and the Macmillan outfit stopped bringing me work, somebody else would. But I did think about the other part of it. I really did. I do work with the guy and we work good together but, damn it, people like us just plain can't afford to let things like that stop us. We have to look out for ourselves—we can't look out for him. That's his worry." He paused, then grinned his wolfish grin. "Besides, we might just as well find out what he's made of."

"Does he know?" Her face was clouded by doubt and worry.

"He does not. Anyhow, he doesn't know from me and he's not likely to."

Why couldn't he see this, she wondered, the absolute necessity to clear every possible path beforehand and then, if they could not all be cleared, the necessity to surrender. How could he, knowing the dark forces which hemmed in every aspect of their lives, challenge those forces so blithely?

"There are two good reasons for not telling him," he went on. "First, going back to what I just told you, it's none of Matt Jones' business where I live or how I spend my money. That's the guts of it."

"But it's his business where he lives?"

"I know that, honey, and that's the second part of it. The truth is, I like the guy, really like him in addition to working well with him. So I can't put that on him. You see, if I tell him he'll have to take a stand. He'll have to be either for us or against us. He can't stay neutral. If he's for us, I'd be lousing him up with his neighbors. They wouldn't like it, natch."

"But if he's against us? What then?"

Now he was entirely serious, even solemn.

"I told you, honey. I like the bastard—and I don't like many white men—and, whether I want to or not, I value his friendship." He paused. "The truth is I don't dare put the pressure on him. If he went bad on me under pressure—and the pressure on him would be terrific, I know that—then, bam, I'd have to hate his guts."

"But he's going to find out anyhow—in the end."

"That's the difference. In the end. But so long as he doesn't know beforehand, it's impersonal. See? This way it's nothing between us."

4

ON MONDAY MORNING, restored in health and conservatively suited for business, Matt waited at the bus stop under the parkway overpass. Though he labored in Madison Avenue, he had consciously avoided the Ivy League uniform, feeling that, although he might look somewhat out of fashion in his western pleats and moderately padded shoulders, he would feel downright silly in a borrowed livery of narrow lapels and tight pants. "I can't understand how you put up with that waterfall down the fly," Grant Macmillan, the president of Macmillan Associates, had once observed, apparently more in curiosity than in criticism. "Anybody would think you cowboys are too shy to let a lady guess you have balls." "Well, boss, at least the pleats let you sit down without tearing them loose from their moorings," Matt had said comfortably. For the same almost instinctive need of cleaving to his own background, Matt carried a raincoat rather than an umbrella. The habit had led to the loss of numerous raincoats in the baggage racks of New York Central trains, for Matt tended to fits of absentmindedness.

Ordinarily Ellen would have driven him to the station, but this was her car-pool day. She was off already in the Chevrolet wagon, making the first of the four daily round trips required to transport the Gold, Cusack, Cavanidis and Jones progeny to and from their staggered classes at Wacapo Consolidated.

It was a murky morning, threatening rain, and Matt hoped it would hold off until his eleven-thirty appointment with Thurston Young. It could be a delicate business, handling this first meeting between the owner of Glamour-Glow and Lamar Winter, and it wouldn't help matters any to arrive wet, bad-tempered and probably late after the frantic fight for a taxi on a rainy day in New York. With luck it could go smoothly, he reflected; after all, Young did know Winter's work and had as much as asked for him. But there was always this: Young did not know Winter personally, and when presenting Winter to a possible new client, there was always that ticklish moment of first meeting.

And, Matt thought with a chuckle somewhere between irritation and admiration, Winter would never go out of his way to make it easier. He made them take it or lump it. Still, who knew? Maybe that smooth cockiness, with the screw-you-white-man scarcely hidden under the veneer of politeness, was exactly right. Maybe, for a man like Winter, it was the only possible armor.

Matt went over in his mind what he knew about Thurston Young. It was mostly trade gossip, he knew, and mostly only on the surface. Certainly it wasn't enough to predict how he would react to Lamar Winter—saving this: Matt was betting that Young wouldn't react to anything except what he wanted. Young was an autocrat, a man who knew every detail of every phase of his business and delegated decision to no man. Coldly jealous of his product's reputation, he was at the same time perfectly aware of the delicate nuances upon which that reputation must be built and maintained. A strange, harsh figure to bulk so large behind a dollars-and-cents business whose essence was as fragile as its façade in the make-believe land of feminine beauty. Incongruous, of course, but you couldn't deny success. Glamour-Glow was a name to rank with Chanel or Guerlain; there was none greater in the cosmetics business. A hard man to handle—and fatal if you let him see you were trying to handle him. That, I suppose, is the reason why Simmons & Quinn lost him and why we may have him now, Matt warned himself; also the reason why I could lose him too.

Absorbed, he only half noticed David Bronson's last year's Buick back out of the drive and come up the lane toward him. With no resentment he watched the Buick pass without slowing, Bronson hunched low to the wheel, seemingly nearsighted and unseeing. Bronson never sees anybody, he thought, half amused, as the car passed out of sight into the narrow curving road through the park land toward the station. I wonder whether it's that he really doesn't see, being so bound up in himself, or that he'd rather not see. A strange customer, he thought. A moment later John Ainslie Outerbridge's conservative black Packard came through the underpass, slowed and stopped.

Matt crossed the road, circled behind the car and, as he slid into the seat beside the lawyer, said, "Morning, John Ainslie. Thanks. You're early—making the seven thirty-three?"

"Yes. Business." Outerbridge hesitated, pursing his small mouth. He always spoke with deliberation, seeming to test his words for weight before permitting them to escape. They did not always turn out to be worth all that pondering. "It is a business, I believe you will find, which concerns you as well as myself. Indeed, it concerns us all."

"How so?"

"You may not have heard that Bronson has his house on the market—and that he is reported to have had an offer?" It was a statement, offered as a question, and Outerbridge turned to give Matt a look so weighted with portent that Matt had to stifle an impulse to giggle.

"I heard. Some talk he aims to sell us down the Swanee River."

"Yes." Again Outerbridge paused, weighing his words. "What do you make of it?"

"Sounds screwy to me," Matt said. "He may be sore at the place, probably is. He may even be sore at us. But I doubt if he's that sore."

"I think he is," Outerbridge said. "And I think he means it. I propose to discover whether we can exert any legal remedy. Deliberate injury is actionable."

"Well, hell, he's probably just fooling around for the fun of scaring people. Besides, why would a colored man want to live with us?"

"I am afraid more is involved here than will be readily apparent to you." Matt did not need to be told that Outerbridge held a doubtful opinion of other men's acuity. "Bronson has been vengeful ever since the parkway was built. He knows, naturally, that he is helpless against the state. His neighbors are another matter. Motivated by malice, he will strike at those he knows he can hurt." Again Outerbridge paused and seemed to consider a statement both for its meaning and for the other's capacity to understand it. "You ask why a Negro might wish to live among us. I do not believe that is the question. A Negro who could afford it might well wish to better his surroundings, but if it were merely a matter of moving into an average white community I doubt if the question would arise. I do not wish to seem to voice anything that could smack of prejudice, but I am quite sure you know, if you will reflect, that a Negro, seeking to invade a white community, would make the effort only where there are a significant number of Jews."

"Huh?" Matt said. "Come again."

"Yes," Outerbridge said pedantically. "He would know that Jews are susceptible to invasion. They make common cause—for reasons of their own—with the so-called liberal movements. They align themselves in public and, as a result, become vulnerable in private. Additionally, I think you will agree, few Christians would subject a community to this sort of injury. You and I, Mr. Jones, are now imminently threatened with the penalty for living among Jews."

"If you mean Bronson is a Jew and is out to clobber the Christians, I don't think I buy it," Matt said. "I got the idea—or my wife did—that the Bronsons are Unitarians."

"I hope you have not been deceived," Outerbridge said. "A Manhattan jeweler? Would you be likely to find many Christians in that business? Surely not. Then the name, Bronson. I believe, if you care to trace that name, you will find that it was changed from Braunstein at about the same time Bronson became a Unitarian."

Matt grunted, feeling uncomfortable, vaguely sickened.

"You trace it. I'm not going to bother. In my family there's already enough trouble with genealogy. There's a rumor that one of my grandfathers was a quarter-breed Sioux. It's fairly widespread in Wyoming."

Contrary to expectation, the train was on time, and Matt, having gone through the convention that the man given a ride buys a *Times* for his host as well as himself, settled down beside Outerbridge on the narrow seat. Feeling a faint obligation to stick with his host and knowing Outerbridge would abhor the smoker, he resigned himself to getting along without a cigarette until 125th Street. They did not speak again, for it was also a convention, indeed a code among commuters, that once the newspapers were open, conversation was dead.

Matt was still going through his mail when Grant Macmillan's secretary called, asking him to step in. Macmillan professed to own a sense of other men's dignity and had refused to tie his executives to him by the efficient but peremptory umbilical cords of an intercom system. Bland, good-humored, wearing the casual air Matt knew to mask the essential ruthlessness which success in their intangible craft demanded, Macmillan looked up and grinned as Matt came through the door.

"A nice recovery." He smiled. "You went at that party the other night as though you were sore at yourself." Macmillan, one of Grassy Tor's founders, still ruled its membership committee. Matt still occasionally wondered how much it had been his urging which had brought the Jones family to live on Peaceable Lane and then, something they could not quite afford, to become members at Grassy Tor.

"I was," he admitted with a smile. "Or, rather, I was sore at the tax assessors. But I paid for it. All day yesterday."

"I picked up a bruise or two myself," Macmillan said reminiscently. "But I don't think I was sore at anybody—although you're right about the taxes. Awful, aren't they? But I think I was congratulating us—and you—for fetching Glamour-Glow. You're seeing Young this morning?"

"Yes. You know, he isn't quite fetched yet," Matt said. "Or if he is, it won't be easy to keep him fetched."

"You'll do it."

"I hope so. They say he's a bastard."

"He's also prestige. That's his real value. Glamour-Glow won't be our biggest account, although it's big enough. But it's a top-quality account. Everybody in the business knows he's hard to hold. The agency that can get him and keep him gets an automatic DSM for diplomacy—clear through the business."

"You know it'll get the college try," Matt said. "The presentation is ready, including the implication that it's all Young's own idea in the first place—which is not entirely a lie; he knows pretty much what he wants. I called Winter. He's meeting me there—sketches and one finished painting."

Macmillan frowned. "That's the getaway point that bothers me. You sure it has to be Winter?"

"I don't see any way out of it. He talked about Winter's work. If I don't produce Lamar he'd likely think I couldn't get him."

"Maybe you should have told him first, given him a chance not to get on a hook."

"I thought of that but decided against it. First, he'd have considered it butting in, trying to make a decision for him. Second, from what I know about Young, he won't ever consider himself on a hook. If he doesn't want Lamar he'll say so—to his face."

"Had you thought it might be simpler all around if Young and Winter never saw one another?"

"I thought of it, sure. But I doubt if Young would stand for that. He wants personal contact. And I know Winter won't work in the back shop either. He likes to be up front with the boss."

Macmillan sighed. "I suppose you're right. But two bastards to deal with at the same time in the same place seems one too many."

Matt felt a familiar unease at Macmillan's use of the epithet. He knew that "bastard" applied simultaneously by Macmillan to both Young and Winter were slightly different things. What he felt wasn't mere discomfort; it came closer to resentment, and that was a little ridiculous, he thought. Often enough he had, himself, considered Winter an ornery bastard. Winter was cocky and sometimes a damn nuisance; if that were all that lay behind Macmillan's dislike, it would be understandable. But he had sensed something deeper and uglier in Macmillan's antagonism. Macmillan was shrewd; he handled difficult talents—and most talented people one way or another contrived to be difficult—with unruffled aplomb and got the best out of them. He was too intelligent to demand deference from one of the profession's major creative artists. But deep within him, Matt suspected, Macmillan's sense of natural order was offended that a colored man should first possess such talent and, second, maintain it in such insolent assurance.

The subterranean strain did not actually hurt the firm. Macmillan was too thoroughly in possession of a sound and healthily avaricious business sense to let that happen. All the same, Matt thought, it was a damn shame, this business of race intruding itself stealthily into professional and personal relationships which were complicated enough without it. In Macmillan it was ludicrous, but disturbing too. And, no doubt, it had contributed its share to making Winter as objectionable as he often undoubtedly was. But in a curious, left-handed way, the orneriness seemed to make Winter likable. You could understand and even admire a man who refused to let a built-in handicap daunt him and had fought his way to eminence against it—even if it did, unfortunately, leave him with a hangover of exasperating combativeness. Fairly often Matt felt an impulse to belt the artist into the middle of next Tuesday, but perhaps, since any human relationship is too complex to be unraveled in detail, it may have partly explained his genuine affection for him as a man.

The weather held, and the taxi delivered Matt at the richly unobtrusive entrance on upper Fifth before Winter arrived, as he had intended. He was waiting outside the door when another taxi drew up and the artist, with that curious litheness and control of physical movement, slid out to the pavement, carrying an ungainly picture case as jauntily as a swagger stick.

Together they entered the decorously gleaming salon which was

Glamour-Glow's face before the world. It was a place, Matt reflected wryly, designed to make the insecure feel like a bastard at a family reunion. Shortly thereafter, passed from one retainer to another, they waited while a secretary announced them to Thurston Young. This was it—if it was going to be anything. Matt felt the tension in the sudden dampness of his palms and angrily wiped them dry on the seat of his pants.

The secretary beckoned, and Matt, waiting for Winter to enter first, came up close beside the artist. He was aware of the tenseness with which he was watching for a sign, trying to read the face of the small, bald man who rose from behind a vast desk as they crossed toward him. He felt an impulse to take Winter by the arm, to indicate before this formidable man that the Negro was his responsibility and in his trust, but he did nothing, knowing that Winter would feel no need of and, indeed, would dislike the gesture.

"Mr. Young, this is Lamar Winter," Matt said as they came to the desk. Now he was trying to read behind the sheen of Young's pince-nez, but the eyes, the whole alert, composed arrangement of the sharp features, healthily glowing with the effects of sun lamp and expensive barbering, were impassive. There was nothing here to read, no sign, no flicker of either surprise or offense.

Matt was also aware, and half resented without wanting to, that Winter, beside him, was as self-possessed as Young himself. Not merely self-possessed—debonair, poised, and probably, damn him, enjoying himself. He knew that Winter enjoyed these moments of tension and that he probably felt Matt's anxiety and enjoyed that too.

"How are you, Mr. Winter?" The voice was dry, precise and carried no undertone, neither reservation nor—what would have been worse—an excess of cordiality. The touch of hands, one white and carefully groomed, the other brown and slender and corded with muscle, was firm. So it was going to be all right then? All right unless Lamar decided to turn mischievous and bugger it. Matt knew Winter was capable of it, but he also knew that the artist knew that this was important to him, Matt, and for this reason he would probably play it straight.

Young waved them to chairs and went back behind the polished plain of his desk.

"I am sure we all know what I intend to do?" It was couched as a question, but Matt felt that Young meant no question. He would know beyond doubt, and equally beyond doubt Young would not be wasting time on them unless he believed they knew too.

"I think so," Matt said carefully, feeling his way. "The heart of it, as I understand your concept, is elegance."

"That's the guts of it," Young said dryly. "The Cadillac approach —on a higher level. Pure snob."

"I don't know how much you are prepared to spend on me—that is, if you decide I'm your man," Winter said. "But there's something I've wanted to try and have experimented with enough to know it could work for television. I can animate the paintings—a kind of Mickey Mouse business except on a lot higher technical level. I warn you, though, it would cost like sin."

"Yes?" A flicker of interest lighted the controlled features. "How much like sin?"

"Enough. Even with farming out the rough stuff—movement of fabric and the like—and doing flesh—hands, faces, arms and so forth—myself, it would run up the bill maybe four times as high."

"I assume you are fairly expensive at any level."

"Fairly." The Negro's quick grin was a burst of sunshine.

"Well"—Young paused, impassively thoughtful—"I may try it. It's an interesting idea. That is—if I like your paintings. May I see them now?"

Matt watched, observant, alert, interested, as Winter arose and zipped open the picture case. But now there was none of the apprehension that had attended the first contact between Young and the artist.

"This is the only one I have finished," Winter said, drawing out a canvas on wooden stretchers and bending to free the tapes holding its protective paper cover. Confidently, without bothering to gauge the pale light of the overcast day, he laid the painting before Young. Placing his elbows on the desk and his finger tips together, Young studied the painting.

Well as he knew this work, Matt could not resist rising to look at it again, to try to see it through Young's eyes. That luminous, glowing quality he knew so well and never ceased to wonder at. The blond girl looking up at them was radiant, the small smile seeming almost tremulous with life, lighted with inner gaiety, invested with mystery.

"The dress?" Young's voice was dry.

"Dior. This year's collection," Matt said.

"So? Does Mr. Winter usually dress his models in Paris?"

Winter grinned, enjoying his moment.

"No. The dress is her own. She has a closet full."

Young frowned faintly, but Matt knew, with sudden unease, that here was a warning of danger.

"You must be aware that this girl—or some girl—will be carrying Glamour-Glow in her hands. Personally, I mean. We are not dealing with a so-called man-of-distinction series. There will be only one woman, and her distinction will have to be unmistakable and above challenge. I will have no dealings with a tramp, Mr. Winter. Not even a beautiful tramp—and that, I grant you, she is."

Winter looked at him, smiling triumphantly, and Matt knew that the artist was standing back, letting him administer the *coup de grâce.*

"She's no tramp, sir. Her name is Alice Collins, and she is a graduate of Barnard. She's being married this summer to the top of the class at Annapolis—who is a son of the chairman of the board of General Metals. Her family owns a good share of the pineapple and sugar cane in Hawaii. They've been there, roughly, from the time of Captain Cook."

Young stood over the painting, the thin, sharp face inscrutable. At length he spoke.

"I do not doubt the dossier, Mr. Jones. But I am curious. Why is a girl of her background posing commercially?"

It was coming now, Matt knew with quick dread. He heard Winter drawl the words deliberately, a calculated invitation to trouble.

"If you mean why she is posing for a nigger, Mr. Young, I'll be happy to tell you. She poses for me because she knows I can paint."

Young came to his feet with deliberation and with an expressionless gaze measured the taunting, dark face beyond the desk. At length he spoke.

"Those are your words, Mr. Winter. They are not mine. I am curious about this girl. I do not propose to invest several hundred thousand dollars in someone I know nothing about. But I ask you to believe"—the voice was passionless—"that I do not have the slightest interest in whether you are a nigger—your word again—or a Finnish fisherman. One thing more—I, too, know you can paint."

Young picked up the painting and walked around the desk with it. He handed it to Winter and made a small dismissing gesture.

"I do not propose to make a decision on this one painting. I expect to see you both again, as often as I think necessary as you develop a program." He smiled thinly, without warmth. "I suspect you may be able to give me what I want."

Young's interlocking chain of retainers passed them back from gloved hand to gloved hand until they emerged into daylight which, though still gray and lowering, now seemed magically luminous. They did not have him yet, clearly, but they had not lost him either.

"Looks like we made it," Winter said as they stood at the curb waiting for a cruising taxi.

"You damn near made a mess of it," Matt said sourly, unwilling to admit the confidence he felt. "Someday, lad, you're going to cut loose with one of those carpetbagger cracks and find yourself looking right down the barrel at a real Suthunuh. Then what'll you do?"

"Spit in his eye."

"Natch. And be out on your ass. As you should be. And me with you. For God's sake, can't you ever unload that telephone pole off your shoulder? You're getting lopsided."

Winter grinned at him. "Yassuh, boss, yassuh. Whatever you say, boss. But he took it, didn't he? Man, he sure took it."

"I'm not so sure he took it," Matt grunted. "It looked to me more like he fielded it and left you looking a little silly."

Winter turned to him, suddenly contrite.

"Don't be sore, Matt. I know I'm ornery and sometimes I regret it. But I wouldn't cross you, you know that." He was serious now. "This is a kind of game with me . . . but necessary. I've got to get things level right away so I know where I stand and where the other guy stands. What you probably don't see is that I'm careful about it. I don't needle a man unless I see he's big enough to stand the needle. That's a big one."

"Okay, Lamar," Matt said, letting his resentment boil away. After all, they hadn't lost Young. Instead, they had got all, perhaps more than they could have hoped for, out of this first visit. And perhaps Winter was right; if they were big enough the needle might not matter, doing no real harm, serving only the artist's touchy self-esteem. "But take it easy, you Harlem Hairbreadth Harry. Someday you're going to guess wrong, and all I hope is I'm not there to see it. How about lunch—with about three Gibsons to get it off the ground? We probably earned them."

"You might even be able to afford them—once this is wrapped up and ready. Where you want to take me, white man?"

"Want to make it Shor's? And sit downstairs with the first-class citizens?"

"Okay, if you think you want to take a whack at it. Those folks could be nasty . . . if they've a mind to."

"For nasty, I'll put you up against them any day."

5

BUILDER RICCETTI had put a lot of money as well as good sense and sound craftsman's heart into Peaceable Lane. He had been relieved as well as proud when, in the spring of 1948, it was nearly ready for occupancy. For months every reasonably pleasant Sunday had been bringing streams of lookers up from the city and the lower suburbs. As always among such pilgrims, there were many more wishful daydreams than tangible assets. Riccetti, who had long ago learned to tell a genuine prospect from a foundation kicker, was polite to all but gave his real attention to those who seemed to stand a fair chance of getting up a down payment and closing costs.

The first house, a white colonial under a slate roof at the

entrance on the left as one entered the lane, went to a Manhattan jeweler named David Bronson. Seeing his name on the mailbox, the settled exurbanites speculated uneasily and wished they had pressed Riccetti harder in the matter of restriction.

But they were mollified when John Ainslie Outerbridge, an Ivy-suited junior member of a firm venerable in corporation law, took the house across the road and put his family up for membership in the Congregational Church. Outerbridge, a younger son of a Cleveland family steeped in railroading and orthodox Republicanism, had been brought into the New York firm through family connections. He might not have bought in Peaceable Lane if Bronson's name had been stenciled on the mailbox in time to warn him. Surely he would not have bought there if he had known some of the names which were to appear later. But at the time he was preoccupied by the desirable nearness of Grassy Tor. The Outerbridges were accepted by the club almost as promptly as they were by the church.

The lane was filling up all that summer and fall. They came from various backgrounds and at first they did not have much in common beyond a desire to live in the country, a well-founded appreciation of the soundness of Riccetti's houses, and the ability, though it took straining for some, to raise a down payment averaging $10,000.

Peter Yale had built a following on the West Coast as a late-night disk jockey and occasional commentator on public affairs. His half-righteous, half-scornful assaults on the entrenched order had won him an income almost large enough to let him join the entrenched order himself. The residual vestiges of privilege and discrimination afforded, in the time of Peter Yale, enough nearly moribund targets of reaction for a young man with a rasping delivery to build a profitable reputation as a fighting liberal without the risk of offending many sponsors. Duly taking note, one of the networks had brought him East.

Yale came to live on Peaceable Lane. But he came against his will. His working hours were outlandish, well outside those of ordinary mortals and ill-adjusted to the New York Central's commuter schedules. But, in a moment of weakness, and probably unwary in the flush of new success, he yielded to his wife Annabelle, who had visions of gracious country living and could not abide the thought of their daughter Liz in the streets of Manhattan. As time passed and he missed more late-night and early-morning trains, Yale became less and less inclined to forgive his wife for his misjudgment.

Yale's name was another which set up a flurry of speculation among the exurbanites, but they were never able to decide about it to their satisfaction.

As with Annabelle Yale, a compelling factor for most of those who came to live in Peaceable Lane was the thought of their children and the hope that, on broad lawns and breathing air untainted by the city's miasma, they would grow tall, strong and virtuous. Gordon Draper was the youngest man on the lane. He bought because his pretty, pregnant wife Shirley wanted their first child to get off on the right foot with country rearing. He was able to buy because his father, a successful contractor with large interests in Westchester County, produced the down payment much as he had already set up Gordon with a Chrysler franchise in White Plains.

Then came Dr. Wolff Abram, who was on the staff at Mount Sinai Hospital and well on the way to professional rehabilitation as a neurologist, although his careful English still carried the flavor of Vienna, from which he had contrived to escape in 1938. Ever since those days, when he was just out of medical school, Dr. Abram had been uneasy in cities. He felt an oppressive sense of threat in confined streets and blank but watching windows.

Steven Cavanidis bought because he wanted these surroundings for Nicholas and Angela, the children of his first marriage. His new wife Cyd would have preferred to remain in Manhattan within convenient reach of the Slenderella people, who were already beginning to have trouble preserving the glossy blond good looks which had moved Cavanidis to take her out of the Latin Quarter chorus in the first place. Cavanidis, who was indulgent with Cyd as long as what she wanted did not conflict seriously with what he wanted, paid her protest the compliment of an absent-minded grunt before he completed the deal. When he thought of her at all, Steve thought of Cyd as a decorative testimonial to how far and fast he had come since he had been born Stavros Kavanodopolos, the son of a fisherman of Piraeus, the port of Athens. Usually steaming receptively, she was also a receptacle for his occasional carnal urges.

Steven had still worn his original name when he jumped ship in Charleston in 1932 and got a flunky job in a textile mill while he learned English. He had joined the textile workers' union in those early years because he felt a bewildered need of protection. He remained to profit by the connection. He had become a shop steward, then a roving organizer. Soon after arriving in New York as a vice-president of the international, he had got rid of his undecorative first wife and acquired Cyd. Somewhere along the line he had gone to court and got rid of his unhandy name as well.

"Nobody can even say Kavanodopolos," he said. "Anyhow it's too goddam Greek. Cavanidis is a lot easier to handle."

Solomon Weissman was the oldest man on the lane. The small Wall Street brokerage in which he was a partner had prospered during the war and after, and Weissman hoped he was near retirement. He owned a passion for growing things and, studying horticultural works in the New York Public Library, had become a knowing gardener even when the only soil he could muster was a window box on the fire escape of a walk-up in Brooklyn. He chose the sunniest acre in Peaceable Lane and laid out most of it in breeding beds for hybrid tea roses. When he did retire two years later, he set out in earnest to develop a new red and promised his wife Rachel that, once the bloom was perfected and accepted by the All-American Rose Selections committee, it would be named for her.

Paul Cusack was an investment counselor in the trust department of the Surety National in Manhattan, and he had his sights relentlessly set on a vice-presidency. He calculated that, keeping his nose clean and choosing both friends and enemies prudently, he could make it in another fifteen years. Meanwhile he could see advantages in Peaceable Lane. Here was a good upcounty area within reach of the kind of people who could do his career nothing but good. As an investment expert, he knew a good buy when he saw one and was confident that property values in the uniquely sheltered lane could only go up. Although neither Paul nor anybody else much liked his thin, spiteful wife Laura, he agreed heartily with her determination to win acceptance by Grassy Tor's membership committee.

Jerome Kelly and his family moved up from Mount Vernon. He was a young dentist with an office in Rockefeller Center on the twenty-second floor of the Time-Life Building. The three children, Hilary, Eileen and Marie, had made it clear that a five-room apartment, however pleasant and adjacent to parochial school, was no longer adequate. Jerome and Claire Kelly chose the only four-bedroom house Riccetti had built, but when the succeeding years brought Paddy and then, dismayingly, the twins, Suzy and Sally, the Kellys were forced to explore for even roomier quarters. They took to roaming lower Connecticut on weekends, hoping to find a farmhouse built in ampler times and combining the attractions of space, low cost and low taxes.

"The trouble with our religion and Claire's fertility," he once ruefully explained to Zachariah Gold, "is that a man is likely to screw himself out of house and home. I'm afraid that I've almost done it."

Nobody on Peaceable Lane loved its roomy serenity—whether somnolent under a July sun or picture-postcard-swathed under January snow—more genuinely than did Zachariah Gold and his quiet wife Beth. It was true that Gold mowed his lawn because he could not afford to have it done, but he knew that even if he could have afforded it, he would have continued to tend his own grounds simply because this was his and he found satisfaction in the feel of it. He was no scientific husbandman like Solomon Weissman, but he was something more—a man who loved his land for its own sake. The Golds basked in sun, air, the green earth, and even mud when it rained; here was blessed release from a prison of brick, exhaust fumes, the angry strivings of too many people too close together. It had taken the Golds a long, hard road to reach this haven. Even Gold's law degree from Columbia had demanded monumental struggle, considering the slum point from which he had started.

Matt and Ellen Jones were the last two to arrive. With some misgiving he had accepted transfer to New York from a comfortably successful career, first as a salesman, then as manager of the Chicago office of Macmillan Associates. New York was frightening, and if Matt and Ellen were sure of anything, it was that they could not live in it; even less would they consider installing their only son within the maw of this stone monster. Matt asked Grant Macmillan's advice and came to Peaceable Lane.

"There's a nice little street of new houses only a couple of miles from my place," Macmillan said. "It's even less from my club—and that's something you'll want to think about, too."

"Probably too rich for my blood," Matt said doubtfully.

"I don't think so. I doubt if you'll do as well for your money anywhere else. There's only one thing."

"What's that?"

"It isn't restricted. You would have some Jewish neighbors." Macmillan eyed Matt speculatively.

"What of it?"

"Some people don't like it, and you may feel that way. Still, you won't have to stay. You'll be moving on in a few years, and that's good property up there, worth what they're asking now and bound to be worth more."

"We'll look at it—maybe next Sunday."

"Good. I'd like having you and Ellen near." This, Matt realized only later, was as close as Macmillan ever came to saying in so many words that Matt was being watched, possibly even groomed as Macmillan's successor. Unexpectedly, never quite able to forget his roots in Wyoming, Matt found that he liked and was stimulated by his job in New York. But it was still a place to visit, even if the visit was made five times a week on the New York Central. When it came to living, he was glad he had chosen Peaceable Lane.

Most of Peaceable Lane's original eleven families were fairly young. They had substantial employment in executive, creative or professional pursuits, and they considered, generally with good reason, that the future held promise. The spirit of their times was one of optimism. Their commitment to Peaceable Lane was adventurous, made at the maximum level of optimism—even to the point, for Gold, Kelly and Jones, of exhausting the loan value of their life insurance. They did not expect to inherit the earth, but they did expect and intend to be able to pay off their mortgages.

They were justified in their hopes and intentions, but only barely so. The fire of optimism, or perhaps a lack of sophistication, prevented their foreseeing the need of margin. Owning real estate, they were to discover, entailed unknowable but inevitable small calamities, all of which would be expensive. But their roots in this soil, although young, were vigorous. Each owned a fierce, fond pride in his share of Peaceable Lane, and this, more than any other thing, they held in common. Slowly the lane developed into a community. Those men who owned a second car or whose wives got up early enough to drive them to the Chappaqua Station fell into the habit of picking up others at the bus stop. Car pools came into being. The consolidated school was four miles distant and operating on split shifts. To the wives it seemed vastly more sensible to endure one day of virtually unbroken taxi service for as many as seven children than for each to suffer through a more limited agony five days a week for her offspring alone.

Socially, in the summer, the swimming pool furnished a center of communal activity, and the numerous children—Jerome Kelly called the lane "Fertility Row"—exercised a right of eminent domain over the entire lane all year round. But, curiously it seemed to Matt Jones, the lane never did become a clubby place in the sense of many close personal friendships. There were a few cocktail parties, and there was the ceaseless round of children's birthday parties, but that was about all. Once, as they sat over a backgammon board beside the Gold fireplace, Matt voiced his curiosity.

"We get along all right," he said. "But we don't neighbor much. Back where I came from, about all we had was neighbors. Of course, television hadn't been invented."

"We don't need each other much," Gold said. "We all work in town. This is only where we sleep. We don't even have two men in the same line of work—barring Outerbridge and me."

"Sure, but we sleep pretty close together."

"Not the way I understand close," Gold said. "We had too many neighbors too damn close where we were. What we came after was elbow room and a reasonable chance to keep the kids from learning how to handle a zip gun."

"Well, yes," Matt said. "I guess you could even take it a little farther. We sure don't have the same backgrounds. You're New York born, lower East Side, you've said. Except for accident I'd still be in Wyoming punching the cows I grew up with. I wouldn't know the lower East Side if you put me down in the middle of it."

"Count your blessings," Gold said.

"You think religion makes a difference?" Matt asked. "We're a mixed kettle of fish."

"I doubt it," Gold mused. "Twenty-five years ago it probably would have. You and I might not have been enemies because of religion, but we'd have been skittish. I'll admit I was a little apprehensive about it when we came here. Not a chip on my shoulder—but ready all right, ready. But it hasn't worked out that way. Even if it had at first, the kids would have fixed it."

"They fight though."

"Kids always fight. But I never heard a fight around here that had much to do with religion."

Even if Peaceable Lane did not practice intimacy, it was to learn, within five years of its founding, that it could unite militantly against common danger. They learned of the danger when the New York Thruway Authority announced its intention to implement a long-pending project to convert the old Mount Kisco-Ossining trail into a cross-country parkway link.

John Ainslie Outerbridge, who saw the announcement in the second section of the *Times* and traced out the proposed route as skirting the southern fence of his property, undertook a personal investigation. He called a meeting at his house; it was the first time that anyone but the Paul Cusacks had been in the Outerbridge home.

John Ainslie was angry as he reported his findings. Outerbridge had a smooth, round face, with a small mouth and small eyes behind gold-rimmed spectacles. Any such forthright emotion as anger looked a little silly on him.

"You understand, of course, that I will be the primary victim if this outrageous project is carried through." Only John Ainslie, Matt thought, would use a word like "outrageous." "They propose to widen the roadbed fifty feet. This means they intend to condemn a twenty-five-foot strip along the boundary of my property."

"Where's the other twenty-five coming from?" Cavanidis asked.

"Out of the watershed," Outerbridge said.

"How about me?" Bronson asked worriedly. Watching, Matt

thought that Bronson always looked worried. Now that he stood to take a real beating, he didn't look much worse oppressed than usual. "I'm up against that road too." His tone was querulous.

Outerbridge acknowledged the claim with a dismissing, distant nod.

"None of you will escape entirely, of course. To begin with, the construction—bulldozing and blasting—will continue for a minimum of six months. We'll be living in dust, mud and noise for at least that long, not to mention the riffraff who will do the work. That will be only the beginning. The cutoff is expected to carry five thousand vehicles a day. I need scarcely point out what that means in terms of noise and litter."

"Obviously we won't like it," Matt put in. "But what can we do about it? We'd have to buck the state."

"It wouldn't hurt to talk to Riccetti about it," Cavanidis suggested. "He strikes me as a sharp hand at finagling."

"A small-time Italian contractor?" Outerbridge was looking skeptical.

"Small-time he may be, John Ainslie," Solomon Weissman broke in, smiling at Outerbridge with a small, sly light of good-humored malice. "But he kept this street from being restricted."

"Yes, so he did," Outerbridge said. "I prefer not to talk in terms of fixes," he went on. "This project is an outrage and a waste of tax money. It will have to be fought in Albany. An injunction first, I should think. But it will cost money. I suggest we enlist the help of the club. There are men like Mr. Strauss, important men, men with influence."

"Grassy Tor?" Cavanidis was chuckling. "That's not a fix?"

"I think John Ainslie is right," Paul Cusack said crisply. "Call it a fix if you want, but the right man in the right place is what counts. If Grassy Tor can help, why not?"

"Only this," Weissman pointed out. "Where it runs along Grassy Tor land, it will only take a strip of woods and rough that the club doesn't use anyhow. They even stand to pick up a few thousand dollars out of the condemnation. That road isn't going to hurt anybody but us. I'll go along with anything the rest of you want to try, but I'll tell you in advance that you won't get much help from Grassy Tor."

Nor did they. To John Ainslie's chagrin, Grassy Tor's attitude toward the new road was complacent.

"Naturally, we're sorry that you're being put to an inconvenience, Mr. Outerbridge," he was told by Grant Macmillan. "You know the clubhouse is more than a mile from the road. Nothing the club uses comes near it except the fifteenth fairway, and we can relocate that with little trouble." Macmillan smiled. "I personally regret your being put out temporarily. But I can't see the members going into a thing like this, especially since, as you must know, a lot of them are none too sympathetic toward some of the people you have down there."

"Yes." Outerbridge's tone held an unmistakable note of reproach. "And if some of you people up here had had the consideration to warn me in time, I wouldn't be down there now."

"Oh, now, John Ainslie," Macmillan said.

The lane raised fifteen hundred dollars among its members, and for nearly a year, taking turns preparing the briefs and in court, Zack Gold and John Ainslie Outerbridge fought a delaying action against the power and majesty of the state of New York. They were defeated, but John Ainslie contrived to win a small internal victory which somewhat soothed his personal defeat. The Thruway Authority modified its plans slightly and, when building the half cloverleaf connecting Peaceable Lane to the parkway, put the access loop in David Bronson's back yard instead of, as originally blueprinted, in Outerbridge's.

It was a long time later that John Ainslie discovered, through connections in Albany, that the senior stockholder in the construction firm which held the prime contract for the $24,000,000 parkway cutoff was Harry Strauss.

6

For what seemed the thousandth time and may in fact have been the hundredth, Matt was finding himself at issue with his son's unbridled zest for expanding horizons. The issue was joined by Ellen's summons to an exercise of parental authority while driving him home from the 6:02 through the woodsy dusk of the watershed park land.

"Billy was down here today—with Jerry Gold," she said. Matt recognized that taut crispness in her tone, and his wary subconscious began to throw up its defenses.

"I know you suspect me of saving these things for you," she went on. Now the tone had that calm reasoning quality that warned him no defenses would work. "But I don't. I try to do my part, but all my talking goes in one ear and out the other—no pause between."

"On their bikes? Again?" Matt asked wearily.

"On their bikes, of course," Ellen said. "Lord knows I don't want to spoil their fun, but you know this road is dangerous—so narrow and twisty. You'll have to have a man-to-man talk with him."

"The trouble with my man-to-manning Bill is that I suspect he is inclined to take me for the junior member," Matt said. "I shudder to think of the day I'll have to tell him about sex—he'll be telling me."

"Matt, it's not something to joke about. His coming out here on that bike terrifies me."

"I know, kid," Matt said gently. He was himself feeling the familiar, sickening wrench of panic that swept over him whenever he thought of the myriad dangers—drowning, mad, unseeing dashes into streets full of homicidal drivers, a fall from a tree, any one of the wild excesses that seemed normal to nine-year-old play—that could deprive them of their only child. "It's hell, though. I don't want to sissify him. There just isn't any way I know how to tell a kid he's irreplaceable."

"I know and it's awful. Left to myself, I'd probably try to keep him on a leash." Her laugh held more nervous tension than mirth.

"I'll have a go at him," Matt promised.

For once Bill was matching his own serious demeanor and even gave outward signs of listening. Looking at him, the close-cut hair, somewhere between Ellen's clean gold and his own mouse brown, fitting his head in a crisp helmet, the wide-set gray eyes, now so solemn and so like his own, Matt felt the swell of pride and love. It was hell's own problem getting him, he thought, but you got a good one when you did it. It was an effort to stay on the level of sternness he had decided to adopt.

"How many times have I told you to stay away from that woods road?" he said.

The gray eyes were direct. The real question, Matt reminded himself, was whether the eyes were being man-to-man or simply facing up to the periodic recurrence of an incomprehensible adult insistence on hedging a kid's life with restrictions.

"Lots of times, I guess. I forgot." The tone was reluctant, but Matt could detect no undercurrent of resentment.

"You scared the daylights out of your mother," Matt said. "Do you think that was fair?"

Lordy, he thought unhappily, what's required here? Do I tell him, aged all of nine and a fraction, that there were three miscarriages to precede him and that, now, there wouldn't even be the hope of a miscarriage to follow him? How can you make a kid take the responsibility for his own safety on the grounds that he is unique, that you couldn't do him over again if you tried for a thousand years? Where do you draw the line between his rights as a human being and your cowardice for him, between a kid's necessity to expand and your unreasoned, instinctive, overpowering, jealous love for him? And, for that matter, whom do you blame for the incomprehensible fate that two people who enjoy being in the sack together as much as you and Ellen do could, out of all your love, produce this one child and no more? The knowledge of their strange incapacity had made cowards of them, he knew.

"No-o-o, I guess not. I just forgot."

"And Jerry, too. Did he just forget? You've both been told plenty of times to stay here inside the lane."

"His mother said his father was going to tan him. Do you want to tan me too?"

The offer was straightforward, an honest attempt to pay for injury inflicted. Matt had trouble with his voice before he could go on.

"No, son, I don't intend to tan you. I don't even intend to punish you, although I'm tempted to take your bike away."

An instant of panic flashed in the gray eyes.

"Honest, Pop. I am careful. I know the rules—they teach us at school."

"Rules aren't going to save you from some knucklehead driving like a crazy man on that woods road. Cars go around those curves like a bat out of—like a bat. It's bad enough here in the lane. Even here I've seen you flying blind, going down that driveway like a bat out of—like a bat." Matt paused for a lame moment. "Do you know which side of the road you belong on?"

"Sure, on the right side, just like the cars. Jeepers, you think I'm dumb?"

"No, I don't think you're dumb, son. But let's get squared away on this—for the last time. I don't want to sound tough, but I mean this—next time out of the lane and there'll be no more bike. Understand?"

"All right. But, gee, how do we get down to the lake if we can't take our bikes?"

Here was something new. Matt recognized it, felt the urge to jump in and seize it, suppressed the impulse and went at it more carefully.

"Well, I just don't know." He paused to consider. "The lake, huh? Any special reason you have to go down to the lake?"

The boy's face lighted with the excitement of discovery and the delight of communicating discovery.

"We found an island. It's right near the shore, and there's a big old dead tree you can get across to it on. It's our own island, Jerry's and mine; the other kids don't know about it."

Man-to-man reasonableness rushed out of Matt Jones with a roar. He was working up to a yell of outrage when Ellen's call summoned him urgently to the telephone. His mind was far less on Solomon Weissman's voice over the wire than it was on a vivid image: Bill and Jerry Gold cat-footing it lightheartedly along a swaying, root-rotted log high above deep and waiting waters. He could almost hear the sudden, startled yell, the deadly splash, and then the choked, childish cries that would never be heard. Brother! he thought. Here's something Zack and I sure better get together on. I will tan him till he barks like a fox!

"Matthew?" Weissman said. The retired broker had a curious, archaic liking for formality in address. "Matthew, if you're not too busy I'd like to have you come over this evening after dinner. We're having a little meeting here."

"What about, Sol?" Matt asked absently, his mind still the image of his son in peril.

"You probably know already, and I'd rather not say over the phone. Anyhow, I think you'd better come. Bring your wife if you like." Peaceable Lane's telephones were on a party line.

"I'm afraid she'll have to stay here with the kid," Matt said. "He's in hock."

"What has he been up to this time?" Weissman asked, an indulgent chuckle in his voice.

"Oh, you know. Kids," Matt said. "But all right, I'll be over."

Weissman's pert, knowing eighteen-year-old daughter, Lana, answered Matt's ring with an impish smirk.

"Come in and join the mourners," she said, and Matt, still preoccupied with the baffling mysteries of childhood, wondered if all kids these days, even freshmen at Barnard who ought to know better, were smart-alecky to their elders.

Mrs. Weissman, plump and fussy and always anxious in the duties of hospitality, was bustling about the bright, painfully neat living room. She brought Matt a chair from the dining room, and Matt, always uncomfortable in an upright posture, squirmed unconsciously, seeking ease on this unlikely perch. He reached automatically for a cigarette, paused in the act of lighting it to make a quick, fruitless survey for an ash tray. He started to crumple the unlighted cigarette back into his pocket, but Mrs. Weissman, with birdlike alertness, caught him fumbling and hurried to the kitchen and back, bringing a saucer.

"I always forget because Papa doesn't smoke," she said apologetically. "You go right ahead." Uneasily, almost not wanting it now, Matt lit the cigarette and was awkwardly careful with the ashes.

The room was crowded; most of the lane's men and some of its women were already there. Solomon Weissman, cherubic with his brown, smiling face under its halo of white hair, surveyed his neighbors. He sat at ease in a favorite chair with the top two buttons of his chino gardening pants open as a favor to his belly.

"If you don't know why we're here, you haven't been keeping your ears open," he said. "But since we're all in this, we thought we might as well get together so we all know the same things and can decide what to do—if we do anything."

"If I may interrupt, I . . ." Outerbridge broke in. Matt turned toward him, thinking that the lawyer's seat on the only other easy chair probably indicated he had been the first one here.

"You go ahead, John Ainslie," Weissman said. "You've been doing the investigating. I was going to call on you anyhow."

The lawyer pursed his small mouth and looked around their circle, weighing his opening remarks.

"A week ago what we have heard about Bronson might have been mere gossip," he said. "However, I—some of us—thought the gossip worth investigation. I have made certain inquiries, and I am now under the painful necessity of reporting to you that he has, indeed, been dealing with a White Plains broker who specializes in obtaining properties for Negro clients. The broker is a white man."

"A white man? What the hell goes on anyhow? Is he nuts?" The voice, rasping in angry bewilderment, was Peter Yale's.

"No, quite sane, I should think, Mr. Yale. But greedy, yes, greedy indeed," Outerbridge primly acknowledged the interruption, then went back to his own theme. "I am informed, through reliable sources, that the broker has given Bronson an offer from a Negro—and that Bronson is seriously considering it."

The collective gasp was almost inaudible, broken now by Laura Cusack's sharp, indignant, "He wouldn't dare!"

"I do not, in fact, know whether he will dare or not," Outerbridge went on. "I hope there will be legal means to prevent it.

Meanwhile, I believe we must all understand the implications if he does go through with it."

"If it means I am going to have to live with colored people, I can tell you right now I'm not." That was Laura Cusack again, shrill and furious.

"Let him talk, Laura." Paul Cusack's interruption of his wife was couched in weary distaste.

"I have consulted several of the most reputable brokers in Westchester," Outerbridge said. "I can tell you, as a basic fact, that each of us stands to incur a considerable financial loss if Bronson sells to a Negro. Even the brokers are unable to estimate the loss. The most conservative placed it at an average of around eight to ten thousand dollars. But there is another factor even worse. Purely as an experiment to test the implications of Bronson's situation, I offered to list my property with the Chappaqua broker who handled my original purchase."

Why does he always have to talk like a law-school professor? Matt wondered.

"I must report to you that the broker, and every other broker in Westchester, was aware of what Bronson was doing long before we knew of it. They were polite, but it was also apparent to me that they were frightened. What it came down to was that they would not list my house—under any circumstances—until this Bronson matter is disposed of."

"If you mean we're now unsalable, I'd be curious to know who of us—not counting Bronson—is selling anyhow?" The voice was Zack Gold's. The voice was calm, curiously inquiring, and Matt turned and saw the big man sitting on the divan between Gordon Draper and the tidy, almost invisibly retiring figure of Estelle Outerbridge. "I came here to live—not to get scared out," Gold went on.

"That is another matter and no small one, I assure you," Outerbridge began again. "If Bronson should go through with this . . . this scheme, we can expect to be subjected to a reign of terror. Reputable brokers will not touch us, but the disreputable will be on us like vultures."

Slowly, one by one, Outerbridge's gaze ranged the room, and

the glint of his gold-rimmed glasses did not conceal the measuring, searching suspicion of his inspection.

"I expect you mean some of us are likely to get a ground-floor offer to be the next one to sell out to a shine?" The question came from Steve Cavanidis, sitting beside Matt, relaxed on the stiff dining chair, saturnine, alert behind his mask of relaxation. "That's the blockbuster technique."

"Precisely." Outerbridge's gaze again circled the room, heavy with warning. "I hope nobody here needs to be advised of the danger of panic. Perhaps one or two could save themselves—if they were quick enough—but they would enjoy no guarantee that they were quick enough."

"You weren't toying with the idea—when you experimented with offering your house for sale?" This was Peter Yale, scowling, suspicious.

Outerbridge flushed, and the tiny mouth pinched tighter.

"Mr. Yale, I resent that remark. I am reporting on the situation as I see it. My inquiries have been in your service as well as my own. I need not, I think, point out that I was under no compulsion to communicate what I have learned."

"Okay, sorry. Just making sure," Yale said. The voice carried a gibing undertone and no hint of apology.

Matt was wondering. What was going on here? Was it so easy for suspicion to sprout, corrosive and ugly, in this street? Did Yale really believe that Outerbridge, that veritable mother lode of solemn rectitude, would be saying these things and simultaneously planning to cut and run, save himself at others' expense? He looked around the room, trying to read his neighbors. What was in each heart here? Zack Gold, hulking and solemn, saying little, but attentive. Gordon Draper looking bewildered, and pretty Shirley, as always, somewhere far behind any thought more adult than a sale at Bonwit Teller. Jerome Kelly clearly trying to adjust himself to a new and unexpected burden, but then, hell, with six kids, Jerome was always coming up against new burdens, and, down deep, they were probably no more unexpected than the kids. They just kept coming. Steve Cavanidis, poker-faced as always, seeing everything, hearing everything, revealing nothing, while his sleek wife Cyd, so improbably blond, sat there and mirrored nothing more than ever-present awareness of her sex.

His eyes drifted to Dr. Abram and he wondered, as he had idly wondered before, how this man could endure and endure with such outer quiet the tensions which seemed always to strain his slender frame. He thought now that he would swear if he were called on to bear witness that Dr. Abram had not uttered one word since saying his careful, precise greeting at the door. When you thought about Dr. Abram, you were likely to think of him as consciously striving for invisibility, and yet, somehow, he never achieved it. You might, it was true, forget him or fail to see him for long moments. But then, with a kind of shock, you would feel the agony of his striving not to be seen or heard or noticed, and then, moved to look at him intently, you fancied you saw the raw twitching just under the rigid surface of his composure. Doc's a strange one, Matt thought, as he had before. A strange one and a disturbing one. He hated to look at the doctor, always feeling that even a glance somehow caused pain.

Lana Weissman's young, patronizing voice cut into the room's collective concern. "I don't see why all the fuss. What's so terrible about Negroes? I had Negroes in my Girl Scouts and I've got them now at school."

Sol looked up at his daughter with resignation. "Shut up, sister," he said, not unkindly. "You can talk when you know what you're talking about—or paying your own bills. If you think your father can take a ten-thousand-dollar licking and still keep you in Barnard—with Negroes or without—you've got another think coming. This is a question of money—not of Negroes."

"Well, I certainly can't speak for you, Mr. Weissman." Here was Laura Cusack's sharp, irritable and irritating voice again. "But as far as I am concerned, it certainly is a matter of Negroes."

"But"—the voice was timid, colorless and, coming from Estelle Outerbridge, totally unexpected—"have we any right to interfere with Mr. Bronson—or to say who may live where?"

Matt caught the quick frown behind Outerbridge's shiny glasses as they turned peremptorily toward his wife. Matt could almost feel her submission as the lawyer spoke again.

"I fear we are digressing. Bronson has not yet sold his property, and I am sure we would all rather prevent trouble than anticipate it. I want to say that I have also done some research into the legal ramifications. Should he sell, knowing beforehand that it would injure us and perhaps with a degree of malice, which would be probable, we may be able to apply a legal remedy."

"What remedy?" Gold's question was professional.

"If deliberate financial injury is demonstrable, it is also actionable," Outerbridge said, a hint of impatience here for the failure of another professional to see his meaning immediately. "Say Bronson's action costs you ten thousand dollars. You have a case against him, have you not?"

Gold frowned and answered slowly.

"I don't think it would work, John Ainslie. First, in order to prove damage, you—or one of us—would have to sell at a loss. Then he would have to prove that Bronson's action not only caused the loss but was deliberate."

"And you think that would be difficult?"

"Perhaps not. But you'd have to take it to a jury and, with the temper of today's times, it would take luck for a jury to find for you."

"You may be right, of course. But we are talking about preventive action, exploring the possibilities. I submit that the threat of suit alone might be serviceable in dissuading Bronson—that is, if he actually intends to go through with it."

"Well"—now there was a smile on Weissman's cherubic face—"I've been wondering whether we haven't been getting the cart a little ahead of the horse. Before we do anything else, why don't we make sure what Bronson is up to? He talks to me—you all know that—and I don't mind discussing it with him. All the same, I'd like to have somebody with me. You people want to name a committee?"

Matt knew the room's eyes were going expectantly toward Outerbridge, waiting for him to make the offer. And indeed, the lawyer seemed ready to speak again, gathering himself to present his qualifications, but the voice of Steven Cavanidis cut in.

"John Ainslie, how about you skip the pleasure? I know you're smart. But I also happen to know you personally irritate the hell out of Bronson. Probably something to do with that cloverleaf in

his back yard—no use making him more nervous than he is already. Personally, I'd like to see either Zack or Matt go with Sol. They're both his neighbors, and they got another thing going for them"—Cavanidis smiled pleasantly—"they ain't as touchy as some of us."
Gold stirred, hesitated, spoke with obvious reluctance. "If you don't mind, I'd rather not." He turned to Matt, and there was regret and apology in his voice. "Do you mind, Matt?"

I mind all right, Matt thought. There's something distasteful about this business, indefinable yet, but certainly distasteful. Still, Steve was obviously right; surely Outerbridge was not the man for the job, considering Bronson's sore and probably accurate suspicions about the parkway access.

"Okay," he said reluctantly. "I doubt if I'll be worth much to this business, but if you all want, I'll tag along with Sol."

"You sure didn't have much to say for yourself," Matt said to Gold, as the two walked back along the lane from Weissman's in the cool and fragrant starlight.

"You were something less than gabby yourself," Gold said equably.

"I know, but there was enough to gab without me. How do you like that Cusack? She gives me shivers every time she opens her trap. That dame is plain mean."

"Crotchety all right. Matt, what do you make of this—really, I mean?"

"I don't know for sure. It all sounds screwball to me. Like a bum joke. In the first place, I can't quite believe Bronson really means this. In the second, what if he does? Anyhow, I wasn't paying the attention I should have. Zack, do you know where the kids were today—Jerry and Bill?"

"Yeah, Beth told me. I took a hairbrush to Jerry; he won't be sitting with any comfort tomorrow."

"I don't know whether that's the answer or not. I've got more than half a mind to whop Bill, but you can't tie a kid down entirely just because he scares the bejesus out of you. Besides, if we lick the idea of the lake out of them, it'll just be something else. Remember the time the hellions got over the fence to the pool?"

Gold chuckled.

"That's why we got them all this space. They're going to tempt fate wherever we put 'em: I'd rather have 'em doing it on Peaceable Lane than in the Bronx."

Matt grunted. "There's that, too. The lane didn't sound so peaceable there at Sol's tonight. I've a feeling this could work up into quite a storm."

"You mean a hebe-goy storm?"

"No-o-o, not that. At least not necessarily that. But I had the feeling that what was in that room mostly was fear. And when people are scared they can get dangerous."

"What about you, Matt? Are you scared?"

"I don't think so. Maybe I'm too dumb to get scared or as scared as I ought to be. The whole thing is so screwy that it's hard to take seriously. I don't think Bronson means it, and even if he does, I wonder, in a half-assed way, whether I'd rather have him or some decent Negro family living next door. Of course, if it's true—and maybe it is—that I would stand to lose eight or ten thousand bucks, that's another matter. I wouldn't pay that to live next door to the Eisenhowers."

"I can't either." The big man's troubled sigh was unexpectedly loud. "But I've got another little problem—which was why I stuck you with the committee duty."

"What problem?"

"Being a Jew." Gold's laugh was a short, mirthless gust of sound.

"What's that got to do with it?" Matt was genuinely puzzled.

"Plenty, but it's hard to explain. It sticks me with knowing where I stand on things like this, or at least where I ought to stand. It doesn't necessarily make sense. You could call it a kind of built-in race instinct—maybe even an obligation."

"I don't think I get you."

"Well, put it this way—you remember those Levittown race riots a few years after the war—the trouble that began popping when the first Negroes moved in?"

"Yeah?"

"Well, I got into it, right up to my ass and over. It wasn't my business. I didn't have a client within ten miles of the place. What pulled me, I think now, was when the goons began equating the Negroes with communism, then equating communism with Jews, and finally equating Jews with anybody who wore horn-rimmed glasses. You know what kind of glasses I wear. As I say, it was none of my business, but the next thing I knew I was out there one night to see if anybody wanted to take a poke at my glasses." He chuckled.

"Somebody did?"

"Damn near everybody I met, the way I remember it. Of course, if I'm driven to be honest in retrospect, I suspect I invited it. If you're going to wear horn-rimmed glasses, it's a good thing to weigh a hundred and ninety, I always say."

"Well, if you got clobbered, you were asking for it."

"I didn't get clobbered—the other way around, if anything. But that's not the point. It isn't even the point that I enjoyed it because I was big enough to wear horn-rimmed glasses and get away with it. The real point is that I was there because I was a Jew."

"You're leaning on it too hard, boy. More likely, like mowing your lawn, you were just bored and needed the exercise."

"Some of that, I admit. But something else too, Matt. Something that you goys don't know about because you don't have to. A Jew just naturally gets himself fouled up with intensities."

"Like sticking your nose into somebody else's hassle about who lives where?"

"Exactly. Or other things. It doesn't have to be a race riot. Everybody gets bored with where he is or what he's doing, but it seems to me Jews are likely to get bored on a nuttier scale."

"If you're preaching me Jewish race superiority by putting reverse English on it, the hell with it. You may be bigger, smarter, braver, or cleaner than I am, lad, but it ain't because you're a Jew and I'm a goy."

Gold's chuckle grew into a boom of mirth.

"All right, you bastard. I was beginning to sound like John Ainslie. It's true all the same—a Jew is more likely to get hotted up—sometimes for the damnedest reasons. Did I ever tell you about the time I was going to quit the law and turn chicken farmer?"

"No, but I'm prepared to believe it."

"The only thing remarkable about it was that I almost did it. I imagine nearly everybody has some farmer in him somewhere, but—here I go again—with a Jew it's more vestigial, maybe a race memory of his great-grandpap not being allowed to own land in Poland."

"Okay, have it your own way, you racist in reverse."

"No, I mean it. A Jew really gets a burn for the soil. Take Sol and his roses. Anyhow, I was going to give it a whirl, get out from behind the lawbooks and back to the land. Visions of outdoors and sunlight and a million hens unloading eggs."

"I assume you were saved in time."

"Sure, by the Department of Agriculture. I got an armload of free bulletins and set out to do it scientifically. But that's what did me in. The more I studied, the more I could see that chickens were subject to so many ailments that it would take a Pasteur Institute to keep one alive long enough for it to grow a suit of feathers. It was so obviously not my racket that I finally gave up the idea. I suspect I was secretly relieved."

"Well, it doesn't seem to have much resemblance to a race riot or, for that matter, to who puts the arm on Bronson."

"I don't know about that." Gold's voice was troubled again. "Maybe more than you think, maybe even more than I think."

7

SOLOMON WEISSMAN telephoned Matt at his office in midmorning.

"Matthew? I wanted to tell you that we are going to have a little breathing spell. I went over to Bronson's this morning. Thought I'd catch him before he left for the office and make a date for us to go to the mat with him. But he wasn't there."

"Flew the coop, huh?"

Weissman chuckled. "No, his wife said he went out to the jewelry convention in Chicago. Won't be back until Sunday. We can probably catch him then."

"Well, it gives us a little time to figure how we're going to handle it. Then, too, we might get lucky—maybe he'll get on an airplane that crashes." Matt regretted the bad joke almost as quickly as it left his lips.

"Yes. Well, anyhow, we can breathe for a few days. He can't very well sell us down the river while he's in Chicago."

Matt had scarcely hung up when his secretary buzzed him again to announce that John Ainslie Outerbridge was on the line. Oh, oh, Matt thought as he waited for the call to be switched on, he's getting anxious; can't wait to find out if Sol and I have messed it up already. But, though the lawyer did ask whether a date with Bronson had yet been made, his errand was another matter.

"I wanted to let you know that I have engaged a young man for the pool."

"That's fine, John Ainslie. Just in time to save me from getting in the doghouse with the neighbors. Who is he?"

"Oh, a fine young man. Princeton. He has been on the swimming team there."

I could have bet on it, Matt thought.

"When can we have him?"

"This weekend. He will be coming up Friday night, and I have made the usual arrangement for him to live in my home. He'll work for me part time, keeping up the grounds, to pay for his board and room. Oh, by the way, his name is Mark Cotten."

Mark Cotten, when Matt met him Saturday morning, proved to be a sleepy-eyed, crew-cut, startlingly handsome young giant. He and Matt, with an excited audience of a dozen of the lane's offspring, spent the day washing down the pool, cleaning out its winter accumulation of dead leaves, rigging the diving board and life lines which had been stored for the winter in the dressing rooms on the pool deck.

The water had scarcely begun to flow through the filter when Bill, Jerry Gold and Benjy Abram charged through the pool's screen of tall rhododendron, all wearing bathing trunks and clearly ready for action. Cotten turned a white-toothed grin on them.

"Not so fast, fellows."

"Aw-w-w! Why not?" This from Jerry.

"Because I don't want to deal with a set of cramps my first day. Do you know how cold that water is?"

"Heck, we don't care if it's cold." Bill turned an imploring look on him, and Matt realized that here was an appeal to higher authority, going over Cotten's head. If he lets them get away with this, he thought, they'll run him ragged all summer. Carefully he said nothing and waited for the younger man to establish his authority—or surrender it.

"I do." The grin was still there, amiable but firm. "And I say no swimming for at least two days—not till the water warms up."

"Aw-w-w-w!" The wail of protest came from all three at once, but, Matt recognized with satisfaction, it was a wail of acknowledged defeat.

"Thanks for not butting in, sir," the boy said later.

"That's all right. They have to know who's boss," Matt said. On the whole, he thought, Cotten seemed likable enough, except for that habit of sirring him, which he thought, half resentfully, was an unnecessary way of reminding him of his age and the fact that his own muscles, while not gone entirely to flab, were by no means the superbly conditioned young meat of the boy from Princeton. There was one other thing which gave him a moment of unease. Lana Weissman had come from across the street to watch them work, and he was aware that Cotten had eyed her shorts-clad figure with the quizzical, measuring look that meant active young male speculation. That's one thing we don't need, he thought, a stud horse on the street. This may bear a little watching.

Matt had trouble getting to sleep that Saturday night. The prospect of the next day's interview with David Bronson preyed on him. Any interference with another man's life was abhorrent to him, and in the case of Bronson, who had always seemed so expectant of injury, it seemed like kicking a man who was down. And that, he thought, is ridiculous; if anything, it's the other way around: we're down and Bronson is fixing to give us the boot.

But how silly we'll look if it turns out to be a false alarm, that Bronson is either just indulging a queer way of amusing himself at our expense or, worse, if it turns out to be nothing but a neighborhood pipe dream.

In any case, it wasn't likely to be easy. Bronson was a hard man to talk to under the best of circumstances. And the worst of it was that Matt was by no means sure that what Bronson did was any of their business. It was his house, wasn't it?

They found the jeweler watching the first inning of a Giant-Dodger game. He didn't appear to show any interest in the game but he didn't turn off the set either, and they had to talk over the announcer's baseball chatter.

"I don't suppose I need to explain why we're here, David," Weissman said without preliminary.

The jeweler nodded glumly, without speaking. Studying him—the down-turned, disappointed mouth, the hot, wet eyes, somewhere between chronic grief and expectant wariness—Matt realized that, rather than feeling anger toward this misfit man, he had a kind of irritated pity for him. He realized that Bronson did not intend to volunteer anything; if this interview got anywhere, it would be because Sol Weissman knew his man.

"We don't want you to think we're interfering, David," Weissman went on. "You know your own business. But naturally, since we live here too, we're interested. We'd hate to see you do something we might all—you, too—regret later."

Still the jeweler sat morosely silent, his hot eyes shifting from one to the other of his callers, then drifting away, as though a direct look was too much of a burden.

"Let's just say this is a friendly inquiry," Sol said.

"Friendly! Don't give me that crap. Say what you've got to say, but don't give me any crap. I know you hate my guts." The outburst fell somewhere between a hiss and a wail.

"That's not it, Dave," Matt broke in. "Nobody hates your guts. But we've heard certain things and we hope you won't think we're butting in because we'd like to know the truth."

"If it's not butting in, maybe you'll tell me what it is," Bronson said hotly. "But all right, since you seem to think it's your business—I am selling. I've been trying to sell the damn place for three years."

"I know you have, David," Weissman said sympathetically.

"But who would want it, the way it is? The middle of a damn noise factory. Just listen to it, that's all—just listen!" Bronson's outburst was a shrill wail of anger. Over the television, turned to the top of its volume and the announcer's inane chatter, Matt thought, they could be taking a column of Patton tanks by on the parkway outside and you couldn't hear it. He wondered if that was why Bronson turned the volume up—deliberately getting even with the parkway or trying to drown it out.

"Three years and they all say the same damn thing. They can't live with that highway in their laps." Now that the cork was out, Bronson seemed pathetically eager to talk, to pour out his grievance. "Three years in this noise box, and every year they tax me more on the damn thing. Schools, they say, they have to have schools. But do I need schools? You see any kids in this house? I should pay for schools? Even my taxes went up once so I should help pay for the parkway. I tell you, the parkway ought to pay me!"

"I know, David. It was just one of those things. You know we fought it, but you can't lick a thing like that," Weissman said.

"And such a fight that was!" The voice was working up to a screech. "Outerbridge!" The name was a snort of bitter contempt. "Don't think I don't know how he fought!"

There wasn't much they could say to that, and they didn't try.

"Three years," Bronson said again, now in a petulant mutter. "Three years and not one decent offer."

"Do you mind telling us what you're asking?" Matt said.

"Mind? Why should I mind? Thirty-six five."

Matt was astonished and started to protest, but Weissman was quicker, mild reproof in his tone.

"Why, David, that's four more than you paid for it. How can you ask thirty-six five when you say yourself the parkway is a nuisance?"

"So why shouldn't I ask thirty-six five? You think I haven't put that other four into it? Storm windows, shrubbery, carpets, my God, what else? And agent's commission! At thirty-six five it's still costing me. You want me to give it away?"

Matt felt the ebbing of his own forebearance and, watching Weissman, he knew the older man's patience was fraying too.

"David"—by the tone Matt knew Weissman was going to lay it on the line—"we hear you've had an offer from a Negro buyer—and that you want to take it. I want to know if that's true."

Now the hot eyes turned away, seeking sightless refuge in the television screen. Now the burst of anger was gone and Bronson was on the defensive and cringing.

"So what if I have? Whose business is it?"

"Our business, David. Do you want to know what you're doing to the rest of us if you go through with this? I'll tell you. You'll be costing each of us somewhere about ten thousand dollars—something like a total of eighty to a hundred thousand dollars—just so you can get more for your house than you paid for it. Do you hate us that much, David, a hundred thousand dollars' worth?"

"Hate? What's hate got to do with it? I'm minding my own business. I got a right to get my money out."

"Any way you can, is that it?"

"I got a right to get my money out," Bronson said again, clinging to it stubbornly.

"Look, Dave, is it just because you want to get your money out? Is that all of it?" Matt asked.

"What else? I got the right."

"What if we could help you get it out some other way?" Weissman asked.

"Help! That's a laugh. Help, maybe, like Outerbridge helped keep the parkway out of my back yard?"

"Now, David, that's done with, and anyhow, I've never been sure Outerbridge had anything to do with it. No, here we are, ten men with a lot of connections. There's no reason why the ten of us can't find you a buyer—especially if you'll reason it out and cut that price to a reasonable figure. It's a nice house, and there ought to be plenty of people who wouldn't object to the parkway."

"You think you're going to be able to find a sucker when I couldn't find one in three years?" Bronson's voice was scornful.

"Not at thirty-six five," Weissman admitted. "Maybe at thirty-four or even thirty-three."

"I got a right to get my price," Bronson insisted mulishly.

"Well, David"—there was now contempt, scarcely veiled, in Weissman's voice—"maybe we can do something about that too. Say we get you a buyer—at the best price we can. Maybe the rest of us could make up the difference so you get everything you think it's worth. I don't know about the others, but Matt and I can take it up with them."

"I'm not trying to hurt anybody—not even Outerbridge." Bronson was whining now. "But I got a right to get my money. If you think you can do something, go ahead and try."

"You haven't taken any money from the Negro yet?" Weissman demanded. "You're not putting us on a wild-goose chase?"

"No, no. Just the offer, that's all."

"Well, then, let's handle this like business. In effect we want an option to get you a buyer. How much time are you willing to give us?"

"I don't know," Bronson said sullenly. "A week, two weeks?"

"That's damned little time. You've had three years."

"I got to have the money," Bronson said miserably.

"Well, David," Weissman said, rising, "we'll see what we can do. We'll let you know."

8

"No!"

In the years he had known Grant Macmillan, Matt had never seen such chop-fallen astonishment on that controlled face. He suppressed an impulse to chuckle, an impish pleasure in seeing Macmillan's bland surface ruffled. He had just now, with only a vague preliminary twinge of hesitation, told the president of Macmillan Associates and chairman of Grassy Tor's membership committee that Peaceable Lane and its environs, including Grassy Tor by extension, now lay open to a colored invasion.

"God Almighty," Macmillan breathed, still wearing that pole-axed look.

Now Matt did laugh, though a little uncertainly.

"What's with this Bronson? Is he nuts?" Macmillan asked.

"Could be. But I think mostly he's hungry."

Macmillan was frowning now.

"You know, I never did like that place," he said. "These days everybody's under pressure, and it comes from every side. But you're never ready for it in your own back yard. I don't mind telling you some of us tried to get that street restricted when the builder—I forget his name now—pulled his fast one on zoning. Place made me uneasy from the first, but this . . . I admit I didn't expect this."

Matt held back an urge to remind his boss that, to any dispassionate observer, there might seem to be some inconsistency between this remembered unease about a street and that earlier urging it upon a junior as a suitable place to live.

"Is Bronson Jewish?" Macmillan asked abruptly.

"I don't know. He could be. But if he is, he now has, there on Peaceable Lane, some of the sorest coreligionists he ever saw. Anyhow, does it make a difference? Think we ought to burn a cross on his front lawn?"

Macmillan's eyes narrowed, and Matt felt, with a flicker of uneasy awareness, that his boss was taking this news seriously. It was baffling; his own telling had been in the spirit that this was interesting, wryly amusing, but scarcely cataclysmic, news. Brother, he thought in bafflement, this is a canoe you can't touch without teetering it. But the temptation had been offered, and he couldn't resist it.

"If it turns out he's Christian, maybe I could fix it for the Jewish neighbors to burn a star of David for him." He grinned.

If it was a joke, Matt saw at once, it wasn't going to score.

"I wouldn't take this too lightly if I were you, Matt," Macmillan said, still frowning.

"Grant, honestly, I'm trying not to," Matt said. "But it isn't easy —not when people suddenly turn as walleyed as a balky mule just at the mention of it."

"They have a right to. Do you have any idea what this is likely to cost you personally if it goes through? I'm not even mentioning what it'll do to the whole area. It doesn't get to the rest of us—not right away anyhow."

"I've been told, and I admit it sounds pretty scary," Matt said seriously. "On the other hand, I can't really convince myself it'll actually happen. We still have something going for us."

"What do you mean?"

"We had a talk with him . . . that is"—Matt could not resist using a little needle—"one of my Jewish neighbors and I had a talk with him. We—my partner mostly—talked him into giving us a couple of weeks to do something."

"Do what?"

"Peddle his house for him—to somebody we're willing to certify as white."

"It's not much time." Macmillan frowned. "There are a couple of real-estate men in the club. Let me talk to them. They ought to be as much interested as anybody—more, if anything—in keeping the area from going to pot. And keep me informed."

"Yassuh, bossman, yassuh," Matt said with a grin. Then the grin faded foolishly at the memory, vagrant but somehow disturbing, that he was caricaturing Lamar Winter's sardonic caricature.

Irritably, all through the day, Matt was aware that the talk with Macmillan was riding him. There must be something here that's not getting through to me, he thought. He remembered the almost palpable feeling of tension in Solomon Weissman's living room, the venom in Laura Cusack's face and voice, the measuring look of Steven Cavanidis. Angrily he shook it off. This was all too silly.

Wednesday was staff-conference day. He was in no measure prepared for what happened when the four of them—Larry Washburn, Ed Roberts, Al Kauffman and himself—assembled at the big table in Macmillan's office. With the other three, like himself account executives in the Associates, Matt maintained an amiable relationship, a kind of corporate togetherness periodically rededicated in ritual six-to-one martinis before lunch. They were all friends but, under this outer teamsmanship, Matt knew each man kept up a shield of sharp awareness against being stabbed in the back and an alert eye cocked for careless chinks in the others' armor. It did not necessarily mean that any unguarded opening would instantly invite a stiletto; it was merely that, in advertising's frightening jungle of intangibles, it was tribal good sense to stay awake.

They were there to ponder over and test out—using one another's brains for backboards—ideas for a new account the Associates had just acquired, a small Swedish auto whose success in Europe had encouraged its makers to invade the American market. The ultimate responsibility would fall on Al Kauffman—any peculiarities Grant Macmillan had about other people's religions were cut off sharply at the gates of Grassy Tor—but at this preliminary stage they were all in it.

They did not, that Wednesday morning, ever get to the business at hand. The fault lay with Macmillan himself, for as they settled down, he chose to aim at Matt a greeting whose jocular tone covered an edge of icy inquiry.

"Anything new on Darktown Lane, Matt?"

Probably it was the edge in his voice, more than the word, that brought the others alert. Matt was aware they were all looking at him with quick interest. It was Ed Roberts who spoke.

"What's this Darktown business? What've you been up to, Matt, changing your luck?"

"Oh, nothing much," Matt said, unaccountably uncomfortable. "Little neighborhood problem."

Macmillan laughed, but the edge was still there. "Matt thinks it's nothing much. He has culluhed folks moving in on him."

"No!" The explosive sigh came from Washburn, and Matt thought, inconsequentially, how similar it was to Macmillan's reaction to the same news. It gets to them, he thought, every damn time.

"What the hell—a blockbuster—up where you live?" Roberts sounded incredulous. "In that rarefied atmosphere? You're kidding."

"He probably wishes he was," Macmillan said. "But he isn't."

"It'll probably come to nothing," Matt said uncomfortably, wishing Macmillan had not brought the subject up. "Let's get to work."

But they did not, for the others would not let it drop. Instead they worried it, fascinated, tugging at it, turning it over and over. You'd think they were stuck with this personally, Matt thought. Their interest was curiously prying, prodding for detail. Once or twice one or the other tried to be funny at the expense of it, but, Matt realized, under the surface, and not far under either, was deadly seriousness. Each man here, Matt realized, was seeing himself in Peaceable Lane and similarly vulnerable, and feeling instinctively that the vision was by no means impossible.

"It probably wouldn't be so bad," Washburn mused, "if it was a judge or a teacher or something like that. The hell of it is you get the judge first, but then people get scared, and the next thing you know you got a big policy wheel or the kingfish of a marijuana ring. Pretty soon you're likely to be right in the middle of the Brethern and Sistern of I Will Arise. God Almighty, Matt, I'm sorry to hear it."

"Well, it's not quite the same as a funeral," Matt said, wishing they would turn it off.

"It's happening everywhere, of course, more and more all the time," Al Kauffman said seriously. "Sooner or later, I expect, it's something we'll all have to stand up and be counted on. But that doesn't make it any easier when it happens. My sister in Baltimore, she had to face up to it years ago, and I still don't know whether she was right."

"What happened?" Macmillan asked sharply, clinically intent on how this problem might have been met before, now that, devastatingly and incomprehensibly, it had become a visible cloud on the sheltered horizons of Grassy Tor.

"She didn't think it was any problem," Kauffman said. "She's always been hot for things like the Anti-Defamation League—a real dedicated do-gooder, my sister. She not only didn't fight it; she got out and actively worked for the guy. Duty and all that, matter of principle."

"I think I can just about guess what happened," Washburn said.

Kauffman shot him a curious, measuring glance.

"Maybe you could at that, Larry," he said. "It's almost near the classic case. That was five years ago. Now my sister's family is the only white one on the block—and her kids have nobody to play with because the little colored kids won't have anything to do with them. But do you think my sister would back down, even yet? Not her, no sir."

"You might give that a thought while you're at it, Matt," Macmillan said meaningly.

"Don't ride me, Grant," Matt said testily, forgetting to be judicious. "I'm the one that lives there." Why can't they leave it alone? he thought impatiently.

Ed Roberts, watching with knowing eyes, felt it was time to take the heat off. He chuckled.

"The guy that fixes my car in Port Washington had a good one the other day. He lives in one of those places they call a changing neighborhood. Like yours, Matt, only it's a lot more changed—around ten per cent changed, and changing more all the time."

"Mine's changed enough to suit me already," Matt said.

"No, listen. This mechanic has a kid around six or seven, and his kid got to playing with one of the new colored kids. This garage-man, he says what the hell, maybe he don't like it much, but on the other hand, is there any harm in it?

"So then one day his kid wanted to bring the colored kid home for lunch and asked his mother if it was all right. There wasn't much the mother could do about it, because the kid had brought the colored boy in with him to do his asking.

"So the mother thinks, what hurt can it do? Maybe she'll give him a talking-to later, but now she tells the kids to go wash while she cooks them up a mess of hamburgers. So finally the two kids are sitting there at the kitchen table and the mechanic's kid dives right in. But the wife notices the colored kid isn't eating, and so she says, 'What's the matter—don't you like hamburgers?'

"So the colored kid looks at her, big-eyed, and says, sure, he likes hamburgers fine. So she says, why don't he eat? The kid looks at her and says—get this—'Ma'am, isn't somebody going to say grace? Besides, I haven't got a napkin.'"

It wasn't very funny but it had come at the right time. The laughter was explosive, and Matt, looking at Roberts, was grateful. Ed, he thought, has a nice sense of timing; he didn't have to do that, but I'm glad he did—and thankful too. There's something you'd better watch from now on, he reminded himself; I knew it was interesting, but there hadn't been any way to know people would get that tangled up in it. Macmillan, for example—why was it getting to him this way? Normally Macmillan took things about as calmly as they could be taken; this edge, this heat, wasn't like him.

The next time, the pressure came from Laura Cusack and was exerted against an unexpected target. Ellen was scarcely back from taking Matt to the station one morning when the chimes summoned her and she found Laura at the door.

"You're just in time." She smiled. "I was just going to lush it up with another cup of coffee. Will you have one with me?"

"That wasn't what I came for," Laura said. "Ellen, I want to talk to you."

"What about, Laura? Has Bill been up to something?" Ellen's manner was pleasant, concerned but not too concerned. She was accustomed to Laura Cusack's angers and emergencies. It paid to be on guard about Laura, but it wasn't necessary, in the end, to take her too seriously.

"Paul and I had dinner at the club last night." Laura's tone was already accusing. "The Macmillans were at the next table with the Strausses. I wasn't eavesdropping." Laura was getting her disclaimer in early. "I couldn't help overhearing."

"Yes?" Ellen's fine brow was puzzled.

"Ellen, I don't think your husband's sense of humor is very funny." Laura's eyes were turning beady as she bored in on her grievance.

"Matt? What does Matt have to do with the Macmillans and Strausses having dinner?" Ellen was baffled.

"If he has no regard for himself, or for you or your own position, he still has no right to involve the rest of us." Laura was getting shrill.

"For heaven's sake, Laura, what is this all about?" Ellen had not yet lost her temper, but she was finding, as often before, that Laura Cusack furnished the temptation.

"Mr. Macmillan was talking about us, about this street, and that means all of us."

"Please, Laura, come to the point!"

"He couldn't have heard it from anybody but your husband. After all . . ." Laura's look was sharp, prying and spitefully triumphant in having nailed her enemy.

"Heard what, for heaven's sake? Stop beating around the bush!"

Laura Cusack sucked in her breath and let it go, and Ellen found herself wondering whether a flare of smoke and brimstone from those pinched nostrils might not seem appropriate.

"Mr. Macmillan was talking about a Negro moving into Peaceable Lane. Laughing about it—I don't need to add it was a nasty laugh—and calling it, calling us, a 'nigger town'!"

"Oh, no . . ." Ellen breathed.

"I'm not lying," Laura said sharply. "I don't know whether your husband was trying to be funny—funny at our expense. But he was certainly stupid."

"That's enough, Laura," Ellen said, still stricken, but now frankly losing her grip on the temper. But Laura wasn't through yet.

"You live here too," she bored on. "Do you want this to get around? Do you want the whole county laughing at us? I couldn't finish my dinner. I couldn't stay there. We—we—we slunk out!" That at the end was a despairing wail.

"Laura"—Ellen had her second wind now and her voice was crisp—"I will not have you sneaking in here behind Matt's back and making your silly accusations. I doubt if I relish people gossiping any more than you do. But if you think you can keep people from finding out what's going on here, you're even a bigger fool than I think you are. And don't try to blame Matt for it. Not one word! I've had enough!"

She had had enough, indeed, but the hurt was there even after Laura's indignant back had departed. A hurt compounded, not only of the remembered tones of that whining, nagging voice, but of something else, something hauntingly threatening. The premonition of fear? She did not know and tried to shrug it off.

The visitor Matt received, late in the week, was as worried as Laura but under better control. John Ainslie Outerbridge had a warning to issue.

"I realize, Matthew, that you probably have a sound reason for discussing this with Mr. Macmillan," he said ponderously. "After all, he is your superior. And, if worst should come to worst, the officers of the club surely should be warned. They too—not only the club, but all their homes—will be affected."

"John Ainslie, don't you think this is getting a little out of hand?" Matt broke in.

"I do, indeed. But perhaps my meaning is not yours. I feel that now, in this early stage, it is premature to let this—this problem go any further afield than absolutely necessary. If, as I say, we are unable to forestall Bronson by ourselves, it may be advisable to inform the club officers and enlist their help. Meanwhile, I feel very strongly that spreading it beyond the street itself is extremely ill-advised."

"Oh, balls," Matt said inelegantly. He had found himself, in the course of a few days, wearied almost to nausea by David Bronson's intentions, whatever they might be.

"No, Matthew. There is very real danger. I am not afraid of gossip, though I do not like it. But I can foresee worse things than gossip. There are organizations—things like the NAACP or the Urban League—do-gooder organizations." His voice took on a tone of faint asperity. "Matthew, you and I have no familiarity with how such groups work. What or how or why they choose a target. I suggest that we don't want to find out. I urge you—for all our sakes—be discreet."

9

MATT AND LAMAR WINTER were standing at the long layout table arranged in Matt's office so that the north light fell on it. Four paintings, in different degrees of completion, stood on the table, propped against the wall.

"She's a lovely dish, isn't she?" Matt mused.

"Nothin's too good for the United States Navy—or for us or, for that matter, Thurston Young and his perfume works. There's only one thing that worries me a little."

"What's that?"

"Whether the midshipman's likely to get snotty about her posing after they're married."

"Has she said anything about it? We'd better be clear on it before we get Young committed too far."

"Nope, she hasn't. And I'm not really worried—just cautious. You take a young guy and expose him to four years of Southern air at Annapolis—plus the Navy itself, which is pretty stuffy—and it occurs to me he just might forget even the armed services have been integrated."

"I suppose it's a possibility all right. We'd better nail her down to a contract."

"Wouldn't hurt. I'll make a date for you, and you can talk to her about it. Think we ought to ring the sailor boy in on it?"

"Not unless we have to. No use putting ideas in his head."

Matt walked along the row of paintings, studying them, while Winter lit a cigarette and slouched in one of Matt's leather guest chairs.

"That thing in the negligee is terrific. Solid sex and at the same time as innocent as Ivory Soap, if that makes any sense."

Winter chuckled.

"Don't ask me, boss. Ask the sailor. I only paint her."

"I wasn't asking. Just ruminating—and slavering a little."

"Slaver away. That's what I was shooting for."

"I wonder a little about the one in the tennis outfit. D'you think perfume goes with tennis?"

"Sure. Anyhow, it ought to. Like basketball—you'd think then they'd need it worse than ever. You know the old gag—if you don't use our soap, for crissake use our perfume."

Grant Macmillan came in, unannounced, and shook hands with Winter.

"Hello, Lamar," he said. "This the stuff for Young?"

"Part of it," Matt said. "Great, isn't it?"

"Hmmh," Macmillan said and gazed at the paintings with an abstracted air. Puzzled, Matt watched him and wondered at his lack of animation; normally Macmillan would be intent, absorbed in the detail of creating a new advertising campaign. Now he seemed incurious, even impatient.

"Nice, Lamar," he said. Then abruptly he turned to Matt. "Step into my office for a minute, Matt."

"Sure, we'll be through pretty soon," Matt said.

"No, now. I'm taking a noon plane to Washington and I'll have to be leaving in a few minutes."

"Of course, Grant." Matt's voice revealed a puzzled concern at Macmillan's unaccustomed sharpness of tone. "You'll excuse us, Lamar?" He was vaguely uneasy about walking out on the Negro, knowing very well that the painter was capable of reacting with quick anger to cavalier treatment. Macmillan's interruption had been nearly rude.

"Has your group made any progress on that house deal?" Macmillan asked, wheeling to face Matt as they entered his office.

"Nothing yet, why?" Matt said, taken aback.

"You're about out of time, aren't you?" Macmillan said. "Two weeks was all he gave you, wasn't it?"

"That's right. We're supposed to come up with something by the end of this week or the first of next." What, Matt wondered, is the cause of all this in the middle of a business day? Anyhow, where did Macmillan fit into this, butting into something that wasn't really his affair?

"Well"—Macmillan spoke heavily—"I've got some bad news for you—for us. I want you to know it before I get out of town. I'll be gone most of the week, and by the time I get back it may be too late."

"Bad news?"

"Yes, bad news." There was an edge of impatience in Macmillan's voice. "I told you I'd try to get some action at the club—through Sloane or Kern—they're both in real estate. It isn't going to work."

"Why not? They're wheels in the business, aren't they?"

Macmillan's face was coldly angry, at what or at whom Matt could not guess.

"You people down in that little interracial village of yours are going to have to face up to something. Unless you can get this Bronson business settled by yourselves, you might as well have leprosy. Nobody'll touch you with a ten-foot pole."

Now Matt himself, prodded again by outsiders' incessant concern over Bronson and his intentions, was growing angry.

"Well, it isn't leprosy, and Sloane and Kern damn well know it—and so do you, Grant. It's just a house and it isn't contaminated with anything except Bronson wants to sell it, and you and just about everybody else don't want him to sell it to a colored man."

"That, by God, is what contaminates it."

"How? I'd think Sloane and Kern would be just as anxious as you seem to be that the Negro doesn't get in."

"They are, oh, they are. Just so it's somebody else—not them—who keeps him out." Macmillan was caustic.

"I don't get it," Matt said. "I just do not get it. If they're so anxious to keep the area white, why don't they get off their fat pratts and sell it to a white man? That's the business they're in."

"Because they're scared."

"Of what?"

"Oh hell, don't be naïve," Macmillan said. "They're afraid of the Urban League and of the NAACP and of their own shadows, for all I know. Every broker does business with Negroes—in Negro areas—and they're scared blue what will happen to their business if they get mixed up in this. I want you to know, before it's too late, there's no help there."

"What does that make us? We're only ten guys on the lane. If the biggest brokers in the county won't touch us, what're we supposed to do?"

"You're there. It's your street, your house, your family," Macmillan said grimly. "You're responsible for it."

Matt suppressed the impulse to remind Macmillan how he had come to live in Peaceable Lane. He hid the uprush of anger in a baffled shake of the head.

"All right, what do you want us to do? Burn the house?"

"Don't talk like an idiot." Macmillan's usually bland face was drawn and his voice peremptory. "You have those other Jews down there. Get them on him—it takes a Jew to outsmart a Jew."

Matt looked at his superior levelly, without trying to hide his distaste.

"Some of us are Jews, yes. What do you suggest they do? So far as I know, Bronson is not."

"The hell he isn't. Scare the bastard. He's vulnerable somewhere. I tell you, Matt, if he puts this over, we're all up for grabs, the whole area."

Matt spread his hands in resignation, hoping to turn this off. "The time's not up yet," he said, "but short of shooting Bronson, I confess I don't know what we can do."

"You'd better do something—and damn fast," Macmillan said coldly.

Winter was still sprawled in the leather chair, smoking and reading a magazine, when Matt returned to his office. The painter looked up with curious, appraising interest.

"What's eating Macmillan?" he asked. "Or what's eating you? You look like you've just been reamed."

"Nothing much," Matt said shortly. "Personal matter. Sorry I was gone so long." He was trying to force his mind back into the groove of Winter's paintings and the campaign that would center around them.

"Seemed pretty uppity to me," Winter said, smiling the tight, hard smile that probably meant he had been toying with the idea of walking out. "Macmillan usually minds his manners better than that."

You don't have to be so cocky about it, old cock, Matt thought; Macmillan usually minds his manners with everybody, not just with you because you're such a touchy bastard. Then, irritably, he regretted his own edginess, resenting that Peaceable Lane's tensions should follow him, like tentacles, into this other life where they had no right to intrude. Damn, this is silly, he thought. If I had any sense I would ask Lamar about it—or tell him about it. If there's something this mess needs, it's a different point of view. At least Lamar might be able to shed some light on the part that baffles me; why any colored man in his right mind would think for a minute of moving into the nest of tarantulas that Peaceable Lane is turning out to be. But he smothered the temptation. He was learning caution.

Later, on the train clattering toward Chappaqua, he found his mind prodding at that obscure hesitation to seek from Winter the understanding he could probably find nowhere else. One thing he did know: it wasn't because he was white and Winter was not. There were no taboo subjects between them. They had settled that long ago, so long ago that Matt knew he no longer thought of the difference of color between them except when it was obtruded by others, as in meeting Thurston Young for the first time, or in choosing a restaurant where nothing would set Winter's ready hackles on end.

It had not been easily or quickly done. When Matt had first begun to work with the artist six—no, by now it must be seven—years ago, it had been difficult. Nearly impossible. Then, as now,

Winter had carried a chip on his shoulder as visible as a cord of firewood. Aggressive, quick to scorn or mockery, alert for slight and forever ready to strike back at it, Winter had been a hard man to like, and at first Matt had not liked him.

Their relationship had begun warily. It was a brittle professional partnership, held together at first only by Matt's respect for the artist's talent and by Winter's acknowledgment of Matt's abilities. That might have been enough for two men of equal capacity and the same color, but it was not enough between Winter and a white man with whom he had to work closely. Some devilish compulsion drove Winter on to test the bond to its breaking point and once, early in their association, he had gone too far.

Some drawled, studied insult, now forgotten, had jerked too hard on the taut reins of Matt's patience and he had rounded on the Negro.

"You're over your quota with that 'white man' stuff," he said, facing the artist, his eyes coldly hostile. "Let's drop it."

"Surely you ain't against being white," the artist said mockingly, his eyes bright with cold glee at the success of his goading.

"Just against your implying it automatically makes me a slave-whoppin' sonofabitch. I didn't make me white, or you black. I'm fed up with being hit below the belt."

"You could hit back," Winter said softly, tauntingly.

"I could. But for what?"

"Maybe you haven't got the guts."

"Maybe. On the other hand, unlike you, I'm not trying to kick the world in the belly, either."

"I won't argue that. You don't need to."

"You do?"

"Being a gentleman is a luxury. I'll leave that for my great-grandchildren when they're running things and your great-grand-children are shining their shoes. They'll be able to afford it. In my generation it ain't possible."

Matt stared at the artist, wondering at the depth of the brand of bitterness this man wore. Here, he thought, is something you have no way of understanding. No way of doubting, either. It was real. But the goddam shame of it was that it used up so much of the vital force of this vital man. When he spoke his tone was milder.

"Look, Winter, this is the generation we have to live in—you and I. You have a beef all right—anyhow, your people have—though I can't say you seem to be suffering much yourself. But your people have—a big one. But the beef is bigger and older than either of us. You let it lie and I'll let it lie. We've got work to do; let's try to get along."

The Negro's stare was level, calculating, probing into Matt's eyes, searching beyond them. At last some of the hard glitter faded.

"Okay, white man," Winter said, but now he was smiling. "Maybe you mean it. I guess you probably do."

It had begun there, Matt remembered. Somehow after that, so imperceptibly that its passing could not be measured, the undertone of hostility had faded from their working partnership. In the beginning each had recognized the other's professional quality, but slowly their relationship became more than that. Neither had to say it when at length they had come to regard themselves as a single set of minds to create and hands to execute. They had become friends, and if Winter still guarded himself from others, Matt felt that he no longer guarded himself from him. This, Matt came to believe at length, is a man's friendship, uncomplicated, undemanding, warmed by mutual respect. He trusted Lamar Winter, and if Winter still kept some part of himself in reserve, Matt was not aware of it.

But deep within himself, Matt knew, there remained some instinctive residue of guilt. The guilt was his only by inheritance, through the color of his skin, but nonetheless he felt its weight. And gradually he came to feel that he could understand, though he wished it otherwise, how the extension of that guilt had forged the anger and the uncompromising arrogance of this proud man, Lamar Winter. He never voiced any of this, for he felt instinctively that any overt effort of his to atone for the poisoned legacy of the white man's way with the black would invite Winter's cold rejection. Winter, he knew, would accept patronage from no man, not even a friend.

And so they let it lie. Winter kept the chip on his shoulder for most of the world. Matt thought he no longer wore it for him.

10

LAMAR WINTER had been prowling the tall white studio living room and now he stopped, fists locked behind his back, and stared moodily at the Rouault. It was the best of other painters' paintings that he had admired and bought even when he could not afford them. Now that he could afford them, they still nourished him. Next to his wife Margo, the paintings gave him a greater sense of pleasure and fulfillment than anything else in his life. Winter was not quite sure how he felt about his son Tod. He loved the boy, of course; he assumed the fact of love automatically, not knowing how to be sure of it. But Margo and the paintings were somehow less of a problem. They were beautiful and they bent easily to his will and they were under his protection, his to admire, his to cherish.

The trouble with the boy, if he could ever bring himself to define it, was that he was too much like the paintings and Margo. Womanish. Yielding. He would not say it aloud to himself, but he knew that he would even have welcomed defiance in the boy. Winter had had to fight for his rights; as far back as he could remember, he had fought. He knew a dark foreboding that his son would have to fight too. It was not fitting that a boy—a boy of his race—should be gentle and malleable.

Margo Winter, bright and decorative in black toreador pants and a yellow sweater, sat on the zebra-skin divan that filled all of one wall opposite the painting. Even without Winter's restless pacing, the room would have seemed alive, somehow exciting. Like its master and his woman, the room was vivid and handsome, virile and exuberant.

"Can't you calm down?" she asked, a frown plucking at her creamy forehead. "It's no good letting it eat at you."

"Somebody's fiddling with it. I want to know who," he said abruptly, not moving from his stance before the painting.

She wanted to soothe him; she feared the violence which seemed always to seethe just beneath his surface. She did not fear it for herself but for him, for where he might sometime let it lead him.

"It has only been a couple of weeks," she said.

"Honey, don't be naïve," he grunted. "No, I'm sorry, but something's going wrong. Fox should have him tied up by now."

"Fox?" For a moment she was puzzled. "Oh, you mean the broker."

"Yeah." He stared at the painting. "I think I'll move this. The light's better on the other wall," he said with a quick, incongruous change of subject.

"Lamar, we don't have to have that house," she said. Once again she felt the shadow of ancient terrors. They were rushing headlong into unknowable dangers and she longed desperately for safety; the house had been a delicious dream, but now she feared it. "I'll be almost relieved if we don't get it," she confessed.

"I don't want to be relieved," he snorted. "I want the house. I want you out of here. And I want Tod out—Tod's got to get out, you know that."

He began again to pace the room, moving back and forth with controlled, feline grace, fury in it. He stopped at a window and stared out at the street, blurred now in afternoon rain, but not so blurred as to soften its dreariness, the spiky forest of television antennae on its rooftops like the bunched skeletons of winter-killed weeds, the litter of blown paper and empty cans, the shoddy debris of despair.

"Pigs," he muttered. "A goddam race of hogs." He swung toward her abruptly. "Where's Tod?"

"I let him go to a movie," she said.

"By himself?"

"I took him and left him there. Who could he go with?" she said. She felt apologetic but wearily helpless.

"I know, I know," he said. "What else can you do? The park? What park? The playground? Not unless you're in the right gang. The street? Christ, no! I tell you, Margo, we have to get him out of here." Sorrow and despair wrenched at him as often before. "He isn't tough enough for this, not tough enough."

She wanted to say that toughness wasn't the answer—anyhow, not the only answer. There was room for gentleness in the world, somewhere in the world. But she knew what he would answer:

somewhere perhaps, not here. He turned from the window and began to pace again, to the Rouault, pause, turn, back across the shaggy white rug toward where she sat behind the broad, dully gleaming black expanse of the ebony cocktail table.

"Why do you think something has happened with the house?" she said.

"Bronson," he grunted. "The pigeon's turned into a weasel. When we were out there he was drooling. But he's been stalling ever since—his lawyer's out of town, or he's not home, or he had to go to Chicago, or he thinks maybe he won't move after all. He's stalling, the little jerk."

"Why are you sure?"

"That's what I want to find out. Maybe he thinks he can hold me up for more. If he thinks that, he's probably right—a little bit more, anyhow. But if the rest of them have caught on, they may be putting the blocks to him. That's the possibility that galls me."

"It's his house, isn't it? Does he have to ask the others?"

His laugh was short, sarcastic, a snarl.

"They're crazy if they don't make him think he has to ask them." The mood that now flashed momentarily across his mobile face was one of gleeful malice. "You know, honey, if I was in their place and knew what Bronson was up to—you know what I'd do to the bastard?"

"What? Shut off his gas?" She had learned to respond to these mercurial changes.

"I'd fix him better than that. I'd castrate him with a rusty saw."

"If you feel that way—or feel they feel that way—what do you think they're going to do to us?" She was back again to the unknown, the atavistic terror of venturing into a forbidden place.

"Forget that. Once we're in, we're in. They can't touch us."

"Oh, Lamar, how can you be so sure? Remember what's happened other places. Bombs, pickets—they could drive us out."

"Not that bunch, baby." The grin was wolfish. "This is a different kettle of fish. They won't like it, but they'll have to take it. They got a disadvantage compared to Levittown; they're upper-class white folks and they're stuck with being civilized." His tone was contemptuous.

"Darling, darling, I want that house as much as I ever wanted anything in my life." She was deadly serious. "But I'm scared."

"There's something else," he said. "Fox—he tried to talk me into getting some organization to work on it. I told him to go to hell. But I wouldn't put it past him to try to do it on his own."

"Why not let him? They could do a lot. Both now—and after."

"That's it, or it's part of it. I don't mess around with that organization stuff, you know that." He was frowning, considering something he didn't like. "I've always gone my own way." He smiled, a swift, unexpected burst of light. "Did I use an organization to get you?"

"No." She smiled back briefly. "But I was practically round heeled. But, really, Lamar, why couldn't they help?"

"They could, natch," he said. "But I'd rather stay clear of them. First, I don't like them. Second, I like to do things my own way. Third, once you tie up with them, you're just a pigeon for them. You don't belong to yourself." Now, again, his expression was contemptuous. "Let those do-gooding dynamiters get their hands on you and you ain't a man any more; you're an exhibit, a laboratory specimen for civil rights. Honey, maybe I do things a hard way, but I'll be a nigger sonofabitch if I'm going to be put on the road in a Westchester side show of *Uncle Tom's Cabin.*"

Solomon Weissman, gnomishly rotund in chinos and T-shirt, the sun-soaked ruddiness of cherubic face and glistening pate rendered even more flamboyant by contrast with the fringe remnant of white hair, found Matt tinkering sweatily over the lawnmower in his garage. It was midmorning on Saturday and the loosely defined period of grace with Bronson had nearly run out.

"You look displeased, Matthew," Weissman said.

"Only mildly, Sol. It won't start."

"I would offer to help, but I'd only make it worse. Machinery is not my forte. Now, if it was a matter of fertilizer . . ." The older man smiled and dusted his hands together, and Matt realized that, as usual, Weissman was giving off a faint, not unpleasant redolence compounded of bone meal, dehydrated sheep manure and aphid spray.

"I know. You'd have it blooming," Matt grunted. "Anyhow, probably all it needs is a new spark plug."

"That ought to be easy."

"It ought to be. Easier, anyhow, than yanking my arm out of the socket on this starter rope. What I'm doing is giving an advanced course in the lunacy of laziness. I keep on yanking rather than go to the easier trouble of getting the car out and driving down to the village for a new plug. What's on your mind, Sol?"

"Bronson, of course. We have come up to the time when we have to act—or decide not to act."

"What do you want to do, Sol?" Matt thought of reporting Grant Macmillan's failure—and anger at his failure—to persuade Grassy Tor's real-estate dealers to venture into Peaceable Lane's crisis, but he decided to wait. He was, he realized rather grumpily, growing wary of discussing the problem, even with Sol, who was as directly affected as himself. It was just too touchy.

"None of us can act alone in this, Matthew." Weissman had one foot up on the tire of the lawnmower, rolling it pensively back and forth. "We had better call the street together again. Today, if possible."

"You'll never catch them all on a Saturday morning. Yale'll still be sleeping off his early-morning show. I saw Cusack heading out, looking like golf. I wouldn't bet on a quorum before sundown. But they'll all come if they know something's really cooking."

"This time we'll need them all. Do you think we can get them all at my house by, say, eight o'clock?"

"I expect so. Let's split the calls. I'll take this side of the street."

Bronson again—and the lane. Matt tried to remember that it had once seemed almost a joke. Now it was an issue, and it had grown, in its few weeks, to bulk threatening and close, oppressing every thought and action. It was another pleasant day, fragrant with early summer, but the brightness had gone out of it for Matt as he abandoned the lawnmower and went into the house. Hearing him, Ellen came from the living room, where she had been guiding Clarice, the once-weekly colored maid, through the operating intricacies of a new vacuum cleaner.

"That was Mr. Weissman, wasn't it?" she said. "Was it this thing again—about Mr. Bronson?"

"Yeah. He wants a showdown meeting tonight. I guess he's right. Where's the keys, honey? I have to run down to the village."

"Matt, this is getting to be a nightmare. Laura Cusack has been driving me mad. When is it all going to end?" She was keeping her voice down self-consciously, with something more than the housewife's normal alertness to the whereabouts and possible eavesdropping of a servant.

"I don't know. Nor how, either," he said glumly. "People keep picking at it." He glanced meaningly toward the living room, where the cleaner had begun to hum. "Next thing you know, she'll be talking about it."

Ellen's gray eyes were frightened. "She has already."

"What! For God's sake, where did she pick it up?"

"Sshh, she'll hear you."

"Well, hell," he said disgustedly, "the maids must be having a gay time of it. She probably knows all there is to know already. You didn't tell her?"

"No, of course not. But I'm afraid Bill did."

"Oh, no," Matt groaned. "Can't he ever keep his trap shut? That kid. Brother!"

"Please, Matt, you can't blame him. He can't help hearing about it and he can't help being interested. And you know he hasn't any inhibitions."

"Inhibitions! He's about as inhibited as a hurricane. What'd he say to her?"

"I'm not sure. I think he asked her if she'd like to work for the colored people when they moved in. But I don't think that was the first she heard, because she seemed to know about it already. She told him if those people thought they were going to get a colored girl to work, they had another think coming."

"She said that?"

"That's the awful part about this," Ellen said miserably. "It's not so much what is happening. It's people prying at it, whispering about it. You can feel them, like fingers plucking at it behind your back."

Suddenly Matt was angry. He yelled, "Hey, Clarice! Come here!"

He half heard Ellen's startled, breathy "Oh no" as the vacuum stopped and the maid, stout and dark, attentive but unreadable, came into the kitchen.

"Yes, sir?" she said, her face impassive.

Just then Matt became acutely aware that, in the two hundred some Saturdays he had known Clarice, they had never once exchanged any thought or human communication more meaningful than "good morning" or "good night" when he delivered her to the bus station. Abruptly, in remembered embarrassment, he recalled that long ago when Clarice had first come to work and had missed her bus he had driven her all the way home to White Plains. Getting out of the car, Clarice hesitantly had asked what she owed him, seeming to take it for granted that no service such as this could come from a white man without a price tag.

"Yes, sir?" Clarice said again, waiting.

"No, I'm sorry, Clarice. It was nothing. I . . ." It was lame and he knew it sounded foolish, and he felt foolish flapping his hands in embarrassed dismissal. He realized, helplessly, that if he had never before learned to communicate with Clarice, he certainly could not now.

The Jones acre was half mowed in midafternoon when Matt, sweating and more than willing to listen to persuasion, yielded to his son's insistence that he come along to the pool and bear witness to Bill's accomplishments as future Olympics material.

"You're getting a pretty good tan," Matt said as, stripped for the pool, he and the boy walked along the lane. The remark was prompted as much by envy—he was aware of his own office pallor—as it was by admiration for his son's allover mahogany tint.

"Yup," Bill admitted complacently. "More'n you."

"You don't need to get uppity about it. If I didn't have any worse problems than the fourth grade has, I could get out in the sun too. Anyhow, at least my shorts fit."

He regarded Billy's oversize trunks, bundled up around the waist to keep them from falling off his narrow belly and flapping around his knees.

"You look like a Tibetan tribesman. Why don't you con your mother into buying some trunks that fit?"

"She says I'll get bigger so I fill them."

"That may be," Matt said thoughtfully. "But I doubt if you'll get big enough fast enough to catch up with them. Your mother is an admirable woman and on the whole I approve of her heartily, but some of her notions of economy baffle me."

"What's economy?"

"A virtue, son. One which—if your mother did not practice it so assiduously—would leave us no place to go but the poorhouse." Matt sighed. "Still and all, that pair of trunks does look ridiculous."

The pool was out of sight behind its screen of rhododendron, but they could hear the uproar of the young before they got to the gate. Responding to this tocsin of his kind, Billy began to hasten his steps and soon was almost running.

"Take it easy, son. The pool will keep," Matt said.

They passed through the gate to the tune of more yells and splashing, went through the screen of bushes, and Billy began to scamper, by now on full rocket power and out of control. Matt reached the top of the ladder to the pool deck just in time to watch his son race madly across the deck and leap for the water, legs flailing, one hand pinching his nose and his face contorted in ecstatic terror. Matt grinned.

Olympics, huh? he thought. If I ever saw a belly flop in reverse, that was it. He looked around the deck and felt his jaw drop in astonishment.

There in the sun, far enough from the water to be safe from the juvenile splashing, Cyd Cavanidis lay on a red towel. Gawd-amighty, he thought. The total area of the blonde's white bikini suit, counting both ends of it, could not have much exceeded the square-inch total of the dark goggles which shielded her eyes. My gosh, he thought, chop-fallen, one wiggle and she'll be out. He realized that he was staring and, feeling the surge of color to his face, tore his eyes away.

Wow, he thought, remembering that Ellen had told him that Cyd was a Slenderella patron; if that's going to seed, I wonder what she looked like when she was fresh. Steve ought to keep that under lock and key.

He dived in and swam the length of the pool. Hauling himself out at the far end, he sat on the coping and watched Mark Cotten trying to work some co-ordination into the determined flailing of Angela Cavanidis. At eight, dark-eyed Angela was both fat and awkward and, working with her, the young Princeton giant wore a look of bored but patient despair on his handsome face.

Cotten clasped his hands around Angela's chubby waist and tossed her up on the coping. "That'll do for now, sis," he said, giving her a friendly pat on the bottom. He drew himself up and squatted on the coping beside Matt.

"If that one ever even learns to dog paddle, it'll be a miracle," he said.

"She's got a built, but it sure isn't the built her ma has," Matt said. "How're the kids doing?"

When Cotten did not answer immediately, Matt turned curiously and saw that Cotten's eyes were on Cyd, who had rolled over and was now presenting her smooth and barely confined buttocks to the sun and the world at large.

"She sure hasn't," Cotten mused.

"Bill learning anything?" Matt asked.

"He's coming along all right. The problem with all of them is keeping their minds on it. They'd rather play."

The same could be said of you, Buster, Matt thought. Just then a whoop from the other end of the pool pulled their attention.

"Hey! Pop! Watch me, watch me, Pop!"

It was Bill. With a thrust of panic, Matt saw him teetering on the outer edge of the high board. He opened his mouth to yell a warning, but Bill beat him to it, again screaming, "Pop! Hey, Pop! Watch!" Bill seized his nose in one hand and went thrashing down, more or less in a sitting position, to disappear in a horrendous splash.

Matt was on his feet as the boy's head came up.

"Boy, am I going to tan his fanny!" he muttered grimly.

He turned abruptly at Cotten's burst of laughter.

"He's all right. Don't worry." Cotten choked his laughter as he saw Matt's face darken in anger.

"Don't worry! The fool kid could break his neck. Do you let 'em get away with stuff like that?"

The young man eyed him levelly. "Let them get away with it? No, Mr. Jones, I taught them to do it."

"You better unteach them, then. Do you want a dead kid on your hands?"

"It's up to you, Mr. Jones." The boy was unabashed. "I'll keep Bill off the board if you want him kept off."

"Damn right I want him off."

"But I hope you'll change your mind." Cotten was unperturbed. "I admit maybe that looked a little wild, but it wasn't really. The most dangerous thing that can happen to a kid in the water is lack of confidence—next to overconfidence, that is."

"You don't think that was overconfidence?" Matt's tone was growing milder as his scare subsided.

"No, sir, I'm not teaching your boy to be reckless. But I hope I'm teaching him to know how much he can do and do it without fear."

Cotten's confidence and earnestness impressed Matt in spite of himself. He glanced once more at the water and board and suppressed the impulse to yell at Billy who, he saw, was halfway up the ladder again. Slowly he sat down again.

"Maybe you're right," he said. "But he scared hell out of me all the same."

Cotten chuckled.

"Don't worry about Bill," he said. "He can look out for himself better than you think—and, where he can't, I'll look out for him."

"Yeah," Matt said. "I expect you will."

Later, as he was dressing after a shower, Ellen came into their bedroom.

"How was it, Tarzan?" She smiled.

"Pretty good—it gets the barnacles off." He laughed. "Pretty stimulating place, that pool. Cyd was down there taking a sun bath practically bare-assed."

"You don't have to be vulgar."

"She was, though. I could hardly keep my hands off her."

"You'd better keep your hands off her, mister," Ellen said. "And your eyes, too, if you don't mind."

"That's quite a lot to ask of a man."

"Don't think she doesn't know it," Ellen said grimly. "She's out there in that—that fig leaf—every day."

"So? What do you suppose she's after—aside from catching a cold on her bare lungs?"

"Trouble, natch!" Ellen's reply was an indignant snort.

11

You wouldn't need a barometer to measure the pressures building here, Matt thought as he entered Solomon Weissman's living room after dinner. The tension could be felt in the timbre of their voices and read in their faces. They were nearly all there, all the men, anyhow, and most of the women. Ellen had stayed at home to steer Bill's reluctant steps through his homework, and he supposed some others of the women were similarly engaged.

He found himself again perched on the stiff chair, torn between wanting a smoke and reluctance to provoke the bustle with which Mrs. Weissman would search out something to serve as an ash tray and would thereafter watch in birdlike anxiety lest he miss it. His eyes went to Outerbridge. He guessed the lawyer had made it early again, for once more he had laid claim to Sol's second easy chair and sat primly upright in it, his hands folded over a brief case. Beside the lawyer, on a chair as stiff as Matt's and clearly as uncomfortable in it, sat Dr. Abram; as always, he was struck and briefly fascinated by the sorrowful and somehow uneasy look on the physician's narrow, sensitive face. He was not likely to miss Cyd Cavanidis either, not after that scene at the pool. Now in red, the blonde lolled—sprawled was closer to it—on the divan between the somber bulk of Zack Gold and the small, colorless presence of Estelle Outerbridge. Even with clothes on, he thought, Cyd carries the air of a bitch.

Weissman sat back, his round belly, as usual, getting the benefit of two compassionately open buttons, and ran his bright, inquisitive eyes around the circle of his neighbors.

"We've run out of time," he said without preamble. "You all know it. We're here tonight to decide what to do about it."

"That maniac ought to be arrested." Matt wondered why Laura Cusack's voice must always carry that shrill saw edge.

"If you mean David Bronson, as I suppose you do, Mrs. Cusack,

I doubt if there is anything in the statutes forbidding the sale of a house," Weissman said mildly.

"Each of us, in the last two weeks, was supposed to canvass his contacts, hoping that one of us might find a buyer. I can tell you that I have made no progress. I am assuming that if any of you had had any luck we would know it already. If otherwise, does anybody have anything to report?" Weissman ran his eyes around the room again.

Paul Cusack cleared his throat.

"I thought I might have something going with the broker who sold me my house in the first place. First time I talked to him he said he'd be glad to help; he'd even cut his commission if it would help keep the area white. But by the time I called him again, he'd gone shifty on me, couldn't pin him to anything. After that I couldn't reach him—every time I called, his secretary said he was out." Cusack paused, frowning. "The yellow jerk!" he added in a voice nearly as venomous as his wife's.

"Anybody else?"

Outerbridge took off his glasses, rubbed them with a handkerchief and restored them primly to his nose. "You will all recall that I warned you of this before," he said. "No legitimate broker wants to or, I may even say, dares to involve himself. This attitude on their part is disappointing and, I feel, shortsighted. However, it exists. I believe Mr. Macmillan offered to explore the possibilities at the club. Mr. Jones, would you know what response he got?"

"No different." Matt spoke shortly, feeling they all might as well face up to it now. "We're untouchable."

There it was—out in the open for all of them to look at, to recognize. They would get no help from outside; they were on their own, all together or each separately, according to his conviction, his need, or the shrewdness of his enterprise. What goes on here? Matt wondered. Fear first—certainly fear now came before anger—but anger was still there, at Bronson, of course, but also, steadily growing, at one another, at their collective helplessness. Panic could come now.

"Anybody else get an offer to sell to a jig?" Peter Yale's voice, bringing this last thing out into the open to be seen and measured, was brittle. His light eyes, usually mocking, were hard now, moving from one to another around the room. "Anybody here ready to run? To pull the plug?" For a time nobody spoke, and all around the room eyes darted from face to face. Gold's sigh was a troubled rumble.

"I did, Pete, if you need to know. Or, anyhow, I suspect I did. I got three calls from people who said they were brokers and they'd heard I wanted to sell. I guess it couldn't have been anything else." He turned his brooding gaze on the broadcaster. "If you're curious, I'm not running."

Outerbridge was on his feet.

"Please, gentlemen. Mr. Yale, you have voiced similar suspicions before. Against me, the last time. They serve no purpose here."

"They serve plenty if somebody's getting ready to bolt. I don't intend to be left holding the bag," Yale said angrily.

"You talk about it a lot, Pete," Matt put in softly. "How about keeping your finger off the panic button?"

Cyd Cavanidis stood up, using Gold's big thigh for support a second longer than necessary. She yawned, and the lifting of her arms raised her breasts provocatively against the red cloth.

"You all talk about it a lot." Her throaty voice was bored. "Just talk. I'm going home. G'night all." She moved lazily, undulating out the door into the night. Cavanidis watched her go, an amused glint in those narrow eyes.

"That's my Cyd," he said expressionlessly. "She's against talk."

Still on his feet, Outerbridge watched her go with pained disapproval. He had withdrawn papers from his brief case and was waiting for their attention.

"A certain amount of talk is necessary," he said, seeming to address reproof to the departed Cyd. "Our talk has served some purpose. It has served to clarify the limitations on our freedom of choice. If you will bear with me, I will review the choices we still have. I have taken some trouble to verify my information."

"Lay it out, John Ainslie." Cusack sounded impatient.

"We can, of course, withdraw and permit Bronson to dispose of his property as he sees fit. I think we all know now how he proposes to dispose of it. I do not intend to discuss here the pros and cons of having a Negro in this neighborhood . . ."

"If there are any 'pros' about having your home invaded and

turned into a slum, they certainly escape me," Laura Cusack snapped.

"Your individual feelings about having Negroes on the street may vary, and I imagine they do to some extent." John Ainslie was not to be distracted. "I propose to address myself only to the realities. I have checked this with reputable and responsible authorities. A Negro moving in will cost each of us somewhere between one fourth and one third the value of his home. That is true, of course, only of those who choose to sell." Outerbridge paused, small mouth pursed, to let it sink in. "From the feelings I have heard expressed here, I imagine there will be those who will want to sell, whatever the loss." His small eyes, behind the glinting spectacles, flicked quickly toward the Cusacks. "You will, of course, learn the exact extent of your loss only when you do sell."

"Just a minute," Kelly said worriedly. "We haven't found a buyer, and you say we probably can't. Where does that leave us anywhere to go from here?"

"I am coming to that," Outerbridge went on imperturbably. "We have one alternative. We can buy the Bronson house ourselves—as a syndicate."

"Holy Christ!" Kelly's sigh was explosive. "What are we going to do with another house? I'm strapped every month now the way I am."

"None of us is likely to enjoy this, Dr. Kelly," Outerbridge went on remorselessly. "However, we are no longer choosers—if, indeed, we ever were. I think, however, that I need not point out to you that taking on the burden of one tenth of a house"—here again he paused to survey the room individual by individual—"will be significantly less costly than losing one fourth or one third of a house."

"But . . . but—oh hell," Kelly said helplessly.

"And I think I ought to point out to you, Dr. Kelly," Outerbridge continued relentlessly, "that in your case the penalty may be imposed more quickly and more severely. You have said that the—ah—size of your family has already forced you to seek a suitable house elsewhere. Are you prepared for the sacrifice of making a forced sale on a street whose values have been radically altered by the presence of a Negro owner? Are you?"

"Don't rub it in," Kelly said. "You know I'm not." He fiddled nervously with his hands in his lap, and it struck Matt that Kelly looked even more harassed than usual. "Right now it's even worse—we've got a binder down on a house in Connecticut . . . near Greenwich," he added irrelevantly.

"You see?" Outerbridge said pedantically, as though driving home a point.

"If it wasn't for that we could stay here if we had to," Kelly said, revealing his perplexity as he picked at it with words. "We're crowded. The kids are, but they'd survive . . . I guess."

"With nigger children?" Now that she had at last, in the urgency of outrage, got the word out, Laura Cusack found it easier to use the second time. "Jerome Kelly, are you willing to see those little girls of yours playing with niggers? Well, if you are, I'm not! If Paul Junior associates with niggers, it will be over my dead body, I promise you!"

Damn that shrill, hysterical nag, Matt thought wearily. This might be simpler if you didn't have to keep reminding yourself that, whatever you're in, you're in it with Laura Cusack. If she would just shut up, it might be easier to understand what we're dealing with and what it implies.

"Let's get down to cases, John Ainslie," Yale broke in. "Are you suggesting that we buy that house—saddle ourselves with it—and just keep it because no broker will touch it? What do you think we are, Rockefellers?"

"No, I don't think that is indicated," Outerbridge said. "I think that once the basic situation is changed—once, that is, that the house is no longer on the Negro market, even by implication—the curse will be off. I have been assured privately that if we buy the house we can expect help in disposing of it."

"Whose help? What kind of help?" Yale's question carried the hard note of challenge. Looking at the taut face and angry eyes, Matt wondered why, of them all, it should have been Yale who first yielded to this hair-trigger touchiness and—yes, he remembered—should be the first to voice distrust of the others. Wasn't this a startling change in the surface of a man? And how much deeper might the change run? How could you square this angry, distrustful neighbor Yale with the deft, glib public Yale who so smoothly rode the radio waves in favor of popular causes? Whatever else you could say about it, this was surely no popular public cause they were here engaged in. Maybe the answer lay there somewhere . . . maybe.

"I am not at liberty to reveal that. But I can assure you it will be competent professional help. I can tell you that, once we have purged this situation of what some might call the onus of discrimination—but which I prefer to describe as something else entirely—most of the real-estate board will be ready to help."

"And how long will that take? A week? Ten years?"

"We will have to be ready for it to take some time, a few months. This situation is known and talked about all over Westchester. It will take time for the talk to die out. People are easily frightened when they are buying homes."

"And you think that we ought to put up the money for a down payment, carry the mortgage, pay insurance and taxes, stand a new title search and legal fees and go on with it for God knows how long—while the place stands empty, getting rotten—on the basis of a half-assed promise from some joker so vague that we're not even permitted to know his name? How crazy do you think I am?"

"Mr. Yale, you persist in challenging my statements and my judgments and my good faith as well. You are under no compulsion here . . ."

"No compulsion, balls! There's been nothing but compulsion, herding us into this corner ever since this first began. Compulsion—what do you call it?"

"Frankly, Mr. Yale, I don't think you have much choice."

"I don't either, Peter." Solomon Weissman stood up and tucked his hands inside his pants and under his belly for further support. "But you do have a choice of language. Mamma isn't used to cussing in this house. She doesn't like it—also I don't." Weissman's manner was still mild, but the edge of impatience had begun to show. "A little while ago Mrs. Cavanidis walked out on us because we talk too much. I agree with her, and we are not going to get to a decision by wrangling—or by cussing. We all know what's involved. It's not a choice between win or lose—but a choice of which way and how much we lose."

Weissman stood in the center of the room and once more let his bright, inquisitive look roam the circle of his guests. Then he sat down.

"I am standing up to be counted," he said incongruously. "I am for buying the house. I will put up my share of the money. I am not going to make a speech about it. I can tell you my reasons in one sentence. I worked for thirty-five years to get a nice place for Mamma and me and to give my daughter a decent start in life, and I do not intend to give up a big piece of it simply because somebody I have never laid eyes on has a whim to live here."

"But, Daddy——" Lana Weissman, who for once had spent half an hour in silent attention, started to speak.

"Shut up, sister," Weissman said wearily. "I have heard it all before."

"I do not think you need to guess what my feelings are," Outerbridge said. "Mr. Weissman is correct—it is time to stand up to be counted. I favor the procedure I have recommended. Nor do I believe a speech is necessary to indicate why. However, if it may help clarify some of the confusion surrounding this situation, I should like to say a few words about discrimination." The word brought a start of heightened awareness into the room's already palpable tension. Outerbridge paused, marshaling thoughts and arguments behind his careful face.

"It is fair, I believe, to warn you all that any action we take will invite criticism in some quarters. It would be foolish to ignore the possibility. I hope we can avoid publicity, but it may not be entirely possible. It will not be possible at all unless each of you—all of us—avoids discussing whatever action we take." The small eyes behind the glinting glasses carried the warning around the room, and Matt felt a small, illogical spurt of relief that Outerbridge had not singled him out as an example of the loose lip.

"But, even if we should be subjected to attack or embarrassment, the only question we really have to answer must be addressed essentially to ourselves. Is this really an act of discrimination? I say it is not. Like Mr. Weissman, I have no knowledge of the person or persons with whom Mr. Bronson has been dealing. My action here is purely defensive. I am defending myself against a deliberate act of malice conceived against me, with intent to injure, by Mr. Bronson. Nothing more, nothing less."

"Who's next?" Weissman asked.

There was an uneasy stir in the room, and Matt, glancing from one to another, was caught by the sight of Estelle Outerbridge, sitting tiny and almost unnoticeable in the shadow of Zack Gold, nervously chewing her lips and staring with bright, frightened eyes at her husband.

"Mr. Cusack?"

Cusack ran a finger around under his stiff white collar as though it was too tight. The Cusacks had been dressing to go out when Matt's summons had caught them at seven o'clock.

"I'll buy it," he said. "It's the worst investment I've ever recommended to anybody"—he sighed—"but I'll go along. I don't see what else we can do."

"Well, I should hope so——" Laura began shrilly.

"Shut up, Laura," Cusack said wearily.

"Dr. Kelly?"

The dentist frowned and twisted his hands together, trying without success to carry his worry gracefully.

"I . . . I don't know. There's a lot of money involved here. Has anybody figured it out? How much for each—the costs and all?"

"Not precisely," Outerbridge acknowledged shortly. "Roughly two thousand each to close—that will be the first cost—then keeping it going until we sell."

"If we sell, don't you mean?" Yale broke in sarcastically.

"It will sell, Mr. Yale. Please, I am trying to answer Dr. Kelly's question. When we sell, of course, you will get much of the total back. How much, of course, will depend on how long we need to sell and the price we can get. In the end it will cost each of us something, a few hundred dollars."

"I would feel better if I knew how many hundred," Kelly said. "And raising that much cash all at once . . ." He paused unhappily.

"Cheer up. Don't you ever read those car cards on the Central? Young executives—can you use twenty-five hundred dollars? Phone for our courteous, confidential service . . ." Yale's voice was jeering.

"Keep out of this, Yale," Kelly snapped with a flash of spirit. "You tend to your problems—I'll take care of mine." He turned then toward Weissman. "I'll come in, of course. I know it's necessary." He sighed. "But I wish it wasn't."

"That's what we all wish, Jerome," Weissman said. "Mr. Draper?"

"Well . . ." Draper, Matt thought, always looked absurdly youthful, although he knew that that boyish face, so easily driven to baffled indecision, must have known well over thirty years. "I don't know whether my dad will put up the money. Maybe he will. I guess he wouldn't want us in a colored neighborhood . . . I just don't know . . . I'll ask him . . . well, that is, if he will . . ." Pretty Shirley Draper clutched at his arm.

"Oh, Gordon," she said, "the children!"

"He'll put it up. I know he will," Draper said firmly, seeming to speak more to his wife than to the room at large. Weissman nodded, then turned quizzically toward the broadcaster.

"Mr. Yale?" There flickered, for a moment, in those bright, warm eyes a glint of malicious pleasure, as mocking as Yale's own. The broadcaster stared back at him, a look of smoldering anger.

"This is blackmail. . . ." He spat the words.

"We all know it is blackmail, Mr. Yale." Weissman's voice was expressionless.

"I am goddamned if I enjoy being whipsawed, either by you or that conniving bastard at the end of the road or whoever the blue bastard is that's trying to crack this place open."

"None of us enjoy it, Mr. Yale."

"There's one thing more. I know the sonsofbitches. I ought to." Yale's laugh was bitter. "There've been times when I worked with them . . . schools and stuff. Maybe this way they're paying me back." He laughed again, balefully.

"What thing, Mr. Yale?"

"You people shush me when I talk about somebody else selling out. All right, be naïve if you want to. But I tell you this—it's no single nigger trying to bust in here by himself. Those people are organized. Now, you listen, it's ten to one we're not finishing it here—just by buying Bronson's house. If they—I mean the whole blasted black lot of them—are out to bust this neighborhood, they won't rest until they do it."

"It is possible. We are not entirely naïve, Mr. Yale."

"I hope not." The tone was jeering. "And you'd better not be. I'm coming in—not because I want to, but because I've been screwed into a corner where I have to. But I want something for it, and if the rest of you have any sense, you'll want it as much as I do."

"And that is?"

"A written, signed, witnessed pledge from everybody here that he will not, under any circumstance, sell out to anybody until the sale has been investigated and reviewed by a committee of members represented by a lawyer"—he glanced first at Gold, then at Outerbridge—"an outside lawyer."

"Why?"

"Why! Don't be a child. Whoever is out to bust this block—it doesn't matter a damn who—won't give up just because we screw them out of the Bronson house. Don't be saps."

"I suggest the same restraint to you, Mr. Yale. I think both Mr. Outerbridge and Mr. Gold will bear me out. Such an agreement would be without legal effect. Is that right?"

Outerbridge nodded. "Valueless," he said.

"Mr. Yale, whether you believe it or not, everybody here is aware of the dangers you are so sure we are too stupid to appreciate," Weissman said. "Each of us, no doubt, might be somewhat easier if he could enjoy an absolute guarantee that nobody else, accidentally or otherwise, would sell him out. Unfortunately, that is impossible. I suspect it may go against your nature, Mr. Yale, but I suggest that you are up against the necessity of putting some simple trust in your neighbors. Faith, they call it."

"Faith, balls!"

"Once more, before I throw you out, Mamma does not like cussing. Now"—suddenly the pleasant, chatty voice carried a whiplash sting—"in? Or out?"

Yale eyed the older man sullenly.

"In," he muttered. "But, by God, if anybody in this room pulls a double cross . . ."

"I don't think anybody will. Dr. Abram?"

The doctor's face was pale, a thin and tortured mask. He stood up and began to pace, the short, spasmodic steps of a puppet and as little under the conscious control of his will.

"I . . . gentlemen . . . forgive me. I do not wish to make a speech, but I must explain, I feel I must. I am coming with you. I wish I had the courage for some other choice, but I do not have it. But . . ." His look around was imploring, full of pain.

"Yes, Doctor," Weissman's tone was gentle. "Whatever you want to say."

"I do not want to say anything because . . . because it will sound like special pleading." The thin face was wretched. "And . . . and I know that that is what it is. Those among you who are Jews"—he bobbed his head painfully, first at Weissman, then at Gold—"may understand more what I say—and understanding, you possibly will also despise it. I come in with you, I join in buying the house, because I am a Jew. This is ironical, for it is the denial of what a Jew should do. It is only understandable because I am not only a Jew—I am also a Jew who has been taught cowardice." He stopped and looked at them, and the wretched eyes pleaded for understanding.

"Yes, Doctor?" Weissman said softly.

"I do not want to recite to you the story of Vienna. You know it anyway. What I must convey to you is what such a thing as Vienna was can do to a Jew—make him an orphan, a corpse, a hero; fill him with nobility and with death; or strip him of dignity and leave him only life and cowardice. For a Jew in Vienna, a Jew in a secure place, respected, substantial, owning a useful place in society and feeling himself an accepted member of that society—I speak of myself—suddenly, without reason, and knowing I was guilty of no offense, finding every hand in that society raised against me . . . I cannot explain . . . only that it was more than I could stand. I must tell you, I could not stand it again. No, I could not." The eyes were dull now, blinded by memory.

The room was deathly still. The doctor passed a hand across his eyes and spoke again.

"I think you ask yourselves what has Vienna to do with this? You are entitled to ask, but I cannot answer. Here in this America, how is it that a Jew still carries cowardice? I cannot tell you. I can tell you only that in Vienna there was a time when a Jew felt as safe as he does here today. And then it was changed. What makes a community turn against its Jews? I cannot answer. I can only answer for myself that, being a coward as well as a Jew, I have not the courage to do any act that might offend—again—the community around me.

"What we do here, I know in my heart, is wrong. Having been denied and rejected, I should be the one among you, above all others, who would refuse to deny or reject another man. But I deny him. I tell you—because I must—I cannot again bear the burden of being a Jew."

He fell silent, and the silence around him fell as an oppressive weight upon them all. The breaking of it came from a source so unexpected and unbelievable that they all gaped and Matt saw John Ainslie Outerbridge's tight little mouth open in astonishment. Tiny, mouselike Estelle Outerbridge was on her feet.

"Dr. Abram, you have indicted yourself. With all my heart I grieve for you, for what has been done to you and for what you have done to yourself. But I cannot help you. Nobody can.

"But there is something more and something worse. You have indicted us, all of us. You must answer for your soul. I must answer for mine."

"Estelle . . . Estelle." Outerbridge was frowning and, though still in the grip of astonishment, his voice carried a commanding, peremptory edge. "This is not the place——"

"Don't stop me, John. Please, John." It was a plea but more than a plea, a convulsive will to be heard. "We are Christians, John—I am a Christian. Dr. Abram has made it clear. Being a Christian is not just words, not just going to church, not just Sunday is a day of rest." Her eyes ran swiftly around the circle, pleading, demanding. "Can't you see what we have almost done? Are we so selfish and blind? Can we refuse this man—whoever he is—sight unseen, close our doors against him—and ever again enter a church without guilt?"

"Estelle!" Outerbridge was on his feet and moving toward her. "Estelle, I want you to go home now."

She looked at him wildly and, for a moment, a trembling exaltation seemed to illumine her until, held and stared down, submission swept over her and, with a sob, she turned and ran out of the house into the night. Slowly Outerbridge went back to his chair. Weissman's voice, when it came, was a harsh break in the silence.

"Matthew?"

She had shaken him, Matt knew. She had shaken them all. And Abram had shaken them before her. And now it was up to him. Almost dazedly, needing an effort, he shrugged away the sight and sound of them and steeled himself to deal with the issue. For weeks he had first laughed at, then tried to ignore, waited for the issue to go away. But inexorably it had closed in on him, and now it was there. The time had come to put up or shut up. And what was the issue? Whether Dr. Abram had suffered by being a Jew and quailed at the fear of suffering again? Whether Estelle Outerbridge feared to betray her religion but feared to defy her husband even more? Whether Sol Weissman could claim as a right the protection of the substance he had toiled a lifetime to accumulate? Whether this was merely a matter of ten families banding together to protect themselves against a malicious act, and the Negro who wanted to move among them was not a man of flesh and blood, but merely a disembodied idea? And what did it mean to Matt Jones himself, to Ellen Jones, to Bill Jones? He shook his head, seeking to clear it. Where the hell was his obligation? To a vague, bodiless, debatable principle—or to his wife, his son and—to a real extent—the people among whom he lived? He looked at Weissman and spoke briefly.

"I'm in."

"And you, Zachariah?" Weissman was coming up to the end of his roll call, but if he felt a sense of triumph in the unanimity of his support, he did not betray it.

The big man had been silent, somber, offering no word. But now Matt was aware that Zack's big fists were tight and his forearms corded across his knees and that, when he spoke, the words came up in his throat through a terrible choking reluctance.

"I never knew"—the words came ponderously—"I would never have believed . . . that in this day . . . in this country . . . within the framework of humanity . . . a man might have to make a choice of what to betray." He stopped, raised his eyes dully to Weissman's. "Count me in."

"There wasn't any other answer, Zachariah," Weissman said gently. He turned to face the last man. "Mr. Cavanidis?"

The watchful face was as expressionless as ever, and the lean body, when Cavanidis brought it upright, was as relaxed and controlled.

"Maybe you should have got to me earlier," Cavanidis said. "Count me out."

"You dirty Greek sonofabitch!" The voice was Yale's, crashing into the shocked silence. Yale was on his feet, livid, contorted, moving furiously in on the controlled, watching man.

"Don't try it, sonny. Don't try it." It was softly, clearly spoken, but the voice carried such calculated, concentrated malevolence that it brought Yale up short. Cavanidis inspected them all, carefully, slit-eyed, one at a time.

"I owe you no explanation," he said at last. "But, because I've been sitting here this long, I'll give you a quick one. I don't like jigs any better than you do." He nodded at Laura Cusack, sitting openmouthed. "But I'm a tall man in a big union. Someday I'll be the tallest. But it's a democratic union, which means the officers are elected. About thirty-five per cent of my members are jigs. Good night."

12

"It's late," Matt said, "but we got some talking to do, chum. Come in and have a drink."

"I need the drink. About four fingers in a washtub, if you're feeling generous," Zachariah Gold said, turning with Matt from the street and onto the flagstone walkway to the Jones front door. The big man sounded depressed, and Matt wondered, as he had been wondering ever since the astonishing final act of the meeting in Weissman's living room. It was astonishing only because of Gold's part in it, but this was still incomprehensible.

Cavanidis had left, leaving them but nine, now adjusting themselves angrily or in unhappy resignation to the idea that each must bear not only the burden of one tenth of a house but must take on, in addition, one ninth of the share Cavanidis had spurned.

"There is one thing more," Weissman had said tiredly. "To do this right—that is, to share the responsibility as equally as the costs—we all ought to be out in front where we can be seen. But it just isn't practical. If nine people sign their names jointly as buyers, this deal will look as phony as it is. Somebody here, one of us—or at the most two—has got to front for all of us. Whoever it is ought to know beforehand that he is going to be the target in the shooting gallery."

He paused, once more surveying the strained, silent faces of his neighbors.

"That is why I am tempted to suggest that two should do it," he went on. "It may look a little strange, but at least it will give those two company in their misery. I don't think any one of us ought to be stuck with carrying the load all alone."

Once again he paused and ran a quick inspection of the room.

"We could vote on it," he said. "Or we could take a volunteer."

The room was silent and, looking around, Matt realized that this hush was the lethargy of fear. Their faces were withdrawn, reluctant, aware now that, however necessary they believed it to be, the conspiracy to which they had lent themselves was somehow ignoble and liable to censure.

"Oh hell," Matt said, on an impulse that he could not at once define. "I'll take it."

Afterward, probing at his own motives, he thought the impulse had been close kin to that which had sometimes moved him to evident rashness long ago, when he had been an infantry platoon leader. That drive, he had felt whenever he tried to examine it, was the simple one that, when there was dirty work to be done, somebody inescapably had to do it. It was quicker, cleaner and in some obscure way more satisfactory to do it yourself than to force it on somebody else. Especially on somebody who might flub it out of reluctance or sheer panic.

He could almost feel the tension of the room relax, but in this relaxation, he knew grimly, there was more plain relief than gratitude. Then, with no preparation, the astonishing thing happened. Gold stood up and spoke, still in that choking reluctance which made him seem to hate his words.

"This business needs a lawyer. If it's all right with Matt, I'll go along with him." He turned to look at Matt. "Okay?"

Now they were together in the Jones living room, and Matt watched curiously while the big man splashed bourbon lavishly into a glass and then, without waiting for water or ice, sucked hungrily at the potent stuff.

"Don't take me for a buttinsky, Zack," Matt said, "but tell me, why the hell did you do it?"

Gold took another pull at the drink and sat for a time, wrestling with it.

"To be honest, I don't quite know," he said. "That is, I know and I don't know, and if I say anything, like Abram, it's a self-serving statement. I could give it a try here, with you, but I will be a ring-tailed sonofabitch if I would have tried it there, in front of that Cusack woman."

"You don't have to try it here either," Matt said. "I admit I'm curious. If there was anybody in that room, including both Doc Abram and Estelle Outerbridge, that did not want any part of this, it was pretty plain that the not-wanter was you. So what are you doing, on your own, sticking yourself in it up to the ass?"

Gold fished a handkerchief from a pants pocket and mopped his glasses, then took another pull at the drink and pondered.

"That's fair. But I could ask you one. What are you doing in it?"

Matt grunted. "That's easy. First, I think I've got enough sense not to bugger it, and I'm damned if, for example, I would have as much confidence in Yale—or John Ainslie, either, for that matter. Second—it may be stupid of me—but, honest, Zack, I'm not carrying any conscience about this—at least not up to the level that I think you are carrying it. This seems fairly open and shut to me—somebody is out to screw us, and I'm trying to keep from getting screwed. But you, you get it up on a plane that's above my operating altitude. It chews on you. I can see that, so for God's sake, if you think you're stuck with it, why didn't you let it give you the minimum sticking and leave it there? You didn't have to rub your nose in it."

Gold smiled, a brief, painful twisting of the lips.

"All right, Matt, I've got to rub my nose in it. If you're going to get dirty, you might as well get filthy. I was dirty when I said yes. I was even dirty when I began to think I might say yes." He sighed. "And so, since I am dirty in front of ten people, I ain't getting any dirtier in front of ten million."

"You poor, goddam, crazy, conscience-ridden bastard," Matt murmured.

"No"—Gold sighed—"don't try to noble it up. I came along for the same reasons I think you did—because eight or ten thousand bucks is more of a whipping than I think I can take. The only difference is I'm a long way from sure the reason is good enough. Necessary, yes, but good, no."

"There's a worry closer than that one," Matt said crisply. "They're all in—or say they are . . ."

"Except Cavanidis," Gold reminded him.

"Yeah, except Steve. Boy, did you see the way Yale backed down?" He shook his head wonderingly. "Steve gave us a reaming all right, but, you know, I half admire the bastard. He's tough, if that's a virtue, and he's practical."

"If, by tough, you mean he's as dangerous as a rattlesnake and if, by practical, you mean he's as sentimental as the snake, I'll go along with you."

"Well, he's out. Now we got to worry about the ones that are in."

Gold grunted.

"There's a couple I wonder about. Yale's one, Draper's another. I guess I don't worry about Kelly. It's going to be a strain on all of us, but I think worst on him. But he'll do it."

"I'm not going to have any fun raising it myself," Matt said grimly. "We still got a few war bonds, but I hate to dump them."

"Nobody's going to have a picnic," Gold said. "I imagine our first chore is to tackle Bronson. Somehow, I hate——" The doorbell chimed, and they both started.

"Now what?" Matt said, getting up. "It's after midnight."

He went to the door quickly, both curious and anxious to stop the bell's chiming before it should wake Ellen and Bill. He switched on the porch light as he opened the door.

"Turn it off," Steve Cavanidis said crisply. "I'm here, but I ain't advertising it."

Automatically, with his finger still on the switch, Matt responded to the Greek's imperative tone and was annoyed with himself for obeying. He stepped back.

"Come in," he said, knowing that his irritation showed. "What's on your mind?"

"I'm already in." Cavanidis smiled his tight, controlled smile. "You're the front men, aren't you?" He nodded toward Gold, silent and watchful in his chair.

"How did you know?" Matt's tone was sharp.

"Elementary. I waited until your little prayer meeting broke up and called Sol."

"I'm surprised he told you."

"So was I—a little," Cavanidis admitted, permitting the smile to broaden slightly.

"We're having a drink," Matt said. "Can I offer you one—worth roughly two thousand bucks?" It had occurred to him that this man, now come so casually calling in the middle of the night, had just cost him a lot of money he couldn't afford.

"No, thanks. I'll speak my piece and beat it. I wouldn't want to be caught here, and it wouldn't do your reputations much good to be caught lushing it up with the local Judas."

"Just as you say. What's on your mind?"

"This." Poker-faced, the Greek reached into his right-hand pants pocket and withdrew a wad of bills. He dropped them negligently on the coffee table. Matt caught the figure 100 on the outer bill under the rubber band binding the money into a wad. "There's three thousand in that," Cavanidis said. "You can count it if you want."

"What's that for?" Matt asked stupidly.

"You're buying a house. It takes money."

"But you've already dealt yourself out." Matt was puzzled, but beneath the bewilderment something else was taking form. Anger? He didn't know yet.

"That was for the peasants. In a bunch of scared blabber mouths like that, d'you think I'd be nuts enough to go along with something that every newspaper in the county is likely to have its hands on in a couple of days? Not me. I got to live and I intend to." Cavanidis spoke casually and did not again even glance at the roll of bills.

"Three thousand bucks is more than one share," Gold put in.

"I doubt it," Cavanidis said. "It may not even be a full share. You haven't seen any of Yale's money yet, have you?" He laughed shortly. "Don't hold your breath till you see it."

"That's a chance, of course. And you—any conditions on how we might use this?"

"Only one," Cavanidis said. His lips scarcely moved. "Just this—don't ever tell anybody where you got it. You ever try to hook that money to me—and I'll call you a liar." His eyes were slits.

Matt picked up the money and tossed it thoughtfully. He turned to Gold.

"What do you say, Zack? Does this square with what we're stuck with doing? Do we let a man pay his money but take a free ride every other way?"

The big man stared musingly at the impassive Greek.

"Sure, take it. It's money and money we're going to need." He paused, then nodded toward Cavanidis, his voice as toneless as the Greek's. "Any way you slice this, it's a mess. The least we can do is let a man pick his own way to get dirty."

Bronson's querulous voice cut through the uproar of the television set, a resentful squeak playing an obbligato to the announcer's enthusiastic baritone.

"You've had two weeks. Now you want more time. What do you think I am?"

"I don't want to go into that in detail," Matt snapped. His patience had worn thin while the television howled and the jeweler squirmed. He got up, walked to the set and switched it off. "Let's at least be able to hear each other," he said.

The jeweler watched him angrily, the hot eyes following him to the set and away from it.

"That's pretty highhanded—in a man's own house," Bronson said.

"Everything that goes on in this house is beginning to seem pretty highhanded," Matt snapped. It's dangerous to push this little rat around, he warned himself; easy does it, lad, easy does it.

"We're ready to set a closing date right now," Gold said. "And there"—he nodded at the money in Matt's hand, still wadded in

Cavanidis' rubber band—"is a binder to show we mean business. We're only asking a reasonable time to raise the rest. The stuff still doesn't grow on trees."

"I got the other people to think about," Bronson said evasively. "They're ready to close now."

"Two weeks ago you gave Matt and Sol to understand you were going no further with that deal," Gold said quietly. That Zack, Matt thought, he's a mountain of patience. I feel like wringing the little bastard's neck.

"I made no promise," the jeweler squealed. "They came here with nothing but talk. Now you are here and, except for that"—he bobbed his head at the money—"you still have nothing but talk."

"That's money. It takes time to raise it," Gold said. "You ought to know that better than anybody."

"You want me to wait forever? Don't tell me how it is with money! I know. And I know it's a good chance you can't raise it at all. Then what do I do? Shoot myself, maybe, and tell my wife first she should not forget to thank you all for the flowers at the funeral?"

"We'll have it in a week," Gold said doggedly.

"Meantime, what am I supposed to do about those people? Committees, phone calls, letters? Do I see any of you helping with them?"

"What people?" From weary irritation, Matt was suddenly alert.

"The organization people, of course." The jeweler's face and voice were hot with grievance. "Don't tell me you don't know they've been here?"

"No," Matt snapped. "I didn't. What's their pitch?"

"What would it be? Why don't I go through with the deal? Why am I waiting? They never stop—and do any of you people help with that? Ask me, go ahead ask me."

"Dave, I give you my word," Matt said, appalled, "I had no idea—none of us did—that they were after you."

"Why wouldn't they be?" Bronson complained. "That's what they're for—to hound people."

"I'm sorry to hear it," Matt said, "but if anybody invited them in, you did. If you'd never begun this damn foolishness, you wouldn't be getting pushed around now. Quit fiddling around."

"Well"—Bronson's eyes were crafty—"they don't talk promises. The money's ready."

"One week and our money will be ready," Gold said again.

"Promises, promises. What's to prove your word's any better now than it was two weeks ago?"

Slowly Gold rose from his chair and moved toward Matt. Watching him, Matt realized that some sudden and fearful transformation had come over the big man. He was still calm, but this was the wooden calm of fury. The forebearing patience at last had drained out of Zachariah Gold. He took the money from Matt's hand and turned toward Bronson, stopping in front of the jeweler's chair, where he seemed to tower ten feet tall.

"That," he said, dropping the money at Bronson's feet, his voice icy. "That proves it. Pick it up!" The command was brutal, slashing in its anger. He stood looking down at Bronson with a strange, cold stare. Fear glittered in Bronson's eyes, and he seemed to cringe into the chair, huddling into the protection of its depths.

Deliberately Gold put out his right hand and grasped the jeweler's throat, gathering shirt front and necktie into his great hand. He lifted Bronson up and, frozen, Matt watched the jerky contortions with which Bronson came upright until he seemed to dangle, with only his toes touching the rug. The act seemed effortless, but Matt saw the bunching and cording of muscle in the huge man's bare forearm. He heard the strain and rip of seam and cloth as Gold jerked his victim forward and held him still, eyes bulging and only inches from his own eyes.

"You creep." The calm of Gold's tone seemed incongruous against the brutality of his act. "You creep, I am tired and sick of listening to you. Now, listen to me."

Bronson flopped and gasped in Gold's grip.

"Shut up. I want you to listen. Do you know what is being said about you? I do. It is said that you do this because you are a Jew. I do not know whether you are a Jew, and it does not matter. It matters that it is said you are a Jew."

Gasping, Bronson tried to speak, but Gold held him as though hanged on a gibbet of steel.

"You malicious little bastard. You crybaby. You blackmailer. I am not calling you names—I am describing you."

Matt heard the croak of Bronson's struggle for breath. He felt frozen to his chair, fascinated and horrified.

"Shut up," Gold said softly. "I have not finished. You have done more than blackmail. You have poisoned this street. You have set neighbor against neighbor, Christian against Jew. The street reeks of you."

Gripped in a vise of flesh, the jeweler now hung quiet, staring up into the cold eyes behind their glasses.

"You have done more. You have brought shame and fear. We stink with your stink. You have found the stink in me, and I could kill you for it."

Abruptly the huge hand opened and Bronson fell back into the chair. Gold stood over him, looking down broodingly at the huddled figure. The sound of Bronson's rasping breath was loud in the room.

"There will be no more of this," Gold said quietly. "We close a week from tomorrow." He paused and turned to Matt. "You finish with him, Matt," he said. "He sickens me—I sicken myself." Gold turned and walked out into the night.

13

"I TOLD YOU I didn't want any part of the do-gooders in this business," Lamar Winter said coldly, eying the lanky, long-jawed man sprawled in a swivel chair with his feet on the scarred desk top. The desk, the chair, a bank of wooden filing cabinets and a liquor-store calendar displaying an astounding pair of breasts comprised the furnishings of the shabby office.

"I didn't call them in." Alexander Fox studied his caller under eyelids lowered far enough to forestall being studied in return.

"They're in," Winter said crisply. "Somebody did."

The broker, a wary man, stirred slightly and shrugged, delicately indicating mortal man's immunity to responsibility for acts of God.

"They deal themselves in sometimes," he said. "They watch things like this and they decide to move on their own. Nobody needs to call them in. To tell the truth"—his eyelids rose suddenly, and he gazed at the artist with such transparent lack of guile that Winter felt a conviction that Fox never did tell the truth if he could reasonably avoid it—"they just mess things up usually. Do-gooders." He drawled the word contemptuously. "They're more hurt than use."

"Well, let's deal them out," Winter said. "I don't want anybody messing this up. It's a straight proposition—there's a house for sale, and I want to buy it."

Fox considered his client thoughtfully. Somewhere at the back of his mind he felt the tug of resentment at the cavalier way Winter was treating him. Ordinarily Fox prudently refrained from making anything special of his own white skin in dealing with his clients; the special kind of service he was skilled at rendering was too delicate to permit any appearance of condescension. Still, he wasn't used to being condescended to either. Generally the people who needed his help and could afford to pay for it were so anxious that they seemed subconsciously to defer to him. But not this one. Still, he reminded himself, he was a businessman and no businessman worth his salt let personal touchiness stand in the way of a commission. He wondered how far he could go with this hard man without losing him.

"It's not simple," he said cautiously. "You have to keep that in mind. It's not simple."

"Nobody said it was," Winter said impatiently. "That's why I came to you."

"I thought we had him." Fox sighed. "But he's getting slippery on me. I admit that. It could be money . . ." He hesitated, having, by long habit, acquired a delicate hatred for talking bluntly about money: it scared too many people. You never knew when they would bolt, but then, he reflected, this one might be sterner stuff. He hadn't flinched yet at money talk.

"All right," Winter snapped. "Find out how much more."

"What if it isn't money?" Fox said, feeling his way with caution. "What else?"

"His neighbors. Those people can make it look pretty rough to Bronson . . . if they find out."

"Hell," Winter grunted. "You never thought they weren't going to find out, did you? I figured that long ago. That's what you're for—to figure a way around it." The artist's triangular, strong-jawed face had hardened. Fox saw and knew that he would have to choose his way with care: talk of money might not lose this man, but a confession of incompetence could lose him—and fast.

"You know, Mr. Winter, you're a tough man," the broker said carefully. "In some ways I'm a tough man too . . . as tough as I need to be. But . . . sometimes it isn't enough for just one or two men to be tough. There are times when you've got to go outside. . . ." He let it rest a moment, but Winter was not ready to let it rest.

"You're getting back to the organized helpers," he said shortly. "Don't try that back-door stuff with me."

"No, I'm not," Fox said with some haste. He brought his feet down from the desk and assumed an earnest look. "I told you they mess it up and I meant it." He studied his client anew and decided that he would have to come to it sooner or later. "You know a man named Francis Barton? Real-estate man?"

"No," Winter said, hesitated; began to look impatient. "I've got one broker—why do I need another?"

"It's a little different, Mr. Winter." Fox was being both earnest and modest. "You're just one and I'm just one. Barton's a specialist. Sometimes being tough and alone doesn't cut the ice that being tough and having company does."

"Let's have it, man. What's his pitch?"

"I guess if you had to call him something"—Fox had to go ahead now, and he wanted to and at the same time almost desperately wanted not to—"you'd probably call him a blockbuster."

Winter studied the broker narrowly, considering.

"So that's it," he said at last. "You want to call in the muscle." His eyes were glinting, and the mobile face wore such a look of malevolence that Fox hated to look at him; he could feel this slipping away again.

"No, no. Not muscle," Fox said hastily. "But consider this. Sometimes being alone—even if you're tough—isn't enough."

"Hmm." Winter had turned thoughtful, considering. "I don't like to lose," he said.

"I know that," Fox said. "You ain't the kind of man who loses easy. And I don't want you to lose."

"Natch. Ten per cent of thirty-six grand is thirty-six hundred dollars. Of course you don't want me to lose. Tell me how this Barton works."

"Depends. Persuasion, I guess you'd call it."

Winter snorted. "Persuasion is what the NAACP would call it. Reason. Justice."

"I think Barton might do better than that."

"Cut the double talk. How? What's his pitch?"

"Well," Fox said, feeling his way, "he might go see some of those people first. Jiggle them a little. Talk about the newspapers, maybe about the churches, their own consciences, look for the weak spots. There's always a weak spot, someplace, that'll give."

"Sounds kind of weird," Winter said. "This kind of thing do any good?"

"Sometimes a lot of good. The world may be changing faster than you think. And take my word for it, this man Barton's pretty effective when it comes to hurrying it along."

"What's he get out of it?" Winter asked abruptly.

"Mainly satisfaction; anyhow, that's what he says. Says he believes in it."

"Look," Winter said decisively. "I'm not sure I like this and I'm damn sure I don't like the way you weasel it. I'll go this far: you can talk to this Barton, get an idea, then let me know what he says."

"Sure, sure, I'll talk to him."

"But there's one thing." Winter's face was hard again, granite-like and malign in the dark sheen of skin taut over bone and muscle. "No muscle stuff. None. Not one goddam bit. I intend to live there, and I don't intend to move into a shambles. No rough stuff. You get it?"

"Yeah, yeah, I get it," Fox declared.

14

Jerry Gold and Bill Jones were sitting on the curb of the Outerbridge acre with Benjy Abram, who was trusted by them in most matters. They were almost in the shadow of the tunnel under the parkway cutoff and were, therefore, up to but not across the point of being off limits. In their nostalgia for a paradise no longer accessible, they had confided to Benjy the big secret of the island in Wacapo Lake. They were now discussing the feasibility of violating the interdiction placed on the island by the men who held themselves to be boss in the Gold and Jones families.

"Heck," Benjy said, "my dad wouldn't care. What're we waiting for?" The island and its tree-trunk bridge were news to Benjy, and the explorer's fever flamed within him.

"You say that because your dad doesn't know what you're thinking about," Jerry said out of hard-earned wisdom. "Wait'll you get paddled when he finds out."

"My dad doesn't paddle me," Benjy said with a certain air of superiority.

"Who does then?" Jerry said cynically.

"My mother," Benjy admitted. "But she's not so tough. Anybody can take her lickings."

"Mostly I get talked to," Bill said. "But I'd just about rather get tanned."

"Good gosh, why?" Jerry exploded, clearly regarding this as nonsense.

"When they tan you, they're sorry afterward and you can get about anything you want," Bill said reasonably. "But when they talk they never stop."

"Here comes the slob," Jerry said suddenly, jerking a warning thumb toward where a figure had appeared, pumping a bicycle slowly up the slope from the lower depths of the lane.

"Ugh," Bill said, freighting the word with disgust. He turned on Benjy with quick, fierce vehemence. "You keep your trap shut about the island, you hear!"

Paulie Cusack, big-boned and heavy for his thirteen years, the feared natural enemy of all his juniors on the lane, was aboard the bike. The three watched his approach warily, hoping he would pass. But he did not, and an instinctive uneasiness tightened their muscles for action as the bigger boy lazily swung his wheel toward them and dropped one foot to the pavement.

"What're you punks doing?" Paulie asked. Even when he was being good-natured they didn't need to be told that Paulie regarded them as vassals without rights.

"Nothin'," Bill said evasively. "Sittin'." There was always a chance that Paulie, disdaining them, would go on about his business and leave them in peace. The thing was not to pique his interest, if you could manage it. But this was not the day for it; Paulie was bored, and in boredom he was likely to become either playful or abusive, either of which the three smaller, slighter citizens of Peaceable Lane regarded as objectionable.

Paulie kicked down the stand of his bike and took a place in the row on the curb, hulking over the smaller boys. He looked up and down the lane cautiously, then took a long cigarette butt from his shirt pocket and lighted it with a dashing air. The three smaller boys watched with fascinated alarm, not unmixed with envy.

"Boy, you're crazy," Bill said. "What'll you do if your ma catches you?"

"She won't," Paulie said with confident superiority. "I smoke all the time."

"Broth-err!" Jerry said in awe. He, too, surveyed the lane furtively. "Can I take a puff?"

"You're too little, punk," Paulie said in disdain. "You'd just get sick and tell your mother, and she'd squawk to mine and I'd get blamed."

"I ain't either too little," Jerry said indignantly.

"You better look out anyhow," Bill said. "If old lady Bronson sees you, she'll tell your ma anyhow."

Paulie stared at the Bronson house across the street contemptuously.

"The hell with her. She won't tell because my mother won't even speak to her. Those nigger lovers!"

"Who's nigger lovers?" Benjy asked with the highly absorbent interest of being eight years old. "What's that mean, Paulie?"

"The Bronson's are nigger lovers," Paulie said. "They tried to sell their house to niggers. How'd you punks like that, living next door to niggers?"

"My dad won't let me say 'nigger,'" Jerry said, wearing a troubled look. "He heard me call our maid a nigger once, and that's the worst licking I ever got."

"He's crazy," Paulie said disdainfully. "Niggers are niggers, but anyway they're not going to move in here."

"What makes you so sure?" Benjy demanded. "You can't stop them if they want to."

"My dad can," Paulie said in superior confidence. "Even my mother can—she said she'd get the Bronsons put in jail."

"Haw!" Jerry snorted. "You said my dad's crazy, but your mother's the crazy one."

Paulie dropped the half inch of remaining cigarette into the gutter and, almost casually, reached out and took Jerry by the nape of the neck and then, with a vicious jerk, pulled the boy's head toward him and, with the other hand, pushed upward across Jerry's face from chin to eyebrows, flattening his nose.

"Don't talk about my mother, punk," he said.

Bunching his muscles, Jerry tore himself free and jumped to his feet. In hurt and fury the tears had started to his eyes, but when he spoke, his voice was tight and low and savage.

"You big slob," he grated. "Someday you'll get yours."

Bill, too, was now on his feet, moving instinctively to form a solid front with Jerry. His face was white and he was scared. It had, once again, come unexpectedly and with little warning, this casual callous cruelty of the older boy. But he knew there was nothing to do but face up to it; it was a battle he and Jerry had had to fight before, and he knew that they would probably, this time once again, lose it. But sometime they would win. Until that day came there was nothing they could do but avoid it when they could and fight it when fighting was inevitable.

Grinning confidently, Paulie stood up and moved toward them. "You asked for it, punks," he said easily. Suddenly he sprang and, though they tried to duck, he got them both by the neck and, ignoring their flailing arms and legs, pushed their faces together and rubbed them hard. Jerry's nose, which bled easily, began to spout, and Bill could taste the salt blood as it mixed with his own spittle. Through the pain and humiliation he heard Paulie's derisive laugh, and his mind went white-hot and blank with the will to murder.

Suddenly they were flung apart, falling onto the hard pavement, too consumed with fear and rage to be conscious of ripping cloth and the harsh scrape of the concrete on hands and knees. As they gathered themselves and vision cleared through the tears, they saw Paulie mounted on his bike, laughing back at them as he pedaled away. In blind fury Jerry started to pursue, then turned back and stared at Bill as the bike left him easily behind.

Bill stared back at him, face white, eyes hot with hate and resolution.

"Someday we're going to get that bastard . . . good!" Bill said, gritting out the words.

15

THE THING was taking shape, Matt reflected as he sat at the desk in the playroom Tuesday evening, going through the envelope with its sheaf of checks and Bronson's receipt for $3000. That had been Cavanidis' cash, and the accepting of it, he hoped now, had bound Bronson beyond escape or further squirming. There were two new checks now—Outerbridge's and Dr. Abram's—which Gold had left for him with Ellen, explaining that he and Beth were going out and could not wait until Matt got home. He had also left a note and now Matt frowned at it.

"Outerbridge wanted a receipt—naturally," Gold had written. "I gave him one. I expect John Ainslie is one man who can be trusted not to flash it around like a Purple Heart—though it is one, in a way. There's something else: I wouldn't want to say that Yale's trying to take a powder on us. But you ought to know that he's out of town—and left without saying anything about the money. His wife said he was called out in a hurry for some network chore in Washington—and maybe he was. She said he ought to be back this weekend. I hope he is, but you can make your own guesses."

Anyhow, it wasn't hard to guess what Zack thought; his belief that Yale was trying to slide from under was implicit in the note's sardonic phrasing. And Yale could be at that, Matt thought, remembering the commentator's rage. Now he wondered if it was just the money. He knew little of Yale's financial condition, but he supposed that Yale knew the pressing burdens common to all of them and that getting up $2000 would be as little fun for him as for anyone else. But there was something else about Yale. There, in the comparative privacy of the lane's people, he had been nearly as rancid as Laura Cusack in his objection to Negroes. But, it now occurred to Matt, Yale could have reasons as compelling as Cavanidis had for not getting involved here; a man who had made himself a crusader in causes where he had no personal stake might well fear being exposed as a conspirator in one in which he did.

But, if that was the case, why not say so? Cavanidis had said it boldly. True, he had come afterward and put up his money on the sly. At the thought of the Greek a faint smile tugged at Matt's mouth. You could probably—in justice—call Cavanidis a schemer, but all the same he had a kind of integrity, a cold, pirate's consistency in protecting his own interests—all of his interests at once when it was possible. It wasn't necessarily admirable, but you couldn't help respecting the case-hardened toughness of the Greek's fiber. This thing of Yale's, this slinking out, was something else. He didn't like the taste of it and, Matt acknowledged to himself, he didn't like Yale either.

Oh well, he thought, if Yale was indeed pulling a sneak, there wasn't much they could do about it. They had no claim on him beyond the lane's agreement to defend itself—and that could not be held binding on him. They could make it without him. They had Cavanidis' money, and that gave them a cushion. Now, if Yale had run for cover, they were only back where they had been when Cavanidis had made his grandstand withdrawal.

There were six checks now, his own and Zack's, Weissman's—

the first to come in—Dr. Abram's and John Ainslie Outerbridge's and that curiously pathetic half payment from Jerome Kelly. He recalled uncomfortably the apologetic manner with which the dentist had asked him to wait for the rest.

"I don't like to do it this way, Matt," Kelly had said almost pleadingly. "But if you'll take this much now, I think I may be able to raise the rest from Claire's people by the end of the week." The check had been for $1,057.50, and Kelly saw the surprise and curiosity with which Matt noted the odd figure. "I had to unload the kids' war bonds," he said wretchedly.

Matt thought that almost any other man would have settled on the round figure of a thousand and held the rest back, but he knew that for a man with Kelly's conscience it would have been unthinkable to withhold a penny. "I hate to put this on Claire's folks," Kelly went on. "But, honest to God, I don't know where else to turn."

"I know, Jerry. None of us likes it. But we seem to be stuck with it."

"Stuck is the word," Kelly had said.

Once again Matt was trying to come to grips with himself and with the issue. He was still plagued by a sense of unreality, still having difficulty believing that he was actually involved in an expensive and questionable conspiracy. It was embarrassing to remember, too, the means by which he himself had raised his share of the money. Literally taking Yale's sneering advice to read the car cards offering the New York Central's upcounty commuters easy credit, it made him uncomfortable to recall his awkward explanation to the loan-company official that he needed the money for home improvement. It was true, but not entirely true, and, anyhow, how would you go about explaining to a professionally cheery credit manager that the precise way you wanted to improve your home was to keep a colored man you didn't know from moving next door?

You don't need to have any illusions about it, he thought. He was scared; they were all scared. That was the only thing that could have driven them to it. And, he acknowledged, with a community like the lane—ridden by the manifold demands of mortgages, taxes, school bills, dancing classes, piano teachers, the endless proliferating avalanche of bills that smothered all of them alike—they would have had to have the bejesus scared out of them to measure it at a price of $2000 each, cash on the barrelhead. It had to be fear.

But what exactly was it that they feared? It hadn't been the money alone; he knew that. Was it Negroes as such? Would he really, if that were the only issue, object to living next door to a Negro? He had never had to think about that problem; indeed, until these last few weeks, the very idea that he might have to think about it would have been unthinkable. Now he liked to think that he wouldn't care, that the color of a man's skin made no difference in the essence of the man. But was he so sure at bottom? Was there in him, hidden so deep that he honestly didn't know it was there, a primitive, atavistic revulsion? Was it possible he would feel, perhaps, a little tainted, a little degraded, imposed on and resenting it?

He shook his head angrily and fanned out the checks on the desk. No, he thought, if the revulsion was in him, it probably had to be something he had learned unconsciously. It couldn't have been inherited. He thought of his boyhood in Wyoming, on the ranch in the foothills of the Rockies—the space so empty that no man would have found it possible to believe another man's nearness could press upon him, be resented, be anything other than welcome. There had been one colored boy in his class in high school, son of the man who doubled as porter and bootblack in the town's one hotel. But now he could find no remembrance of prejudice against the color of Sam Bates's skin. Indeed, he remembered, the colored boy had been less of a curiosity than the blind, albino white girl who, though forced to live and learn in the black world of Braille, had come out at the end the class valedictorian.

If what was in him now was, unknown to him, the secret detestation of another human's pigmentation, it had to be something he had learned since, soaked up in the cities where his profession had brought him.

It had to be a product of cities. And yet he could not recall anything about the cities he had lived in which might have sunk the hot iron of hate into him. When they were first married and he had gone to work for Macmillan Associates, he and Ellen had lived on Chicago's near north side, on Astor Street. He knew, of course, that a colored "problem" existed in Chicago, and he knew that one of the infected areas lay only a few streets away in the soot-grimed jungle along the car tracks on Wells and Franklin. It had moved stealthily, with the grinding pressure of human blood and nerve and sinew, until it had reached, in his time, as far toward the lake and sunlight as LaSalle. But it had not touched him personally and, he thought he could say confidently, had not infected him. And yet, he ought to remember, it was in Chicago that he had come to know the meaning of the words "blue" and "jig" and learned—maybe this was the dangerous thing—to accept them casually.

Oh hell, he thought, let's try to keep this simple. It had seemed simple enough, and he had thought he was responding to an exact, calculable necessity: the necessity of measuring two thousand dollars against ten thousand. Where was it complicated? The problem here was not a man, not a family, not one set of nerves and fibers and ambitions which might or might not clash with his own. The enemy was disembodied, faceless, shapeless, even colorless, only tangible enough to be calculated on an adding machine—the simple difference between ten thousand dollars and two.

Ellen came down the steps from the main floor and put an opened bottle of beer, frosty with cold, on the desk before him. He looked at her and smiled, pleased, as always, by the clean handsomeness of his wife. Youth and freshness seemed to cling to Ellen and, even after fifteen years together, it still made him glad to be with her. She frowned as she looked at the checks.

"How many more?" she asked.

"Three. Draper, Cusack . . . and Yale. Only Zack thinks Yale is trying to get out of it."

"Why would he?"

"I can think of several reasons. The most likely one is simple—money."

"I wouldn't think he would dare. After all, they live here. I wouldn't think—if he did that—he could look the rest of us in the face afterward—or Annabelle either."

"I'm not real sure any of us are going to be able to look ourselves in the face right away."

"I know. Why did it have to happen?" Her eyes were unhappy.

"I don't know." He sighed. "It does seem to have the earmarks of a dirty trick, doesn't it?"

"It all seems dirty. I keep wondering if we're doing the right thing. I know it's necessary and that we can't do anything else. But it all seems so messy. I don't know what I mean; it's so—so uncivilized. Everybody on the street upset and nervous and angry and suspicious of each other."

The doorbell rang. Matt started up, but Ellen was already on her feet, looking surprised.

"I'll get it," she said. "I wonder who . . ."

A moment later, her voice calling his name brought Matt to his feet, startled by the thin note of urgency and alarm. He almost ran across the room and up the steps. He found her standing in the hall, one hand on the latch of the screen door, as though unconsciously barricading the portals of her home. Two men were standing beyond the door, bareheaded under the porch lights. Matt saw that they were Negroes. He moved to the door, putting himself between Ellen and the men.

"Yes?" he said, trying to keep the stiffness out of his voice.

"You're Mr. Jones?" the taller and older of the two men asked. He was heavy, almost portly, and probably in his fifties. He wore a dark suit and, despite the heat of the night, a vest across which sparkled the links of a heavy gold watch chain. The smaller, younger man had a thin, curious face, a nervously smiling face with restless eyes behind thick spectacles.

"Who are you?"

"I am Francis Barton, an attorney," the older man said. His voice was dignified. "This is Edward Smith. Here is my card—this is a professional call."

This is it, Matt thought with a thrill of apprehension. It was an effort to keep his voice level.

"What can I do for you?" he asked guardedly.

"I think you know, Mr. Jones," the big man said calmly. "There is a matter we have come to discuss with you. It concerns the Bronson house. May we come in?"

The thought flashed in Matt's mind that he could refuse them entrance, and he was tempted to do so. But instantly he warned himself that barring them would be both churlish and childish.

Wasn't it better, if this was the face of the enemy, to know what went on behind the face? But watch yourself, lad, watch yourself, he thought as he swung the door open. He led them into the living room and indicated chairs.

"If you will state your business, Mr. Barton," he said cautiously. Unsmiling, but composed and seemingly at ease, the Negro studied Matt a moment before replying.

"We understand that you represent a syndicate and that you propose to buy the Bronson house."

"Not a syndicate," Matt said flatly, lying because he felt that he must, and feeling resentfully that this stranger had no right to force him into lying. "I am buying it. Mr. Gold, an attorney on this street, represents me."

"So?" The big face was expressionless. "If you choose to pretend that you are alone, I cannot prevent you. May I ask you, why are you buying it?"

Resentment tugged at Matt's mind again, but he put it down. Take it easy, take it easy, he thought.

"I could say that my reasons are private," he said levelly. "I'll say this much—I'm buying it as an investment."

"So?" The big man studied him again, and Matt felt the stir of uneasiness under that calm inspection. "Would it be fair to say that by 'investment' you mean you are hoping to maintain or enhance the value of this house"—the big man glanced around the pleasant room—"by preventing a colored man from moving into the one next door?"

Once more anger stirred in Matt, but he checked it. He realized that he was being deliberately invited to lose his temper.

"You said that, not I," he said shortly.

"Yes, I said it. But believe me, I am not inexperienced. It serves no purpose to lie to me, and to do so merely affronts my dignity as well as your own. I know that you are not alone. I also know that a man in your position does not, as a rule, buy houses as investments. If I may say so without offense, I doubt if you could afford it."

The smaller man, who had been sitting silent, his eyes darting here and there in the room, snickered, then abruptly fell silent.

"You're pretty careless with your words," Matt said stiffly.

"No, not careless," Barton said. "I merely sought to bring the sparring to an end. We will only get somewhere when we begin to speak frankly. I urge you to do so."

"I don't want to be offensive either," Matt said. "But you will forgive me if I say that I fail to see how my intention to buy this house is your business. You spoke of getting somewhere—where, precisely, do you hope to get?"

"That's better," Barton said with unemotional approval. "I hope to persuade you of the truth of several things. First, I hope to persuade you that your fears are groundless. A Negro moving into the Bronson house will not, unless it drives you people to panic, reduce the value of your properties. I hope to persuade you that my interest is as much in your behalf as in that of the prospective Negro buyer. I hope to persuade you, if you persist in going through with this purchase, to, in turn, sell it to the Negro who wishes to buy it—perhaps at a profit, instead of at the loss you will otherwise take. Finally, I hope to persuade you that if you go through with this act, as you now plan it, you will surely regret it."

Matt studied the man. Here, he thought, was a pretty impressive figure. He wondered whether this man himself was the person who had tried to buy Bronson's house, to live in it? With wry amusement he wondered whether, for a neighbor, he wouldn't have preferred this man to Bronson. This one is no slouch, he thought; this one is in the major leagues. Aloud, measuring his words, he said, "Is the last of your 'persuasions' a threat?"

"Not entirely. It is a threat only in that it represents an experienced prediction. You will regret it, first, within yourselves. This is a community of educated, sophisticated and, I hope, largely intelligent persons. I suspect that, even now, you are moved to this act with reluctance, with some shame. I warn you, the shame will not grow less. The times are not what they were. Overt acts of racial discrimination are no longer acceptable in the light of public opinion. You will be criticized by your own world—the white world." Barton smiled. "I know that you will think this criticism—in a church perhaps—is unfair, because you will feel that the preacher, who is not himself being hurt, has no right to speak against you because he doesn't know what he is talking about. You will think that it is not his ox being gored. And you will be right.

But being right won't silence him—or others. The world is cruel, Mr. Jones, and its level of understanding other men's fears is a low one. My people knew that a long time before your people began to have occasion to find it out.

"Also, the act you propose, if not itself illegal, comes close to it. It offends the spirit of the law which has already ruled against discrimination in schools and in public housing. Then there is the matter of the press. Here again, it will be your ox being gored, but to the newspapers it will be just another story—one that you will not like to read or to be read by others. No, Mr. Jones"—Barton sighed—"I must tell you this. You can't get away with it."

"You mean you propose to sic the newspapers on us?" Matt asked, now with no feeling of anger, more in curiosity at this man's monumental assurance.

"If it becomes necessary, yes. There are also other means, less palatable, but useful in times of necessity. You would not like them. We hope it will not be necessary to use them. Believe me, I greatly prefer to convince you of the truth that you are acting against your own interest and that your fears, which I will grant are genuine, are groundless."

"I don't think you're going to get far trying to bulldoze me," Matt said. "I don't share your conviction that my fears are groundless."

"They are, and I am prepared to prove it. Doesn't it stand to reason that a man capable of paying Bronson more than this house is worth would not be likely to let it turn into a slum? Run a policy wheel there, perhaps? Sell marijuana? A whorehouse? Throw gin bottles on the lawn? Rape his neighbors' wives and corrupt their children? Surely that is not what you apprehend?"

Matt grinned in spite of himself.

"No, I don't think anybody expects that exactly. But aren't you getting off the point?"

"Oh," Barton said, comprehending, "you mean the property values. That bogey has no foundation. We can prove that, in cases where Negroes have moved into all-white communities and where the whites have not yielded to panic, property values have not gone down. Believe me, the Negro who wishes to buy the Bronson house is not a fool. He would not be stupid enough to invest a good many thousand dollars in something which would immediately become worth many thousand dollars less. Would you like to know who he is? I can tell you."

For a moment Matt allowed temptation to tug at him. It would be interesting to know the man's name and description, to have the faceless enemy reduced to human terms. But, no, he thought, what would be served? If he was going to fight him—in a fight which he acknowledged to himself was something less than admirable—wasn't it better to keep him faceless?

"No, I think not," he said. "Since I'm not likely ever to meet him, I don't think I'm curious about his name."

"That may be another error. Having made the one, you and your neighbors seem bent on compounding it."

"That may be, but I doubt it. If your man is such a substantial citizen, why doesn't he come out here himself instead of, to put it bluntly, hiding behind your skirts? This business of yours, using the big stick on us, would be extremely unlikely to increase the guy's popularity around here."

"I doubt if he would come here either seeking or expecting neighborhood popularity."

"That's what baffles me. Knowing that he's likely to be disliked, why in bloody hell would he even contemplate moving here? What kind of a man do you have to be to deliberately surround yourself with people who will hate your guts?"

"Tell me, why did you move here?"

"That's easy—because neither my wife nor I can stand cities. But I don't see where that applies."

"Don't you? Isn't it conceivable to you that our man, too, might dislike living in a city? Do you imagine that a liking for fresh air, sun, space, trees, grass and flowers is the exclusive province of souls wrapped in white skin?"

"No-o-o. I didn't say that. But I still can't understand a man who, in order to get those things, is both willing to damage his potential neighbors with a heavy financial penalty and, in turn, accept the penalty of their resentment."

"You won't see, will you? You will not believe that the financial penalty is a figment of superstition. You will not understand that a man might be willing to risk your temporary displeasure in order to claim his fundamental rights as a human being."

"What makes you think my displeasure would be temporary?"

"Because, inevitably, you would begin to get over it once you saw it demonstrated that he was not here to injure you. Maybe this will convince you: I would not pretend that our people are more tolerant, more moral, more sensitive to the rights of other men than you are. One of the compelling reasons why this man wants to move here is to get away from Negroes, from colored slums. This is an attitude we understand and, although we do not condone it, we are willing to help him—even though his intent is selfish—because every Negro moved into a better community makes it easier for the next one.

"No, this man is not coming here to destroy Peaceable Lane. Just the opposite. Indeed, if he comes and then if, in panic, several of you sell to Negroes and the street begins to deteriorate, our man will be the first to move again."

"Doesn't that make him something of a sonofabitch, even in your eyes?"

The portly Negro smiled gently.

"Nobody pretends that being a sonofabitch is the exclusive prerogative of the whites."

"Well," Matt said with finality, "it fails to increase my enthusiasm for having him next door. We're wasting one another's time."

"You're just asking for it, white man." Matt turned to look at the slender young man whose voice, shrill and malevolent, was now raised for the first time. Matt eyed him, feeling the anger rise in himself, fighting to keep it down.

"I told you before that I don't like threats," he said. "Mr. Barton, I don't think we have anything more to say. I'll have to ask you to take this junior-size bad man and get out of here."

The portly man rose, a monument of calm.

"I had hoped you would be amenable to reason. Since you have chosen otherwise, I regret it. I must say to you once more, you, too, will regret it."

"It's time to go," Matt said thinly.

16

On Wednesday, Matt met Paul Cusack for lunch at Billy the Oysterman's downtown. Beyond a perfunctory hello, they were silent until they were seated at one of the bare tables in the dark, old-fashioned dining room. Already curious about Cusack's request which had brought him so far from his normal midtown haunts for lunch, Matt noted that an air of unease was showing through the banker's usual reserve. Cusack's well-manicured fingers tapped on the table top while they waited for the first round of pale martinis and, when he lighted a cigarette, he began nervously folding and refolding the book of matches.

"What's on your mind, Paul?" Matt asked, as the drinks were set down and they had taken the first icy sips off the top.

"That mess out at the lane, naturally," Cusack said. "A couple of things. One—I have the money here. Would have had it sooner if I could. But something else I want to chew over with you—I wonder what we've got ourselves into."

"Why, what's different?"

"I don't know exactly. That's the trouble."

"I don't think anybody is easy in his mind about it. But you know what we all—or most of us—thought. We have to do it."

"Oh, I know that, all right." Cusack's voice was impatient. "But somebody's fooling around with it, and I don't like it."

"What do you mean?"

Cusack took a deep breath, almost a gulp.

"Laura called me right after I got to the office. She got a phone call. The dirty bastards!" Cusack looked angry and baffled and, Matt realized, fearful.

"What happened?" Matt was puzzled, but underneath, he realized, he somehow knew what it would be.

"I couldn't make much sense out of what she said—she was hysterical. But I gathered he had her mesmerized. She just held onto the phone and listened, probably with her mouth open, until he hung up."

"Who was it? What'd he say?"

"How do I know who he was? But he let her have it. Called her everything he could think of, the real low-down four-letter words."

Matt looked at Cusack with concern, feeling the rise of anger and—yes, in him too—fear. He remembered the slender young man with the malign, shifting eyes behind thick glasses.

"It could have been a nut. What was said about the house—anything?"

"That's the baffling part. Nothing was said about the house. You know how he finished? He said as long as I was away, he was coming over and give her a screw she would remember. For Christ's sake! You know Laura—not even a nut would be nutty enough to want to screw her."

Cusack stared at him, baffled, almost accusing. Despite the outrage welling up in him, Matt felt a small, guilty jolt of delight at the macabre image of Laura Cusack, thin, bitter, sexless, physically as unattractive as he thought a woman might manage to be, getting propositioned over the telephone.

"Do you really think it was the house, Paul?"

Cusack stared at him, anger and apprehension fighting behind his eyes.

"Don't you?"

"Yes," Matt admitted. "It probably was. There'll probably be more of it."

"We'll have to put a stop to it."

"How?"

"Christ's sake! A man has rights, doesn't he? You don't have to put up with that kind of abuse. What right have they got to mess with it? I'll tell you what I'm going to do. I'm going to call in the police."

Matt sighed, feeling helpless, half pitying and half angry at Cusack's impotence.

"You can't police the telephone lines, Paul."

"The hell you can't. They can put a bug on my line and trace any call that comes in."

"If they call from a pay phone, and they probably do, it'll do a fat lot of good to trace a call."

Cusack slammed one fist down on the table, causing the martini glasses to jump and tinkle.

"I wish I knew how far they're ready to go. One sure thing, I think we got to go to the county or state police and get a full-time patrol in the lane until this is finished. If they'll pull a thing like they did on Laura, they'll probably do anything."

The afternoon became a nightmare for Peaceable Lane and the rest of the week grew worse by the hour. The telephones rang repeatedly. An incongruous terror ran through the pleasant houses in their sylvan setting. Sometimes, when the receiver was lifted, the line would seem dead until the listener became aware of a soft, panting breath, unspeakably menacing. Sometimes voices came over the wire, gruff or cold, abusive, scornful, and sometimes, perhaps worst of all, came a peal of high, jeering laughter. In one house, the Cusacks', the telephone shrilled every quarter hour until Laura, beginning in fury but at last reduced to shuddering terror, ripped the instrument from the wall with the convulsive strength of hysteria.

In fear or fury the wives called their husbands. Each train, through the early afternoon, brought more of the men home. Matt reached Chappaqua on the 4:32, tense with nameless foreboding. Unwilling to wait for the bus, he took a taxi and leaned forward on the edge of the seat, urging haste, until the driver lost patience with him.

"Take it easy, Mac," the driver said. "We'll get there if you'll leave me be. You wanta get us both killed?"

The house stood serene and lovely, garlanded in the scarlet of climbing roses, drowsing in the golden light of early evening. He hadn't known what to expect, but he had known that he was afraid. The serenity was deceptive, he knew, when Ellen met him at the door. She was composed, but her gray eyes revealed the strain.

"They called you?" he demanded.

"Twice. Matt, it was . . . unbelievable!"

Rage tore at him, corrosive in his helplessness.

"What was said?" His throat felt tight and his jaws stiff, so that it was hard to get the words out.

"There's no use repeating it. Anyhow, I couldn't . . . don't want to." It was almost a wail, but she got herself under control. "Matt, do you think there'll be more?"

"I don't know. I'm going over and talk to Zack. Try to figure out what to do."

When the big man came to the door, his wife Beth, dark and pretty, a *zoftik* girl whose eyes shone with recent tears, came with him, and Matt saw that Gold was holding her hand.

"They're after us, Zack," he said. "Now what?"

"They can't kill us with a telephone," Gold said grimly.

"They can hurt us though. How do we fight it?"

"We can't—except by keeping the girls and the kids away from it. If they try something more than the telephone, they'll be in trouble. We can get our hands on them then. Anyhow, it's only three more days. We close Saturday, and then they're licked."

"We could cave in. Do you want to? Do you think anybody else does?"

The big man's face was set and the eyes, behind their owlish spectacles, were cold.

"I might have been willing to back out before—for other reasons; you know what they were. But not now. I'll see them in hell before I quit now. And I'll see that nobody else does either." It was, Matt knew, a savage, solemn promise.

"I don't see how we can hold anybody who wants to bolt."

"Oh yes, we can." Gold's voice was hard. "The deal's in our hands, yours and mine. And the checks are certified. They'll have to ride it whether they like it or not."

"I got Cusack's check today. But there's still Draper—and Yale."

"No, only Yale. I came home as soon as Beth told me what was going on. I stopped in White Plains and nailed Draper down. I was afraid he'd turn jumpy if I didn't get to him before they did. Good thing I thought of it too." A thin smile tugged at Gold's lips.

"Why?"

"It wasn't more than an hour later he was out here, scared white and wanting out. Shirley had got a call threatening to beat her up. I tried to talk some backbone into him. Maybe it didn't work, but it doesn't matter. Here, I'll get you his check."

The telephone rang, and Matt saw Beth gasp and pale as she turned toward the summons.

"Don't, Beth," Gold snapped. "Stay off that phone. I'll take it."

Tautly Matt watched the big man lumber across the kitchen

and lift the receiver from the hook and heard him say calmly, "Yes?"

He stood there, impassive, listening. Across the room, reduced to an incomprehensible cackling by distance and the muffling of being held against Gold's ear, came the sound of a voice. There were no words to be distinguished, but Matt knew what it was: the confused gabble came hoarse and thick with the feeling of hate. Softly, almost gently, Gold put the receiver back on the hook.

He took his wife's hand gently and patted it.

"You see, Beth? It's just a telephone and a voice. Only I don't want you to answer it. I'll be home until Saturday."

Like others in the lane, Matt stayed at home until Saturday. The telephones continued to ring, and Paul Cusack, who had had the instrument repaired that morning, stood guard over it. Now when it rang he leaped for it and raged back savagely at the tormenting voice. His violence brought only a jeer of laughter, but he could not bring himself to ignore the endlessly repeated summons to abuse. He asked the Chappaqua police to monitor his line, but each effort to trace a call led only to the blank, unidentifiable cul-de-sac of a pay booth.

It was sometime after midnight Thursday. At first, shocked from sleep into consciousness, Matt did not know what had awakened him. Then he became aware of a hideous, ululating blare of sound and, his heart thudding in response to the unknown, he was out of bed and on his feet, fumbling for shoes and trousers. He was aware of Ellen, tense and cold beside him, reaching for him.

"What is it?" she breathed. "Oh, Matt!"

"Go stay with Bill!" he commanded. "No, first I'm going out. Lock the door behind me."

In the hall he grabbed up the old putter he kept behind the door for back-yard practice and then he was out, half naked, stepping into a crazy cacophony of noise. It was a moonless, starless night, but now he could make out the bulk of autos passing in front of the house, one after the other, lightless, moving slowly. Their horns were blaring, and from somewhere among them came an inhuman screech of human voices.

The cars were passing now, the din moving on down the lane.

Vaguely he could see bits of white fluttering from them. He started across the lawn, but now the blast of noise was returning, swelling again to an insane bellow. The cars, nearly unseen, had turned the circle and were coming back. The pent-up pressures of these two days of standing helpless under the torrent of telephoned abuse broke through. He was suddenly, savagely glad, eager now to give battle to a tangible enemy. He ran toward the street, his fists locked on the steel shaft of the putter. The first dimly seen car came abreast as he ran into the street. He felt the exultant, wordless roar of his own voice as he swung the club and heard the brittle crash of breaking glass. The car stopped.

Matt felt, rather than clearly saw, its doors swinging open and half-seen figures spilling out. Suddenly he was engulfed in a bewildering, surging wall of human flesh. He reeled under a blow, blinding hard, against the side of his head, and the salt taste of blood welled in his mouth. Then the blows came from all sides, a battering, smothering rain of violence. He struggled to get free to swing the putter's steel blade. Agony knifed into him as a hard knee came up into his crotch. Then he was down in the street and he felt himself going under as a heavy foot smashed against his temple.

He was fighting back toward consciousness as the last car passed him and, wallowing to his feet, he had started after it when he felt an arm go around him and take up his sagging weight.

"Let 'em go, Matt! Let the filthy bastards go!" It was Gold.

Friday morning, early, Annabelle Yale telephoned her husband in Washington. Yale's voice, at 7:00 A.M., was quarrelsome, but Annabelle was in no mood to submit to captiousness.

"Peter, you've got to come home. Right away," she said.

"Come home! What for? You know I can't come home until this job's finished. Why the fuss?"

"Matt Jones was beaten up last night, here in the lane."

"Beaten up? What's it got to do with me? Who beat him up?"

"Peter, listen to me! He was beaten up by a gang that came here and filled the street with leaflets attacking everybody on this street—by name—for buying the Bronson house."

"Jesus Christ, Annabelle, what the hell am I supposed to do about it?"

"Peter! Our names are on that list too."

"Damn the lane! Why did you have to drag us out there to live anyhow?"

"Peter! And there's something else. You listen to me and get back here fast, because you're in this as deep or deeper than anybody. People have been getting these telephone calls. I got one last night and it was for you personally."

"Well, what was it?" Yale's voice was tight with anxiety.

"They said it was a reminder. They said you shouldn't forget your contract with the network comes up for renewal in eight weeks. Is that true, Peter?"

For a long while there was no reply and Annabelle Yale waited, knowing what her husband would look like, sitting there on the edge of his hotel bed in Washington, shaken, scared and bitterly resentful.

"Annabelle, listen to me and get this straight! First, I'm not coming back until that business is finished. No, I tell you, listen and don't argue. I'm not coming back, not, repeat, not! I tell you, damn it, don't argue and listen. If you get another phone call—listen to me now—you talk back and tell them I—I mean we—have nothing to do with this deal. We're against the deal, see?"

"Peter, you can't. You're in it too. You promised." She had finally squeezed her protest into the rush of his demands.

"Don't be a damn fool! Promised, my ass. Do you want to starve? How long do you think I'm going to last with the network if I'm pinned with this thing? Now, listen, and do what I tell you. Oh, that lousy, lousy, stinking street—your stinking street!"

At noon Friday, stiff in every muscle, still gut sick from the blow at his genitals, wearing a bloody scrape across his face, Matt found the card left behind by Francis Barton and called his Manhattan number. Dialing the number, he asked for Barton and, after a brief wait, heard the measured voice courteously asking after his health.

"You probably know my state of health as well as or better than I do," Matt said. "I'm just calling you to let you know that I am buying the Bronson house tomorrow and that I do not, from here, see how you can stop me. Maybe it's giving you more of a break than you deserve, but just in case you think you can still do it, there's a state patrol car in front of my house, another at Bronson's, and two county radio cars are patrolling the area on twenty-four-hour shifts. That doesn't leave you much but the telephone, does it, Mr. Barton?"

"No, I agree with you, Mr. Jones." The voice was still calm, unemotional, courteous. "It may have been an error. There was not enough margin. It is possible that we tried to do too much in too little time. I regret your injuries, Mr. Jones, and I wish you a speedy recovery."

With a soft click the line went dead.

17

THOUGHTFULLY, absently fingering the ring of keys that symbolized possession of No. 1 Peaceable Lane, Matt stood with Zack Gold at his driveway entrance Saturday afternoon, watching a moving crew load the last of Bronson's possessions into a van. The lane wore an unwonted air of quiet. No children played in the street or on the lawns and no others, either men or women, were visible outside the houses except Matt and his big silent companion and the movers. Bronson and his wife were already gone. They had driven away in the Buick as soon as the packers had arrived.

It was finished. But the street had been changed. It had felt the iron of fear and hate and, though Bronson was gone, he had left his brand on them. Instinctively the people of the lane kept indoors and, by some indefinable reluctance, kept apart from one another. They had been in it together; they had risked and endured and won out together, but the ordeal had, instead of binding them close in spirit, driven them apart. Here, each one sensed, they had been exposed to a malignant infection and now, each sensing the disfiguring and destroying stain in the other, they shunned contact. Even the children had felt it.

Their faces were somber as they watched the crew foreman close the van doors and the truck moved away.

"Well, let's go over and give it a look," Matt said as the van grumbled up the ramp toward the parkway cutoff. "Not that we'll be able to do much about it if he decided to kick in the plaster or take a hammer to the furnace just for a reminder. But we have to lock it up and we might as well look."

"Yes." Gold sighed. "Let's wrap it up."

They found the house bare, wearing an air of desolation. It is strange, Matt thought, how a house once lived in but then stripped of its furnishings has the shabby, derelict feel of a dead man's clothes, empty, shapeless and lifeless, but still marked by the comings and goings and habits of the dead. There were cigarette burns in the worn carpet beside the indentations left by a heavy chair, and Matt remembered that Bronson had been a chain smoker. With something like surprise, Matt noted that the brick lining of the fireplace was as white as when new; clearly no fire had ever been lighted there, and somehow that sign of exclusion from use seemed pathetic. It was, he thought, almost an instinct with man that he should make a place his own by lighting a fire within it. Though Bronson had owned this house for eight years, somehow he had never taken possession of it, never really settled into it as his own.

"It'll need a coat of paint and I guess we might as well have that carpet ripped out. It's pretty far gone," Gold said appraisingly. "Otherwise they left it in pretty good shape. No damage anyhow. I don't know whether I'm surprised or not."

"He left quietly enough," Matt acknowledged. "Maybe the bastard wasn't so bad after all. He had his troubles, God knows."

"Yes," Gold said somberly. "But he left his mark on us all the same. The thing I hate having to remember is that he opened up the weakness and meanness in all of us. He's gone and I don't have to despise him any more. I wish I could say the same for myself."

"Get the monkey off your back," Matt said shortly. Because Gold was his friend and he knew that he was a good man as well, Matt hated to see him troubled. There was no question about the goodness, he thought; Zack was a big man in more than mere physical size; he radiated warmth and generosity and a tolerant regard for his fellow men. But, though Matt knew Gold's distaste for what they had done was deeply and sorrowfully felt, he knew he did not understand it, and because he did not he was impatient with it.

"Look," he went on, "you said it yourself once—sometimes you have to make a choice. The choice this time was simple. Here was a guy who was out to do us in, and we stopped him from it. That's all we needed to know about him."

"Was it? We knew he was a man too. It isn't what man he was but the fact that he was a man. I don't really care a damn who he was. What bothers me is that I helped deny a man his right to live where he wants to."

"Oh, balls, Zack. Does any goon have a right to go where he wants to, just because he wears pants and walks on his hind legs? It was a fight, yes, but remember this, it was the other side that fought dirty—not us."

"Maybe." Gold sighed. "I'd like to think that. I don't know, Matt. Maybe I'm wrong; I hope so."

"I know one thing," Matt grunted. "If I ever did have any conscience about this, getting kneed in the nuts jarred it out of me."

"I wonder if there'll be any more of that?" Gold mused.

"I dunno. I'm going to stick around home the first part of the week—just in case. But I think they're finished. At least with the rough stuff."

They checked the locks throughout the house, let themselves out by the front door and started up the drive in the breathless quiet of the late afternoon. Except for the squawking of the jays high in the trees and the sibilant hum of cars on the cutoff, the day was silent.

"Quiet, isn't it?" Matt said. "It's uncanny. Not even a kid bellowing."

"That's another thing he left us," Gold said. "I know this feeling and I expect you do too. I got it first early in the war. I was a reserve j.g., a red-assed junior gunnery officer on a cruiser when Halsey made his first strike at the Marshall Islands. Never been shot at before and couldn't have imagined what it would be like.

We stirred 'em up and then had to take two hours of bombing. Scared liquid, scared yellow. And, when they finally let up on us, it was like this. You hardly knew whether to breathe or light a cigarette for fear it would bring them back. And, knowing how scared you had been, you hardly dared look at anybody else for fear he'd see it in you. And you didn't want to see it in him, either."

Matt found Bill in the playroom, sprawled in a chair, aimlessly fiddling with a pitcher's glove, his eyes vacant with the occasional utter supine emptiness of youth. The depression had closed over them all, even as Gold had said, including the kids. Remembered anger stirred in him.

"Come on, skipper, snap out of it," he said with false heartiness. "How about a swim?"

"Naw, don't feel like it," the boy mumbled.

"Come on, kid. This isn't the Johnny Weismuller I know. Get your trunks on."

"Unh, unh, Pop." Bill squirmed and scuffed a foot back and forth on the tile floor. "It wouldn't be any fun."

"Brother." Matt sighed. "That's a brand-new attitude on your part."

The boy looked up at him and, with a kind of delayed shock, Matt recognized the fear and unhappiness in the boy's eyes.

"Pop?" The boy hesitated and then plunged into it. "I'd rather stay in the house. I don't want to be outside and maybe the niggers might come back."

The word struck Matt like a blow.

"What did you say?"

"I'm afraid of the niggers," the boy confessed miserably. "I don't want to go out."

"Bill, Bill," Matt said earnestly, "where did you get that word?"

"Mom," the boy said. "When Mr. Gold brought you in the house and we were waiting for you and I was bawling and Mommy was crying and cussing—I never heard Mommy cuss before—and cussing the niggers that hit you."

"Oh." Matt felt a sickening weight. "Mommy was upset. She wouldn't say it otherwise, and she didn't mean it. Listen to me,

Bill, and don't forget. I don't want you to use that word, not ever. Understand me?"

"I don't care!" Bill flared. "They beat you up. They're niggers. I'll kill 'em!"

"Bill, listen to me!" Matt roared. "I told you not to use that word again. And you can listen to this too! I don't know who beat me up. I never saw them. I don't know who they were or what color—and you don't either!"

Matt stayed at home Monday and Tuesday, reluctant to go to the office. But Wednesday morning, unwillingly, he got into his working uniform of gray summer silk and had Ellen drive him to the station. It could be put off no longer, he told himself, and, in any case, his presence had not measurably helped shake off the lethargy in his own household, to say nothing of the lane as a whole. The kiss he planted on Ellen's mouth was lingering, warmer than the usual hurried station leave-taking. The heaviness of a sense that he might be needed here still hung over him.

"Call me if anything comes up," he said in a voice carrying the extra impact of an order. "Don't wait."

"I will, but I think it's over," she said, smiling at him.

He wouldn't have gone to the city even now, he told himself on the train, but the Glamour-Glow work wouldn't wait. This layout session with Lamar Winter had been scheduled for more than a week. There were at least six hours of concentrated and important work that had to be done today. Young wasn't a man to be stalled off and, for that matter, neither was Winter. For a painter, Winter was an extraordinarily businesslike man, a compact, controlled talent, sure of its powers, as impatient with lack of assurance in others as it would be with uncertainty in itself.

18

When his secretary came in to announce Winter's arrival at eleven, he rose and was walking toward the door when Winter came in briskly, carrying the flat, heavy picture case. They shook hands and moved toward the layout table, where Winter dropped the case with a solid thud. He turned toward Matt, the dark face composed, sure of itself. Then Matt saw Winter's look change suddenly to one of surprised consternation.

"What hit you, man? Your face looks like it had gone through a meat grinder. And the limp? Your wife been working you over?"

"I got beat up," Matt said shortly. "I'll get over it."

He looked at the artist and was suddenly baffled by an expression he had never seen there before. Doubt, question and a curious kind of anger ran fleetingly across the dark features. Abruptly, with only a fleeting sense of caution, Matt decided to talk. The haunting questions in the back of his mind still demanded answer. And here might lie the means to get the answer. Winter might be able to tell him what he still could not figure out for himself—the dark, compelling, mysterious and baffling why behind it all. Why had it happened?

"Let's let the paintings go a few minutes. Sit down, I got something on my mind. I need your advice.

"Now, look, Lamar," Matt began, feeling his way into it, "what I want to talk about has nothing to do with you. But it has something to do with a kind of thing you could know about. You may not like some of the things I'm going to tell you. Probably won't. I'm ready for that. But I've got to dope this out for my own satisfaction and I need help doing it, and I don't know who else I could talk to. If I make you sore, all right, tell me and I'll drop it, but we know one another well enough for you to know I'm leveling with you. It isn't business—it's personal."

"It might surprise you to hear I think I know what you got on your mind, boss man," the Negro murmured.

Intent on his need to make Winter understand and, in turn, to draw understanding from him, Matt missed the meaning in the artist's words. He began to tell the lane's decision and ordeal in a flat, unemotional voice. He recited the facts, leaving out nothing, putting nothing in to embellish or extenuate what the lane had done. He watched the attentive, impassive face across the desk, seeking subconsciously to read the effect of his words upon this man to whom, as a Negro, he was now appealing for a Negro's special knowledge.

"And that," he finished, "that is how I got clobbered. But that's not what's bothering me particularly. I'm not trying to ask you whether I—we—were right or wrong; that's something I hope to figure out for myself eventually. There wasn't time to do it then. But, Lamar—since you must be aware of things like this in a way I haven't any way of understanding—I thought you might be able to help me by explaining how a thing like that would come up in the first place." There was appeal in his voice, a plea for light. "Just tell me, if you know or can understand it, why the bloody hell would a colored man want to come in there with us—with a bunch of whites—in the first place?"

Abruptly the painter rose from his chair, strode to the layout table and, for a moment, tinkered pensively with the clasps of the picture case. He lit a cigarette, inhaled deeply, then let the smoke drift through widespread nostrils. Matt could sense the tension in Winter, but the composed face was bafflingly without expression.

"It's too bad you got beat up. I didn't have any part in that and I sure would have stopped it if I had known they'd do it. That stuff gets you nothing. But now I guess you might just as well know it all. I was the guy who was buying Bronson's house . . . until you diddled me out of it."

"You! Sweet suffering Jesus!" Matt breathed. He stared at the painter, aghast. With an effort, seeing a sardonic grin creep across the dark face, he got his mouth closed.

"I doubt if He had much to do with it. Nossuh, boss man, there sure wasn't no Jesus mixed up in the way you white folks operated. No, suh, moah like ol' Beelzebub, I'd say."

"Cut the comedy, Lamar," Matt managed to say. "You're no Uncle Tom." He shook his head. "I don't get it. I just, by God, don't get it."

The dark face was mocking him. The voice carried a taunt.

"You just brood about it long enough, white man, and it may come to you. You'll catch on."

"What're you going to do?" Matt asked, suddenly aware of the weight of what now lay between them. He glanced involuntarily toward the picture case, and the Negro, watching him, caught the look.

"Why, boss man, I wasn't figuring to do anything except get on with this here job. I wasn't aiming to quit, if that was what's worrying you. Don't need the money for a house, maybe, but I'll find something to spend it on. Maybe another mink for Margo. Yes, sir, might be just the thing to take the taste of white people out of her mouth."

Book Two

1 MATT STARED into Winter's dark, contemptuous face and at first felt nothing but disbelief. But the taunt in the artist's eyes was not there to be misread for long. Belief came and rage came with it. This familiar face, known, respected, trusted, even loved in the affection a man may give to a friend. Friend? This was the face of the enemy, as stripped of friendship as though it had been stripped of flesh. Now he felt a lust to strike, to give back hurt for hurt. He was on his feet and had started toward Winter when revulsion swept over him, and he stopped and was only able to say, "Get out. Get out."

"Sure, boss man. Sure enough," Winter said easily, wearing a tight smile as he moved gracefully toward the door, without haste. He turned in the doorway and waved a hand at the picture case.

"I'll leave that," he said, still smiling. "You might want to look at it when you get tired feeling sorry for the white folks."

Grief has few words to express itself, bewilderment even fewer. Matt exhausted nearly their entire vocabulary as he gazed at the empty doorway. "Jesus Christ," he said and shook his head as though to clear it.

Though he kissed her warmly at the station, Ellen knew at once that something in this day had withdrawn Matt from awareness of her. He had three martinis before dinner, which was one more than usual, as she well knew but noted without comment. She was aware of the frown which was more a puzzled shadow in his gray eyes than a physical expression on his lean face. She was curious but she said nothing, believing that sooner or later he would tell her. He always had.

After dinner he made a halfhearted attempt to read but soon put the book aside. He turned on the television set and ran around the dial until he found himself in the fifth inning of a night game but, although the Yankees were three runs in arrears, he could not summon enough of his usual bias against the team to wait and watch them take a whipping. He flipped the set off, and Ellen, who was finishing up the kitchen, watched in silent astonishment while he poured a double bourbon and tossed it off.

He left the house and prowled the yard in the dark until he barked a shin on a lawn chair and kicked back at the offending object in absent-minded resentment. The act made him feel foolish. He sat down and, although his throat was already raw from the cigarettes he had smoked that day, he lit another and drew the smoke deeply into abused tissues.

Once he got up and started across the lawn through the hemlocks but, almost on the Gold terrace, changed his mind and went back to his chair. The same obscure reluctance which had stopped him on the brink of telling his wife now held him back from confiding in Gold. He could not have explained why.

I've got to find my way into this, he thought doggedly, fighting his mind's reluctance. There had to be a handle somewhere that he could get a grip on. That was the first thing. But where was it? Where could he even begin to fumble for it? In this bald, new knowledge that a friend had betrayed him, slyly and viciously gone behind his back? In the truth that a man he knew, liked and believed in had callously and with intent done him injury? Who had probably, indeed—the idea was staggering—paid to have his wife cruelly harassed, his son terrorized, himself slugged and kicked? All right, the facts were there; Winter had been the enemy. He felt the exhausting weight of knowledge, but did it help him understand what he needed to understand? No, it only proved that he had not known his man. Demonstrated his stupidity, not Winter's evil.

His anger had drained away. He wanted to summon back the

clarifying fire, but strangely it would not come. He shook his head; where was the manhood in him, the simple human will to hate an enemy? But instinctively he knew that no answer lay there. It might be desirable, once a friendship was proved bankrupt, to dismiss it with contempt, to foreclose it as though it had never been. But it wouldn't work, he knew. If he was forced to liquidate whatever he had invested in it, of heart or spirit, he had to understand. That was the first requirement. He needed to probe the root of his own misjudgment. A man did not give friendship casually, nor, once given, could all its traces be erased at a moment's notice. He had to know why he had failed and to know that he had to fathom why Winter had failed him.

If that was the real Winter, this sneering man who had confronted him today, why hadn't he recognized it long ago? "Wuff!" He expelled the smoke from his lungs in a spasm of disgust. How could he have been so goddam dumb?

What had there been between them that he had mistaken, misread, failed to see? He had never before been driven to ask that question, never felt any slightest need of it. He would no more have asked the question about Winter than he would about Zack Gold; either a man was a friend or he was not.

But, no, it wasn't that simple. Now the question was necessary. Grant Macmillan was his friend, for example. But Macmillan was also his boss, a man who held certain powers over him. For master and servant to be friends, they needed a degree of mutual pretense, a sham of equality that both conspired in and both knew was false. Those who rose above the need were rare birds indeed.

Nor was it the same thing as camaraderie with his colleagues in the office, Kauffman, Roberts and Washburn. They were equals. They could respect or even envy one another's skills, enjoy one another's jokes, borrow money from one another. But beneath the surface each had to know that they were rivals, striving for the most part fairly, but striving nonetheless for position and power.

Neither competition nor one man's implicit mastery had affected his relationship with Gold. His friendship with Gold was transparently simple and satisfactory. Boil it down, and it came to the simple pleasure of liking a man and being liked in return. No problem there, no unspoken reserve bred of inequality, jealousy or ambition.

But had not the same thing been true of Winter, or had he not at least believed so? Only the events of this day could have forced him to the effort of definition. There had been early mistrust and hostility, but it had survived. And it had grown into respect for one another's capacities and from that into admiration. No rivalry detracted from it; no master-servant relationship flawed it. It was a full and effective partnership. They were a team. There had been pride in it. And shouldn't this friendship have been even more secure than, for example, the totally uncomplicated companionship he shared with Gold?

It should have been, yes. But clearly it had not. Why not? Where lay the flaw—in Winter or in him—that rendered Winter ready to strike him down in his own home? Had he failed Winter in something without knowing it? He picked at it, and a thought swam up out of the past: he was white and Winter was not. Was that it? Ridiculous. His tired mind dismissed it but then, obstinately, came back to gnaw on it. That ghost they had long ago laid to rest. Long ago. Even when he had been aware of it, it was only a flash in the pan. It was Winter who had made a point of it once, not he. He had forgotten it, long ago ceased even to be aware of it. Was that true? Yes, true, damn it, entirely true. Was it true of Winter? Of course, why not? Winter was intelligent, sensitive, acutely aware of the world around him. He carried a chip on his shoulder, yes, but the chip was as much a theatrical prop as it was anything. It wasn't for Matt; there was no reason for it to be there for Matt.

Weariness sat on him like a drug. His mind rebelled from clawing at the unanswerable. He got up and went to the house. Not wanting it, he took another drink straight from the bottle and climbed the stairs to their darkened bedroom.

"Matt?" Ellen said sleepily.

"Yes."

"Do you want to talk?"

"No," he muttered, shrugging out of his clothes and letting them drop. He was too tired to be aware how stiffly she lay beside him, coiled tight in the spring of her curiosity and concern. Sleep came down on him heavily. When it abandoned him an hour later, he was ready to talk but she was asleep, breathing quietly. He fumbled on the bedside table for a cigarette and lighted it and then, not wanting to disturb her, rolled out of bed and, navigating on Braille, found his way woodenly to the lower floor and the kitchen. Hopefully he gulped two aspirin and drank a glass of milk and then, detesting the taste, lighted another cigarette. An accusing stare at the kitchen clock told him it was already two-thirty.

He was still sitting in the living room with a book in his hands when dawn filtered through the draperies and the birds began their hungry twitter. Dully tired, eyelids grainy and hurting, he showered, shaved, dressed and forced himself to eat a breakfast he did not want as necessary therapy against the sour reminder of cigarettes he had smoked in the night.

2

MATT'S CURIOUSLY humble and defenseless report on what had taken place in Peaceable Lane had touched off Lamar Winter's old hard habit of disdain for white men. It sustained him long enough to get away from the offices of Macmillan Associates with his scorn intact. But then, suddenly, he lost it. The memory of Matt's scarred face and dragging leg brought down on him an insistent and humiliating reminder that his side of the battle had been fought with foul weapons. It was a damn fool mistake when I let that slippery chiseler con me into letting Barton into this, the artist acknowledged. If I'd been using my head, I should have guessed they'd go at it with a baseball bat.

He had not only lost, which probably had been inevitable anyhow, but having let Barton's muscle loose left him in a position no more defensible than the lane's whites—perhaps even less defensible. Nor did it help to remember that he had fatuously forbidden violence and expected the ban to work. Let yourself get too eager, he reflected sourly, and you wound up looking like a gorilla.

Also, it had left him with a score to settle. The difficulty was to decide with whom or how it was to be settled. With Fox? He dismissed that. The broker was a small-time schemer and hardly worth the trouble. With himself for having been a fool? Probably —his lips twitched—but that was a more or less lifelong process and not very fruitful at best. With Barton? Of course. But how? He had to acknowledge there wasn't much he was likely to be able to do to Barton. But suddenly he decided he had better see him face to face. He had been a fool to neglect that earlier, leaving it to Fox. It was time to make an estimate of the man; he had a feeling they were not yet done with one another.

His anger was still there but he had it under icy control when he reached Barton's office in a building not far from his own in Harlem. He had not come to brawl; that was useless now. But Barton was obviously a formidable man, and he intended, even at this late date, to see what manner of man he was and, if possible, test the degree to which he might be involved with him.

Measured against the decrepit shabbiness of the building which housed it, the quiet taste of Barton's outer office surprised him. It was also a little unsettling that he should be admitted almost immediately to Barton's presence; he had half expected a brush-off. He was on guard, curious but warily alert, as he crossed the spacious room toward a dully gleaming expanse of desk. He could see that the man seated there was big, but he could not at first make out his features; Barton had the advantage of the light, which came across his shoulders through half-open blinds and left his face in shadow.

Barton stood up, a portly figure carrying itself with calm assurance in oddly old-fashioned dress, and offered his hand.

"I thought you might be coming in," he said. "We should have met before."

Now that he could see clearly, Winter was struck by the composure of this man's face, matched by a quiet tone of grave courtesy.

"I agree. We should have," he said. "But I didn't come to congratulate you."

"Naturally not," Barton said. "We failed, but that is sometimes unavoidable, particularly when there is not enough time. But there may be another opportunity—there—or elsewhere."

"I didn't mean that," Winter said crisply. "I meant sending your goons into Peaceable Lane. I told Fox I wanted no rough stuff. And if it had worked, I still wouldn't have been here to congratulate you. I'm curious. Why did you do it?"

Barton eyed the younger man pensively before he spoke. "I suspect that you are new to this, Mr. Winter," he said at length.

"Not entirely . . . if you mean me moving into a white suburb. I tried it once before—Long Island."

"Do you mind telling me what happened?"

Winter's laugh was mirthless. "About what you'd expect. I had a deposit down through a broker. The seller never saw me until it came to closing. It was quite a shock to him when he did." He laughed again. "Shock enough so we didn't close. But I'm more sophisticated now."

Barton let his thick fingers march along the edge of the desk while he regarded his visitor. "Mr. Winter, at the risk of offending you, may I observe that you are not yet sophisticated enough for this sort of thing?"

Winter's voice hardened. "Possibly not. But I think I'm sophisticated enough to know it wouldn't have done me much good to move in there after you made a battlefield out of it. I wasn't going there expecting to be popular, but I didn't see any use at all moving into what was left over from a suburban-style Iwo Jima."

Barton's composure was imperturbable. "Forgive me if I say again that your experience is negligible. And I imply no boasting when I say that mine is considerable. I have been doing this for many years and I ask you to believe me that vigorous, if unorthodox, measures are sometimes necessary. My goons, as you choose to call them, did not go into Peaceable Lane intending violence, although they were ready for it if it became necessary. It is true they were there, so to speak, to disturb the peace. The uproar they were there to make was deliberately intended to precipitate even further an already developing panic, to take advantage of fear of the unknown. But violence, no. That was forced on them by the rashness of one of the residents. You believe this to be distasteful and I agree. But in fighting a war—which this is—one cannot afford squeamishness about weapons. A defensible end justifies indefensible means."

"I don't agree," Winter said. "You hammer a place into panic first, and what's left for the colored man who moves in? The panic's still there. The guy moving in starts with a double rap against him. So then, if it blows up in his face, what has he gained?"

Barton again paused to ponder his visitor in monumental calm. Barton was a complex man who contrived to harbor within one body contradictory elements of fierce idealism, passionless savagery, clear-sighted realism and calculating greed. Once he had been—and still held himself to be—dedicated only to the triumph of his race in an agelong war against white men, and no means toward that end offended him. He would scheme, connive, deceive, bribe, compromise, persuade or bludgeon as circumstances indicated. He was thinking now that in some ways men like Winter were useful to his ultimate end: they had ambition, courage and capacities that raised them above the general level of men and made them persuasive exhibits for the thesis that the black man was in every sense the equal of the white. But also they had a grave weakness which, in Barton's eyes, made them suspect: they were out for themselves. They would fight like tigers to advance their own position, but they would not acknowledge that they were inextricably a part of the larger issue, that was all men of their color against all men of white skin. They were loners. Loners could be used, often to advantage, but they were unreliable tools simply because they were loners. Barton would help them, and use them when he could, but he would never trust them very far. By his measure, a loner was already half a traitor.

"I am going to ask you a question," he said at last. "I stipulate that I think I know the answer in advance, but I wish to ask it anyhow: by moving into Peaceable Lane, were you hoping for eventual peace—so much peace, let us say, that you expected and intended to remain the only colored man there? Were you, in short, attempting to make a private escape which would benefit your personal circumstances and, by the same terms, prevent any other colored man from moving into the same street?"

Winter grinned coldly. "Not exactly," he said. "Although, to be frank, I wasn't thinking in general terms of the race. A guy has to look out for himself, you know that. I take it you want to be realistic and I'm willing to be. I say if you take a place like Peaceable Lane and crack it wide open and drive all the whites out and fill every house with colored men, you've just created another little Harlem."

"Doesn't that make your view a little narrow, Mr. Winter? A little selfish? To be seeking a privileged position–and denying it to the rest of your race?"

"Maybe," Winter said and paused. "But practical, too. I think you might agree that people in our position have to be practical before they're anything else."

"Perhaps. But I think I may say that I take a larger view of practicality. I agree that placing one colored man in Peaceable Lane is a certain advance for all colored men. But I also submit that the problem is larger than individuals. And I say that, no matter how favorable a position one individual like yourself might achieve, neither you nor colored men generally will be safe until the whites have been forced–and force is necessary–to grant all colored men their rights."

"Well," Winter said, "it's noble. I'll give you that. But I don't think I'm ready to wait for the millennium. And I don't think you're going to live to see it either. So now let me ask you a question."

"Yes?" Barton said smoothly.

"It takes organization to do what you do, and that takes money. It also takes money to maintain an office like this. Do you mind my asking–since you seem to claim that your only interest is the good of the race–how you finance this kind of operation?"

"You are too acute for me to waste your time or mine on nonsense," Barton said calmly. "I agree that these things take money. I will acknowledge that my activities, in addition to serving people of my color, also make money. Sometimes a good deal of money. Let us say, for example, that Peaceable Lane could be broken and driven to flight. The first two or possibly three houses sold to Negroes would cost a good deal more than their true value. But there would be at least eight others which, in the end, I would buy for a song."

"I see," Winter said. "I think I also see, Mr. Barton, that your moral position ain't a hell of a lot better than mine."

3

AT THE OFFICE Matt shuffled unwillingly through his mail and pushed it aside, unread. His secretary came in with a container of coffee and he sat sipping it, disliking its cardboard flavor. His gaze drifted back to the discarded mail, and this time he saw Glamour-Glow's severe letterhead among the others. He knew what that would be—polite, no doubt, but unmistakably imperative, Thurston Young's command for a progress report. So, there was that, too: the necessity to decide whether he could continue to work with Winter, the need to find a new basis on which it would be possible for them to work. The old solid foundation was gone. Well, there was no putting it off; whatever outrages time chose to inflict, it was still always there, at your elbow and impatient. Abruptly he reached for the telephone and dialed.

"Lamar, this is Matt," he said when he recognized the artist's voice. "I want to talk to you."

"Yeah? So talk, man." Winter's voice was light, easy, carrying none of the tightness Matt felt in his own.

"Not on the phone," Matt said. "I want to see what I'm talking to."

"Okay, but I'm busy. You want to come up here? Neighborhood's kind of culluhed, but I don't guess it'd rub off on you—not much, anyhow." The tone was cheerfully bantering.

"Oh, give it a rest," Matt grunted.

The chuckle over the wire was rich and gleeful. "Kind of touchy, ain't you, boy?"

"Maybe. What's the address?" Matt said shortly. Winter told him, giving a street and number which Matt recognized as uptown near the 125th Street Station. "I'll be there in half an hour," he said and hung up.

Matt had been in Harlem before, but now, as the taxi threaded through dingy streets, sometimes revealing a litter of accumulated trash in alleys and vacant lots, he was sharply aware of his surroundings and repelled by them. Almost consciously he tried to rid himself of a feeling that he was intruding on foreign and forbidding soil. The dark faces of people on the sidewalks or waiting for the lights at corners, as the taxi moved northward, somehow seemed closed in, watchful and hostile. He found himself wondering how it would be to live here. His heart recoiled at the image of his son in a world bounded by laundry-hung fire escapes and the drive and press of humanity hemmed in by angry traffic and grimy stone.

The building was old, its entrance sandwiched between a butcher shop and a gaudy neon-fronted saloon, but the narrow hall leading to the elevators was clean, its linoleum surface waxed and shining. It did not, at this moment, occur to him as strange that he had never been here before in seven years, or that he had to search the mailboxes to learn that Winter's apartment was the only one listed for the sixth floor, which seemed to be the highest. The elevator came down to him with a decrepit, descending whine, and he got in and pressed the button for six.

He was astonished when the elevator let him off beside large, sunny windows, through which he could see an expanse of graveled roof, open-air furniture and potted plants. Farther away on other roofs a forest of television antennae sprouted. He found the door at the end of the short hall and stood for a moment of indecision. He became aware of the sound of a piano and, though he had no ear for music, he recognized both that it was "The Blue Danube" and that the instrument was being earnestly and amateurishly pounded. Finally he pushed the bell.

Nothing in his seven years of association with Lamar Winter could have prepared him for the striking beauty of the woman who opened the door and stood smiling a careful welcome.

"I'm Matt Jones," he said and felt uncomfortably that he was both stammering and staring.

"I know," she said. "Come in. Lamar expects you." She stood back, waiting for him to enter the high white room. His eyes were drawn to the black bulk of a grand piano, now silent, and a small head and dark, inquiring eyes regarding him through the triangular space under the instrument's upraised cover.

"Tod," she said softly, "come here and say hello to Mr. Jones." She turned to Matt. "It's his practice time," she said. "It's hard to keep him at it."

"I heard him," Matt said. "He's doing fine." He felt that the observation probably sounded as awkward as it was, because he wouldn't have known whether the boy was doing well or not. Matt was off balance and he needed time to get it back. He was now, in this moment, under the impact of realizing that, however well he had thought he knew Lamar Winter, he might have been on another planet for all he really knew about him. This strikingly handsome dwelling isolated in Harlem's human anthill, this breathtaking woman, this slender boy—about Bill's size—now doubtfully but dutifully coming around the piano toward him—hell, he thought, I never knew he had a kid.

He took the boy's offered hand with awkward heartiness, wondering at the same time how much these two, mother and son, knew about Peaceable Lane and what had happened there. If they did know, they weren't showing anything. The woman's smile was pleasant, the mark of impersonal hospitality, nothing more. He followed her across the big white room and into another where Winter, in shirt sleeves and dungarees and with a brush in his hand, stood pondering a canvas on a tall, smeared easel. He put down the brush and wiped his hands on a rag smelling of turpentine.

"Hello, Matt," he said, smiling slightly. "You've met Margo?"

"Yes. And the boy," Matt said. Now that he was here, he was wondering rather desperately how he was going to get into it. The Negro's manner, easy, controlled, revealing no sign of awareness that anything had changed, was baffling, somehow irritating. "What are you working on?" he asked, nodding toward the easel, knowing as well as Winter did that the question had nothing to do with his presence here.

"Alice Collins, natch," Winter said. "Another hunk of glamour for Glamour-Glow." He turned to his wife. "Honey, would you whip up a pot of coffee? I don't know about you, Matt, but I don't function right until I'm on my tenth cup. Navy habit, I guess. Were you in the Navy?"

So he takes it for granted we're going on with it, Matt thought, as he moved to the easel and glanced at the golden-haired girl coming to life on the canvas. "No. Army. I didn't know you did time in the Navy."

"That's a fairly accurate way to put it. I was a mess boy on the *Enterprise* for three years." Matt glanced sharply at the painter, looking for a sign of the man's ever-ready baleful resentment of the white world's impositions upon him. Winter's face was impassive, but it came when he spoke again. "Along toward the end a new gunnery officer decided to make a gun crew out of us nigger boys. Guess he thought it'd improve our morale—or make men out of us or something."

It runs deep, Matt thought, deep and poisonous. Maybe I was nuts—thinking it didn't run against me too. Well, this stalling wasn't going to make it any different. He had to find out sometime, and it might as well be now.

"There are some things I want to know about," he said.

"I figured there might be," Winter said calmly. "Coming clear up here to Harlem and all."

"I got beat up," Matt said. "That was just one of several things. Probably the least. My wife was abused over the telephone by some sonofabitch who didn't have the guts to name himself." He was calm now and, looking at the dark, attentive face, he wondered why the anger was not coming back. It occurred to him that, under certain circumstances, he might be able to kill this man who had been his friend, but that it would have to be done without anger, out of necessity. "The last time around you said you had nothing to do with it. I remember that and I've been poking at it since. Now I've got to say I think you lied."

He would have expected the word to bring swift and savage counterattack. And so he was unready for the change that came over Winter's face. It was startling; no shadow like this ever had fallen over those mobile features in Matt's memory. What was it? Pain, surely, but more than pain. Shame?

"I lied and I didn't lie," Winter said heavily. "I neither ordered nor paid for it and I thought I had that kind of stuff ruled out. But you're right part way. I let it happen. I was stupid."

"How?" Matt asked, wondering. He was used to the ready signs of the artist's bitter anger. But Winter bitter against himself was something else.

"There's a guy named Francis Barton."

"I know. I met him," Matt said shortly.

"You white folks had me pretty well diddled out of the house. I let myself get conned into going along with Barton there at the end. Last resort, sort of. That's his business—blockbusting."

"For money?"

"Depends on how you look at it. I think yes, although I suspect he'd like to have people think it was for love."

"What kind of a blockbuster are you?" Matt's question was truly curious, but also it carried an edge of bitterness.

"Huh? Oh, I see." Winter regarded Matt curiously. "You mean was I trying to open up the street for colored folks generally? No. Just putting a small, personal crack in it, that's all."

"Why? That's one of the things I don't get. Why?"

"Why?" Suddenly the old dancing light of mockery had come back to Winter's eyes and his smile carried a malignant edge. "I wanted to come there and live. That's a pretty nice little street you got there, Matt—even if most of the people on it are pricks."

Now anger, so long drained out of him, stirred in Matt again, but he rode it down. He was here to learn, he reminded himself, not to blow his top.

"We may be pricks, but we had a pretty decent community until you put the whammy on us," he said stiffly. "Maybe you don't know how badly you messed us up."

"I messed you up? Maybe so—if you mean stirring you people up so you took your first real good look at each other. If that messed you up, I guess I did it."

"But why go out of your way to do it? What did you have against us?"

"Look, Matt"—Winter's face was grave now—"you have trouble understanding. But this is simple. There was a house for sale there. I could afford it and I wanted to buy it. You're a white man and there are still some things I don't know about white men—not many, but some—so I don't know whether you can rightly understand this or not. But the simple fact is I had the right to live there—or anywhere else I wanted—and if you come down to the gut of it, it wasn't any of your goddam business."

Matt recognized the abstract justice of Winter's thrust and

winced under it, but he knew also, and knew that Winter knew, that the complex business of living could never be separated into such clear-cut, tidy compartments.

"The street would have hated your guts," he said. "You'd have cost everybody on it more than he could afford. You want to live with hate—deliberately?"

Astonishingly, Winter grinned at him.

"I wasn't counting on the Welcome Wagon. And don't think I don't know everything there is to know about having my guts hated. Man, I grew up on the south side of Chicago. I knew it all by the time I was seven years old. All you really need to know is how to hate 'em back."

"But why? What was the use of it? Going out of your way?"

The Negro studied him and, under that somber, measuring gaze, Matt dimly understood that Winter was appraising him in terms he would not be likely to grant to any other white man.

"You saw my kid when you came in?" The question was incongruous. Wondering, Matt nodded.

"What was he doing? Playing the piano? You think he's any good at it?"

"How would I know? I'm tone-deaf."

"Well, then, take my word for it, he's good. Or will be."

"What's that got to do with this?"

"That's the most thing he's good at." The pain in Winter's eyes now was something Matt could not miss. "My kid is not a fighter. I don't know how far you'd go for your kid—I know you've got one—but I expect you'd go quite a distance. I'll go as far as I need to go for my kid—far enough to get him out of this." Winter turned and looked out the window, across the rooftops of Harlem, and, watching him, Matt somehow felt the hard, straining, brutal struggle for existence that went on, year in and year out, under those roofs. "He's not built for it," Winter said.

The painter turned away and went to the easel and stood looking at his work. Matt watched and wondered what he himself was feeling. Seven years, he thought, seven years of working with this man, matching brain with brain and skill with talent, seven years of steadily grown regard, sometimes failing together but more often succeeding, and sometimes triumphing, trust and confidence grown and firmed and then shattered, and not once, not once in seven years, not once before this had this man let him see into his soul. Nor, he acknowledged sadly to himself, had he, Matt, had the perception or the insight to look.

His own voice was hoarse when he found it.

"You knew I lived there?" he said. There was still this and it had to be dealt with.

"Of course," Winter said. The smile was there, but it held none of the old, ready edge of malice. There was a kind of rueful sorrow in it, Matt thought.

"Why didn't you tell me?"

Abruptly the artist left his easel and came to face Matt and stood looking at him.

"What would you have done if I had?" he asked softly.

The question, so quiet, so searching, carried the force of an explosion. What would he have done? What, indeed? It had seemed clear enough when the enemy had had no face. The difference between ten thousand and two. Was that all? He had believed so. Surely Grant Macmillan's angry anxiety had had nothing to do with it, nor Laura Cusack's venomous prejudice. But was that all? He felt again the dark loom of something none of them had really understood—or known how to deal with—but that had hung silent and sinister over Peaceable Lane, threatening hearth and home, wife and child.

"I don't know," he said. The words were wrung out of him, out of the heart of truth at his core.

"I think you'd have caved in," Winter said, still softly. "Forgive me, Matt, but I think you'd have had to cave in. I didn't want to see it."

4 Matt and Ellen Jones did not often quarrel, and almost never, despite the high decibel rating of Bill's zest for living, did Matt really lose patience with his son. But that day Matt had come from Lamar Winter's Harlem penthouse shaken and gnawed by a sense of the wrongness of man, including his own. That night the Joneses might have had a family brannigan had not Ellen, though she did not know the cause, recognized the signs in time and refused to be provoked.

The trigger was absurd, as Matt knew even at the time. Bill's swimming trunks lay soddenly abandoned in the middle of the master-bedroom floor; all the towels on Matt's rack were wet, and the soap was in the shower drain, turning into goo. His outraged yells were futile because Ellen was in the back yard, beyond hearing. Matt got himself more or less dry with Kleenex after showering off the film of sweat which the Central always left him as a reminder of its summertime passage.

Stumping downstairs and into the playroom, he found Bill collapsed on the floor, his attention riveted to the clatter of hooves and the crash of gunfire on a television western.

"Hey!" Matt yelled. "Turn that blasted thing down! Or off."

Somewhat startled, but still in a glassy-eyed trance, Bill looked at him. "Huh?" he said, barely audible through the machine's blare. Suddenly and illogically angered by the contrast between his mesmerized son and the image of Winter's son earnestly banging away at the piano, Matt strode to the set and turned it off.

"Aw, Pop!" Bill wailed, restored to full consciousness by the outrage. "That's Matt Dillon!"

"And I'm Matt Jones," Matt snapped. "And I've just been wading up to the knees in the swamp you left upstairs. Why didn't you come and get me a towel when I hollered?"

"I never heard you holler," Bill said defensively.

"No wonder!" Matt grunted. "But you hear me now. I want you to get upstairs on the double and clean up that mess."

"All right. I was going to anyhow," Bill said. "But can't I watch the rest of Gunsmoke first?"

"No. I said now!" Matt said. He turned on his heel, leaving Bill to puzzle out whatever logic there might be in an ill-humored addendum which, to Matt, did not seem a non sequitur. "Other kids have work to do. You don't know how lucky you are."

Matt was in the kitchen, manufacturing a pitcher of martinis, when Ellen came in with a half-dozen roses.

"At nine," Matt stated without preamble, "you would think that kid could at least get the first glimmering of an idea that he is not a guest in the house."

"The damn Japanese beetles are back," Ellen said, not really having heard him, since she was stewing over the summer's first manifestation of a more irritating pest. "Filthy bugs—they murder the roses. Matt, this summer you're going to have to spray them —what's that stuff? Chlordane? They make me sick."

"Look," he snorted, "I spend ten hours a week barbering and babying this barnyard. Civilized men play golf. I fight bugs, and when it isn't bugs it's crabgrass or aphids or Clarice loses a hairbrush down the john and I have to spend half a day pulling the thing apart to get it back. You want a real messy piece of exercise sometime, try tearing a john off the floor."

"Well, listen to him," Ellen said. "What got into you? Your secretary get sassy or married or something?"

"Nothing got into me," Matt retorted indignantly. "It just strikes me now and then that, compared to keeping this dump running, the hired man on my old man's ranch had a soft touch. At least he didn't come home and find the bathroom looking like it had been hit by hurricane Edna. Can't that kid ever pick up anything, and, by the way, why the hell don't you try a little discipline once in a while?"

"Don't you swear at me," Ellen said dangerously. "All I said was the Japanese beetles are out again. And you fly off the handle."

"Who's swearing? Now it's your damn bugs."

"*My* bugs!"

"Well, all right, your roses. You want a martini?" Matt asked ungraciously, feeling silly, but still feeling put upon. Since the day had been nearly as muggy on Peaceable Lane as it had in the city, and since Ellen knew, with a touch of envy, that Matt's office was air-conditioned, the temptation was strong in her to explode. But she resisted it and managed a strained smile instead.

"I think I'd better," she said. "With the mood you're in, if you slobber up all those martinis by yourself, you won't be fit to live with for a week."

Matt felt the impulse to yell an indignant denial but didn't do it, remembering in time that he wouldn't be on safe ground. Matt knew bleakly that most times when he fought with his wife martinis had something to do with it. Anyhow, this evening had already been subjected to enough strain to last through, likely enough, all the next day—unless he did something about it. He poured the drinks in gloomy silence and carried them out to the terrace.

"What's eating you, Matt?" Ellen asked as she joined him. She was worried and she was tired of waiting.

"Nothing," he said shortly, taking a moody suck at the drink. Ellen sighed, knowing she would still have to wait. Even yet Matt could not put a finger on his reluctance to confide in her. He knew he was in a fight, but he felt, without knowing why, that he had no right to pass on the burden of fighting it. It would have to be fought and won—or lost—within himself.

Matt knew that he had little of the race consciousness or race conscience that went deeply into the fiber of Zachariah Gold, for example. With Gold, he knew, it was a matter of principle that had little or nothing to do with the individual. Gold had made his painful decision because he thought he must, and the degree of his feeling about it would not have been measurably changed by knowing the name of the man he had helped keep out of Peaceable Lane. But knowing made a wrenching difference to Matt; he wished it did not.

I'm a WASP, he thought, a sure-enough white Anglo-Saxon Protestant. It leaves me with blind spots. But one thing I know is that the level Gold would like to operate on is not for me. That's out of my reach, and I suspect that when Zack really got down to it, he realized it was out of his reach too. If you tried to follow through on that plane of pure, objective justice there would never be an end to it. You would pretty much have to remake the world, and that, he thought wryly, would probably be pretty chaotic, at least for a while. If mankind ever set out to rip down all the barriers that prejudice had put up over the centuries, there would be no stopping place, not if it was to make any sense. You would have Irish forgiving the British and Norwegians fond of Swedes. Russians and Finns would be friends, and the French would quit hating Germans. Even the Arabs and Jews would make up and, among Jews, the Sephardic aristocrats from Spain would begin to think more kindly of Jews from Polish ghettos.

He did not hear Ellen's gusty sigh—although she meant it to be heard and interpreted. He was scarcely conscious of her absence when she finished her drink and went into the house to deal with dinner. Their brief blowup had added its measure of strain.

Winter haunted him. He had liked Winter and believed that he knew him as a man—but not blindly. Matt had come to feel that he understood the artist's angry drive for eminence in a white man's world. You could admire a fighter. That automatically meant that you did not have to pity him or feel much guilt for the conditions which had produced him. It meant that you did not feel obliged to take any more of his touchy guff than you would from a similarly combative white man.

But now look. How well had he really known his man? He had known the professional half of him, all right, known it well. But was that where a man's deepest, most urgent forces drove him? Some men, yes. But not Winter, he knew that now. Then why hadn't he known it before? Because, dammit, he hadn't looked, hadn't even been curious. He had not known even the bare statistics of Winter's life—where he lived, that he had a wife who was also a great beauty, that he had a son, about the age of Matt's own son. He had not known that Winter feared for his son and was weak and vulnerable because of him. That day, for the first time, he had been permitted a momentary glimpse into the hidden place where this tough man still quivered and could be hurt. Here was a kind of cowardice against which no man could defend himself. I know it, I know it, Matt thought. Half an hour earlier he had yelled at his own son's sloppy carelessness. He wished he hadn't, partly because this time, though clearly guilty of being sloppy, Bill had been unfairly pinned as stand-in target for a different distress. Partly because, whenever it happened, he hated having caused that sudden, startled light of alarm. Kids lived in a different world; sometimes, locked out of that world by the weight of years, an adult had no recourse but yelling to summon a kid over into his. He knew he would yell at Bill again. And Winter, baffled and fearful because he could not see his own steely sinew reproduced there, would probably yell at his son. But the yelling was only a surface symptom of an adult's helpless incapacity to do all he wanted for a kid. You wanted them tall, strong, honest, smart and safe. But mostly safe. That first, safe from their dreaming selves, safe from the ravening world. You couldn't do it, of course, but you couldn't stop trying either. Winter had said it: you would go a long way for your kid, go as far as you needed. Go as far as death. And in going, if it seemed necessary, it would be little more than an incident that you tramped on the toes of a friend.

He had claimed Winter friend. On good grounds? Perhaps they were good, but now he knew that they had had little to do with the guts of the man. And he had turned him away. Not knowingly, but he had turned him away. On what grounds? On the difference between an actual two thousand dollars and a theoretical ten. Good enough? Hell, no.

The world in which Matt Jones had been born and grown to manhood and fought honorably in a war and chosen a woman and begot a son had never yet, in all its thirty-eight years, required of him a really hard or lonely decision. Not that he had always thought them easy. He had agonized in his last year of high school in Dubois, Wyoming, before finally settling on Northwestern. He had sweated a little before following a classmate into the advertising business, but not much. Choosing a girl, Ellen, had been as natural and mutual and satisfactory as choosing to breathe. The war had asked hard things of him, but nothing lonely; the war had its own climate and tempo, and when it asked hard things of a man, the demand was natural in that time. He had come out of it with a Silver Star and the rip of grenade fragments down his left side and belly, but he had known, even when making a dangerous decision, that in those circumstances heroes were made by only a small rise above conformity—and that an equally small drop below it made a coward. This was something else. Here was decision in the pure sense. This was hard; it would be shattering and it could only be reached alone.

All the same he had help making it, although he did not consciously ask for help. For a long time that night he lay in bed with Ellen with his brain closed and his belly tight and his soul crying to be rid of problems. In the midst of it, with an alchemy of spirit which had survived and even grown stronger over fifteen years of familiarity, he became more aware of her than of his clamorous mind. She lay beside him, breathing easily, but he knew she was not asleep and that, though she spared him her urgent questions, she knew his aloneness. A wave of tenderness swept him and of remorse for shutting her out. He reached to touch her, drawing a finger down from her lips, over her chin and down her throat to her breasts. She lay still for a moment and then, with quick hunger, moved against him and felt for his flesh. These bodies knew one another well, but knowledge had not dulled but rather had enriched with knowledge the gift they had, one for the other. No frantic, clumsy haste drove these two. It was a slow, tender, absorbed ritual, sweeping upward to a breathless eminence by dizzy spiral paths that were known and beloved by both. Beyond the summit, quiet and clear and luminous, as they both knew, waited the reward, peace of body and peace of spirit.

Matt did not know it, but at some point in this shared act of love, decision was made possible for him. He had set his mind to fight it out, but in the end his mind had refused the test, set itself to balk before a hurdle it would not clear. Now he lay awake, but peace and a calm sureness had come to soothe his exhausted will. In an ancient, unspoken and unjust miracle of the flesh and spirit, a woman had taken into her body not only a man's seed but the burdens he could not support alone as well. It was unjust to her, since she could not know how heavily she would pay for the decision she had made possible. In justice to him, he probably did not know that by this unfair means he had reached decision.

Some few men own minds so orderly, of such clarity, range and power, that they can at once see and coldly weigh all the implications of a complex issue, whether of strategy or of ethics. Matthew Rice Jones was not one of these. He belonged to a more numerous company of those who could, when driven, find their way to the bottom of a problem but who, in seizing on the main point, were likely to relax their grasp temporarily on other aspects of it. He did not think of himself consciously as a just man, although he was one when he recognized one of the many contradictory faces of justice. Nor did he reckon himself a generous man, nor one likely to act on reckless impulse; but he was both of these as well.

When he kissed Ellen at the station that morning, he had not yet warned her what he would do that day, or how deeply he would commit her without her knowledge. In fairness to him, it should be said that he himself did not yet exactly know. But he did know that he would do something.

The decision was made but the act was not yet defined when, in midmorning, he telephoned and asked Lamar Winter to lunch with him. A more analytical mind might have recognized by the way he issued the invitation that he had not only reached decision but had gone farther and was already building a fence to defend it.

"All right, Matt," Winter said over the telephone. "What time and where?"

"Around one," Matt said. "Meet me at Twenty-one."

"Twenty-one?" The Negro sounded surprised. "I've never been in Twenty-one in my life. Man, they ain't going to like it."

"They'll like it," Matt said grimly.

Deliberately he did not make a reservation in advance; he knew he would never again take precautions because of the color of Winter's skin. And so, as they passed the doorman and stepped down from the street, past the jockey statues in their painted silks, the chip had been transplanted from the artist's shoulder to Matt's. His voice carried a note of challenge, scarcely muted, when he told the impassive headwaiter that they needed a table for two. He had been braced for resistance and was almost disappointed when the man nodded and said, "Of course, Mr. Jones," and asked, "That one, there in the corner, that suit you?"

They ordered drinks and food without, at least in Matt's case, paying much attention to the menu. He was ill at ease, feeling the tug of a queer, impatient excitement curbed by a reluctance he could not define. This act, now, was all but done, but he was aware of an oppressive shadow looming over the doing of it. There would be no turning back. He looked at the dark face across the table and wondered how, no matter how well controlled, it had concealed so much from him for so long. He realized that Winter was studying him in return.

"I know you didn't ask me here just for kicks," Winter said at last. "What's on your mind? Let's have it."

So then it was done, quietly and without drama.

"Do you still want the house?" Matt asked. He saw the faint start, instantly suppressed, and then the tightening of the eyes that signaled the quick rise of anger.

"Don't rub it in, boy. I've taken my lumps."

"Take it easy," Matt snapped, feeling his own impatience and something like anger rising in return. "I'm asking if you want the house."

"Why? Why're you asking that?"

"Because you can have it if you still want it."

Winter breathed a slow, hard sigh and sat back and stared at Matt. Suspicion had closed his eyes to glittering slits and for a time they remained so, probing the eyes of the white man across the table. At last they opened slightly and, for an unguarded moment, the taut, dark face wore a look of puzzled wonder.

"Well . . ." the Negro breathed at last. "Well, I'll be damned."

"I asked you if you wanted it." It was out, and now, suddenly, Matt was impatient to have it settled.

Winter continued to study him, almost palpably testing, feeling for the flaw in an offer that must otherwise be incredible.

"I think you mean it," he said softly at length.

"I mean it," Matt said. "You didn't think it was a game, did you?"

"It sure sounded goofy," he said. "It sure did. Who says I can have it?"

"I do."

"You're not alone," Winter said. "It isn't your house." He had accepted it, at least provisionally. But his mind, skeptical by nature, was probing at it. He saw the strain and exhaustion in Matt's face and felt the flash of insight. He's got a monkey on his back, he thought. Conscience? No . . . maybe . . . but something more than just conscience. His mind ran swiftly back over the years of their association, and suddenly he was acutely aware of something which had grown so familiar that he had almost lost sight of its rarity: Matt Jones was the only white man he knew against whom he did not always keep up his guard; somewhere along the road he had stopped measuring Matt primarily in terms of white man–colored man. Why was that? Some unsuspected softness in himself? He doubted it. Something in Matt, something unique? He nearly shook his head in puzzlement. He's a funny bastard, he thought. "You've got a syndicate," he said aloud. "Who else says I can have it?"

"No," Matt said shortly. "They don't have to say it. I'm the buyer of record. You must know that if you cased the place as well as I think you did. I control it. I can sell it."

"To me? Why?"

"Oh hell," Matt said angrily. "Quit picking at it. Let's keep it simple. You say you have the right to live where you want—I agree with that."

"What'll they do when they find out?" Winter's mind was calculating the possibilities. "You looking to get tarred and feathered and ride out on a rail? Trying for a divorce?"

"Knock off that reverse Jim Crow stuff," Matt grunted. "I'm serious and I ain't amused."

"The waiter will be," Winter said warningly. They watched silently, not thinking about food, while their steaks and salads were served. I wished this was over with, Matt was thinking. There ought to be pleasure in this, some big, bright feeling of well-being and a clean conscience. But it's just something that has to be done, and it's hard work and I'm not sure it's not dirty work. But it had been dirty work the other way too. Dirtier, if anything. I wish to hell none of it had ever happened. But it had, it had.

"I think you're asking for it," Winter said, mirroring his thoughts. "You can get into trouble with this stuff, making believe you're God."

"I'm not," Matt said wearily, wishing it were true. "I'm just trying to straighten out a mess before it gets any messier. I don't think you're out to wreck us." That part, at least, had better be true, he thought. He stared at Winter, consciously probing and challenging the intent behind those careful eyes. Then he remembered the woman and the boy at the piano. No, he thought, however Winter might come to Peaceable Lane, it would not be as an intentional wrecker.

"How do you think you're going to handle this?" Winter asked. "You know you can't do it in the open—no matter who controls what. Man, they'd lynch you."

Now there was this to be faced and Matt recognized it. This was the thing he had lost sight of while fighting his way down to the heart of the problem. He saw himself announcing this to a meeting of Peaceable Lane, pleading there for generosity and understanding of another man's need. The image was absurd, impossible. This was the classic dilemma. There was no honest way in which this honest thing could be done. Nor any just way. It had to be recognized. The physical fact of a man's skin color, which should have been meaningless, carried shockingly powerful connotations of meaning: suspicion, fear, superstition, hate, money. There was no possible way to render justice to Lamar Winter, his wife and his son without, in some measure, rendering injustice to Peaceable Lane, his own wife and his own son. But a choice had to be made, had been made already. To make it he had to believe that the injury to Peaceable Lane would be the lesser; that indeed, with time and luck, both hate and fear would fade and there would be no injury at all. If this was playing God, he could find no way to escape it.

"We'll have to sneak it," he said, foreseeing all that the word might mean, hating the taste and sound of it. He had never felt so tired, so wrung out. "Do you want it?"

This is quite a man, Winter thought. I wouldn't have believed he had it in him. He thought he probably knew what it had cost Matt to come this far; he thought he could guess, even better than Matt, how much more it would cost him to go the rest of the way. I ought to be grateful and I guess, in a half-assed way, I am. But he realized that what he really felt, watching that strained white face, was the unfamiliar surge of pity—and a sharp sense of triumph.

"Yeah," he said, "I want it. I'm sorry, Matt, I've got to use you. You're a tame white man."

5

ELLEN WAS PALE and her face, more familiar when it was tender, gay or whimsical, wore a look of stunned bewilderment. Watching her, Matt felt the angry weight of guilt, but even more, man's perennial need to reach into another mind and understand and be understood and the baffled impossibility of accomplishing it. It couldn't be done, even when the other mind belonged to someone beloved. It's strange, he thought. We are close; I know all her moods; I know her more intimately than any person alive; I know every curve and crevice of her body. And we are still strangers in the end.

"I'm trying to understand," she said. "I'm sorry, I just don't understand."

"I know," he muttered. Remembering his own blind groping after truth, he felt the impossibility of communicating it, even to her. It needed an eloquence he knew he didn't have. Whatever he could find to say would only pick at the surface. "You don't know him. That makes it harder. But he's no bum, you have to believe that. He's my friend." Christ, he thought, how feeble and banal it sounds.

"Friend?" Her voice was nearly shrill. "How could a friend do what he did to us, or what he had done the night you were beaten up? Was he one of the people in those cars, hooting and screeching?"

"No," he said somberly, wondering how near he dared come to the truth with this. "He made a mistake, maybe a lot of them. But he didn't have anything to do with that. They got their hooks into him and they used him—the same way they'd use any colored man they could."

"Why didn't he stop them if he's your friend?"

"He didn't know they'd do it."

"That's what he says. How do you know he's telling the truth?"

"Ellen, I've worked with him for years."

"I didn't know you worked with a colored man. You never told me," Ellen said irrelevantly. It surprised him, but it was probably true. He couldn't remember whether he had or had not, but probably not. A man lived on several levels and each, in many ways, was closed from the others. The fact that Lamar Winter was colored had had so little effect on their professional association, one way or another, that it was unlikely he had ever talked about it at home. It was probably a mistake in some ways. The same kind of compartmentalization had kept him from ever knowing anything about Winter's family—or even that he had one.

"How do you think you're going to explain this to Billy?" Ellen went on. Matt had brought this inexplicable nightmare home with him; she felt a wild desire to destroy it before it could become real. "He was terrified that night. He thought they were killing you. So did I." Her face was a mask of remembered loathing. "Oh God, I thought we were through with all this. Now you tell me it's just beginning."

"He's a kid. He's probably forgotten it already," Matt said, hoping it was true. "Anyhow, can't you understand this is different? We're through with the bad part."

"How is it different? It's still a colored family."

"They are also people! Dammit, that's what I'm trying to put across." He realized that he had said it explosively, the absurd way a man may yell when he is trying, by sheer desperate noise, to force understanding into a mind that does not comprehend his language.

"You didn't feel that way before you knew who they were," she said, sticking to the facts with maddening feminine insistence.

"I know," he admitted, speaking more gently. "That made the difference. Before I knew who it was, we were afraid of something that didn't have any name or face. It wasn't even human. It was just an idea that all of us, for some reason, let scare us. A nightmare, a bogey. Herd panic, something like that. Now I know who it is. A man, just that. A man like anybody else, a guy with a pretty wife and a kid that he doesn't want ratting around the streets of New York any more than we would want Bill there. He also happens to be a man I know and respect. Oh hell, don't you see what I'm trying to say?"

Ellen shook her head stubbornly. She loved Matt and most of the time had confidence in him, but she was no spineless wife to take the incredible on faith merely because he asserted it.

"You know him. So now you can say it was panic . . . that we were just a terrified mob. You're not afraid. But I am. You were afraid it would destroy the value of our home. We couldn't afford it. Can we afford it now . . . or have you just forgotten it?"

"No, I haven't forgotten it," he said slowly. He could feel her fear and he wanted to touch her and reassure her, but the rigidity of her whole body forbade it. He struggled with it, longing to be understood. "Ellen, you can't put a price on a man. You can't accept him on every other level . . . work with him . . . trust him . . . then shut him out on another."

"But you can put a price on your wife and son," she said bitterly. Instantly she wished the words unspoken, but even in the quick rush of shame for having said them, she knew that here lay the heart of her bewilderment: what came first, a man's family or this wild, quixotic notion?

"No." His voice was cold. "Sometimes you have to take a chance . . . even with the things you love. Because, if you didn't, the day would come when your shame would shame them too. I won't kid you—this may not be easy, not at first anyhow. But there's no real danger."

She shook her head.

"Matt, I know this isn't just a whim. And I'm not afraid to take my share of something that has to be done. Not even for Billy to take his share . . . if it's right and necessary. But this seems so—so impossible. How about the others? What are you going to do about them?"

"The only thing I can do," he said woodenly. "Cheat them."

"Oh!" she said. She sat frozen, her hands locked so tight in her lap that the knuckles were white. Matt saw her and hated to look. He felt the rise of all men's baffled irritation at the inability of women to deal logically with the logical necessities of man's illogical deeds. He was feeling the despair of a man who knows his position is untenable but knows that it must be defended anyhow.

All right, Matt thought bleakly, don't try to duck it; this is plain fraud, less admirable than holding up a bank or even rolling a drunk. I'm not geared for it, he thought, and clawed futilely for a way out. Only one thing would make it possible: he had to believe it was essentially right and the only thing that could be done. Even so, it was necessary to close off his mind, compartment by compartment, until nothing was left but a cold will to get it done. There were times in the process when he disliked Lamar Winter almost as much as he despised himself.

He learned that betraying those who trusted him presented no problems. For a monument to deception, the mechanics of conveying the deed to No. 1 Peaceable Lane to joint tenancy in the names of Lamar and Margo Winter proved childishly easy.

It was easier because he was in control, the nominal owner in his neighbors' behalf. But he knew the job would have been nearly as easy if almost any one of the others had held his point of vantage. Sol Weissman, Cusack, Kelly, Draper, Dr. Abram or even John Ainslie Outerbridge—any one of them under pressure of the lane's anxiety to be shut of the lane's unwelcome collective responsibility—would have accepted the legitimacy of his discovery of a buyer with little question. To any of these it would have seemed a piece of luck, unexpected, but not to be suspected. It might have been different if he had had to deal with the wary and cynical Cavanidis. Almost automatically Cavanidis would have distrusted any escape from the lane's predicament which promised to let them off the hook with all their money back. Yale, even if he were around, no longer counted. As Cavanidis had predicted, they had never seen the color of his money.

Gold should have wondered, and Matt had half expected it and tried to prepare himself to deal with the big Jew's doubts. But he accepted Matt's news in seeming calm. Matt knew Gold's distaste for what they had done; he put down Gold's ready acceptance to relief that the unpleasant task could be finished and at last put out of sight.

He kept the structure of deception to a bare and—he realized—suspicious minimum. He could not summon the will to embroider his lie and subconsciously he was perhaps almost wanting Gold to unmask it.

A white shill was necessary. Alexander Fox, with the cynical skills he had developed by not letting scruple inhibit him as a broker, furnished a plausible-appearing professional stand-in who called himself Arthur Lakeland. Matt told Gold that he thought he had a prospect. Matt described him as an advertising man who, he understood, wanted to escape Long Island, partly because of the frailties of the Long Island Rail Road and partly because it delivered him to Penn Station, an irritating subway ride from his uptown office. He had met the man briefly, he said, and he had looked all right and seemed to have money, not merely talk it. He thought Gold should handle the details, in any case look the man over, and he had made an appointment for them to meet.

"Fine, Matt. That's good news," Gold had said. "When and where?"

That weekend Gold brought Lakeland out to look at No. 1 Peaceable Lane. The two men went through the house swiftly and expertly and within an hour Gold was taking him back to the Chappaqua Station. Later Gold found Matt in his back yard.

"He seemed to like it," he reported. "Did you know how deep he was ready to go? Pricewise?"

"I didn't talk money with him," Matt said, telling the literal truth, since he and Lamar Winter had agreed, even before Lakeland appeared to play his peculiar role, that if Peaceable Lane must suffer fraud, it must at least be spared financial penalty. Indeed, Winter had offered a premium, but Matt had rejected it as impossible to explain. "I gathered he could manage to pay for what he wanted," Matt said cautiously.

"He made an offer," Gold said. "I told him what we—you, rather, as the seller—had in it. He said he could match that but he wouldn't want to go higher."

"You mean we get out free?" Matt asked, making an effort to simulate surprise and pleasure.

"He said so. You want to take it?" Gold's face was without expression.

"Why not?" Matt said, then added prudently, "If he's on the level. What do you think?"

"He's a buyer. He's the right color," the big man said dryly. "I didn't take a binder, but I will if you agree. It'll be getting out quicker and better than we could have hoped."

"I don't know what there is to wait for," Matt said.

"He went through it pretty fast," Gold mused. "And he didn't bring his wife. Pretty brave man."

The ceremony of any real-estate closing in New York holds a nightmare quality for both seller and buyer. They find themselves mere paying spectators, bewildered and tolerated, but not consulted, at a practiced ritual whose performers are the brokers, the lawyers, the mortgage men, the guarantors of titles. This time Matt found the formalized business of writing and handing checks back and forth and the stylized transfer of documents even more endlessly harrowing than the buying of his own house—and more lately Bronson's—had been. He ached for it to be finished and was sweating when at last they all stood up and shook hands.

"I suppose you'll be moving in soon?" Gold said to Lakeland as they parted. Something extra in his tone, some silky edge of insult, struck Matt's ear, but he dismissed it as imagination. I'm edgy, he thought, and it's no wonder.

"Two, three weeks, I think," Lakeland said lightly. "Some things to settle first."

"Come on, Matt, let's get a drink," Gold said, as they left the mortgage company's office on upper Broadway. It was a muggy day, and the blast of air conditioning was a relief as they found a back booth in a bar and ordered beer.

"That's that," Matt said woodenly. "What's next on the agenda?"

"Getting the money back into people's pockets," Gold said. "I'll make up a statement. There are some details beside what we paid for it and what we got for it. New title search, interim insurance, adjustment for taxes and amortization. We had it less than a month and they don't come to much. At a rough guess, the whole deal cost two hundred dollars—little more, little less." He studied Matt coolly. "I suggest you and I split the loss between us. We can't very well ask the others to take that on."

Matt felt the cold clutch of surprise. Then the surprise went out of him. Who did he think he had been kidding? He met Gold's thoughtful gaze steadily, waiting for him to say it.

"Do you know how much time we have before Lamar Winter moves in?" Gold asked quietly. "It might make it a little easier if we have time to get things cleaned up first. Get people's money back to them."

"How long have you known?" Matt asked. He felt a frozen

curiosity, a need to know exactly how and where this fraud had been transparent.

"Almost right away. I guessed at first. It took a little longer to get the details."

"How did you find out?" When was it coming, Matt wondered: the contempt, the anger, whatever he would have to take?

Gold smiled almost imperceptibly. "Hell, Matt, did you really think I was that stupid? It stuck out a mile. After that it was a simple matter of checking. You didn't really think you were going to get away with it, did you?"

"I'm not sure what I thought. I knew I had to try. And I did get away with it. You could have gummed it up. Why didn't you?"

"That was my first impulse," Gold admitted. "At first I had trouble getting it into my head that was what you were really up to. You're a pretty easygoing character, you know. So I knew something powerful must have been working on you to make you take this on. It was so far out of character that—after the first jolt—I began to wonder what had got to you. At first I even wondered if it was money. I'm sorry."

"No. Not money," Matt said.

"Yes, I understood that almost right away. I knew you must have got a hell of a jar—making that hundred-and-eighty-degree switch—and trying to do it on the sly. Man, you'd been so sure that keeping the colored guy out was the only thing to do. It baffled me."

"Now it doesn't?"

"No. Not after I learned the man was a friend of yours and that you'd just found it out." The big man was silent for a moment. "I still had trouble figuring how you worked yourself up to the point of trying to sneak it. How do you feel now?"

"Like a first-class prick," Matt said grimly. "You knew what was going on. Why did you let it go through?"

"I had myself to wrestle with," Gold admitted. "I'd been through it before. You know that. I'd thought it was settled, that I could buy it the way it was. But there you were all of a sudden—as unlikely as anybody on the street—mucking yourself up even worse to unmuck us all. It wasn't easy. I talked it out with Beth, and in the end I left it up to her. But I told her, God Almighty, if a slob like Matt is willing to wreck himself, dig a hole he may never get out of, and turn crook to do something right that we'd all done wrong, then what the hell would we be doing trying to stop him?"

"She bought that?"

"It scared her, but she bought it."

"So did Ellen," Matt said moodily. "I suspect she thinks I'm crazy but that if she's stuck with me she's also stuck with me being nutty."

"There's a good chance we both are," the big man said somberly. "It's going to be touchy keeping it covered up. With, just for example, Laura Cusack prying away at it. It can get rough as a cob."

"You took a hell of a chance—going along with a madman," Matt said, now for the first time fully aware that this huge, quiet man had come to pick up a share of the load. He was no longer alone. There were damn few who would make that trip, so few they were unique.

"It was a case of when you gotta you gotta," Gold said ruefully. "I'm not worried about myself, at least not so much as about Beth and the kids—although it comes to the same thing. But there's the street to worry about. If they find out—too soon—they could come apart like a firecracker."

"There's still what scared us first. Property values," Matt said. "I'll admit I'd lost sight of it. What do you think?"

"I can't afford a licking now any more than I could a month ago," Gold said. "But I hope there doesn't have to be a loss. I've had a good look at your man Winter. He's a quality citizen if any of us are, and I couldn't find anything that made him look like an organization man. Maybe, with luck, we can keep the lid on and the lane will absorb him. We'll just have to hope and take it easy." He sighed, then looked up at Matt, and a quick grin lighted the heavy face. "Don't feel so crummy about it, crumb. At least your boy's bound to raise the tone of the joint. That'll be the only Jaguar on Peaceable Lane."

"There's something else," Matt said. He had an ally now and he was glad for it, and grateful, but the help had come unexpectedly, generously, from a man who could not know or share his reasons. "You were against the business in the first place, but I doubt if it was because we were keeping out a guy named Winter

—or named anything else. Here we've got a guy—not a principle. How come you settle for this?"

"Yes, there's that," Gold admitted. "And I'll confess I still wish he had never wanted to get in. But he did. It isn't who he was. It's that he did want in and that we were keeping him out—which we had no right to do. Maybe I buy it because you're right—even if you're right for the wrong reason. It doesn't save my conscience, just salves it. Just the same, he's a danger, and I hope to hell there are no more of him."

"You know," Matt said carefully, "you know that the way I did it—and you let me—is crooked."

"Of course," Gold said. "There aren't many ways to get out of being a sonofabitch."

Lamar Winter, with his hands on his hips, stood in the tall white living room in Harlem, considering the Rouault on the wall. Thoughtfully, he reached up and lifted down the painting in its heavy oak frame.

"I'll pack this myself," he said. "Leave it for the movers and all I'll have left will be an insurance claim."

"When are they coming?" asked Margo Winter, decorative though disheveled in blue jeans and one of the artist's old white shirts. She had her arms full of dresses which she put down on the black-and-white zebra skins of the divan. She had just come from sorting a voluminous wardrobe in her closets. Nearly everything more than a season old had been set aside for the Salvation Army, a freedom of choice which would have jeopardized even further her welcome to Peaceable Lane had its women witnessed this profligacy.

"Tomorrow. First load," Winter said absently. He was absorbed in the painting.

"Isn't that rushing it?" she asked, frowning. "I'm anxious, of course. I can't wait. But I wonder if it wouldn't be better to wait awhile. Give Mr. Jones time to, well, to pave the way—if he can."

"It's our house, honey," he said, grinning at her. "The key's in my pocket and the deed's in the bank. Leaving them an empty house to wonder about will just make them curious. They may just as well take a look at us and start getting used to it."

Their son came from his bedroom, proudly and gingerly carrying a bright model airplane. Winter remembered that he had bought the expensive toy the previous Christmas, remembered also the patient hours spent helping the boy assemble it and the pleasure he had got, abandoning artist's brushes for a spray gun, in building up the little craft's coats of burnished lacquer.

"Can I take it?" Tod asked.

Looking at him, Winter's eyes softened as they never did for any other human except his wife. Not even she got under his guard the way the boy did. There was a difference. He knew he could keep her safe. But the inevitable years were already driving Tod into a world where Winter knew he could not follow. Too soon by far the boy would be on his own, and when the time came, Winter's love for him would be as vulnerable as the boy himself. The glow in his eyes was fond and proud, obsessed by fear, fierce with helpless will to stand between his son and the world.

"Why not? There might even be room to fly it out there," he said. He hated these prisoning walls. The most Tod had got out of the handsome toy was to start its engine and listen to the satisfying howl of power in the bedroom—while holding the fragile craft safely tethered from flight and harm. Flight, to get up and go on your own, that was what any strong young thing needed. The boy needed it. Winter needed it for him—and also dreaded it.

"How'm I going to pack it?" Tod asked. "It'll get smashed."

"Never mind packing it," Winter said. "We'll take it in the car."

"I don't think there's room," Tod said doubtfully. "That old back seat is pretty little and this thing is pretty big."

"Don't worry about it, son," Winter said. "If that little old back seat is too little, we'll get a Carey Cadillac and let you and it deliver yourselves in style."

"Gee!" The boy's eyes glowed. "You mean it?"

"He's excited." Margo smiled after Tod as he swoopingly banked the plane to get it safely through his bedroom door. "He's been taking inventory for three days."

Winter shook his head. "I don't know whether I'd want to go through being that young again, but I doubt it. Sure, it's exciting. It's getting the edges of excitement knocked off you that's hard to take—until you get used to it."

"All right, Grandpa." She giggled. "I still get excited. And scared. I still don't think it's true."

"It's true," he grunted. "But it wouldn't be except for Matt."

"I know," she said. "I wonder why he did it and I wonder what it does to us, what we owe him."

He turned toward her quickly and fiercely.

"Get that out of your head. Get it out!" he nearly yelled. "Don't ever think you owe a white man anything. You do that and you're down the drain."

She was staring at him, wide-eyed, half scared.

"Margo, Margo." He was gentler but much in earnest. "I like Matt Jones. I like him on almost any level, almost all the time. I even admire the bastard—he knows his business. He hardly ever works at being a white man. Most of the time I don't notice. But he's working at it now. Do you think he'd be busting his ass to get us into his street today, inviting his neighbors to skin him alive, if he wasn't so conscience-ridden by him being white and us not?"

"You're touchy," she said coldly. "Too touchy, Lamar, and too cold. Would you rather have him busting his ass to keep us out?"

"Almost," he muttered. "Almost. Sooner or later they're going to slug him for it. It'll happen when they get wise to him." Suddenly he was fierce again. "Just don't go sloppy on him when it happens. Never. He's asking for it. He can take care of himself. You have to know this—people like us have to use what we can use. We can't afford to go soft."

Sometimes he scared her. Sometimes she was sorry for him. Just now, with a sudden stab of pity, she had glimpsed something strange. She sensed that he was bewildered and that, comfortable only when he was sure of himself, he was striking out in anger at his uncertainty.

For once in his life, Lamar Winter was struggling with a force he could neither control nor understand. All his life he had fought for what he wanted as well as for everything he believed was his by right. He had come at last to wring a savage joy from battle for its own sake. He had been fully prepared to fight his way into Peaceable Lane, and winning the fight against powerful odds would have meant an extra bonus of gleeful triumph. But he had won without a fight. No, he had not even won. He had lost and then the victory had been handed to him as a gift. One man's gift, offered without condition, made at the cost of honor. Nothing in his life had prepared him to receive warmth or generosity or another man's sacrifice. Instinct drove him to suspicion. And yet a sharp and ruthless intelligence which would spare himself no more than it would an enemy insisted that, in Matt's gift, there was nothing to suspect. Winter had found himself on a precipice of doubt, staring, both fascinated and repelled, into an abyss where the clear, cruel values he lived by suddenly and unaccountably did not hold true.

He's so damn tough, Margo was thinking. So hard. He was ruled by courage and an unbending pride. And yet there was in him such a well of compassion and enfolding warmth. But only, she realized dimly, for herself and her son. She knew he was troubled; she could not know why, nor could she realize that Winter himself did not know.

"We'd better think how we're going to act . . . out there," she said. "Maybe we ought to rehearse."

He smiled, brought back suddenly to a gay confidence.

"Like we owned the joint, honey, just like we sure enough owned the joint. I haven't had much training in the country-gentleman bit yet, but I'll get to it. To start, I'd say we hire a gardener and a maid and buy some outdoor furniture for the kind of gracious country living they show in *American Home.* I'll turn that north bedroom into a studio so I'll hardly have to come to town. If we feel like getting the sun, we'll sit on the lawn and soak it up. And if we don't, we won't. And if the folks come calling"—the smile broadened—"we'll go calling back. And we won't take any guff from anybody. How's that for a program?"

6

"ZACK AND I are going out to peddle our papers," Matt said to Ellen after dinner. He spoke with self-conscious stiffness. He knew what was uppermost in her mind. They had avoided talking about the house, and he did so now only because it was necessary. "The money's in the bank and I've written the checks. We're going to make the divvy before the storm breaks. They may be mad but they'll be solvent."

"Wait a minute," Ellen said. "Wait until I get these glasses in the dishwasher. I'm going along and talk to Beth while you're out."

Beth Gold and Ellen Jones had been on first-name, egg-borrowing, car-pooling, morning-coffee-drinking, bridge-playing, back-yard-gossiping, leaving-the-key-with-the-other-during-vacations terms from the first summer in Peaceable Lane. They were not intimate friends, but they were casually good friends, and that, they both considered, was about as much as you wanted in a neighborhood no more closely knit than this one. Theirs was a woman's friendship, which meant that it was keyed partly to their living conveniently close together, but even more to the interests of their children and their men.

Now they shared an extra and appalling intimacy. They, and no other woman on the lane, knew what one of their husbands had done and the other had connived in. It felt like the shared, unwanted ownership of a hurricane about to break.

Beth manufactured two cups of instant tea and brought them to the kitchen table. "My mother would have made me stand in the corner for using this stuff," Beth said. "She would have said it was lazy. And she would have said it doesn't taste like tea—and she would have been right. But it's easier, and I'm for anything that's easier. There were six kids in our family, and my mother worked from the time my father got up at six until she was the last one in bed at eleven. But with all the dishwashers and automatic washers and driers and vacuum cleaners and rotisseries and deep freezes and frozen food and instant food and six-month floor waxes, I know I wash and iron and cook and clean and pick-up-after as time without end as she did. Anyhow, she didn't have a car pool to worry about—the kids went to school on the subway. You're worried, aren't you?"

"Yes," Ellen said. "Scared silly. And baffled. And I don't even understand why they did it."

"You think it doesn't make sense?"

"Well, does it? First they get together with everybody else and they decide that if these—these people move into the lane, it's over the hill to the poorhouse for everybody. Then we're put through absolute hell by those gorillas. Then the next thing we know they've turned right around and sold it to the very same man. Sense?"

"My mother always said that no man made much sense," Beth

said mildly. "I decided a long time ago if I was going to keep Zack I'd have to keep the part that is—you should excuse the expression —ham."

"How do you mean, ham?" Ellen asked.

"Causes," Beth said succinctly. "Worries about justice. Frets about underdogs. Gets on committees. He thinks it's because he's Jewish, but it isn't really. Only that, maybe, being Jewish increases his exposure to other people's problems. There are plenty of Jews who don't care about anything but number one."

"But Matt was never a cause carrier."

"No? But something then."

"Yes, something all right." Ellen's smooth forehead was puckered and her gray eyes were wondering. "Something, but I don't quite know what. He isn't tough—anyhow, not tough the way Grant Macmillan is tough. He could get hurt by not being tough enough, but I'm glad he's not. But . . . in another way . . . he's being terribly tough about this. I don't know whether to be proud of him or put arsenic in his coffee."

Beth giggled. "You don't look like the arsenic type to me. But it's an idea. This fancy flim-flummery of theirs—what if somebody catches on?"

"Oh, good Lord!" Ellen gasped. "I hadn't thought of that. Laura Cusack! Can you imagine?"

Incongruously she giggled at the frightful image; she couldn't help it.

Peaceable Lane's children and women were suffering an onset of the affliction which kills cats. The painters spent three days in the house at No. 1. Then delivery trucks and plumbers, electricians and carpet layers arrived in waves. They carried in a glittering army of de luxe kitchen and laundry appliances and followed with an enormous roll of carpeting. When the burlap was stripped away on the lawn, the carpet was seen to be luxuriously piled and of a perilously impractical eggshell shade. All this was accomplished without benefit of visible supervision by the new owner, who was, they understood, somebody named Lakeland from Long Island.

"She'll go crazy trying to keep that thing clean," Laura Cusack confided when, after observing the carpet during a reconnaissance patrol, she went to the pool and encountered Cyd Cavanidis, lightly contained as usual. Laura disapproved of Cyd, but she was the only handy recipient for news. On Laura's fact-finding forays she used the Cusack chow for camouflage. This stratagem did not deceive many people, since every other woman on the lane knew that she never walked the dog unless she needed to find out something.

Laura shared discovery of the zebra-skin divan with a stick-ball game being played on the street in front of No. 1. The kids were standing watch too. Laura was walking past the game warily, keeping an eye out for flying bats and flung balls, when the moving van arrived. She stayed to watch the game and was thus in position to bear witness when that striking set of furniture was carried into the house section by section. Her interest did not abate when it was followed by a grand piano, the gleaming black expanse of the Winters' ebony cocktail table, and lamps like Japanese lanterns on wrought-iron stands.

"You wouldn't think Long Island could produce something like that," Laura told Ellen Jones when they met beside the frozen-juice bins in the A & P in Chappaqua. "Those people must certainly be exotic." Ellen winced and toyed grimly with the thought of saying, "Ma'am, you ain't seen nothin' yet."

And so Peaceable Lane was on stand-by alert when at last the scarlet Jaguar slashed down the ramp into the lane. Laura was on patrol at the moment, but all the Jaguar's occupants saw of her was a flashing glimpse of an emaciated, red-haired woman attached by a leash to a red chow as, with a squeal of brakes and facile expertness, the Negro sliced the car around her and whirled into the driveway of No. 1. Feeling exuberant, Lamar Winter jumped out, walked around the car and scooped his wife into his arms and carried her into the house with a flourish.

Half laughing, Margo wiggled and gasped and yelped, "Put me down! You're making a spectacle."

Winter laughed delightedly and patted her shapely bottom.

"They're probably already bringing up the shock troops," he said. "Honey, you just fetch me my musket while I bar the door."

Having been caught on the wrong side of the road and in the Jaguar's line of fire, Laura had had a good scare. The car was already past her and screeching into the driveway before her faculties galvanized and she scuttled over the curb and onto the Outerbridge lawn. She whirled at bay and stood, openmouthed, as Winter flamboyantly delivered Margo across the threshold.

She was still staring when a black Cadillac limousine slid down the ramp and into the driveway with a contented swoosh. A chauffeur in gray livery descended and helped a small boy with an anxious dark face remove a red-and-silver model airplane from the tonneau. The driver saluted amiably as the boy turned toward the house with his treasure balanced in solicitous hands.

Laura was nearly home, yanking at the indignant chow, when she had recovered her breath sufficiently to begin to get mad. It was about then that what she had witnessed began to register. Even then she didn't believe it. She disbelieved it so firmly that only the shattered remnants of her dignity prevented her going back to confirm her disbelief.

By the time Paul reached home she had come around full circle and decided that what she had seen she had seen indeed. By that time the news was widely distributed, having missed only the Drapers, who were spending a week on Fire Island, and Steve Cavanidis, who was out of town on business.

Before dinner Solomon Weissman strolled up the lane. He was making for the Outerbridge home but hoping to supplement the neighborhood grapevine with some first-hand evidence en route. He got all he needed, for Lamar and Margo Winter were in the front yard with Tod, taking a new owner's critical survey of the shrubbery. Winter tossed him a negligent, neighborly wave, and because Weissman was a hard man to catch off base, he waved back.

"So it's true, John Ainslie," Weissman said as the lawyer admitted him. "I had my doubts when Paul Cusack telephoned as soon as he got home and said the new people over there"—he nodded toward No. 1 without looking at it—"were colored. Do you know how this happened?"

"No, I don't. I have only just discovered it myself," Outerbridge said. The lawyer's small mouth was a tight pink rosebud, and his eyes looked agitated behind the pince-nez. "Have you seen Jones or Gold?"

"No. I wanted to make sure first. Are you sure these are the owners—not servants?"

"Would servants arrive in a Jaguar and a Cadillac? In a wild sport shirt like that? Did you see him?"

"No, I suppose not. I understood the buyer was a man named Lakeland—and that he was white. Do you know if that's Lakeland?"

"It is not Lakeland," Outerbridge said grimly. "I saw Lakeland when Gold was showing him the house. I was afraid of this. We were marked for slaughter. Once those organizations set out to break into an area, they stop at nothing—nothing."

"I'll see Gold. Try to find out what happened. He must know—at least have some idea by now." Weissman shook his head. "It's . . . it's unbelievable."

"Frankly, I was suspicious when we got our full price. The place simply wasn't worth it."

"Yes?" Weissman looked mildly skeptical. "You didn't say anything, John Ainslie."

"No," Outerbridge admitted. He was frowning, his mouth pursed in troubled thought. "I can't help wondering. It's so bald. Do you suppose it's possible somebody got to them, Gold or Jones or both?" He hesitated. "I mean with money?"

"No." Weissman was emphatic. "They could have been duped. They may even have been stupid. But they couldn't have been got with money. I'd swear to it." He sighed. "Well, we'll find out. But the damage has been done. The question is what we do now. I haven't thought it all out, but for the moment I believe our safest course is to do nothing. This street needs calm now as it never has before."

"Yes," Outerbridge said thoughtfully. "We'll have to be very careful."

7

Outwardly there was nothing to reveal that Peaceable Lane had suffered a volcanic shock. The street turned a serene and placid surface to the midsummer sun. Lamar Winter was at first puzzled and then a trifle resentful, as a man may feel resentful when he is tensed to resist attack and then finds nothing to oppose him. He did not lower the chip from his shoulder, but after an uneventful week he began to carry it a little less self-consciously.

Matt Jones also was oppressed by the deceptive air of calm and communicated his unease to Gold.

"We could have been wrong," he said moodily. "Maybe we underrated the place. They're taking it better than we thought they could. Maybe we'd better level with them. I don't like this load on my back."

"Come clean and you can head for the hills," Gold said earnestly. "They're still in shock. Let them know we deliberately sold them down the river and this place will blow like a keg of dynamite."

"It may be worse if we try to keep the cork in and somebody pries it out by himself. If that happens we'll have no defense," Matt insisted.

"It's the chance we have to take," Gold said. "Meantime, the only thing is to lie—lie until they call him Old Whirling George Washington, the way he spins in his grave."

"I don't like it."

"Do I? But we're stuck with it. We have to go on pretending it was an act of God. As long as they believe they were licked by an organization too big to fight, they can accept the idea that it was hopeless from the first. That way they won't like it, but they'll take it and learn to live with it."

"I'm not sure you're right."

"Why?"

"It was the machine we were afraid of in the first place. The idea that a machine was out to bust us. If we let them go on thinking it was the machine, maybe somebody will get scared and stampede that much quicker. Then we'd have a real mess—everybody bolting to the nearest exit. Nobody walking, everybody running."

"It's a guess," Gold said thoughtfully. "Maybe a good one, but I doubt it."

"If it is a good one, though," Matt pressed on, "it might be smarter to let them know how and why Winter got here. They wouldn't have to guess and worry. That way they'd know he was here to live, not to wreck the place."

"Maybe, Matt," Gold said. "Maybe later—but right now I'm afraid it would pull the plug. Let's wait a while."

Out of the paralyzing shock of the first week, there came a few sparse but encouraging signs that Peaceable Lane owned at least the nucleus of the strength it needed to survive.

Estelle Outerbridge, so little and quick and quiet that she resembled the wrens which nested in the birdhouse on the maple outside the Jones kitchen window, came to the door as Ellen was pouring another cup of coffee after Matt left.

"You're just in time. Join me," Ellen said.

"Ellen, I want to say something," Estelle said, busying herself with sugar and cream. "Please don't be hurt. But you must know people are talking and wondering how your husband and Mr. Gold could have been fooled by those people."

Ellen stiffened warily and said nothing, waiting . . . gathering her defenses.

"Well, I just want you to know . . . of course, I wouldn't dare say this to John Ainslie . . . at least, I don't dare say it yet. But, Ellen, I'm so pleased . . . so happy . . . I can't tell you."

Ellen looked at her, astonished.

"I hope your husband doesn't feel badly about being fooled." Estelle's face was—there was no other way to describe it—radiant. "I really believe it was meant to be . . . God sometimes saves us from ourselves . . . I hope your husband understands that and can accept it and be thankful."

Ellen's first impulse was to say that the big knucklehead understood all too well, but the sight of the earnest little face was too much for her. She got up and went around the table and took the small creature in her arms and murmured, "Thank you, Estelle, thank you very much." The fact that her own eyes were misty made her long to plant a spike heel somewhere south of Matt's equator.

The conviction which Dr. Abram expressed to Zack Gold, though less inclined to credit divine intervention, was not otherwise much different.

"I wish to congratulate you," the doctor said. "Somehow, by good luck or bad management, you have saved us all from a sickening crime. I do not wish to seem effusive, Mr. Gold, but I must say this—for the first time in many years, at no cost to myself, I feel like a brave man. I must thank you."

The doctor went back across the street with a stride springier and more carefree than Gold had ever seen that thin, bent and intensely introverted man achieve. Gold watched him go with somber eyes.

There was that much. It was not enough. It was not enough, either, that Solomon Weissman returned placidly to his roses or that John Ainslie Outerbridge, finding a greater degree of fatalism than he had suspected inside his pudgy body, reasoned his way to a conclusion that, the battle having been lost, abiding patience was needed to win the war.

The lane had been stunned. It had not been knocked out. Slowly, beneath the surface, almost imperceptible at first, began the subterranean stirrings leading to avalanche.

Steve Cavanidis, who occasionally looked upon his lush, blond wife with urgent lechery but otherwise held her in faintly amused indifference, mortally offended her when he returned from a conference of union business agents in Cleveland. He got off a plane at La Guardia and took a taxi to 125th Street, where he caught the 6:10 for Chappaqua. He happened on Paul Cusack in the smoker and settled beside him and there learned the turn of events in Peaceable Lane. A poker player born and later polished, Cavanidis received the news with the merest show of interest, just enough to milk Cusack dry with an occasional, seemingly casual question. Cusack didn't know much, but Cavanidis' offhand manner irritated him enough to tell it all and offer everything he speculated as boot. Cavanidis merely nodded.

Cyd was at the door when he came from the taxi with his bag.

She smelled muskily of Tabu and glowed healthily in a strapless white summer dress, held up by a cantilever principle which Steve could have understood but was confident he could circumvent without research. She came to kiss him, and he slid an arm around her and down over her buttocks and caressingly discovered, as he had expected, that the silky white cotton covered flesh—not pants.

"R-r-r-row," he observed. "Now? Or five minutes from now?"

"Quit it," Cyd said archly. "Don't you ever think of anything else?"

"Now and then," Steve said. "Which is more than you can say."

"Smart aleck," Cyd bridled. "All right, but we'll have to hurry. The kids are over at Kelly's, but they'll be back for dinner in twenty minutes." She started upstairs, reaching for the keystone of the improbable dress.

"It's a form of activity I don't like to rush," Steve grumbled as he followed her. But nothing came of their intent, for Steve, pulling off his shirt, called to Cyd in the bathroom, "Cusack tells me we got some new neighbors. Kind of blue, he says. You seen them?"

"They're blue all right," Cyd called back. "The man's a handsome brute and the girl's a dazzler. She's got every woman on the lane seeing green—except me, I think. I'll know for sure when I see how you act when you see her."

"I don't think I'm about to change my luck. One blonde is about all I can manage at my mileage. Anybody seem to know how they weaseled in?"

"Unh unh," Cyd said. "I heard that Mr. Gold said they got fooled by a dummy buyer. You know I don't pay much attention to things like that. Anyhow, I've been busy getting ready for the decorators. Wait'll you see the paper I picked!"

"Hmmm," Steve said, remembering that just before leaving he had yielded to Cyd's long-standing petition to have the house done over in colors to accent her personality. He had given in out of sheer ennui with Cyd's marathon wheedling, even though he suspected that the result was more likely to prove garish than livable. Even in the act of surrender he had speculated that he must be getting soft; he could remember when he had been tougher about being conned out of a thousand clams—or more.

"They're going to start tomorrow," Cyd said, undulating out of the bathroom, starkly and breath-takingly naked.

"Hmmm," Steve said again thoughtfully, sitting on the edge of the bed with one leg of his pants off and tugging at the other. His face wore a veiled, abstracted air and, although she was long since accustomed to his often mysterious but always calculating thought processes, Cyd was slightly offended at his failure to respond to the view. She knew he would respond vigorously enough when he got around to it, but it would do a girl's heart good if once in a while he'd be a little more spontaneous about it. Snort, maybe, paw the rug, or at least whistle.

"It's early yet," Steve said. "You can probably catch that boss painter at home. Call him and tell him the deal's off."

"Off! Are you crazy, Steve?" Cyd's voice held sheer, stricken disbelief. "For heaven's sake, why?"

"Off," Steve said equably. "I'm not crazy. Not crazy enough to stick any money into this joint until I see what happens. It doesn't need decorating anyway, and it sure as hell doesn't need it if the place is going to blow up. Your personality might make a terrific impression on the nigger we might be selling out to in the next few months, but I'm not about to speculate on it. See if you can get him now. I don't want to have to run the guy off after he gets here with his ladders and brushes." He struggled out of the second leg of his pants and, reaching to the bedside stand, handed the telephone toward her.

Cyd stood immobile, a voluptuous work of statuary, more lush and considerably more available than marble. But her face was pinched into a mask of shock, anger and rejection.

"Steve Cavanidis," she yelled, "if you think you're going back on your promise, you're not going to get away with it! I won't have it! I've waited long enough to have this gloomy dump fixed up decently." The tears began to flow copiously, and her nose, as it always did under these circumstances, turned instantaneously red. "What kind of a cold-blooded damn goon are you, anyway? Trying to make me call up a perfect stranger when I haven't got a stitch on!" Outrage incarnate, she flounced to her closet and came back struggling into a wrapper with such anguished tugs that it ripped.

"Steve, you promised!" she wailed. "And just when—what are you, anyhow? A man . . . or a fish?"

Steve sighed, reached for his pants and started pulling them on again.

"What's his number?" he asked through the uproar of her sobs. "I'll call him—just as soon as I get my pants on—so he won't think I'm not modest."

8

WHEN LAMAR WINTER first felt the tensing of Peaceable Lane's forces of rejection, the attack seemed mere spite. Expensive, inconvenient, irritating, but that was all. It was nothing conclusive and nothing he couldn't handle.

He had wanted to be rid of his Harlem studio. He liked to work at home and, when he had first seen the Bronson house, he had noted that the north bedroom could be converted into an admirable studio. He had envisioned ripping out the wall and part of the roof, to be replaced with what would be, in effect, a huge dormer mainly made of glass. He had sketched an approximation of what he wanted. Soon after they moved, he went looking for a craftsman to create it for him.

He sought out a Negro carpenter. Margo might be looking for a white maid, but Winter took an obscure pleasure in showing the lane that, for enduring work, he preferred a man of his own race. He found Sam Stapleton in White Plains.

Stapleton looked at Winter's sketch doubtfully. He pointed out that the big dormer would be visible from the street in side elevation and that it would not particularly agree with the architectural harmony Riccetti's designers had shaped into Peaceable Lane.

"Never mind that," Winter said. "I'll get a tree moved in there, and the first thing you know it'll be out of sight."

"You know what you want," Stapleton said. "And that's what I'm here to deliver." Shortly he appeared with a helper, and in two days they tore out the wall and roof. Each night he covered the hole with tarpaulin.

"Lot of rain this summer," he explained. "No point ruining the floor and the plaster underneath."

Gordon Draper came back from Fire Island and saw the carpenter's truck in the Winter driveway and recognized Stapleton's name stenciled on the sides. He knew the man and, moreover, knew that Stapleton's usual occupation was to work for his father whenever the senior Draper had a job under way, which was most of the time.

He mentioned the alterations in progress at No. 1 when his father, Clarence Draper, stopped in at the Chrysler agency during the day.

"You say the black bastard's got Sam working for him?" the elder Draper said thoughtfully. "Tearing the side of the house out? What do you suppose the jigaboo is up to?" Gordon told his father that he wouldn't know exactly, but from the looks of things it was an eyesore already and promised to become more so.

"Hmmm," said Draper, Sr. "I'd better look into this. You young punks don't seem to know how to look out for yourselves."

That night, when he knew Stapleton should have pulled in from the day's work, Clarence Draper telephoned him.

"Sam? You busy? I want you to drop over here to my place after supper. Got a little job I want to talk to you about," he said.

By and large, Clarence Draper held a low opinion of his son's acumen, and he had been irritated to learn of Peaceable Lane's change of status. It was just like the stupid little jerk, he thought, not to have better sense than to buy into an area that was going to be ruined this way. If he'd had the brains God gave a goose, he would have known that living next door to all those Jews was bound to result in something nasty. Damn fool kid. It's always up to the old man to bail him out of a jam, he thought, always had been, always would be.

Stapleton's pickup pulled into the Draper driveway obediently in the dusk. Hearing it, Clarence came from the house and put one foot on the running board and one elbow on the window sill. "Sam," he said, "I hear you got a job going up there on Peaceable Lane. Tell me about it."

Stapleton was puzzled, but he knew that when Mr. Draper asked questions he wanted answers.

"Well, there's this new guy up there," he said. "He's a painter, he says. So he's making that north bedroom into a studio. God-damnedest, biggest goddam dormer you ever saw. But that's what he wants and that's what he gets."

"Not from you he don't," Clarence Draper said succinctly. "I want you to drop that job, Sam."

"Drop it, boss? What for? He knows what he wants and it's his house, and as long as he got the money, why should I drop it?"

"Just drop it, Sam," Draper said evenly. "Don't worry about why. Just drop it."

"But, boss, you ain't got any work for me just now. What's this all about?" Sam Stapleton had not mistaken the hard edge of threat in Draper's voice, and he knew Clarence Draper well and he knew that he wasn't going to push this very far. But all the same he was puzzled, and he hoped Draper would explain, a little anyhow. Sam Stapleton knew with experienced clarity exactly which side his income was buttered on.

Draper was not in an explaining mood. It would have been strange if he was.

"Just get off the job," he said. "Tomorrow. I'll be putting you to work next week anyhow. Got those new apartments coming up in Greenburgh."

"Look, boss." Sam Stapleton was ready to fold; indeed, he knew that he had folded already, but his artisan's conscience was bothering him. "What in hell am I gonna tell the guy? I got his place all open to the weather and I sure do hate to walk out on him that way."

"You're walking though," Draper said. "Tomorrow morning bright and early. And take your tarps. Let him worry about the weather, and I hope to Christ it rains."

"All right, boss. Whatever you say. I sure hope that Greenburgh job comes up like you say," Stapleton said in surrender. The next morning he obeyed orders, mournfully taking down the tarpaulin, gathering up his tools and neglecting to ask for two days' pay. To Winter's first bewilderment and then quickly flowering anger he returned only a mulish silence. After all, what could he say? Admit that he had been bullied by a man whose will, he knew with dull resentment, was incomparably stronger than his own?

The Cusack dog had never had it so good. But to pay for all the walks he took, he did have to put up with more ill-tempered jerking on the leash than he liked whenever developments at the Winter house proved too much for his mistress's sensibilities. He had an easy day of it when Laura bore witness to the stoppage of work on Winter's big dormer. Shirley Draper had warned her that it was about to happen and she was there to see. But it was as much as a dog could bear two days later when she watched the project start up again. It had not rained and Winter had found another carpenter. This time the artist researched his man with care and offered no hostages to race pride. The carpenter was white and Winter had had to go all the way to the Bronx to get him, and another five hundred dollars had been tacked on the price. But this time, learning his lesson, Winter had his man on a contract; if the job stopped, somebody would have to pay for it.

Peter Yale was a nervous man in a nervous profession and he owned an acutely developed sense of personal injury which nothing about life in Peaceable Lane had tended to soothe. He suffered the exasperations common to all commuters. But they were worse for Yale: from him the penance of three hours a day on the train, five days a week, was exacted at unlovely hours when the Central's trains to Chappaqua were few and far between and made up of its oldest, creakingest, moldiest and most dismal coaches. He was denied the joys which some men thought made the sacrifice worth while, for he abominated rural surroundings and longed for the city. Injury mounted upon the back of insult while, year after year, the assessors revised upward the taxes he was forced to pay on the acre he hated.

And now this had happened. He learned it as soon as he returned, after a prudent period, from the Washington foxhole where he had believed it wise to sit out the battle of Peaceable Lane.

He was having a conference with his wife, or rather, he was using Annabelle as a backboard on which to bounce the causes of his just complaint.

"There's something about that deal that stinks," he said. "First, the nigger's shut out and everything is under control. Under control, my ass. The next time I look, there he is, right under my nose."

"Well," Annabelle said mildly enough, "I don't see where you stand making an objection."

"Oh, you don't, don't you?" Peter said, wondering why she always had to slop around in those crummy, garden-stained jeans and shirts. She had certainly let herself go to pot from the smart, svelte dish he had picked out of the cast of a Hollywood television show nine years before. And those snot-nosed kids, forever squalling. "I don't suppose it means anything to you that having that jig down the road is going to cost me ten thousand bucks? Don't tell me I don't have a beef!"

"You'd make one anyhow," Annabelle said wearily. It was quite a while now, she reflected, a matter of years, since she had abandoned her last illusion about her mate. "I suppose it's unfair to remind you of where you were when the roof fell in."

"What did you expect?" he shouted in exasperation. Why were women so stupid blind to reason? "You knew they had me by the balls. If I'd got caught in that deal, you know where you'd be now—out on your fanny in the dusty street."

Well, it was probably true, she thought. The network was touchy, excessively sensitive to criticism where its minions were concerned. She wondered again, as she often did, whether life wouldn't be pleasanter all around if she divorced him. Still, you had to be realistic: how did a girl as long out of the profession as she was go about supporting two kids? She sighed.

"I don't see what there is to do about it," she said, not quite sure whether she meant his grievance or her own.

"Oh, don't you?" Peter snarled. "Maybe you like living in nigger heaven. You probably do. It was your idea to move out to this insane Sleepy Hollow in the first place. Country life for the kids! Don't throw money away in rent! Invest in something real! I'll never understand what made me listen to that crap. Now look at your fine investment—straight down coon alley."

"They tried to stop it," Annabelle said reasonably. "You can't blame them."

"Can't I?" Yale snorted. "I could have bet something would go sour, letting the deal be handled by that Gold do-gooder. These people must have been out of their minds."

"Well, you weren't out of yours," Annabelle said. "You ducked in time. Congratulations."

"Ahhh," he said. He went to the picture window and stared moodily at the Jones house across the lane. "I just wonder . . ." he muttered.

"Wonder what?"

"Wonder if Jones and Gold got paid off."

"Oh, give it a rest." Annabelle sighed. "You ought to know better."

"No," Yale said. Annabelle had seen that slit-eyed, calculating look before; it irritated her. "One thing sure," he went on, "they're not catching me in this wringer. If this stinking street comes unstuck, here's a lad who isn't going to be here when it happens."

"Yes?" Annabelle said, without much interest.

That morning was misty and unseasonably chill, one of those days which can never decide whether to rain in earnest. Matt and Paul Cusack, both feeling grumpy under the thrust of weather, walked up the lane together and stood at the bus stop, drearily contemplating a dreary day. Normally they could have hoped to pick up a ride before the bus arrived, but this was the vacation season and few of the regulars would be going to town. Ellen was off early, taking a load of small fry to day camp, which accounted for Matt's lack of a chauffeur.

Lamar Winter's Jaguar swished under the overpass and started up the ramp. Then it bucked to a stop in a squeal of brakes. Winter had seen them.

"Hi," he called. "Want a ride?"

Matt saw Cusack stiffen and his face set in a banker's mask. Well, he thought, here we go. Rootity-toot.

"Sure," he called. He turned to Cusack with the best approximation of a careless grin he could manage. "Come on, Paul. It's a free one."

"No, thanks," Cusack muttered, looking at him incredulously. "You're not going to——"

"The hell I'm not," Matt said clearly and crossed the road. Winter let the Jaguar roll back down the slope to meet him. Matt got in and glanced back as Winter put the red car in gear and gunned it. Cusack looked stunned.

"Kind of standoffish, your buddy back there, wouldn't you say?" Winter asked, throwing Matt a sardonic grin.

"Well," Matt said, "I wouldn't call him one of your strongest boosters."

The grin spread wider and Winter laughed aloud. "That's the understatement of the week. You've been seeing too many British movies. I know what my ration of boosters is." He took his right hand from the wheel and held the index finger erect and alone. "One."

"You haven't been doing your homework," Matt grunted.

"Huh?"

"The way you check things, I'm surprised you didn't know," Matt said. "It wasn't just me. The deal never would have worked if somebody else hadn't stood aside and let us slide it right through him."

"I'm damned," Winter said, suddenly serious. "Who? I wouldn't have thought there was another Samaritan in the county."

"Zack Gold," Matt said. "He knew what I was up to . . . and let it go."

"Why?"

"I'm not sure I can explain him. I think he thinks nobody has the right to interfere—with you or anybody else."

"He's a Jew, isn't he? That could explain it—if he's the conscience-ridden kind."

"I don't know." Matt shrugged. "He's a Jew, but I doubt if that explains it. He's an extraordinarily decent guy."

Well, there it was, Winter thought. Something else to ponder about and take account of. Another thing he couldn't have foreseen or allowed for. It was good to know though, possibly useful. But was it either wise or necessary to do anything more than take note of it and remember it? He didn't think he would ever fathom the offhand affection with which a man like Matt could bestow that casual, admiring accolade: "decent guy." And probably meant it, too. These white men with their easy, uncomplicated likes and dislikes. Well, he shrugged inwardly, they could afford it.

"How're you making out?" Matt asked. "You're still a tenderfoot —wait till you get your first tax bill."

"It's all right . . . so far," Winter said, bringing his attention back to the moment. "Had a little hassle with a nigger carpenter I hired. Somebody got to him—one of the folks, no doubt. You know, no yellow bastard makes me quite as sore as a black yellow bastard. Why can't they stand up and fight for their rights?"

"Like you?" Matt asked.

"Like me," Winter said flatly.

"I wouldn't fight it too hard," Matt said seriously. "The street is touchy and will be for a while, as if you couldn't guess. You're going to live here, and I don't need to point out that in a fight you're outnumbered. Take it easy."

"How ain't I taking it easy, boss?" Winter grinned. "Been here a week already and I'll guarantee nobody's smoked a reefer in my house yet. Haven't even hardly raped any white women yet."

"Ah, put the fence post down off your shoulder."

"I may need it to defend myself." Winter smiled. "Who's that underweight redhead that does guard duty up and down the street? She's got a chow as red as she is and nearly as big as me—and he doesn't look so peaceable either."

"Laura Cusack," Matt grunted. "She'll be the last one in the neighborhood to decide you're a great man."

Matt had not noticed the Jaguar's pace. But as they rolled from the cutoff and straightened out on the Saw Mill Parkway, he became conscious of its powerful rush. He looked at the speedometer, blinked and looked again. The needle held to the hundred mark, shuddering slightly.

"Hey!" he yelled. "Look at that! What the hell are you doing?"

A happy grin flashed across the dark face.

"Just going into town, boss. Thass all, yassuh, jus' goin' t' town."

"Come off it, you poor man's Fangio," Matt snarled. "You get a ticket and I never saw you before in my life. Slow down, boy! You tired of living?"

"Calmly, lad. I can handle this thing like I was born in it."

"You'll die in it," Matt said. "If you're just proving you're smarter than white men, let me point out white men built the Jaguar. Slow down!"

9 It was early when Macmillan's secretary asked Matt to come in. Macmillan had just arrived and was at the window, looking out at the gray day. Matt saw that his mail still lay untouched on his desk. When Macmillan turned and came toward him, Matt saw the shadow of agitation and something more —anger?—on the blandly self-assured face. What's up? he thought uneasily. It was unlike the boss to let much show on the surface.

"What's going on down on your street?" Macmillan demanded abruptly. "What happened? How did it happen?"

So that was it; he might have expected it. "We've got a new neighbor," Matt said cautiously. "I suppose you heard he's colored. He is. How did you find out?"

"How could I miss it? Or anybody miss it? That skinny redheaded magpie, Mrs. Cusack. She was blabbing it all over the club last night," Macmillan said, then added incongruously, "I can't stand that woman."

Matt couldn't resist a grin. "If you had to make the choice, who would you pick for next door? Laura? Or a colored family?"

Macmillan shot an impatient look at him.

"This is nothing to joke about, Matt. You ought to know. You're hit first and worst. What's so funny?"

"I didn't say it was funny," Matt said a little stiffly. "But I don't see that blowing my stack will change anything."

The look Macmillan bent on him was baffled and angry and carried something less than full approval of his favorite junior executive. "I thought you people had that situation under control. You had charge of it yourself. Somebody must have slipped damn foolishly. How did it happen?"

Matt shrugged. Lying was getting easier. "We were taken," he said shortly.

"Taken how?"

"As John Ainslie Outerbridge says, you can't fight an organization. They put in a ringer on us."

"I should have guessed it," Macmillan said and shuffled his mail with impatient gestures. "But you should have too. How about that lawyer of yours? Didn't he investigate?"

"As much as he could," Matt said cautiously. "It was a neat job."

"Neat!" Macmillan snorted. "Neat and dirty and damn dangerous. Do you realize that's the first break-through in this part of the county? And now they're in, they won't stop there." He stared gloomily at the wall; Matt could not know that Grant Macmillan was seeing the crumbling of carefully erected, seemingly impregnable barricades that had, all his life until now, withstood humanity's vulgar pressure upon a way of life which seemed to him not so much privileged as sacred. Now, in regretful hindsight, his mind went back to remember when all this might have been prevented, if Grassy Tor's members had only had the foresight and the plain guts to bring tougher pressure on builder Riccetti.

"I don't think it's the beginning of a big break-through," Matt said carefully, feeling his way, because he knew Macmillan had to be told now, but recognizing the danger in what he must say. "It sounds as though you don't know who it is. If you knew you might have less reason to worry."

It took the words a moment to penetrate Macmillan's angry preoccupation. He looked up sharply. "I know? What do you mean?"

"Lamar Winter."

"What about Winter? What's he got to do with this?"

"Winter's the man who moved in."

"What?"

"Yes. That's why I don't think it's the start of a flood." He considered how to go farther, as far as he had to go on this dangerous ground. "He had organization help, that's true. Had to have it. But you know Lamar. He's no hot-eyed crusader. He was doing what any man would have done to get his wife and kid out of Harlem."

"Winter? I don't believe it," Macmillan breathed, but, staring at Matt and reading confirmation in his face, he rallied to probe this new knowledge. "What made him think he could get away with it?"

"He did get away with it," Matt reminded his boss. "He says he has a right to live anywhere he can afford the tab. I can't quarrel with that."

"Didn't he know you lived there?"

"He probably did," Matt admitted, guarding himself against saying too much. "He's the kind who would have investigated."

"He never said anything to you?" Macmillan muttered. "What guts! What colossal guts!"

Matt permitted himself the edge of a smile. "If you'd been in his place, would you have said anything?"

"You take this pretty lightly, Matt," Macmillan said. "I wonder if that's why he did it." His eyes had come alight with quick suspicion.

"How do you mean?" Matt said warily. He knew what Macmillan meant and recognized the danger.

"Because you lived there. Knowing you work together. Knowing how much work he does for us. It could be—by God, I'll bet it is! I'll bet he counted on you—on us—for protection."

Matt snorted. He was getting impatient, and the edge of anger was rising to support him in this distasteful and dangerous role of liar. "How could I help him?"

"I don't know. I don't know," Macmillan said impatiently. "You think you know a man but you never do. You don't suppose he really thinks I'll let him get away with it?"

"There isn't a lot we can do," Matt said. "If we had to have one, I'm glad it's Winter. If we can keep people off the panic button, there's a chance we can absorb him and get back to normal."

"Don't be a horse's ass," Macmillan snapped. "I do not propose to tolerate being double-crossed and made a monkey of by a man in my own organization."

Matt knew it was reckless, but he didn't like being talked to that way, didn't like Macmillan's tone and, in the upsurge of anger, he didn't like Macmillan and didn't care if Macmillan knew it. But he made an effort to keep a grip on self-control.

"Winter is not in our organization, Grant," he said. "And, the chances are, if you still want Glamour-Glow, you can't have it without having Winter too."

"Perhaps," Macmillan said grimly. "Just perhaps. I have yet to see an indispensable man."

The Cusack chow suffered his worst indignities—and consequently made a serious error of his own—on the day Laura Cusack discovered the white maid Lamar Winter had hired for his wife. In the role of protective coloration, the dog was being led up the lane when Laura saw a solidly built Nordic blonde on a stepladder washing windows at No. 1. Laura wheeled and hauled the chow toward home so savagely that, when his warning growls failed to relieve the painful and humiliating pressure on the leash, he forsook restraint and bit her on the seat.

Panting, Laura turned on him. She shortened her grip on the leash and lashed him into submission with the lead-weighted grip. She hated the beast, anyhow, because he shed hair badly and could not be bullied into staying off the overstuffed divan.

Safely home, she harried him into the basement and then went to the bathroom and, in some pain and embarrassment, anointed the wound with iodine. After that she turned out Paul's desk until she found the chow's shot record and made sure his rabies inoculation was up to date. She considered calling a doctor but decided it would be too humiliating. In any case, a second and searching inspection of the damaged area, accomplished with the aid of a mirror, indicated that the fangs had merely bruised her.

She decided the chow would have to go. Never mind that impressive pedigree, and twice never mind the fact that Paul foolishly adored the monster.

Then she went to the telephone. She needed a dozen calls to discover which White Plains agency had furnished the Winters' blond servant, but it was worth the effort. She gave the agency a dressing down in no uncertain terms and had the satisfaction of assuring the manager that it would be a long, cold day before she or anyone she knew brought him any business. Her sense of accomplishment was slightly dampened by the manager shoehorning in the last word and craftily hanging up before she could finish him off.

"Madam," he shouted into the telephone, "you can make your own beds and lay in them till hell freezes over!"

The next development in the affairs of Peaceable Lane was serious. Matt was closing in on the last swaths of the front lawn on Saturday morning when he saw Jerome Kelly come up the lane and stop expectantly at the curb. Matt shut off the chattering lawnmower engine and crossed the freshly mowed greensward to meet the dentist.

"Hi," he called. "What's with you?"

"I wonder if you would help me with something," Kelly said. "Advice . . . sort of." He looked depressed, Matt thought, but then he usually did. With that many kids, what could you expect?

"I'm a lousy source of advice," Matt said. "But sure. What's on your mind?"

"You're a member on the hill," Kelly said, and then rushed on with it. "If you can arrange it, I would like to meet Mr. Sloane or Mr. Kern—you know, the real-estate men. I know they're pretty important."

"I know them," Matt said. "Not so well you could call us buddies. What's on your mind?"

"You know I had my house listed with the MacCauley agency . . . for months. Only now they don't want to handle it. I had a letter saying they were releasing it, so I called them up and they meant it, all right. I'd like to talk to somebody about it . . . you know, somebody who knows about these things."

"They give any reason?" Matt asked, but he knew the question was rhetorical; he had already felt the quick, painful stab of what was coming.

But Kelly was a deliberate man with a slow habit of speech, and he wanted to lay it all out in order.

"Well, there was the letter first. They said they were sorry they hadn't been able to move my place, but with the market slow right now and the taxes so rough here, they hadn't been able to locate a buyer. But they knew I was anxious to sell, so they had decided to release it and they hoped I would do better with some other broker."

"You bought that?" Matt asked, wondering why some men were custom-tailored for hard luck and how some, like Kelly, managed to develop such patience to endure it.

"Not exactly," Kelly said. "I didn't see why people like MacCauleys would think somebody else could sell a house if they couldn't. They're supposed to be the top. So I went to see MacCauley himself. He finally admitted the real reason."

"What was it?" Matt asked automatically. But he knew it already and felt the cold, sick weight of it.

"That," Kelly said. He turned and nodded toward where the slate gables of Winter's house and the raw frame of the new dormer were visible above the shrubbery. "MacCauley did a lot of hemming and hawing. But what it came down to was that, because they are the top and intend to stay there, they won't handle a deal in what he called 'questionable and unstable circumstances.' I suppose what he means is, they're scared."

"The jerk," Matt said. He did not need to be told how richly his own hot sense of guilt was contributing to the anger welling up in him. He had overlooked this, somehow forgotten to take account of Kelly's hostage to fortune, now exposed to peril because Lamar Winter had come to Peaceable Lane. That's mine, he thought grimly. Don't try to duck it. But it's not only me. See how they run! Was Winter a man—or a plague? Take MacCauleys. The firm had grown old, respectable and rich dealing in Westchester real estate. "Questionable and unstable circumstances" be damned. Who owed the county and its people a larger debt of stability and confidence? Who held a greater stake in refusing to give way to panic? Who, more than a venerable real-estate broker, had a greater responsibility to recognize that men like Winter could not be denied forever, or a greater responsibility to make a sane adjustment to that knowledge? Yellow, he thought bitterly, plain yellow. His voice came thickly through his anger.

"What do you want to do, Jerry?"

"Whatever's best. That's why I want to talk to somebody about it. We're crowded, but we can manage if we have to. The only thing is, it leaves me in a box. I had already put down earnest money on the place we were dickering for in Connecticut."

"I'll talk to them. See if anything can be done," Matt said.

Stripped to the waist and sweating in the combined heat of the sun and his Saturday chores, Zachariah Gold rested on a bale of peat moss and listened to Matt in somber, thoughtful attention.

"He put down fifteen hundred on the Greenwich deal," Matt said, finishing his report.

"Sort of reckless," Gold said, "ponying it up on a new place before he was out from under the old one. Still, I know he was anxious to move. Taxes, all those kids, and everything. Normally it would have worked too. He wouldn't have been the first man to tie himself to a new house before getting rid of the old one."

"What's his chance of getting his deposit back? Legally, I mean."

Gold shook his head.

"Not much. That's what a binder's for. Earnest of good faith. Sign of intent to go through with the deal. If he doesn't, the other man is entitled to keep it."

"He can't afford it," Matt said.

"I know."

"You never know, not soon enough, how tough it is to level with everybody," Matt said heavily. "Even just those that deserve to be leveled with. I did this to the poor bastard."

"Not just you," Gold said quietly. "I told you it was next to impossible not to be a sonofabitch. We lost sight of this one . . . but even if we hadn't, I don't know what we could have done to avoid it."

"But we can't let it slide either," Matt said.

"No. I know that." Gold sighed. They looked at one another and each knew what was in the other's mind. Here was another burden, one they hadn't counted on. But it was inevitably their own, because they had exposed themselves to it and because there was no one else to take it up. Kelly, that inoffensive man, must not be punished for their deeds. That was unthinkable. And running desperately through each man's mind was his own perennial lack of margin, the relentless, proliferating pressures that made another $750 bulk so huge. But there was no ducking it.

"It'll take a little time to get it up," Gold said. "I'll have to borrow it."

Looking at the heavy, thoughtful face, knowing it bore worry and concern, but no trace of resentment, Matt felt the warmth of his affection for this big man. There aren't many like this guy, he thought, almost not any.

"So will I. But that ain't all. How do we handle it? We can't just give it to him." He had a sudden image of the two of them walking up to Kelly and handing him a check for fifteen hundred dollars.

He could see the dentist's face as they tried to explain. The wild incongruity of the scene was too much and he had to grin. "Can't you just see the sad-eyed bastard?"

Suddenly Gold was laughing back at him.

"Cut it out, you silly sonofabitch. I'll figure a way to handle it. If we tried that he'd be sending for the crazy wagon."

10

WINTER'S STUDIO DORMER was finished in midmorning of one of the summer's sultriest days. He was delighted with it and eager to see it ready for work. He had abandoned the Harlem studio and had, himself, solicitously ridden up the parkways with the truck bringing the easels, canvases, cans of brushes, boxes and bottles of paint and thinners and varnishes—all the disorderly paraphernalia of his craft. Now he felt the stuff had to be moved up from the garage—at once.

"It would make more sense to go fishing," Margo protested, as he staggered up the stairs with the first load. "Don't you know what the radio says? It's going over ninety."

"I want to see what it looks like," he said.

"I'll bring you a picture of what it looks like at the hospital." She sighed. "But, okay, I'll join you in the loony bin. What goes first?"

"You stick to hausfrauing," he said. "The big stuff is too big for you, and the little stuff Tod can handle. Do me a favor and pry him away from TV. He's big enough to give the old man a hand."

The job was finished in midafternoon. Sweating and content, Winter stood at the big easel on which, as though to ease the radical change from Harlem, rested a half-finished portrait of the Glamour-Glow girl. Winter studied the work, trying to decide if this light was different and how much the difference meant.

"Looks good, hey, Tod?" he said.

"She's pretty," the boy agreed soberly. "You want me to call Mother?"

"You can if you want," Winter said, "but it's not necessary. One of the things you need to understand about women—and will eventually—is that they don't know much about men's work and care less. They're not geared for it."

"Well, gee . . ." Tod said. Winter laughed and gripped his shoulder.

"I've got a better idea," he said. "Let's give her a surprise and take her swimming. She might not need it, but we do. I've got to get this place air-conditioned."

"Swimming?" The boy's face lighted. "Sure, wait'll I tell her." He bolted, yelling, "Mother!"

Winter found Margo in the living room, wearing a bemused expression and listening to a distant clamor.

"Where did he go?" Winter said.

"His swimming trunks," Margo said. "He came through here yelling we were going swimming, and then, whoosh, he was gone. Where do you think you're going swimming?"

"Where'd you think, honey? The pool, of course."

"What pool?"

"You're a good-looking babe," Winter said, "but as a real-estate buyer, you don't keep track of your marbles. Didn't you know there's a pool on this street? And that we own a hunk of it? Read the deed."

"You're not going there!" She had forgotten where they were; now, suddenly, she remembered and was afraid.

"Sure. Why not?"

"Lamar, are you crazy? Are you just looking for trouble?"

He saw the quick lift of terror in her eyes and spoke soothingly, as though to a child. "Honey, honey, we're never going to make it walking soft and babying these folks. They'd make us go second class forever if we let 'em. There isn't any halfway. Where're our suits?"

The habit of obeying him was ingrained in her, which may be as good a way as any of saying that she trusted him.

"All right," she said, though uneasiness lingered in her eyes. "I'll look for them. I don't think they've been unpacked."

"Wear the bikini." Winter smiled. "Start in high gear."

"Oh, no, you don't," she said. "If I'm going to be lynched, I am not going to do it naked."

And so, for the first time, the Winter family crossed the lawn and moved down the lane toward the pool to whose use and enjoyment their deed clearly entitled them. Margo wore a long terrycloth robe concealing her white suit and the contrasting grace of her slender brown body. Walking between husband and son, each with a towel across his shoulders, she was almost quiveringly conscious of the names on the mailboxes: first Outerbridge, then Jones and Yale paired, then Gold and Abram, and then, between Kelly and Cusack, the gate through the rhododendrons. She was acutely aware that she knew none of the faces behind those names, and she dreaded the day she would encounter them.

She could feel hidden eyes on her. But only two pairs were watching, in fact. One pair belonged to Lana Weissman. These were alert and curious rather than hostile as Lana, in a new skin-tight skin-colored suit which she fervently hoped would make lifeguard Mark Cotten's eyes bug out, strolled up the lane from the opposite direction. The other pair, concealed behind organdy curtains in the picture window and wearing a look of baleful dismay, belonged to Laura Cusack.

The sound of splashing and juvenile shouts and screeches came to them. The scream of a police whistle cut piercingly through the uproar. Flinching, Margo felt Tod stiffen beside her, and Winter felt a prickly tightening of skin as the whistle shrilled again. Wary by habit, Winter instinctively connected the whistle with their presence. He was right in a way that no other resident of the lane could have understood. Anybody else on Peaceable Lane would have dismissed the two long blasts and one short as an ordinary, unalarming code message in the community's mother-child signal system. Both sender and addressee were instantly recognizable. The message meant that Paulie Cusack should get home on the double. But Laura would not have been blowing the whistle if she had not known that Paulie was in the pool and that the Winters were en route to it.

Cyd Cavanidis was on the pool deck dressed in languor and little else. Lana Weissman, with firm young hips and strutting young breasts, was just behind the Winters. Mark Cotten, the object of both Cyd's lazily speculative concupiscence and Lana's urgent adoration, was halfway along the pool, trying to co-ordinate Ruth Gold's kicks and strokes. Ruth was fat like Angela Cavanidis, but she had a sense of timing and Cotten had hope for her. The pool was raucous. Jerry Gold, Benjy Abram, Bill Jones, four of the uncountable Kellys, Nicholas Cavanidis and Paul Cusack, Jr. were in the deep end or bounding in and out of it. Angela, the larger of the two Drapers and both Yales were splashing in the shallow end. Cotten was keeping one eye on them lest they get too brave. The noise was close to insupportable, most of it emanating from the larger boys. Paulie was so intent on exercising the prerogatives of size and age that he did not hear the police whistle. He was an old hand in the art of not hearing.

Cotten saw the Winters come up on the deck and thought there would be hell to pay for this. Still, I don't know what I'm expected to do about it, he thought, shrugging, as he turned his attention back to Ruth. Cotten's foreboding was accurate, but the payment was to be deferred yet awhile. All in all, if Lamar Winter felt he had to bring his family to the Peaceable Lane pool, this was as good a day as any.

Winter dropped his towel and mounted the high board. The kids were startled as the lithe, dark body knifed down among them in a clean, hard dive. But they were too intent on their own uproar to be more than momentarily abashed by the alien presence. After a moment's staring silence the noise began again. Cyd rolled over on her towel and watched Winter come up the length of the pool in a fast crawl and spring lightly up to the deck, but Cyd was too lazy to hate anybody, particularly a man with shoulders and legs like that. Lana was too intensely and alertly curious to hate anybody but Cyd.

Winter moved toward his wife and son, dripping and grinning. "Come on, it's great," he said.

Margo shook her head slightly but managed a taut smile. "Don't rush me," she said. She was still in her robe and felt an anguished conviction that she would never be able to take it off. Winter knew and felt the stir of impatience but knew she could not be bulldozed in this. He turned to the boy, seeing with annoyance how closely he sat against her, but he kept his voice softly cajoling. "Come on, kid. Last one in's a white baby."

He saw eagerness and doubt struggling in Tod's eyes and, in a kind of despair, saw doubt winning. He knew how cruelly the boy was being tested. But it had to be done. Angrily he wished it possible, by sheer effort of will, to fuse some of his own reckless courage into the boy. He knew Tod could not summon the resolution to plunge into that shimmering water among those kids he did not know. He felt an impatient impulse to reach down and seize the boy and fling him into battle.

Lana Weissman saved him from it, which was not as strange as it might have seemed. Lana irritated nearly everybody on Peaceable Lane, including her parents. She smoked ostentatiously and openly enjoyed the dismay this caused her mother. She dressed flamboyantly. When she was not being smart-alecky, she cultivated a grating air of weariness with all adult opinion. These qualities successfully concealed from most onlookers the fact that Lana was not only pryingly interested in the world around her but also owned an all-inclusive fund of sympathy for anything in it that was hurt or weak. She had temporarily forgotten Mark Cotten and his reaction to her swimsuit. She had settled down behind and to one side of the Winters and had been covertly studying them. Margo's fear and Tod's reluctance, controlled just short of bolting, were not secrets to her sharp, young eyes. She slid over and squatted beside Tod and grinned at him.

"Can you swim?" she asked.

Caught off guard, Tod answered before he could decide whether the bright, wise eyes held threat or friendliness.

"Sure," he gulped.

"Okay." Lana grinned. "I'll race you from here to the board and back. Come on." She grabbed his hand getting up, and before Tod knew it he was in that alien water. Winter stood staring after them, then slowly settled down beside his wife. "Well, I'll be damned," he said. The dark, intelligent face wore a baffled look.

Suddenly the police whistle sounded again—two long blasts and a short. It was louder this time, piercingly loud and shrill and furiously imperative. Laura had come out of her house and across the lawn to the street, and the summons, like the scream of an enraged and terrified animal, came from just beyond the concealment of the rhododendrons. Not even Paulie's long experience in the arts of convenient deafness could ignore this one. Startled and sullen, the boy climbed out on the deck, retrieved his towel and disappeared.

"Wuff! What a stinking day," Matt groaned, as he stepped off the station platform and planted the sweat-sticky seat of his pants in the station wagon beside Ellen. He loosened the knot of his necktie. "I sometimes wonder what sabotaging sonofabitch planted all the major cities of America in the country's worst climates."

"Sorry, darling," Ellen said, looking at him sympathetically. "You'll feel better after you've had a drink."

"First things first," Matt grunted. "I'm going to have a swim—then a drink."

"You have a surprise coming. You can't swim."

"I'd like to know why not."

"The pool's being drained, that's why."

"The what?"

"The pool's being drained. Mr. Cotten is letting the water out. Bill told me."

"Nuts! I wonder what went wrong." Matt looked puzzled and irritated. "Whatever it is, I'll bet it's expensive. I'll have to go down and find out."

"I don't know. You could ask Bill. He was there most of the afternoon." She paused and then spoke again with a curious tone of excitement. "Do you know what?"

"Know what what?" Matt asked absently. He was trying to think what costly part of the pool machinery might have failed.

"Bill said the colored people were there today—swimming. I'll bet it took some working up their nerve—the first time."

"They pay their share," Matt grunted. "Why not?"

"I know," she said. There was a little worry crease in her forehead. "But, Matt . . . I wonder . . . could it cause trouble?"

Changed into an old pair of shorts and a loose shirt, Matt felt better but a long way short of contented. He found Bill in the back yard in a game of three-cornered catch with Jerry Gold and Benjy Abram.

"Don't you kids understand heat—or do you just don't care?" he asked enviously. "What's this about draining the pool? What happened?"

"I dunno. Nothing happened. Mr. Cotten chased us all out and said he had to drain it," Bill said, smacking the ball into his glove, impatient to get back to the game.

"It was right after the new kid left," Jerry Gold offered. "The colored kid. Mrs. Cusack came over and talked to Mr. Cotten. They were arguing, and then Mr. Cotten told us to beat it."

"Oh?" Matt said. "Mrs. Cusack, huh?" He turned away. "All right, kids, back to your sunstrokes." Damn that woman, damn her vicious eyes, Matt thought. He strode toward the pool, walking fast and oblivious to the heat. He knew now what he would find and why he would find it.

Cotten, in bathing trunks and dangling a long-handled scrub brush across his knees, was sitting on the coping, moodily watching the water level go down. The pool was half empty.

"What for?" Matt demanded as the young man looked up.

"Mrs. Cusack told me to do it," Cotten said gloomily. "I knew there'd be trouble."

"There is trouble. Since when do you take orders from Mrs. Cusack?"

Cotten shrugged. "She's one of the owners. She raised hell. I didn't see what else I could do."

"She may be one of the owners," Matt snapped, "but she's not running this pool. Not this summer. I am. Shut off the drain and start filling. Now!"

"You're the boss," Cotten said, getting up and moving wearily toward the control box. "But I hope you'll square me with Mrs. Cusack. She's a determined woman."

"Don't worry about Mrs. Cusack," Matt grunted. "She'll have enough to worry about. You've dumped a hundred bucks' worth of water and it's going on her bill."

Matt turned, jumped down off the deck and passed through the rhododendrons and started swiftly up the Cusack walk. Almost to the door, he changed his mind. What the hell am I doing? he thought disgustedly. Picking a fight with a woman. Better wait until Paul's home—and I cool off a little. But I'd love to wring her scrawny neck.

"Matt, you can't talk to my wife that way!" Under a strain, Cusack's face was likely to turn mottled.

"All right, I don't want to act tough, and if I have I apologize," Matt said. "But let's make sense, Paul. If everybody is going to decide the way that pool's run whenever they take a notion, you can get another chairman. I told Cotten to fill it again and I want it understood that it's going to stay that way."

"Not if those people are going into it again!" Laura said. Her voice lost none of its asperity by being muffled in the handkerchief into which she occasionally sniffled furiously. "You can just tell them to stay out, since you're the chairman."

"I'll tell them no such thing," Matt said flatly. "They own a house here; they have the same right to that pool as you do."

"I don't get this. I don't get it at all," Cusack said. "What are you doing, Matt, taking their side against your own neighbors?"

"Come off it, Paul," Matt said wearily. "Neighbors, shmeighbors. The Winters are just as much my neighbors as you are. If you doubt that, read your deed. You can't rule them out of the pool. What's the matter with you people anyhow? D'you think the color washes off—or if it does, that it'll wash onto you? Let's show some sense. The street is daffy enough already."

"Now, look here," Cusack said. "You're taking a damn funny attitude. First you and Gold go to sleep and let this colored man stick it into us. And now, you're not only sticking up for him, you're even riding into town with him. Anybody'd think you're trying to make the black bastard feel right at home."

Matt stared at Cusack, hard and level.

"It's not a bad idea at that," he said finally. "Meanwhile I want that pool left alone, and I hope you both understand I mean it."

"You bet your sweet life it'll be left alone," Laura snuffled through her handkerchief. "It'll be left so strictly alone that, when you get around to collecting the assessment, you can just get it from your black friend. Don't come here for anything." Suddenly Laura lost the remainder of her composure and emitted a keening wail.

"Oh, why couldn't those horrible people leave us alone? Why, why, why?" As Matt rose, she collapsed on the sofa and began to sob convulsively.

11

IN A GENERAL WAY Matt had expected Peaceable Lane to resist Winter and his family. He had been prepared for suspicion and resentment. He had even considered the possibility of violence, although he thought it unlikely. He knew danger was implicit in the act. He and Zack had gone ahead with it because each, for his own reasons, had believed it both necessary and right. They had hoped that with time the lane would become reconciled to Winter in peace.

But it wouldn't wait. That ugly business of the pool had made it clear. The lane wasn't a particularly sociable place, but it was too tight a community to keep any one acre set apart in a hermetically sealed cell. Lives bumped into one another whether their owners wanted it or not.

Something was needed to break through the mesmerized grip in which fear held the lane—and quickly. And it was fear, he thought, fear bred of the bogey of ignorance. Winter was a threat because nobody knew what he would do. You couldn't change the color of his skin, but perhaps something could be done to make him seem ordinary, a man like other men. It wasn't something Winter could do himself; in the lane's present frame of mind anything he did would be branded with suspicion. Somebody else had to take the first step to strip away the sinister aura of mystery.

Well, hell, he thought, what would you do about any other new family in town—if they happened to be the same color as everybody else? Give a party for them. Natch, what else? The notion was so ridiculous that he laughed aloud, picturing the pursed, disapproving lips of John Ainslie Outerbridge, the nervous bumbling of Gordon Draper, the solemn and transparent cordiality of Jerome Kelly, and then Laura Cusack, bridling at the threat of contamination, alert for insult or the opportunity to inflict it. That would be, of course, in the inconceivable case that Laura came at all. It would be some show. But, okay, let's quit being funny.

Wait a minute. Maybe it wasn't totally insane. The Winters needed to be humanized in the eyes of the lane. Perhaps the lane could concede them some small but essential measure of the quality if somebody the lane knew accepted them as such. And did so in plain sight, in the most ordinary and informal manner possible. Simply asked them over, as you might any other newcomer. Not something inside a house, which could be considered hidden and therefore furtive. But simply, informally, out in the open where anybody could watch.

Of course, you would never fetch the likes of Laura Cusack with that guff. But the lane was a long way from being pure Cusack. There were solid people here; give them a chance and they would settle down—just half a chance.

He was unprepared for the resistance he encountered.

"Matt, are you out of your mind?" Ellen said. She looked dumfounded. "Have them here? To dinner?"

"Why not?" he insisted doggedly. "They're people. They are new here. They have to get dovetailed into this street sometime." He thought a moment and then added a clincher. "Besides, I know them. It not only looks damn funny, but it is funny, to pretend they don't exist."

Ellen shook her head. "Matt, we live here too. Not just you, but I live here and Billy lives here. We have to go on living here. It's . . . it's impossible."

"I don't get it," he said. "It doesn't sound like you—simply because they're colored."

That stung. "Oh, Matt," she said helplessly, "you know better. It's not because they're colored. It's . . . don't you understand? . . . with people already suspicious . . . prying . . . insinuating. You don't know how these women are."

She remembered longingly and helplessly how easily and simply she and Matt had always understood one another—almost instinctively. But in these few weeks a crevasse had opened between them, and she could no longer find her way across. He seemed so sure, so stubbornly sure that he was right. But why couldn't he understand that her fears were real? How could he plunge ahead, blind to danger? And how could she communicate across that imperceptibly widening and deepening gulf the doubt and foreboding that tormented her?

"They're just people," he said again. "A few cuts above most—including some of our neighbors. I'm not suggesting we make bosom buddies out of them. That would be silly. But somebody has to take a little of the scare out of this street. It's important."

You took a man—for better or for worse, the book said. You cooked for him, slept with him, bore his child, loved him. You shared his triumphs and his disasters—the most harrowing of the second being the one you shared most fully. That was the heartbreaking incapacity which had denied them any more children after Bill. You thought you knew the man, gentle, passionate, considerate with most people, but never likely to become deeply immersed in their affairs, generous and even indulgent with his family when he was not harassed by money worries. Surer than anything, you knew his proud, protective love for their son. This you knew—or thought you knew. Then this: an entirely new, almost totally inexplicable and frightening side of him. Willing to perjure himself and betray a trust for the sake of an outsider. Money worries gone by the board, forgotten—just like that. Willfully courting danger for himself and—this was unbelievable—thrusting wife and son onto the balance.

"Matt, why does this man mean so much to you?" she asked. "Is he so good a friend? Do you think he would do this for you—if things were the other way around?"

"Huh?" he said. "Do what for me?"

"Would he go out on a limb for you—the way you have for him?"

He looked nonplused. "That's a goofy question. How could it be the other way around? White Protestants don't need help—not this kind."

"But if it was, do you think he would?" she persisted.

"I don't know," he said honestly, looking her full in the eyes. "But that's not the question."

"What is then?" she asked desperately.

"Well, it isn't easy to keep it from sounding nutty—or just sloppy." He stopped and then, frowning, went on. "It's roughly this. When we first shut out a colored buyer, I didn't feel much about it one way or another—except that if somebody was out to rook us, I was for stopping him. Then I found out it was Lamar. I don't think of Lamar as a colored man especially. I think of him as a guy with a lot on the ball. Later I found out about his family. So then—oh hell, Ellen, it's really simple—it struck me, what right have people like us to stand in the way of people who want the same things?"

"And that's all? Standing in their way is one thing. Taking these awful chances for them is something else."

"You get started on a thing like that and it's hard to find a place to get off. It wasn't as though Lamar was the closest friend I ever had. I know he's a hard man to like—even if I think I know what made him that way—and that comes into it too, of course. Hell, how I bobble it! But what I mean is, for example, I didn't like him any better than Zack—if as well—and I knew that if I succeeded in slickering the street I would also be slickering Zack. I know it sounds crazy." He stopped.

"But when Zack found out, he helped you," Ellen said helplessly.

"Yes," he said. "Zack did—he would."

"But he didn't know them."

"That's it. With Zack there wasn't anything personal in it. Zack just thinks, all right, there's a man. He has as much right to live and grow and be free as I have. I have no right to get in his way. What's more, because I'm a man, too, I have an obligation to help him." He stopped, and amazingly his face took on a sheepish expression. "I suspect that before I got through I was thinking like Zack. It wasn't so much the personal part any more—at least that wasn't the most of it." He stopped and finally finished lamely, "Oh hell, Ellen, you know I was never a do-gooder. I just ran out of excuses for being a jerk."

In the end, caught in confusion between pride in him and the temptation to crack his skull, still unwilling and ridden by dark and unshakable foreboding, Ellen consented.

Ellen had not wanted to do this. She felt it was both reckless and useless. Asking them to bring the boy scared her even more, because that involved Bill. She had nearly balked at that. It was one thing for her to venture perilously; asking a nine-year-old boy to do it was something else. But she was committed and she went ahead with it doggedly, though in dread.

She did not know, although she might have guessed, that Margo Winter came to it in equal apprehension. But both young women had unsuspected capacities for grace under pressure, and probably because of them the evening went off fairly well on the surface. Still there was about it an air of unreality.

It began with the front-door chimes. The sound was oddly upsetting. If the Golds—or any other neighbor—had been coming to an outdoor summer dinner, Ellen would have expected them to drift in unannounced, and the man would surely have been as sloppily dressed as Matt. But here, formally waiting for her on the doorstep, stood this handsome, dark-skinned trio, dressed superbly and with care.

"This is Margo and I'm Lamar Winter," the man said, smiling easily. "The boy, here, is Tod."

"I know. Please come in." Ellen smiled. She had a nightmare sense that this could not be happening. Here she stood, Ellen Jones, a proper suburban housewife, smiling and bidding into her home three alien strangers who, she knew, were feared by most of her neighbors and hated by some. She wondered if her smile looked as idiotic as it felt. It didn't; it looked easy and welcoming.

"I'm so glad you could come," Ellen went on, persisting in the lie because she knew if it was to be done at all it had to be done gracefully. "Matt's in the back yard with Bill," she said to Winter. "Why don't you and Tod go on through?" She nodded toward the open door leading to the terrace. "I'm afraid we live outdoors—until it snows."

"I should have known." Winter smiled. "It's what the magazines call gracious country living. I've painted it often enough."

"You'll find Matt a messier chef than the ones you paint." Ellen laughed. "Go see for yourself."

Winter, jaunty and showing no sign that his handsome dark silk suit, white button-down shirt and small-figured tie were more than the occasion demanded, turned toward the terrace door with the boy close in his wake. "Out this way?" he asked.

"Through there and keep going," Ellen said. "You can't miss Matt. He'll be the one in a dirty shirt."

"I'll tell him what's wrong with his technique," Winter said over his shoulder.

"Better not. He resents it," Ellen said. She turned toward Margo and, making a quick appraisal, was not deceived by the simplicity of the yellow linen dress. It was plain; it looked cool; it was undeniably perfect, and Ellen knew absolutely that it had cost at least twice the price of the best formal in her own closet.

"What a lovely house," Margo said, taking in the room's air of lived-in quiet and comfort and space.

"It's shabby," Ellen said dishonestly. "And it's not very orderly. It's probably my fault, but I prefer to blame Clarice."

"Clarice?"

"The maid." For no reason that seemed to make any sense, Ellen was suddenly embarrassed by remembering the color of Clarice's skin. "But she only has one day a week to undo the damage," she said quickly.

Winter found Matt beside the grill, inspecting a two-inch-thick slab of dark, fat-veined meat. An ice bucket and a tray with bottles and glasses were close at hand.

"That's a handsome hunk of cow," Winter said.

"Hi, Lamar. Got it at Manero's in Greenwich. Only place I know that has really prime beef. But it's a long drive over."

Matt turned to Bill, who had been waiting, wondering what was required of him. Bill had seen Tod in the pool and had even raced against him in wordless competition. The memory of the bad night had faded, but still he knew this situation was unprecedented and that it probably wouldn't do to go at it slapdash, the way he would with any other kid. "Bill, how about fetching me the charcoal? This fire needs hotting up," Matt said. "Take Tod along—he can help bring some Cokes. And why not turn on the lights? You could play croquet."

"I'm overdressed," Winter said, as the boys left obediently but warily. "All right to shuck my coat?"

"It's about time," Matt grunted. "I was beginning to feel like a slob. Better shed the tie too. The butter off a cob of corn doesn't do much for a Sulka."

"What'll I do with them?"

"Toss them in the living room. I'll make a drink while you're at it. Gin and tonic?"

It was easier for Matt and Winter. They knew one another. The women had no such bond to ease their way in an unknown and fearsome place. Each was oppressed by a sense of isolation on an island of light exposed to the hostile dark. Unwillingly, by an act of will, they had become castaways together, but unlike castaways of chance, neither could take comfort in the other.

The boys made a better job of it. They had felt the strain, but argument helped them through it. The issue was whether Bill was entitled to drive Tod's ball into outer darkness after a successful collision shot.

"It's the rule," Bill bellowed. "You want to see the book?"

"How about when I hit you back there?" Tod complained. "How about that?"

"I wasn't through the first wicket then. You couldn't do anything. That's the rule too."

"Some rule," Tod muttered.

"Sounds like the start of a race riot." Winter grinned. "Think we ought to call the cops?"

"Doubt it," Matt grunted. "They'll probably settle it this side of the Supreme Court." Ellen wondered irritably how they could talk that way, toying lightly with something forbidden and not to be acknowledged. Angrily she brushed the thought aside. She wasn't being logical. Probably they were right. Probably it was the only way: take it out in the open and make fun of it and see it vanish for what it was–nothing. Why did she permit her nerves to jangle so? It was stupid.

But she was relieved when Matt went to prod experimentally at the steak and lifted it, smoking, from the grill. "Come and get it," he said, wearing an infuriating air of self-satisfaction.

It was easier while they ate. There were things to be done with hands and mouth, and the silences did not fall with such deadly weight. But both Ellen and Margo still felt the uneasy sense of talking too much, chattering too brightly, laughing too quickly.

"Have you seen the school?" Ellen asked once—and instantly damned her foolish mouth. With any other woman this would have been a subject of absorbing mutual interest. Why should it be something else with this woman? But she knew it was.

"Yes, it's a lovely school," Margo said. "But it seems so far away." She sensed the peril, too, but was as helpless as Ellen to keep out of quicksand. "Do they have to leave early?"

"It's complicated," Ellen said. There was no help for it; she was in it now and she pushed on bravely. "They're on split sessions. The morning is better if you can work it out. It means getting started awfully early, but then they're home early in the afternoon."

"Is there a school bus?"

"Yes, but it's a disgrace. We're at the end of the line. First to be picked up and last to get home." Ellen hesitated, aware of the yawning trap, knowing it could not be avoided. "We do better with car pools."

All right, dammit, Margo thought, I'll have to face it sometime. I can't escape it any more than she can. She had an odd, sorrowful feeling of sympathy for the blond woman across the table. She knows this is tricky, too, Margo thought, but she's not trying to get out of it. Suddenly she found herself longing for the familiarity and safety of Harlem. What had possessed them? What insanity had driven them to flee, with Tod, from that to this?

"How are the car pools arranged?" she asked, trying to keep her voice normal, lightly curious and nothing more.

"We work it out among us," Ellen said steadily. "I'll let you know when I know more."

Something like real ease came with the coffee. The endless evening was ending. Soon there would be privacy and the chance to put aside the aching mask of pretense that this was normal. They warmed to the approach of escape and, feeling the nearness of relief, warmed to one another.

"It was a lovely dinner. I stuffed myself," Margo said. She was surprised by the thought that now, unbelievably, Peaceable Lane had granted her that cachet of acceptance, a social obligation. On the heels of the satisfying notion there came a rush of panic at the prospect of fulfilling it. Then she started involuntarily as, from somewhere far off and hidden in the darkness, came the shrill, wild cry of a police whistle.

Beth and Zachariah Gold had finished dinner more than an hour earlier. Since then, in moody silence for the most part, they had been sitting on their back terrace, acutely aware of the glow of light in the Jones back yard and the occasional murmur of voices.

Gold stirred and sighed. "Well, Matt went and did it," he said. "I hope they live through it."

"I suppose he thought he had to," Beth said softly. "It must be hard. I'm sorry for Ellen, sorry for all of them."

"He's crazy," Gold muttered. "Turn Matt loose and sometimes he's nuttier than the most conscience-driven Jew you ever saw. Asking for it, daring the hurricane." He fell silent, but then a rueful chuckle rumbled up from his big chest. "But you have to admire the knucklehead. He's crazy, but he isn't crazy enough not to know what he's doing—and doing it anyhow."

"The tongues will be wagging," Beth said. "I can almost hear them."

"They're wagging, all right," Gold said moodily. "Rattling's closer to it. Even ours."

Gold knew he was in a struggle, caught between the contradictory demands of conscience and common sense, in dispute between the drive to reckless courage and the plain need to refuse senseless risk. There was too much at stake, too little to gain. But he felt like a deserter, an unreasoning and galling sense of cowardice.

"I didn't tell you he asked us too," he said abruptly. "I turned him down."

"Oh," she said. "I didn't know." She paused and then said unhappily, "Oh, Zack, I don't know whether I'm glad you did or not."

"I know," he grunted. "I tried to talk him out of it, but he wouldn't be talked. He said it had to be done. Claimed you couldn't let Winter and his family in and then pretend they didn't exist.

Said it was ridiculous to expect people to stay bottled up like poison on a shelf. He's right—but he's wrong too. I don't think it can be done this way."

"Is there any way to do it?"

"I don't know. Time, maybe. Patience." The chair creaked under the restless shift of his weight. "I don't know . . . I know he's crazy but I feel like a heel—safe here in the cyclone cellar."

"Zack"—her voice was thoughtful—"we're not safe either. Are we really? If Matt pulls himself down?"

"No," he grunted. "But nothing ever is. What Matt and I did isn't buried so deep it can't be dug up. I know that. But sometimes I'm not sure that trying to play it safe is the answer either. Now, listening to them, under the lights and stage center, trying to pull it off by sheer guts, I'm not sure. It's crazy but, by God, it's wonderful too."

Somewhere down the street a police whistle sounded—two longs and a short.

"Whose is that?" Gold asked, raising his head.

"Cusacks'," Beth said, wondering. "It's late too."

The whistle called again.

"Kids!" Gold muttered. "Does anybody ever know what they're up to?" He rose, looming huge in the dark. "I'm out of my mind, but I'm going over there and do a little neighboring." She felt his eyes on her in the dark. "Are you daffy enough to come along?"

Beth Gold had strong within her a woman's instinct to protect her own. It was in her nature to walk softly and inconspicuously. She was not one to seek challenges and she could not have said why she accepted this one.

"All right," she said. "I'm messy, but I'll come." They started toward the pool of light beyond the trees. They were walking softly, hand in hand, when they became conscious of some furtive presence among the hemlocks and then saw a sudden, jerky movement. A brittle crash and a startled cry came from the pool of light.

For a moment they sat frozen, staring at the dark stains, as dark as blood, slowly spreading on Margo Winter's yellow dress. A splintered coffee cup lay on the table and, in the moment of silence while shock still held them, the sound of coffee spattering on the stone terrace was loud in their ears.

Ellen saw the smooth round stone lying beside the broken cup and reached for it in stunned curiosity.

Matt was on his feet. For a moment he stood staring into the blind darkness beyond the lights. Then he started forward as he heard a brief thrashing among the hemlocks and sensed movement coming toward him into the light.

Then he stopped. The great bulk of Zachariah Gold was striding toward him. Looped effortlessly into the crook of one big arm, he carried a struggling, bawling bundle.

"Here it is," Gold said disgustedly, dropping his burden in front of Matt. "Just in case you want to do anything about it."

"What is it?" Matt asked.

"Paulie Cusack. Junior Klansman, home style."

Matt looked into the tight, frightened, tear-stained face staring up at him. Here it is, he thought. Here is the poison, the sickness, the hate and the stink of hate. Here it all is, all wrapped up in the scared, sniveling, bared-tooth, pants-wetting rattiness of a caught thirteen-year-old boy. Here it is; look at it.

Demanding, angry, fearful, the police whistle screamed in the night.

"Get up, Paul. Go home," Matt said. "Your mother's calling you."

12

FRANCIS BARTON had infuriated, inspired, intimidated or puzzled many men, but he did not puzzle himself. He remembered nearly every step of the path he had trod. The only blind spot he suffered was that in maturity he had deliberately chosen to forget the clean, hot zeal of the young man who had first set foot upon it. The son of a preacher, he had drawn upon all the respect his father enjoyed in their Michigan community to win acceptance in law school. Aware of the uniqueness of his fortune, he had slaved his way through—both at his books and at the eight-to-midnight lunchroom job that fed him and paid the tuition. He had emerged, afire with ideals and ambition, just in time to collide headlong with the great depression. It was a time which broke some men and sent others off on the trail of heady political millennia they would learn to regret bitterly in twenty years. Barton had not been built to be broken and, while youthful ideals and his acute knowledge of his skin color might have tempted him into political extravagance, the rigid discipline of ambition forbade it.

He had been on relief. He had been a public defender, partly because his poor shingle could bring him no more lucrative clients but mostly because, in that time, it was politically useful for the machine to have a few carefully selected Negroes in the public pay. He had become, in Detroit, a minor relief administrator concerned with housing. The job had driven home something he already knew: that of all America's unfortunate citizens in those years the least favored were the Northern urban Negroes from whom he had sprung. He had got involved in the fringes of the CIO's organizing drives of the thirties and, attending union meetings and Youth Congresses, had stayed up late, smoking too much and drinking bad bootleg alcohol, fiercely talking social justice.

There was a hot pride in breaking his first block in Detroit, thereby loosening by a little the white strictures on the colored ghetto. He broke others thereafter and became skillful—and ruthless—at the work. For a long time he felt himself a conqueror. He had begun by being tormented by rage at the insensate white mass which stood between him—and his like—and the right to live as a full man. The enemy's superiority of number and power had seemed invulnerable. But, much to his astonishment, he had learned that the enemy could be beaten—and with that knowledge the passion began to drain out of him.

Somewhere along the road he had not so much lost the passion as deliberately abandoned it in favor of ambition. It may have been because, recognizing his own steely strength, he also realized that the pity he felt for the weak was more than half contempt. He learned that once a white block was broken, its remainder tended to crumble quickly—especially if fear could be planted in it. And he discovered that he knew how to move more quickly and surely than either his beneficiaries or his victims. He kept on breaking but he began to buy for himself just at the point of breakage—just behind the spearhead of panic—and even he was surprised to learn what profit could derive from the point of crumbling.

Barton was a raider. His tactics were those of the guerrilla: concealment, surprise, swift and savage action. He was also a patient man, full of experience and craft. He had learned to lose skirmishes with grace. But he did not like to lose campaigns and seldom did. He regarded Peaceable Lane as a lost skirmish. The fact that Lamar Winter had got a house did not satisfy him. His own raid had failed. Winter's possession of the house represented the gift of soft-headed white men. In any case, Barton did not approve of Winter, for Winter had been a less than satisfactory tool. Peaceable Lane was still a campaign that Barton intended to win. It was vulnerable now, and Barton, calculating the potentialities, decided it was time to move.

He summoned Edward Smith, the slender, owl-spectacled man who served as his scout and also, when Barton deemed violence necessary, commanded his troops in the field. An abiding hatred of the whites smoldered in Smith. He was also clever and observant. The combination rendered him valuable.

"I want you to look over Peaceable Lane again," Barton said. "You know the one. That one-street community near Chappaqua where the colored artist bought last month."

"The usual?" Smith asked laconically. He knew his job and did not need to waste any words with his boss.

"Yes. Information only—for the time being. I think you may find a soft spot. There should be one by now."

"You want to finger one? Any special favorite?"

"Not yet. Any one of several might serve. I know you remember the most likely ones."

"Want to run over them again? You remember more things than I do. Sometimes it scares me, the way you remember things."

Barton smiled faintly. "There is no need to flatter me, Edward. Your memory is not to be despised. At the time, however, I estimated four possibles. There is a Dr. Abram. He is a Jew. During the war he escaped from a German concentration camp in Austria. I believe he can be frightened. There is a young man, Gordon

Draper. He is weak and dominated by his father who, I suspect, considers him a fool. You are aware of Peter Yale, the commentator. Yale has already demonstrated that he is susceptible—since he reneged on his commitment to the neighborhood conspiracy when we threatened getting at him through his network. There is the banker, Paul Cusack, an ambitious man with social aspirations. His wife hates niggers."

Edward Smith's eyes glittered behind their thick spectacles. "Getting to that kind is a pleasure," he said.

"I understand your prejudice, but do not let it affect your judgment," Barton said quietly. "I want the easiest and surest one, the weakest link. It may not be Cusack. He strikes me as a man who could develop scruples at the last minute."

"I suspect you like one of the others better."

"I dislike influencing your judgment. But take a particularly good look at Yale."

"No scruples, huh?"

"None that I am aware of."

"I see," Smith said. "Anything you want me to do with the pigeon when I decide which one it is?"

"I'll let you know when I want him brought in," Barton said pensively. "I'll want to try a lever on him."

"Money, huh?"

"Money, of course—in the end. But I have something else this time which may be useful. Shock treatment, you might call it."

Smith, retiring behind his spectacles, studied over his briefing and decided there was something he needed to know more about.

"What about Winter?"

"I advise you to keep clear of him. Winter is a question mark. He is proud and he is probably now finding his pride abused by his new neighbors. He is not a friend of white men—or rather, he believes that he is not. But the two are not precisely the same thing. I doubt that you would find him useful. He might even prove an impediment. He does not belong to us either. He is not friendly to me. He felt that our efforts in his behalf were—if I may state his attitude mildly—offensive."

"It'll be a little touchy with Winter there. I'll need to keep low and quiet," Smith said.

"Of course. But you always work quietly. They all have maids, but you may find that the servants are still frightened and not especially useful. I suggest you try out that broker—Alexander Fox. He knows a good deal and knows how to find out more—when it is worth his while. Fox is a rascal—but a useful one."

Smith stood up and moved to the door of Barton's office. "I think that's all I need to start," he said. In the doorway he turned. His face was alight with eager malice. "You know, Mr. Barton, I'm glad we're going into this one again. There's one out there who thinks he's tough, that Jones we went to see one night. He's on my list. That last night when we went out to jiggle them a little, Jones came out with a golf club. He smashed my windshield. Then before I got him held by the boys and kneed him in the nuts, he was the one did this to me." Smith opened his mouth and pushed his lip higher with a careful forefinger to reveal a gap in the gleaming façade of his upper teeth.

Barton regarded him thoughtfully. "You will refrain from personal animosities, Edward," he said softly and clearly. "This is not your private feud."

13

"WHAT ARE WE going to do about that boy?" Ellen asked. They were alone at the breakfast table in the sunny kitchen. Bill had bolted his orange juice, eggs and cereal and was already away on some demanding business of nine-year-olds. Ellen had spent a weary, tossing night, unable to rid her mind of the humiliating and somehow horrifying image of the dark stains slowly spreading on Margo Winter's dress. Her smooth face wore the traces of sleepless strain.

"There's not much point squawking to the Cusacks," Matt said dourly. "They'd probably congratulate him. On the other hand, Paulie can't be sure of that. He's probably worried."

"You can't just let him get away with it."

"He isn't, exactly. Let him sweat. He can't be sure we won't spring it on him, or what he'd get if we did. Anyhow, he won't be back." Matt sighed. "He's a nasty little piece."

"I'm ashamed. It was so barbarous . . . so indecent." The shadow of unhappiness was dark in Ellen's eyes. Matt saw it and felt the weight of it.

"Try to forget it," he said, reaching across the table to touch her hand with a brief, warm pressure. "Kids are kids and, mostly, they aren't much of an improvement on their parents."

"I wish it was that simple," Ellen said darkly. "Laura's a bitch . . . but she lives here . . . and has to be lived with."

"I'd like to kick her behind," Matt grunted, "but I suspect I'd end up busting a toe on her bones."

Ellen shook her head. "I can't help being afraid there'll be more of it," she said.

"It won't last and it isn't important anyhow," he said, wanting to believe it. "There are only so many Cusacks, and the rest of the neighborhood is taking it pretty well. What did you think of them?"

"The Winters?" She had expected the question—and dreaded it, because she wasn't sure what she thought.

"She's nice . . . I think." The word was banal and she knew it, but what could she say? What could she possibly know of Margo Winter—or think of her? "She was nervous. But what else could she be? So was I."

"And Lamar?"

"I don't know, Matt, honestly. How could I? There's something strange about him. He's pleasant enough—and sure of himself. Maybe that's it—too sure. There's something hard about him—and cold."

"If you think he's hard, you're right," Matt admitted. "He is. He's a colored man in a white man's world. He had to be hard to make it. Any white man with half his talent would have got as far as he is, or farther, on the cushions. No sweat."

"I know it must be difficult for them," she said somberly. "But, Matt, it's difficult for us, too. We didn't invent this race business. We just inherited it."

He looked at her with a sudden grin, proud and warm. "You did a lot to disinherit yourself last night," he said. "You're quite a woman."

"You set a pretty fast pace," Ellen said ruefully. "Honestly, Matt, now that it's over, do you really think it did any good?"

"Someday I think you'll agree that it did," he said somberly. "Notwithstanding that little heathen and his rock. Anyhow, it had to be done."

"I still think it was reckless," she said decisively. "This is our home and I don't want to be driven out of it. I don't want to drive myself out of it." Her nerves were jangling again. She hoped they were done with this—this wild careening over forbidden territory. She was pleading now. "Matt, you can't make people over—just like that. Can't you see, they won't stand for it?" She sat silent, staring moodily down at her hands twisted in her napkin. "I hope we're not going to be tarred and feathered."

He grinned at her, refusing to share her fear. "We won't. And you kind of stuck your own foot in it with that car-pool talk. You're really on my side and don't know it."

"Oh Lord," she breathed, aghast, remembering. "What can I do about that? Everything's running away with me. It's mad."

It was mad. And it got worse. If Ellen had feared there would be more, she was right. And for the next few days it all belonged to her. It came to her first at the meat counter in the A & P. Trundling up with her basket, she saw Shirley Draper and Laura Cusack talking to the butcher. Because Paulie's outrage was still fresh and humiliating in her mind, she was tempted to turn away. She suppressed the notion, dismissing it angrily as childish. Laura did have to be lived with. And so when Laura turned toward her companion and showed somewhat more than a profile, Ellen smiled and offered a cool "Hello." There was no answer, but Laura's head was turned away so quickly that Ellen made the mistake of thinking she had not heard.

In all her life Ellen had not had much practice at being snubbed. She wasn't quite ready for the reality. And so she repeated the greeting when all three met in the aisle between the salad dressings and the canned dog food. Shirley looked startled and unhappy and began a small, jerky smile and even seemed about to speak. But Laura first looked through Ellen and then turned to fix Shirley with an intimidating glare somewhat colder than the frozen codfish cakes Shirley had picked up the second aisle over.

Ellen's face stiffened. Experience or not, she knew it when she saw it. In cold fury, she wheeled her basket with such abrupt and possibly intentional violence that it collided with Laura's and toppled the top hamper of Cusack groceries into the aisle with a horrendous clatter. Happily, the accident and Laura's outraged gasp were enough to cushion Ellen's shock and send her away up the aisle filled with evil glee. A quick glance backward at Laura scrabbling about on her knees, retrieving the wreckage, and Shirley fluttering above improved Ellen's outlook even more.

The next time she met it, it had spread farther afield than she could have believed and in a direction that dismayed her. Ellen was not much for committees, but that year she had agreed to help plan and produce the annual Halloween children's party at Grassy Tor. She had been bidden to a lunch on the hill with the committee's seniors, Mrs. Harry Strauss and Mrs. Grant Macmillan. Mrs. Strauss was fat and full of good works and reminded people of cartoons of club women in the *New Yorker*. Sybil Macmillan was svelte for fifty, expensively and attractively turned out, and had been to Europe four times. Usually she kept her claws almost sheathed in a velvety and solicitous manner—but never so well sheathed that an attentive victim didn't know and bleed when she was scratched. Because Sybil was Matt's boss's wife, Ellen tried to like her and so far had managed to conceal the truth that she did not.

Grassy Tor activities were always planned well ahead. Halloween was far away in the bracing autumn, but this was still sultry summer. Ellen parked the Chevrolet and leaned toward the rear-view mirror to make sure her lipstick was on straight and that she didn't look as sticky and shiny as she felt. Getting out, she smoothed the blue linen dress over her still-slender flanks and heartily but silently cursed the sweaty tug of her garter belt. Like everybody else, she no longer wore seams, but the habit of years twisted her into a knock-kneed, heels-out stance for a last precautionary look at her stockings. Then she went through the castle's mighty oak door and found the two ladies already seated at a shaded veranda table laid with Grassy Tor's heavy linen and ponderous silver.

"I'm late," she said. "I'm sorry. I was sure I had time, but that old devil rat race never gives you a fair chance. At the last minute, Bill——"

"Forget it, dear," Sybil said sweetly. "I know it's awful having to do all your own work—even in that tiny house—such a doll's house, really." She inspected Ellen lightly but searchingly. "And with all that, you do keep yourself up beautifully. Your hair is lovely—did you do it yourself?"

All right, Ellen thought grimly, so it's going to be like that, is it? She struggled with and put down a temptation to observe that Sybil would need a remarkable memory to recall much about work—considering the years and all.

"I'm lucky. It curls naturally," she said, trying not to be short about it. And I might add it's still its own color, she reflected savagely, but secretly taking in the improbable blue tint of Sybil's expensive coiffure.

"There's the waiter," Mrs. Strauss said quickly, not quite sure why she felt uneasy. "Don't you want a drink, Ellen? We have ordered."

Ellen shot her a grateful look but then watched doubtfully as the waiter placed martinis before the two older women.

"I don't know. It's too warm for gin and me in the same package. I think I'll have a daiquiri."

"I think you're wise, dear," Sybil said. "You'll probably have to drink more gin than you can stand from now on—without doing it here at the club too."

"Huh?" Ellen said inelegantly, completely baffled.

"Your new neighbors," Sybil said sweetly. "Do they drink anything else?"

"Oh!" Ellen's gasp was involuntary. It felt exactly like being kicked in the stomach.

"New neighbors?" Mrs. Strauss looked perplexed.

Sybil turned to her a countenance as open and transparently guileless as a baby's. "Oh, didn't you know? The new family in Peaceable Lane. Ellen and Matt had them for dinner."

"The colored people!" Mrs. Strauss's contented round face was suddenly chop-fallen, thoroughly dumfounded. "My God, Ellen, did you?" With an effort, she began to assemble the fragments of her composure. "Oh, how brave you are," she finally said.

"Oh, now, Ethel," Mrs. Macmillan said briskly. She could see the thin, cruel edge of the initiative being blunted in shock and she didn't intend to let that happen. "It isn't that hair-raising. In Europe it's done all the time. Even mixed couples, and nobody makes anything of it. Perhaps, for Westchester, it's just . . . advanced."

Mrs. Strauss was getting herself in hand which meant, in part, that her normal abundant curiosity was surfacing again.

"Tell us about them, Ellen," she said, almost breathlessly. "What was she like?"

It had happened. It hurt. But the numbness was wearing off. Ellen was down but she wasn't out, and cold rage was welling up in her.

"Like any of us," she said coolly, looking at Mrs. Strauss but tailoring this for Sybil. "She's very pretty. She was at Vassar—Daisy Chain, you know." She was sure about Vassar, although not quite sure about the Daisy Chain, but she thought coldly that neither of these would know or even know how to find out. "Before she married she was a professional dancer. A night-club star—you probably remember." She hoped that was true but she didn't really care, because she knew the next part absolutely was and she aimed the stiletto with devilish accuracy. "She wore a stunning new Givenchy dress," and then turning to Sybil with a smile that beamed, she asked, "Isn't that your Givenchy, dear . . . that you got year before last?"

Sybil had been stabbed and knew it. She was an old campaigner and recognized good knife work when she saw it. But she was tough too.

"How fascinating," she said. "I hear they have a son—Billy's age," she said with what looked like affectionate concern. "Billy's such a fine youngster." She turned to Mrs. Strauss. "I know you've seen him. He's so lively. Grant and I are so fond of him." There, Ellen thought grimly, is a bald-faced lie if I ever heard one. "I hope this hasn't embarrassed him—with the other children."

"He doesn't seem to be," Ellen said carefully. It wasn't simple anger now; it was closer to hate. She knew it was reckless, but this was a war in which the aggressor chose the weapons and the defender had to accept them—or die. "He liked him. I could bring Tod Winter to the Halloween party . . . as Billy's guest," she said sweetly. "Would you like that?"

It wasn't a victory, but neither was it total defeat. And the duel had been forced on her. But sick regret swept over Ellen that she had let herself be provoked into enlisting Bill. I'm getting as reckless as Matt, she thought disgustedly.

She was to learn, too quickly, that the enemy could not be disengaged and that there was no hope of keeping Bill out of it.

One thing the women on Peaceable Lane were glad to forget for the summer was the car-pool system which transported the lane's young to and from Wacapo Consolidated during the school year. It was less complex than dispatching the New York Central System, but it was intricate enough, taking into account that it had to be adjusted to split sessions, grocery shopping, bridge days, club meetings, dancing classes and fetching and delivering maids and husbands.

Now it was time again. School was only three weeks away. Subconsciously Ellen had been putting it off. There was the Winter problem, and she confessed to herself that she did not know what to do about it. But school would not wait, and she began cautiously to feel her way toward a solution.

She telephoned Cyd Cavanidis. Cyd's stepchildren, Nicholas and Angela, had been part of a job lot including Jerry and Ruth Gold, Paulie Cusack and Bill the year before. She realized that calling Cyd was incongruous; Cyd was no mover and shaker or organizer. But she felt oddly hesitant to involve Beth Gold in an onerous obligation and she would be damned if she would call Laura on this or any subject. Cyd was at least a place to start.

"Why, honey, I thought you knew," Cyd said. "It's all set up. Laura arranged it, as usual."

Ellen caught her breath. She would have needed to be a lot less intelligent than she was not to recognize this. But she couldn't spare herself the details.

"I'm sorry, Cyd," she said. "I seem to have missed it somehow. Do you mind telling me what was set up—that is, if you have Laura's permission to say?"

Cyd could smell strife when it raged around her, but she was lazy and did not intend to let herself be drawn into it.

"Somebody must have goofed, honey." She chuckled. "I could guess who, but I didn't at the time. I surely didn't. Laura just said things needed to be rearranged this year—with the Draper kids starting. She suggested splitting up into smaller groups—and that's what we did. There'll be Paulie Cusack and the Drapers and our kids in one car. She said she understood the Yales and Kellys were working out something."

"Did she?" said Ellen. "I assume she disposed of the Gold children too?"

"She didn't say. But I suppose she thought you and the Golds and . . . that new youngster . . . well, you know."

"I know," Ellen said. "Indeed I do. All right, Cyd, thanks."

Ellen started to stab the receiver savagely onto its hook. She checked herself and hung it gently in place. Then she lifted it again and started to dial the Gold number—then stopped and replaced the instrument and slowly walked into the living room and sat down. After a while she realized she was shivering.

"Live with her," she thought dully. "Live with her? I'll see her in hell."

Or take the road Laura had so pointedly left open to her? Commit Bill, all unarmed, to an adult war he had not started and could not understand? No, it was not possible. No, no! Her shoulders slumped wearily but she could not cry.

14

MATT WAS THINKING that, no matter how many times you went through it, it was always an adventure, that suspenseful moment when you submitted to another man's judgment the work you had done in pride and believed was good. You knew he could destroy you. This time the suspense was multiplied by what Thurston Young was and by what he meant to Macmillan Associates.

Nobody approached the consummation of a million dollars' worth of business in boredom. There was no boredom in Matt or in Winter when they kept their noon appointment in Young's office to present an advertising campaign built upon Winter's portraits of Alice Collins.

The paintings were propped against the walls of Young's office and the floor was spread with page proofs, separated by lanes of dark red carpet to facilitate Young's inspection. Young took his time. Right elbow cupped in left palm, chin propped on doubled right knuckles, he moved deliberately from one painting to another. His face was unreadable.

Matt wondered at the power in the man. He was short; he was bald; he was physically frail. But he shaped and molded the tastes of a million women—no, ten million—to his will. That was where the answer must lie—in his will. That dominating, inflexible, steely insistence on perfection. You could hate him. Many people did. But you could not deny him admiration.

The artist sat, smoking, in one of Young's deep chairs. Matt envied his catlike relaxation but could match it with outward serenity only by staying on his feet. He paced the lanes of carpeting, looking for flaws he did not believe existed. Tension pulled at every nerve and sinew. He knew what they were showing was good; it was far more than good. But he also knew that he had no guarantee that it would strike the hard, sure chord of Young's decision. He, Winter and Macmillan Associates had a lot riding on whatever was going on behind Young's glittering pince-nez and cold blue eyes.

He found himself staring at Young's back, trying to read the set of those slender shoulders under the costly dark cloth. If he doesn't break pretty soon, he thought, I am going to blow a gasket. This had been going on for an hour, and never a grunt or mutter out of the great stone face after those first clipped words, "Let me see them."

At last Young left the paintings and moved into the paths between layouts. It was all that Matt could do not to dog his heels, trying to see afresh through those relentlessly critical eyes. Illogical dismay swept in on him. Suddenly the plan and execution were shabby, pretentious and tawdry.

Young turned out of the last aisle of carpet and came toward them.

"I would like the first of these to appear in October," he said. "The second week. I want the series to build up impact toward the Christmas season." He eyed Matt. "Can you schedule space in *Life* that quickly? I doubt if there will be a question with *Vogue* or the *New Yorker*, but *Life* may be difficult."

"What kind of space?" Matt asked. There it was. Click. Like that. No drama. It was done. And the paralyzed brain began to work again at familiar equations. "Four-color, of course. Six weeks for processing. But where do you want it in the magazine?"

"The inside front cover, if it can be managed. If you can't, the back cover—a maximum compromise. Preferably the front." Young smiled, a flicker of humor. "They ought to thank us for it. Having this at the front would give tone to the entire magazine."

"You know the rates?" Matt said cautiously, with an eerie feeling that this was getting out of hand. If Young was serious about that kind of space, it was time to begin revising the estimate upward.

"I am aware of the rates," Young said, dryly dismissing astronomical costs as meaningless in terms of what he wanted. "Can you do it?"

"I think so," Matt said cautiously. "But that is premium space. We will need to guarantee continuity. They won't let us touch it on a one-shot basis."

"Naturally. I know their standards." Again the cold smile flickered, its mirth, if any, concealed behind the eyeglasses. He nodded toward the paintings, a gesture nearly without movement. "But you are not empty-handed. There are twelve. Twelve successive weeks, four-color and cover—front or back—should render even *Life* amenable. It is possible that the series will be enlarged and continued. I assume you men are prepared to go on with it." It could have been a question, but Matt knew it was not.

"I guess you like them," Winter said, breaking a long silence with a contented smile.

"Did you think I might not?" Young asked without expression. "Were you concerned?"

"Not much." Winter grinned. "But it's pleasant to hear it."

"They are superb," Young said. "They are what I intended they should be." Wow, Matt thought, nobody except this bald-headed bastard with mercury in his arteries would have the gall to say "intended" instead of "hoped."

"There shouldn't be any question at *Vogue* or *New Yorker*," he said aloud. "I'll work out a schedule with them. *Life* is another kettle of fish, as you know. But it can be done."

"I am sure it can," Young said. He turned to Winter. "Will you leave the paintings here overnight? I want to have my people see them. And I want to decide whether to begin with that"—he gestured imperceptibly toward a painting of the girl in a black evening dress—"or that," indicating her in a beaver coat, radiating the excitement of a brisk autumn against the background of a stadium.

"Either one." Winter nodded. "The thing in the Dior might have more whump."

"Mr. Winter, the degree of whump is identical."

"You going back to the office and spring the news on Macmillan?" Winter asked as they reached the street.

"He isn't there," Matt said. "He has some wheel in town from a Chicago account—electronics outfit—and he took him out home to soften him up on the golf course." Suddenly it hit him. He had not realized how the tension had built up, like a slowly coiling steel spring, in the weeks of preparing the Glamour-Glow campaign. Now, without warning, the catch was disengaged and the spring leaped free. For a moment it left him limp. Then came the rush of exultant certainty. They had Young, the next to impossible. They had it made.

"Office? That's for peasants." He beamed at the artist in delight. "Come on, lad, let's howl!"

Two hours later the frame of mind induced by Thurston Young, combined with certain chemical reinforcements, had left Matt, for once, immune to the way Winter drove a car. Through a rosy glow of contentment he noted that the Jaguar had left the parkway in a vertiginous swirl and was straightening out on the cutoff toward Peaceable Lane.

"What'd you say?" he yelled above the exhilarating rush of wind around their bare heads.

"I said, with Young in your pocket, you're blue-ribbon vice-president material," Winter yelled back. "You want an office boy?"

"Never mind that. You've got work," Matt shouted. "For an office boy I'll get Michelangelo."

The car swooped over a hill and started the long roll down toward the entrance to Peaceable Lane.

"Whoa up!" Matt yelled. "Stop this fire wagon."

"What's your trouble?" Winter asked owlishly as the car slowed, rode up on the grassy shoulder and stopped. "Forget your wallet? Scared to go home smelling the way you do?"

"No, it just occurred to me I could stand another. Let's go up there and have one. I haven't been giving them enough business lately."

"Up where?" Winter asked.

"Up there to the club," Matt said, waving airily at the castle crowning the hill above them. "I'm a member. So's Macmillan." Another happy idea hit him. "He might be back in the locker room by now. If he isn't, he soon will be. Let's go hand him Thurston Young—all tied up in ribbons."

Suddenly Winter made the quick, bleak descent from their carefree cloud. He stared at Matt, slit-eyed and cold.

"Are you anywhere near sober?" he asked at last.

"Too close," Matt said happily. He felt like giggling. "That's what I'm trying to get away from. For a man of your per—per—what I mean to say is, for a man of your perception it ought to be obvious."

"That isn't all that's obvious," Winter said. "So you wanta go up there and give Macmillan the Santy Claus bit, do you?" He eyed Matt grimly. "Make the boss happy, huh? So what else do you think's going to happen—when you show up there with me?"

Matt was not sober and knew it. He also knew both that this was reckless and that probably only the twin glow of triumph and booze could have led him into it. But deep underneath, with the bright edge of clarity that liquor sometimes brings, he knew that it was inevitable. He had gone too far in his championship of Winter to draw any line short of all the way. He knew perfectly well that defeat might lie ahead, but it would not come to him because he had hesitated or cried stop, enough. He was serious and deadly certain when he answered.

"We're on the roller coaster, Lamar. There isn't any place to get off. You know that." He considered for a moment. "I can't think of a better time—with a million bucks' worth of business in our pockets. Macmillan is no dummy. He knows as well as I do that you're the reason we got that business. Sooner or later he has to decide what he's made of. Let's go."

"Okay, white man," Winter said savagely. The Jaguar spun into a U-turn and went into the white road up the hill in a lash of flung gravel.

When they left the men's bar two hours later, Macmillan had not appeared. It would not have been a good time for it if he had; they had let down their guard again. With the imperturbable aplomb acquired in twenty years behind Grassy Tor's bar, the steward, known to the membership only by the name of George, corrected their course, steered them successfully away from the locker-room door and out to the Jaguar.

"Yes, sir, Mr. Jones," he said, closing the car door, "I'll tell Mr. Macmillan to call you." He turned to Winter and spoke in an altered tone, sharp with command. "Take it mighty easy down this road, boy. They's a lot of folks coming up this time of the evening. You hear?"

"I hear you, Pappy." Winter grinned. "Don't worry. Just you get back to your white folks, nigger."

15

SEATED AT HIS DESK in massive calm, Francis Barton looked up as Edward Smith came from the anteroom and turned to close the door carefully behind him. Smith was smiling, alight with excitement. Barton waited quietly and wished that Smith could hold his emotions in firmer check. Still, he thought, Smith was valuable and effective, a man of deeds; it was a regrettable flaw, but supportable, that he sometimes let face or manner betray more than was desirable. Barton was too wise to expect more from a man than was possible for him.

"I brought him," Smith said. "Are you ready for him now?"

"How is he?" Barton asked.

"Jumpy." Smith let an edge of contempt creep into his smile. "Real jumpy. He ain't sure why he's here."

"Jumpy enough to bolt?"

"No-o-o." Smith considered. "He's nervous . . . but curious. I don't think he'll run."

"If he does, we can always get him back," Barton said comfortably. "Let him stew ten minutes, Edward. A little sweat won't hurt him."

Smith turned and let himself through the door while Barton sat back and let his thick fingers do a slow and thoughtful dance along the edge of his desk. He enjoyed the feel of the rosewood; more than any other object in the austere luxury of his office, the hard, dry polish of his desk, softly gleaming but as unyielding as steel, complemented and confirmed his sense of power.

"Mr. Barton will be with you in a few minutes," Smith said in the anteroom, addressing the slender man sitting forward, elbows on knees, in the deep chair Barton provided for his guests.

Peter Yale looked at him and the frown tightened over his eyes. "I don't have all day," he said sharply. "He asked for me—I didn't ask for him."

"It won't be long," Smith said soothingly. He settled himself in another chair and began to thumb through an old *Esquire*. The shiny mask of thick spectacles hid his observant eyes. He heard Yale's jerky sigh and watched with satisfaction as Yale crushed out a half-finished cigarette, immediately lighted another and sank stiffly into the chair's depths.

"What's he want?" he asked abruptly, mashing out the new cigarette in an onyx tray.

Smith performed the small, elaborate business of seeming to be absorbed in the magazine. "Pardon me?" he said, looking up with an apologetic smile.

"I said, what's he want?" Yale repeated. "What's all the mystery?"

"I'm sorry, Mr. Yale. All Mr. Barton told me was that you would be interested in what he has to say."

"Why doesn't he say it then?" Yale said. He didn't like any part of this: the air of mystery, the hints, the sly, knowing look on Smith's face, the suggestion of threat; and most of all, he didn't like being kept dangling like some bum come to beg a favor.

Yale had been on his feet for two minutes, pacing the narrow room. Abruptly he made up his mind and swung toward the door. "I'm going," he said just as a discreet buzzer sounded. Smith arose quickly with a soothing smile.

"Please, Mr. Yale. Mr. Barton is free now," he said. It was hard to conceal a grin. The slick old sonofabitch, he thought admiringly; sometime he's going to guess wrong.

Barton wore a smile of disarming warmth as he rose and came forward with hand outstretched. "I know you, Mr. Yale," he said. "I know you well. I seldom miss your broadcast. Let me say that you—and the few men like you—are doing more for this country than perhaps even you are aware. It is a privilege to meet you."

A little of Yale's tension melted in the open warmth of Barton's approval. He was taken off guard, but a warning depth of suspicion was still there.

"You didn't ask me here to talk about my show," he said.

"No. Although I should like to," Barton said. "Perhaps someday we can. But your show has something to do with it. Because of your show I know something of the man you are. It has made me feel that I can—and should—confide in you."

"What do you mean?" Yale asked. There was something here that needed caution. He could feel the force in this big, quiet man and, wary by nature, he probed for it nervously, watching the composed face, sensing some danger beneath its benevolent calm.

"It will take a little time," Barton said, still smiling. "Please sit down." He waited until Yale sank into the leather chair beside the desk and then went back to his own. Yale seemed composed, but Barton knew and was pleased to know that he was not. Barton did not believe that this thin, taut face held many secrets from him. It wasn't all intuition, but a good part of it was. He had researched his man, but the choice of the man to research had been dictated by a sure instinct for detecting weakness—even when it was deeply buried, as it was not in Yale's case, he thought with satisfaction. He felt this man's insecurity, his fears, his petulance, his greed and his vengeful sense of injury. Yale ought to be easy. Still, the hard body of experience wrought in two decades of fighting white men warned him that it was not necessarily so. Even the worst of them, the most venal, could go sour at an unexpected moment, suddenly remember that they were white and retreat into the dark burrow of tribal taboo. Fear could do it, or the long habit of racial arrogance, or both, inextricably intertwined. Well, sooner or later you had to find out. He decided to go at it boldly. "Do you know anything about me, Mr. Yale? About my profession?" he asked.

"Some," Yale said cautiously. "I've heard of you." For an impulsive moment he toyed with the notion that he could shatter this man's monumental composure and take command of the situation by naming Barton for what he was. Barton denied him the opportunity.

"We can be frank, Mr. Yale," he said. "The word 'blockbuster' is inaccurate, but it does not offend me."

"I didn't say it," Yale said shortly. Watch it, watch it, he warned himself; this guy is dangerous.

"I would expect you to know my reputation. You are a man of breadth and awareness," Barton said comfortably. "I would not insult you with pretense. Therefore I admit at the outset that I have asked you here on a matter that is in my interest. I ask you to believe that it is also in your interest—perhaps to a greater degree in your interest."

"How do you mean?" Yale said.

"Permit me to state it bluntly," Barton said, leaning forward slightly. "You live in Peaceable Lane. Six weeks ago a colored man bought a house on your street. There was some resistance. I believe it was felt, among other considerations, that his coming would damage property values for the rest of you. There was a conspiracy to keep him out."

"I didn't have anything to do with it," Yale said. "Not a damn thing!" Yale had felt the icy thrust of fear. Christ! he thought; you're over a barrel any way you move, and something like hate welled in him at the memory of Annabelle's insistence that they buy the house.

But Barton settled back in his chair again and smiled at him.

"I am aware that you had nothing to do with it, Mr. Yale," he said. "I remarked before that I know you. Believe me, it was not idle chatter." Yes, he was thinking, I know you, Yale. I know you better than you know yourself. "I know that it would be impossible for a man of your views to join in an ignoble conspiracy," he said aloud.

Jesus, Yale wondered, what's he getting at?

"I told you I had nothing to do with it," he said. "So what do you want of me?"

"Six weeks have passed," Barton said. "I am curious. Mr. Yale, what is the climate of the street after six weeks?"

"You ought to know—you created it," Yale blurted. He knew it was foolhardy but, damn the bland black buddha to hell, he was tired of this cat-and-mouse business. "The place is in a panic. What did you expect it to be? You cost everybody on the street around ten thousand bucks—including me."

Barton folded his thick fingers across his vest and sat regarding Yale in pensive calm. He's coming along, Barton thought. He's frightened, but he's beginning to remember where he hurts. And he hates being hurt so badly that even he, the rat, is almost ready to fight back. He wondered if it would be wise to goad him further. You could carry it too far, he knew.

"I regret your loss," Barton said. "Had it been possible, I would have avoided it."

"Well, then, why the hell didn't you?" Yale snarled, letting caution go. "You people have had a lot of help from me and you know it. You're too damn well organized not to know I lived there. So when you had to pick a place to move in on, why move in on me? Why go out of your way to clobber a man who helps you? Did you think I had ten thousand dollars to throw away?" Even through his anger Yale knew he was racing into peril but, for the moment, in the bedeviling sense of injury, he didn't care.

Barton's expression did not change, but he raised one hand, palm out, to stem the rush of words.

"That is why I called you here, Mr. Yale," he said. "I brought you here to tell you that I had nothing to do with the Bronson house being sold."

"Didn't have anything to do with it!" Yale blurted. "What kind of fool do you take me for? You trying to tell me those weren't your gorillas driving the place out of its mind?"

"The gorillas, as you call them—yes, they were mine," Barton said. "Sometimes, as you know, vigorous methods are necessary in liberal causes. Not all men, Mr. Yale, are as enlightened as yourself." Barton paused and considered and decided he might as well rub this one's nose in it a little more. "But I must tell you this. Despite all we could do—I include you in this, Mr. Yale, since you refused to join in the conspiracy and were therefore, I assume, on our side—despite all we could do, we failed."

"Failed?" Yale's mouth was open, gasping at the big man's massive effrontery. "Failed! Do you think I'm blind? The guy lives there!"

"I know," Barton said silkily. "But not through my efforts—nor through yours, Mr. Yale."

Yale shook his head. "Jesus Christ," he breathed. "Am I out of my mind? Or are you?"

Barton sat impassive, considering again, wondering whether the time was ripe to let him have it. The man was punch drunk already, he thought—reeling. Yale didn't know what he was dealing with, which was what Barton had intended, but he was scared and angry, aware of some nameless force that had hurt him and might hurt him again. I think it's time, Barton decided.

"The conspiracy succeeded, Mr. Yale," he said aloud. "Your neighbors bought the house."

"Then how the hell did the ni—how did Winter get it?" Yale asked helplessly.

"That is what I called you here to tell you," Barton said. "You will understand that I tell you only because you were not a member of the conspiracy. You refused to join it. Therefore, as I told you earlier, I regret your loss." He paused. "No, Mr. Yale, you were sold out inside the lane. Your neighbors placed it in the hands of Jones, as you probably know. Jones arranged the sale to Winter—with the connivance of Gold."

"No!" Yale breathed.

"Oh, yes, Mr. Yale, exactly that."

"I don't get it," Yale said.

"You will," Barton said. "And when you do, you will probably also understand that it was not the sort of transaction which meets my approval. It was done out of sentiment—and sentiment does not advance my purposes." Barton sat forward and stared at his guest. "Mr. Yale, do you want to sell your house? Make good the loss you have suffered? Perhaps better than merely make it good?"

16

BILL JONES and Jerry Gold were deep in the serious business of shooting baskets into the hoop Zack had put up for his son against the back wall of the Gold garage. Since this was a pursuit demanding a man's full attention, it was only by accident that Bill happened to see Tod Winter watching from the hemlocks. He happened to glance in just the right direction at the right time to catch a glimpse of a dark face and furtive figure.

"D'you know that new kid?" Bill panted, as Jerry dribbled out from under the basket and circled back toward where he would pivot and give him the ball in a short, hard pass.

"Nope. Why?" Jerry puffed.

"He's over there in the trees, watchin' us."

"Let him watch."

Bill was having one of the flashes of perception which come oftener to children than they do to adults. He knew why Tod was there and he also knew why he was hanging back. He felt something of the strange boy's loneliness and the frozen reluctance that would probably keep him from doing anything about it unless somebody else made a move. He did not consciously decide what his move would be. In Bill's nine-year-old world, cliques and ententes formed, shifted, dissolved and re-formed in constantly changing patterns, meaningless to an outsider but intensely, even passionately, important to those who lived within them. It was possible to be welcomed with openhearted pleasure—and equally possible to be shunted coolly aside with the effect, though not the intent, of cruelty. It could have gone either way.

"He was over at our house one night," Bill said. "He's all right, I guess."

"Nobody said he wasn't."

"Well . . ." Bill hesitated, bouncing the ball against the flat of his hand. He didn't really expect resistance from Jerry, but he was conscious that this was a little strange—not much, but a little—and anyhow, it was an instinctive matter of protocol to consult one partner before adding another. "You care if he comes over and shoots a few baskets? He ain't having much fun."

"You'll catch it if your mother hears you saying 'ain't.' I don't care. Tell him to come on over. If he's any good we can call ourselves the Harlem Globe Trotters. Hey! How's that for an idea?"

"Shut up, dope. He'll hear you." Still bouncing the ball, Bill peered toward the hemlocks. "Hey, Tod! Wanta shoot baskets?"

All three were still there an hour later, following the inane, endless, tired but tireless and highly important circle. Take the ball, dribble in fast, go up in a tight, hard spring and shoot, retrieve the ball, dribble out, pivot and pass to the next, still-puffing shooter. They could have kept it up until they dropped and might have done so had not Paul Cusack, Jr. come around the house. There was no time to tighten a defense against him. Paul charged in, tipped Bill's shot off the rim of the basket and, blocking the smaller boy aside with hips and elbows, recovered the ball.

"Come on, creep!" Bill bawled his indignation. "That's my ball and my turn. If you wanta shoot, get in line."

"Dry up," Paulie said. "It *was* your turn—now it's mine." He pivoted away and dribbled around the circle, ignoring Tod, who was next up and waiting with hands out to take the ball. He dribbled in under the basket, shot, missed, grunted angrily, picked up the ball in a fast dribble and circled around for another shot.

"Come on, Paulie, pass the ball," Jerry yelled. "It's Bill's ball and my house. Come on, pass it!"

"You dry up too," Paulie told him and spun away as Jerry charged in, trying to knock the ball from under his dribbling fingers. Bill tried it and was fended off with such force that he lost his balance and went sprawling. Here again was the familiar, bitterly resented outrage of heavier bone and stronger muscle, and the two smaller boys rose to it with familiar, unplanned and impotent fury. For a few wild seconds Bill and Jerry fumbled madly, trying to wrest the ball from the older boy. Paulie kept possession and laughed at them, mockingly dribbling toward them, then swinging away to the basket, using his heavier body in ways that were meant to hurt.

"You big lunk!" Bill yelled. "Give me my ball. Nobody asked you here. Why don't you go swim or something? Or drown?"

The bigger boy stopped dead, holding the ball. For the first time he seemed to pay attention to the Negro boy. Tod had been standing uncertainly aside, unsure of the role he should or would be permitted to play in this. He had been joyfully but unspokenly grateful for the last hour of fun, granted unexpectedly and seemingly without reservation. But now, in an agony of doubt, he had been brought back sharply to the realization that he did not know these kids. It was not a reasoning process; there was simply the knowledge that he was different and an instinctive fear of trespassing where he was not wanted. Here was some part of the prudence and diffidence that had baffled and disappointed his father.

Paulie stood, patting the ball up and down. "The reason I'm not swimming is him, if you want to know," he said, staring at Tod with cold hostility. "That's where I would have been instead of fooling around with you punk kids. Except for him. Just him, that's all." The stare was contemptuous and accusing. "My father says I can't go in the pool again until he moves away from here. How do you like that, huh? What do you think of that?"

"If you ask me," Jerry said, "I think you're a creep. What's he got to do with the pool?"

"He's a nigger. That's what he's got to do with it." Paulie's eyes were malevolent. "A nigger."

Suddenly the three white boys became aware of Tod. Throughout their squabble he had been standing aside, abashed, wanting not to be seen. But now he was moving toward the taller, heavier boy. He moved with dragging feet, stiffly, with terrible reluctance.

His face had gone pale under the dark skin, frozen but for a faint trembling of the chin. It was as though he was driven against his will by a force that not even terror could deny. Slowly, jerkily, he moved forward. But out of the pinched, fear-raddled little face, Tod's eyes blazed hatred.

"I'm going to kill you," he said. The words came in a thin, sobbing gasp. He moved forward as though mesmerized, never taking his eyes from Paulie's face.

"Why, you little nigger punk," Paulie said. But Paulie was startled. It showed as he dropped the ball and let it roll away. He spread his feet and dropped his shoulders and, bunching his muscles, put his hands out, wide apart and half clawed. This was Paulie's meat; taking this little nigger would be a pleasure. But Tod was moving forward, step by jerking step, and suddenly Paulie shivered and felt an illogical impulse to bolt. There was no doubting the crazy, scary intensity of the eyes staring out of Tod's tight little mask of fear. This kid meant to murder him.

"Come on, punk. Come and get it." It was intended to be a jeer, but it sounded uncertain, even to Paulie.

For as long as Bill Jones could remember, the humiliations and injuries inflicted by Paul Cusack, Jr. had been followed by vows, sometimes pledged through blubbering tears, sometimes through the snuffling of a bloody nose, to get even with him someday. He and Jerry had planned their vengeance more times than they could remember. It had never worked. And yet they knew the time would inevitably come when they would take him.

And suddenly Bill knew that it had to be now. Somebody was about to get hurt, and badly. He had been in battle often enough himself, as often as was necessary to maintain his self-respect and that of his peers. Usually they had been battles fought in quick, hot anger. But never, in all his nine years, had he seen a look like that on the Negro boy's face, that blank, burning, terror-ridden will to kill. Something bad was about to happen here and he knew it had to be stopped.

"Jerry!" Bill yelled, and Jerry looked at him, tearing his eyes away from the hypnotic fascination of Tod's slow advance. Wholly absorbed in one another, neither Tod nor Paulie gave any sign of hearing. Jerry nodded and pointed. They did not need to talk. They both knew where and how they would interfere. They had planned it too often and Paulie had been their target too long.

Moving softly but swiftly, Bill ran in behind Paulie and dropped to his hands and knees. "Hit him!" he yelled. Jerry, slipping first into Tod's line of advance to cut him off, suddenly flung himself forward, throwing every ounce of his slight, bony weight against Paulie's chest. Paulie was down and then engulfed in a blinding, flailing, squirming, desperate tangle of arms, legs, fists and butting heads. Almost at once, in shock, outrage and sudden fear, Paulie knew he was going to be licked. Almost simultaneously, in sweet exultation too long delayed, both Bill and Jerry knew it too.

Dazed, still held by the spell of what he had intended to do, Tod stood and stared at the struggling tangle of bodies. He realized that he was panting, gasping for breath as though he had been running and was ready to drop. As though from far off he heard Bill's voice rising out of the thrashing melee in high-pitched command, "Keep out of this! He's ours."

And Paulie was theirs for one minute and thirty-seven seconds. At the end of that time the advantage of size and weight, multiplied by the sheer force of panic, heaved him up out of his unbelievable Waterloo. One eye was closed; his face was smeared with a fairly even mixture of his own and Jerry's blood; his exploring tongue would gingerly discover later that he had two loose teeth and his right ear had been torn by an agency which probably could have been identified by the Jones family dentist. Sobbing in the great, anguished gasps of the mighty brought low by midgets, Paulie fled.

"Well . . ." Tod Winter's eyes were on the floor. He looked up only when he could no longer bear not taking a furtive glance at his father. Lamar Winter, warned by Matt Jones, who had been advised by his wife, who in turn had been advised in vituperative detail by Laura Cusack, was trying with pain and patience to extract from his reluctant son an eyewitness version of Paulie Cusack's downfall.

"Well, what? Now listen, Tod, I want to know what happened.

And I don't want you to try to cut any corners with me. Did you gang up with those two kids and beat up the Cusack kid?"

"No, I didn't. I told you that. How many times do I have to tell you anyway?"

"His mother says so. She says the three of you got together and beat him up. With clubs, she says. Why?"

"I tell you," Tod said, twisting in an agony of embarrassment, "we were just playing and he butted in."

"So you clobbered him?"

"I did not either clobber him." Then the boy's head came up and he looked his parent in the eye. "But I was going to . . . and I wish I had! He called me a nigger."

"Well . . ." Winter breathed. Here was news indeed. His soft son, this lad who was good at the piano but shunned the harsh reality of lifelong combat that had been imposed on him by the color of his skin. This kid who had never been in a fight in his life, who had always walked softly to avoid battle and fled from it when it was forced on him. This youngster, so slender and young and easily hurt, now rising up unbelievably to face a challenge. Facing up to it even when the odds were impossible, when he knew he had to get hurt. By God, Winter thought suddenly, maybe the best thing I ever did was bring him out here! Tod had never fought in Harlem, among his own. But this . . . somehow that white kid's sneer had brought him to his heritage. Pride and sheer delight surged up in Winter, and even deeper, he knew, came the profound wave of heartfelt thankfulness: somehow Tod seemed to be finding it, the hard, gritty guts he would need to survive. It was an effort to conceal his joy.

"So you were going to take him on, were you?" he asked softly. "You know he's about twice your size, don't you?"

Remembering the agony of that stiff, dazed, terror-driven compulsion pushing him forward, knowing that he would be mercilessly beaten, knowing also that he must smash and claw the sneer from Paulie's face, even if he died doing it, Tod shuddered.

"I couldn't help it," he muttered.

"Yes, boy, I know," Winter said softly, yearning to pull the boy onto his lap and comfort him, but knowing that he must not. "I know and it's all right."

Tod could not look up. "But, I didn't," he mumbled. "They wouldn't let me."

"Who wouldn't let you?" Winter asked sharply.

"Bill and Jerry. They made me stay out. They beat him up—I never touched him."

Winter stared at him, trying to understand. There was something more here, something still hidden and baffling, and he had to get a grip on it. "Do you mean to tell me those two kids ganged up on young Cusack and beat his teeth in just because he called you a nigger?"

"I don't know." Tod's face reflected an agony of doubt. "That's when they beat him up. But I don't know if that was why they did it. They were already mad at him."

"Christ!" The exclamation burst from Winter without his knowing it. He had a wild, illogical impulse to smash something, somehow to batter his way to understanding. Everything about this denied everything he had lived by. Black was black and white was white, and there was no middle ground. His son must fight, not only for the right to live his life as he would, but for life itself, and all his life he must fight alone and against long odds. That was the way it had been ordained, whether by God or by man did not matter. It was the simple, diamond-hard equation by which Winter himself had lived and triumphed. There was no room in it for mercy, for any kind of yielding, for any kind of generosity. But, goddammit to hell, this business of Peaceable Lane kept refusing to live by the rule, kept skirting around it, kept fuzzing it up. Who knew whether the rule held or did not hold? That was when they did it, Tod had said, but he didn't know if that was why they did it. And who did?

For a moment Winter felt the rush of terrible fear for his son. The kid could get lost here. Less than half formed, with a mind still tender and malleable, a prey to doubt, he might lose sight of the one sure thing he had to know: that everything white was his enemy and that he must struggle against it to survive. It was a lesson that Winter believed he himself had known from babyhood, but he feared his son might not learn in time. He might never learn it here. Not with kids who did things and you didn't know why they did them.

He shook his head in bewilderment. How could he explain this to the kid when he did not know what was happening to his own sure image of fact?

"All right, son," he said softly. "Don't worry about it. You did all right, and I'm proud of you."

17

THE THING WRONG with knowing where the body was buried, Peter Yale reflected sourly, was that it stuck you with the burden of deciding when and under what circumstances it would be safe or useful to dig it up. Not that he wished himself rid of the secret Francis Barton had confided to him. Far from it. He did not doubt that he would use it; the question was how—and when.

He had left Barton's office hugging the knowledge with vengeful glee. His first impulse, as Barton had suspected it would be, was to use it immediately to cut Jones and Gold down to size, the self-righteous bastards. But his natural calculating wariness had reasserted itself in time to keep him from going off half cocked. Barton had suspected that this would happen, too, but he did not greatly care. He knew that sooner or later Yale would use what he knew, and he did not see how his use of it, in whatever context, could do anything but serve the Barton purposes.

Of course, Barton had reflected placidly as his guest departed, the most satisfactory result would be for Yale to rush off and tattle immediately. With Peaceable Lane as close to panic as it was already, that might be just the thing to start the stampede. He could picture Cusack and Draper trembling on the edge of bolting—and then doing it. Barton was shrewdly aware of how profoundly the lane had been shocked; he thought it extremely unlikely its people would ever again be capable of rallying together to resist a common enemy. There would be an extra dividend of satisfaction if Yale proved vengeful enough and reckless enough to set the thing off prematurely—and was himself trampled in the stampede. Barton had studied Yale thoroughly and despised him in an unemotional way.

Still, the pleasant prospect that Yale might wreck himself as well as the lane was mere egg in the beer. Barton suspected that Yale's instinct for survival was too sharp to let it happen. And, taking the long view of what he intended to accomplish in Peaceable Lane, it did not really matter. He felt confident that he would get Yale's house and that, in itself, would bring Peaceable Lane close to the jumping-off place. Then, if Yale chose to spill what he knew after first saving himself, that ought to do the rest. Even sitting alone, ruminating behind the smooth expanse of the rosewood desk, Barton's big, calm face did not betray the satisfaction he felt.

As Barton had foreseen, Peter Yale's thought processes made their way safely past the immediate pitfall of temptation and settled down to essentials. First things first. And the first thing, naturally, was to insure his own safety. After that there would be time for the luxury of letting Jones and Gold have it.

But the longer he thought about it, the more he could perceive how tricky that first objective could become. Just as a starter, there was the question of Annabelle. The deed was registered in joint tenancy; it would be impossible to sell the house without her consent and co-operation. He felt the familiar upsurge of resentment and frustration at the prospect of having to deal with her stubborn resistance. Still, he thought, it would probably be possible to bulldoze her into it. Despite her dislike of him, about which he had no illusions, and despite her absurd attachment to the house and her even more ridiculous sense of obligation to the neighbors, he knew that Annabelle was susceptible to threat. After all, she knew she couldn't make it on her own—not with two kids. But she would make it as difficult for him as possible, that he knew.

But then, probably far trickier than handling Annabelle, was the question of the lane itself. Even before the summons from Barton had opened these dazzling new avenues of action, Yale had toyed with the idea of blackmailing the lane as Bronson had done before him. He had hesitated, knowing as sharply as Barton how deeply its people had been disunited by the coming of Lamar Winter; in order for the lane ever again to serve as a fitting victim of blackmail, it was first necessary that its members trust one another enough to act in concert—and this, he strongly suspected, was no longer possible.

Well, then, why not go about it the simplest way? Why not just take Barton's offer to buy—at a premium—take his money and run? It was a mighty temptation, and Yale thought that sooner or later, when he had worked out all the angles to his satisfaction, it was probably what he would do. But he wasn't going to rush into it pell-mell. Something about Barton's offer had roused Yale's deepest, most powerful instincts for self-preservation.

Yale could never forget his profession. It needed a crafty, calculating, constantly alert intelligence to avoid all the pitfalls lurking in the frantic, hypersensitive, ruthlessly cowardly world of broadcasting. There was nothing so chronically scared as a network, nothing so hysterically ready to chop off one of its fingers to save its neck. It had been through his fear of the network's fear that Barton's telephone tactics had scared him off in the first go-around on Peaceable Lane. He had been vulnerable, particularly so because the foundation of his reputation and his rating was as a champion of liberal causes. But he did not have to kid himself and did not; he knew as well as anybody that the network's real roots were sunk into and nourished by money, not liberalism. He had no illusion about it; his selling out to a blockbuster, if it were known, would certainly offend money—and there was a lot of it around here in upper Westchester, just up the hill on Grassy Tor, for the closest and probably most sensitive example. Goddammit, he thought, it was a dandy little box he had been stupid enough to let his wife trap him into.

Nor, despite all that easy, cajoling talk, did he trust Barton to help him out of it. Barton had suggested that he use Alexander Fox as his broker. Fox, Barton had said, knew every trick in handling a deal as sensitive as they both knew this one would be. But, on reflection, Yale had realized that that was just the trouble; Fox knew the tricks all right, but he was also known to too many people as the man who knew the tricks. Getting caught dealing with Fox wouldn't be much safer than putting up a billboard on the parkway cutoff to advertise the fact.

He knew there must be other ways to do it, but the trouble was that he did not know how to go about it. One way and another Barton was probably right; he would need Fox's special knowledge, but he damn well intended, insofar as it was possible, to keep Fox invisible.

When he made up his mind, he moved as cautiously as he knew how. He took the trouble to drive into Chappaqua to call Fox from a pay telephone in a drugstore, to avoid the hazard of the lane's party lines. He protested when Fox said that it would be necessary for him to inspect the house before committing himself. When Fox insisted, Yale in turn made sure that he would come only at night and only when he could be sure of being alone. In the end, he made an opportunity by persuading Annabelle to take the kids to a Disney movie in Mount Kisco, pleading that he needed the time and solitude to work over a ticklish script.

All the same, he was jumpy by the time Fox's cream-colored Dodge slid into the driveway, and he let the broker into the house without turning on the porch lights. It was already after nine, and he was all too acutely aware that, unless they stayed through the second feature, Annabelle and the kids would be back before ten.

"I thought you were coming at eight," he said sharply as the tall, long-jawed broker came through the door. "We won't have much time."

"I'm sorry, Mr. Yale, I really am sorry," Fox said apologetically. "I had to meet a man and got hung up. But don't worry. This won't take long, and after that we can go out in the car and talk where it's private." Fox paused and considered whether he ought to warn Yale and decided he might as well. "I guess we have to go out anyway," he said. "The man I had to meet was Barton's man, that Smith. I think he wants to talk to you."

"Talk to me? What about?" Yale said sharply. "You didn't bring him here?"

"No, of course not," Fox said hastily. "We'll meet him down the road where it's private." This one's pretty fidgety, Fox thought; I hope they've got sense enough not to push him too hard.

Alexander Fox had been dealing with men, both white and colored, in furtive circumstances for more years than he liked to think about. The process had given him a chameleon-like quality of wary invisibility; he could never rid himself of the feeling that the anomaly of a white man working stealthily between the white world and the colored made him dangerously suspect in both. I sure hope they don't shove him too hard, he thought again. Fox never really enjoyed getting involved in one of Francis Barton's deals, although he knew perfectly well that they needed and complemented each other. It had begun a long time ago with his recognition of the need and his finding Barton with the intent of using him. He still liked to think that he was using the big, impassive colored blockbuster, but he could never quite be sure it wasn't the other way around. Fox knew he was interested in money; he knew the same thing about Barton, which should have soothed him. But it did not; Barton made him nervous.

"I don't know why Smith should want to see me," Yale said. "Barton said to deal through you."

"Oh, I don't think it's anything much," Fox said soothingly.

"And I don't know why you thought you had to see the house either," Yale went on irritably. "It's here and you know it's here and Barton knows it's here, and it's his money."

"It won't take long," Fox said. "Just so I get an idea of the layout and the general condition." Deliberately he made it sound pompous. "After all, a man in my position has a responsibility to his client."

"Responsibility, my ass," Yale said shortly. "All right, let's look and get it over with and get out of here." If Alexander Fox felt that Yale hustled him through the house with indecent dispatch, he gave no sign, and twenty minutes later they were drifting along the woods road through Wacapo Park toward Chappaqua. If Annabelle beat him home, as she probably would, Yale thought, it would be easy enough to explain that he had gone out for a walk to clear his mind to deal with the script.

"How do you want to handle this?" Yale demanded as they rode.

"Seems to me it's more a question of how you want to handle it," Fox said cautiously. "You're selling; Barton's buying. I'll handle it any way that's agreeable."

Yale considered warily how much it would be safe to tell this man. One thing he did not want to do was to surrender any more hostages than absolutely necessary to the discretion of other men. You could never be sure who suffered from a loose lip, nor—he winced inwardly at the thought—was it entirely impossible that somebody might take it into his head to blackmail *him.*

"I have reasons for wanting this done quietly," Yale said, putting out a feeler. "I don't want to advertise the fact I'm selling."

"What you mean is you don't want to advertise the fact you're selling to somebody who might let a colored man get the house, isn't it?" Fox said quietly. "You can't very well hide the fact you're selling."

Yale was startled. Damn him, he thought angrily, this man knew too much already and knew it too fast. He felt a petulant but, considering his own intention, entirely incongruous resentment that this white man had chosen to work with colored men against the interests of whites. He started to protest, but Fox was speaking again.

"Don't let it scare you, Mr. Yale," he said. "I've been handling these things too long not to know what the score is. Most people don't want it advertised."

He might have known, Yale thought disgustedly. Fox was an old hand and so was Barton. And the only way to keep from leaving cracks through which—sometime or somehow—somebody might get at him was to keep out of a deal like this entirely. He had found out about Gold and Jones, hadn't he? What was to guarantee that this, too, wouldn't be dug up sometime and flung in his face? In a moment of panic he thought of backing out, right now, quick.

"Don't you worry, Mr. Yale," Fox said again. "Maybe that's something you ought to ask Smith about." The way this one was fidgeting, Fox thought, it would have been better to keep Smith out of it. Smith just naturally scared people. But he didn't see how he could, not at this point. "He'll be waiting along here."

Yale's uneasiness did not abate when they drew up beside a waiting car along the shore of Wacapo Lake and the slender, owl-eyed Smith ducked quickly through the headlight glare and into Fox's car. Unease drove Yale, more abruptly than he liked, into flinging his concern at Barton's lieutenant. Tensely he swung to face Smith in the back seat.

"Before this deal goes any further," he said, "I want a guarantee it'll stay covered up afterward. You ready to give me that?"

Smith regarded him calmly. It would be a pleasure, he thought, to let this scared bastard know what he thought of him. But he wouldn't. There were Barton's orders, for one thing, and, for another, he recognized panic when he saw it.

"It'll stay covered up," he said quietly. "There's nothing to be concerned about, not in your case."

"The other deal didn't," Yale reminded him. "Barton told me about it. What if Barton—or him"—he jerked a thumb toward Fox beside him—"gets an idea it would be fun to rat on me afterward—or you do?" There was a whining snarl in Yale's voice.

"You don't understand," Smith said. "There was a reason for telling you. Barton figured you had a right to know. And that other wasn't Barton's deal. We don't talk about his deals afterward. It stands to reason, Barton's in business and intends to stay there. It wouldn't help him any to have word get around that we don't protect people who co-operate."

"I'm not sure I believe that," Yale said tightly. "I don't think he'd wait a damn minute—not if he thought it'd help him crack the rest of the lane open."

"No." Smith paused for a moment. What he had to say now was what Barton had sent him to say. There was a message he had to get across, but it had to be done just right. He had to scare the bastard, terrify him, in fact—but he knew it could go exactly wrong. It was dangerous. This was where they had to be sure of their man, sure the guy was greedy enough not to do a flip-flop and suddenly remember he was white and owed a duty to the white man's protective association. But Barton had said the man was ripe, and he trusted Barton's judgment. Just ram it into him, he thought, ram it in; let him know what was what. "Mr. Barton wouldn't need that to crack the rest of Peaceable Lane, Mr. Yale," he said, letting the very quiet of his tone carry the menace home. "If Mr. Barton doesn't get your house, he'll get somebody else's. And with Winter already there, the street'll go fast from then on. Take my word for it, Peaceable Lane is going to go. You couldn't stop it if you tried. The only thing you can do is get out first, nice and easy and free, like Mr. Barton told you." He sat back to let it sink in. "That's your guarantee. Mr. Barton does not need to rat on you."

Yale shivered. Damn Barton and his crew to hell anyhow; once they took out after you, you were done for. He did not have the slightest doubt that what lay in store for Peaceable Lane was precisely what Smith said.

"Got me over a barrel, haven't you?" he said, trying and failing to make his voice sound tough.

"Oh, I wouldn't feel that way about it," Smith said easily. "You're lucky Barton likes you." That, he thought, was one of the blackest white lies he had ever told. "How would you like to be some of those other folks?"

Yale shivered again and sat silent. He's hooked, Smith thought, looking at the hunched shoulders. He said good night pleasantly and slipped out and returned to his car and drove away.

Fox, still wishing that Barton and his men would take fewer and less brutal chances, but breathing a silent sigh of relief at the thought that it had worked, started his engine and wheeled the Dodge back toward the lane.

"I still got to know how you're going to handle this. Keep it under cover," Yale said stubbornly as they moved along the winding woods road. "I got to know." He tried and failed to keep the whine out of his voice.

Fox told him carefully, deliberately trying to soothe his fears, knowing now that Smith had planted the barb deep and that the man was hooked.

"You see," he finished, as he started to swing the car into Yale's driveway, "it'll all be covered up right from the start and, like Smith says, there'll never be any reason for Barton to pull the plug on you. Here you are, home, and take my word, Mr. Yale, there's nothing to worry about."

"No," Yale said sharply. "Take me down a couple of houses. I'll walk back."

Obligingly Fox drove on past Dr. Abram's house and stopped along the curb of the Cavanidis lawn. Yale quickly opened the door, winced skittishly as the automatic dome light winked on, slid out and quickly closed the door.

"Good night, Mr. Yale," he heard Fox say softly. "I'll see you middle of next week. And congratulations."

"Arrgh," Yale said disgustedly, as the car slid away and he turned to walk back up the street.

Yale was not to know it for yet a while, but he was unmasked in the brief seconds the car door was open and the dome light illuminated both his face and Fox's. It probably would not have materially affected his dismay to know that he was undone by love, and love alone.

Steve Cavanidis had been away for two weeks on another of his long swings around the country in behalf of the union. During that fortnight, the preservative skills of the Slenderella people, the brevity of Cyd's bathing suits, and her languorously steamy air of being in heat had finally won out over the firm young flesh and the coltish overavailability of Lana Weissman. Steve's refusal to permit Cyd to redecorate the house after Winter's arrival and Cyd's smoldering resentment may also have had something to do with it. Thus, by indirection, did the tentacles of Peaceable Lane's crisis extend themselves even further, although it must be said, given Cyd's temperament, it might have happened anyhow.

This was the fourth night on which Lana, her overburdened young heart bursting with unhappiness and hate, had kept her lonely vigil over the Cavanidis house. Unable to bear the pain, equally unable to spare herself the lash, Lana was lurking among the rhododendrons, waiting to see how late it would be before Mark Cotten came out.

She did not think it would be soon. Once, in a fever of desperation, she had ventured across the lawn and crouched in the shrubbery beneath the open ground-floor window of what she knew was the Cavanidis master bedroom. The room was dark, but the murmuring sounds of endearment and activity within had cut off the little hope she had of doubt. She had crept away, sick and trembling, blind with rage.

Even yet she could not find it in her heart to blame Cotten, though she went far enough to think him a blind fool. No, he had been trapped by that fat, phony blond bitch. And so she crouched, in her pain and humiliation, and made and remade lurid plans for vengeance.

She was there when Fox's Dodge drifted to a stop along the curb. For a moment she felt a wild surge of hope that this was Cavanidis, unexpectedly home and about to take his wife in *flagrante delicto;* almost instantaneously the hope was drowned in a flood of terror that Cotten was about to be trapped and killed.

Then the door opened, the dome light flicked on, and Lana's staring eyes recognized Yale and saw the man he was with. Instantly Lana recognized Fox; like every other child on Peaceable Lane, she had seen that face more than once in the touchy weeks while David Bronson was first negotiating to sell his house. Not even in the depths of her passionate preoccupation with the Cavanidis house could Lana Weissman have been described as less than bright. These two men together, Yale's doubtful state of grace with his neighbors, this furtive delivery two hundred yards from his own house. Lana knew how to put two and two together and promptly did so.

The next morning Lana told her father, at the same time wishing in a red passion that providence would grant her as deadly a tool as this to deal with Cyd Cavanidis.

18

EVERY INSTINCT warned Ellen Jones that the act she was here engaged upon was foolhardy, shot through with the ingredients of disaster. And the utterly incomprehensible part of it was that this time the whirlwind she was daring was one that could engulf her son. And so why, she asked herself helplessly, was she doing it? It was difficult to answer. Somehow the bewildering rush of events in Peaceable Lane seemed to have trapped her. She had laid herself open first with that nervous, unguarded talk about the school on the night of the Winters' visit. That had been followed by the hysterical bitchery of Laura

Cusack and the smooth, calculated savagery of Sybil Macmillan. Then the shocking knowledge that the school year's car-pool system had been planned without her. She had felt herself driven beyond the tribal pale; her instinct had been to rise against it in defiance, and to that extent she had trapped herself. Even so, she did not believe she could have brought herself to challenge the whirlwind by these things alone.

But Matt had wanted it and pressed his advantage, making light of her fears, appealing to the warm compassion he knew was hers. And then the fight had come and Bill and Jerry had come home in a warrior's triumph after vanquishing a superior enemy at last. She had not quailed under Laura's rage and, when she looked upon her tattered, bloody and suddenly grown-up son, she could have burst with pride. And so, somehow, here she was.

With Beth Gold and Margo Winter she was sitting in the Gold kitchen, sipping coffee and working out a complex rotation in units of three weeks—fifteen school days—to arrive at an even division of the burden of transporting their progeny to and from Wacapo Consolidated.

"That gives each of us a one-day stint every third week and two days each the other two," Beth said. "It will work out all right if we can get them all into the morning session, but it will be a real headache if we can't."

"Have you ever done this before, Margo?" Ellen asked, still feeling odd to be calling her spectacularly handsome and also, in other ways, different new neighbor by her first name. But, she thought grimly, if we're all going to be second-class citizens together, it'll look pretty silly to try to be formal about it. And I'm not so sure we're second-class either.

"I'm afraid not. But what's hard about it?" Margo asked.

"Nothing—if you're prepared to use a baseball bat," Ellen said. "You establish that you're boss in the car the first day—or you never will be. Otherwise you'll just be hostess to a riot and work up a nervous breakdown. By the way, how do you hope to pack four junior-size tigers into that sporty go-buggy?"

"Oh, that." Margo laughed. "I should have told you. Lamar's getting me a car of my own."

"A Cadillac?" Beth asked curiously.

"Why, yes. How did you know?"

"A rough guess, that's all. But if you don't mind, I suggest you talk him out of it. If you can manage two cars, a police van would be about right for our youngsters."

"Well," Margo said wistfully, "if you're sure. You ought to know. I'll see what Lamar says." She looked from one to the other and spoke again in an impulsive burst of warmth. "I think I ought to thank both of you . . ."

"It might be more accurate to thank Mrs. Cusack," Ellen said with a dash of acid.

"I doubt that," Margo said. "I'll stay with it this way if you don't mind. I do thank you, both of you."

Matt was involved in the deep August curse of rooting out crab grass. For several optimistic seasons he had rotated from one to another chemical preparation, each bearing a fearsome name and labeled with a glowing description of its selective death-dealing properties. The trouble was that the stuff always either killed everything or killed nothing. Matt, disillusioned and impoverished, had resigned himself to fight the good fight by hand. This year, after propaganda intended to trap his son into the illusion that work was fun, he had succeeded in acquiring an unpaid assistant—more or less.

This was not an unmitigated triumph. Bill developed a suspicion that he was being had and with it a tendency to dawdle. Moreover, he suspected that an adult willing to spend a month every year, one of the best months at that, on his hands and knees, blistering his fingers, to favor one kind of grass over another must be less than bright. What with one thing and another—the blasting sun, the stubborn roots, the unbelievable expanse of lawn still to be done and the plain impossibility of ever doing it all—plus the depressing knowledge that it would all have to be done over next year—Bill had despaired of the present. But, because life must go on, he was developing a corrective philosophy for the future. As one more clump resisted his effort, he settled on his haunches and looked on the scene with disgust.

"Why do people have to have grass?" he asked.

"I sometimes wonder," Matt grunted. "Gives you kids something to play on. That's one reason."

"I'd just as soon play on crab grass as any other kind. Besides, how can you play when you have to spend all your time pulling it?"

"Son, you have hit on something profound, but I'm afraid I don't know the answer. And I doubt if any suburbanite ever will discover it."

"What's a suburbanite?" Bill thought he could glimpse the beginning of a conversation if he could just keep it going. And that, while falling short of an ideal situation which would involve something really rewarding, like football, was preferable to this.

"What we are. People who live in the country and work in town."

"If we lived in town we wouldn't have to pull crab grass, would we?"

"No-o-o. But then you wouldn't have a place to play either."

"Well, heck, I'm not playing. When I grow up I'm going to live in the city. Let the squares pull the crab grass."

"How many times have I told you not to use that word 'square'? Anyhow, if you live in the city when you grow up, where do you think your kids will have to play?"

"I'm not going to have any kids. They're too much trouble."

"Hm-m-m," Matt said. "There speaks a traitor to his class. What have you got against kids?"

"We-l-l-l." Bill furrowed his brow; this was holding up better than he had hoped. "Nothing much, I guess. Only they are a lot of trouble. That new kid, he told us his family went to all the trouble of moving here just for him."

"He did, huh? Did he say why?"

"He said his mother didn't like to have him going to school in the city or playing on the street." Bill paused to consider and uttered a dark forecast. "He'll find out. Next thing his pop will have him pulling crab grass and he'll wish he was back in the city."

"Somehow I don't think his father is the crab-grass-pulling type," Matt observed. "He's more the hiring type. He'll get somebody else to do it."

"Why don't we do that?"

"That's easy, bub—I can't afford it."

"I guess then Tod's father has more money than you have?"

"Just between us, I suspect Tod's father has more money than any two people on this street." It occurred to Matt that this conversation had taken a fortunate turn and here, without laying too much stress on it, was an opportunity to take a whack at the mysteries of what went on in his son's mind.

"Do you like Tod Winter?" he asked and found himself watching Bill's face narrowly for a clue to more than he might say.

"I guess so," Bill said indifferently. "He's pretty good with a basketball."

"It doesn't make you feel strange, I mean, playing with him?"

"Nope. Why?"

"Well, no reason." Matt hesitated, weighing his words. "Son, there's something I've been wondering about."

"About me?"

"Yes, you and Jerry. You two took quite a chance lighting into Paulie Cusack. He's bigger than both of you together."

"He's not so tough," Bill said shortly, speaking from the newly discovered eminence of the victor.

"Well, I don't recommend toughness just for the sake of being tough. Sometimes you have to fight, but I wouldn't go looking for it. I keep wondering why you decided to take him on. After all, I know you've taken a pushing around from him before."

"I know it. He's a bully," Bill said.

"I wish you'd tell me this," Matt said earnestly. "This all seems pretty strange to me. Did you beat him up because he called Tod Winter a nigger?"

Bill looked at him in astonishment. "Heck, no! What do I care what he calls the kid?"

"I thought you said you liked Tod," Matt barked in exasperation.

"I do, but what's what you call him got to do with it?" Bill said, in the patient tone of one who has learned to expect a certain imperviousness to reason in adult skulls.

"Well, then, tell me this," Matt said in bafflement. "Why in the name of—why did you beat up Paulie?"

"He had it coming," Bill said reasonably.

"I know he had it coming," Matt yelped. "What I'm trying to find out is why you picked that particular time."

"Well," Bill said thoughtfully, "he took the ball away from us.

He's always taking stuff from kids. Besides, he was paying attention to Tod, and it looked like a good chance to get a head start on him. We'd been waiting for him a long time."

"And that's the only reason you whipped him?" Matt asked, baffled once again by the processes of juvenile reason.

"Well, no, maybe not," Bill said, studying his feet and looking, Matt suddenly realized, embarrassed. "It was kind of scary. The kid was awful mad, and Paulie might have hurt him pretty bad."

"Oh," Matt said.

"Besides," Bill said seriously, "Jerry and me would have looked silly if that little kid had licked Paulie before we did."

"Oh," Matt said again.

19

PETER YALE did not enjoy the process of worrying, but he worried, nevertheless, and resented it. Fox had assured him that the necessities would be taken care of by the middle of the week. But he could not help remembering the cool, menacing terms in which Edward Smith had described what was going to happen to Peaceable Lane. Nor could he shake off the fear that Francis Barton might have found a more suitable vantage point to apply his lever and tip the lane and its people over the edge of the cliff—and him with them.

And always, despite the blockbuster's assurance, there was the nagging contrapuntal fear of being found out.

His relief was profound when Fox called him at his office in Manhattan and asked him to stop off in White Plains that afternoon if it wouldn't be inconvenient. Yale, aware of and disliking the overeager haste in his voice, assured him that it would not be inconvenient.

"This business is shaping up nicely, Mr. Yale—yes, sir, nicely," Fox told him when he arrived at his office.

"Fine," Yale said, trying to conceal the relief in his voice. "But how do you mean nicely?"

"Well," Fox said slowly, perfectly well aware of Yale's relief and wondering whether it might be possible to jigger things around a little somehow in a way to take advantage of it, "there are a few formalities yet, you know. Always are, of course. Damn fool real-estate laws. And the lawyers always have to get their hunk."

"I thought you said it was coming all right," Yale said sharply.

"I did, I did indeed. It is." Fox decided that jiggling Yale a little wouldn't hurt anything. "I trust your wife agrees to our little deal?" he said.

"Goddammit," Yale blurted, against his better judgment, but went on with it because Fox had left him no other place to go. "You know I can't nail her down to it until you produce a buyer—one she'll go for, I mean," he finished lamely.

Fox permitted himself a smile. "You mean a certified white buyer—and nothing funny anybody can wonder about, of course," he said silkily. "Don't worry, Mr. Yale. Barton will never appear on the surface of this and neither will any other colored man until you're long gone and in the clear. In fact," he added unctuously, "I won't even show myself—just in case somebody might remember me from that Bronson business." You're damn good and well right I won't show, he thought privately; there's a buzz saw somewhere in this business of Barton's, and the last man that's going to get caught in it is Alexander Fox.

Yale stared at him balefully. All right, you slick bastard, he thought; I'll watch you fry in hell yet. He decided to be a little reckless. "I don't like this stalling around. Does Barton want the house—or not?"

Oh, oh, Fox thought, so he's going to get uppity, is he? He could make him sweat, he thought, but maybe it would be better to handle it the way Barton wanted it handled and lay off fiddling around the edges. This one could bolt even yet, unlikely as it was.

"He wants it all right, Mr. Yale," he said soothingly. "Don't get yourself in an uproar. I got a buyer—perfectly respectable man named Greenwood, white as all get out. Even got a white broker to look as though he represents him. Nothing to it."

"So why the diddling around?" Yale said coldly out of the remainder of his anger and panic.

"Diddling?" Fox asked innocently. "Nobody's diddling, Mr. Yale, don't you ever think it." He sat forward behind his desk and looked at Yale earnestly. "It's practically all set. I've got some people making the title search—that's necessary, you know that. The script is all written and cleared. My people will be around your neighborhood about ten tomorrow morning. Will you be home?"

"I can be," Yale said cautiously.

"It'll be better if you are," Fox said. "Not much point in starting with Mrs. Yale. You know, you've got to handle that end."

"I know," Yale said shortly.

"Well," Fox said, settling back comfortably, "if you can handle your end all right, I don't see any reason we can't close a week from Saturday. Do you?"

"No," Yale said, wondering, probing his own mind. Fox had been pretty damn snippy and smart-alecky at the beginning of this. Why had he come so butter smooth all of a sudden? "No," he said again, "I'll handle my end."

"There's just one thing more," Fox said. He had a chore to do for Barton and, while he could not detect any danger in it for himself, he rather resented being asked—really told—to do it. Barton always had a way of entangling a man in his intricate machinations, and Fox didn't like it. If it wasn't for the money, he thought for perhaps the hundredth time, he would stay clear of Barton entirely. The man could be poison.

"What's that?" Yale demanded, suddenly alert.

"Barton asked me to tell you something. He likes to time things so they fit together just right," Fox said. "He wants you to know he would think it was real good of you—now that you're all set up—if you'd just nudge those other people up there about now."

"Nudge them?" Yale asked. "How?"

"Well, Barton thought this might be just about the right time to kind of get the word around what happened to the Bronson house. You know, how it was fixed for Winter to get it."

Yale's eyes narrowed, calculating, suspicious.

"I intend to," he said shortly. "But I'd rather wait until I'm in the clear."

"Don't worry, Mr. Yale. You're in the clear already—all but the shouting. Barton said he'd give it to you in writing if you're worried. But he would like that word to get out right about now."

Yale was far too acute to miss the threat in Barton's relayed message. Fox's diffident manner did nothing to disguise it. Barton could find another way to move in if he chose not to play ball; that had been made clear. He was hooked, that was certain. All right, then, if a certain amount of risk was implicit in doing what Barton wanted and when he wanted, he no longer had the power to tell him to go to hell. Anyhow, he probably couldn't lose at this stage by humoring Barton and, in any case, it was something he had wanted and intended to do.

"All right," he decided. "I'll see the word gets out. Tonight."

And he did, with nearly as much relish as he had expected. He called on Paul Cusack and explained how Lamar Winter had come to be invited to buy a house on Peaceable Lane.

Zachariah Gold was a big man, and it took anger a long time to fill him to where he spilled over. Even in anger, it struck him as odd and sourly amusing that for losing his temper the second time in one summer he had picked the same locale as the first. Here they were, Matt Jones, Lamar Winter and himself, in the playroom where some weeks before he had hauled David Bronson contemptuously from his chair and held him dangling. The memory of that absurd scene still embarrassed Gold. The big man felt subconsciously that the possession of great physical strength imposed upon a man an obligation of equal restraint.

Now he was angry again and wished he was not. It was even worse because, he admitted to himself, he was not quite sure of the target at which his anger ought to be aimed. The spill-over point had come with the profoundly disturbing news brought to him that day by Solomon Weissman. One trouble was that the news, though clearly menacing, was still too inconclusive to be acted on. But it had brought to a head the related uneasiness which had been growing in him for weeks.

"What's on your mind?" Winter asked, sitting relaxed and regarding him calmly.

"I came over, and brought Matt along, because I've got some things on my mind I think you, both of you, need to consider," Gold said ponderously.

"Okay. Shoot," Winter said lightly, "and I'll consider."

Gold hesitated, wondering how to get into it. He was embarrassed because he knew what he had to say would sound ridiculous and petty in almost any other context. It could be saved from absurdity only if they would give him serious hearing, and Winter's faintly mocking air made him fear they would not. But he knew it was serious and had to be said. They were all in danger. Flushing a little, hating to say it, he turned directly toward the artist and went at it bluntly.

"I think you're being too goddam conspicuous—for your good or anybody else's," he said, and then, turning to face Matt, "and I think you've been compounding it."

"Huh?" Matt said, dumfounded. He knew Gold well enough to know that this was anything but capricious and that only a compelling and laboriously reasoned conviction could bring him to interfere in the lives of other men. But what the hell could have got to him?

"Well, now, that's interesting," Winter said banteringly. Glancing at him, Matt saw that the dark face was still smiling but that now the smile was taunting and malicious. Gold saw, too, and felt the turgid stirring of his anger.

"It is," Gold said. "And that cocky grin isn't making it any less so."

"I don't think I grasp what you're driving at, Zack," Matt said seriously. "It doesn't seem to me Lamar has been doing anything but mind his own business. I know you mean it, but what is it?"

"Yeah, man, lay it out," Winter said.

"All right," Gold said with heavy reluctance. "I will—chapter and verse, all in one package." And while Matt and Winter listened, the one in mounting incredulity, the other with a chilly grin, he did so. "I'll go along with you that this is all Winter's business—or would be in any other circumstances. In these, it's everybody's. But here it is, all of it. One, the minute you moved in you built that glass monstrosity on your house. Some people think it's an eyesore —and a deliberate one. Two"—Gold hesitated, then sighed and plunged doggedly on into what he hated to say—"you pop down to the pool the first time it occurs to you—and offend the mortal hell out of Mrs. Cusack, as you knew it would. Three, we all have kids here, as you do, and they play all over the place, but you drive that silly-ass foreign hot rod of yours like an accident in a hurry to happen. Four, you and Matt, doubtless Matt's idea, turn up at Grassy Tor half stewed and leave quite a lot more than half stewed. Five, in some way that I still don't understand, but that I know involved your kid, our kids"—he nodded toward Matt—"beat the stuffing out of the Cusack kid. The fact that I'm proud of them for doing so doesn't alter the fact that the Cusacks later tried to bring an assault charge against you—until the Chappaqua cops talked them out of it. In short, you've given this street to understand that it can like you—or lump it."

"It can," Winter said coldly. "Precisely."

"I don't get it, Zack," Matt said in a puzzled tone. "That's all true, of course, but don't you think it sounds a little silly? Picayune?"

"Let me tell you what I think of it," Winter broke in with brittle scorn. "Piece by piece, just the same as you, Gold. One, that monstrosity, as you call it, is where I make my living—and I'll be glad to match incomes with anybody you want to name around here. Two, my deed says I own a piece of that pool, and I couldn't care less if some white lady—I give her the title free—thinks the water's so contaminated it needs draining. Three, I don't tell anybody else what kind of a car to buy or how to drive it, and nobody's going to tell me. As for driving, your kids are a lot safer with me at the wheel of that hot rod than they are with the way some of your bubble-headed female neighbors handle a car. Four, why should you worry if Matt and I hoist a few at Grassy Tor? You ain't likely to be a member much sooner than I am. Five, it was your kids that licked young Cusack, not mine. I don't know why they did it any more than you do, but I got the distinct impression he had it coming." Winter sat back comfortably and stared at Gold with a look of cool derision. "Anything else I can do for you, white man?" he asked in a tone intended to be insulting.

Gold flushed, a deep, slow color compounded of embarrassment and anger.

"Yes," he said steadily. "Quit pressing. I know you're within your rights. But I know that you know you're an irritant on this street. The place is ready to fly apart like a busted flywheel. This stuff is petty; I admit it. But the place blowing up wouldn't be petty. Give the place some time to figure out if it can relax and enjoy it."

"Would you care to estimate how long that might take?" Winter asked.

"Forever, if you don't stop shoving," Gold said.

"I would have thought forever in any case," Winter said. "So I don't figure I have much to lose."

"I don't know what you're made of, Winter," Gold said. "I expect I'd be a fool to expect any kind of compassion from you. It's not only what you might lose. There's also a question of what the rest of the street might stand to lose."

Winter's grin dripped ice water. "A bunch of folks who, a couple of months ago, were putting up dough to keep me out? I'm supposed to worry about them? Don't make me laugh."

"But you're here now. You're part of the street whether you care or not, whether the street likes it or not."

"Yeah, I'm here. But only because you and Matt here went soft. In the pinch you didn't have the guts to be the bastards you'd intended to be."

"All right, put it that way if you want to." Gold sighed. "The point is that you accepted it on those terms. That puts an obligation on you, the same as it does on Matt and me. You owe the street something."

"Owe it what?" Winter asked bluntly.

"To go easy. Not to scare it. And not to wreck it."

"Scares mighty easy," Winter said, "if this piddling stuff you're talking about is what it takes."

"I know it sounds silly," Gold said stubbornly. "But it's true. Any Jew would know it automatically, and don't tell me you don't."

"Sure, I know it. All us second-class folks got to know our place. Can't go around upsettin' the quality." Winter's tone was light, but the sneer was unmistakable.

"Look, Winter," Gold said in a tone that was somber but as cold as Winter's, "this wasn't a bad street a couple of months ago. Not what you'd call an ideal American community maybe. Petty maybe, less than generous, weak the way people are weak, and maybe even, in some ways, vicious. But it was livable and we got along. Everybody here had strained a gut for what he had and took pride in it." Gold gestured angrily, helplessly. "Now we're at one another's throats."

"My fault?" Winter asked silkily.

"Not entirely. But you could put on a little less heat."

"Get myself bleached maybe? Would that help?" Winter's tone was mocking.

"Don't be a damn fool," Gold said impatiently. "Just give us a chance, that's all."

Matt had been listening intently, recognizing how reluctantly Gold had driven himself to a distasteful task, realizing the force of conviction that must be behind the effort.

"Look, Zack," he said at last, "I know you don't go off half cocked." He turned to Winter. "And I think you ought to know he doesn't either." He turned to Gold again. "I don't say you're off your rocker, and it might make sense for Lamar to go out of his way to lay low for a while. But also, I think you may be overestimating this. Except for the Cusacks and one or two others, it seems to me the street is settling down better than we could have expected. Where's the panic?"

"You haven't been doing your homework," Gold said grimly. "Yale has some kind of deal going with a crooked broker." He nodded coldly at Winter. "The same guy you tried to use. Fox. Whatever they're doing, you may not like any better than I will."

"Yale is?" Matt looked astonished.

"Yale is," Gold said. "You got any idea what happens to this street when the second colored family moves in?"

"Who's Yale?" Winter asked with alert interest.

"The only guy around here who ducked from under putting up money to keep you out," Gold said flatly.

20

Life would be a lot easier to manage if a man could accurately foresee the consequences of his and other people's actions, Lamar Winter was thinking, as he switched on the television and stared at a horse opera without seeing it. But you never really knew the complications lying ahead. White people's complications; subconsciously his mind shaped the words with a sneer. The trouble was that here on Peaceable Lane he was inextricably involved in white people's complications.

All right, he acknowledged to himself, let's say I upset the street, as Gold says. So what? Most of the people on it are jerks who need upsetting. Now he was here—with the same rights, privileges, scenery, pool, back-yard barbecue, Japanese beetles on the rose-bushes and taxes the rest of them had. But did that make them neighbors? His lip curled; not in any ordinary sense, it sure as hell didn't. He knew they didn't want to live with him and he certainly did not yearn to live with them. All he asked of them was that they let him alone. And he intended to see that they did.

Well, then, did he, as Gold asserted, owe the street an obligation to be inconspicuous merely because he was there? He rejected the thought. He had not come here to kiss anybody's backside and he was not about to begin.

Was that enough? Simply to let them know that they could go to hell? He scowled at the flickering screen and got up and turned it off. Maybe not; it was never as simple as you would like it to be. A man had to face the realities, and Winter knew he was not afraid to face them. One reality was that Matt Jones and that big bastard Gold had stuck their necks out a long way to get him into the lane. But what of that? Any man who had fought Winter's lifelong battle had to know that he would occasionally encounter white men who could be used by a colored man. White men who, because of nagging conscience or some other unrealistic or reckless fund of softness, were almost traitors to the tribe. Matt and Gold were such men, and he had used them knowingly, callously. He knew, if they did not, that the struggle was too age-old and blood-deep to leave any room for compassion on his side.

He would not consciously wish them hurt. In any case, he liked Matt and he thought it possible he might come to like Gold. But they were white and therefore they could take care of themselves.

All the same, he was not satisfied. Somewhere along here there was something amiss. All his life, because he must to get the things his pride and ambition demanded, he had lived by a harsh code which neither asked nor granted quarter. Now, against his will, the clear outlines of that code were being fuzzed. He had not asked for quarter; no man had seen him humble himself; his stiff pride was intact. Or was it? Dammit, he was no longer certain that in some obscure way he had not permitted his pride to be compromised. He had asked for nothing; that was true. But hadn't he taken quite a lot? Yes, but that was within the code; you took what you could take. But had it been too easy?

And then there was that still deeply disturbing question of what had occurred between Tod and the three white boys. He still did not know, and it bothered him. He knew perfectly well that dealing with people, hard and tough and relentless, was one thing for him and quite another for Tod. Tod, who was in many ways defenseless, had been defended. If he was going to face realities, he might as well face that one too.

He let his thoughts find their way to Yale and whatever Gold's report that Yale had made contact with the crooked broker, Fox, might portend. This would involve him, too, he knew, and he was impatient with the thought that he could not yet foresee the nature of his involvement. He had no illusions about what might happen to the lane if Yale actually did sell to a colored man. The place was jumpy already. But where did that leave him? How was he involved? Or if he were involved, there was still the question of what he could or should do. If Yale was going to sell to a Negro, he was going to sell, and that was all there was to it. If one more colored man was going to make it the hard way, why should he either help or hinder? Although, of course, he thought with a wry smile, it was obviously going to be easier for the next man because he was already here.

Naturally, he had to know that if the place went to hell in a hand basket, he was going to suffer too. But those were the chances a man had to take and he, at least, could afford to take them. One thing he was pretty sure of: he couldn't see him taking sides with the whites to keep another colored man out. Hell, it was a fundamental contradiction in terms: he was coolly curious about Yale's prospective customer, but he felt no sense of kinship to him.

"Lamar!" It was the third time Margo, standing in the door of the playroom, had called and he had not heard. "Lamar, are you asleep?"

"Huh?" he said. "What is it, honey?"

She laughed.

"Boy, when you go away, you go the full distance."

"Just thinking," he said. "Where's Tod?"

"Where would he be? It's nearly ten—he's in bed."

"What's on your mind, honey?"

"Well," she said, sitting down and looking both serious and pretty, "I was wondering about the car you're getting for me."

"Wondering what? Anything wrong with a Caddy convertible? You want to change the color?"

"I was just wondering. Could you change the order?"

"Sure, I guess I could, but it's supposed to be delivered next week. What's wrong with white?"

"It's not the color, Lamar." She hesitated, then blurted it out. "Don't you think it's kind of flashy—for the neighborhood, I mean?"

Winter looked at her in astonishment. "You, too!"

"Me, too, what? I'm just talking about the car."

"That's what I'm talking about. I just listened to an hour's bawling out about flashy automobiles and a couple other things."

"Honey, I'm not bawling you out. All I'm saying is I'd rather not have a Cadillac if you don't care. It's not really because it's flashy; it's just too big. What I need a car for mostly is getting kids to school, and Ellen Jones and Beth Gold both said a fancy car is no good for that."

"What's the difference? And what kids? Tod isn't going to squawk about a Caddy."

"It's not just Tod, honey. It's a car pool. I'll have four kids to take—on my days. Anyhow, we're in the country now. It snows here.

They said I ought to get a station wagon—with snow tires and chains too."

"Look, baby"—Winter regarded his wife in puzzled inquiry—"I guess maybe you better explain this. You mean you're not just hauling Tod, you're hauling other kids too?"

"Just on my days. The Gold youngsters and the Jones boy. Mrs. Gold and Mrs. Jones will be driving the other days."

"You mean they're letting their kids ride with Tod? Are you kidding?"

"Of course not. Why? Ellen Jones called me and said the others on the street had already divided up and, since we were the only three left, we might as well divide it up as well as we could."

"Well, I'll be damned!" he said at last. "Does Zack Gold know about this?"

"I suppose so. Why?"

Suddenly Winter laughed. "So now who's being conspicuous?" he murmured.

"What do you mean?" Margo asked. "I swear, Lamar, sometimes I don't know what you're talking about."

"I swear sometimes I don't know myself."

"Well, I was asking about the car."

"Okay, honey," he said. "We'll get whatever kind of car you want—or they con you into getting. Paint it gray, too, if you're worried about being too visible." He sat for a while, pondering, staring at her moodily. "Baby," he said at last, "I'm curious about something. Those two kids, Jones and Gold, whacking the Cusack kid around. You got any better idea than I have why they did it?"

"Only what Tod said. I didn't see it, you know."

"I wonder," Winter mused. "I just keep wondering."

21

"I SUPPOSE you know the charge you're making is serious," Grant Macmillan said, staring sourly over his drink at Paul Cusack, who sat with him and John Ainslie Outerbridge around a scarred oak table under the antlered heads on the walls of the men's bar at Grassy Tor. "You'd better be able to prove it."

"I know it's serious," Cusack said, bridling. "And it can be proved."

"You can prove it?" Macmillan shot at him.

Cusack flushed. "Not if you mean did I see them do it. But Pete Yale swore it came from a solid source. They might have the guts to deny it, but it could be dug up."

"Who's Yale?" Macmillan asked brusquely.

"The man who brought this to me. He lives in the lane."

"Why isn't he here then? Or, for that matter, why are you doing his tattling for him?" Macmillan glowered at the man across the table, thinking that he had never liked Cusack and wasn't liking him now, even though the knowledge he was bringing, if true, was important and would have to be acted on. Macmillan was both depressed and angry. It wasn't merely injury, although God knew that was enough, coming from a man he had trusted. Almost worse was having to face up to the fact that you had misjudged a man. Dammit all, he had treated Matt Jones as a son. Took pride in him, pushed him into deep water out of the sheer pleasure of watching him make his way. To do that you had to believe in a man's capacity. You had to put a lot of yourself into him—not merely trust him with your money and your prestige, but, even more, trust him with your belief in yourself. You had to believe his judgment was damn near the equal of your own.

He stared at Cusack, not really seeing him, but disliking him for what else he had forced him to see. But why hadn't he seen it earlier? He wasn't blind; he'd been judging men for over thirty years and had built a signal success on that judgment. How could I need a pip-squeak like this to tell me what was plain in front of my eyes? he thought angrily. Even if I couldn't guess long ago, I should have when Matt pulled that fool stunt of bringing Winter in here to get drunk.

"Precisely why are you here with this tale? What do you want out of it?" Cusack looked surprised, taken aback by the cold savagery of Macmillan's demand.

"Why, because it concerns you, too, obviously," Cusack protested, thinking angrily that if he'd known he would have to take this abuse he would have stayed away. "We got hit down there on the lane first, of course. But it concerns the club, too, and you. Believe me, Grant, we don't take this lightly—not knowing what it costs us, what it costs the whole area."

"Don't call me Grant," Macmillan snapped brutally, and turned to Outerbridge. "Where do you fit into this?" he demanded. The pudgy lawyer had been sitting silent, watching the other two through his polished glasses, lips pursed, taking no part.

"I am not here by choice, Mr. Macmillan," the lawyer said. "I would have preferred that this interview not take place. I came with Mr. Cusack—first, because he asked me—but second, in the hope of dissuading you from any rash action. The situation is bad enough, I believe we all know, without further precipitate or ill-judged action."

Macmillan snorted. "It seems to me there's been enough bad judgment loose around here to sink the county."

"That is precisely what I have in mind. Therefore, I hope we, at least, can bring some rationality to bear on this situation."

"Pretty late to start," Macmillan said.

"Granted. But perhaps not too late. Let us consider the facts. The Negro is now in the lane, in the area. That is a fact, however much we may dislike it or deplore the means that were used to place him there. Now what?"

"Well, what?" Paul Cusack said angrily. "Are we supposed to just take it? Do you think Macmillan here wants to take it?"

"Slowly, please," Outerbridge said. "I have observed this situation with care, as you may imagine. This is something that is taking place all over the country. In a word, you might say it is inevitable. Now, I don't pretend to enjoy it and I surely do not condone the connivance of Jones and Gold with this man. But I have had

Winter investigated thoroughly. I am fairly well convinced that he is not, as you probably fear, the forerunner of a wave of invasion. He is out for himself and, in some senses, he may actually prove to be a protection against further invasion, since I think that, out of self-interest, if nothing more, he may resist it."

"But we've still got him! For God's sake, John Ainslie, he's there and he's black. So we've already had it," Cusack burst out, and then turned to Macmillan. "Look, sir, both of these men are employees of yours. They depend on you for a living. I tell you, I can't even conceive of the brass it took for that man to move in on top of you and think he could get away with it. But the thing is, he can't stay if you tell him to get out."

"Just a minute. I'm sorry, but I wasn't finished," Outerbridge broke in. "What I began to say is that we must face up to the fact that Negroes are moving into white communities all over the country. Now, as I say, I have investigated Winter. He is a man of substance and background. I admit I would prefer not to have him across the street from me, but I do want to say that if I must have a Negro in the neighborhood, I prefer him."

Macmillan, broodingly silent, had been thinking that when a man destroyed your faith in him he inevitably destroyed a part of you as well. Think what you would about it—listen as long as you like to these two—you couldn't change that. And that, by God, was unforgivable.

"I don't own Winter and I don't own Jones," he said abruptly. "And I don't own Gold. And I don't like your street or the mess you've made of it. Good evening, gentlemen. I'm going home."

Lamar Winter told himself it was mainly curiosity that led him to leave his studio and drive to White Plains to see Alexander Fox. But it wasn't idle curiosity; he had learned long ago that the man who best protected himself was likely to be the man who was best informed. Not that he expected Fox to be generous with the truth, especially not if Yale was actually preparing to bolt and the broker was involved in the process. Still, he thought, if he handled it carefully, he might get something. Winter liked to know where things were and in what directions they might move. He had no plan. Not yet.

"I thought there might be something going on up there where I live," he told the broker pleasantly. "Something you might know about and I ought to."

"What sort of thing, Mr. Winter?" Fox asked with a carefully casual air of inquiry. Fox had not expected this visit, but he wasn't particularly surprised; long experience told him that things had the damnedest way of getting out even when they had no earthly reason to do so. Winter might know something—or guess something; he decided he had better handle this carefully. "Something worryin' you?"

"Not exactly," Winter said easily. "I was only wondering if somebody might be doing something to somebody else—and if they were, what it was likely to cost me." His tone had sharpened almost imperceptibly.

"Cost you?" Fox's expression was one of innocent curiosity. "What sort of thing could that be?"

"Oh, like knocking the props out from under what my joint's worth," Winter said. "Something like that."

"Well, sir, I would sure be surprised to hear anything like that," Fox said. "We certainly thought your interest would be safe when we got that property for you. Yes, sir, that's as fine a piece of property as there is——"

"Save the guff for white folks," Winter said bluntly. "You know that I know how safe that place is. Also, you didn't get the property for me. What you got was a commission. If it hadn't been for a pair of tame whites . . ." He broke off and then went on without heat. "But that's not the point. I expect you did your best. What I want to know now is whether something new is going on—chapter and verse and punctuation marks."

"You got something to go on?" Fox asked cautiously. "Anything that makes you think something might be happening?"

"Enough to know I'm curious," Winter said crisply, aware that the broker was dodging, but thinking he might go along with it, a little longer anyhow. "There's a guy up there, radio type, name's Yale. Peter Yale—one of my neighbors."

"I know who he is." Fox nodded thoughtfully. "He's the one ran for cover when they were all fixing to keep you out."

"It wasn't because he loves my big blue eyes," Winter said.

Fox paused and pondered. He didn't have to guess any longer; this one did know something. The discovery made him uncomfortable. Fox was a businessman, which meant that he was interested in making money; he did not mind that the peculiarities of his business occasionally required sliding around a few shady corners or leaving as devious a trail as an agile mind could devise. That was part of the game. But, he remembered ruefully, he was more likely than not to run into some kind of discomfort whenever he got involved in something Francis Barton was trying to accomplish. The trouble with Barton, he reflected, was that he always had purposes beyond, or below, or to one side of Fox's own simple and clean-cut interest in money. Fox knew that his own feeling about money was one of devotion, but he recognized that it was a feeble thing compared to the dedication which Barton brought to the subject. Barton could get rough if he thought he needed to and, personally, Fox had a strong distaste for rough stuff. As far and fast as Fox wanted to go, he didn't think that was necessary.

"What about Yale?" Fox said cautiously. It occurred to him, as he peered at the artist's taut, triangular face with its challenging eyes, that this one could get rough too. He thought getting caught between Barton and Winter would probably be mighty unpleasant; he shuddered inwardly and instantly hoped it had not showed on the surface.

"I suspect he's thinking about taking a powder," Winter said. "Probably fiddling with the idea of taking a fast buck and running before I ruin the white folks' country." He grinned; Fox's involuntary flinch had not escaped him, and he thought he might as well put the prod in a little. "I wondered what you could tell me about it."

"Me? Why me?" Fox asked, a little too quickly.

"Well, I just thought you were, generally speaking, the man who was likely to know about it when a white man got to thinking about selling out to colored folks," Winter said blandly. "You did when Bronson had the idea," he added reminiscently, "went out of your way, as I recall, to help Bronson—and me too." Winter was sure now that Lana Weissman's conclusions, relayed first through her father and then to himself and Matt by Gold, were perfectly correct. Still, he had no plan; for the moment he was content to needle the broker and watch him squirm.

"You know I was glad to help you, Mr. Winter," Fox said uneasily.

"Any gladder than you would be to help Yale?" Winter asked blandly.

"Well, of course now, you know it's a broker's duty to do the best he can for any client," Fox said righteously. Then, feeling the quick start of Winter's alert interest and feeling he might have trapped himself into error, he added hastily, "Not that Yale is, you understand."

"Oh, sure," Winter said.

Fox rallied his faculties and made an effort to feel his way into this mocking man's mind a little. "But just say, for example, that this man Yale should be thinking about selling out. Would that interest you?"

"It might," Winter said calmly.

"Hm-m-m," Fox said. "Was there something you had in mind you wanted me to do?"

"I might. I might want you to shop around a little and see what you hear," Winter said amiably. "You know, nothing much, just service to a former satisfied customer."

Fox watched as Winter let himself out the door, moving with sure-footed grace.

"Whew!" he said, when he was sure the artist was gone.

22

GRANT MACMILLAN had long ago decided that distasteful necessities were never rendered palatable by delay. He had no intention of shirking this one. In part he was sustained by smoldering anger, but Macmillan did not want to probe the sources of his anger too deeply. He was aware of disturbing depths. It was simpler to keep it on a level where he was sure of himself; the issue here was loyalty. In his business only confidence could sustain you. And, because you must trust men, confidence could have force only so long as men were trustworthy. When he chose men unwisely, which he felt he seldom did, Macmillan knew that the fault lay in his judgment. He could not compromise in the cure; when he recognized that his judgment had been faulty, he must tear it up and begin again.

Pushed to it, Macmillan might have agreed that his correcting errors of judgment could sometimes bring cruel results to other men. Still he believed that weakness or delay would in the end prove an even greater cruelty.

In this case more was involved than the rooting out of error. What had happened and was continuing to happen on Peaceable Lane affected Macmillan personally; it was a matter of where he lived and how his way of living was affected. He loathed the idea of Grassy Tor and its gracious environs going to pot. But business was involved here also. Success with intangibles depended in part on the value other men put on his prestige. It could hurt professionally to be made to look ridiculous by men in his employ conniving to undermine his dignity. Macmillan had no illusion that what had happened in Peaceable Lane would long remain secret in the gossipy milieu of the advertising business.

Now that he reflected, Macmillan felt that he had made the original error years before. It was he who had brought Matt Jones to live in Peaceable Lane. He had been planning Matt's future. It went to show you, he thought now, how long an error of judgment could lie fallow.

This could be costly. The rooting out of old error must inevitably jeopardize his firm's new and valued relationship with Thurston Young and Glamour-Glow. Nor would Young feel bound to him if he lost the ability to deliver what Young wanted. Macmillan, no readier to spare himself than another, recognized that what Young wanted was Lamar Winter's talent.

It was testimony to Macmillan's uncompromising belief that, knowing the probable cost, he knew what he would do. It was also characteristic of him that he did not wait for the unpleasant chore to come to him; he went to it.

Nevertheless, he was taken aback on Monday morning when he walked into Matt Jones's office, unannounced. He had not expected to find Winter there, but he was. The artist and Matt were at the layout table, studying the engraver's color corrections. Macmillan shrugged inwardly. Maybe this is better, he thought. Take it all up at once, out in the open.

"Hello, Grant," Matt said easily, a little surprised, but not at all alarmed. "I'd have been bringing this stuff in soon, but since you're here . . ."

The easy, smiling attentiveness of the younger men surprised Macmillan. He was so full of his own decision that it was difficult to imagine they were not aware of it. Still, he thought sourly, if a man had the guts to betray you, only a fool would expect him to stammer and boggle like a schoolgirl when the fact came to confront him.

"Let them go for now," he said. "I have something else I want to say."

Winter came quickly alert at his tone. "If it's private, I'll go," he said, turning toward the door.

"No," Macmillan said. "You'd better stay. You're concerned in this."

Matt had not missed the hard undertone, but even now he was not warned.

"You want a chair, Grant?" he asked, wondering what was coming.

"No, I won't need one. This won't take long," Macmillan said. "Winter, what is your understanding of the rights to the Glamour-Glow paintings?" Matt winced at the brusque use of the artist's surname. Winter was quick to resent anything that seemed cavalier. And Winter had not missed it either, he saw by the quick tightening of the artist's eyes.

"Same as always," Winter said quietly. He knew something was coming and was preparing to meet it. "When they're finished and Young accepts them—and I get the money—I release the rights to you as Young's agent. Except, of course, the basic right to forbid misuse or mutilation. Otherwise they'll be in your control. Until then they're mine."

Macmillan's sigh was barely perceptible. He was thinking that he could have waited the few days or few weeks until the deal was complete. But the reflection was only vaguely tempting; he would have felt that to play with time to advantage was a violation of his own integrity.

"That's the deal we always have," Matt said.

"I know. I just wanted it clear before I start," Macmillan said. "What I have to say has nothing to do with the paintings . . . although it may affect them. I want it understood I recognize that possibility."

"Well, I don't understand it," Matt said in a puzzled tone. "Not yet, anyhow."

"I think I do," Winter said, and Matt was astonished to see the malice suddenly bright in his smile. "Just in case you want to change your mind, Macmillan, I can tell you your guess is correct. It will affect the paintings."

"Even knowing that it means in the neighborhood of forty thousand dollars to you?" Macmillan asked, regarding the Negro in icy calm.

"It will mean more than that to you." Winter grinned. "Besides, I'll still have the paintings."

"I was prepared for it." Macmillan sighed, openly this time. "Do you want the rest of it now?"

"I could maybe listen to a couple of stanzas, just to sample your delivery. But, since I've heard this sort of thing before, I may not stay for the whole show," Winter said.

"I'll give you the punch line first if you're in a hurry," Macmillan said. "You are through at this agency." Thinking back, thinking ahead, reckoning the cost, coldly hating the man before him, he spoke again. "Do you want reasons?"

"Briefly, white man, briefly," Winter told him.

"I'll keep them brief. I believe you presumed on your relationship with this agency and its personnel to move your home . . . next door to him." He nodded dismissingly toward Matt. "Doing so, you knew you would damage that street and the area in a manner that could not be repaired. In order to do so, behind my back, you entered into an act of collusion." Again he nodded toward Matt. He eyed first one, then the other without expression. "Neither of you are children. Therefore, I assume these were knowing and willful acts. I recognize that I was responsible for permitting the existence of the circumstances that made them possible. That makes me responsible to the area for the damage that has been done to it. Do you want more?"

Matt had been listening in fascinated disbelief. Now he began to feel the slow, sour upwelling of anger and outrage. He had respected Macmillan, admired him and liked him. But there were areas in a man—his right of choice, his essential dignity as a man—which could brook no trespass. Certainly not this coldly bitter scorn. He had trouble finding his voice.

"You'll be getting around to me," he said. "You may as well know that you haven't left me much choice."

Macmillan turned toward him. "I have left you even less choice than you imagine. Your contract calls for a year's salary in advance if the firm wishes to break it. The check and the necessary papers will be ready when you are."

Macmillan walked to the door. With his hand on the knob he turned toward them again, and now, suddenly, the bland face was drained and weary.

"You have always understood that I will not tolerate disloyalty," he said. Then he left.

Except in monosyllables, when she could not avoid it, Margo Winter had not spoken since he had come home with the news. The artist didn't think he was being punished, at least, not precisely that, but he did think she was getting more mileage out of silence than the occasion deserved.

"Come off it, honey," he said. "I'll get you a drink. Gin and tonic?"

"Unh, unh," Margo said. "I don't think so." She stared at her toenails, glistening with an iridescent, metallic paint.

"Quit it, kid, the world hasn't ended," Winter said. Impatience was moving in on him.

"Lamar." She looked up suddenly, and he saw with irritation that her eyes were brooding and even, it struck him, fearful. "How did Mr. Jones take it?"

"Shook—after the mad wore off a little and he had a chance to begin thinking about it. Trying to pretend he wasn't—but shook all right." He chuckled.

"Lamar, don't!" The passion in her voice took him by surprise.

He had never heard that tone from her before. "Don't joke—you'd joke about death."

"Why not?" He cocked an eyebrow at her. "Although this isn't death exactly. Just a white folks' falling out. A man doesn't often get a ringside seat for that."

She stared at him, disbelieving.

"Come on, kid," he said. "Let up. There's no tragedy. Matt just got stuck with a predictable result of holding the unconventional notion that a colored man is a human being. He sticks around me long enough and he'll get used to taking his lumps."

"Lamar, stop it! Don't joke any more. Don't you have any feeling, any at all?"

"For white men, baby?" He gazed at her coolly.

"Yes, yes, for a white man! For a good friend!" The words were tumbling out almost incoherently. "What are you—stone? Doesn't it mean anything to you that this happened to him because he wouldn't turn you down?" She continued to stand and stare at him, and tears spilled down her cheeks.

Winter gazed up at her from his seat on an ottoman beside the ebony cocktail table, where he had been playing solitaire while he waited for her mood to clear. His eyes were slaty.

"Let's not kid ourselves just because we live on this charming street among these charming folks. We're still colored. We'll always be colored and they'll always let you know it—and I don't give a damn how many white kids you'll be driving to school. Don't make the mistake of going soft on them—you'll just get kicked in the belly."

"Who got kicked in the belly this time? Tell me that!"

"Matt did," he said coolly. "I told him he would when he first stuck his big soft head into this. So he did. So he should have known he would."

"And you laugh about it!"

"Now, stop this a minute," Winter snapped. "Now listen. I'm neither as stupid nor laughing-boy happy as you seem to think. But I'm a realist. I knew this would happen—or if not this, something just as rough. He was asking for it. He got hurt because he got deeper into something he didn't understand than he knew he was getting. But he isn't killed. Nothing that can't be cured. People have been fired before."

"Only because of you—of us," Margo wailed. "What's going to happen to him now—to his family? Oh, Lamar . . ." Margo's voice trailed off.

Winter grinned again. "Well, he won't starve, if that's what you mean. He's sitting on a year's salary, which he may notice after a while."

"And after that?"

"Something else a long time before that." He smiled at her. "It probably never occurred to you, but your old man happens to be Thurston Young's favorite painter. And Thurston Young has a million bucks' worth of business to do that he can't see his way clear to do without my paintings." The grin, chill before, was now sunny and delighted. "And, it's a funny thing, but old Pappy Winter can't paint a lick without the advice and co-operation of Matthew Rice Jones."

Gleefully, as his words sank in, he watched the glow of relief grow on her face—but then doubt darkened it again.

"Do you think he'd take it?" she asked. "Wouldn't he think it was charity?"

"It wouldn't be," he said flatly. "Not even Thurston Young would think so. He'd be lucky to get Matt and he's smart enough to know it." The grin lighted up again. "Nope, there's no charity in this. But I won't deny I'm getting a belt out of the thought of being able to do something for a white man—just for a change. Been getting kind of itchy the last few weeks—taking it the other way around."

But Lamar Winter was shaken, too, more deeply than he knew, far more deeply than he could have brought himself to admit, even to himself. It was true that he had foreseen that Matt would somehow be made to pay for the unorthodoxy of taking his side against the white world. It was also true that he had warned him of the cost to come. But now, dimly, he knew that it wasn't enough. Foreseeing the likelihood of trouble was one thing; the reality was quite another. He had watched the wrecking of a man's career and had seen the shattering of his pride. Now, somehow, it did not help enough to know that it had been inevitable. Nor did it help enough to know that, once he had accepted what Matt and Gold were willing to do, the die was cast and nothing he or Matt did thereafter could have altered the way it would fall. It did not even help enough to know that he held the power—through Thurston Young—to repair the material damage Matt had suffered. A man could be crushed in more and worse ways than material security. Winter had said he was a realist, and he nearly was. He was realist enough to acknowledge that Matt had let himself be destroyed for his sake; he was not quite realist enough to see that his own hard code that the colored man owed no quarter to the white had been shattered as well. His cross was here to be borne; he took it up rebelliously, for once not sure of himself.

Matt Jones had never been fired before. He was trying to find the grace to live with it, but it was a paralyzing business. At first the shock saved him from really feeling it. Then anger helped for a while; the sonofabitch, he thought, the unbelievable, megalomaniac sonofabitch. But this was frail armor; it began to crumple under the withering blast of humiliation.

Bill met him in the road as he walked blindly home after getting out of the Jaguar at Winter's driveway entrance. It was plain bad luck that Bill, as he often did, had a pressing personal need on his mind.

"Pop, I gotta have six dollars," Bill bawled, coming across the yard at a dead run.

"Don't say gotta," Matt said absently. "Why do you need six dollars?"

"New football helmet," Bill yelled, bouncing up and down with the excess of energy which afflicts nine-year-olds and the urgency which seems to attend all their needs.

"What's the matter with the old one?" Matt asked. "You had a new one last year."

"Aw, that's a baby's helmet. I want a regulation one. Can I, Pop? It's only six bucks."

"And don't say bucks either, say dollars. What do you mean, baby's helmet? It fits, doesn't it?"

"Well, gee, sure it fits. But it's not regulation. Gee, don't you understand that?"

"Not exactly, but I understand six dollars." And then it hit him. The whole works. Mortgage, taxes, insurance premiums, groceries, car payments, doctor bills, the orthodontist, water bills, gas and light and telephone and the milk bill, the speed with which a nine-year-old boy's shoes wore out, train fare, the worn place in the living-room carpet with its threat of inescapable replacement, even the jangling of the Good Humor man's bell. All at once, there it was. The grim ghost. Fear.

"Aw gee, Pop," Bill plowed ahead on his single-minded course. "Gee, Pop, I need it!"

Matt did not intend to speak sharply. His roars at his son were usually tempered with such transparent good nature that Bill seldom took them seriously and, indeed, tended to regard a bellow as the normal prelude to surrender. But now, rising out of the sudden, blinding terror of not being able even to feed this chattering mouth, Matt's voice came loud and harsh.

"No!"

"But, Pop," Bill plunged ahead blindly.

"I said no! I hate wheedlers." Matt's voice was grating.

Startled, looking up at the taut, tired, angry face, Bill saw something he had never seen there before; he didn't know what it was, but he knew he was scared. Numbly he followed Matt into the house; the day had suddenly lost its zest.

Later, after three martinis, which he had stirred with a guilty feeling that he shouldn't be wasting the money, and a dinner for which he could summon no appetite, Matt sat stonily quiet, hearing his wife, wishing wearily that she would stop talking and let him think.

"I wish you hadn't," he heard Ellen say, and realized that very little of what she had said had registered.

"Hadn't what?" he asked.

"Hadn't flown off the handle at him. He's in his room, crying." She looked forlorn. "I haven't heard him cry for two years—except when he got in a fight."

Matt resisted the tug of remorse. "He just hit me at the wrong time. When he wants something he never lets up."

Ellen was sitting stiffly with her fists balled in her lap; her face wore a strange, frozen look.

"Matt, what has happened to us? What is happening?" she blurted. He heard the appeal in her voice and the sad worry.

"Isn't getting fired enough?" he grunted.

"I don't mean that," she protested. Then, seeing his quick, challenging stare, she hurried on. "Oh, yes, I do, of course. But there are worse things."

"What things?" he asked harshly. "It takes fifteen hundred a month, take-home pay, to keep this place running. Do you have some notion what to do about that?"

"Don't," she pleaded. "You know I'm not making light of it. But other things are worse. We never used to be like this, so tense, so ready to hit at one another."

"I doubt if getting canned ever made anybody more sociable," Matt said coldly. "Please, Ellen, I've got to think."

"Please, Matt, don't shut me out like that," Ellen said. After a moment she spoke again with sudden passion, "I wish they had never come here. I wish you hadn't brought them."

"Who?" he demanded challengingly. She had got through to him.

"You know," Ellen went on doggedly. "The Winters."

"You too?" he said.

"Matt, don't. You know better."

"It doesn't sound like it," he said, feeling the familiar anger stir in him. Wherever he turned, this resistance awaited, this blind, unreasoned, destructive fear—even here. "Ellen, I cannot see how a reasonable mind can hold a man responsible for the sonofabitchery of others," he said coldly.

"I know," Ellen said steadily. "I know it's not their fault. I know it's cruel. But we have to live, too, and we have to live in the world the way it is. You can't change it all alone. It's too much to ask; he shouldn't ask it of you."

"He's not asking anything," Matt said shortly.

"I know," Ellen said again. "But see what has happened. The children are fighting. Half the people on the street hating or afraid of the other half. The Yales probably getting out and who knows what wreckage they'll leave behind. Now this, you having to start over after nearly twenty years. Oh, Matt, what's happening to us?"

He shook his head wearily. "Ellen, there wasn't anything else to do. Zack knew it; his wife knew it, and you knew it. Once you saw it, there was no way to duck it. Either the guy was my friend . . . a man as much as I was . . . or he wasn't."

Matt made an impatient, dismissing gesture. But he knew it was all true. It was butting your head against a stone wall until you bled, or worse, were crazed. He had gone too far to give in to weakness now. But, unbidden and unwelcome, the doubt was growing. When you knew you were right and had invested nearly everything, how was it possible to go on and on, through blow after blow, and never reach the break-through point where you would win? Matt had suffered a paralyzing shock and he could not help knowing that it was he, his wife, his son—not Winter, or Winter's wife, or Winter's son—who had paid the price. He would never admit, even to himself, that he wished this burden had not chosen to fall on him. And he would not, even now, seek to lay it down. But, more and more often, the weight of it seemed insupportable. Matt felt that he was close to the bottom.

Restlessly, he got up and started toward the door, heading for the dark solitude of outdoors. His foot struck something that rolled away, clattering against the playroom tiles. Automatically he bent to pick it up and straightened up with Bill's football helmet in his hand.

"Oh," Ellen said, seeing a bemused expression cross the lean face. "Oh, I told him to put it away." It had startled her.

He stood looking down at the garish red-and-yellow globe of plastic, running his fingers over the scars and scratches that marred its shiny surface and told of battles fought with a full heart, joyously won or lost. It's not the same thing, he thought. Or is it? Ellen, watching anxiously, saw the tired lines smoothing out as his face relaxed. In his mind's eye he was seeing the fierce, fearless, and fearfully dirty young face peering out from under the visor of this battered but undaunted crest. He looked at Ellen quizzically.

"It is kind of beat up, isn't it?" he said musingly. "And it sure as hell isn't regulation." He jiggled the helmet thoughtfully in one hand for a moment and then turned toward the door. "I'll be back," he said.

Fifteen minutes later he came down from the kitchen carrying two opened bottles of beer and put one in her hand.

"Here," he said. "Nightcap. Great for the hips." He looked at her and a slow grin grew on his face.

"What happened?" she asked.

"Oh, he put up quite a battle," he said. "Claimed this one was all right. Didn't need a new one. Wouldn't consider it. But he finally broke down."

"You gave him the six dollars?" she asked.

"Six bucks." He grinned. "He's asleep."

She got up suddenly and came to him, unsure whether she was laughing or crying. It was all right; he had come back.

"You're out of your mind." She giggled against his shirt. "He didn't really need it and we can't afford it."

"Can't afford to get his skull cracked either," he said. "If we're lucky we can make a pro out of him and he'll support us."

"Matt, how bad is it?" she asked, suddenly grave again. "Will we have to sell the house?"

He was still smiling. The weight was there, but his strength was coming back. This was his woman, and up in the bedroom was his son, his and his to do for. No light burden, but one to be carried lightly, in pride and love. His laugh had the ring of mirth.

"We probably couldn't sell it if we wanted to"—he smiled—"considering everything. We'll just have to keep it."

"But we'd better be careful. No more football helmets just because he takes a whim." She felt the return of confidence and, feeling safe in it, was grateful. If there were burdens, they could be shared.

"Sure," he said easily. "Cut out the frills. We could get out of the club, for example."

"That ought to be easy," she said, sobered again. "On top of everything else we had a letter from the club. The board of governors."

"What do they want this time?" he grunted. "New assessment for restoring the gun room or a fund for caddies' honeymoons?"

"No. They asked us to resign."

23

THE FACT THAT Alexander Fox had been mortally certain Lamar Winter would come again failed to render the sight any more enjoyable when he heard his office door open and looked up to see the artist coming toward his desk. Fox was not given to poetic imagery, but he was struck by the chill notion that Winter made him think of a tiger on the prowl. Fox was a devious man and knew it; generally he was able to think his way around corners more quickly and surely than most, and he felt, not without pride, that this faculty gave him an advantage over other men, even the crafty ones. Being ahead, he was often able to look back and understand what they were up to, sometimes even before they did. But his self-confidence had an unsettling way of deserting him with Francis Barton, and lately he had been learning that the same thing was true with Winter. Both men gave him a feeling that he was being stalked. In an inchoate way, he resented it. It struck him as somehow unfitting and indecent that he, a white man who had done well skillfully manipulating the fears and ambitions of both white and colored, should now find himself intimidated, of all things by two Negroes. But he didn't intend to show it if he could help.

"Hello," the broker said with cautious cordiality. "Glad to see you again."

Winter's dark face was unreadable as he hooked a toe under a rung of the straight wooden chair beside Fox's desk and pulled it away. He felt like surveying the broker in depth; a little distance might make the process more intimidating. He sat down, tilted to balance the chair on its rear legs, folded his hands, and regarded Fox pensively.

"What can I do for you?" Fox asked, his unease growing under the other man's scrutiny.

"Just dropped in to see what you've found out about that matter," Winter said mildly. He knew he was going to be lied to and was curious to know how long Fox was prepared to keep it up.

"What matter's that, Mr. Winter?" Fox said, hoping rather

illogically that if he refused to give house room to what he suspected, it might go away and never come back.

"You know what matter," Winter said. "Yale."

"Oh, that," Fox said. "Yeah, yeah, I remember."

"I thought you might," the artist said dryly.

"I've been pretty busy . . ." Fox's voice trailed off apologetically.

"I can see that," Winter drawled. "You think things might move a little faster if you took your feet off the desk?" The tone was placid, but Fox grunted as though he had been struck and only managed to keep his heels in their well-worn grooves on the scarred wood by a mighty effort of will.

"I think better this way," he said reproachfully. He was aware that Winter had nearly provoked him into a ludicrous scramble to straighten up.

"Well, then, try thinking about this," Winter said, his tone suddenly crisp. "I told you I think Yale is getting ready to sell out to a colored man. Say he does it." Winter lowered his chair to all fours and his eyes turned cold and watchful. "What happens next?"

"How do you mean, happens next?" the broker said, stalling because, for the life of him, he couldn't think of what else to do.

"You know exactly what I mean," Winter snapped. "What happens to the street when the second colored man moves in?"

"I guess that would depend on a lot of things," Fox said.

"What things?"

"Well . . ." Fox hesitated, wishing again this cold bastard would let up on him, knowing that he would not, wondering in anguish how far he was going to be pushed and whether he could keep from betraying himself. "I guess it would depend on who the colored man was, for one thing. And, of course, it would depend on how those people out there would take it. Nobody can tell about that."

"I can," Winter said. "Except for one or two—maybe three or four at most—they're ready to come unstuck."

Fox had what he thought might be a saving inspiration. He still didn't know what was on Winter's mind, but he thought, which was natural to Fox, that it might be money. If it was money, there was a chance to get Winter off his neck by showing him how to save his own.

"You ever think about maybe getting out yourself, Mr. Winter?" he asked, probing cautiously.

"Get out?" Winter asked. "What for? I just got there."

"Well, if the place is as touchy as all that," Fox said, still feeling his way, "it might be a good idea to pull up stakes. If Yale is going to sell, I might be able to get you a real good deal by doing it fast before he does."

Winter stared at him so long that Fox had to look at something else and made a virtue of inspecting the bountiful pair of breasts on his calendar.

"You mean run first?" Winter said. "Let somebody else pick up the pieces?"

"Exactly," Fox said, feeling eagerness grow in him. "You don't owe anybody there anything, and what's the point in getting hurt if you don't have to?" In the pleasure of conviction that he had hit on the right answer, Fox decided to do something he seldom did and tell a customer some of the truth. "I'll tell you this: if Yale sells to a colored man, that street will be a turkey. Yes, sir, a frazzle-assed turkey. You could get out ahead." Damn, Fox was thinking, why hadn't it occurred to him sooner? He must be getting slow, or being pushed by those two ornery men must have addled him. Here was the perfect solution. Barton wouldn't object. In fact, he'd be pleased. Barton had never liked the way Winter had got the house anyhow; a colored man befriended by whites was a situation Barton just didn't trust because it made the colored man surrender so many hostages that, in the end, he couldn't be trusted to remember his color. But if Winter could be persuaded to give up and get out, it would be dandy. Then the place would be wide open and Barton could control the avalanche any way he liked. Moreover, it would get this mean-eyed bastard off my back, Fox thought. It occurred to him, last but not least, that it would also mean an extra commission.

He turned away from the calendar to bend the warmth of his inspiration upon the artist. The glow faded and clicked out like a light. Winter was staring at him with such intent and icy malevolence that Fox shuddered and felt a wild impulse to get up and run.

Lamar Winter had decided to quit playing games. Hearing the truth had flicked him harder than the lies. Slowly he arose and stood by Fox's desk, staring down at him. His voice was savage.

"Just in case you still have any doubts about what I know, I know Yale is making a deal. I also know who is making it for him." He paused, watching the rush of panic to the broker's eyes, feeling the lift of evil glee as the long legs tightened convulsively and the feet came off the desk and hit the floor with a thud. "And I think I'll put a spoke in your wheel, you slippery sonofabitch."

Winter turned and walked out.

Francis Barton put the telephone on its cradle, sat back in his chair, and his finger tips made a thoughtful march along the hard edge of his desk. Barton never panicked and made his infrequent decisions on rash action only after a meticulous calculation of risk against gain. What he had just heard had warned him that his purpose to convert Peaceable Lane from a lost skirmish into a victorious campaign was in jeopardy. He let his mind run over the possibilities. He had known Winter was a hard man, but he thought he knew, better than Winter did, the powerful softening pressures to which the artist was being subjected. Winter was now set in a pattern which Barton could have predicted; the question was whether it was necessary or worth the dangers implicit in reversing the pattern.

He had made up his mind by the time Edward Smith reached the office in midafternoon and he called the slender, spectacled young man to receive his instructions.

"I had a call from our friend Fox this morning," he said. "Fox is frightened."

"Of what?" Smith asked.

"Of Winter. The artist. Winter let him know that he has found out that Yale is selling his house and that Fox is his broker. How do you suppose Winter discovered it?" he said musingly.

"Winter's pretty sharp," Smith said. "And there are always places where things can leak."

"I am aware of it. It was idle speculation, thinking that it would be easier to predict what Winter might do if I knew what he knows. However, I know enough. He threatened Fox."

"With what?"

"Nothing specific. I don't think he knows himself yet. I want you to change his mind before he has time to decide."

"Me? Change his mind? How?" Smith looked owlishly puzzled.

"What is the weather forecast?"

Smith was used to the idea that Barton's mind would take unpredictable bypaths without warning and, although he was always startled when it occurred, he tried to be ready.

"Showers, cloudy, hot—upper eighties. Why?" he asked.

"The moon?" Barton asked.

"Last quarter. Almost none. It'll be a dark night," Smith said. He had the glimmering of an idea now; Barton wanted something done and, although he did not yet know what, he could sense the process of working out an operations plan behind that placid face. He began to feel the taut thrill of impending action; it was one of the most rewarding things about working for Barton.

"Listen carefully," the big man said. "If this is done properly, it will work. If you slip, it will be worse than useless."

Smith had learned long ago that Barton's plans, while often intricate, always had a direct and simple purpose. But this time he was baffled and his bewilderment showed as Barton set forth the order and timing of the steps he was to take. Barton, aware that his lieutenant would understand what, decided that for once it would be wise to tell him why as well.

"It is not absolutely essential to implicate Fox," he said. "But it will help to keep him in line—now and in the future. If you're afraid to use him, tell me, but if you think you can keep him under control, I much prefer that you use him. As for the act, I can see that you are puzzled. You will understand if you try to think as Winter must be thinking—feeling, rather. He has been through a difficult summer. He and his family have been under a strain, subjected to tension, insult and injury. On the other hand, he got there and has been able to stay through agencies he could scarcely have believed possible. He has accepted help from white men, more help than he could have expected. This puzzles him.

Right now Winter is a bewildered man. He could go either way. What you are going to do will remind him that he is a colored man—inescapably one of us."

"But . . ." Smith was still baffled, fumbling for words. "But, holy hell, boss . . . what if this drives him out?"

Barton smiled gently. "I don't think it will, but if it does, I do not greatly care. Winter may not know it himself, but he is already corrupted. I intend to turn that street colored and I do not propose to take the chance that Winter might stand in my way. If this cures him of vacillation, well and good. If it breaks him and drives him to flight, it doesn't matter." He paused, and when he spoke again, his voice had taken on a chilling emphasis. "From this point on, I intend to control whatever takes place on Peaceable Lane."

24

IT WAS A restless night, muggy and dark, with an intermittent flicker of lightning around the horizon and thunder muttering in the distance. The heavy air was still and hot, and Matt was sweating as he sat alone in the back yard, trying to strike a balance. There was no bitterness in him, but he knew that he and his had been heavily damaged. Now he was trying to decide whether to allow his son to risk even another hurt.

He wondered whether Ellen was scared. She probably was, but since she had committed herself—even though he remembered that she had done so reluctantly—she was probably prepared to stick it out. There would be other forces working on her: the awful tendency of anything once begun to keep moving on its ordained course, the knowledge that the Golds were also involved with the added burden of steadfastness that implied, a real sympathy for the Winters, the fear of putting more weight on him when she knew he was already heavily laden.

The trouble was that there was no sure way to protect the boy. No matter how an adult might long to keep a kid safe, there was really no doorway by which he could enter a kid's world. The dangers there were real enough and awful enough, but they belonged to kids and could not be delegated to an adult. But this was different. Dangers that a kid found for himself were one thing; dangers that you thrust him into were another.

He could get that far, but it wasn't far enough. What about the Winter kid? The thought of Tod Winter's sensitive, careful face —eager to be as young and carefree as Bill, but knowing, even at ten, that he had to walk softly—struck at him.

He got up and started toward the hemlocks and Gold's back door. Zack's in this, too, he thought. The girls had cooked it up themselves, but he was a long way from sure that it ought to be left that way.

"I've been thinking about it," Gold said a few minutes later. "I hate to throw them into it, and a couple of times I almost called you to say nothing doing. On the other hand, oh hell, I hate to see the little guy try to make it on his own."

"It can be rough. There's a thousand kids in that school and a normal percentage are mean as copperheads," Matt said.

"If they take it into their heads to let him have it, they'd be likely to let our kids have it at the same time. I hate the thought of those four—bucking a thousand. And the alternative is to toss the Winter boy to the lions on his lonesome," he added after a moment. "That's lousy too."

"When's school start?" Matt asked. "I've been so goofed up I've lost track."

"Right away. Tuesday—day after tomorrow."

"That soon? I thought there was another week."

"I haven't taken much of a whipping yet," Gold said heavily. "You have. Some of it might have been your own fault, but you've put a lot on the line already. I don't think you ought to be asked to put your kid on the line too."

"Nobody asked me," Matt said sharply. "Or you. If we put them up to bat, it's our own decision."

"Does it have to be?" Gold asked softly. "Have you talked to Winter about it?"

"No," Matt said. "It's too much like hitting below the belt, letting him know I'm worried about Bill in the same car pool with his kid. He's like the rest of us—if you want to kill him, hit him where his kid is."

"No," Gold said. His voice was somber. "He's big enough to stand some hurt. You've taken your share. Winter's no world-champion humanitarian, but I doubt if he'd think our kids owed it to his kid—or to him—to take a beating. Anyhow, I think he ought to know about it—and know that we know the size of the risk."

"All right," Matt said at last with deep reluctance. "Let's go talk to him." Not speaking again, sunk in brooding thought, they started across the dark lawn toward the Winter house. It was as close as Matt would ever come to losing his resolution to stand by Lamar Winter and his family.

They moved silently in the still, oppressive night, scarcely conscious of the heat, hardly aware that the lightning was brighter and the rumble of thunder louder.

Beyond the darkened lawns and across the street John Ainslie Outerbridge, feeling the restless pull of the approaching storm, had come out of his house and stood under the trees on his front lawn, trying to estimate whether the squall would pass. He hoped the rain would strike; it had been a dry summer and they needed it. He saw the lights of a car approaching through the underpass tunnel. Suddenly he was alert and curious. The car had stopped along his curb, across the street from Winter's place. The lights were switched off and he heard a car door close softly, but he was conscious that the engine was still running.

Edward Smith was happy. He never felt better than on the edge of or in the midst of action; too often the things he was called upon to do by Francis Barton were merely intricate or devious or time-consuming. Smith preferred the harsh, bloody taste of violence. But Smith's cool mind would never let his sense of pleasure interfere with doing the job efficiently.

Now that he understood what Barton was about, it seemed crystal clear and simple. It was the classical thing, the ultimate act of rejection that Winter, or any Negro in his position, could expect from the whites around him. Therefore, unless Smith flubbed it badly, which he did not expect to do, it was practically foolproof. When a colored man was burned out, he didn't have to think twice to decide who had burned him out. That was what made Barton's intent beautifully logical. Smith was so accustomed to accomplishing Barton's purposes that it never occurred to him to think that it was also beautifully ironic.

He called Fox from the office, telling him no more than was necessary. Smith was no more fooled about Fox than Barton was; he knew the man would bolt like a scared rabbit if he had any idea what was afoot. It was all right to make him curious; it was even safe to keep him nervous; he would hold still so long as he could see a profit in the offing. But he had to be kept from panic until he was so deeply involved that he couldn't get out.

When Smith's train pulled in at White Plains at ten o'clock he picked up the package, which he had kept in his lap rather than trusting it to the baggage rack. Down on the platform, he walked briskly with the crowd. He would have liked to raise the package to his ear and shake it once more, but he knew that would be conspicuous and he knew it wasn't necessary; he had filled it with care; there would be no betraying slosh.

Down the stairs and through the grimy station, he emerged on the brick plaza and, as he had expected, saw Fox's cream-colored Dodge among the cars parked in the roundabout.

"Sorry I kept you waiting," he said as he slid into the front seat beside the broker.

"I'm used to it," Fox said in resignation. "It's the New York Central and it's mostly late. I don't blame it on the passengers." Smith, as he expected, had seen the broker's curious eyes go to the package. "What's that?" Fox asked.

"I don't know. Something Barton told me to stop and give Winter on the way."

"What's Barton doing giving things to Winter? I thought Winter was sore at him," Fox said suspiciously.

"How would I know?" Smith said negligently. "You know how the old bastard goes around in his own tricky circles. Maybe he's trying to make friends with him."

"Why didn't you drive out yourself?" Fox asked. He was uneasy; wary as a weasel, he felt something wrong somewhere, and the sensitive antennae of his caution were quiveringly in search of it.

"Couldn't," Smith said, keeping his tone casual. "Car's busted. Anyhow, you ought to be there when I lay it out for Yale. We'll be closing Tuesday." Smith smiled to himself; he could almost smell Fox's jumpiness, and he enjoyed it. Just wait till the bastard knows what he's let himself in for, he thought with pleasurable contempt.

Fox fell silent, letting his mind range nervously like a searching radar, and Smith, knowing exactly what was to happen, enjoying the prospect and feeling no wish to chatter, shared the quiet. They swung out of Hawthorne Circle and onto the Saw Mill Parkway for the run up to Chappaqua. Far ahead the lightning danced over the wooded hills, and they could feel, rather than distinctly hear, the grumble of thunder through the purr of the motor.

Fox turned the Dodge onto the parkway cutoff, and they were rolling down the long grade and almost at the ramp leading into Peaceable Lane before Smith spoke again.

"Just stop down there across from Winter and I'll run in with this. You can wait—I won't be more'n a few minutes, and then we'll go down to Yale's." Smith knew that neither he nor Fox would be going to Yale's house that night, but it was essential to keep Fox thinking they were. He had debated the wisdom of having Fox go down around the circle and park heading outward, but had decided against it rather reluctantly. Heading out would have assured a faster, more certain getaway; on the other hand, he could foresee a possibility that Fox would bolt once he realized what was happening. If Fox had to go down to the end of the lane and around the circle, Smith could still catch him coming out if he did try to cut and run. The hard weight of the pistol in his shoulder holster reassured him of that.

If it wasn't for Barton wanting to entangle Fox in this, he thought, he would have preferred to do the job alone. You were always better off when there was only yourself to trust. If you did have to trust somebody, this bunny rabbit would be his last choice. Smith didn't like Fox, never had liked him. Secretly, he held the broker in contempt. But he knew Barton considered him necessary, and it was his habit to suppose that Barton was right. He would prefer to have nothing to do with him. But—he shrugged inwardly—what Barton wanted, Barton got.

The car whispered to the curb along the Outerbridge property across the street from the walk to Winter's front door. Fox switched out the lights and Smith slipped out, carrying the package, and turned with a grin. "Be right back," he said. He closed the door quietly and was gone. For a reason he could not have explained, Fox left the motor running. Smith, walking rapidly away, heard the engine's idling mutter. Maybe it's just as well, he thought. We could have to leave fast. Only I don't like him being that jumpy; he isn't supposed to know we'll be leaving in a hurry.

Moving up the walk, keeping to the grass to avoid the thud of heels on flagstone, Smith felt a few heavy drops of rain and was conscious that the storm was closer. He didn't think it would matter. This would all be over quickly and, anyhow, it would take a real cloudburst to seriously dampen what he was about to do. He reached the house. He avoided the door and slipped among the sweeping, pungently fragrant branches of a blue spruce beside the entrance.

Concealed by the shrubbery and darkness, John Ainslie Outerbridge, not knowing why he was both curious and cautious, moved silently across his front lawn toward the idling car. In the leaden dark he could make out only that the car was light in color. He stood there, waiting.

Silent and swift, Smith tore the paper wrapping from the package and unscrewed the cap of the gallon can it contained. The smell of gasoline rose to his nostrils. Hurrying but unhurried, he began to spill the stuff in small splashes, first the lower branches of the spruce up to shoulder level, then against the wood of the front door. The house was faced with brick and the roof was slate; he thought it unlikely that the main structure would go. But that was not necessary. Barton had merely wanted him to drive home in Winter's mind the white man's ultimate insult to the black.

He was nearly ready. It was none too soon. The lightning was brighter by the moment, the thunder now nearly booming, and he could hear the first soughing of the wind that would bring the rain. All right, he thought, it's time; get it finished and get out.

Matt Jones and Zachariah Gold, as was normal to them, had taken the short cut through the hemlocks and across the darkened back yards. Walking silently through familiar territory, they skirted the trees without really needing to see them. Matt wondered if they were too late and half hoped they were. He could see no lights in the Winter house and thought that it must be well after eleven.

Halfway across Winter's yard they shifted direction, circling toward the front door. They were within twenty yards when lightning shot across the sky—and they stopped dead. Something was moving there by the door, between the door and the tall spruce, something furtive. And then they smelled the sweetish, metallic odor of raw gasoline.

The spruce exploded with a soft, sucking whoosh and brilliant light. Instantly it was a tower of flame and roiling smoke, leaping tall among the trees, beating against the brick, tumbling over the eaves, searing the paint from the door.

Smith was moving away swiftly across the lawn. Only he was immune to the paralyzing shock of the great torch suddenly come to life.

From the house came a woman's scream, thin and breaking with terror.

Gold yelled, a harsh and wordless roar. His great body galvanized into action and he lumbered toward the side of the house where he knew there was a tap and, probably, a garden hose.

Frozen for a moment, Matt saw a hunched, running figure, now heedless of noise, pelting along the flagstones to the street. Without thought, he plunged after it.

Across the street an idling motor roared to powerful life; lights switched on the car lunged ahead, flinging gravel from its spinning wheels. Fox, all his native sense of something wrong triggered to instant panic, was not waiting. Transfixed by the fire, John Ainslie Outerbridge was shocked to awareness by the motor's sudden roar. He started as the lights leaped up and turned his eyes to the moving car. There was only a flicker of time as the car gathered speed, but the lawyer's eyes went automatically to the rear license plate in its illuminated frame. "VV," he thought, as the car sped down into the lane. "VV—what? Six or nine, the first figure." He couldn't be sure. "What was the second?" He couldn't tell; it was only a blur now—and then it was gone. John Ainslie turned and trotted as fast as his short legs would carry him toward his garage, where he kept a five-gallon fire extinguisher.

Smith grunted a curse when the car leaped into motion while he was still a hundred feet short of it. Running, he fumbled inside his jacket for the gun; he did not intend to let Fox get by him when he turned the circle and came back up the lane.

He was in the street now and stopped and settled the gun in his hand. Either the sight of it—or a shot across his bow, if that was necessary—would stop Fox.

But then he heard feet pounding behind and, turning, saw Matt's unidentifiable figure, silhouetted against the fire and bulking larger than it was, running toward him. Instantly he decided: there was no time to wait for the returning car, and his mind rejected the risk of using the gun on anybody here. He was in trouble, but it wasn't worth a shooting—not yet. Sonofabitch! he thought, and turned and sprinted up the lane toward the underpass tunnel.

Gold found the hose against the house, tangled in shrubbery. Savagely he tore it free and knelt to couple the hose to the tap and spin the faucet wide open. This side of the house was away from the fire and dark, but lightning revealed the nozzle writhing and leaping under the pressure of released water. He jumped for it and got it and ran around the house with the spurting hose.

Then he stopped, frozen. The rain had become a downpour, and Gold was incongruously conscious of how the great drops hissed in the torch of the spruce. Lamar Winter was down on one knee in the light of the fire, and the flames set up a dancing flicker on the barrel of a gun as he raised it to his shoulder. In a brilliant rip of lightning Gold, dimly through the blurring lash of the rain, saw two figures running toward the underpass and the muzzle of Winter's gun swinging to follow them. Gold dropped the hose and dived, hitting the kneeling man with all the force of his more than two hundred pounds. He heard Winter's sodden grunt, and there was a numbing blast in his ears as the gun went off.

Fox went around the circle fast, the Dodge's outer springs sagging as the weight came down on them. The car was accelerating all the way up the lane and was flicking toward seventy when it passed the fire. In panic, staring into the lash of rain, Fox never saw Outerbridge staggering across the street with the heavy extinguisher. He nearly ran him down and would have, had not the lawyer dropped his burden and flung himself, sprawling over the curb.

Fox had a glimpse of two men running ahead of him into the tunnel. He knew one must be Smith but, if he knew anything else at all, it was that he did not intend to stop. And Smith, with Matt pounding closer behind him, knew there wasn't time to wheel and face the broker down. He ran on, knowing he was losing the race.

Gold got to his feet, his ears ringing from the blast of the gun. Winter still lay sprawled, but he could see the artist's chest heaving and hear the harsh gasp of his breath. Cold-cocked him, he thought grimly—and none too damn soon. He found the hose still spurting and turned it on the fire. He was not particularly surprised when John Ainslie, panting audibly, appeared beside him and turned the extinguisher's foam nozzle on the flames. Together the pelting rain, the hose and the foam were too much for the great torch. Hissing, flaring, fighting back, the flames began to die.

It was dead black within the tunnel. Matt could see nothing of the man he pursued. But he could hear the labor of his breath and the thud of his feet, and when he sensed that he was near enough, he went for him in a running dive. His clutching hands closed on cloth and muscle, and they were down together in the blackness. Instinctively Matt rolled to get on top and smashed a fist down into an unseen face. He felt a satisfying crunch of flesh and bone; Edward Smith had lost another tooth. But then Matt felt nothing more as light exploded in his skull; Smith had swung the hard weight of the gun. It was a glancing blow against the side of his head, but it had behind it all the desperate force of Smith's savage panic. Matt's weight collapsed soddenly across him; Smith rolled from under it, staggered erect, and ran into the darkness of the woods road.

In Chappaqua, exhausted, certain that he did not dare show his puffed, bloody and now numbly painful face, he ducked into a streetside phone booth. It was only then that he realized he had lost his thick spectacles; he could not read the numbers and only by memory and touch was able to dial Barton's number. He was deathly sick, wet and weary when, at four in the morning, the car Barton sent picked him up in the shadows near the railway station.

Matt had no idea how long he had been out when consciousness and, with it, blinding pain came back to him. Fumbling to his hands and knees, his right hand encountered something smooth and angular and, without thinking, he kept a grip on it as he staggered to his feet. He reeled and nearly fell, but, summoning his will, he began to move out of the tunnel and back into the lane.

Numbly he realized that the fire was out as he stumbled over the curb and walked toward the lighted open door and window of Winter's ground-floor playroom. He reached the door and sagged against the frame, seeing the four people in the room as a frozen tableau. Margo Winter, clutching a robe around her, stood in the other doorway. Her eyes were huge and blank with fear. Sodden, streaked with mud and soot, John Ainslie Outerbridge stood pudgily just inside the door, lips pursed in an expression of disapproval. Winter was slumped in a chair, elbows on knees and head drooping. Gold, bulking huge, stood over him with a double-barreled shotgun broken open across one arm. In his hand he held two shotgun shells, one spent.

Gold turned at the sound of Matt's footsteps, and Matt blearily saw a look of concern cross the heavy face, overlaying its sternness.

"What happened to you?" Gold asked.

Matt raised his left hand and pressed it against the pain that filled his head and, drawing it away, saw the blood.

"Fought," he grunted. "He got away. I always lose my fights."

Winter's head came up at the sound of voices. He looked dazed and broken.

"Man," he muttered, "you hit like a ton of brick."

"Sorry," Gold said. The shadow of a wry smile twitched his lips. "I was in a hurry."

"Why?"

Gold jerked his head toward Matt in the doorway and a somber anger settled in his face and voice.

"One of those people you were gunning for was Matt," he said.

"Matt?" Winter muttered. Then, slowly, full comprehension grew in his face and, with it, shock and horror. "Matt? Holy Christ! Hit me again."

"I'd have hit you anyhow," Gold said somberly. "What you were doing was murder."

The artist stared at him, and for a moment bitterness flickered in the drawn face.

"Murder?" he said. "Murder to defend your wife and kid against murder? That's murder?"

"That's murder," Gold said. "Listen, Winter, I know you've been through hell. I don't excuse it. But I don't excuse you either. You're not the law."

"No," Winter said, as a little of the old mocking and scornful malice lighted his eyes. "I know who the law is, all right. White men are the law. They're the law even when they're burning out a nigger."

"Shit!" Gold said in sudden, explosive disgust. "Talk sense! There's also a law to handle the people that tried to burn you out." He turned to Matt curiously. "Who was the guy you tangled with? Any idea?"

Matt shook his head and gestured wearily. "It was dark, black as a pocket. I never saw him."

"What's that in your hand?" Gold asked sharply.

"Wh——" Matt started to say, then looked down at the thing he had picked up in the tunnel and then forgotten. It was a pair of horn-rimmed spectacle frames. He held them up; one lens was gone, the other smeared with mud, but thick as the bottom of a beer bottle. Not much sense found its way through the thundering waves of pain in his skull. "His, probably," he muttered. "Whoever he was."

Outerbridge moved for the first time. He stepped toward Matt and took the broken spectacles from his nerveless hand and held them up to the light.

"Very nearsighted," he said thoughtfully. "Nobody from around here. It may be possible to trace them—by the prescription, of course," he added, falling normally and naturally into pedantry. Suddenly he remembered the wild, lurching start of the car. "There's something else," he said. "I saw the car start up. I got part of the number. It began with VV and the first number was either six or nine. Not much to go on, but it could help. I was disconcerted by the fire," he said primly, as though in extenuation for lacking a complete report. "It was a light-colored car," he added. "With fins. Probably one of the Chrysler line . . . DeSoto, Dodge, Plymouth . . . one of those."

"Hmmm," Gold said. "It's something to start on anyhow." He dropped the shells in his pocket, stood the gun against the wall, and turned to Matt.

"Look, fella," he said with concern. "You better hit the sack. You're beat."

There was a queer, fumbling smile on Winter's face as he looked up again.

"Yeah," he said slowly. "Beat it, Matt . . . and thank you." He turned to Gold. "And you." A bemused expression crossed his dark face. "How is it every time I look around I find you two up to the ass in my business?"

"I dunno," Gold grunted and grinned wryly. "Maybe because there's so much of your business."

25

MARGO WINTER had slept little and she was haggard, her whole body feeling slumped and defeated, when she went down to the playroom in the morning and found Winter sitting with the broken spectacles in his hand. He had been there all night but, strangely, felt no fatigue.

"Lamar," she said. He looked up and his eyes warmed with sympathy and concern.

"You had a tough night, honey," he said. "Try to relax. You got any sleeping pills?"

"Lamar, I can't take any more," she said out of the depth of desolation. "They've beaten us. Please, let's get out of here. Please, right now, today!"

"Don't lose your nerve, honey," he said gently. "Nothing worse can happen."

"How can you say that?" she said wildly. "They won't stop anywhere. Can't you see that? They won't have us. They won't!" She was near hysteria. He got up and went to her and drew her into his arms, feeling her smallness, sensing how fear had shrunk and broken her. He tilted her chin and kissed her; his eyes held a quizzical expression.

"Who do you think 'they' are?" he asked.

"Oh, Lamar, who else? These people. They won't have us! Next time it'll be worse."

He released her and when he spoke his tone was brisk. "I've been thinking. Listen, I'm going to check something. Right away. You take a pill and get some rest. When I get back I'll know whether we ought to leave. If you're right, we will. I promise you."

"But . . ." she said helplessly. Was there no end to this man's obstinate defiance, to his iron will? Was he utterly blind to defeat? Must they be crushed flat?

"No buts," he said, turning her around and propelling her gently toward the door. He went to the extension telephone and dialed and, after two rings, recognized Zachariah Gold's voice.

"Zack," he said crisply, "this is Lamar Winter. I think I'm going to need a lawyer. Does your pride permit you to work for a nigger?"

"That's a hell of a question," Gold's voice said sourly. "What's on your mind?"

"I'll be able to tell you in an hour," Winter said. "Can you give me that much time before you leave for the office?"

"I could, yes. But why the mystery? You got something to say, say it."

"I will," Winter said. "Just as soon as I make sure about something. Will you wait?"

"All right," Gold said. "But don't stall. I got an appointment in town."

Winter got the Jaguar from the garage and, driving slowly for once, took the Saw Mill and then the Bronx River Parkway toward White Plains. He seemed self-possessed, but tumult raged in his mind. So far as he knew, Winter had never shirked a fact; he would not shirk the one the long night's agony of thought and memory had brought him to confront. He realized now that for weeks his way had been set upon an unbelievable road, and now, in the crisp, rain-washed clarity of this morning, he could see its incredible, inevitable destination. Behind him the uncompromised, uncompromising and merciless beliefs of a lifetime lay shattered.

He found an open parking space within a block of his destination and walked toward Alexander Fox's office, watching for the broker's car. He found the finny, cream-colored Dodge parked in front of the building. One quick, confirming glance gave him the license number—VV-6916. He was not surprised; he was already convinced that he had been dealing with memory—not imagination.

Catfooted, calm, sure of himself, he walked in. Fox, as usual, sat slumped in his swivel chair with his heels in their familiar grooves on the desk. But Fox's cultivated habit of self-possession had deserted him; one startled glance galvanized the lanky body and brought his feet crashing to the floor. Winter grinned wickedly.

"Kind of jumpy, ain't you?" he said mildly.

Fox stared at him.

"Take it easy," Winter said. "This is a social call—sort of. I want to give a guy something he lost and I thought maybe you could help. Ever see these before?" Still smiling a smile alight with deadly malice, he reached into his shirt pocket and held out the broken spectacles.

Without actually moving, Fox seemed to recoil in every nerve and fiber. Winter smiled more broadly.

"Take 'em," he said. "They won't bite. They're Eddie Smith's, aren't they?"

Abruptly the artist moved toward the desk. Fox's feet kicked out involuntarily, driving his chair back toward the wall.

"You don't need to come unstuck, man," Winter said. "You seem kind of tongue-tied, and I thought I would save you the wear and tear. I just want Francis Barton's phone number." He picked up the memo pad on the desk and thumbed through it, grunting with satisfaction when he found what he sought. Picking up the telephone and beginning to dial, he flicked a grin at Fox. "Mind if I use your phone?"

Barton answered. Winter knew the voice. "This is Lamar Winter," he said.

"Of course, I recognized your voice." Over the wire, Barton's tone was unruffled, courteous and assured.

Winter felt a flicker of admiration; whatever else you may say about him, he thought, you can't question the old pirate's nerve.

"I'm calling from Alex Fox's place," Winter said. "We were having a chat." He paused deliberately. "About arson."

"That's curious," Barton's voice said calmly. "It occurred to me that you might be, but I hardly thought this quickly. My congratulations. What can I do for you?"

"It's more a matter of what I'm doing for you," Winter said. "I doubt if Alex here or Eddie Smith—or, for that matter, you, as an accessory—would much enjoy a stretch in Sing Sing. I just called to suggest that you get your fingers out of Peaceable Lane—and stay out."

"I was already reconciled to something like that, Mr. Winter," Barton said. This time there was a perceptible pause and though Winter could not be sure, perhaps the suggestion of a sigh. "You can't win them all."

"No, I guess you can't," Winter agreed. He glanced at Fox and spoke again. "There is one thing you can do for me, Mr. Barton. Just hang onto the phone and listen a minute." He put the instrument on the desk with the mouthpiece facing the broker. He stood over him and spoke crisply and loudly, but without emotion, "All right, you white yellow sonofabitch. Stand up!"

Fox stared up at him and seemed to shrink even further. Winter reached out a sinewy hand, grasped the broker by the shirt front, and pulled him to his feet. Holding him upright with his left hand, he cocked his right, measured the target with an appraising eye, and sent a short, vicious blow to the belly. Fox went backward into his chair and crashed against the wall and lay gasping.

Winter picked up the telephone. "That was just about what it sounded like," he said pleasantly. "By the way, if Eddie Smith wants his glasses back, I'll have them for him. Any time at all."

He hung up and left. Hurrying northward in the Jaguar, he felt some small regret for the brutality with which he had cut down the broker. It had been almost too easy, but the night's violence and his present contempt had demanded outlet and he had done it. Barton, Barton, he knew that was where, if anger's demanding hunger was to be fed, he should have satisfied it. Barton had made those other two his tools, using one's weakness and cupidity and the other's rancorous resentments. If he had to hate somebody it ought to be Barton. But then, he thought, mere physical violence would never hurt Barton in body so deeply as he had already hurt him in pride. Defeat was Barton's real punishment and Winter knew he had defeated him. It was enough.

An hour later, his appointment forgotten, Zachariah Gold stood in his own living room, gazing down, in sour contempt, at Peter Yale. Yale's thin face was livid, his eyes angry but nervous. Winter sat aside, relaxed and silent.

"You're here because Winter thought it would be better," Gold said. "Nobody wants to give you a break particularly, but he doesn't think there's any point in rubbing your wife's nose in it. She probably knows what a prick you are anyhow."

"You can't talk to me like that," Yale snarled.

"I can and I am," Gold said. "How much was your deal with Barton?"

"Forty thousand," Yale said defiantly. "That's what it's worth, and if he thinks he's going to buy it"—he jerked his head toward the artist—"that's what it's going to cost him."

Gold looked inquiringly at Winter and saw him nod slightly. But then he shook his head in angry rejection and turned back to Yale.

"It is not," the lawyer said crisply. "He might be willing to pay it, but I don't intend to let him. That was a blockbuster price and we all know it. The blockbuster has decided not to go on with it. He has decided that owning your house is not worth a prison term. If you doubt that, I'll get him on the phone and you can ask for yourself."

"Then I'll keep it," Yale said doggedly.

"You will not." Gold was inexorable. "You've worn out your welcome here. I know what you paid for the place—thirty-four. That was eight years ago and it isn't worth that now, but you've put something into it—storm windows and so on. So I'll let Winter settle for that. No more, no less. You be in my office tomorrow afternoon at four with your papers. Bring a lawyer." He paused, then added an afterthought. "At that you're lucky. No broker's commission."

"You're not going to blackmail me," Yale said hotly. "I'm not going to be pushed around by any goddam shyster and his nigger client."

Gold glanced at Winter with a look of inquiry. "If you want to hit him, I'm not looking," he said. Winter grinned and shook his head. Gold turned back to Yale.

"You're already pushed," he said. "If you think you're not pushed enough, I can arrange the full treatment. I don't know whether I could make a conspiracy charge stick, but I promise you I could give it a hell of a try. But I don't need to. A blockbuster deal, that's enough. Where do you want me to start? With your wife or with the network? And would you want to write and tell me how you're getting along when you get work again?"

Staring up balefully into the brooding, contemptuous face, having no room left for doubt or any room left for maneuver, Yale knew he was beaten.

"Four o'clock. You understand?" Gold said.

26

LAMAR WINTER thought he ought to feel more amazed at himself than he did, in fact. Sometime later, he thought, the jolt might hit him and he would be forced to assess the implications of what he had done already and was preparing to do further. Winter could no more escape honesty with himself than he could escape the color of his skin. He knew that, by his own standards, he stood in an impossible position: he had surrendered something kept impregnable for thirty-seven years, the defiant armor of his race. A month ago, he knew perfectly well, he would have looked on this present self as contemptible. A tame nigger was worse than a tame white man because he could not claim conscience for his excuse.

But it hadn't caught up with him yet. Instead he felt intensely alive and alert and sure of himself, taut with singing inner excitement. It was going to be a busy day.

But something else had to be done first. He had to see his dark-skinned son off to his first day in a white school. It was an act which should have been commonplace, and he intended, so far as it was within his power, to make it seem so—both to the boy and to his mother. But he knew that, far from being commonplace, this first day of Tod's in Wacapo Consolidated was an enormous gamble. Here was the core of it, the reason why he had violated the fierce integrity of a lifetime. It was a legacy. He had staked the essence of Lamar Winter on the gamble that one day the act of Tod Winter leaving home for Wacapo Consolidated would become commonplace in fact.

Winter was no jackass in rose-tinted spectacles. It would be a miracle if the gamble paid off today, in the fifth-grade classroom to which Tod would report. It might not pay off at all in the fifth grade, or even next year in the sixth. But he had to believe that someday it would. For Tod's sake he hoped it would be soon. Knowing the boy's vulnerability, he feared for him. But he also knew he could not follow him into the classroom to protect him. All he could do was this that he had done and was doing, betting the essence of himself that it would work.

Ellen Jones had volunteered as car-pool chauffeur for the first day of school. In fact, she had insisted. She had felt instinctively that this venture into the fearful unknown was something she had to share with Bill.

When the Jones station wagon, with Bill and Ruth and Jerry Gold already aboard, stopped at the foot of the walkway, Tod was ready. Margo stood with him at the door and, although by instinct she knew as well as Winter that this ought to be kept casual for the boy's sake, she could not resist stooping for a last fierce and fearful hug as the horn tooted and Tod opened the door.

Winter wanted to be doing the same thing, but he would not permit himself the luxury of revealing his concern. He forced himself to keep his chair and newspaper and to restrict himself to a cheerful, "So long, kid. Be good," when he heard the horn.

But he could not ignore the dark well of concern in her eyes when Margo turned toward him wordlessly as the station wagon drove off.

"Relax, baby," he said. "He'll be all right." He hoped his voice carried the conviction of easy confidence he intended that it should.

Then, suddenly, he was impatient to get on with the day. He dropped the newspaper and strode across the living room and took down the Rouault.

"Guess we'll have to put something else here for a while," he said, surveying the bare spot. "Might even get biggity and hang one of my own."

"You're really going through with it?" she said.

"Sure," he said lightly. "Gonna get right up there with the landed gentry. We can always buy this back."

Margo looked at him gravely.

"I know why you're doing it," she said in an unexpected rush of words. "I can't tell you . . . Lamar, I'm so proud . . . and so scared."

He grinned. "Relax, baby, the old man's just being logical."

He cradled the painting in its heavy frame and, jutting his chin awkwardly across it, kissed her. "Hold the door for me, baby," he said. He went around the flagstone walk to the garage. She was still standing in the door as he backed out in the Jaguar.

"Honey," he called, "I'll be gone all day. You'll tend to that, won't you?" He pointed at the black, bristling spine of the burned tree and the scorched door and heat-cracked glass of the picture window. "I don't want to have to look at the damn thing."

"What shall I do?" she called.

"You can look up a window man and a painter in the telephone book." He grinned. "Get the highest-priced help you can—I'm going to send the bills to Barton."

"Get the gardener up here. He can put in a new tree by tonight."

He backed into the lane and swung the Jaguar. Then he was gone. An hour later he left the car in the Waldorf-Astoria garage and, juggling the painting, took a taxi to the elegant gallery of a renowned Park Avenue dealer. It was not yet eleven when, having watched the dealer's helpers hang the Rouault and felt no pain at the sight, he pocketed a check for $20,000.

"I'll hold it for a year," the dealer said. "You can have it back within that time for a thousand more. You could hardly do better at a bank."

"I know it." Winter grinned. "You're my favorite hock shop."

"Hock shop?" the dealer asked with a lifted eyebrow, then looked up at the painting. "It's a handsome thing, isn't it? I wish I could afford it for myself."

"So do I," Winter said. "But while I can't, it's in good hands."

It was a short walk to the Chase Bank in Rockefeller Center, and soon the artist left the bank, feeling rich and powerful. There's something useful to a man's spirit, he thought, in having in his pocket a certified check for thirty-four thousand clams—even when the check was made out to somebody else and you'd had to hock a Rouault and jolt your bank account to get it. It was a satisfying feeling to look around at all the handsome, well-dressed bums on Fifth Avenue and reflect that probably not one in a thousand had $34,000 cash—in his pocket or anywhere else.

It was still only eleven-thirty. It struck him that this day had the feel of going right. Why not clear up the whole shebang while things were clicking? He had made an appointment with Thurston Young for later in the week, but now, on impulse, he went to a telephone booth in the International Building lobby. It worked; things really were going right. Sounding only slightly surprised, Young agreed to see him immediately.

"So that was it?" Young said, coldly expressionless, as Winter finished talking. "I had wondered." He smiled thinly. "Enough to break another appointment to see you. I had only a telegram from Jones that he had been removed from the account. Nothing more. No word from Macmillan."

"My impression was that Macmillan thought your business was up the flue anyhow—since I own the paintings," Winter said. "I think he knew that was the price and was ready to pay it."

"Jones might have been more explicit," Young said coldly. "Why wasn't he?"

"He had been fired," the artist said with equal coldness. "He had notified you. It seems to me that was the limit of his responsibility. Getting canned can preoccupy a man. Besides, he was busy."

"Busy?" Young asked.

"Ours is a busy neighborhood. Things like people trying to burn my house and Matt getting beat up trying to catch the guy who did it."

"Oh?" There was something like genuine curiosity in the cold eyes behind the pince-nez. "Some objection to your presence there?"

"You could put it that way," Winter said. "But I think it's finished now—due to Matt and one or two others. It's time now to get back to work on your campaign." Thinking about this interview, the artist had wondered how best to get to the crux of it. Now, suddenly, he believed this was the only way; indirection would get nowhere with this hard man.

"Perhaps," Young said. "However, my contract is with Macmillan Associates."

"And they have abrogated it, since they can't deliver the paintings for which you contracted."

"That is how you understand it. Do your lawyers have a similar opinion?"

"He does." Winter had laid the question in Gold's lap the day before. "I own the paintings until and unless you buy them and I accept your terms—or I sell them somewhere else."

The sharp face permitted itself a thin smile. "You don't seem to doubt your ability to dispose of them."

"I don't," Winter said simply. There was no boastfulness in it. "For ten years no painting that I had to sell has gone unsold."

"What does Jones plan to do?" Young asked suddenly.

"He'll have to work with me on this," Winter said. This was it, but there was still no way to go at it except boldly. "He planned it and organized it. My work stops at the easel. His begins before that and continues after it. For the last five years I have worked almost exclusively with Matt."

"A team?"

"Exactly."

"Macmillan is a fool," Young said. The tone was so quiet, the frosty face so impassive, that the artist was startled.

"Huh?" he said.

"To let valuable men escape him on an issue of personal prejudice."

"Oh." Winter studied the cosmetic king's expressionless face. Then he smiled. "Not necessarily a fool," he said without malice. "Not by his lights, anyhow. He probably can't help the way he thinks."

"I won't debate it and it doesn't matter. Now I want this program to go ahead without any more delay. Will you send Jones to see me about a new contract?"

"I would rather not," Winter said.

Young darted at him a quick, imperious glance, carrying an icy edge of annoyance.

"I mean I would appreciate it if you sent for him yourself," Winter said hastily. "Getting canned doesn't do much for a man's morale. Matt's is all right now, I think, but a little boost wouldn't hurt it."

Young's face, for once, carried a diluted but unmistakable hint of warm amusement.

"Of course," he said. "I should have thought of that myself."

"One other thing." Winter was grinning at him in open delight. "Do me a favor, sir. Don't tell him I was up here first."

"I never reveal a confidence, Mr. Winter. Particularly one involving an associate." Then Young did smile.

Winter's step was jaunty as he reached the street and went swinging south along the avenue. The big check was crisp in his pocket and, from his present point of vantage, the world looked nearly as crisp and satisfactory—and certified—as the check. Matt and he would divide something on the order of $150,000 from the Glamour-Glow campaign. There would be that even if Young, in the end, decided not to extend it beyond the original program of twelve paintings in three class magazines. And after that, who knew? But, in his present mood, it didn't seem likely it could be anything but good.

He still had three hours before he was due at Gold's office. He was hungry and felt like an expensive and leisurely lunch. If Matt was with him, he thought wryly, it could have been Twenty-One with no problem. He discarded the temptation to try it on his own; he was in no mood to mar an otherwise pleasant day by getting sore at anybody. He hailed a cab and had the driver take him to the United Nations' gleaming tower beside the East River. It was by no means the best food available in New York, but it wasn't bad, and—considering all the shades of color, from Ghana's blue-black and Indonesia's tawny yellow to Sweden's pale blond, that would be feeding themselves in the Delegates' Dining Room—he thought it unlikely that anybody would make an issue of his. The idea amused him.

The day had begun drenched in warm sunshine. In Manhattan, where Lamar Winter pursued his successful works, he was too pleased with the way things were going to notice or care when clouds rolled in above the city's towers. Far to the north above the Chappaqua hills the wet clouds massed even more darkly. A spattering of rain came and passed on in midmorning, but shortly before noon a violent squall broke over Wacapo Consolidated. Thunder crashed and reverberated, and lightning lit the modernistic glass-walled classrooms with dazzling glares. There were some tears, some fearful huddling around teachers, and a few shrieks of outright terror, but for the most part the thousand young citizens of Wacapo responded to the storm's violence with an awed, exciting absorption that shut out interest in anything else, whether teachers, assignments or a small, dark alien in their midst.

The lash of rain turned the school grounds, churned and torn all summer by trucks and bulldozers at work on the new wing, into a soupy quagmire. There could be no outdoor recess, and Wacapo's student body was kept inside through the lunch hour, its myriad noses pressed against the glass to watch heaven's artillery in action.

All this was just as well. Playing second fiddle to the storm, Tod Winter had a better, less eventful day than he or anyone else had really hoped.

He did not, of course, pass entirely unnoticed. Despite the storm's distraction, the school was aware of him. He was under continuous, curious, furtive inspection. Peaceable Lane, acutely aware of its own summer of discord and discontent, would have expected this sly appraisal. It would have been greatly surprised, however, to know that for the most part it was not hostile. To most of Wacapo's thousand, the dark, alien presence was an object of intense curiosity . . . but not of hate. Perhaps, in some ways, the storm was a misfortune; if it had not absorbed so much of the school's attention, Tod might actually have received some overt sign to show him that most of Wacapo, given time, would accept him, even welcome him.

It was a real misfortune, but inevitable, that this was not universally true of the thousand. Wacapo, like any other assembly of human beings, harbored its quota of hooligans. Tod was unaware that one of them saw him, gauged him, and marked him down for attention. Within the building, the staff, from principal to janitor, had been alerted and was on guard. Wacapo's small fry, from teacher's pet to hooligan, owned a lively sixth sense for adult surveillance; their instinct for it was as sensitive as radar. And so the peace was kept.

It held until three o'clock, when the dismissal buzzer sounded and the doors swung open and the canopied plaza beside the driveway suddenly swarmed with shrieking, undersized humanity. The rain had subsided to a spitting drizzle, but it was still penetrating enough to keep Wacapo's young citizenry massed and jockeying for position while they waited to be picked up.

Ellen Jones had dreaded this day. She had waited through the storm with a rising sense of unease and foreboding that she could not shake off. As three o'clock approached, her anxiety increased. She was torn between a reluctant fear of learning how the day had turned out and a harrying anxiety to get it over with. Feeling that she was being silly, trying to enforce nonchalance upon herself, she waited until a quarter of the hour before getting out the station wagon and driving through the wet afternoon to the school.

She made it in good time and jockeyed the Chevrolet into the melee of cars crawling up the driveway toward the canopy. It was a slow, disorderly business and highly competitive, for most of the cars were driven by mothers preoccupied by the thought of muddy feet and hopeful of getting up to the paved plaza in time to forestall a wild dash through the mire. Normally Ellen would have felt the same concern; today she merely wanted the four kids inside the car as quickly as possible.

She made the plaza at last and saw them gathered in a knot at the curb. They seemed quiet—perhaps abnormally quiet—and somehow apart from the mass, but even her anxious eyes could read no sign of hurt or danger into that. She breathed a sigh of relief and, stopped at the curb, she tooted a short summoning blast on the horn and leaned over to lift the locking buttons on the right-hand doors. They came tumbling in; the doors slammed. Ellen rolled her window down and turned her head out into the rain to watch for oncoming cars as she inched her way into the moving traffic.

She never saw it coming, though Bill did and yelled a warning. A figure had darted out of the crowd, across the pavement ahead of the car and onto the mud of the torn lawn. Trying to watch both ways, only aware of the scurrying figure as a half-seen flicker of movement, Ellen jammed on the brakes to avoid it. She did not see it bend down and scoop up a handful of mud. She did not see it thrown. She took the gooey, gravel-seeded blob full against the side of the face. Through the shocking pain and blindness she heard a jeering, hysterical shriek, "Nigger! Nigger!"

She heard Bill mouthing curses she had not known he knew, heard the rear door slam open, heard him yelling, "Come on, Jerry! Come on!" She struggled out of the car, mopping the mud away on her sleeve. For a moment she could not see from her stinging eyes. Then she saw Bill plowing into the crowd, head down and elbows flailing. Jerry was just behind him and then, she realized, so was Tod Winter. The three of them were a flying wedge boring into the mass of children.

She stopped them. Afterward she never knew how. She got them back into the car. It was a physical struggle to handle Bill; his face was contorted and he was sobbing in rage. Jerry was muttering, pale with anger. The Negro boy subsided into the seat without resistance, saying nothing, with a set face and burning eyes. A high, screeching taunt came from somewhere in the crowd where the mud thrower had taken refuge. Stiff of back and face, ignoring the excited, indignant flapping of a teacher, Ellen drove away.

"Stop it, Billy. Stop it at once!" were the only words she uttered all the endless, aching, longing-to-weep-and-to-curse four miles back to Peaceable Lane.

27

It was six o'clock, and Yale, his lawyer, the representative of the bank which had held his mortgage, and the man from the title-guarantee company were gone. It was finished. In the quiet office, with its tall cases of somber and serious-looking lawbooks, Winter sat pensively in the black leather chair beside Gold's mahogany desk. He was holding the deed which signified that he was now sole owner of No. 10 Peaceable Lane—as well as No. 1.

After a while Winter looked up at the lawyer, who had been silent, thoughtfully regarding the bronze bust of Lincoln which was the only ornament on his desk. A slow smile grew on the artist's face.

"He was pretty tame, there at the end," he said.

"Yale?" Gold said. "Yes, it was time for him to be tame." The big man looked tired, Winter thought.

"Then there's this," Winter said. He withdrew a folded paper from his inner breast pocket. "I don't know if it's legal—I wrote it up myself. But I guess it might be if you got your girl to witness it. Maybe it has to be notarized—I don't know."

"What is it?" Gold asked curiously.

"You know already. I don't know what you'd call it—a conveyance maybe. Names Matt manager of the property—with full authority to rent or sell, as he sees fit, bearing in mind his sole judgment of what serves the best interests of the community. No strings attached." He grinned. "No salary either. The bastard'll have to do this for free."

"You didn't have to put it in writing," Gold protested. "You know I was ready to take your word for it. And I know Matt would."

"I just thought I'd rather have it all wrapped up and tied with a bow. In case I got tempted to change my mind—or slipped on a banana peel or something."

Gold eyed him quizzically. "I can't see you slipping on anything," he said at length. "You look like about the most nonskid client I ever had."

"Thanks." The artist chuckled and then, turning serious, added, "I don't know about that. I have a feeling I've skidded a hell of a way from where I was."

"You may have, at that. Have you said anything about this to Matt?"

"Not yet," the artist said. "I wanted it all nice and clean before I handed him the duty. You know, in one way it's a dirty trick to stick Matt with something like this. He never struck me as a civic-father type."

"Why did you then?" Gold was curious.

"Damned if I really know," Winter said ruefully. "Maybe because most of the neighbors probably think he made such a mess of it when he sold the Bronson house to me—and you did. Give him a chance to show them he can do better." He pondered a moment. "No, that's not right. The plain truth is that you and Matt are the only people around there I could give the job to."

When Gold spoke again, his voice was heavy with a curious, hesitant reluctance.

"Listen, Lamar. I know what you've done and what it means and I don't have to tell you I'm grateful that you did it. Why you did it, I suppose, is really none of my business. But I'd like to know . . . if you feel like saying . . ."

The artist sat silent, gazing at him thoughtfully.

"What I mean is," Gold went on with obvious difficulty, "well, I mean, you never struck me as a man who'd put himself on the line to do something like this . . . save a white community from blowing up. Frankly, I don't get it."

"I don't know that I do, not entirely," Winter said at last. "But I don't mind telling you . . . at least as nearly as I can figure it out . . ." He fell silent again, thoughtfully tapping the deed against the desk.

"I'm a colored man," he said at length. "I don't propose to make a lecture on what that means in full, but one of the things it does mean is that you work uphill. You learn early that people, white people, are going to slap you down. Then, if you're the way I am, you slap back. You do better than that—you kick and claw and gouge, and, I dunno, maybe after a while you get so you enjoy it."

"I thought you still did," Gold said.

Winter grinned briefly. "I wouldn't be surprised," he said. "When I decided to do this I could hardly stand my own amazement. I thought, why, by God, that's a mighty strange spectacle, Ol' Marse Winter, a tame nigger." He sat up suddenly and his voice turned hard. "Only the truth is I am not a tame nigger. I still stand ready to slap, kick, claw or gouge whenever I think it's necessary."

Gold gestured helplessly. "Why did you do it then?" he asked. "The street hasn't given you many reasons to quit gouging."

"Don't I know it?" Winter said wickedly. "You could say my being in Peaceable Lane—so far—has been damn near a total failure—despite the best soft-headed efforts of a few tame whites like you and Matt."

"All right, all right." Gold sighed. "I'm getting a little sick of being called a tame white, but have your fun."

"I'm sorry," Winter said quickly. "I really am. Being a bastard just comes natural to me, maybe too natural. But let's look it in the eye. I jolted the living hell out of that street and they've jolted me back. But that's only one thing. I can take it and dish it back as long as they want to keep it up. But it isn't the only thing. The other is the reason I made up my mind."

"What do you mean? You lost me there," Gold said, puzzled.

"The other thing is the kids," Winter said. "You take my kid—he isn't a born gouger or kicker. I used to be scared because he wasn't." In amazement Gold saw the artist's eyes go soft. "Now I'm beginning to wonder. There have been a few things around there that got to me. Things I couldn't understand. You know the day I went down to the pool and Mrs. Cusack raised so much hell? What you probably don't know is that Tod got into the water that day. That Weissman gal, pretty little kid, got him in before he knew what was happening. Then your kid and Matt's kid treating him like any other kid on the block. I've even seen him playing with one or two others. I keep my eyes open, man, and I'm around there more than you are." The artist paused and a puzzled light came into his eyes. "There's one thing that still baffles the hell out of me, though."

"What's that?" Gold asked.

"That fight. The day your kids clobbered Paulie Cusack."

Gold smiled wryly. "He'd had it coming for quite a while," he said.

"I expect he did," Winter said. "The point I'm trying to make is this—I doubt if Peaceable Lane is going to enjoy having me for a neighbor if I live to be a hundred. And I doubt, barring a couple of exceptions, that I'm going to lose much love on Peaceable Lane. But I've seen enough to make me think the kids might make it. There's a chance they can solve a problem that our generation is too old and ornery to deal with. That's why I did it."

"You mean that's why you kept Yale's house out of Barton's hands?"

"Yup. I know Barton. He wasn't fixing to turn that street mixed. He was fixing to turn it colored. If he'd got Yale's house, the place would have come apart like a hand grenade—and the kids never would have had a chance to see whether they could work it out."

"I see," Gold said. He gazed at the artist for a long time before he spoke again. "Tell me something. That must have been a hell of a decision to make. Considering your background—uphill all the way against the white man—did it bother you any that, to give the kids a chance, as you say, you had to take the side of the whites and keep another colored man out of Peaceable Lane?"

"Some," Winter acknowledged somberly, but then he smiled. "You ought to know how it is. You've done some of that yourself. Take one thing with another, it's pretty hard to avoid being a sonofabitch."

He stood up, dropping the deed on Gold's desk blotter. Then he reached for the other paper, signed it, and dropped it with the deed.

"You can handle this stuff better than I can," he said. "It's been a full day and I'm calling it one. Want a ride home?"

"No, thanks," Gold said. "I've got a meeting in town tonight." He smiled warmly. "At that, I'd probably turn you down anyhow. I still don't fancy the way you drive that red fire wagon."

Twenty minutes later Winter tipped an astonished parking attendant five dollars and tooled the Jaguar up the slope to the street and slipped into the evening traffic toward the west side of Manhattan and the Henry Hudson Parkway. The traffic, the lights, the pedestrians swarming heedless in each intersection filled him with impatience.

He breathed a gusty sigh of pleasure when, at last, above the cutoff draining the bulk of traffic away to the Cross County Parkway, he was able to give the Jaguar its head. Mindful of police and traffic, ready to give way to necessary lets and hindrances upon his progress, but only those that were necessary, he raced up the Saw Mill as free as and far fleeter than the wind. The controlled sweep of power under his toe had its answer in a mood that was close to exultation.

In spite of the dark, unsightly bruise on his left cheek and the cut in his scalp above the ear, souvenirs of Smith's clubbed gun, Matt had gone to the city that morning. His calls were exploratory probing along Madison Avenue; the quickly melting brevity of even a year's salary haunted him, and he felt demon driven to get to work again. Now in the dusk he had come home and was seeing his own scars mirrored in the gravel scratches of flung mud left on the face of his wife. Rage, thick and sickening because it was helpless, churned up in him.

In his mind's eye he could see the humiliating splatter and in his mind's ear hear the childish yell of scorn. A child, he thought, a fourth- or fifth-grade baby. Clean in its slicker and saddle shoes and fresh-bought cowboy shirt and jeans for school. Clean in its bed, clean in its home, protected, safe, sanitized, fed with comic books and Grade A homogenized milk and fresh-squeezed orange juice and vitamins. Rotten in its corrupted, spoon-fed-with-reasonless-hate little mind.

"Why didn't you let the kids take him?" he asked harshly. He wanted to be tender and not harsh, but the anger was too much in him. He wanted to soothe away her brittle, breaking look but did not know how. He was trapped by knowing that, however little he had foreseen what would come out, it was he who had turned the key to open this Pandora's box of ugliness.

"No, Matt. There has been too much of that," she said stonily. "Too much of everything."

"Dammit all," he said bitterly. "There are times when a man has the right to fight, when it's wrong to stop him. Even a kid."

"No, Matt," she said again. The frozen look in her eyes and the pale, set face frightened him.

"I know who it was," Bill said from the doorway. His voice startled them; they had thought themselves alone with this beast of knowledge. But the boy had been there, silent, watchful, wounded, plotting revenge.

"Who was it?" Matt asked sharply.

"Kid named Jim Pierce. Sixth grade. I'll get him tomorrow."

"No!" Ellen's voice rose, sharp and forbidding. "No, you must not. Do you hear me, Billy? I forbid it!"

"I'm going to get him," Bill said again. The young voice was tight with sullen promise.

"I said no!" Ellen was on her feet. A passion of rejection was welling up through the numbness. "Billy, do you hear me? I forbid it! I will not have it. Brawling through that school, trying to whip every child in it. Listen to me, you don't know. That's what it will be, having to fight every child in school."

"Aw, it won't either," Bill said stubbornly. "It was just Jim. He's a jerk. The other kids didn't do anything."

Bill had put his finger on it. There was the essence of Wacapo Consolidated and its relation to Tod Winter. But Matt and Ellen were too overwrought to catch it. It was just Jim Pierce—and perhaps a few more. It was a tragic thing to miss.

Ellen turned to Matt. He had never seen her smooth face so drawn and almost old.

"Matt, this has got to stop. First you, then all of us, now Billy. It cannot go on!"

She was right, of course, he thought. However bitter his anger or fierce his will, the kid couldn't be set free to try to hammer an entire school into submission. It was impossible and ridiculous. People could not live that way. And still Matt himself felt the same savage need to strike out at and smash a shapeless, insensate enemy. It was a man's need, and a kid could be driven by it as passionately as a grown man.

"Dirty sonofabitch! I'm going to get him," Bill raged, driven to burst the bonds of a pain too big to be contained.

"Billy!" Ellen shouted hoarsely.

"I don't care. I'm going to get him," the boy muttered. The anger in him would not tolerate silence.

"Bill!" Matt exploded. "Shut up! Go to your room. I don't want another word out of you. Now!" There was too much here, grief, rage, an enemy beyond understanding or reach. And his nerves had been drawn too fine. Here was the helplessness of all men brought face to face with the ultimate knowledge that there is a cutoff point between the world they control and can protect and another world from which they are excluded, but where their young must find their way and move alone.

"But, Pop, I know him," Bill said stubbornly.

"Go to your room, I said. Now!"

Silently, keeping his head down to hide the shaming tears, the boy turned and went.

Hunched, resistant under the load that had fallen on Peaceable Lane, himself, his wife, his son, Matt wondered where the breaking point would come. One thing he thought he knew—it had gone past the point of no return. They were committed; he had committed them. They had to win now—or be smashed.

He looked at Ellen and wished he could comfort her. Her body was slumped, stiff with fatigue and drained of strength. But her eyes were strange, bleak, somehow cold, appraising him as though he was a stranger. She stirred, tiredly straightening herself.

"I can't take this any more," she said. "I'm going away."

"You're what?" he said woodenly.

"I'm going away and taking Bill. If it was only the two of us, I could stay. I can't let this be done to Bill."

Outside Chappaqua, racing up the Saw Mill, Winter was struck by a notion and, delicately touching the brakes, slowed the Jaguar's flight and slid off the intersection and into town. He stopped in front of a liquor store. Sooner or later, he thought, there was likely to be a reaction, but now that queer, high-strung mood of exultation still held him. I may be a sonofabitch by my own lights, he reflected, but at least I've damn well settled something.

"Got any champagne? Chilled, if you have it?" he asked the

somnolent man behind the counter. His curiosity might have been stirred if he had known this was Harry Easton who, in a way, was responsible for Peaceable Lane and thus, by extension, for everything that had happened there. This was the man who, after nearly three hundred years, had sold the Easton homestead for development by builder Riccetti.

"Mebbe," the storekeeper said, eying his customer curiously.

"*Cordon bleu,*" Winter said.

"Whazzat?"

"Blue ribbon," Winter said with a smile, feeling good will even toward this sleepy dullard.

"Got some Rheingold on ice," the man said. "No Blue Ribbon. Budweiser, maybe. Want me to look?"

"I said champagne, man," Winter said. "Wine."

"You were talking about beer," Easton said reproachfully. "Anyhow, I haven't got any champagne. Got a little California burgundy if you got to have wine."

"Okay, okay," Winter said impatiently. "Give me two bottles."

Back in the car, he put the bottles on the seat beside him. Well, hell, he thought, who needs champagne? He started the engine and gunned the car, slinging gravel from the wheels before the Jaguar bumped over the New York Central tracks and dove into the labyrinth of the road through Wacapo Park. Despite puddles of water in the neglected pavement and a slick wetness of the surface, the car felt obedient and sure-footed under his touch.

Puzzled, feeling slapped and driven out, locked in combat with forces he had never known existed and knew no better than his elders how to defeat, Bill Jones trudged from the playroom and, so far as his parents knew, went on up through the split level to his room. Instead he stopped in the kitchen and stood for a while, undecided, scuffing his sneakers angrily on the polished tile. Abruptly he went out the garage door and, yanking impatiently to free it from a tight squeeze between the lawnmower and a garbage can, got his bicycle out onto the driveway.

The worry and bewilderment were enough. Hurt and anger were enough. The urgent longing to hear Jim Pierce bellow for mercy and thus wipe out the insult and injury to his mother were more than enough. But there was something more, this knowing somehow he had and they all had got into conflict with something too big to understand. He felt puzzled and battered. Now this—his mother's strange, frightening violence and Matt's incomprehensible, brutal rejection. He did not know what he intended to do, but he knew he was not going to his room.

It was almost dark as the bike coasted down the driveway and he turned toward the top of the lane. He was going somewhere, maybe to the lake in the woods with its island and the secret fallen-tree-trunk bridge, where a warrior could nurse his wounds in solitude and grow whole again. He was almost upon him before he saw Tod Winter sitting on the curb, hunched with his arms around his knees, staring into the street.

"Where you going?" Tod called. Bill flipped his heel down on the coaster brake and tipped the wheel expertly to a stop beside the other boy.

"I dunno," he said. "Why?"

"Just wondered," Tod said. His voice was dispirited.

"I'm damn near ready to run away," Bill said.

Tod's voice was suddenly fierce. "I'll tell you one thing—I'm not going back to that school. I don't care what my father says, or my mother either."

"It's all right for you," Bill said. "I'll have to go back. I live here."

"Where do you think I live?"

"You don't live here. You just moved here, that's all. You don't have to stay. I've been here most of my life."

"I never asked to come here and I don't want to stay." Pressed down by the weight of loneliness and defeat, burdened with the tears that he knew Margo was shedding alone in her bedroom, wondering half resentfully why his father was not at home to help, Tod had had more than he was ready to handle. "I won't stay here. If they won't go, I'll go by myself."

"I think you'd better. You damn well shouldn't have come," Bill said in sudden flaring anger.

They would never afterward know why they fought. These two had been on the edge of becoming friends and would have, had the world left them alone to go about their business. Reason had nothing to do with flinging them at one another. But, there in the rain-wet street, it all came to focus: the pain, the humiliation, the inexplicable failures of the adult world and the reasonless savagery of the child world. They had suffered the same blows by the same enemies, but now somehow for each it was all bound up in the other. Passion built so high had to have an outlet, and in a world so full of mad confusions that no enemy could be named, it was now suddenly impossible to find any other outlet but the other's flesh. They were a tumbling, straining, sobbing tangle of arms and legs and thin, strong bodies, aware of nothing but the need to smash and pound and thus, somehow, drive out the fear and hurt within. In the long history of man's helpless stupidity there had been few fights more senseless than this. But they had to do it and they were blind and deaf to everything around them.

But the world was not quite blind or deaf to them. Reluctantly yielding to a repeated order by his mother, Paulie Cusack was out in the street, giving the Cusack chow his evening walk. He heard the panting, scuffling struggle from a distance and, curiosity aroused, hurried along toward the noise. Paulie, well versed in the sounds of juvenile battle, recognized them for what they were; he was curious to see who it was and, still conscious of his advantage of size and strength despite the licking he had taken, approached the scene of conflict with interest but no alarm. It might be something he would be tempted to take a hand in.

The light was almost gone, but he could make out the tumbling figures in the gutter ten yards before he reached them. It needed a closer look to identify who they were. With the chow sniffing uneasily, Paulie approached almost within reach of the flailing fists and feet and stood peering curiously down at the two small, heaving bodies. Then he recognized them. His start of surprise was followed by a slow, pleased grin. Well, he thought, it would be pleasant to know what brought this on, but, meanwhile, he could think of nothing more satisfying than to stand and watch and see how it came out. Great, he thought, just great; the nigger and that snot-nose, smart-aleck Jones punk.

He moved back a little to stay clear of the melee so that he and the straining chow were standing almost in the middle of the street.

Racing around the blind curves of the Wacapo road, thinking about the day's work, anxious to get home and tell Margo about it, going fast but not worrying or even thinking about the car or the road because his touch at wheel and brake operated with such sure instinct, Winter drove the Jaguar through the underpass tunnel and slashed into Peaceable Lane. He was almost home, a place, he thought now, which might someday become truly home.

Then he saw them. There was the tumbling, thrashing movement of bodies near the curb. Ten feet away in the middle of the road, now jerking his head around into the sudden glare of the headlights, stood a boy and a dog. The writhing confusion of the fight was near the curb, and he might have got by it safely but for the other boy. His mind told him instantly that it was a fight, but, since both boys were covered with mud, there was no way of knowing who they were. The other, standing, paralyzed and staring into the glare of his head lamps, he may have recognized. Lamar Winter could not have said whether he consciously made up his mind. He wrenched the wheel savagely to the right, and the Jaguar, obedient to the end, leaped the curb onto the Outerbridge lawn and hurtled toward the bole of the biggest oak on Peaceable Lane. He did know, whoever they were, that he had missed them.

28

AT DUSK, after they had returned from the funeral in late afternoon, Matt walked across the back yards and found Gold waiting for him on the terrace.

"Have they left your house yet?" Gold asked.

"They're with her now," Matt said. "Zack, I hate to put her through this." Half an hour earlier Beth Gold had appeared at the Jones house, and she and Ellen had left together to escort Margo Winter to a meeting of the lane's people in the home of Solomon Weissman.

"She's stood up under everything so far," Gold grunted. "And this is necessary. She committed herself, but it was only on our say-so. She ought to have the chance to see how it is firsthand—she might want to change her mind."

"You've made sure she can afford it?" Matt asked.

Gold grunted again. "Winter must have been one of the most insured guys in Westchester. Even he must have suspected he drove that damn red wagon too fast—every life policy he carried was double indemnity."

"How much was there?"

"When it's all cleaned up, expenses and all, quite a hunk. He paid cash for the Yale house. There's a mortgage rider on one policy that takes care of the other. So she'll own both clear and, on top of that, the cash will run close to two hundred thousand."

"I knew he made a lot. I didn't know he'd stashed that much away," Matt said. "And there's still more to come in."

"How's that?"

"Thurston Young saw it in the *Times* and called me in. He owns the account Lamar and I were working on when I got fired. He wants me to carry through the campaign, using Winter's paintings. Her share of that will run seventy-five, maybe even eighty thousand."

"Bails you out, too, doesn't it?" Gold asked.

"It sure as hell does," Matt said somberly. Suddenly, feeling the pain of grief and the uselessness of it, he drove his fist savagely against the solid wall of Gold's house. "Why did the crazy bastard have to drive like that?" he exploded.

"He was a hard-living guy," Gold said. "That way and every way. Come on, let's get over there."

It occurred to Matt as they entered that the scene had not been much different outwardly the last time he had been in this house. Now, as then, Mrs. Weissman was bustling about in hospitable anxiety. Sol sat relaxed in an easy chair, wearing his look of a bright, inquisitive cherub under the fringe of fluffy white hair. Steve Cavanidis was silently, cynically watchful, missing nothing. Gordon Draper looked youthful and undecided, Jerome Kelly kindly and concerned, Dr. Abram inwardly brooding and sensitive, John Ainslie Outerbridge primly erect and faintly disapproving.

Was there a difference beneath the surface? If so, had it reached into the depths of Laura Cusack? He looked at her and wondered whether what he saw on that pinched, acidulous face might be a shadow of confusion, of doubt.

There was one difference, certainly. Margo Winter, drawn but composed, sat on the divan between Ellen and Beth Gold.

Weissman stood up and tucked supporting fingers between belt and belly and ran his sharp eyes around the circle of his neighbors. "Most of you know why we're here," he said. "I suppose we could have left it without all this formality. But perhaps it will be better if we all know the same things at the same time. Also"—he turned his bright eyes toward Margo—"it is about time that Mrs. Winter has a look at us." He paused and nodded toward Gold. "You don't need a speech from me, but I think you'll want to listen to Zachariah."

Gold, balancing on a dining chair that looked perilously fragile under his huge weight, did not stand up. He took off his glasses, polished them on a handkerchief, restored them to use and peered owlishly around the room.

"I won't take much time," he said. "But you should know this —in my office, on the day he died, Lamar Winter bought Pete Yale's house. He paid cash for it. It belongs to Mrs. Winter, as does the Bronson house they bought earlier."

The room was silent, waiting.

"You all know somebody tried to burn his house. He decided to buy Yale's house when he learned why the fire was set. At first he believed that the fire was started by white men to drive him out—that was what he was intended to believe. But he learned —don't ask me how—that Yale was actually dealing with a colored blockbuster and that the blockbuster arranged the burning as a deliberate ruse. He wanted to convince Winter that the whites were still and always would be his enemies—as they had been."

He stopped again and still the room was silent.

"The blockbuster intended to drive you out—all of you—and make this street colored. Winter decided to stop him. He did not make his decision especially out of sympathy for the people in this room—a fact"—the lawyer's voice turned dryly sardonic—"a fact which I think most of you will find understandable."

Gold stood up then, looming over the room. His voice had grown hard and grating.

"I come now to the point. Winter did not believe it likely that you—we—would ever accept him as an equal. He did not believe he was ready to accept us, either, on those terms. But he did believe something else enough to buy Yale's house and keep it and all of us out of the hands of the blockbuster. He believed that his son and our children had at least a chance to find a way to live together in peace—possibly even in friendship." Gold stopped again and let his eyes rove the room from one to another. "I believe that he was correct. Moreover, I believe that if we are to have any hope of keeping the world we live in livable, some such belief—or hope, if you want to call it that—has to be correct. I —some others, Mr. Weissman and Mr. Outerbridge among them—have asked Mrs. Winter to stay here and give his child and ours the chance he meant them to have." Gold sat down, imposing an improbable load on the fragile chair.

Weissman stood up, tucked his fingers under his bellyband and looked around once again.

"Any comment? Any dissent?" He waited calmly, but nobody stirred. "All right, I take it we agree. Anything you want to say, Mrs. Winter?"

Margo's eyes were swollen and her beautiful face showed the strain. A handkerchief in her hands was wet with sweat, alternately balled into a hard lump and pulled into a soggy string. Few things life had ever required of her—the hardest of all had been to watch the coffin disappear into the earth that afternoon—had been harder than coming to this meeting. She knew things had changed profoundly on Peaceable Lane, but these people were still white, and from now on, shorn of Winter's strength and courage, she would have to face them alone—she and Tod. She didn't want to speak; she wanted to flee into the shell of her grief. She bit her lips, trembling, then got control of herself with an effort. Then she spoke.

"My husband was a bold man . . . and not a patient man . . . and often he made me afraid. Coming here was one of the things I feared . . . but wanted to do . . . especially for my son. . . . After we came I was even more afraid . . . and you know it has not been easy . . . either for you or for my family." She paused, shuddering, then, almost gasping, went doggedly on, "I am still afraid. And strange. I hope you will forgive me . . . but I must say that the fear of you—of white people—is very old in me . . . and very deep. I wish it was not true . . . but I cannot help it. I know I would feel safer somewhere else . . . with my own people. But it is true that some of you have done things—kind and generous things—that made it seem possible after all. I must say the truth—I would rather run away. But I trusted my husband—I still trust him. He wanted this to work . . . for Tod . . . for your children. I will do what he wanted . . . I will stay . . . with Tod."

"Thank you," Weissman said. "I think the kids will get the chance he meant them to have." Then he turned to the room and spoke crisply. "There's something else you need to know. Winter put the Yale house in the keeping of Matthew. You should hear what he proposes to do with it. Matthew."

Matt looked around the room, measuring Peaceable Lane's people one by one. Most of them know what I'm going to say, he thought, probably all of them by this time. All I'm doing here is giving them a chance to beef in front of one another if they've got the guts. And I don't think they have. He thought of Bill, safe and warm in his bed. He wondered about Laura Cusack—but not much. She knew; she knew where her son was and why he was there instead of dead. He didn't bother to wonder about Draper; there was pressure enough to keep him in line. He felt again the upsurge of grief a man may feel for a lost friend, and he was impatient to be done with this picking over his dead bones and let him rest. His voice was harsh.

"Lamar Winter was a tough man. He was intolerant, impatient and cynical. He did not have much affection for white men and he had even less trust of them. But he was willing to bet on our sons.

"In the end he bet his life on them. He would not have bet on us. Probably not on himself either. He may have been right, anyhow at first. There is not much question that both he and we began this summer the kind of slobs he suspected we were. Partly by accident, he got down to something better in the end. It would be a damn shame if the rest of us hadn't too.

"It has been suggested to me by more than one of you—I don't think it's necessary to say which ones—that we ought to find out right away what we're made of by deliberately looking for another colored family to take the Yale house. But Winter left the Yale house to my judgment—and I'm trying to exercise some. You might stand for it now, while we're still in shock, but then when we came out of shock—and if we hadn't really changed—it might all go to hell in a hand basket.

"Maybe our maximum capability is what Winter thought: giving the kids a chance. Maybe he gave us less than our due. It's not easy for people to tell about themselves—even when they're trying. I propose to give us a chance to try. I have asked Mrs. Winter and she's willing. We're going to keep the Yale house empty for a while. Six months from now—or a year—if we turn out to be better or braver—or maybe even smarter than Winter suspected—well, then, we ought to be able to figure out a way to demonstrate it."

"It may be risky," John Ainslie Outerbridge, sounding prissy even when he wasn't visible, said to Steve Cavanidis as they walked toward home in the dark. "It may not even work, but I suspect that this summer has showed us all that it has to be tried. We can't keep the world shut out forever. Gold and Jones are right in that. And it seems to me that it is far better to accept it and try to make it work than to try to fight a losing battle against it."

"Yeah, I guess so," Cavanidis said laconically.

"I confess I was a little surprised at your accepting it," Outerbridge went on. "Excuse me for saying it, but I always felt that you were not a man who would take chances. What I mean is, it seemed to me that you would always want to make absolutely sure your interests were safe."

Cavanidis gave a short, grunting laugh. "Hell, they are. Way last summer I got the union to buy my house—and give me life tenancy in it." He laughed again. "Free, too."

ABOUT THE AUTHOR

KEITH WHEELER *has, since 1951, been a writer, editor and foreign correspondent for* Life *Magazine. Before that he was a reporter and war correspondent for the Chicago* Times, *now the Chicago* Sun-Times. *As a journalist he has received Sigma Delta Chi, Headliners Club, Newspaper Guild and the Benjamin Franklin Magazine awards as well as Overseas Press Club citations. His previous books include* The Pacific Is My Beat *and* We Are the Wounded *(both non-fiction), and* The Reef *and* Small World *(fiction). He now lives in a suburb of New York with his wife and two children.*